THE
GOLDEN
GLOBE

• • • • • •

JOHN VARLEY

ACE BOOKS, NEW YORK

The films of Jimmy Stewart and the many characters he portrayed served as a continuing source of inspiration to the author.

THE GOLDEN GLOBE

An Ace Book / published by arrangement with
the author

PRINTING HISTORY
Ace trade hardcover edition / October 1998
Ace mass-market edition / September 1999

All rights reserved.
Copyright © 1998 by John Varley.
Cover art by Danilo Ducak.
This book may not be reproduced in whole or in part,
by mimeograph or any other means, without permission.
For information address: The Berkley Publishing Group,
a division of Penguin Putnam Inc.,
375 Hudson Street, New York, New York 10014.

The Penguin Putnam Inc. World Wide Web site address is
http://www.penguinputnam.com

Check out the ACE Science Fiction & Fantasy newsletter
and much more on the Internet at Club PPI!

ISBN: 0-441-00643-4

ACE®
Ace Books are published by
The Berkley Publishing Group,
a division of Penguin Putnam Inc.,
375 Hudson Street, New York, New York 10014.
ACE and the "A" design are trademarks
belonging to Penguin Putnam Inc.

PRINTED IN THE UNITED STATES OF AMERICA

10   9   8   7   6   5   4   3   2   1

ACT
1

"I once played *Romeo and Juliet* as a one-man show," I said. "Doubling with Mercutio won't be a problem."

The curtain was already up, and Dahlia Smithson—our fair sun, the snowy dove trouping with crows, the rich jewel in the Ethiop's ear—had yet to appear backstage. This was not a surprise. The last two nights we'd had to winch her loveliness into the balcony and tie her down to keep her from falling out.

"You're out of your mind," shouted Larry "The Leech" Crocker, our producer-director-stage manager: the wax in the Ethiop's ear. He was bug-eyed with fury, trembling, drenched in sweat . . . and the picture of calm composure next to Dee, the assistant stage manager, who kept pushing Larry's ragged script away from her as if it might bite.

There had been talk of bringing in an understudy in view of La Smithson's recent behavior, but this was not the Schubert Traveling Shows, ladies and germs, this was The Crocker Players, and if you haven't heard of them it's probably because you live within a parsec of civilization. We were chronically undercapitalized (read "dirt-poor") and it fell to the ASM to understudy all the female roles. And while I'm sure Dee would have provided yeoman service as Ladies Montague or Capulet, and could probably have taken a creditable swing at the Nurse, the prospect of Juliet had turned her pale green.

"I don't know all the lines," Dee wailed.

"See?" I said. "She doesn't know the part."

"You're crazy," Larry exploded. "Aren't they onstage at the same time?"

"Mercutio and Juliet never meet," I said. "I know you've put Mercutio at the Capulets' party, but the Bard doesn't demand it, and it can be solved by letting the Prince wear my costume in the scene. Mercutio is masked, and has no lines. However"—and I cupped my ear to the stage—"you'd better make up your mind. Scene two is about to begin, and Juliet is in three. I'll need a little time."

"You're crazy," Larry the Leech muttered again, then jerked his head toward the dressing rooms.

"You'll never regret this," I said.

"I regret it already."

This being a Crocker show, it goes without saying that we were a lot more than forty-five minutes from Broadway. Hell, we were just about forty-five hours from Pluto. That's how long it had taken my last message to my agent to reach the System, and an equal time for the news to reach me that he wasn't answering his phone. No big surprise there; I'd been "on the road," as it were, for almost ten years now, and my agent hadn't been answering when I left. (The question I'd wanted him to answer? Simple, really: *"Who booked me into this toilet?"*)

The plumbing fixture in question was know as Brementon. Who knows why? Humans have this need to name everything, no matter how little that thing may deserve it. When I saw the name on the travel itinerary it brought to mind a peaceful little hamlet. German, perhaps. Happy burghers in *lederhosen*, smiling *fraäuleins* in *dirndls* and pigtails and wooden shoes, cottages draped in *swastika* bunting. In reality, if they'd added "Maximum Security Prison" to the place's name they'd have been closer to the truth. About a quarter of it *was* a prison. We hadn't seen that part as yet, but if it was worse than the rest of the place, the mind reeled. B-town, as the players came to call it, could have provided the very definition of the word "boondock," except that the stop before B-town had actually been *called* Boondocks.

Brementon was a random collection of junk, natural and artificial, welded together in the cometary zone and pressed into service as a "City" by the escaped criminals, madmen, perverts, and other misfits who liked to call themselves Outlanders. Brementon, Boondocks, and ten thousand other similar wandering junkyards constituted the most far-flung "community" humanity had ever known.

As to where it was, that was something that could have mattered only to a celestial navigator. Upon arrival I'd looked for the Sun, and it took a while to find it. We were due to pass within ten billion miles of it in only four thousand years; to an Outlander, that qualified as a near miss.

It was tough to say how big Brementon was. Much of it was tied together with cables and hoses and it tended to drift around. If you'd grabbed two ends and yanked hard you might have stretched it out twenty kilometers or more, but you'd never get it unsnarled again. When I first saw it from the ship it presented a rude circular form about five kay across, like some demented globular cluster, or a picture of a spaceship a few seconds after a disastrous explosion.

One small part of this orbiting traffic-accident-in-progress was a silvery sphere called the Brementon Playhouse. It was tied to a counterbalancing ball containing the municipal sewer works, which gives a fair idea of the high esteem Outlanders held for The Arts. The balls rotated around a common center of gravity. The result was that we didn't have to play Shakespeare in free fall, as we'd done at Boondocks and several previous engagements. *Friends, Romans, countrymen, throw me a tie-down!* Talk about your theater in the round.

But enough about Brementon. Let's talk about me.

I raced up the spiral stairs in the wings and slammed into Dahlia's dressing room. I paused for just a second there, breathing the intoxicating air of the headliner. I'd hate to say how long it had been since I'd rated a private dressing room. I caressed the back of Juliet's chair, then pulled it back and sat in front of the light-girdled mirror and gazed into my face and centered myself.

I'd never actually done Juliet before. No point in telling Larry that. (The one-man show? A comic skit, really, with quick changes, slapstick, clown faces, and japery, lasting twenty minutes when I was really rolling.) No point in worrying him; I knew the part. But line reading is just the starting point, of course. You must get inside the character. All good acting is played from within. I had about five minutes.

It's not enough time, of course. It wouldn't have been enough even if I'd been able to use it to do nothing but think about the part. As it was, I'd need every minute to accomplish the physical transformation. But I did use the mental time to go back over the many, many performances of Juliet I had seen, going right back to Norma Shearer in 1936. As my mind ranged back over Juliets of the past, taking a bit of business here, a word emphasis there, my hands were busy changing hatchet-faced Mercutio into a visage with cheek to shame the fairest stars in all the heavens.

Once I had my own face. Well, I still have it, of course, the specs are somewhere in my trunk, the copyright number SSCO-5-441-j54902. It's a good face, and served me well in the trade for almost thirty years. But it became the wisest course not to use it.

Thirty years ago, with unaccustomed money in my pocket following a long and successful run, I invested in every makeup gadget then known to mankind. This required, among other things, that my entire head be taken apart and rebuilt. My body harbors enough tech wizardry to qualify as a public nuisance. Radios spit static when I walk by. Compasses are thrown off true. But when the part calls for a full-body alteration in a hurry, I'm your guy. Or gal, as the case may be.

My first appearance was a logistical nuisance, really. Juliet says, "It is an honour that I dream not" when asked if she wants to be married. To which the nurse hoots, "An honour! Were not I thine only nurse, I would say thou hadst suck'd wisdom from thy teat." A guaranteed laugh line, which dear sweet Angeline Atkins vamped outrageously, as she did the entire role.

The problem was that the next scene, Act One, scene four, was Mercutio's chance to shine. What to do, what to do?

First things first. I struggled into the costume, stuffing padding in the appropriate places. Luckily, the skirt reached all the way to the floor.

I pulled on a black wig, quickly combed it out, and then picked up the Masque-Aid. It's a nice little gadget consisting of two parts. The first is a thin plastic tube with a snap connector on the end. I fastened this to a matching connector hidden behind my left ear, turned it on, and heard the high hiss as air began to flow through it. The second part is a styling wand, which looks like a pencil with a broad, flat head. Both units are connected to a control console and a switching system buried in my cheekbone. I pressed the flat end of the wand to my face and got to work.

There's nothing real fancy about the wand itself. It contains a powerful magnet that rotates when I press a button with my thumb. When I put it in the right position it causes surgically implanted magnets to turn, which then turn screws . . . which slowly cause various bones or groups of bones to move apart or closer together.

I can vary the distance between my eyes. I can lengthen my jawbone, raise and lower my cheekbones. I can create a brow ridge. In five minutes I can be Quasimodo or Marilyn Monroe.

That's the base. The air hose was taking care of the rest.

There are twenty little air bags embedded in my facial skin. Suck them all dry and I look like Death. Fill them up: Fatty Arbuckle.

The only problem with all this stage magic is it can hurt if done rapidly. Depending on how much I had to do, the pain could be like a mild toothache or a severe beating.

No one ever told me art would be painless.

I was brushing pink spots onto my cheeks when someone began frantically pounding on the dressing room door. "One minute!" Dee called.

"I'll be there." I slashed two bold eyebrows with strokes of a pencil, looked at myself critically one last time. I tasted blood, dabbed at a tooth with a towel, smiled broadly at myself in the mirror.

Larry was waiting for me in the wings, and I savored the expression of bafflement as I approached him. Beyond, Romeo and Benvolio were onstage, the curtain about to come down on the scene. Larry grabbed my arm.

"Listen, babe," he whispered, staring intently into my eyes. "You can't let us down. We're all counting on you, every last one of us. I know it's been a tough road. I know I've been hard on you, but I did it because I knew you had something, darling, some magical quality you can't buy in a store. I want you to go out there and knock 'em dead. When you come back, I want you to come back a *star*!"

"For pity's sake, Larry, get a grip on yourself." He stood there blinking for a moment.

"Sorry. I just always wanted to say that, that's all."

"Well, I'm glad it's out of your system."

From the stage: "What, lamb! What ladybird! God forbid!—where's this girl?—what, Juliet!"

Christ, that was my cue!

"How now, who calls?" It came out in a kind of croak, but at least it was a high-pitched croak. Lady Capulet and the Nurse looked at me strangely, but soldiered bravely on through one of the less interesting scenes in Shakespeare, all about Lammas-eve and other things of minimal importance to a modern audience. I let it all drone over me and concentrated on my vocal cords, which, in the rush, I had neglected to tune. I hummed softly to myself, earning a few sharp looks from Angeline. Finally I thought I had it, and just in time, too.

"It is an honour that I dream not of." Strange. I was sure I'd heard that voice before. Lady Capulet had her back to the audience . . . my god, she was stifling a laugh! I played the line back in my head. Blanche DuBois! I was using the same voice I'd last employed in our production of *Streetcar*.

I frantically cast back through the female roles of my career, looking for something I could slip on like a comfortable shoe. A voice, a voice. My kingdom for a voice!

"Speak briefly, can you like of Paris' love?"

And I said, "I'll look to like, if looking liking move." Damn, that one sounded familiar, too. "But no more deep will I endart mine eye than your consent gives strength to make it fly." Great Caesar's ghost! That was Natalie Wood with a bad Puerto Rican accent! My review of Juliets past had led me down a cinematic byway.

Maybe if I broke into a chorus of "I Feel Pretty" no one would notice.

I had no time to lose. Exeunt all, curtain down, curtain up, enter Romeo, Mercutio, Benvolio, Maskers, Torchbearers, and others. I stood in the wings and went through a transmogrification that would have had Henry Jekyll green with envy while the company entered and stalled, as they'd been warned to do, until I was ready for my entrance.

Off with the dress. Off with the wig. And no time at all for a session in front of the mirror, this has to be *quick,* so with a wince very like a man in front of a firing squad, I jammed my face into a plastic mask and pressed the reset button on the Masque-Aid control console.

I don't recommend this. What happened next felt like I imagine having all your teeth removed at once might feel— if you had five hundred teeth.

The machine went back to square one, at warp speed. In ten seconds I was Mercutio.

The scene went well. In it, I wax fey about Queen Mab, the fairies' midwife. Somehow my pain and disorientation made the lines less stilted than they usually seemed, less a flight of fancy and more an oration of deep meaning to Mercutio, a complex and difficult character. By the end of it, when Romeo calms me down, I was weeping unfeigned tears, shaking with emotion.

It is Larry's theory that Romeo and Mercutio were homosexual lovers. He makes it explicit by having Mercutio kiss Romeo after the line "Turning his face to the dew-dropped south." It is a good-bye kiss, presaging the upcoming assault on Romeo's heart by fair Juliet, and a prescient surrender at the same time. Myself, I have no opinions in the matter. I think it's too tough for a person of our age to really imagine what homosexuality was like in a pre-Changing time. But the scene played well. The curtain rang down to long applause.

And thank god for that, because I don't know if I could have faced the retransformation ahead of me without that sound to buoy me up.

Dee and Larry were arguing about something as I came off. Dee shouted at Larry to shut up—which turned a few heads—and grabbed my arm and pulled me to the stairs.

"I've got you five minutes to change," she said, hauling me along. "I'm replacing you in the dance, and we're doing two choruses. You'll enter, stage left, across from Romeo, while Capulet is talking. I'll cue you."

"I know the spot," I said. "Thanks." I kissed her forehead and entered my dressing room. Elwood was there waiting for me. I nodded to him and collapsed in my chair.

"There's talk of deleting the first scene in the second act," he said. Elwood is a tall man who likes to wear period clothing that hangs on his lanky body like billowing sails. He looks just like Jimmy Stewart.

"That would help a lot," I said. The styling wand was whirring quietly in my hand and Juliet's face was taking shape in the mirror. Elwood sat in a chair beside me and stretched out.

"Yeah, but it sort of cuts the legs out from under Mercutio."

Of course it did, and I didn't need Elwood to tell me. The scene had Mercutio growing increasingly frantic in his search for Romeo, who, we all know, was by then deep in enemy territory and ready to deny his father and refuse his name. Cut it, and Mercutio would look silly in scene four.

"This talk," I said, shrugging Juliet's costume over my clothes. "Who's saying it?"

"Oh, I hear things," Elwood said, with a shrug. Which is all I'd ever get out of him.

I didn't want to cut it. I'd hired on to play Mercutio, and I meant to play him well. And I'd promised Larry I could double the parts, and I meant to do that, too. But Mercutio exits at the very end of scene one and Juliet appears on the balcony at the very start of scene two. If it was only a matter of more pain I'd do it willingly, but for *this* appearance of Juliet I had to have the whole change and I just didn't know if it could be done in a minute.

There are air bladders in my body, too. I plugged the hose fitting from the Masque-Aid into a socket (never mind where; you could search me pretty thoroughly and probably not find it), and warm saline began pumping.

Juliet was thirteen. She had to be covered in baby fat. She needed a slim waist. She needed boobs, and a bottom.

Those last two would have to wait, as they'd look passing strange under Mercutio's tights and jerkin.

Dee was knocking on my door.

I got through the dance without mishap, and without the voice of Blanche, praise all the muses. I don't know where the voice I used came from, but it was suitable to a love-struck teenager.

Then off and wrench my face back during the short intermission between acts, then Mercutio's plaintive search for Romeo ... then I was tearing backstage, tearing off Mercutio's clothes, slapping my face into the Masque-Aid while Dee plugged in the saline hose ... and she was the only witness to what may have been the fastest sex change since Roy Rogers gelded Trigger.

A couple of pints quickly produced a pair of breasts fit for peace to dwell in. Ditto the behind; no sense overdoing it in either place. Suck out a little more juice from the waist, swell the hip, and voilà!

Only one small detail to attend to. Well, not *that* small.

The penis is just skin covering two blood-filled chambers. With the proper operation those chambers can be pulled back into the body, sort of like pulling a sock inside out. Extrude it and you're the leading man. Pull it back in for the ingenue effect. Do it several times quickly and you'll be popular at your next orgy.

My father would have been proud. I came off that stage Mercutio, and appeared sixty seconds later on the balcony, Juliet.

"With love's light wings did I o'erperch these walls," said Romeo, tearing off his shirt. "For stony limits cannot hold love out: And what love can do, that dares love attempt. Therefore thy kinsmen are no let to me." He kissed me as I shrugged out of my own shirt.

"If they do see thee, they will murder thee." I was breathing hard now.

"Alack, there lies more peril in thine eye than twenty of their swords. Look thou but sweet, and I am proof against their enmity." Dropping the Montague britches as he spoke to reveal not hand, not foot, nor arm nor face, but another part belonging to a man. A fair sun, arising! He came into my arms and we fell back together on the bed.

"I would not for the world they saw thee here." Kissing him again.

"I have night's cloak to hide me from their sight; and, but thou love me, let them find me here: my life were better ended by their hate than death prorogued wanting of thy love." And so, into the sex scene.

Yes, I hear you, all you purists out there. What can I say? Given my own druthers, I'd druther do it the traditional way, too. Passionate kisses, doe-eyed looks. But the public demands realism—especially in a backwater like Brementon—and that's what they get.

Or that's what they were *supposed* to get. A minute into the naked embrace, I began to wonder if Romeo had read the same script I had. His bud of love, which by summer's ripening breath should by then have proved a beauteous flower, had proved too like the lightning, which doth cease to be ere one can say, It lightens. In a word, impotency.

O Romeo, Romeo! Wherefore art thou, Romeo? Inconstant moon, that monthly changes in her circled orb, thy love has proved likewise variable.

When I had a chance to reflect on it later, the reason for his trouble was obvious. It's the obvious problems most people overlook. Romeo had an odd sexual quirk. He was a dedicated heterosexual.

I realize they're common enough in the general population, but they are rare in the thespian community. Hell, I'm practically one myself, except on the stage. Perhaps that's why no one really understood that when it came to the sticking point, as it were, his will would fail him. None of us really understood the serpentine logic of his particular perversion.

As a male hetero, he could only get aroused by a female. And though I now gave every evidence of that gender, he had known me as Mercutio, and that's what I stayed, in his mind.

I can laugh at it now. It's become one of those theatrical disaster stories we all love to tell each other, like the prop telephone that rings at the wrong time. (Solution? Pick it up, listen for a moment, then hold it out to your worst enemy and announce, "It's for you.")

There was nothing funny about it at the time.

You wouldn't have known it from the audience reaction, however. *They* were laughing. It's one of the worst sounds you can hear in my business: laughter when you haven't made a joke.

But if you're getting laughs, it's best to keep getting them until you figure out what else to do. Rising from the bed and stalking naked around the stage, I became Kate, shrew of Padua.

"Nay, then, I will not go today. No, nor tomorrow, nor till I please myself. The door is open, sir; there lies your way. You may be jogging while your boots are green; for me, I'll not be gone till I please myself. 'Tis like you'll prove a jolly surly groom, that take it on you at the first so roundly." Suiting action to the word, a frustrated woman trying to please herself.

Romeo sat disconsolately on the edge of the bed, hunting *The Taming of the Shrew* for an appropriate comeback. He looked up at me. "Why does the world report that Juliet doth limp?" he said. "O slanderous world!"

We tossed lines back and forth for a while. The laughter gradually faded—not because they were taking us seriously, but because we could stretch this situation only so far. I had no idea how to salvage it.

Suddenly Romeo jumped from the bed. He embraced me with one arm, his free hand rubbing his buttocks. And I felt his interest begin to rise.

Dee had procured a drug banned on most worlds because of extreme hazard to the male recipient: they often hurt themselves attempting sexual congress with electric light sockets and household pets. She had crawled under the bed and jabbed a needle right through the foam rubber.

"Now, Juliet," he said, "I am a husband for your turn. For by this light, whereby I see thy beauty—thy beauty that doth make me like thee well—thou must be married to no man but me. We will have rings, and things, and fine array. And kiss me, Ka—Juliet, we will be married on Sunday."

And so, at long last, to bed. Where he performed like a trouper and, as if in an effort to make up, tried to jump me again while we were singing the second verse of "Tonight."

And at long last, a scene I wasn't in.

While Romeo poured out his heart to Friar Lawrence (and, this performance only, tried to hump the Friar's leg), I staggered back to my dressing room with a full ten minutes to change back to Mercutio. And who should I find there but Dahlia Smithson, by now neither rich jewel, fair sun, nor snowy dove. I'd say she was closer to an envious moon, sick and pale. That which we call a rose would smell of gin. See how she leans her cheek upon her hand! See how her eyes, twinkling in their spheres, bulge from her head as she points to me and says, "What the fuck are you doing in here, in my costume?"

She bent over and threw up on the floor.

Well, it wasn't my problem, was it? I opened the door and

yelled for Larry. Then I sat at the mirror and did what I'd have been doing with or without Dahlia's reappearance: I turned myself back into Mercutio.

Dahlia Smithson was the only name with any star power in our motley cast. She was a fading star (you can't drink that much, miss that many shows, without entering a steady and inevitable decline), but her name above the titles of our little repertory was all that had drawn the working capital for this marathon mission to bring culture to the hinterlands. Did Larry have the nerve to fire her? Not a chance.

So I sang, "Farewell, ancient lady, farewell—lady, lady, lady," left the Nurse with Romeo, and hurried backstage with three or four minutes to perform my penultimate Capuletization—not knowing if it would be needed, half hoping it wouldn't.

At first it seemed the problem had solved itself. Dahlia was stretched out on the couch, limp as Romeo's willie. Larry, lavender with terror, and Dee, purple with rage, were both tiptoeing around the room.

And Dahlia demonstrated the true resilience of the longtime alcoholic by springing from her resting place and shrieking like something out of Act One of the Scottish play. She was getting her second wind.

"You can't do this to me, you pusillanimous toad," she cursed. "And you! You ridiculous old ham! How dare you stab me in the back like this? Can't get a starring role any other way but stealing it from your betters, is that it? You polymorphous, talentless, scenery-chewing, ass-kissing sorry excuse for a has-been actor! I'll get you. I'll show you, all of you." She stormed from the room, but her voice drifted back. "I'll get you all!"

"And your little dog, too!" I cackled. Dee laughed nervously, but not Larry. He sank into a chair, eyes staring blindly into the distance, where I don't doubt he saw his profits flying.

Well, *really*. Has-been actor, indeed!

I stumbled through the end of Act Two, re-Mercutivated myself, and shambled out into the public square to meet my doom. By then I was a little delirious with the pain. I began to see an actual dusty street in Verona swimming in and out of view. I think it was the one from the Zeffirelli production. I frankly think I outdid myself in the swordplay that followed. I damn sure gave a hell of a performance after I was stabbed. I looked down at my wound—not so deep as a well, nor so wide as a church-door; but 'tis enough, 'twill serve—and realized that in the confusion I'd forgotten to have the target area numbed. In one side and out the back the sword had gone, and damn me but the sucker *hurt*!

"Help me, Benvolio," I said, "or I shall faint. A plague on both your houses! They have made worm's meat of me." And never, dear hearts, were those words uttered in a more heartfelt manner.

Some artists can only work when all is calm about them. I seem to thrive on disorder. The worse things get, the more strongly my craft asserts itself. By Act Four I was solidly in the role. I *was* Juliet. Cast members began to come up to me in the wings and whisper encouragement and congratulations. It meant very little to me; I was living the next scene already.

But at one point I did become aware of a tall, broad-shouldered man holding out a piece of paper to Dee, who was looking at it and shaking her head. He moved on to Friar Lawrence and Paris, who were awaiting their entrance. Paris frowned at the paper, shrugged and shook his head, and went on. The fellow drifted over to me.

"Excuse me," he said, in a voice like sandpaper on a bass fiddle. "I'm looking for a man by the name of Kenneth C. Valentine."

"And who might you be?"

He produced a private detective's license which alleged his name was Manuel P. Garcia, and that he was authorized by the principality of Brementon—an autonomous region of the great Outland Free State—to issue bail bonds, apprehend fugitives, conduct investigations, carry a nonnuclear weapon, and in general skulk, lurk, pussyfoot, slink, creep, and lie in ambush. What it really meant was he'd been thrown off the Brementon police force and was eking out a living the only way he knew how.

"Is he in trouble again?" I asked.

"I just need to talk to him, lady. Do you know where he lives?"

"Right now, in the same hotel with the rest of us. Look, I'm sort of busy here. But I know who might be able to help you." I grabbed my makeup bag from its emergency perch in the wings and rummaged through it. "His name is Dowd. Elwood P. Dowd. Here, let me give you one of his cards." I handed it to him. "Now if you want to call him use that number, not this one. That number is the old one. Or you can hang around for the curtain. I'm sure Mr. Valentine will show up then."

I went out on the stage, fuming. God alone knew what Sparky Valentine had been up to this time. He was always in trouble of one sort or another. Having him hauled off into court would cause the production a lot of trouble.

"Yea, noise?" I whispered. I felt a steely resolve building within me. I could barely see for the tears streaming down my face. "Then I'll be brief. O happy dagger! This is thy sheath." I plunged it into my breast. "There rest, and let me die." I collapsed across Romeo's prostrate body and felt the total relaxation of death steal over me.

God, was I good.

I could actually hear sobs from the audience, that group of tough, semiliterate Outlanders. Well, it may be the saddest story ever told. It's been making people weep for six hundred years.

Could real death be any more peaceful than this? Could an actor get so far into a role as to actually die onstage? I'm not saying I felt death, but I had been so deep in Juliet that some reasonable imitation had taken me. I did not want to open my eyes. I did not wish to get up. When the curtain came down they had to lift me off of Romeo and carry me into the wings.

I was alive enough to take my bows. They'll have to screw me into a real coffin before I miss that.

The applause was deafening.

Unfortunately I wasn't able to stick around for the second curtain call. I hurried up the stairs to the dressing room, where Elwood had my trunk already packed. We wrestled it into the elevator and rode up to the weightless, centrifugal hub, took a moving beltway to a taxi dock, and a taxi to the spaceport, where a high-gee was boosting for Pluto in one hour.

It was a nervous hour, but soon I could see Brementon dwindling on the ship's rear screen, and relaxed for the first time since the curtain rose.

For you see, I am K. C. Valentine. But call me Sparky; all my friends do.

Judy was hollering something about Brick and Skipper, so Punch shouted back.

"You shut up or I'm gonna hit you with this crutch!"

But Judy never shuts up. So Punch started whaling away.

That's not the way it's written, but sometimes you have to punch up a play here and there if it lacks action. For a long time I'd stuck faithfully to the classical Punch and Judy repertoire, putting on everything from *The Brigand Chief* to *Vendetta, or The Corsican's Revenge*. After you've spent three or four weeks staring up Judy's skirt at her wide, flat butt, you get a little desperate to try some new material.

Now Maggie was shouting something about no-neck monsters, which didn't sit well with Dixie. They began to tussle back and forth across the stage. Judy got the upper hand and flung Dixie out into the audience. (I could see fifteen people through the peephole in the curtain; it was the best I'd done all day.)

Even if I could have held my hands above my head for three hours, no one but vagrants were going to stick around that long. Street theater is meant to be performed for people with a little time to kill while going from one place to another. Thirty minutes is about tops. Fifteen is a lot better. So *Henry VI* parts one, two, and three was right out. *A Midsummer Night's Dream* had gone over fairly well, as had *King Lear*. The critics had been cool to *Cyrano,* for some reason; with all the swordplay, I'd thought it a natural.

All the above had needed a little pruning here and there, of course.

But my last performance had left me a little cool to the Bard. I moved on to musical comedy. It turned out Punch and Judy were naturals at it. The children loved the songs, and the adults liked the jokes. I began alternating *My Fair Lady* with Sondheim's *Sweeney Todd* and managed to keep myself diverted for two weeks.

"I'm not dyin' of cancer, Gooper. It's nothing but a spastic colon."

"Of course not, Big Daddy. Have you made out your will yet?"

That's right. It was *Cat on a Hot Tin Roof,* with Punch and Judy as Brick and Maggie, the Devil as Big Daddy, the Crocodile as Big Mama, Toby the Dog as Gooper, and Hector the Horse as Sister Woman. And featuring Tennessee Williams as Man Spinning in Grave. Don't cry for me, Mississippi.

I don't know how many times Punch and Judy have saved my bacon. For an itinerant thespian, the skills of the Punchman can be a heaven-sent alternative to a life of crime, or worse, honest work.

It costs nothing. I have carefully preserved in my trunk six character heads made for me many years ago by a fan. But I make new ones regularly from papier-mâché, the ingredients for which can be mined from garbage bins behind any large food store. For paints, go to a flea market, engage an artist in conversation, and soon you will have the use of a palette and brushes. Costumes can be made from scraps begged from a dressmaker, or scrounged from dustbins, if you're handy with a needle and thread. Any actor who is *not* handy with a needle and thread needs to get out and see the real world more often.

There is a standard plastic packing crate you will locate easily if you haunt the delivery ways backing a mall. Sticks or stiff wire will make a frame to support the box above your head. Cut a hole in front, paint the proscenium with gay finials, arabesques, and dadoes. Now attach the curtain to the bottom edges of the box. If you can't find enough scraps, use your bedroll. Presto! You've just made a castelli, or swazzle-box, which, if you didn't know, is a curtained enclosure the size of a shower stall, with the Punch and Judy stage above it.

As my father used to say, "If you've got some ham, play *Hamlet.*"

And I'd reply, "If you lay an egg, scramble it."

Thus we dined on many a meal of ham and eggs. And in the process, I learned how to make something out of nothing.

· · ·

"I *do* love you, Brick. I *do*!" said Judy.

"Wouldn't it be funny if that was true?"

I pressed on the pedal with one foot, causing the music to swell to a climax, and as Brick went into Maggie's arms I bit the cork dangling at my left and yanked the stage curtain closed.

There was applause, so I pulled the cord on the other side and opened the curtain again, slapping Punch and Judy down into the character rack in front of me, jamming my hands into Hector and the black glove I use to handle Toby, holding them up to take their bows. Toby yapped excitedly, dangling from his harness, six kilos of French ham. He's the only dog I ever knew who preferred plaudits to provender. I dropped him to the floor along with his bucket. He picked it up and ducked under the curtain to work the crowd.

The Crocodile, the Devil, then Punch and Judy. If a Punchman ever figured how to let the whole cast take bows at once, I never heard of it. I'll continue to bring them on in pairs until I grow another arm. I put my eye to the judas and saw the crowd had grown to perhaps two dozen. Toby trotted from one to another in his ruffled collar and pointed hat, holding out the bucket, barking if he didn't think enough was dropped into it, walking on his hind legs for the really hard cases, doing a back flip for the big spenders. Nobody can turn a tip like Toby.

I pulled the curtain closed and waited awhile. Lots of puppeteers reveal themselves at the end, take a bow of their own. I don't approve of it. My hands have done the performing. No need to break the spell. Let them go their separate ways with visions of brightly painted imps dancing in their sugar-plum heads.

While I waited I reached into my mouth and popped out the silver swazzle. I always get a warm feeling when I handle it. It's nearly three hundred years old, and was given to me by my father. Families used to pass along expensive pocket watches, father to son. In my family, it was the swazzle.

It's a simple device. This one had been hammered from two coins, shaped to fit into the roof of the mouth. The two pieces were wired together, and between them was . . . well, I'm not going to tell you. Swazzle-making was a closely guarded secret among Punchmen for centuries, and though

I'm sure no one cares today, it just wouldn't feel right to spill the beans. But I can say it works something like a kazoo. With the swazzle in your mouth (and with a *lot* of practice) you can make that distinctive Punch twang/buzz/screech, like no other sound I've ever heard.

Everybody swallows the swazzle at least once while learning the trade. Getting it back is one of the prices you pay. Nobody ever told me art would be painless.

Toby stuck his nose under the curtain and set his pail at my feet. I lifted the castelli from its sockets in my belt, shrugged the curtain over my shoulders, and set the box on the floor, inverted. All the puppets fit neatly inside, and the curtain folded over it. (The curtain was also my sleeping bag, but since the bag is edged with gold braid and patterned in a comedy/tragedy mask motif, few ever suspected.) As I was doing this Toby nipped at my sleeve. When I frowned at him he looked off to his left, where my following gaze discovered a uniformed policeman leaning against a wall and twirling his nightstick at the end of a leather thong.

"Box, Toby," I said, and the dog leaped in on top of the curtain. I lifted it and walked past the flatfoot.

"Top o' the mornin' to you, Officer," I said, tipping my hat. He nodded, still regarding me thoughtfully, probably comparing my face with the ones he'd studied, pinned to the precinct wall, at the start of his shift. With any luck, he wouldn't make a match.

Or he could have been deciding whether or not to brace me on the matter of a performance permit, or a puppeteer's license, or a canine registration, or any of the thousand other forms citizens see fit to employ to harass people like me. I had no idea if any of the above were required here; it had been a long time since I'd been on this planet. I remembered it as reasonably loose, easygoing, even a little eccentric, like its orbit. But if history teaches us anything it is that frontiers become settled, then set, then rigidly bureaucratized, and the more bureaucrats there are, the more laws are needed to keep them fed. I hadn't been here in many years. It was time enough for lawyers to have sucked the blood from this society.

"Hey, you," said the minion of law and order. They are two of the most dreaded words I know, when coming from a blue suit. Well, Sparky, you can play deaf, you can play innocent, or you can run. But can you hide? I turned, and gave him Tom Sawyer. He made a poor Aunt Becky.

I barely got my hand up in time to snag the spinning coin that was coming my way.

"Good show," he said. A patron of the arts, a possibility I hadn't considered. "Nice dog, too," he added.

"Bless you, guv'nor," I said, tipping my hat again. "Punch thanks you, Judy thanks you, my dog thanks you, and I thank you."

And I sauntered away down the central promenade of a mall that could have been on Mercury, could have been on Mars, but happened to be on Pluto.

Civilization at last.

The high-gee transport in which I made my hasty exit from Brementon was called the *Guy Fawkes*, following an Outlander tradition of naming their vessels after famous rogues. Fawkes was a Norwegian, I believe, who invented some sort of explosive. Our trip outward had been aboard the *Quisling*.

Ships in the outlands fell into three categories, I learned on the long inbound voyage. There were the medium-sized "hoppers" that served local city clusters and returned to Pluto or the Neptunian moons every decade or so. The *Quisling* (named, if I recall, after someone involved in rigging game shows in the early days of television), or Big Q as we called her, was one of these. She had started her days as an inner planet cruise ship, but had been obsolete for that purpose for a century. And she was showing her age.

Then there were the vast, slow cargo carriers, unmanned, that might take seventy or eighty years to reach the markets on Mars or Mercury. You know, I never did find out what it was they carried. You know something else? I never did really care. What I do know is it must be very valuable, and it must be found nowhere else. There's no other possible explanation for people being in the outlands in the first place. I postulate they were shaving the tails off comets. What else is out there?

And last, there were the "zipper" ships, small and fast, like the *Guy*. The *Guy Fawkes* was infinitely superior to the Big Q in one area, and that was velocity. In every other way, it suffered.

Certainly, the *Quisling*'s staterooms smelled bad. Sure, the food was indifferently prepared and usually cold. Yes, the whole cast did come down with an infestation of fleas just short of Boondocks. The tiny bars of soap crumbled in your hand—*if* you could get the rusty water to flow in your shower in the first place—and the toilets muttered menacingly all night and flooded on some sort of lunar cycle. Ah, but a smelly stateroom is better than no room at all. The toilets were unreliable, but they were *there,* one to a room.

There's an old joke about one actor turning to another and commenting on how terrible the food is in this hotel. To which the other replies, "Yes, and such small portions." I'd never really appreciated it until boarding the *Guy*. Soon I was thinking of my cantankerous toilet on the *Quisling* with real nostalgia: a poor thing, but mine own. There was one toilet on the *Guy*, for 150 passengers. There had been two, but one had exploded a few months before. That's right, I said exploded. You could still see blood stains on the ceiling above it. I'll say this: it reduced the waiting time. Most of us stalled until we were dancing, then sort of hovered over it, alert for any premonitory gurgle. Which proved to be a good idea, as one brave soul who actually *sat* became the victim of a "transient pressure deficit," a term I wrote down as soon as the captain told us, it being the best euphemism for vacuum—a word spacers avoid—I'd heard in my many years in space. If you want to know what happened, I propose an experiment for the curious student. Drop a few burning matches into a beer bottle, then set a hard-boiled egg over the mouth. We pried for fifteen minutes before we could get him loose. He described the experience as "like an enema in reverse" and improvised a bedpan for the rest of the trip, as did most everyone else.

I know it's in mighty poor taste to dwell at length on such a subject. Normally I wouldn't, but nothing else could so quickly and succinctly give you a picture of conditions aboard the *Guy*. It had all the stinks, fleas, cockroaches, rats, and rusty water the *Quisling* did, and it was crammed into a much smaller space. It had worse food, and not enough of it. We slept on drawers that rolled in and out of the wall like slabs in a morgue. This put you about a foot away from your neighbors on each side, above, and below, and gave you a unique opportunity for research into the sounds and smells of a class of humanity most people never get to meet.

I did mention that much of Brementon was a prison colony, didn't I? Then it stands to reason that more than half my fellow passengers were parolees, or people who had finished their terms. Mostly the latter, as Brementon didn't get a lot of the sort *anybody* would *ever* trust on parole. So night after night I lay there and listened to conversations that would curl your hair, and to other, involuntary sounds polite society tries to pretend don't exist. So *that's* what a man who murdered his mother sounds like when he farts. Interesting. And that smell, that's the dirty socks of a ritual cannibal.

"It's all material, Dodger," my father used to say when events had brought us to a particularly perilous pass. "You can use all of this. Next time you have to play despair, why, you can just think back to this." And he'd smile, and pinch my cheek.

I said "night after night," but that's misleading, too. Of course, there is no night in space, particularly out where we were. And my sleep period was not even ship's night. We shared the bunks, you see, in eight-hour shifts. And if you think the linen got changed between shifts you haven't been listening. I don't think the linen got changed between *flights*.

And while I've got the chance, I'd like to complain to the management about that transit time of six months. Is this any way to run a railroad? What we did was blast at an ungodly acceleration for what seemed like days (they swore it was more like hours), and then we *coasted* the entire trip, until it was time to slow down at Pluto. I tried complaining to the captain, but he was exasperating about it, as spacers always are. Trying to tell me it was more "economical" to use all our reaction mass in one big kick, as hard as we could stand it, and then another one at the end. I ask you, does that make sense? Wouldn't it be better to boost at a sane, comfortable one gee until we got halfway there, then do the same thing slowing down? Or if we didn't have enough fuel for that (I'll admit I'm a bit vague on some of the details), at least spread the acceleration out. It stands to reason we'd build up more speed that way, and I'm sure we'd get there more rapidly. I'm convinced we were cheated. I shall write my congressperson, really I shall.

Because the kicker to the whole sorry mess was that, for all that uncomfortable "economy," we ended up paying *an eighty percent surcharge on our tickets*! As if that third-rate cattle car were some crack liner! And what did we get for our money? Bone-breaking jackrabbit starts and stops, and six months of free fall with no soap or showers.

That eighty percent fee almost killed me. After beating a hasty retreat from the Playhouse, thinking the hounds were literally nipping at my heels, I trundled my trunk into the spaceport secure in the knowledge that I had a confirmed booking on the next ship out, which was the *Fawkes*. Out of long habit I had made such a reservation, in Elwood's name, on every ship that was scheduled to leave Brementon. This wasn't much of a chore, as Brementon was not King City Interplanetary; arrivals and departures were at an average rate of one every three days. At more civilized facilities I would memorize flight schedules for a selection of possible emergency destinations. At Brementon, it was take it or leave it.

One precept my father put right up there with "always cut the cards" was never to embark on a road trip without your return ticket in your pocket. If you were my best friend, and came to me swearing that without the loan of a fiver your dear sweet mother would die of a horrible disease, and all I had in my pocket was my return ticket, I would look you in the eye and swear I was penniless. I would cheerfully listen to the old broad croak her last, secure in the knowledge I'd done the right thing.

So I thought I was in good shape when I slapped my ticket down on the counter, trying not to look over my shoulder, and that's when I was let in on the closely guarded secret (actually, it was buried in the fine print when I looked, later) that sent me scrambling to my purse to discover that, even with gold fillings in my teeth, I couldn't do better than sixty percent. Not, that is, until I recalled the antique diamond brooch I'd discovered only the day before, carelessly and shamefully neglected upon Dahlia Smithson's dresser top. I'd just been passing by in the corridor, honest, when the thing seemed to call out to me. I feel that when you own something as fine as that you are obligated to be more careful with it. I'd meant to tell her that, too, but events intervened, and here I was shy a bit of cash, so there was nothing for it but to sell the brooch to a larcenous ticket agent for a twentieth of what it would have fetched in any pawnshop in Luna.

All this, mind you, when Larry held a tidy sum in his accounts, two weeks' pay, that rightly should have come to me but which I was by then powerless to collect. I gnashed my teeth, leveled a mighty curse on the ticket agent, his heirs and assigns unto the seventh generation, and boarded ship.

This is why I debarked at Lowell Interplanetary with three dollars and a set of Punch and Judy dolls.

You're probably wondering just what the private detective wanted to talk to me about. I know I was, though I didn't dwell on it. There's nothing to be gained by that, and *certainly* nothing to be gained by sticking around to find out. It was sheer luck he came searching for "Mercutio," armed with his picture from the playbill, and that the poor boy was by then a grave man. Fortune doesn't smile so brightly on me every day, and when she does I don't insult her by asking a lot of questions.

But I'll admit, I did wonder. Was it that business on Boondocks? I swear, I didn't know the girl was the governor's daughter.

This mall that happened to be on Pluto was called Cerberus Place, and that name forces me to admit that, though a mall is a mall is a mall, this one couldn't *really* be on Mars or Mercury. Not unless the Martian or Mercurian mall was attempting a Plutonian look.

It is a major failing of modern society, to my mind, that most of the inhabited planets don't have a style of their own. Oh, there are minor differences, of course, a few things here and there that would lead you to believe you were on Miranda and not on Luna. Mostly these are in the category of monuments, tourist attractions. As on Old Earth the Statue of Liberty was emblematic of New York, the Eiffel Tower meant Paris. There was no Lunar look, as there had been a Japanese, or a Danish, or Mexican, or Nigerian look. No one would be walking around in "Lunarian" costume, living in Lunarian buildings, doing Lunarian folk dances in their peculiarly Lunarian steel shoes. Cultural and stylistic differences were dealt a death blow by the Invasion, which left only one human ethos really viable. That culture has been called Techno-

English by its admirers, Judeo/Anglo/Cyber/NASA/Caucasian and much less flattering combinations by those who love it less. Certainly the Techno-part was indispensable; people who didn't take their machines seriously soon found themselves gulping vacuum.

Pluto was the exception to the rule of uniformity. The first thing you noticed was that there was a definite, strong Plutonian accent. Other planets had slight differences in word choice and pronunciations. Plutonians (or Stygians, or Hadeans, as they sometimes called themselves) spoke with a pronounced twang that could be indecipherable to the untrained ear.

Then there was the architecture. There was a distinct Hadean style, most pronounced in older structures. The remarkable thing was that a Hadean style existed at all. Its reason for being lay in Pluto's unique historical place among the Eight Worlds. For its first century of human habitation, it had been a prison planet.

There's a deep urge in the human soul to send the bad people as far away as possible from "decent folk." On Earth, Australia was a prime example. Post-Invasion, Pluto seemed to fit the bill, and today, it's Brementon. If society succeeds in pushing criminals any farther, we'll find we have achieved star travel.

I don't know what Australia was like. Probably a fairly awful place for urban transportees. In the case of Pluto, the urge for distant exile was purely a psychological one. Living in one place where the atmosphere is inimical or nonexistent is pretty much like living in any other. You burrow underground, you husband your oxygen, you struggle to grow things you can eat, you bear and raise children. As time goes by, all these things get easier. Who really cares if the struggle is on Luna or on Pluto?

Obviously, the early Lunarian voters did. They sent their prisoners there by the thousands over the decades. There must have been a lot of self-righteous satisfaction in shipping your incorrigibles off to a place that was a synonym for hell.

Like remote prison colonies before it, Pluto had developed a convict/citizen society. Sentences were always for life, but could be served behind bars, in labor camps, or in relative freedom, depending on the offense. But even the "free" prisoners despised the guard class and the ruling elite, a social division that survives, in some respects, to this very day. The place is run, by and large, by descendants of criminals. But the richest families trace themselves back to the Regents, as they call themselves. Or "screws," as everyone else knows them.

Had enough history for today? Hold on, I'm almost through.

The Hadeans, as many downtrodden people had before them, eventually made being outcasts a source of pride. Send us to Hell, will you? All right, we'll glory in it. We'll be hellcats, hellhounds, and hellions. We'll be hellacious hell-raisers, hellborn and hellbred.

Aesthetically, the Plutonian style embraced the colors red and black—excessively, to my eye. Shapes were massive, and tended to loom. Fire was a frequent motif, stone a frequent building material. Hadeans were big on obsidian. There was something vaguely Egyptian to it all ... if the Pharaohs had painted their temples glossy black, with crimson highlights.

Philosophically, the obsession with all things Abyssal led to the founding of one of the two great religions established since the Invasion: Diabolism.

Morally, the combination of distance, banishment, and rebellion (the result, I'd always felt, of a planetary inferiority complex) had formed a society viewed as permissive in a milieu not noted for social constraints. It was easier to murder someone on Pluto, for instance, than anyplace in the system. You could mount a valid defense based on a legal principle the locals summed up as "He needed killin'," and if you could prove it, not even pay a fine to your victim's survivors.

And practically, the interactions of frontier vigor, strong competitive instincts, a neurotic impulse to prove oneself better than one's rivals, and something hardly known elsewhere in the system—a solid work ethic—had produced a civilization perpetually nipping at the heels of those old-line bastions, those stuffier, more comfortable, and much more smug rival claimants to the mantle of Center of Humanity: Luna and Mars.

So it was through these infernal environs I trudged after my last show of the day. And I do mean trudged; Pluto's gravity is not much, but I'd been in free fall a very long time and didn't have my ground legs back yet. When you add in the fact that I'd been standing in the castelli for almost six hours with only a few rests, you get one tired polymorphous, scenery-chewing, talentless, sorry excuse for a has-been actor.

Six months later, and that *still* stung!

But I wouldn't think about that now. I'd think about it tomorrow.

Toby had very little sympathy for the pains human flesh is heir to. He trotted along five or six steps ahead of me, pausing every ten or fifteen seconds to look back, impatient but too polite to say anything.

Toby? That's right, you haven't really been introduced, yet, have you?

I picked him up at a theatrical supply shop, it must be forty-five, fifty years ago. Toby comes from a line of show folk almost as long as my own. He's a bichon frise, in theory, which is French for "curly lapdog." His forebears capered in the court of the Sun King. They fared no better in the French Revolution than the Bourbons themselves, and afterward eked out a living in the circus ring. Like many other dog breeds, they were wiped out in the Invasion, revived during the following century from the Genetic Library, and in Toby's case, extensively tinkered with in the process.

He looks just like a standard pre-Invasion Bichon, which is to say he is covered with fleecy white curly hair, has beady black eyes set in a head like the puffball of a dandelion. When combed out and groomed he looks much bigger than he really is, which is about fourteen inches tall. Somewhere in his chromosomes are genes that evolved in squirrels before being snipped out and pasted into the canine species. This enables him to hibernate, with the proper chemical stimulus.

He doesn't seem to grow any older while he's hibernating. This, and a bit more genetic high jinks, accounts for his good health at such an extreme age.

And there's something else in the mix. Some say it's monkey genes, some whisper that it's human—but *that*, of course, would be illegal, so I'm sure it's not true. Ahem. Whatever the source, he does have a remarkable brain. He learns very quickly, responds to over two hundred verbal commands and about as many gestures, and has even demonstrated initiative and discrimination, as when he recognized the idling cop as a possible source of trouble. On the other hand, being from a line of actors, he might have inherited that ability honestly.

He tolerates costumes of all sorts. He knows his part in twenty-five Punch and Judy plays and learns his cues in new shows with no more than two rehearsals. He can prance all day on his hind legs, climb ladders, walk a tightrope, jump through a hoop of fire. He gets horribly depressed if the show bombs and would walk by a raw sirloin to steal that extra bow. In short, a trouper down to his little toenails.

He's also something of a mathematical whiz, being able to count to five. I know this to be true because numbers six and above confuse and depress him. He'll worry for hours about the difference between a pile of six coins and a pile of eight coins. Ask him which is larger and he'll mope all day. But he can make change for a nickel.

I've often thought that, with just double the IQ, he could master the decimal system and become a stockbroker.

I counted the day's take as we strolled the eighteenth promenade of Cerberus Place, and realized this was going to be a big day for us.

"Looks like we've got enough, Toby," I said. "With a few shekels left over for some dinner." He understood only the last word of that, but he understood that word very well, and turned a back flip in celebration. Then he led me to the pushcart on the nineteenth level, no doubt recalling how we'd had to pass it by the evening before, a terrible day for the theater. I bought two hot pretzels and two steaming, juicy bratwurst on sourdough buns, slathering mustard, relish, and a little sauerkraut on the latter. I cajoled the vendor into giving us a cup of water and a plastic bowl, then carried the whole glorious mess to a nearby picnic table, where we sat down, just like citizens, and had our evening's repast.

Well, I sat. Toby stood on the table and watched me cut the brat with my pocketknife and put the slices in the plastic bowl. I added a dab of the pickle relish and more of the mustard.

"Is that enough mustard?" I asked him, and he barked once. "Enough" was the key word there; I don't think he knew "mustard." He knew he liked it, you understand. He just wouldn't recognize the word if I said it to him. Toby likes mustard, can deal with relish, prefers to leave the sauerkraut alone.

The one bark, you may have figured out, meant "yes." One for yes, two for no. Can *you* count to *two,* boys and girls?

"Too bad there's no wine, eh, Toby?" He didn't answer, too busy with his little muzzle in the bowl, chowing down. And I wasn't really complaining. For weeks we'd had mostly rice cakes. Twice I'd splurged on a jar of peanut butter. The brats were straight from heaven.

The business day was winding down around us. Cerberus Place was not a big mall, just another dozen levels above us, possibly half a mile across and two miles long. It looked to have been a natural surface feature at one time, roofed over, pressurized, heated, then terraced like a farmer contour plowing, tunneled, excavated, paved, lighted, landscaped, painted, decorated, and presto! Open for business. What nightlife there was seemed to be concentrated on the upper levels. Down here on the nineteenth the stores were closed, a few employees locking the doors and trudging off to the slideways, patrolbots and a few human security guards making their entrances. The vendor had shut down his grill and wheeled his cart away. Toby and I were left with the little pocket park to ourselves. I gazed out over the mall as I ate, registering nothing really novel. The floor was a manicured park, with tidy trees and streetlights lining the walking paths, a little railroad running around the edges. There were half a dozen freestanding apartment buildings in the park, all fifteen stories high, all mounted on turntables so the residents had ever-changing views. Rents would be high in those sparkling jewel boxes.

I could see a little amusement park down there. A carousel turned, the horses bobbing up and down with no one riding them. For some reason it made me sad.

We finished our meal. I poured a little water in Toby's dish and let him lap it up. He had mustard stains around his mouth, so I wet part of my handkerchief and dabbed at him until he was clean, then combed the hair on his head until it stood out as it was supposed to. He never trusts me on that; he began to bark, so I sighed and took out the small hand mirror and held it up for him. He studied his image until he

THE GOLDEN GLOBE ••• 31

was satisfied he was in a fit state to meet his public, then graciously allowed me to carry the wrappings to a garbage can.

Two of the human security guards had paused as they walked by our table. A person alone is suspicious to the cop mind. Two people together, of course, are probably planning something. Three is a gang, and five is a riot waiting to happen. You can't win. Can *you* count to *five,* Officer?

We set off for the Outland Lines freight office.

The second thing I hadn't counted on in my journey from Brementon to Pluto, after the eighty percent surcharge, was the new Wandering Thespian Harassment Assessment Fee. They didn't call it that, naturally—some bullshit about a Spaceport Improvement Luggage Excise—but that was the effect. There now was a duty on each piece of luggage you brought in to Pluto.

I spent most of my first day on Pluto shouting at an endless series of obstinate officials. Result: no tickee, no luggee. The one bright point was that they couldn't simply confiscate my trunk, though it was plain in their eyes they all viewed this as an unfortunate technical oversight in the law, soon to be remedied. But they could damn sure keep it until I paid the fee. I left there with my tail between my legs—and my dog in my hand. Arguments that the tools of my trade, my means of making the money to *pay* their goddam extortion, were all in my trunk, fell on the usual deaf ears. But I told them that if I couldn't get my hibernating dog out of his box and feed him he would die in a week and I'd hit the spaceport, the city, the county, and most important, *you,* asshole, with a lawsuit the likes of which this stinking iceball of a planet had never seen. They leafed through their books of regulations and found nothing to cover the situation and so, grudgingly, let me open the trunk and get Toby out. While I did it I got my bedroll and my puppets, as well, and no one said anything.

All bunkum. Toby would have been fine for five months.

I was dying to tell one of them that, but when we entered the freight office and announced I was ready to pay the ransom on my belongings, none of the officials there had been present at my disembarking. That's the way it is with these people, you know. You never see the same ones twice. I think they're composted at the end of the day, and new ones spring full-grown from the muck, like toadstools.

"All the world's *not* a stage," my father had been fond of saying. "Only the best part of it. Between shows, you'll need good luggage."

It's good advice, and I've always taken it to heart. In my career I've lived in nine-room hotel penthouse suites and plush-carpeted modular winnies trucked to location sites. I've owned luxury condos and homes in the most exclusive Disneylands. At times I've owned enough things to lease storage modules simply to accommodate the excess.

More often, everything I own could be packed into one trunk. It's a big trunk, granted, but if you think it's easy, look around your own surroundings and ask yourself if *you* could do it.

Remember I talked about a return ticket, when going on the road? My attachment to that ticket would rate as a pale thing indeed compared to the tenacity with which I would hold on to that trunk. Imagine how you'd feel if murdering rapists were holding your children hostage, and you'll get some idea how upset I was to learn I couldn't take my trunk with me on arrival.

Pawnbrokers weep with joy when they see me coming, begin planning that long-delayed rumpus room in the basement or a nice vacation on Oberon. But while the trunk may contain many items I'll cheerfully hock, the trunk itself is sacred. It contains everything of any importance to me.

Don't shop for one like it at your local outfitter. It was custom-made for me thirty years ago by the firm of Signe & Powell, christened the Pantechnicon Mark III. (I also owned the original, and the Mark II, replacing each not so much because it had worn out or become obsolete, but because I had the money, and a few new ideas.) It is waterproof, vacuumproof, fireproof, and proof against most forms of radiation. It's . . . well, it has so many features that any useful description would quickly start sounding like an operator's manual, so perhaps it's best just to mention them as needed. But if in the course of my story the Pantechnicon blacks up, gets down on one knee, and starts to belt out "Swanee River," don't be too surprised.

· · ·

The nine-room penthouse suites were but a passing memory these days. Lately, Toby and I had been sleeping rough in mall service corridors.

You can spend a long life beneath the surface of one of the Eight Worlds without ever visiting a service corridor, unless you are a delivery person or work in the stockroom of one of the stores it adjoins. These are not exactly public spaces, but they're not precisely private, either. You don't need a permit or a security badge to enter most of them, but *finding* the entrance is usually beyond the powers of the uninitiated, at least the sort of entrance I was looking for. Getting to them should have been easy. Simply walk into any store, any retail outlet at all, follow the signs to the emergency fire exit. This will take you through the stockroom . . . where you will be seen, bothered, and usually turned back by some meddlesome employee, especially if you're wheeling a trunk the size of a small asteroid. No, it was seldom that easy in practice. The public and service corridors are like the human circulatory system. Arteries carry goods from the factories to the point of sale, veins carry them back to consumers' homes. The great engine of commerce flows freely at all points, but the two flows never mix.

But if you know how to get back there, unchallenged— and I'd learned it at my father's knee—you will find a Spartan realm free of the madding crowds. It is a place of dim lighting, high ceilings, gray walls, completely utilitarian as few places in the public world are.

It's a dangerous place until you know the ropes. Robot and manned vehicles zip along paths whose system is not intuitively obvious, following signals and signs you may not even see unless you know what to look for. It's a good place to get squashed like a bug beneath a fifty-wheel flatbed goods train equipped with only token lights and brakes; the operator usually will never know he hit you. So don't go back there unless you're with somebody like Uncle Sparky, who knows the ropes, okay, boys and girls?

The great advantage to this huge, unknown city is that people will usually leave you alone once you've gained entrance. This is where the down-and-outers hide from the rousting nightstick and the contemptuous stare. Winos, tramps,

vagabonds, swagmen, and other ladies and gentlemen of leisure drift away from their daytime endeavors to find a private
corner here where one can spread his kip and not be bothered.
Did you ever wonder where city pigeons go to build their
nests and raise their pidglings? This is the place.

This is also the site of that peculiar abode known as the
jungle. By following a few seemingly random chalk marks
on walls, marks that you probably would not even have seen,
and certainly couldn't have read even if you knew there was
information in them, I made my way to a warehouse door.
There was a court seal on it, promising me that if I broke it
I would be subject to a fine and jail time. But the date was
twenty years previous and the printing was almost illegible.
Places like these, full of useless merchandise attached in connection with a bankruptcy dating to when dinosaurs walked
the Earth, were among the least frequented and policed areas
on any civilized planet. Which was just fine with the hoboes
who came here to gather around the fire and swap stories just
as they had in the heyday of the railroads on Earth.

Toby and I picked our way through towering stacks of
dusty crates in the darkness, guided only by a light from the
Pantechnicon. We came to a huge open space, at the far end
of which was a flickering orange light with human shapes
sitting around it. Toby took off, barking. You don't sneak up
on a group of 'bos, but I never had to worry about announcing
myself when Toby was up and around.

I got there to find Boots Lumpkin putting down a plate for
the dog. Toby himself was working his way around the circle,
greeting his friends, some of whom he'd known for thirty
years, others he'd met the night before.

"Easy on the mulligan, Boots," I said, setting the trunk
down on its end. "That rascal put away a sausage big as his
own hind leg an hour ago."

"Gotcha," said Boots, and ladled a bit of stew into the
bowl while Toby threw me a reproachful look. The crazy
hound would have eaten whatever was put in front of him,
though his belly was round as a beach ball, because it's rude
to turn down stew in a hobo jungle, and because that's just
what dogs do.

I was greeted around the circle by those who knew me,
introduced to those few I hadn't met.

"Looks like you finally got your bindle back," Sarge Pollito called out, which was always good for a laugh. While nobody there actually had his goods tied in a handkerchief and hung from a stick, comparing the Pantechnicon Mark III with the canvas backpacks, haversacks, kitbags, portmanteaux, and valises that contained the belongings of these happy mudlarks was comical indeed.

"Will the butler be arriving soon?" someone called out.

"Had to let the blighter go, Skids," I said, ruefully. "He just *wouldn't* keep the silver polished." I accepted a plate of stew, shook my head to the offer of coffee. It keeps me awake.

"Hard to get good help these days," said Rivkah the Jewess.

"You said it, Riv. I'm looking for a new upstairs maid. Interested?"

She punched my shoulder, and I sat on the trunk and spooned up the stew.

One night in 1867, in a railyard in Ohio—so the story goes—a 'bo knocked over a rabbit with a good toss of a stone. He skinned it, chopped in a potato and a few wild onions and carrots he found growing trackside, added some flour and salt and pepper, then tossed the whole mess in his billy and boiled it up. It tasted so good he saved some for the next night, when another hobo offered some venison jerky to add to the mix. The third night he met a man who had some beans and a chili pepper. The night after that it was raccoon. And since that unfortunate coney met his maker, every bird of the air and beast of the earth, every fish that swims in the sea, every creepy-crawlie that wriggles on its belly or burrows in the mud has had its turn in the stewpot. The mulligan had been ladled over chow mein noodles, spooned over eggs, slapped into sloppy joe sandwiches, sizzled with dumplings, rolled up in crepes, and slipped under mashed potatoes. The Eternal Mulligan is boiled anew every night; you donate what you can to the pot, take out what you need—it is always shared with all present.

And somewhere on my plate, I fancied, was the tiniest bit of that jackrabbit who was just a little bit too slow one night in Ohio, almost four hundred years ago, on the poor Old Earth.

Highly unlikely, I'm well aware. But hey, cobber, there's no need to rain on my parade, eh? A sense of continuity is nothing to sneer at in this impermanent world. Does it matter if that continuity is a fable? Is reality that sacred to you?

I put a few bread loaves, scrounged from a bakery's waste bin only an hour before, beside the stewpot as my part of the night's meal. Then I rolled the Pantech into a dim corner and prepared for the night.

The trunk sprouts two wheels and a handle for upright movement, a wheel on each corner if you'd prefer to get behind it and shove. I popped the wheels back into their sockets and opened a panel on what had been the top end before I laid the trunk on its side. An air compressor began to chug quietly, and my tent began to inflate itself.

It's made out of memory plastic. Folded, it adds about an inch to the thickness of the trunk. Deployed, it makes a cube about five feet on a side. Five of those sides are rigid as plywood and much stronger; an elephant could dance on my tent roof. The floor is full of pockets and makes quite a good air mattress.

I shoved my bedroll through the sphincter door that, in a pinch, can be almost as effective as a formal airlock. Then I squeezed myself in, reached out, and snapped on the light. I just sat there a moment, breathing my own air. It was the first time, literally the first moment I had felt safe and secure since the PI tapped me on the shoulder in Brementon.

This was the second thing that kept me sane in the *Guy Fawkes*. When I was feeling the worst, I'd slip down to the cargo hold, deploy the tent, crawl in, and sit there and shake. I'd have cheerfully passed the whole voyage in here, but the cargo area was off-limits to passengers and I lived in fear I'd be discovered and watched more carefully, so I rationed my time. What luxury to sit on my own bed, with my own six walls around me!

I ran a quick systems check, determined that the Hadean Customs Service hadn't managed to wreak any real harm, probably not from lack of trying.

Most of one wall was the top end of the trunk. I lowered a shelf from it, a shelf containing a hot plate and a teapot. I brewed up and poured into a porcelain cup that had once been the property of Judy Garland. Luckily, there was no way of authenticating this, so I was never tempted to pawn it since, in the world of collectible Terriana, provenance is all. I pulled out a drawer and using the spoon and freeze-dried cream I found there, made the tea the proper color. I noticed I was almost out of cream. (Actor: "I'll have a cuppa tea, without cream." Waiter: "We're out of cream, sir. It'll have to be without milk." Rimshot.) Where the shelf had been there was (what else) a mirror lined with strip lights, so the tent could be used as a dressing room. The whole side would fold away, providing me access to the trunk without lifting the upper lid or leaving the tent.

I spread my blankets and took off my coat, and in the process remembered something else I'd filched from the baker's garbage. Toby slipped through the lock as I took the cupcake out of my coat pocket and set it on the shelf. He watched me curiously as I rummaged in another drawer and came up with a single candle. I poked it into the cupcake.

I'd been trying to forget it, trying to make it add up another way, but there was no avoiding it. Today was my birthday. Please, in lieu of presents, send your contributions to Actors' Relief.

It was a rather significant birthday, too.

"How about it, Toby?" I asked him. "Can you count to one hundred?" He barked once, which I'm sure everyone in the class remembers meant "Yes!" Well, of course he could. Toby can count one of anything, including hundreds.

I lit the candle and was about to offer him a piece, but he scratched at the lock and looked inquiringly at me.

Ah, Tobe, what am I going to do with you? For the last week he'd been going out at night, after I was asleep. I suspected he had a girlfriend out there somewhere. That, or he was getting together with one of the packs of wild dogs rumored to live in the service corridors. Probably peeing on everything in sight. Toby is quite the ladies' man. I'd seen him, with more optimism than common sense, mooning over a Great Dane bitch he'd need a stepladder just to sniff. Sure, you can write that off to high hopes. But the amazing thing was, the bitch was looking really interested.

"Oh, sure, party time again," I said. "And may I ask you, young man, when you're going to settle down and make something of yourself?'' He waited patiently. He knows that when I get in certain moods I'm apt to toy with him, take unfair advantage of the fact I know a few more words than he does. "Go, then, and be quick about it," I said. "But so help me, if you come back smelling of strong drink . . ." He was already out the door.

So I blew out the candle, ate the cake, and pulled the covers up around my neck. I left a small night light on for Toby . . . and because I had trouble sleeping in complete darkness.

How about you, boys and girls? Can *you* count to one hundred?

"I still feel so *foolish,* Detective Friday," said the lovely Miranda Mayard-Tate as she rose from her genuine Earth-crafted Louis Quinze settee, a piece of furniture equivalent in price to the Gross Planetary Product of some smaller Uranian moons.

"Don't worry about it, ma'am," I said, in Friday's flat, affectless voice, giving her his flat, unemotional-but-earnest stare, and thinking, *Foolish? Any more foolish and respiration would be a big intellectual challenge, you pathetic screw.* I trust that opinion never showed in my face, and I continued: "You weren't the only one taken in by this bunch. But don't worry. We'll get 'em." I sketched a flat, wry smile, the only sort Joe Friday was capable of. You know Joe, the taciturn, humorless homicide dick from that old warhorse, *L.A. Blues*? I've played him in three different productions. ("Thursday. 8:03 P.M. Went to the Larson Theater, 5543 Main Street. Heard there was a 437 in progress. Acting without dramatic license. The sign said *L.A. Blues*. Went in. Sat Down. Watched the show. Gathered enough evidence to convict four cast members of emoting, hamming it up, chewing the scenery, and felonious gesticulating. Figured out the plot during first act. Issued a warrant for the playwright. The charge: clichés in the first degree. Had to let Ken Valentine go. No basis to the charge of woodenness. Found him to be resolute, implacable, just after the facts."—*Flip City Courier*.) (There was similar schtick the other times I played Friday. Why do reviewers have to be so cute?) Dropping back into Friday for

Miranda M-T's benefit was like putting my flat feet into a pair of comfortable old shoes.

"Goodness! I certainly hope so." What can I tell you? I'm not responsible for other people's lines. I merely report what I hear, even when it contains "goodness" as an exclamation.

A long, gloomy silence settled over the scene. As it threatened to become funereal, or possibly even permanent, I decided a prompt was in order.

"Well," I said, "we can get started on it if you'll just get the money."

"Oh, certainly," she said, getting up and looking around vaguely. It was obvious she'd forgotten where she put it. The rich really *are* different. "I'll just go . . . are you sure you won't have a drink?"

"Not while I'm on duty, ma'am." There was a double meaning to that. Every line Friday uttered screeched teetotaler. He wouldn't drink, on or off duty, not so much because alcohol was evil, but because it would get in the way of his relentless pursuit of crime. You just knew his evenings at home were spent perusing his old notebooks, and his idea of a good time was oiling his gun. As he said in the last line of *L.A. Blues*: "Just the facts, ma'am." That's all he was interested in. Just the facts.

Me, I would have gladly joined Miranda in a glass of something, but when I'm "on duty," playing a role, I never step out of it.

As Mrs. Mayard-Tate fluttered away to unknown regions of her palatial warren, I stood and looked at her parlor closely for the first time. What had caught my eye was a wood and glass display case housing dozens of yellow-white carvings, none much larger than a golf ball. Of all the fabulous riches in that room, the loot of generations, these are what drew me.

I was still studying them when Miranda returned carrying a small canvas bag emblazoned with the name and logo of the Bank of Hell.

"You like them?" she asked, handing the bag to me.

"I was wondering what they were, ma'am," I said.

"They're called netsuke. I've never cared for them, myself. I keep wondering if I ought to sell them. I'm told they'd bring a good price."

She probably had no idea. Any pre-Invasion artifact is worth something, but there is earthcraft, and then there is *Earthcraft*! There are societies that collect mass-produced paper clips and pencils from the twentieth century. These people keep their treasures in glassine envelopes and handle them only with tongs, but they are *not* the same crowd that traffics in netsuke.

"I think they were some sort of hair clip," she was saying, shoving vaguely at her great mass of chocolate hair. "Kind of a barrette. I never could get any of them to work. There was probably some trick to it. I guess I'm missing something."

How about several billion brain cells, darling? Netsuke . . . hair clips? I was tempted to tell her the cunning little wooden-and-ivory objects had been used to suspend items from the ceremonial sashes, or *obis,* of the gentlemen of Japan, as depicted on many a vase and jar, many a screen and fan, three or four hundred years ago. But Friday wouldn't have known that. For that matter, Sparky Valentine wouldn't have known it but for the fact I'd worn one many years before during a production of the Noh opera *Yurigi at the Straits of Awa* (". . . a not entirely successful attempt at mating Akira Kurosawa with Victor Herbert, enlivened considerably by the puckish performance of K. C. Valentine in the role of Yasuhiro."—*Neptune Trident*).

"You seem to be staring at that one."

"Was I? I hadn't realized." But it was obvious which one she was talking about. It was a frog, perched on a human skull. The skull had a thick brow ridge, and the long, bulb-tipped fingers of the frog wrapped around it and into the eye sockets. Somehow, the artist had portrayed a coiled power in the little beast, and had given it a predator's lazy eyes. They looked at you without fear or mercy, and you just knew you couldn't show them anything they hadn't seen many times already.

"Would you like a closer look?" Without waiting for a reply she reached behind the cabinet and produced an oddly shaped piece of metal—copper or brass, it looked like—which I soon realized was an antique key. She opened the case, took the frog and skull, and handed it to me.

It was cool at first, but quickly warmed, seemed almost to

soften in my hand. My thumb automatically caressed the frog's back. I looked up at her and smiled.

"Maybe I will have that drink, ma'am," I said.

Elwood was waiting for me at the edge of the big park that marked the boundary of Miranda Mayard-Tate's upper-upper-class neighborhood. He was seated on a bench, his hands jammed into the pockets of his baggy trousers, his long legs stretched out before him, the gray fedora pushed forward to almost cover his eyes. Toby sat on the bench beside him. Behind them, people in red jackets and white riding breeches and black riding boots sat atop their magnificent steeds and cantered grandly back and forth in a ritual as old as money itself. And the funds of these equestrian dandies were ancient indeed, so old that their primordial corruption served as its own fertilizer, so old that the sweet whiff of its decay overpowered the honest stink of the piles of horseshit that was all most of these people ever produced. And true to the breeding habits of the very, very rich, some of these people made my Sweet Miranda seem a mental giant.

Perhaps those thoughts seem unworthy. I knew where they came from: I was psyching myself up for Elwood, who didn't much approve of my recent activities.

Toby spotted me first, and came scampering in my direction. Elwood followed in his relaxed, shambling gait.

"You get what you came for?" he asked.

"Don't I always?"

When Toby realized I was talking to Elwood and not to him, he started to growl and bark. You don't know what terror is until you've heard a Bichon growling. After you've heard it, you *still* don't have a clue. Back in the park, I'm sure all the squirrels in earshot were helpless with laughter.

It made me sad. The fact is, Toby really can't stand Elwood. Elwood hadn't been around much since our arrival at Pluto. Now he was back, and Toby didn't like it a bit. I had to speak to him sharply, which made his head hang and his tail droop. He fell behind us and trudged along under a dark cloud of gloom, his every movement calculated to wring the last drop of guilt from his pitiless master. The awful thing was, it worked. But it wouldn't do to let Toby know that, so I shrugged my shoulders and tried to ignore him.

"I just don't think that robbing from one of the most powerful families in Pluto is the smartest thing you ever did," Elwood went on.

"Godfrey Daniel!" I exploded. "Getting somebody to hand you money is not robbery. It's a short con. They're two different things. And the fact that the Mayard-Tates are rich and powerful isn't why you object; it's that you object to thieving of any kind, from anyone, *including* these rich old screwish families who wouldn't miss a *billion* if I lifted it from them, much less the paltry and entirely reasonable sum in question."

"That's your father talking," Elwood drawled. "The last of the Wobblies."

"Here's another line from my father, while we're at it," I said. " 'Never give a sucker an even break, nor smarten up a chump.' "

"That has a familiar ring. Could it be he stole it?"

"Of course he stole it! What do you think actors *do*?"

"Always remember, son," he had told me many times. "Authors write. Producers produce. Directors interfere. Angels write checks. And it's all for us. We make the art, and if you need to borrow something to make it work, then borrow it!" Borrow was a euphemism my father used frequently, *steal* being a word he disliked. But he was an anarchist, didn't believe in property or laws.

That's how I was raised, and if it gives you a liberal comfort you can use that fact to explain or forgive my admittedly piratical attitude toward other people's possessions. Or you can think of me as a goddamn thief; I don't mind. I *do* believe in property, and in laws, though as few of them as needed to curb our animal tendencies. I own the things in my trunk, for instance, and would be peeved if they were taken from me. My father never owned anything he wouldn't have cheerfully given away if you asked him for it. Of course, he seldom owned anything worth giving away.

But take the screws. Does it make sense to you that they should have access to these almost infinite amounts of money simply because their grandparents excelled in brutality, bribery, chicanery, sadism, and the nearest thing to chattel slavery humanity has known since the American Civil War? Not far from where we were walking, human beings had been traded on a computerized auction block—though they used the polite fiction that it was the prisoners' labor contracts that were being bought and sold. That's what the old fortunes on Pluto were founded on: cheap and plentiful labor.

My father was capable of going on for hours on the subject.

I myself don't hold to any doctrine concerning wealth, and the inheritance thereof. On the one hand, who has more right to the money one has amassed during one's lifetime? Some opportunistic layabout with nothing more to recommend him than his ease-softened, skeletal, extended hand? Or one's own children? The answer seems obvious. But maybe it should be neither. Well then, how about the state? Why not let the government take it all, and use it for the public good? Mainly because when it's been tried in the past, it merely financed more official thievery.

But it is equally obvious to me that something is badly wrong when one person has billions, and another has nothing.

Damn it all! Miranda would never miss what I had taken.

It's called the Bank Examiner, and some say it was first used by one Lucius the Louse in 113 B.C., when he persuaded an octogenarian widow named Octavia to withdraw thirty pieces of silver from her account at the First Imperial Bank of the Tiber, Circus Maximus Branch, and hand them over to him: i.e., Lucius. But it's said that Lucius learned it from Agamemnon "Aggie Pop" Popodopoulis, a Greek panderer, picaroon, and president of the Athenian Bar Association, who swore he happened upon it while reading a book of Chaldean pornography to pass the time while cooped up in a giant wooden horse during his involuntary hitch in the Greek army.

In a word, it was old. One of the oldest in the book. That it would still work at this late date was a tribute to another adage my father liked to quote: "There's a sucker born every minute, and two to take him." We like to think there's been progress in the human species since the days of Aggie Pop. We like to think we're somehow smarter than previous generations. Hell, we live in outer space, don't we? Don't we build fast spaceships that violate the virgin sky with impulses of villainous saltpeter? Can't we harness the power of the heart of the sun? Don't we know what E—c*cf112* means? (Well, *I* don't, but *somebody* does, okay?)

Yes, yes, yes, and yes. And if you think that makes us one bit smarter—where it really *counts*—than our ancestors, I'd like to drop in on you and discuss the purchase of a fine set of leather-bound Classics of Human Literature, only twenty dollars down, the rest when they arrive. Don't worry, I'll give you a receipt for the twenty.

There was another thing about the Bank Examiner, other than its age, and perhaps we've finally arrived at the source of Elwood's silent reproof and my own uneasiness. It has to do with yet a third adage my father was likely to quote when the vicissitudes of our profession forced us once again into a closer and more personal contact with the audience, and their pocketbooks. When it became necessary to take to the streets for a spot of improvisation. When, in short, it was time to run a short con.

"Dodger," he would say to me, "don't worry about it. You can't cheat an honest man."

Well . . .

I'm not aware of any rules without exceptions, and the Bank Examiner was the exception to that one. With any other of the dodges we pulled, those golden words from Mr. Fields were pure gospel. The Spanish Lottery, the Jamaican Handkerchief, the Priceless Pooch, and Put and Take, the Gold Brick, the Pigeon Drop . . . all these swindles rely in large part on the avarice of the average man. (Did I say the Bank Examiner was old? On a wall of one of the Temples of Karnak there is a line of hieroglyphs showing a puzzled mark looking at the worthless wad of cut-up papyrus in his hand while two sharpies from Abyssinia skedaddle with the real loot he put up for "good faith." Welcome to the Pigeon Drop.)

The mark either sees an opportunity to make a quick profit with no risk, or is offered a foolproof way to steal money from someone else. His greed blinds him to the shenanigans going on right under his nose, and he's left holding the bag. (That's where that expression came from. Really!) The *empty* bag. Often he doesn't go to the cops, because to do so he'd have to explain how he planned to steal from the folks who stole from him. Most citizens could care less about the victims of these scams. The general consensus is, they got what they deserved.

Not so with the Bank Examiner. Here's how it works, reduced to its essentials:

You are approached in or near the financial institution where you keep your money. Someone working at this fine establishment has been pilfering, you are told. I, the Examiner/Policeman/Bank President/Security Officer (or almost any authority figure), am on to this miscreant, and I need your help to gather evidence against him. Would you be so kind as to withdraw X number of shekels from your account?

With the money in hand, I tell you I must take it away to . . . oh, photograph it, say. Just about any explanation will do, because if you have withdrawn the cash at all it is because you have bought me as an authority figure. I'll be right back, I say. That's what Jesus said, too.

Now I can almost hear the creaking as your credulity is strained. Nobody would fall for that, you protest.

The fact is, they do. Year after year after year. I have no idea if the Egyptians really even *had* banks, but if they did, you can be sure somebody really *did* pull this one on the banks of the Nile. Because that's one of only two things you need to make the Bank Examiner work: a banking system.

The other thing, of course, is a mark who is (a) trusting, or (b) stupid. In my own thesaurus, those words are listed as synonyms.

It worked fine when banks wrote their accounts in huge ledgers with quill pens, and it works now when it's all electronic impulses in machines. If we ever go to a cashless society (and don't hold your breath), someone will find a way to make it work there, too. So as long as the human race keeps producing idiots, I'll never be broke.

But wait! There's more!

Technically what I had just educated Miranda Mayard-Tate in was not the Bank Examiner at all, but the second act sometimes known as the Copper Comeback. You see, some marks just exude a charming naïveté that, to a veteran con, screams, "Take me! Take me again and again and again . . . !" It seems cruel to abandon these people to *other* con men who might be slipshod or clumsy, who might not consummate the affair with the proper aplomb. It was for people like these—and my darling Miranda could have been the very prototype—that the Comeback was developed.

The original hit on Miranda had taken place while I was still a month away from Pluto's frigid orb. When her money was not returned after a few days, and when no one called, she contacted the bank, who of course were quite familiar with this scam. The police were called in. The Mayard-Tates being the considerable cheeses they were, no expense or effort was spared by the boys and girls in blue to run frantically in circles, look under carpets and rocks and in toilet tanks, handcuff and question dozens of hapless citizens, shout "Stop, thief!" in a loud, firm constabulary voice, and generally create the impression that something was being done, and that a resolution of the case could be expected at any moment. Then all that wound down and the cops went away, and Miranda was left to realize that it was really all over. That no one was going to be charged with the crime. That, sometimes, money can't buy justice. Ain't it awful?

The people who put the con together let her worry about it for a suitable length of time. Their thinking was that, after she'd stewed about it, she'd be ripe for an opportunity to see the rascals in jail. Enter K. C. Valentine, who just blew in from parts unknown, made contact with one of the swindle ring, and asked if they had anything going suitable to his talents. They steered me to Miranda and off I went, Junior G-Man badge in hand, armed with nothing but Friday's flat voice, stare, smile, and feet.

As it turned out, the waiting time hadn't been necessary. Revenge was the farthest thing from Miranda's mind. The sum of money in question, though large by my standards, had literally been forgotten in the madcap, dizzy fandango that qualified as a life in her circle of friends. I had to remind her that she'd been taken, then keep bringing her attention back from unknown areas as I explained that at last we had a lead in her case and that I, Friday, was the man to run it down. We had learned there really *was* a dishonest teller at her bank, and that he had been in cahoots with the swindlers all the time. Now we intended to catch him dead to rights, and get him to squeal, to rat out his gang of nefarious hoodlums. All she had to do to help us bring this about was to withdraw X number of shekels from her account so we could . . . well, by now you should be able to fill in the blanks with a story of your own.

She couldn't have been more delighted to help. Her guileless, canine eyes danced with excitement when I used words like "squeal" and "cahoots," but went a little glassy at "nefarious." So in the end it was her relentless stupidity . . . sorry, I meant unblemished honesty . . . that led her into folly again.

And so it was that I found myself walking along beside the equestrian park in the richest neighborhood in Pluto, carrying an unaccustomed amount of money, paced by a lanky conscience, and trailed by a pissed-off poodle-dog. I should have been happy, but my heart was, I admit, a bit heavy. But my wallet was about to become even heavier. These things even out.

If only she hadn't been so *goddam* honest.

When a felon's not engaged in his employment or maturing his felonious little plans, where do you suppose he goes?

I went to church. You have to fence the loot somewhere.

If any of you in the audience are true-believing members of the First Latitudinarian Church of Celebrity Saints, better known as the Flacks, you might want to skip this next scene. The fact is, wherever you attend services, from Coronaville to Brementon and points beyond, you have found your way into a den of thieves. The chances are excellent that the fellow standing next to you, helping you hold the hymnal and bellowing "Blue Suede Shoes" off-key in a state of exalted presleyan bliss, is not somebody you'd be eager to see marry your brother or sister. He might very well be . . . well, somebody like me.

A lot of Flackites I've mentioned this to have a hard time believing it. As my father used to say, "Denial is more than a big river in Egypt."

All churches have their share of sinners, of course. You might say that's what they're for. You can't get very far in the redemption business without some genuine sinners. But in other churches they're not organized into a band of brothers. I doubt that most churches often see actual crimes being originated and planned at meetings in the church basement.

It would surprise me to learn that stolen goods were actually being fenced on the grounds of, say, the synagogue down the lane. And aside from a little bingo and the occasional bit of buggery, Catholic churches are relatively free of crime. As for Diabolists, don't ask me. It's all veiled in secrecy.

But if it's a spot of larceny you're after, I recommend the Flackites. Every grifter I know shows up there regularly, to find out what's going down, coming off, falling together. It's where I heard about the Mayard-Tate sting, and it's where I went, swag in hand, to dispose of it.

Uncle Roy is choreographer-in-chief at the Main Planetary Studio, First Latitudinarian Church, Pandemonium, Phlegethon Province, Pluto. As a song-and-dance man he had been only mediocre, and he wasn't exactly setting the planet on fire now that he'd hung up his tap shoes. Busby Berkeley's ghost had nothing to fear from Roy. But he was the guy to see if buying wholesale no longer satisfied you, if what you were seeking was really deep discounts. That is, as long as what you were shopping for didn't require a legal title, and if you didn't mind that the serial numbers had been filed off, there was no owner's manual, and the merchandise might have a few dents and scratches from falling off the back of a freightlorry.

I found him in the studio itself, sitting in the third row with his hands steepled in front of him, watching with great concentration what looked to be a final dress rehearsal. The stage was jammed with sequined chorus dancers, just a-hoofin' their little hearts out, and dazzling spotlights swept them like the fingers of angels. I paused to drink it in. When the houselights go down and the stage lights brighten, a new world is created, a world where I've spent most of my life. It's a magic trick I never grow tired of.

I recognized the show immediately as *Work in Progress,* the musical version of *Finnegans Wake* that had bombed at its opening on the Alameda in King City fifty years ago. I know it bombed, because I was there, in the part of Cromwell. ("Val Tiner turns in his usual competent performance in a production more confusing than its source material."—*News Nipple*) Since then *Work* had developed quite a cult following. I myself had revisited it only ten years earlier, this time in the lead role of Humphrey Earwicker/Joyce. ("overwrung. A charmful water-

loose prixducktion, dacently gaylaboring the auld meander-
thalltale from jayjay's mythink Dyoublong of farago. D'ya
dismember what a mnice old mness it all mnakes? But Hark!
Hark! Tray chairs fur Muster Casey Valentoon in a roustering
vendition of 'Miss Hooligan's Christmas Cake,' the topsiest
mnoment of a quarky under-parformance. Stillanall, the shows
a way a lone a last a long a little''—*Arean Gazette*).

The Pluto studio is one of the largest indoor proscenium
theaters in the system. It seats twenty thousand, which means
the cheap seats are in a different postal zone, and high enough
for a nosebleed. I've been in the last row, and from that van-
tage you might as well be watching *A Doll's House* performed
by a flea circus. From the stage, you can get through most of
Hamlet's soliloquy before the echo of your voice reverberates
the first "to be" back to your waiting ears. There's a fair
chance of a rain delay on account of thunderheads forming
in the fly lofts.

But not to worry. The hall is surrounded by several thousand television screens, from a few inches to twenty feet
across. The people in back see just about the same show you
get from front row center, from a bigger variety of camera
angles.

Not my sort of house at all. Give me a three- or four-
hundred seater and I'm a happy man. Let it be my own leathery lungs shouting down the rafters, or making them lean
forward in dead silence to catch my whispered words.

Uncle Roy glanced over at me as I sat at the end of the
row. I nodded, and he smiled briefly, then stood and started
pacing rapidly back and forth at the edge of the orchestra pit,
pointing at people and shouting things I couldn't hear over
the thunder of the music. The conductor frowned at Roy over
his shoulder, but by this time he must have learned better than
to protest. He hunched his shoulders and continued to saw at
the air with his big, glowing baton.

I don't know Uncle Roy's last name, nor why he's universally called uncle. There's probably a story behind it. If
you hear it, let me know. I love stories like that. He's a big
man who has pegged his apparent age in the late fifties, with
a wrinkled face and receding hairline. He has a shock of un-
kempt silvery hair streaked with black, and eyes of purest

newman blue. His lips are thick and rubbery, and he has a habit of chewing on the lower one when he's thinking. When he's *not* thinking he chews tobaccoid, certainly the least attractive retro fad in the last century, one that's finally showing signs of having outworn its welcome. Forget the occasional brown drool from the corners of one's mouth, or the necessity of carrying around a can sloshing with the vilest stuff imaginable, or the truly disgusting sight of someone spitting into it. The habit kept Roy's teeth stained an abhorrent greenish brown, like fungus growing on a corpse. If the smell of his mouth was any guide, the taste of it must have been unimaginable.

Like quite a few dancers I've known, as soon as Roy left the chorus line he blimped up like a satyriastic's condom, twenty, thirty kilos above his boogeying weight. He claimed it was all by design, part of his scheme to be a more physically commanding presence, the other parts being his high forehead, white hair, and wrinkled face. A director ought to have dignity. I had done a little experimenting myself, the few times I had lowered myself into the director's chair. I'd helmed productions looking like King Lear, and like Shirley Temple, and got about the same amount of respect and attention either way—which is to say, very little.

And there's this about ex-dancers: I think a lot of them are just plain *tired* of being human greyhounds. The girls cultivate exuberant boobs of the sort never seen jiggling beneath a tutu. A lady with a butt like two BBs suddenly lets her hips spread out, finds she has something comfortable to sit on for a change. The guys turn into the spitting image of a nineteenth-century banker: prosperous, corpulent, paunchy, chipmunk-cheeked. The reason for such a delightful word as portly. And all of them like to lounge around like neutered house cats in the sunshine, thinking about supper.

". . . and five, and *six* and *seven* and EIGHT!" Uncle Roy was bellowing over the roar of the orchestra. "And lights *out*! Aaaaaand . . . curtain, curtain, applause, applause, applause . . . okay, stop the curtain. *Houselights,* please!"

From far overhead came harsh, unshielded work lights descended on cords; cruel things no performer would ever let into his house because of the ghastly effect they had on tired, sweating people in pancake makeup. It makes us all look like the charpeople those lights were designed to aid when they descended on the spilled drinks, crumpled programs, and wilted flowers, long after the magic had retired to wherever it is magic goes between performances.

These lights revealed a stage full of people in outrageous costumes, breathing hard, some sitting down, others leaning on friends. The shadowless, sourceless light had no mercy. Gold turned to tinsel, silver to tinfoil, diamonds became rhinestones. Every chipped nail and scuffed shoe was exposed. Pearly white teeth turned out to be flaked with lipstick.

When the magic is over, it's *over*.

"One hour for tiffin, boys and girls," Roy said, leaping onto the plank that spanned the orchestra pit and striding confidently among his players. I followed, more slowly. "Except you, Haynes, and you, Dallman. You get to go down to the rehearsal hall and do it again, and again, and *again,* until you get it right three times in a row. You know the part I'm talking about." A man and a woman, presumably Haynes and Dallman, slumped off to the wings. Roy whistled loudly, looking up into the fly loft. "Mr. Lacon, if you please. If your people can't get the bar set rung off in twelve seconds tonight, I'll tie you to a rope and use you for a sandbag." There was angry shouting from on high, which I didn't understand and Roy didn't listen to. He was putting a beefy arm around my shoulders and guiding me through the bustling wings and through a door with a big star on it, labeled DIRECTOR. He slammed the door behind us, threw himself into a groaning jurist's chair, leaned back, and laced his fingers behind his head.

"So. What did you think?" he asked.

"All I saw was the Flying Dutchman number," I said. "How's your budget? Do you have elephants?"

"I've got elephants."

"Then I don't see how you can go wrong."

"Elephants? Hell, I got ten elephants. I got peacocks and horse-drawn carts, and I got horses guaranteed not to crap on anybody's tap shoes. I have a trained seal. I have thirty-seven set changes. I have three ultracopters to bring people in from the lofts, gonna land 'em right there on the stage. I have a thirty-foot pool, seventeen fountain jets, and eight gals willing to give up sex for the run of the show so we can morph them into mermaids. I got every piece of gimcrackery anybody ever thought of when they were staging this overblown turkey, and I got a guaranteed opening night sellout. I even have a chorus line that can get across the stage without tripping over either of their left feet.''

He paused to draw a breath, then leaned slightly forward and spoke in a more confidential tone.

''You know what I don't have? Ask me what I don't have, Sparky.''

''Leapin' lizards, Uncle Roy!'' I squeaked, in my old ''Sparky'' voice. ''What don't you have?''

He leaned over even farther.

''What I don't have is an Anna Livia Plurabelle who can reach a high C three times in a row without I shove a hot poker up her ass.'' He leaned back in his chair. ''Which I'd be perfectly happy to do.''

I tsked a few sympathetic-sounding tsks.

My sympathies for directors who miscast and then complain about it are severely limited. After all, it's usually *me* out there trying my best to make some pathetic hambone look good, and cursing the moment the little shit got into the mighty director's pants.

''Who is this up-and-comer?'' I asked. ''Was that Haynes?''

''Little Miss Drury Haynes,'' he confirmed. ''Sparky, you know that montage in *Citizen Kane,* the one where the no-talent broad tries to sing grand opera and stinks up the place? That no-talent broad looks *good* compared to Drury Haynes. Or how about the traveling troupe in *The Court of Babylon?* Take the *worst* of those mugs and stand her up against Drury. . . .'' He finally ran out of steam. He glared down at his desk, then looked up at me again.

''I want you to ask me one more question, Sparky,'' he said.

''Roy . . .''

''Just one more. Ask me the name of the Grand Exalted Super-Flack of this particular Studio.''

''Uh-oh.''

''Aloysius J. Haynes is the good worthy's name, and he just couldn't be prouder of fathering little Drury, who thinks the musical theater is simply *ripping,* and who has wanted to be a singer and an actress just *ever* so long. And who has been taking singing lessons since she was three from a series of increasingly desperate voice teachers, at least three of whom can be seen this very moment sitting on filthy beds in the charity ward of Pandemonium General, gibbering to themselves, in restraints to prevent them from driving sharp objects into their ears.

"So when little Drury showed up at the auditions and the word came down that she was to be treated 'just like any other singer,' that's exactly what I did. I treated her just like any other producer's favorite daughter, and gave her the part. 'I can fix it,' I said to myself at the time. 'She'll get better.' We can mike her and cover it up. Or I can pull a *Singin' in the Rain,* have a *real* singer behind a curtain. *Something.* Only when I tried, she went running to daddy, of course. And the Word came down.

"And if you were still asking questions, Sparky, I'd ask you to ask me if I give a free-falling fuck anymore about the Word coming down, and you know what I'd answer? I'd say no. Because yesterday I found myself cleaning out my left ear with a very sharp pencil, and wondering what it'd feel like, and thinking it might not be half-bad. And in my dreams I see them making up the empty fourth bed in that padded ward in the giggle academy, and I see them putting me in it and murmuring 'There, there, Roy. There, there.' "

I admit my attention had drifted. Roy likes to hear himself expound, and this all had the sound of a set piece, one he'd honed on many an unsympathetic ear over the last few weeks. But now he stood up and leaned over the desk, putting his weight on his clenched fists, and he got my attention in about the only way he could have done.

"So how about it, old friend? The part's yours. Say the word."

I opened my mouth to say yes. Folks, unless you have the acting fever yourself you can't possibly know the idiotic things one will do to get a shot at a part he has never played. Or one he's already played, and knows he could do again, and better.

Or a chance to carry a gold-painted wooden spear onto the stage and shout "Caesar approaches!" to an audience of bored schoolchildren.

I am an absolute *sucker* for somebody who says those magic words: "You've got the part." It has got me into more hot water than yearly flows through Phlegethon, the famous River of Fire in Pandemonium Park, not three miles from where I sat. It has made a shambles of my life, this puppy-dog-like eagerness to perform.

So I was a tenth of a second from taking the part, when I looked up and saw that Elwood had silently opened the door behind Uncle Roy just enough to stick his narrow, dour physiognomy through the crack. He was looking at me, pursing his lips in that pensive way of his, and shaking his head.

"I'm not a singer," I managed to cough.

"You're not *primarily* a singer, granted," Roy said. "However, we're not talking grand opera soprano here. We're talking *Broadway,* Sparky, we're talking *musical comedy,* and I don't know anybody in the system can handle that kind of part any better than you. Believe me, you're ten times the singer Drury is. I saw you—what was it, ten years ago? Fifteen?—as Mrs. Lovett. Best I ever saw, and that music is lots tougher than *Work.* Then there was . . . what was it . . . *The Three Masks.* I've never heard Mabel Parsons sung better. Swear to god, Sparky, you had me thinking Streisand."

Well. How bad could it be? I'd already done the male lead for several hundred performances; I could swot up Anna Livia's lines in a few hours' intense cramming. I'm a very quick study. I looked up to say yes . . .

. . . and Elwood was still shaking his head, no. There were frown lines on his forehead now.

". . . I'm pretty much sticking to male roles these days." This was partially true. The memory of my recent painful Juliet was still fresh enough in my mind that I didn't regard a radical body shift in a short time with a lot of enthusiasm.

"Please, Sparky," he said, leaning across his desk with his hands folded. If he came across and grabbed my lapels I'd have no choice but to run like a scared rabbit. There was no other resistance I could offer.

"Please, please, *please*!" he groveled.

"All right," I said. "I accept." Or that's what I opened my mouth to say, but what came out was more like "Awwwrrrgh," followed by a strangling sound I can't transliterate, as Elwood was now drawing a finger across his throat—

—and the full depth of my folly was revealed to me in a blinding burst of temporary sanity. I'd been on Pluto three, four weeks? Already I'd committed at least two felonies— ones I was aware of, though the place had so many new laws now it was likely I'd committed a handful more simply by getting up and going about my daily business. So what did I now propose to do? Nothing but get put down on the shit list of one of the most powerful men on Pluto, in letters ten meters tall and written in fire: The Man Who Wrecked My Daughter's Life.

No thank you! No, I thank you! And again, I thank you!

"I'm really sorry, Roy," I said. "I have a previous engagement on . . . on the, er . . . the *Titanic*."

"Dinner theater? You're giving up Anna Livia for *dinner* theater?"

"At least I won't get trampled by elephants."

"And between shows you can bus tables. I never heard of—"

I slapped the bag of swag onto the desk between us, possibly the only action I could have taken at that moment that would get his attention. He looked at it suspiciously, then took it and zipped it open. He hauled out the wad of crisp, new banknotes and then looked at me.

"Any trouble at all?"

"No trouble. She was just like you said."

He nodded. He'd met her before, having been the original bank examiner in our little true-life sketch. He moistened a thumb and started shuffling through the bills, sorting them into two piles: nine for him, one for me. Hey, I'm not complaining. Ten percent is not bad for coming in so late in the sting. They'd done all the groundwork.

"All right, Sparky. Here's your share."

I pocketed the loot, and placed a small object on the desk in front of him. He frowned at it, picked it up.

"What is this? A chessman?"

"It's called 'Dutchman.' It's netsuke, nineteenth century, dating from a few years after the opening of Japan. This is how the Japanese saw the Western invaders. Notice how his little eyes are slanted?"

"You got this from Mayard-Tate?"

"No, I found it lying in the street. Jesus, Roy."

He frowned at the tiny mannequin while his thumb absently caressed it.

"Reason I asked," he said, "we talked about it before you went in. The Charonese Mafia."

"We sure as hell did talk about it. You said it wouldn't be a problem."

"It ain't. Only I didn't figure on you pinching any sukiyaki."

"Netsuke. What's the difference?"

He rolled his shoulders, nervously rubbed the back of his neck.

"Come on, Roy. Don't do this to me. You said the Mayard-Tates wouldn't bother to tell the Mafia."

"Normally, no, they wouldn't. They'd be embarrassed, for one thing. And it's a small enough amount of money—to them—it's easier just to let it go. In fact, I was gonna ask you if you'd like to be in on stage three of the sting. We're planning to—"

"Not for all the netsuke in Pluto."

"Okay. Just a thought. They didn't do anything after the first sting, and I don't see why they'd do it now, 'cause it's even *more* embarrassing to fall for it twice. Still, I didn't count on you lifting the furniture."

"Get real, Roy. I walk into a house like that, you think I'm walking out with my pockets empty? Would you?"

He grinned. "There's that," he admitted. "What do you want for it?"

"What'll you give?"

He named a ridiculous price. I just shook my head. But instead of making a counteroffer, he shook his head, too.

"I'm out of my element here," he said. "I never dealt in Nipponiana. Let me talk to a few people." He swiveled his chair to the side and started typing on his keyboard, studying the results on a clear glass pane whose angle made the returning answers invisible to me.

"What do you hear these days?" I asked him, more to be making conversation than anything else. "Anything interesting going on?"

"My show's just about it," he said. "A few other revivals

here and there. I don't think there's been three new plays debuted on Pluto this year. Things are pretty dead." He glanced at me, smiled. "Unless you count Polichinelli coming out of retirement to direct *King Lear*."

Sure. I returned his smirk. "And I heard Hitchcock's come back from the dead to direct John Wilkes Booth in *Our American Cousin,* too." Both events were about equally likely. If there *was* something good coming up, Roy wouldn't tell me. He wanted me for *Work in Progress.*

His attention had returned to his screen.

"I hope those questions aren't going out over the public cables."

"Don't teach grandpa how to get under a skirt, little boy," he said. "This is encoded nine different ways. The police could never trace it. Of course, if the Charonese are looking for you, nothing's gonna help."

Did he have to bring that up? I expected Elwood to stick his nosy phiz back through the door again and croon, *Don't say I didn't warn you.*

He had warned me, not that I'd really needed it. The hardest part of the Mayard-Tate sting had been knocking on that front door with the red handprints on each jamb, like the fresh lamb's blood beside the doors of the Israelites. Those prints meant, to anyone who had spent any time on Pluto, "This residence protected by the Red Hand." I read them in a more colorful way: *Burglar, pass by this place.* Had a more Biblical sound, and the Charonese Mafia was nothing if not Biblical.

After the end of the penal system on Pluto and the establishment of democracy, there was never much enthusiasm for the institution of police. Too many voters—ex-transportees—had nothing but negative associations with the color blue. No very large society can get along without *something* in the way of law enforcement, and Pluto did have police, both municipal and planetary. But they were weaker than on any other major planet.

The trouble was that crime doesn't stop just because the people don't like cops. The resulting gap between an anemic constabulary and a healthy and growing—some even argued *genetically predisposed*—criminal class was filled, as such gaps always are, by free enterprise, in the form of vigilance committees, posses, and protective associations. And of these sellers of protection, the greatest and most feared was the Charonese Mafia.

If you'd like an historical parallel, there's a good one from the Old Earth. The nation of Italy had organized crime, like many other countries. But in one particular province, known as Sicily, the Cosa Nostra, or Black Hand, was far more ruthless and relentless than in any other region. They were so good at what they did that they ended up actually exporting their brand of gangsterism to other countries, particularly America. I know this because I had to study it when I played in *The Martian Godfather* ("Valentine is effective in the role of Don Tharsisini, mugging and brandoing his way through some lines that might have choked a less professional thespian. Go see it, or I'll break ya fuckin' kneecaps."—*The Quicksilver Messenger*).

You'd think being an inmate in a planetary prison was about as low as one could sink. You'd be wrong. In any prison there is a hierarchy. It may be topsy-turvy to outside eyes—murderers usually got more respect than embezzlers, for instance—and it varies from culture to culture, but there are always those who the run-of-the-mill convict views with the same contempt that civilians view *him*. Baby killers, for instance. Cannibals. Crazed serial murderers. Try to parole such people into a population of ex-transportees and you'll get the same uproar you'd get anywhere. So Pluto found itself in need of a prison planet of its own, and the logical choice was forlorn, useless, and neglected little Charon, Pluto's largest moon, named for the ferryman of Hell.

Taxpayers are loath to squander a lot of money on the care of people such as they were exporting to Charon. They must have air, water, and, Charon being from two to four billion miles from the sun, a certain amount of heat. Those things were provided, though not generously. As for food, they could learn hydroponic farming or they could damn well eat each other. I think the Plutonian electorate had the Kilkenny cats in mind: throw them together, stand back, and in a little while there would be just teeth, hair, and eyeballs left.

But politics has a natural ebb and flow. Regimes came and went for nearly two hundred years. Sometimes standards relaxed and genetic criminals were sent to Charon. During a brief right-wing coup any number of political prisoners were transported. There were times when no one went to the rock, as do-gooders tried one more futile time to "reform" the worst of the worst with some new "therapy," or as more pragmatic souls scrambled offenders' brains with the newest lobotomy equivalent that left them happy droolers, or, as the pragmatists would have it, "perfect citizens."

It had been over fifty years since the penal colony was closed and Charon became a more-or-less-equal member of the Plutonian Fed. But in the century before that something had been bred that, save for Areoformed Martians, was nearer to a subspecies of human than anything yet seen in this tired old Solar System. They were the Charonese.

They looked like normal human beings, though they tended to a choleric complexion and red hair. Where they differed from the bulk of humanity was not so visible. This difference has been described in a dozen ways, depending on what sort of expert you're talking to. They were said to be empathically dysfunctional. That, or they lived their lives according to an antisocial cultural ethic. Or they suffered from a planetary traumatic stress syndrome. Or, as my father had once put it, "They are mean sumbitches."

Traumatic, dysfunctional, antisocial, deprived, depraved, depraved on account o' being deprived, genetically abnormal, or just plain mean, I lean toward a simpler explanation. They had no souls.

I know it's not scientific, but I never laid claim to a rigorous point of view. Don't ask me to define a soul because I can't. But I know one when I see one, and the Charonese don't have them. I have one. Uncle Roy does, though we're both not very nice. Toby has one, and I'll bet you do, too.

Basically, all Charon had to export was viciousness. And they made a hell of a good living at it. There have always been people who have need of really tough guys.

Charonese were often referred to as "ferrymen."

This was all unprofitable reflection, and I was glad to be drawn away from it when Roy turned from his screen and named a much more satisfactory figure. I might as well admit it: I had no idea what the thing was worth. I was merely following another valuable piece of advice from my father. "Never take the first offer," he said. "It makes you look hungry." A corollary to that was to try not to take the second offer, either, so I named a higher figure and, sure enough, he came up a little bit.

I'm sure we would have ended up splitting the difference if we could have spent the next hour haggling, but he was due back onstage, and he didn't know something, which was that he would have to do this twice more.

"Deal," I said, and put a lovely little recumbent water buffalo on the table between us. "Now how much for this?"

The rest of our negotiations were quickly concluded, on terms a bit more favorable to me, I like to think. Then he was hustling me out of his office, into the breathless rowdy-dowdy, randy-dandy, rollicky-ranky that is backstage at a major musical before the second curtain. He guided me to the stage door, which disgorged me into the end of the traditional long, dark alley, the door lit by a single overhead bulb. With the door already closing behind him, he stuck his head out again.

"You want to come tonight and catch the opening? I'll leave a ticket at the box office."

"No, thanks," I said, with a tip of my hat and a bow. "I'll come tomorrow night, and catch the closing."

He extended his middle finger, then smiled and waved.

"Break a leg!" I shouted as the door clicked shut.

For the last ten days I had been staying in modest quarters at the Lambs Club. For the last three of those days I had been making my entrances and exits while the front desk was not occupied, or when the clerk was busy with something else. A few times I'd been reduced to the back stairs and the freight doors. At the Lambs they know actors, you see, most of them being either aspiring or ex-actors themselves. One of the things they know is that an actor with a hit series or a big part in a picture doesn't stay at the Lambs. Another is that an actor lies. It's his business. They have heard every variation on I-Shall-Positively-Pay-You-Next-Tuesday. Your best story about how your saintly mother needed the dough to pay off an unsympathetic bookie will be met by a stony silence. They will regard your crystal martini mixer, said to have belonged to Shirley Temple, with sneering disbelief, and direct you to a pawnbroker known to have a heart of pure flint. Or they'd simply point to the big sign behind the front desk: ALL ROOMS TO BE PAID FOR *IN ADVANCE*.

Yesterday I'd been ready to throw myself on the mercy of a desk clerk. There was one who looked like Mickey Rooney. Could such a man be a rogue?

Today I swept into the seedy marble-columned lobby in my best black cape and top hat. There was a shine on my shoes and a melody in my heart. I don't think I mentioned it, but when I smile, I can look a lot like Fred Astaire. That thought so cheered me that I actually danced a few steps, past the eternal contingent of office boys, barmaids, and young mechanics who come from Chillicothes and Paducahs with their bazookas to get their names up in lights. And they end up sitting hunched in the Lambs' shabby novodeco armchairs with their attractive but worried faces buried in copies of *Casting Call* and *Pluto Variety*. I grabbed the hand of one comely lass, pulled her from her chair, and we Fred'n'Gingered through the dusty potted palms, up the seven steps from the lounge, where I rolled her into my arms and planted a kiss of purest em-gee-em on her rosebud mouth.

I was striding by the front desk on my way to the elevators when I suddenly stopped and looked thoughtful, as if remembering something . . . just as the clerk held up a finger and opened his mouth. (I admit it. I was watching from the corner of my eye for just such a moment.) I hurried to the desk, taking out my wallet as I went. I let him see the stack of bills inside as I peeled off three large ones and placed them on the blotter.

"I believe this will cover any arrears, my good man," I said.

The clerk (not Mickey Rooney) gave me a sour look that told me he'd been anticipating my ouster with relish. But he took the money and turned to his computer. I dug in the pocket of my cape and removed Toby and set him on the counter. He sniffed at the inkwell, and promptly knocked over the "No Pets Allowed" sign. I told him to sit, which he did.

The clerk's already prunelike mouth wrinkled even further when he turned from his ledgers with my change.

"I'm afraid no pets are allowed in the guest rooms, sir," he said.

"Toby is not a pet. He is a performer." I put my palm flat on the blotter between us.

"Nevertheless, I'm afraid . . ." He had finally noticed the edge of the twenty sticking out from under my hand.

"Seems there's a *lot* you're afraid of," I said. "You'll have to stop going around in such a frightened state." I pushed the bill a little closer, and he took it, making no effort to be discreet. A bribe's a bribe, as far as he was concerned.

"No need for any change just now," I said, airily. "We shall be checking out tomorrow morning, and I may be charging some interplanetary calls to my room. Tomorrow I shall need my bags delivered to dockside, H.M.S. *Britannic,* in time for the afternoon sailing."

"Of course," he said, making a note. Then he looked up, sneering. "Shall I have them sent to the crew deck?"

"And have your mother drop them over the side? You should let that old woman retire. No, no, send them to my dressing room. It's the one with the star on it."

I picked up Toby while the clerk was still sputtering, and swept away to the elevators.

It's always a melancholy time when I must once more put Toby down. Melancholy for me, not him. He always knows it's coming because for the two days prior I stuff him with food. A full belly extends his downtime and makes him recover more rapidly from the effects of hibernation, but the real reason I do it is guilt. It's entirely self-induced. Toby never offers a word of reproach.

I'm sure dogs don't experience the passage of time in the same way we do. He's sharp enough, I think, to know a hibernation is not the same as a regular night's sleep. While there are no actual seasons in our modern environments, there are periodic daily, weekly, and quarterly changes in temperature, humidity, pressure, and so forth, because it's been found people do better that way. Toby surely noticed those when awakened. But I doubt he had any notion of how much time had passed. So it was no skin off his nose, right?

I just hated treating him like a little, warm machine. I'd never thought of him as property. A dog sticks to you out of loyalty. And, pragmatically, because you're his meal ticket.

I called him over and tossed the sleepy pill in his direction.

THE GOLDEN GLOBE ··· 63

He leaped into the air and caught it. I heaped praise on him, which he took as only his due, clever dog, *smart* dog. Then, old hand that he is, he sat down and waited. He used to stagger about, run into things. He didn't like to be held at such times, as he sometimes became delirious, hallucinated. Once he bit my hand, and felt rotten about it for days after I woke him up. So he just sits there, and pretty soon he begins to nod. Sometimes he growls at things I can't see. But in no time his heart rate is falling, along with all his other metabolic signs.

He fell over and I scooped him up.

When I bought him he came with a little hard-sided carrying case, about the size of a hatbox. It was a hideous aluminum color. I had it covered with the finest crocodile skin, replaced the plastic handle with leather. I put him in the case, curled into a fluffy ball, and pasted a sensor to his pink belly. Green lights came on in the lid, which I then snapped closed. If anything went wrong, alarms would sound, and if I was close enough to hear I could rush him to a vet. Nothing had ever gone wrong.

I packed him into the Pantechnicon, laid out my clothing for the next day, then showered, brushed my teeth, put on my nightgown and cap, said my prayers, and crawled into the narrow, lumpy bed provided by the Lambs.

I heard the door squeak open on rusty hinges.

"I don't want to talk now, Elwood," I said. I could see his shadow on the floor. He nodded, and closed the door quietly. He knows I'm moody when I've just packed Toby.

Soon I was asleep.

About an hour later I sat up, instantly awake. I had the terrible feeling I'd forgotten something important. Something *impossibly* important. I cast my mind back over the day, which had been a fairly eventful one. I could come up with only one thing, and it was silly.

Surely he had been kidding. Surely . . .

There was nothing for it but to call the union. I got a computer. Don't tell me PFPA never sleeps. I showed my union card to the screen, which agreed I was a member in good standing of the Pluto Federation of Performing Artists (luckily for me you can still be in good standing though in arrears on your dues), delivered a canned lecture concerning the matter of P$795.03 due and payable or we are entitled to deduct said sum from any residuals received by this office (don't hold your breath), and asked what it could do for me.

"Search announced productions. Stage. *King Lear*. Polichinelli."

There was a short pause, and the computer was sorry to inform me no such production had been billboarded. Not on Pluto, not on Charon—

"Not Pluto, you idiot. Polichinelli never travels. Check the Luna listings."

"Inner-planet bookings are not handled by this office, sir. Please call—" Which I did, only to be answered by an identical computer voice. After the same rigmarole (oddly, this office felt I owed them P$795.13), I asked the same question.

The pause was even shorter.

"General casting call, all parts, *King Lear*, by William NMI Shakespeare (b.1564, d.1616). Production announced E-day 1/1/38. Casting begins 10/1/38. Venue: Golden Globe Theater, 2001 The Alameda, King City, Luna. Director: Kaspara V. Polichinelli. Producer—"

"Lear! Lear!" I was shouting. "Has Lear been cast?"

There was that little gurgle a voice program sometimes makes when shifting protocols.

"Dramatis personae," it intoned. "Lear, King of Britain: TBA. Goneril, daughter to Lear: TBA. Cordelia—"

I broke the connection so hard I almost broke my finger as well. Then I was fumbling with the card by the room phone, trying to find out how to call Luna. I got the hotel computer—the same voice I'd just heard from the union; a very good program salesman had been through here at one time—which regretted to inform me that such calls must be paid in advance.

After a bit of shouting I figured it out. That goddamn clerk was trying to pocket the change from my payment!

I stormed into the lobby in my dressing gown and slippers. Naturally the blackguard was not on duty. The night clerk looked up, doe-eyed, from a large crossword she was working on. I throttled my anger; she looked like a sweet kid, probably a drama student. She had enough heartbreaks in her future without me adding mine.

"I would like to send a telegram to Luna," I said.

"A what?"

"Eight letters, starts with *T,* a Western Union wire. Good lord, child, haven't you ever read about Flo Ziegfeld? He used to send them from stage right to people standing at stage left, because they made an *impact*. I want to send a written message. A fax, if you please."

"Okay." She shrugged. "But you can get voice and picture at the same price."

"Polichinelli dislikes telephones," I said.

"Polichinelli?" she whispered. Apparently she had heard of Polly, because her lovely fawn-colored orbs grew even wider. "You're sending a fax to Kaspara Polichinelli?"

I sighed, and lifted the flap in the counter and came around to stand beside her. I selected a pen from a great pot full of them, and pulled a sheet of white paper from a cubbyhole. I held them up for her to see, then pushed up my sleeves and rested my elbows on the counter. I chewed on the end of the pen for a moment. She leaned close to watch as I wrote the following:

Kaspara Polichinelli
c/o Directors Guild of Luna
1750 The Alameda
King City, Luna

We two alone will sing like birds in the cage. When thou dost ask me blessing I'll kneel down and ask of thee forgiveness. So we'll live, and pray, and sing, and tell old tales, and laugh at gilded butterflies. You have found your Lear, and he draws nigh.

K. C. Valentine

I handed the paper to her, and she read it unabashedly. Then she read it again. When she looked up her eyes were misty.

"That's beautiful," she breathed. "Did you write this yourself?"

Perhaps she should consider a career in hotel management. Drama school hadn't taught her much. I took the paper from her and put it on the desk, placed a bill on top of it.

"This should cover the cost of the telegram," I said. I took her tiny hand and kissed the back of it, then turned it over and pressed a shiny new ten dollar piece into it, folded the fingers over the coin. "This is for your trouble. And this"—I put my arms around her, gabled my eyes down into hers for a moment, and said—"this is for me." I gave her a long, black-and-white kiss: that is to say, no tongue. Her lips were very warm. She made no resistance. How could she resist, and call herself an actress?

It begins to be silly in a minute, with nothing to fade out to, so I broke the kiss, and smiled at her.

"Wish me luck," I said.

"Break a leg," she whispered.

There was going to be no chance at all of getting any more sleep.

The room had no chair. I dragged the bed over to the single, narrow window, which I cranked open. I sat on the edge of the bed and looked out over Pandemonium's neon hell.

This was the notorious Thirteenth Avenue. Two blocks to my left was Pluto's equivalent of the Great White Way, the Rialto. It was six blocks of exclusive shops and restaurants, and about a dozen legitimate theaters. If I stuck my head out the window I could almost see it. But what was the point? It was late; the last show had let out hours ago, and the tasteful marquees were dark. Most of the restaurants were empty, too, their patrons on the trains to the suburbs or already snuggled in bed. Anyone who still wanted to party had to come here, to 'Teenth. If you want a parallel, think of Forty-second Street in little old New York. Naughty, gaudy, bawdy, sporty; the 'Teenth was all of that, and more. Here the lights still flashed, urging one in to baser amusements. At one end was the slash-boxing arena. Ten blocks away, beyond the Rialto, was the Motorpsycho racetrack. In between were dozens of orgy rooms, virtuality dens, rough bars and spike bars and squeeze bars and cyberpunk bars, dance halls, bordellos, live sex shows, and the Salvation Army mission. There were other theaters, too, the stepchildren of the glittering palaces around the corner, our modern equivalents of vaudeville and burlesque, revues and skit houses and stand-up comedy stages.

There was an actual old-fashioned strip show. There were three or four experimental theaters, though most of that was farther downtown, sub-Rialto. Across from my room was the menacing edifice of the Grand Guignol, granddaddy of the Theater of Cruelty. Headlined in flashing lights: *The Garden of Torture.* I decided to skip that one.

It was "summer" in Pandemonium. The bright, hot overheads were out, but the air was still balmy. My room was on the fourth floor, just one below the roof. I sat on my bed and watched the traffic in the street.

It was a colorful bunch. I saw people being led around on leashes. A group of motorcyclists thundered by, on their way to a competition at the velodrome. Directly below me, two naked whores laughed and chatted with a beat cop, cool in his summer khaki.

I looked at the clock with the skull face and the skeletal hands across the street at the Grand Guignol. It had been three hours since I sent the wire. At *least* another three hours to go. With any luck, Polly should be getting my message just about then.

I can't imagine why no one has yet done anything about this speed-of-light business. To think that in this day and age we have to wait *three* hours for a message to crawl to Luna, and three hours for an answer to return. No amount of bribery will get it there any faster. My father, for one, never believed that. All his life he was convinced that rich people had a faster way, and that they kept it from the populace out of spite.

My thumb caressed the little frog-and-skull netsuke there in the semidark. At the last moment I had decided not to set it on Roy's desk. Don't ask me why. I opened my hand and looked at it, pulsing red and blue, pale washes from the neon outside. A truly evil little thing. The frog looked back at me impassively. *He* wasn't impatient. He had plenty of time. A fly would drift by sooner or later.

I heard the door creak behind me, then a soft sound as it closed. I knew I wasn't alone.

"I don't much feel like talking, Elwood," I said.

"Who's Elwood?" came the soft whisper. "Are you gay?"

"How can you ask that of a man who kisses like that?"

"Good." I heard soft footsteps, and looked to my left. She

was across the room, by the dresser, nude, with some sort of wrap in her right hand. With her left she was placing something on the dresser, something that glinted in the next flash of blue neon that turned her from a gray shadow to a magical dolphin girl. I saw the sway of her hanging breast as she bent over the dresser, and again as she straightened and turned toward me, dropping the gown, hips moving, a bit pigeon-toed, her pubic triangle bold and black as her skin now burned the red of smoldering coals. I looked back out the window. I'd seen enough; I was in love. She'd put the ten dollar coin on the dresser so there would be no question of the nature of the coming transaction.

I heard springs creak and felt the bed move as she put first one knee, then the other, on the mattress. I felt soft hands on my shoulders, massaging gently.

"My name is Margaret Sawyer," she whispered. I wondered if she always whispered, or just around me. "People call me Peggy." Everyone has a cross to bear. "Are you having a hard time waiting for your answer?"

I gestured at the dark room. "These luxurious surroundings go a long ways to soothe my anxieties."

"Mine enemy's dog," she said, "though he had bit me, should have stood that night against my fire; and wast thou fain, poor father, to hovel thee with swine and rogues forlorn, in short and musty straw? Alack, alack!"

Alack indeed. "Do not laugh at me, for as I am a man, I think this lady to be Cordelia." I tried to look at her over my shoulder, but she kept massaging me. "And not the ignorant bumpkin I took her for."

"I've been reading the last few hours," she admitted. "And I've been wondering if you're old enough to play King Lear."

"Pray, do not mock me," I quoted. "I am a very foolish fond old man, five score and upward, not an hour more nor less."

She pressed herself against me, all softness but for the stiff brush of hair against my spine, all firm but for the pillows of her breasts on each side of my neck. Her hair fell around me, smelling of soap and jasmine. She still wouldn't let me turn as her hands moved over my face, chest, belly.

God, it had been a long time. What had happened to my

sex life? Miranda didn't count, of course. That was business. Before that, the brief run as Juliet, and I'd been catching, not pitching. Oh, yes, of course. The governor's daughter. Sweet as she'd been, I realized I hadn't really stopped running since that goddamn gumshoe tapped me on the shoulder, way back in Brementon. I certainly hoped little Peggy Sawyer didn't come with so many strings attached.

"Your father isn't a member of Congress, is he?" I murmured.

"My father was two cc's of white fluid in a test tube."

"The best kind." I twisted, took her in my arms, pressed her against the bed. She wrapped her legs around me and looked up with flashing eyes.

"Lord, you feel wonderful," I said. There's nothing like a woman's body. She must have been reading my mind.

"Why are our bodies soft and weak, and smooth, unapt to toil and trouble in the world, but that our soft conditions and our hearts should well agree with our external parts?"

Good question. It had always seemed to me to strike at the heart of the eternal mystery of sex. And she was no shrew.

I could have bid her kiss me, Kate, but I'd used that line in more comical circumstances, and besides, another was at hand.

"The wren goes to it, and the small gilded fly does lecher in my sight," I told her. "Let copulation thrive."

And it did prosper mightily there on that short and musty straw.

Eventually we repaired to the facilities down the hall to see if anything could be done about the damages. I examined myself in the mirror while she got busy at the bidet. There were a few bite marks, nothing a little maxfac couldn't cover up. Lips a bit swollen. Hair . . . well, perhaps a good beautician could give me a cost estimate.

"Once again, my father was right," I said.

"How's that?"

"When he urged me to brush up my Shakespeare. Claimed it was the quickest way to get girls in the sack. 'Just declaim a few lines from *Othella,* and they'll think you're a helluva fella.' "

"Well, it's the first time Shakespeare got *me* in the sack."

She looked up, suspiciously. "Are you sure that was your father's line?"

"Dad stole all his best lines," I admitted. "But he only stole from the best. In this case, Cole Porter."

She shook her head; never heard of him. And to think, I was considering asking her hand in marriage.

By the time we got dressed and I was packed, "day" was dawning on the street outside, and there was still no reply from Polly.

Cordelia followed me as I trundled the Pantechnicon to the lobby and out onto the street. We embraced there, kissed, and I told her I'd drop in again as soon as the cruise run was over. And I would have, too. . . .

That's when the bellboy shambled up, pillbox hat askew, shirttail out, and pressed an envelope into my hand. He turned on his heel and left us standing there, apparently never dreaming I might actually tip him.

I tried not to let my hands tremble as I opened the envelope and unfolded the yellow paper within.

If thou wert my fool, Nuncle, I'd have thee beaten for being old before thy time. Thou shouldst not have been old till thou had been wise. Sparky, if you can make it, Phileas Fogg was a piker. But, as the Bard says:

The sweet and bitter fool will presently appear;
The one in motley here, the other found out there.

If he says you can do it, maybe you can. Lear is yours.

I modestly took my place as the one and only bass. I would have been tickled pink to oompah my little heart out except I had somehow neglected to take sousaphone lessons in preparing for a life on the stage. Though I knew it was rumored that if one pressed the middle valve down the music would go 'round and 'round and come out way up there somewhere, I had no personal experience of this. Hell, for the first two hours of rehearsal I'd worn the thing on the wrong shoulder. It still looked more like some plumber's catastrophic mistake than a musical instrument, but at least now, after a dozen performances, I knew where to blow.

Or pretend to blow. The sound system backstage took care

of the actual music. My job was simply to be in the right place when the sousaphone was dropped from the fly loft, like a human horseshoe peg.

The ''Seventy-six Trombones'' number was the climax of the twenty-minute ''Sounds of Old Broadway'' piece we did twice a day, at six and eleven. At seven and midnight, it was ''Caribbean Rhythms,'' where I got to fake it at a set of steel drums, dressed up like Carmen Miranda.

So when's the last time *you* demanded *Oedipus Rex* on a cruise ship? It was legitimate stage work, and I was glad to have it.

So I continued my high-kicking march step, in place, waving my Panama straw hat and grinning like mad at the audience as the music thundered to its conclusion and the curtain dropped down before me, seventy-six trombonists, a hundred and ten cornet players, and more than a thousand reeds.

Close enough. There were actually three 'bone pickers, four cornets, and five woodwinds. As Busby Berkeley is rumored to have said when informed he could only have twenty chorus girls for a dance he was staging, ''That's all right. I know how to make twenty *look* like a thousand.''

The way he did it was through artistry and film editing. The director of this particular turkey had used a holographic echo generator. The images of my dozen chorus kids was picked up by this gizmo, and a computer introduced variations in height, skin color, facial shape, and so forth, then endlessly replicated the first row—the only row I had—into twelve infinitely long files, vanishing into the distance of a stage that was actually no deeper than a starlet's intellect.

Don't bother notifying the union about this, you dirty snitch. The contract plainly states that hol-echoes can be used for crowd scenes in medium-to-small houses. Nobody ever called Sparky Valentine a scab. Not under my real name, anyway.

I waited in the wings while the boys and girls took their bows, then bounded out as the spotlight picked me up. People were standing, but not, I was forced to admit, in an ovation. They had drinks in their hands waiting for the aisles to clear. I bowed as the music swelled, gestured to the maestro, who turned and smiled as one hand continued to conduct his three-piece augmented orchestra. I knew the applause would not extend for long, and besides, I'm not one of those pathetic hams who milk it beyond that Zen moment of one hand clapping. I bowed once more, and the curtain came down.

This was not, in point of fact, the *Titanic,* as I had told Roy, but her sister ship, the *Britannic*. A third ship, *Olympic,* completed the trio, faithful external copies of the White Star Line behemoths of the early twentieth century. It was a very Plutonian thing, to name a cruise fleet after such an ill-omened trio. Everybody knows what happened on that Night to Remember back in 1912; it's passed into the language as a synonym for catastrophe, and hubris. *Titanic* proved all too sinkable. Less familiar is the sad story of *Britannic,* converted to a hospital ship during a war and sunk by a mine. Would you believe there was actually a woman, Violet Jessop, who had the bad luck to be aboard both ships when they went down? And the incredible *good* luck to survive both disasters. It was in the tour brochure.

I'm as superstitious as any actor—a notoriously twitchy lot. I didn't know what to make of it. I know my father would never have set foot aboard either vessel. He made many an astrologer rich during his lifetime. He believed in hexes, hoodoos, and bad karma of any description. My own life seems more like Violet's: depressingly regular disasters followed by perilous escapes that made Pauline of the silent melodramas seem tame.

Two flights of spiral stairs took me a bit closer to the engines, which I had expected to throb but instead made a deep humming sound. Pluto White Star's devotion to authenticity didn't extend to coal-fired steam engines. I gathered the vessel was propelled by some infernal nuclear contrivance, probably generating a pure sleet of insalubrious particles to career through my unprotected body every instant I spent in my dressing room. However, I try not to think about things I can't see, and the dressing room *did* have a star on the door.

I kicked it open and edged in sideways because of the sousaphone still slung over my shoulder. The big silver horn had to be the most awkward single object ever invented by man, and for a week now I'd been stuck with it between shows. The property manager said there simply wasn't space in the narrow flies of the shipboard theater for all the gear needed for our two shows, so would I just be a dear and pitch in . . . ? I'd foolishly agreed, not yet knowing there is absolutely *no* good place to store a sousaphone.

I nudged the door shut with my knee, and put my lips experimentally to the mouthpiece, puckered my lips, and blew. All I got was the same merry flatulence I'd produced on my first attempt. It had been days before a guy from the ship's band had played a tune for me on it . . . and I'd been amazed to discover it was *supposed* to sound like that. Now I shrugged it off my shoulders and attacked the screws that held the monstrous bell onto the loops of silver tubing, wondering once again where they had found such a ridiculous item. The flea market of Hell, no doubt. It was supposed to nest inside a case that might have held two moose heads side by side, but there I had put my foot down. It actually took up less of my limited space if I hung the bell on a clothes hook above the door, then put the rest on the bed. When it came time to sleep, the instrument was propped against the door, where it made a nice informal burglar alarm. You never know, with all the crooks around these days.

In addition to the bunk there was a makeup table with lighted mirror and a chair mounted on casters. And there you have the catalog of my furniture. In the wall opposite the table were two doors, one leading to a coffin-sized head, the sort where you stood on the toilet to take a shower, and the other to a locker where I stored my costumes between shows. The architect hadn't planned on the occupant bringing something the size of the Pantechnicon with him. I had to roll it in front of the head to get in the closet, and vice versa. Three people in this cabin was a considerable crowd. Add a fourth and you had the stateroom scene from *A Night at the Opera*.

I was glad to have it. The chorus bunked together in a room not much larger than this. If they all inhaled at once the door burst from its hinges.

I pulled the chair around and opened a desk shelf on the side of the Pantech. Speaking a pass phrase—which I don't think I'll mention here, thank you very much—caused a small drawer to spring open. I took out the thin stack of large bills inside the drawer and thumbed through them. Sadly, they had once more refused to mate and multiply. I took a dinner menu

and an eyebrow pencil and a well-thumbed booklet of interplanetary rates and schedules, shoved my straw boater back
on my head, and once more tried to make my bankroll add
up to a trip to Luna before October. Improvise! I told myself.
Rhapsodize! Steerage is fine, no problem, but the ships had
to be reasonably fast.

It just didn't compute. I had enough for passage, but not
in any reasonable time. Or, I could get as far as the Jupiter
trailing Trojans by early May, only to arrive dead broke.

I took the little netsuke frog from the drawer and set it
beside the stack of money. I sighed. It just didn't make sense
to keep the thing. Not that selling it would get me to Luna in
time, but it would provide me with some walking around
money when I reached the Trojans. Perhaps something would
turn up there. I really had no choice. Time was the operative
factor.

There was a knock on the door, and I hastily stowed my
valuables back into their hiding place and sealed it up. I put
on my dressing gown and opened the door to find a man
standing there, looking up at me with a faint smile.

"Mr. Valentine?"

"Yes?"

"You wouldn't happen to be Sparky Valentine, the guy I
used to watch on *Sparky and His Friends*?"

"Careful," I said. "You're dating yourself."

"You are? Really?"

"Guilty."

"I knew it, I just knew it," he said, his grin growing
wider. "I told my wife, 'That's just *got* to be Sparky Valentine,' I said, but she didn't believe me. Isn't she going to
be surprised? She said everybody knew you died years ago."

"Those rumors were greatly exaggerated."

"That's what I told her. But no, she insisted you'd been
murdered in some back alley in Luna forty, fifty years ago."
His smile faded a little. "To tell you the truth, I'd heard that
story, too."

"I'm not surprised. I've heard it as well. Once these stories get going they turn into urban legends. Who knows how
they start." Well, this one started because I got it going
myself, having a great need at the time to avoid a certain

THE GOLDEN GLOBE ··· 75

party who just wasn't going to stop looking for me short of the grave . . . but that's another story.

There followed an awkward moment of the sort I used to be quite familiar with, but which had become infrequent. I used to be recognized all the time, stopped on the street, buttonholed, quizzed, importuned. Mostly complimented, because Sparky was beloved to a whole generation of children. You never become completely comfortable with it. Somebody is standing there telling you how much he admires you, or your work. Sometimes, it's that he frankly idolizes you, that you've changed his life. Even *saved* his life. I'm not going to try telling you it isn't enjoyable to be told things like that. If you hate compliments you should never get into show business. But it is awkward, and soon you find yourself standing there with a false smile on your face listening to the fan extol your virtues and wondering how quickly you can gracefully get away. The more effusive the praise, the tougher this is. I soon begin to wonder, if my work in that long-ago series changed your life, what sort of pitiful life do you have? Are you going to bend my ear all day long? And most important, are you stalking me?

I'd stopped really worrying about stalkers years ago. I had plenty of more concrete things to worry about. So I wasn't really uneasy as I stood there in the doorway, listening to him gush about how much he'd enjoyed the show, how he still caught it every chance he could in reruns, how he'd loved me and all the other characters in Sparky's Gang. I figured the nicest way to give him the bum's rush was to offer an autograph, and was trying to figure how to slip the offer into the stream of words, when he said, "Say, would you mind? I went back to my cabin and got this. I found it in the Tokyo gift shop and I'm going to give it to my son. Could I get your autograph on it?"

He was holding out a book. I took it and flipped through the pages. It was a reprint edition of *Sparky and His Gang,* something I hadn't seen in decades. I quickly sought the copyright page, only to discover no date or copyright information. *Printed in Brementon,* it said.

The nerve of the guy! This was a pirated edition, printed by convict labor, of a book to which I still, theoretically, owned the rights—for all the good it had done me the last seventy years.

... But what the hell. The guy probably had no idea I'd written the thing (well, ghostwritten, but I'd *paid* the ghostwriter, and now it was *mine*). Trying not to clench my teeth, I took the book and pencil from him.

I guess I bore down too hard, because the point broke off. He started patting all his pockets, looking for a pen. I knew that to get rid of him I'd better find one myself, so I turned around, and the back of my head exploded.

The thought processes must keep going during unconsciousness. As I swam my way up through sluggish depths toward a distant light, it all came clear to me, so that when I opened my eyes and saw that my straw hat had landed on what looked like a dead cat, I knew exactly what it was. I knew just what had happened, and it's hard to say if I was more frightened or disgusted.

He just happened to have bought a copy of *Sparky and His Gang,* which he just happened to have in his room? Unlikely. That should have alerted me. His rubicund complexion I had taken for the flush of too much liquor. But it was the wig that should have tipped me, should have warned me never to turn my back on him.

I reached for the straw hat with an arm that had grown to be six meters long. The crown was crushed where his cosh had hit it. It just might have cushioned the blow enough that I only stayed out for a few minutes, instead of the several hours he had intended.

And that could be the difference I needed, if I could take advantage of it. I took a deep breath. I didn't want to look up, but I had to, so I did.

Sure enough, he had a dazzling red head of hair. Mister Carrot-top. The wig had come off as he swung the blackjack, and my hat had landed on it.

Unforgivable! Incredible stupidity. I had known it was a rug from the first moment I opened the door. Civilians don't know how to wear toupees, they always get it wrong. This one had not even been gummed down around the edges; he had worn it so loosely that simply swinging his arm overhead had knocked it off.

"I really did enjoy *Sparky and His Gang*," said the diminutive agent of the Charonese Mafia. He had moved my chair in front of the door and was sitting in it, feet flat, back straight, bright and alert. He had a pistol of some sort, and it never wavered. I had no doubt he could pick which of my eyeballs to hit, shooting from the hip.

"I'd like to get up and give you the frog," I said.

"Just stay where you are. I'll take care of everything."

That's what I was afraid of. With the Charonese there were usually only two options: a quick bullet, or prolonged torture.

"Should I order a drink?" I sighed. Don't imagine I was as cool as I sounded. The line and the attitude belonged to Nick Charles, from *The Thin Man's Last Stand*. (". . . nobody could be quite so cool as Mr. Charles in the face of the many dangers he stares down, but Casey Valens had a grand old time making us believe it."—JMMT Channel 70 Minute Reviews).

"Just wait awhile."

"Don't want to make a scene?" I asked.

"It's best to keep these things quiet. When we dock at Honolulu a friend of mine will be coming aboard. You'll leave with us. I can give you a drug to keep you docile if you make it necessary. But I hate to use it. It's annoying. When I'm annoyed, I do things you wouldn't like."

"It won't be necessary," I said. "I'm . . . say, you never told me your name. Or is that an annoying request?"

"Comfort," he said.

"Beg pardon?"

"Isambard Comfort."

I looked at him dubiously, but he gave no sign he was kidding. I'd asked his name not so much because I wanted to add him to my Christmas card list, but in hopes he would refuse to tell me. Traditionally, if they don't care about you learning their names, it means they plan to kill you. "He can identify you in court, Rocko. Better wax him." However, this was Pluto and the Charonese Mafia, who did more or less what they pleased. His distaste for taking and disposing of me publicly had more to do with decorum on the part of the ferrymen.

But I had a plan.

"I'm going in there and splash some water in my face,"

I told him. He made the slightest of shrugs, so I struggled to my feet. I stood there swaying, looking down at the hat in my hands, then set it on my head. The impression I wanted to give was of someone still woozy from the blow. Part of my tortured mind was howling in pain and I was keeping it rigidly under control. I knew how to do this since I once did the last two acts of *Hamlet* with a broken arm, sustained in a fall backstage. ("The Prince of Denmark is one of the more tortured figures in the theatrical canon, but never have I seen so much naked pain brought to the stage as in Mr. K. Valentine's portrayal last night at the Metro Forum. As he lay dying, poisoned, I wanted to leap from my seat and call for medical attention. Bravo, Valentine!"—Liz Harcourt, *The Oberonian*.)

I washed my face in the tiny sink in the head, then staggered back out toward the dressing table mirror, where I leaned forward and studied myself.

"God," I said. "I look like Macbeth in the last act. *After* Macduff cuts off his head." I prodded around my left eye, which seemed to be swelling up. I must have hit something on my way down. " 'Let fall thy blade on vulnerable crests,' " I quoted. " 'I bear a charmed life, which must not yield to one of woman born.' "

He knew little of the theater, apparently, but he was sharp. Oh, so sharp. I saw his eyes narrow and dart around quickly. I suppose they teach them, in Charonese survival schools—of which there are no better in the solar system—to beware the inconsistent, the unexplained, the unexpected. Something about my lines must not have rung true to his predatory ear.

I didn't give him a lot of time to chew on it, though. Nor did I betray, I trust, the rising tension in my body as I looked down at my crumpled hat, sighed, and tossed it on the bed.

Sharp? Hell, yes. And *fast*!

I didn't even see the tanglenet as it flew from the tiny hole in the Pantechnicon. I did see the line of red laser light that hit his weapon. Saw it, heard it sizzle, and pretty soon smelled it in the form of ozone and the stink of crisping flesh.

Nothing went quite the way it was supposed to. He was so damn *fast*!

The laser shouldn't have been on more than a fraction of a second. It's supposed to locate a weapon, hit it, heat it very quickly, and that's that. It would melt the lead in a bullet. I could see his finger pull the trigger until the finger was sliced off as the laser ray passed through it.

He was trying to rise from his chair. He got halfway out of it, but the force of the expanding tanglenet hitting him threw his body back against the door . . . with one arm still free. The net was *supposed* to hit him so quickly that both arms would be pinned to his sides, but that snakelike speed had enabled him to keep his gun arm out of its clutches. Now that free hand was a blackened mess, all his fingers off, only the thumb intact.

That's when I got a bit of luck. The force of his impact knocked the sousaphone bell loose and it fell over his head. He stumbled and went down tangled up with his chair.

I knew it wasn't over yet. Casting about for a club of some sort, my hand fell on the other part of the great horn. I grabbed it and turned around, in time to see him shrugging off the bell, his free hand at his side ready to lift him to his feet. I swung the heavy metal tubing over my head and brought it down around his shoulders.

And it *still* wasn't over. I could have wished for a tighter fit of horn and body. The only way I had to keep him within the circle was to move in close and keep it jammed down around him. That gave him a chance to use his feet and his knees, and to gnash at me with his teeth, which had been filed sharp. I will never forget that sight: those teeth snapping closed inches from my nose, and those eyes, showing no pain, no fear . . . no emotion at all but a determination to do his job, to kill me.

What we did then was a violent close-quarters ballet, a road-show version of the famous fight in the cabin of the *Quantum Belle* from *The Pusher's Return*. It's thirty seconds of mayhem in a five-sided shoe box, based on a similar situation on the Orient Express from a much earlier movie, and they said it could never be done on boards until Dixon de la Nash and I made it the spine-tingling centerpiece of that year's smash hit of the Alameda season. ("Look for the names Sparkman and de la Nash when they draw up the list of this year's Alley nominees. Their incredible fight in the cabin has to be seen to be disbelieved, and is merely the capstone of two of the best performances of this or any other year. If there's any justice, they should *both* get the award.''—*The Alamedan*.)

Friends, *Pusher* ran six months, eight shows a week, and if I hadn't been there for the whole run I don't think I'd have come out of that *Brittanic* cabin alive.

With one hand almost off, one arm stuck to his side by the tanglenet, the other arm held by the ring of brass tubing, six inches shorter and fifty pounds lighter than me . . . even with all that about the only edge I had on him was the weight. I could horse him around by tugging on the horn, while at the same time being sure it stayed down around him. I wrestled him to the bed, all the time soaking up a punishing series of kicks to the shin and a jackhammering of his knees to my crotch. I scrambled among the bedclothes, meaning to strangle him if possible, managing only to jam a sheet down over his head and shoulders. His kicking lost some accuracy, but never let up. I hurled him face-first into the makeup mirror, pulled him away, and then did it again now that it was broken and jagged. The sheet over his face turned red. I searched for his eyes with my thumbs and felt something squish, but that gave him a chance to shrug the tuba up over his free shoulder and he began flailing at me. He used the arm as a club, getting in one ringing blow that almost broke my collarbone, then another to my side, before bringing his forearm down like a swung baseball bat on the edge of the makeup table. Face powder blossomed into the air, and both bones in his forearm snapped like dry spaghetti. I thought I heard him grunt a little from that, but it never slowed him. He kept swinging the arm, which now bent in three places, the mangled and blackened remains of his fist like a grisly mace at the end of a bloody rope.

But I managed to jam the horn back down over him. Fumbling behind me, I came up with a big jar of cold cream and swung it up and over and down, as if trying to pound a stake into the ground. I heard something crack, and he stopped moving for a moment, staggered, and almost fell down. Then he began moving toward me again, blind, almost immobilized. I heard a high, shrill sound that I thought was some sort of Charonese war cry, then realized it was me. I couldn't stop making the sound. I hit him again and he went to his knees but still wouldn't fall over. I hit him a third time.

When things became clear again I was on my knees in front of him looking at bits of matted, bloody hair sticking to the edge of the cold-cream jar.

Nick Charles would have shrugged off being sapped, shinned, and drop-kicked in the crotch. He'd have straightened his tie, dabbed at a trickle of blood with an immaculate handkerchief, and delivered a trenchant line. Well, folks, I am an actor, and the thought of Nick and others like him from violent melodrama had kept me going through the fight—me, basically a coward and not the least bit stoic—but when it was over I did what most humans do. What you would most likely do. I howled like a dog.

Everything hurt. Getting sapped, in particular, is not at all what it seems in the comic books.

One thing that didn't hurt was the family jewels. That's because they were in a safe-deposit tube in a Lunar hospital, near absolute zero. My father taught me that testicles were God's joke on the male species, good only for procreation and the delivery of agony. Testosterone comes in pills.

I got to my feet. When I turned my head a team of horses clattered over the top of it. I thought I might throw up, but mastered the urge. I stood looking down at my vanquished foe, then at the Pantechnicon. I *told* you not to be surprised at what it might do.

I banged my fist on the top of it, and with an apologetic little *sproinnnng!* the collapsible billy club popped out of the side and clattered to the deck.

"Where were you when I needed you?" I asked it, then fell down and slept.

It should have been one, two, *three*!

One, the laser, and two, the tanglenet, arriving almost simultaneously. Then, with him disarmed and restrained, the steel shillelagh pops into my hand and I belabor him about the head, shoulders, and any other sensitive parts that strike my fancy.

All for want of a spring . . .

The ejection mechanism worked fine when I tried it later. No doubt years of disuse and infrequent testing had frozen it just enough to nearly get me killed. It wasn't the Pantech's fault, but my own.

When designing the thing I'd given a lot of thought to a lethal attack. The laser was quite capable of slicing heads from shoulders like lunch meat. But killing is a step you can never draw back from. Nor can you ever be sure you might accidentally set your infernal machine into motion. I had been as careful as I could, requiring that the Pantech get not one but two cues from me. In this case, in the dressing room, the quote from *Macbeth* had primed the mechanism, jacked a shell into the chamber, as it were, causing the Pantech's brain to come alert, size up the threat, locate the weapon, if any, and await further orders. Which came when I tossed my hat onto the bed. Both these are things an actor never does in the dressing room. Had I been elsewhere there were other signals, which will remain within my own purview. There are enemies lurking everywhere, and who knows but that you might be one of them?

Thank God for *The Pusher's Return*. It wasn't the first time my craft had saved my life. One day I might even put my sword-fighting skills to good use.

And by the way, there is no damn justice. Dixon de la Mare won that Alley Award, *stole* that Alley Award. It's the same old story. I played the villain so well the voters subconsciously didn't like me.

When I woke up I did so all at once, nearly falling off the bed as every muscle in my body jerked. I'd dreamed he was hovering over me, the bloody ruin of his face twisted into a deadly grin, his white, sharp teeth getting star billing. I looked at the floor and he was still in the same position.

Bad mistake, that, not taking the time to check him out. But I'd really had little choice. I looked at him now.

All right, Sparky. You've cleverly lured your prey to you, and you've vanquished it. Now, do you stuff it and mount it in the den, release it back into its native habitat, or eat it?

Maybe I didn't have much choice. Maybe he was already dead. I reached down and pinched his nostrils together. In a moment a breath came bubbling from his lips, a comical sound in another situation.

Good. He might still die—I might yet decide I had to kill him, for that matter—but it's always best to have a choice. And Father always used to say you should never kill anyone unless it's absolutely necessary. Of course, he viewed getting a bad review as fulfilling that condition.

This might be one of those times. The Charonese had a bulldog reputation for pursuit. There was no way they were going to let this matter remain in its current state. They would be coming after me. I was not safe on Pluto, or the Neptune or Uranus systems. It was said the ferrymen had considerable clout as far sunward as Saturn's orbit. Beyond that I didn't know.

So step one was to depart the balmy shores of Pluto. Five minutes from now would be about right, I thought. It would take me a bit longer in actual practice.

What about Isambard Comfort, then? Could that really be his name? Should I let him survive to inflict its ridiculous syllables on other innocent ears? I frowned down at him again. Under a flap of detached scalp I thought I saw a gleam of metal.

I nudged the skin aside with the tip of my billy club. It looked like a stainless-steel egg in there. There were broken bits of skull bone but beneath it all he seemed to have encased his brain in a protective shell.

I'd heard of it, but never seen it. We monkey with our bodies these days—Lord knows I'd done enough of it myself, for professional reasons—but there are a few hard constants that resist our best efforts. That wrinkled, red-gray, be-veined and be-flustered mass known as the brain was one of them. You could augment it with crystal memory, wire it for radio reception, or bronze it for posterity, as Comfort had done, but if you tampered with it too much it simply stopped working. So I knew that, whatever he had done, it hadn't been proof against repeated blows from a jar of cold cream. That sphere of metal would prevent the gray matter from being penetrated by a knife or a bullet, but nothing could alter its inertia, and slamming it against the inside of the shell produced a concussion, and you were *out*. Worse, the not infrequent sequella of concussion was brain swelling, which could be fatal even in our current state of medical grace. Isambard's brain would be swelling now, with no more place to go than if it had been in a standard-issue skull.

As I came to that conclusion I saw a tiny network of cracks appear in the metal carapace. The whole construction grew by about a quarter of an inch. It was now more of a fine metal mesh than a seamless helmet.

This was commando stuff, I realized. Damage-control circuits were coming into play.

That's when I realized I wasn't going to kill him. Mainly, it was the conclusion that killing him would not further my cause in any way.

And he'd said he liked *Sparky and His Gang*.

For well over twenty years *Britannic* had been cruising a triangular route meant to simulate a trans-Pacific voyage. The original ship could not have made the crossing in less than two weeks. The Plutonian copy did it in four days. This was no great feat of speed, as the entire journey took place in the hundred-kilometer bubble of rock deep beneath the planetary surface known as the Pacifica Environmental Park, still the largest disneyland in the system.

It was a voyage in both space and time, and don't ask me how they did it. I mean, the ship when under weigh always seemed to be making good speed, cutting smartly through the blue water, leaving a long, straight wake behind. It stood to reason that she was actually either tethered in place, or going in large circles, but you couldn't tell it by looking.

The trip started in Edo, in 1853, the year of the arrival of the Black Ships in the bay of what would become Tokyo. Passengers embarked after sampling the culture of feudal Japan, sailed out with magnificent Mount Fuji in the distance as Commodore Perry sailed in.

The next morning brought them to Tahiti in 1789—a very cute trick: two thousand leagues south by southwest, and sixty years into the past in about eighteen hours. *Britannic* would drop anchor at Papeete alongside the *Bounty,* met by dozens of outrigger canoes filled with happy, naked brown people throwing tropical flowers, and the passengers would be ferried ashore for a day of sensual pleasures in the sun, surf, and sand. They'd feast, frolic, and fornicate (all included in the price of your ticket, no tipping, please!), have their pictures taken with Fletcher Christian and Captain Bligh, then stagger back to feast and frolic and fornicate most of the night, until the morning, when the ship arrived at Pearl Harbor on the morning of December 7, 1941, where the Pacifica disneyland management had prepared a little show for them, which the less hungover among the vacationers might actually watch. Even those you might have thought dead to the world were usually awakened; the show was very noisy.

From there the ship sailed for San Francisco, arriving in time for the earthquake of 1906.

I said the trip was triangular, and you might have noticed this triangle seemed to have four corners. No real mystery this time: San Francisco Bay was actually just a few miles on the other side of Fuji. During the night the ship was brought around through a tunnel under the mountain, ready for another group of revelers. Actually, the trip through the tunnel, which the passengers never saw, was as interesting as the Great Quake, in my opinion. I'd gone through it twice.

This schedule allowed *Titanic* and *Olympic* to follow at twenty-four hour intervals, which meant that every fourth day Pearl Harbor was spared, Frisco didn't burn, and the Clark Gable and Charles Laughton clones and all the other actors in the four locations got a day off. (Not the crews. We worked thirty days, then had a ten-day furlough.)

Not this time, though. My hiatus would last a bit longer, as I was about to bid an informal good-bye to *Britannic*.

It was not the first time I'd had to abandon a show in the middle of a run. In fact, thinking back, it had been some time since I'd been able to *finish* one. There'd been two more before my hasty departure from Brementon. I never felt good about it. The show must go on, don't you know. You hate to let your fellow troupers down. But there was no point in sticking around if you were about to be sent to jail, or the grave. Any way you looked at it, it was understudy time.

Dawn was just breaking as we rounded Diamond Head and steamed into Pearl Harbor. Just down the beach I could see rows of resort hotels that had not been there in 1941. Even at this hour I could see a few fanatics out in the water perched on fiberglass boards, engaging in a Hawaiian version of attempted suicide known as "surfing." I'd tried it my last time through. If God had intended me to surf, He'd have given me gills.

Disembarking was going to be something of a problem. If I waited until we tied up at the wharf, I'd be sure to encounter whoever M. Comfort had intended to meet. I felt I could elude him or them with a suitable disguise, but there was no good way to disguise the Pantechnicon, and somebody was bound to wonder why that odd-looking fellow was stealing my luggage. Embarrassing questions were sure to be asked, attracting unwanted attention.

That meant an unceremonious dunk in the drink. Even that presented problems. It would be a good idea not to be seen. With the Day of Infamy about to begin, the decks were jammed with spectators. My one lucky break was that the port side offered much the better view of the festivities, and the stewards had advertised that fact. That was also the side that would tie up to the dock after the show, so the crew preparing hatches and ramps were over there, too. I had found a big cargo hatch near the starboard bow and in the fifteen minutes I'd been standing there, watching the water flow by twenty feet beneath me, not a soul had come down the passageway. Until now.

"Good morning, Elwood," I said. He was ambling toward me, hands jammed down into his pockets, hat jammed down on his head. I hadn't seen much of him during the voyage. No doubt he was spending his time at the bar, telling his tall tales to anyone who would listen.

" 'Lo, Sparky," he drawled.

"Feel like a swim?" I asked him.

"No. No, I think I'll pass on that one." He leaned on the pole that blocked the open hatch door and gazed out at the gray Navy ships, dozens of them, clustered around the dry docks and repair yards of Keanapuaa. All the bigger ones, the behemoths, the battleships named after political divisions of the old United States, were on the port side.

"I looked in on that feller in your dressing room," he said.

"How's he doing?"

"Gonna be a close thing," he said. "A real close thing."

"That's what I thought, too."

He turned to squint up at me.

"Didja have to hit him so hard?"

"You didn't see the fight, Elwood."

"No, you're right. I didn't see it. He must have come at you really hard, for you to do that to him."

"Actually, he didn't come at me at all. He was just holding me at gunpoint."

He looked surprised. "You don't mean it. What was he, some sort of cop?"

"In a way. Private security."

He shook his head slowly and looked down at the water.

"It's usually not a good idea, beating a cop half to death."

"Didn't have much choice. He was going to kill me."

"He said that, did he?"

"Well, not in so many words."

He gave me another long look, and this time I looked away. Sometimes I wish Elwood would just go away. He's always second-guessing me.

"What did you want me to do?" I protested. "Wait around and see?"

"Now don't you get all excited. I'm just asking, that's all. I don't want to try to run your life for you."

"Sure you do."

"That's not true, Sparky. I'm just looking out for your welfare. If that man dies, you know good and well there'll be more trouble—"

"Getting killed isn't your idea of trouble?"

He looked me over again, then nodded. I was beginning to hear a low, droning noise, still distant but getting nearer. Elwood looked up. The sky was blue, and still clear.

"All I was gonna suggest," he said, "is when you get ashore, would it hurt anything to give a call and have somebody go get him? It might make a big difference."

"They'll find him soon enough."

"Maybe, maybe not." He kept looking at me.

"All right. I'll call."

"That's good." He looked down at the water again. "I'm glad I won't be diving into that. Looks cold to me."

"Are you kidding? This is Hawaii. It's warm as soup."

"Yeah? Seems to me there's a nip in the air."

With that the droning noise got a lot louder, and the first wave of torpedo bombers of the Japanese Imperial Navy appeared over the pineapple fields to the north. I gave Elwood a sour look, and shoved the Pantech over the side. When I hesitated for a moment, he planted a foot encouragingly, and I tumbled into the water.

• • •

The next half hour kept me busy as a one-man show of *Cast of Thousands*. It wasn't nearly as dangerous as it looked . . . or so I kept telling myself.

Pacifica's Pearl Harbor spectacular, known in the trade as a Vegas, employed every trick in the book to make it seem life-sized and historically accurate, including one of the more subtle tricks I know: having parts of it actually *be* life-sized. The aircraft were all exact replicas, powered by real gasoline engines. The torpedoes they dropped were to scale, but had no warheads, explosions being provided by charges already in place. The battleships themselves were also big as life . . . on the side the audience saw, anyway.

The show employed a cast of several thousand. Most of them simply had to run around shouting and pointing. Others did actual stunts, from simply swimming through water dotted with burning oil slicks, to being blown from the deck of an exploding battleship. There were fire gags, with sailors running around engulfed in flame, and bomb gags, where men bounced off concealed trampolines at the moment the gas and flash powder went off.

Only about a hundred of these were full studio-certified expert stunt performers, and they were clustered near the center of the action. The rest were journeymen, getting extra wages because of the marginal dangers involved, but not qualified for the more exacting gags. My plan was to stay in the areas where these guys were assigned, and try not to get my hair singed off.

The Pantechnicon is equipped to deliver motive power in a variety of mediums. Today I'd rigged a small propeller to a shaft that would normally power a set of wheels, and I trailed behind at the end of a three-meter cord. The Pantech is about as streamlined as a brick. Its progress might best be described as wallowing, but it managed a steady three knots, which would eventually get me there.

I'd seen the show twice before, so I had some idea where the biggest effects were produced. Still, it could get dicey. The best thing I had going was the clarity of the water, at least before the worst of the explosions roiled the bottom and filled the water with foamy bubbles. I could duck my head under and see where the charges were placed.

My worst moment came when I felt a vibration in the water, turned my head, and saw a torpedo headed straight for me. I saw it pass about ten feet below, a lethal silver shark, then the water all around me turned to foam and my clothes filled up with air for a while.

But a few minutes later I ran aground on a concrete shore to the south side of Ford's Island. I dragged myself and my luggage out of the water and sat down to await the end of the show.

If you think the sinking of the *Arizona* is spectacular, you should see the raising.

Britannic had gone to her berthing point before it was over, all the fire and noise and fountains of water and planes crashing in flames. Then the heavenly director shouted, "Cut, that's a wrap," and it all stopped for a moment . . . then went into reverse. Torpedoes bobbed to the surface, then headed for a submarine tender like schools of fish. Half a dozen enormous gray metal battlewagons were lifted from the bottom, still smoking, paint blistered. Sailors who had gone down with the ship spit out breathing tubes and broke out the paint cans. Everywhere water cascaded off buckled "wooden" decks, which now started to unbuckle along the invisible hinge lines. All over the harbor little boom skimmers darted, corralling the black bunker fuel, sucking it into big tanks.

Everybody went about his business without a single cheer being raised, nor a solitary high-five exchanged. They call it theater, but it's not, to my mind. I know it's hard to maintain enthusiasm after a long run. The solution to that is to *get out* when you no longer feel excitement as the curtain falls. This particular Vegas had been running for twenty years. Some of the people around me were the children of the original cast. Their own children would no doubt take over the jobs when this generation moved on to something else. I found these disneyland shows overproduced and cheerless. If you want a history lesson, a holograph movie would serve.

Ah, well. It created a lot of jobs in the system's number-one industry: tourism. I'll confess I've played in them when at liberty from more rewarding projects.

No one gave me a glance as I found my way to the freight elevator that took me down into the bowels of Pacifica and deposited me at the employees' train station, which in turn dumped me at the spaceport fifteen minutes later. Even on the train car I drew no curious stares as I dripped Hawaiian water onto the red seats and black carpet. Plutonians are a mind-your-own-business crowd, one of the best things about them.

One more train ride and I was at the freight terminal at the most remote point of the spaceport. If I'd come there two weeks before, I could have avoided a great deal of trouble, and Isambard Comfort could have missed a monumental headache.

I hadn't come here for one big reason. It scared me to death. Now the alternative was worse, so I marched resolutely up to the express counter of Pillock and Burke Interplanet Carriers and inquired as to the cost of mailing myself to Uranus.

I didn't put it in just those words, of course.

"What's in it?" the clerk asked, with a big yawn, looking without interest at the Pantech, sitting there seeming as new as the day it was built, having shaken off all signs of its recent adventure like a duck's back sheds water.

"Personal effects," I said. "Tools of my trade." I knew that would get me a discount, under the Interplanetary Artists' Convention.

"Anythin' t'd'clare?"

"No contraband. There's a bichon frise inside."

"A what?"

"A dog. Here's his license. I'll need Oh-two and H-two-Oh feeds, and a two-twenty power connection." I didn't really need the power, since the Pantech has its own internal source, but it was illegal to ship that power plant without having it inspected and certified, and why bother them with all that red tape? Better to pay for the power hookup and not raise any questions.

Such as the one he now asked.

"What about food? The dog gonna need food?"

"He has his own." He looked at me and raised an eyebrow. "He doesn't eat much," I explained. "It's a small dog." I could feel myself getting too elaborate. My father always said to keep your lies simple, and never answer a question you're not asked. But he kept looking, so I shoved the license closer to him and let the P$20 bill peek out from under it. His eyes shifted, and he picked up the license and shoved it into a machine. The bill was gone. He handed the license back to me with a new stamp on it. I really hated to do this, since anyone who knew about Toby might be able to trace me through him, but I had no choice.

He took a yellow form from a stack and started filling it in with a pencil. It was almost Dickensian, and a blatant waste of time since he had a voice-capable computer at his elbow, but Pluto, like most planets, had some archaic and fiercely protected labor laws. Reading upside down, I saw him fill in the spot for *breed of dog* as Bitching Freeze.

Finally he slapped a shipping tag on the side of the Pan-tech, and I watched it trundle away on a conveyor belt into unknown depths.

Now I was in a big hurry.

There was a convenience store at the train station. I filled a grocery bag full of granola bars, jerky, honey, corn syrup, and as many other items of concentrated fat, sugar, and carbohydrates as I could carry. Then I set off in search of the sort of merchant you can always find hanging around a spaceport. The sort who doesn't display his wares on shelves, or hang out a sign.

She wasn't too hard to find. Most drugs are legal on Pluto, and even the ones they try to control are readily available if you know where to look—as has always been the case. I was directed to a back booth of a coffee shop on one of the lower levels. I sipped a hot chocolate while we haggled about price, then she left and I sat looking out a big picture window overlooking the freight-sorting yard. Millions of crates and parcels slid down ramps and along conveyors until they fetched up at the doors that would soon open and disgorge their loads onto shuttle trucks.

The pusher returned with a small plastic envelope, and told me the quickest way to the yard.

This place was probably more dangerous than Pearl. The mechanized mayhem of the Vegas was predictable, most of it was smart, and programmed to be on the lookout for fragile humans getting in the way. Not so in the freight yard. If you didn't stay on your toes something might roll up behind you and crush you like a bug under silent wheels. I moved quickly, following the homer beacon in my pocket, and soon I was standing where the Pantechnicon had come to rest, midway down a line of larger crates.

I was about to activate it when a movement in the corner of my eye made me stop and duck down. I looked up cautiously . . . and let out a deep breath. Two lines over a man was on his hands and knees, crawling under the metal frame of a conveyor. This was all right with me; cops never crawl, and they never look furtive. Neither do yard bulls. They can *sneak* just fine, but they do it with entirely different body language.

In fact . . . I thought I knew this guy.

I gave a low whistle, three notes known to hoboes throughout the system, and he looked up at me and grinned.

"Sparks," he said, in a husky voice.

"Lou? Is that the uke man?"

"You don't believe me, I'll play you a tune."

Ukulele Lou was a legend in his own time. He was rumored to have some sort of brain damage, which made his conversations a little hard to follow, and he was crazy as a mudlark. But his memory for music was amazing. He claimed to know words and music to fifteen thousand songs, and I'd never doubted him. He was wearing a battered pressure suit. His precious ukulele was in his hand.

I swear, the helmet faceplate had a crack in it. It made me sweat just to think about it. Lou and some of the other 'bos *always* traveled this way, and without the comforts of top-of-the-line luggage.

"Where you bound?" I asked him.

"Where else? Uranus." He pronounced it your-*an*us.

Where else, indeed? I'm largely ignorant of these things, but my understanding was that due to orbital dynamics, nearly *all* the outer planet commerce for the last decade, and for a few decades to come, was the triangle of Pluto, Uranus, and Neptune, then back to Pluto, in that order. It had to do with the relative positions of the planets. Pluto had for some years been at the lowest point in its orbit, which meant it was closer to the sun than Neptune. Uranus was about sixty degrees ahead, and Neptune clear around the sun from Uranus. *No* orbit in the outer planets that gets you there in a reasonable time is a truly economical orbit, but going *against* the direction of planetary motion is the least economical orbit of all. It's like stepping off a moving train. Before you go anywhere else, you first have to kill your own motion.

"What about you?" Lou asked.

"Uranus," I confirmed. I pronounced it *Ur*ine-us. Was there ever an orb so inelegantly named? Nobody's ever agreed on how to say it, and *both* ways stink.

"The Bard's World?" he asked, with a cackle.

"Where else?"

"Can't get them stars outta your eyes, is that it? Gonna stand at the corner of Columbia and Paramount and gawk at the names in the pavement? Buy a map to the stars' condos? See how your feet fit in Henry Collyer's footsteps?"

I ignored the ribbing and saluted him. "Good luck, Lou," I said.

"Break a leg," he urged. Then he pried up a corner of a three-story packing crate and squeezed himself inside. I could hear him working, faintly, as I activated the shelter on the Pantech.

I did a little research on tramps and hoboes while struggling through an ill-advised update of *The Grapes of Wrath*. ("Kenneth Valentine struggles through this ill-advised update as Tom Joad, an asteroid miner thrown out of work when the 'Tailings Crisis' of '86 shuts down all operations. He would have been better off playing this material for laughs, of which there are many, few of them intended."—*Daily Cereal*.) Back then it was boxcars on freight trains, and you would weep in terror to know what these men went through. They rode in them, on them, and *under* them—"riding the rods"—their bodies inches from the murderous wheels.

Then, as now, the owners of the railroads were aware of the informal passengers, and then, as now, they didn't like it much. What they did about it depended largely on where you hopped the freight, or where you got off.

The clerk I'd bribed had been fully aware of my real intentions. Declaring a live animal was the most common ruse to obtain air and water en route. He'd heard that story about the dog before. (Ironically, I really *had* a dog, of course, but he would not need any consumables.)

Maybe that clerk meant what he said when he wrote "bitching freeze." It would be one *hell* of a bitchin' freeze if anything went wrong with any of the Pantech's systems along the way. Or any of the freighter's systems, for that matter, and let's face it, they just aren't as careful about things as they are in even the worst passenger liner. You lose a passenger and it's lawsuit time. If the Pantech sprang a leak I'd be little more than spoiled freight, who shouldn't have been in there in the first place. Like those old 'bos who fell off the rods; gathered up, bagged, and tossed in a hole in potter's field. Maybe a token effort to contact the kinfolk.

We are used to a high standard of safety, and fear of vacuum is the most common phobia, one I share with eighty percent of humanity. Though I believe I have it in a greater degree than most.

Then there are the old space rats like Ukulele Lou. Cracked faceplate and all. He seemed immune to the fears that now began to bore into my spine like an electrified dental drill.

I heard him as I squeezed myself through the lock and into the newly deployed shelter half-made of memory plastic. He was doing what you might expect a guy named Ukulele Lou to do: singing.

The memory plastic can remember a variety of shapes. This time, since the Pantech was standing on end, and since we'd soon be in vacuum, it was best to be spherical. From the outside it looked like a cubist's idea of an ice-cream cone, and from inside, the hatch I could open to gain access to the interior was now under my feet, the Pantech becoming my basement. I lifted this hatch and fiddled with the environmental controls, preparing it to accept the external air and water feeds when they were hooked up, just prior to loading aboard the ship.

Luck. I'd need some of it. The trip would be eighty-four days. I had enough food to stretch for about thirty . . . *if* I stayed awake and my metabolism worked as usual. I didn't plan on staying awake.

I broke open the package I'd bought from the pusher, took out two of the pills, and swallowed them.

I heard the vacuum alarm going off outside, and I took a deep breath. I realized I'd been taking a lot of them. Now the huge doors to the outside started to rumble up toward the ceiling, and the sound died away as the air puffed out into space.

I felt like I was choking. My tongue seemed to swell until it filled my mouth, and became dry as an old wool sock. I could see the curved wall of my tent bulge outward the tiniest bit, and I was suddenly drenched in sweat.

"To be, or not to be," I gasped. "That is the question. Whether 'tis nobler in the mind to suffer the slings and arrows of outrageous fortune, or to take arms against a sea of troubles, and by opposing, end them."

That felt a little better. The conveyor began to move. I was bumped along quickly, and soon loaded onto a cargo pallet. Small robot handlers were climbing all over the pressure crates, metal spiders no bigger than my hand, stabbing shipping labels with red laser lights. I watched as they snapped lines to the pallet's air and water tanks. I saw the two yellow lights at my feet turn to green; I closed the basement hatch and sat down in lotus position as the shuttle truck lumbered out onto the dark surface of Pluto at high noon of a midsummer's day.

I was reminded of a postcard I once saw. Christmas in Vermont. A horse-drawn sleigh wound down a lane between leafless trees, snow-covered hills in the background. Out here the sun cast about as much light as the full moon in that postcard. Dozens of distant, skeletal cargo ships might have been Vermont maples designed by a mad geometer. There was a tractor moving along beside mine, pulling a cargo pallet on skids, that could do for a one-horse open sleigh . . .

No, sorry. Let's face it. This wasn't Currier and Ives. Those snow-covered hills were massive bergs of frozen methane. The glaciers coming down the sides were solid oxygen and nitrogen—pollutants, actually, not present on Pluto's crust until man arrived. On a busy day at the spaceport the rocket exhausts sometimes melted parts of these glaciers and they became murmuring streams. What a shame no Plutonians actually came out here for a sleigh ride, or to picnic by the little brooks a-gurgling.

I was choking up again, and didn't feel the least bit sleepy.

"Speak the speech, I pray you, as I pronounced it to you, trippingly on the tongue: but if you mouth it, as many of your players do, I had as lief the town crier spoke my lines."

A movement caught my eye. On the next crawler the corner of a packing crate had popped open from the inside. I saw Lou scramble out and start moving like a scuttling crab, over and around and under the other crates.

Jesus, Lou! He was holding one hand over the crack in his faceplate, and I fancied I could see a fine mist of oxygen snow like a halo around his head. Baby, it was *cold* outside. Midsummer, and the weather forecast was for another scorching day at 370 below zero. Something must have been wrong with the first crate to force Lou to change his lodgings this late in the game. A problem with the hookups, a defective seal, who knows? But there wasn't a thing I could do to help him.

Like a swimmer in a Siberian lake, you only get a couple of minutes. No spacesuit yet built protects well from frozen methane, and Lou's was an antique.

I watched him pry up the corner of another crate and slither inside. The corner was pulled back into place . . . and I realized I wouldn't know for another eighty-four days whether or not he was alive or frozen stiff.

When I turned away I seemed to be moving in slow motion. That's when I realized the drugs had started taking effect. It was a pleasant feeling, a warm heaviness in my limbs. My breathing became slow and deep and relaxed. I smiled. I closed my eyes.

I heard a distant wind blowing. There was the sound of dry leaves being swept along. I saw a great hourglass, grains of sand the size of houses rolling silently through the narrow neck. Slowly, the glass turned, the sand tumbled from the bottom to the top, and began to flow quickly in the other direction.

And I'm sorry as hell about this, but I can only report what happened. I'd been watching old movies all my life, and when it came time to flash back on my own life there was no way in the world it would come to me as anything but a black-and-white montage of whirling clock hands and fluttering calendar pages going backward, backward, ever backward in time. . . .

ACT
2

The warm water filled his ears. It made a deep roaring sound. He heard splashes that sounded far away, and he heard his own heartbeat. Air trickled from his lips and nose.

Friends, Romans . . .

Looking up, he saw the shimmery surface of the water, and beyond that, the dark figure with the ceiling light behind his head, making a halo.

Maybe that's what God looks like, he thought.

Sometimes he could almost see through things. Sometimes things seemed to shimmer, like the water, and he could see beyond them, to some shapeless otherness he could never quite remember. Was he dreaming when he saw these things? Was it remembering?

Remembering . . .

Friends and Romans and countrymen and ears and . . . something something something, *not to praise him.*

Quicksilver bubbles rose toward the looming, dark face. Strong hands on his shoulders. Strong, loving hands, good hands. *I only want the best for you, Dodger.*

It felt good to lie here. It was warm and it was safe and it was wet, and this is what a baby must feel like in its mommy's tummy.

His heart was pounding louder now. It wasn't fear. He just needed some air, that was all. Babies in their mommies' tummies didn't need air. But once you took that first breath, you sort of got used to it, air got to be something you needed.

Friends Romans lend me your praise him.

A big burst of air broke free and he began to struggle. He didn't want to, he'd been so good, so good so far, but his arms and his legs just wanted to move, and his lungs ached for a sweet breath of air. His small naked shoulders squirmed under the big hands, the good hands. He was so ashamed of himself. Maybe he should just take a big breath of water. Maybe he could learn to breathe water again, since he couldn't seem to learn the *important things*.

He'd heard it three times now. What was *wrong* with him, that he couldn't remember after hearing it three times?

It wasn't so bright now. Things were getting dim around the edges. The last of his air leaked from his nose, making hardly any sound at all.

And he had it. He became still as a stone and felt it all burst up from whatever depths it had fallen to when he lost it, and it flowed through his mind and his body, and he was nodding frantically as things got darker and darker.

He was pulled into the air and made a tremendous croaking sound as he filled his lungs and began to spew it out, like vomit.

"Frens romans countrymen lend me yerrears I come to, come to, come to bury Zeezer not t'praze'm," all the air was gone again, so he gasped in another breath, "lives after dem d'good 'soft enter'd with their bones." Pause. Breath. "The noble Brutes has tol' you Zeezer was . . . was . . ."

He breathed in and out frantically, staring down at the water, at his legs beneath the water, at his penis.

"Ambitious." The voice came from above. He was flooded with gratitude and love. Everything was going to be all right.

". . . was 'bitious if it were so it were a grievious fault and—"

"Grievous."

"Huh?" He looked up into Father's face, searching for signs of anger. "Isn't that what I said?"

"*Grie*-vous," the man intoned. He had a wonderful voice. It filled the small room. It made the water vibrate. "*Grie*-vous," he boomed again. Then he wrinkled his nose and upper lip and made his voice nasal, tinny, ridiculous. "You said *gree*-vee-ous. Where did you learn that?"

"I think Gideon Peppy said it."

"I think so, too. No more television for you, young man,

especially the *Peppy Show*. That man is single-handedly destroying the language."

The man lifted his son from the bathwater and set him on the mat. He wrapped him in a big fluffy white towel that said THARSIS HYATT on it. All their towels had the names of hotels on them.

"Now, take it again, from 'it were a grievous fault, and . . . ' "

". . . and grievi—and grie*vous*ly hath Zeezer answer'd it." The boy continued through Marc Antony's funeral oration, happy as a kitten with a bowl of cream, stumbling only over "Lupercal" and "coffers." As he spoke his father's big hands pummeled him and rubbed him dry through the big towel, powdered him, sprayed him, combed his long yellow hair.

"Very good, Dodger," he said, after the boy had gone through it three times. "But you must never say it that way again."

"All right."

"You must never 'say' it at all. From now on you will *hear* the words. You will learn what each word means, and what they mean together, and you will make the words live. Memorizing is all very good, but we are not phonographs, are we?"

The boy agreed, having no idea what a phonograph was. Then he was lifted, still wrapped in the towel, and brought to his tiny bedroom, where he stood shivering—the landlord, through some misunderstanding, had stopped providing heat three days before—as his father found a pair of blue flannel pajamas with fluffy tassels on the feet, two sizes too small, and held them while his son stepped in and zipped them up in front.

"We'll get you some new ones next week," his father said. "You're getting to be a big boy." He put his son in bed and tucked the big comforter under his chin.

"Good night, Dodger," he said.

"G' night, Father." The man left the door slightly ajar, as he always did, knowing his son was prone to bad dreams.

Dodger lay there in the dark, looking at the sliver of light on the ceiling that came through the door, and thinking about

Junior Zeezer, Octopus Zeezer, Marcus Bootless, Mark Anthony, Cashless, Sinna, Kafka, and the Smoothsayer. He knew those names were wrong but he found it helped him remember them to think of them that way. The real names made no sense at all to him. Neither did the play. That didn't bother him; *none* of the plays Father read to him made any sense, except *Titus Andronicus* (Tightest and Raunchiest, in Dodger-speak). Now, *there* was a story, with guys chopping off hands and pulling out tongues and stabbing each other with swords and stuff. It was almost as good as television.

But not *Junior Zeezer*. Oh, there was all those guys stabbing Junior in the Senate (also in the heart and the back and the gut, if Dodger understood it right), but most of it was no better than *Hambone,* which other than a neat ghost and some sword fighting didn't make much sense to Dodger, either.

His trouble was that, though he had a vocabulary ten times larger than most children his age, he didn't know what half the words meant.

Now his father said he was supposed to *hear* the words. Know what they mean, one at a time and all together. The prospect excited Dodger. All his life he'd been hearing these stories by Shaky-Spear, stories none of his friends knew, stories he couldn't tell his friends because he didn't know what they meant himself.

Now he would know. He suspected that learning what they meant would involve more time underwater.

But maybe that was just for remembering. He was getting so good at remembering now that some bath times went by without getting dunked at all.

The boy shivered, and pulled the covers more tightly around him. Soon he was asleep.

Dodger was four years old.

It's me again. Mister First Person.

And who are you? I might hear you ask. A certain amount of confusion at this point would be only normal.

"Your name is just something to put up on the marquee," my father always said. *"It doesn't mean a thing." He proved his point by giving me a handful of them: Kenneth Catherine Duse Faneuil Savoyard Booth Johnson Ivanovich de la Valentine, to mention just a few. Alias K.C., Casey, Ken, Cat,*

Kendall, Kelly, Kenton, and Kelvin. A.K.A. Valencia, Valentine, Van den Troost, and Jones. In various combinations of these and others I may have neglected to mention, I had enough noms de théâtre, de plume, *and* de guerre *to make a list longer than the memory of most big-city police computers.*

"It gives you options," said my father, a man who was known throughout his life simply as John Valentine. *"I have an enormous ego,"* he would say, with a twinkle in his eye. *"I can't stand for the applause to go to anyone but John Valentine. But I am able to do the jail time, when it comes to that."*

Well, I can't *do the time. I've never stayed in jail longer than it takes to make bail, get new paper, and catch the first available transport to a distant planet. This has prevented me from compiling the sort of credits that might lead to critical adulation, but after all, as my father also used to say, "The performance is the thing."*

But as I said earlier, all my friends call me Sparky.

Or, before that, Dodger.

But speaking of the printed page, here's a request to the typesetter:

Could we lose the italics?

Thank you.

I've noticed that, in books, when the point of view is switched, the new part is often set in italics. Well, I don't like italics much, and I'm just going to assume that you, the reader, are smart enough to know when I'm in first person and when I'm using third. Hint: examine the pronouns.

There is this odd thing about me: I usually dream in the third person. Frequently the dreams are in black-and-white, not Technicolor. The dreams are thus a little like out-of-body experiences. I see myself doing things, rather than seeing the things I do. I've spoken with other actors about this, thinking it might be an occupational disorder resulting from spending so much of my time thinking about how a motion or gesture would look, about makeup and staging and presence and all the other aspects of my craft. I found only one other actor who dreamed like I do. Shortly after he told me that he put a bullet through his head, and I stopped asking the question. I didn't like the way people looked at me when I asked, anyway.

That's why I'm putting parts of this in the third person: because I dreamed it. And the reason I'm back in first is, I woke up. Far too soon.

I didn't know it at first. Apart from the grogginess natural to the dosage of "deadballs" I'd taken, there is nothing in space to give one cues as to elapsed time, particularly in the Outer Planets; Pluto would have vanished from sight during the first hours of acceleration. After that, there was nothing visual to show time's passage until arrival at Uranus.

But among the Pantech's equipment is a clock, and I soon became alert enough to fumble open the protective hatch and consult it. I found we'd been gone for only three days.

I was alarmed.

The illegal mixture of drugs sold on the street as deadballs enabled the human body to do something it was never designed to do: sleep for a week, with few deleterious side effects. Hibernate, if you will (or estivate, take your pick, since there were no seasons in space).

Why ban a drug? After all, this isn't the Dark Ages. Getting high isn't illegal on any civilized planet—not that deadballs made you high.

My father's explanation made as much sense as any.

"Profit, Dodger, simple profit," he said. "Ninety percent of interplanet travel is tourism, people running away from their humdrum lives to experience humdrum amusements far from home. And every mile of that travel is the most boring experience imaginable. The owners of the ships that make these useless trips realize this, and devise endless amusements for the passengers—*not* included in the price of the ticket. A comatose passenger doesn't do any gambling or eating. We can't have that, so deadballs are illegal."

Cynical? Perhaps, but then why are deadballs sold legally to people traveling on errands for the government? Why do the staterooms of high-powered business executives on high-powered fast courier ships remain closed for days at a time? The people who do that other ten percent of space traveling usually do it on hibernation drugs, from the movers and shakers to the immigrants stacked like cordwood in the steerage holds of many a cargo ship.

(Oddly, I never could find a deadball in my hasty flight from Brementon. Judging from the waking state of my fellow

passengers, neither could anyone else. In a place where every
drug known to man could be had simply by walking up to a
guard and paying for it, deadballs were unknown. Apparently
the living hell of the trip to and from the prison station was
seen as part of the punishment.)

A more legitimate reason for banning them was the informal type of travel I found myself indulging in at that very
moment. Without deadballs, only the shortest ride on the rods
was survivable.

Now I was beginning to wonder if I would survive this
one. Adding it up, it didn't look good.

I had expected to awaken during the course of the voyage;
I estimated between ten and a dozen half-day surfacings
would be about right. When you wake from a deadball you
either need to urinate very badly, or find you have already
done so. Though your metabolism has been drastically
slowed, you will be very hungry. Usually, a bowel movement
will not be necessary. (After the trip you will with great heart-
break deliver yourself of a hard, dried . . . but let's skip on
over that part.)

You can do two weeks of deadballs standing on your head.
A month is no real problem. Two months . . . you would really rather not, for reasons of both comfort and health. Three
months, four months . . . you're pushing it. A few people have
survived six months of continuous deadballing, but most
would rather not speak of it, like victims of torture.

I had plenty of air, heat, and water. In a cramped environment like the Pantechnicon, or a packing case, food becomes
the dearest commodity. Try packing even very light rations
for ninety days into a space you can't even stand up in. Just
try it. Even if you could, are you able to endure ninety days
of solitary confinement? No shuffleboard courts or slot machines. Just you, squatting in the dark, watching your toenails
grow.

But if my deadballs had been cut with something, I faced
forty or fifty days of that. I would probably not starve. Part
of the price of the ticket is the loss of thirty to forty pounds.
With bad drugs, I might expect to lose a hundred or more on
the Miracle Deadball Diet.

"If you've learned your part cold," my father used to say,
"then you've got nothing else worth worrying about. Just take

the rest as it comes." Or, don't fret about things you can't do anything about. The future will deliver up its load of misery in due time.

With that semicomforting thought, I began treating this as just a normal, expected comfort stop. I set about tidying my small space and preparing a cold meal of beef jerky and maple syrup. It's better than it sounds, when you haven't eaten anything in three days.

I dialed the shelter to transparency.

The first thing I saw was a thundering herd of horses.

The drugs, right? No, I never even thought of that, though they can cause hallucinations. These horses were frozen in attitudes of great speed, as though they had galloped through a puddle of liquid helium. The freezing was certainly plausible, given the outside temperature. But they were carved from wood. I had been stowed next to a cargo of merry-go-round horses.

They were hanging from racks inside a large packing crate that, for some delightful reason, was transparent. I assumed the case was pressurized and heated. When I played my flashlight over them a thousand jolly colors leaped out at me. I was enchanted.

Where were they going? Who had made them? I never found out.

Like most miscellaneous-cargo vessels, this one consisted of the bare minimum. Basically, it was a central core that contained the drive and the life support systems for cargo and crew—typically, only two or three people. It was over a mile from stem to stern, and along its length it sprouted long composite racks, not much different from a pole you would hang your clothes on. The cargo modules, including the Pantech, had standard couplers that simply and easily snapped over the "horizontal" poles—they were horizontal at launch, anyway—where it was free to swing and sway and orient itself according to the direction of thrust: "riding the rods," just like the Old Earth hoboes. When the ship landed, the rods would be depressed slightly, and the modules would slide off the ends and onto ground carriers. It was a simple system, in use for decades, standard throughout the inhabited planets.

The Pantech was the last module on a rod near the front of the ship. I'd paid a small premium for the outside berth, since I get claustrophobic if I'm stacked in the middle, surrounded by heavy crates that could crush me if they swung in the wrong direction.

I soon saw something odd. It was the crate Lou had abandoned on our way out to the ship. It seemed to have sprung a leak.

I could see it a few rings forward, and one rod over. The corner he had pried up to get in and out now sported a long, white tail. It reminded me of a picture I'd once seen of a tapestry from the Middle Ages. The artist had represented a comet as a many-rayed star with a long tail to one side as it arched across the heavens. This tail was ice of some kind—hard to tell what; hell, *everything* froze out here. For a while the leak had been in one direction as the ship accelerated. Then, in free fall, the liquid had seeped out in all directions, making a rather pretty Christmas-tree ornament.

I chose to take it as good news. Lou had detected something wrong with his proposed abode before it was even loaded on the ship, like a squirrel finding a leak in his hollow tree just before turning in for his winter's snooze. I hoped his new home proved a little more solid.

Of course, he might be freezing or starving or slowly dying of thirst and there was absolutely nothing I could do to help him.

So I drank a second dose of deadballs, turned the shelter opaque, and curled up in a warm blanket to sleep for a week. I hoped.

"Father, is this the Emerald City?"

John Valentine chuckled and squeezed his son's hand.

"It will do until something better comes along," he said.

They were riding in a half-full tramcar that traced the edge of Hyginus Rima, in the southeast corner of Mare Vaporum, known far and wide as the entertainment capital of the system. Had they taken the tram to the end of the line, young Kenneth would actually have seen the Emerald City, pretty much as Dorothy, Toto, and company had approached it in 1939 on a yellow brick road that was partly on a Metro-Goldwyn-Mayer soundstage and partly in the box of tricks of a process cinematographer.

There were those who called the Hyginus Line the Yellow Brick Rail.

The official name of the sector they were now entering was the Route of the Stars. The builders had taken their cue from the city fathers of Hollywood, U.S.A., but everything they did had to be a hundred times as large, a thousand times as spectacular—and even less substantial than the original.

Where the stars in the sidewalk on Hollywood Boulevard had been nothing more than small squares of masonry and brass, the ones in Hyginus were holographs the size of billboards, easily seen and read from a speeding tramcar. The giant stars seemed hammered out of pure gold, and in the center of each was a forty-foot fully animated three-dimensional image of the honouree. The stars' names were spelled out in diamonds bigger than watermelons.

"So it's really Hollywood?" the boy asked.

"Son of Hollywood," said his father. "Not much around here that's all that original."

The real name of the area was the King City/Mare Vaporum Artistic and Industrial Park, but no one called it that. The King City part was gerrymandering of the most blatant sort. The actual city was over a hundred miles away, but the city limits ran on each side of the Hyginus rail until it reached Vaporum, where it ballooned to include all the area zoned for industry. The only real benefit reaped by the businesses there was the privilege of paying King City taxes.

As for industry, the only industry in Vaporum was The Movies. Whether anything "artistic" was happening was endlessly debated among the more acerbic critics back in the city.

Those who worked there called it The Park, The Vapors, or Hollywood, the Sequel. They spoke of going out to The Rima, or The Edge, or Yellow Bricktown. Everybody else just called it Hollywood. Since the original Hollywood was a memory, there was seldom any confusion.

"And besides," John Valentine said to his son, "Hollywood was always just a state of mind, anyway."

Young Kenneth pressed his face against the window beside his seat and watched the passing spectacle. The stars were only the beginning.

Behind them were mountainous holograms of the logos of motion-picture studios, past and present, solvent and defunct.

Dodger knew they were holograms, but since he had no idea what a hologram was, they were as real to him as the car he was riding in. The apparent heights of these juggernaut illusions could be measured in miles.

There was a tapering iron tower sitting on the north pole of a half Earth globe, spitting stylized sparks and spelling out, letter by letter, A RADIO PICTURE. Next to that was a snow-covered mountain surrounded by drifting clouds and haloed with a starry diadem. A mile-high lion's head roared in the middle of an elaborate scroll of old-fashioned motion picture film, and then yet another globe, hanging suspended and massive above the barren plain, being endlessly circled by a winged machine.

"An airplane, Father!"

"That's right. Universal."

"Look! Look!" the boy shouted, pointing to one he was more familiar with. "Sentry! That's where we're going, isn't it, Father?"

"If you don't knock the train off the tracks with all your commotion. Settle down, boy."

Dodger contained his excitement, and watched the armored warrior and bursting firework trademark of Sentry/Sensational Pictures. The gigantic figure went from attention to a position of challenge, his huge weapon held out before him at port arms. But soon he was fading into the distance, replaced by a circle and golden sunburst saying TOHO and a word he couldn't read. A horse with wings charged the tramcar and leaped over it. Dodger looked, but the Pegasus never landed on the other side. A gargantuan rooster flapped its rust-colored wings and ruffled its neck. A dozen multicolored flags snapped in a nonexistent breeze under the towering legend FILMWERKS.

Dodger wished he could fly over this wonderful plain. Recently Father had him memorize the script for *Swift!*, and he supposed it must look as if a child of Brobdingnag had upended his toy chest and then abandoned his mammoth fripperies out here in the wilderness. Actually, from above he would have seen nothing at all. It cost more to project a holo in all directions, and the designers of the Route of the Stars understood a principle known since the days of D.W. Griffith: make sure your budget gets on the screen. The Hyginus route was the electronic equivalent of dusty old western streets walked by William S. Hart, Tom Mix, and Roy Rogers: false fronts propped up with two-by-fours.

They were just getting into the part of the route devoted to scenes from classic movies when the train pulled into the first Vaporum station. Dodger didn't really want to get off, but when Father took his hand he stood and followed him off the car.

They went down a slideway with a curved, transparent roof, right between the hairy legs of a giant gorilla chained to a big wooden cross. The beast followed them with his eyes, and father and son both looked up as they walked under him.

"Let's hope he doesn't have an upset tummy," John Valentine said, and his son collapsed in helpless giggles.

John Valentine led his son to a wide sofa in a big, nondescript waiting area outside the casting offices of Sentry/Sensational studios. There were many other couches, mostly filled with people. He sat him down, and then squatted in front of him.

"Now, I may be a while, Dodger," he said, straightening the big yellow bow at the boy's neck. Current fashion for young men was a quasi-Victorian look, with knee breeches and frock coats and lace at the cuffs. When Dodger was dressed up like that John called him Buster Brown. Since this was an important audition, father and son were dressed in their best, which if examined closely would have revealed loose threads where the tags reading PROPERTY OF NLF COSTUME DEPARTMENT had been removed. Young Kenneth had golden hair that hung past his shoulders and framed a face with wide-set blue eyes, apple cheeks, and a prominent pair of front teeth with a wide gap between them. He wore a floppy brown velvet beret.

"I want you to wait right here until I get back," Valentine said. "There is a water fountain over there, and the rest room is just around that corner and down the hall. You've got your script"—he took a tattered copy of *Cyrano de Bergerac* from his briefcase and set it on the sofa—"and I brought a lunch for you." He produced a brown paper bag, opened it, and let Dodger look inside. The boy saw something wrapped in waxed paper, and smelled a banana. "Peanut butter and jelly, your favorite. Now, can I trust you to behave?"

Dodger nodded, and his father pulled the beret down over his eyes, tickled his ribs lightly, and stood. He headed for the door marked CASTING DEPARTMENT.

"Father?" Dodger called out, and John Valentine turned.

"Break a leg," the boy said. Valentine gave him a thumbs-up, and went through the door.

Dodger was pretty good at waiting. This wasn't the first time he had gone along for a cattle call, though never before at a motion-picture studio. His father didn't have a very high opinion of the movies, though he worked in them when there was nothing else happening and the rent was overdue.

"Never extra work, though, son," he would say. "If you don't get a line, it's not acting. You might as well hire yourself out as scenery."

Dodger wouldn't have minded being scenery, sometimes. Scenery didn't have to memorize so many plays.

This one was pretty good, though. By the second act he had assigned his own names to all the characters: Cyranose, of course, and Rockshead, who reminded Dodger of a chorus girl they used to know. Pretty, but dumb as a mime. If only she'd been like a mime and stopped talking every once in a while. Then there was Christian the Noodlehead, the Comedy Grease, and Raggynose, the pastry cook.

It was jammed full of sword fighting, which was great, but it also had lots of words he didn't recognize. He dutifully underlined each one, as his father had taught him. He would learn them later. *Popinjay. Jobbernowl. Ambuscaded. Mountebanks. Buskin.* And what was he to make of *Hippocampelephantocamelos*?

From time to time an adult would hurry by, usually far too busy to notice the boy sitting in the farthest corner of the lobby. Then someone would pause, look back at him uncertainly. Dodger would give him or her his most winning smile. If that wasn't enough, he would say, "It's all right. My father is meeting with Mr. Sensational." Jack Sensational was the head of the studio. Nobody asked any questions after that.

He ate half his sandwich and all the banana. He visited the facilities his father had pointed out, and decided he was bored to death. What would it hurt, he wondered, if he did a little exploring?

· · ·

The sign TO SOUNDSTAGES A-B-C-D had lured him farther afield than he intended to go. Now the huge door he was passing read SOUNDSTAGE H-2, and he knew he was lost.

He also knew he was going to be in big trouble. But there is a defense mechanism in dogs and young children that prevents them from worrying too much about future consequences once it is clear that it is too late to avoid them. *What the hell?* Dodger thought. *If I'm going to catch it, I might as well make the crime worthy of the punishment.*

So he wandered along the wide corridors, dodging heavy equipment hauling props and scenery, and groups of actors and extras in outlandish costumes chattering among themselves.

He knew just enough to avoid any door with a red light over it, since the light meant actual shooting was going on. But when he opened another door and stuck his head in enough to get a glimpse of a huge ballroom set swarming with carpenters and electricians he was shouted at, and beat a hasty retreat.

But he viewed an open door as an invitation to come in.

The first one he entered was a soundstage populated entirely by six-foot-tall blonde women wearing pink high-heeled shoes and pink ostrich-feather headdresses that towered another four feet over them. There must have been a hundred of them. They were just standing around, doing nothing. Before them were a hundred champagne glasses filled with bubbling liquid, big enough for the women to take a bath in, and behind that was a towering blue backdrop. One of the women glanced at him, then went back to contemplating her long, pink fingernails. For five minutes nothing at all happened. Nobody noticed him and nobody asked him to leave, and it was all incredibly boring.

And that seemed to be what moviemaking was about. He visited three more stages, and in all of them people were standing around doing nothing. Nobody was shooting at anybody, there were no sword fights, no action of any kind. Dodger tentatively decided against a career on the silver screen.

· · ·

He was getting tired by the time he wandered into Soundstage F-5, and wishing he could find his way back to his half a peanut-butter-and-jelly sandwich. But when he entered F-5 he forgot his hunger.

The other stages had been large, but difficult to see because of false walls standing here and there at random, and lights hanging from the ceilings. This one was empty and the overhead lights were turned off. Dodger didn't need them, because most of the floor of the stage was a vast blue pool of water, lit from below. It was smooth as glass. Tied up not far from him was a full-scale pirate ship, sails furled, whose masts towered a hundred feet high.

This was more like it. Maybe there was magic in the movies after all.

His footsteps echoed in the big barn as he went to the ship. He reached out and touched it, and the ship bobbed slightly, sending out concentric waves that turned the even play of light across the distant ceiling into a magical pattern of diamonds. He pushed harder against the ship, heard an anchor rope creak against a piling, and the pretty pattern of lights was shattered even further. He wondered how he could tell Father about this. There must be words for it. There were so many words.

"Hey, what are you doing?"

He jerked guiltily and looked up. There was another boy standing in the open door of the soundstage, but it was not he who had shouted. An angry-looking woman in the red-and-yellow uniform of Sentry Security was holding the boy by the arm. She was about to pull him out into the corridor when she looked up and saw Dodger.

"You, too," she called out, beckoning. "Get over here. You kids were told not to go wandering. I ought to kick you off the lot."

Dodger thought of running, but didn't immediately see any other exit doors from the place. There was absolutely nothing to hide behind. So he hurried to the guard and she grabbed him, too.

Without another word she hustled them across a busy corridor and through a door marked STUDIO 88. Someone had taped a notice to it: *Auditioners and Parents ONLY!*

Inside was chaos. It was not an entirely unfamiliar scene to the Dodger. He had witnessed casting calls for the legitimate stage, and knew what happened when you got a hundred precocious youngsters and their indulgent parents together at one time. Some of these kids had yet to hear the word "no" issue from their parents' mouths. They were the ones running in every direction at breakneck speed while Mom and Dad looked on with simpering approval and told everyone in sight that little junior was just so damn talented they didn't have the heart to repress his creative impulses. Sometimes these creative impulses took the form of hitting another talented child with a handy blunt object, and in these cases the police frequently had to be called to prevent murder among the battling parents.

The rest were of another sort entirely. Dodger knew them well. They had spent most of their short lives learning to actually *do* something—singing, ballet, accordion playing—and had achieved some success at it. They were as spoiled as the first group, but quieter about it. Most of them sat serenely with stage mothers and stage fathers, and the only noise they made was the hideous sounds that issued from their kazoos, harmonicas, and Jew's harps.

"Damn all aspiring Shirley Temples," John Valentine had once said, at just such an audition. "Children on the stage are a necessary evil, I suppose, if you're reviving *Annie*. God forbid. But they should be locked in a trunk and stored in the wings between shows. Take them out, feed and water them, let them do their turn, and lock them up again."

But he reserved the worst of his scorn for the parents.

"Gypsy Roses, every one of them!" he sneered. "Frustrated, talentless, hams *by proxy*. They mouth lines along with their brats, and dream of their names on the marquee. They eat their young. If the first one doesn't work out, you'll see the same faces five years later, with a new brat in tow."

Dodger, who had witnessed this routine of his father's several times, would say nothing, remembering the *first* time he had heard it, when he had innocently asked if he himself wasn't something like that, what with memorizing all the plays by Shakespeare.

And his father would put his hands on Dodger's small shoulders and look intently into his wide blue eyes.

"That's not for you, Dodger. No tap-dancing dog-and-pony shows for my boy. You're learning your *craft,* and it's the noblest craft of them all. It's the only thing in the world worth doing."

"Where's your release form?"

"Huh?" Dodger looked up into the face of a pretty young woman with a clipboard and a harried expression.

"Here," she said, and thrust a printed form at him. "Have your father or mother fill this out and then wait until your name is called. And *please,* don't lose this one." She was gone as quickly as she had appeared.

Dodger found his way to a table that was heaped with food. He'd seen nothing like this at theater auditions. Once again his opinion of the movie business moved up a notch.

Much of the food seemed to have been used recently as ammunition in a truly epic food fight, but there was still plenty left in bowls, on platters, and even on big steam tables. He slapped a hot dog into a big bun, squirted mustard, topped it off with three spoonfuls of relish, then grabbed a can of Coke from a barrel of ice and pulled up a chair. He took a big bite, then swept the tablecloth in front of him clear of crushed potato chips and bits of cupcake and part of a melting ice-cream bar. He put the release form on the table and studied it. It seemed simple enough. He glanced around, saw that no one was paying him any attention.

Name? He filled in *Kenneth C. Valentine.* Stage name (if any): *The Artful Dodger.* Parent or Guardian: *John B. Valentine.* Age: *8.*

He filled in all the blanks, after first checking the bottom to see if there was any penalty for *perjury,* a word he had learned a few days ago. His father had cautioned he should always look for it previous to signing anything. And there was a space at the bottom for a signature, but they didn't want his, they wanted his father's. He looked around again, then accurately reproduced the flamboyant loops and incisive angles of his father's autograph: *John Barrymore Valentine II.*

He finished his hot dog and handed the form to the lady when she came by again. He didn't think anything would come of it, since it would obviously take some time to work through this many children. As he waited he overheard enough to realize this was the first cull from a much larger group. Most of the day's attendees had already been sent home with that ancient kiss-off ringing in their ears: "Thank you for coming don't call us we'll call you."

He looked around at the seventy or eighty remaining. Then he looked at the table where the lady had put the stack of forms.

Hmmm.

A group of kids had been running around the table since he sat down. On their next pass Dodger carelessly stuck his foot out in front of the leader, who went skidding on his face. The others fell down on top of him. The shrieks were deafening, and in no time a frantic gaggle of parents had congealed into an explosive mass, volatile as nitroglycerin. In no more than five seconds the first punch was thrown, and soon after that four fathers were bloodying each other's noses. Dodger strolled toward the casting director's table as everyone else hurried the other way. Glancing around to be sure everyone was either watching the fight or trying to stop it, he lifted the stack of paper. There it was, his application, on the bottom. Hell of a place for it, he decided. He made a small adjustment to the stack and stepped away.

In a moment yet another woman emerged from behind the curtain. She picked up the top form.

"Kenneth Valentine? Kenny, where are you, dear?"

Dodger tugged at her skirt.

"Oh, there you are. Well, you can come with me, and your parents must wait right . . ." She looked around, puzzled. "Where are your parents, dear?"

"Oh, over there," he said, pointing. Then he smiled and waved.

"Yes, well . . ." She looked confused for a moment, then brightened. "Well, that *is* different. Usually I have to bar the door, and then guard the room to keep them from sneaking back in. Very well. Come this way, please."

He followed her through the curtain, then through two doors. The noise didn't completely die away until the second door shut behind him.

"Over here, kid," said a gravelly voice.

It was a large room, almost filled by a long conference table with a dozen chairs on each side and one on each end.

On the walls were posters from the *Gideon Peppy Show*, bright and cheerful and primary-colored, most featuring the maniacally smiling host of the top-rated children's show on three planets, Gideon Peppy. Directly across from Dodger three people sat together near the middle of the table. At one end was an unsmiling woman sitting rigidly upright, hands folded on the table, "a broomstick up her ass," as his father would say. At the other end slouched a man it took Dodger a moment to realize was Gideon Peppy himself.

"Take a seat, little guy," said the man on the left of the triad, a portly fellow with a big shock of blond hair and a plaid shirt. "My name's Lawrence Street, and I'm the casting director. Do you know what that is?"

"Yes, sir." Dodger fought the impulse to hurry over to the table. "Keep your movements slow," his father had told him many times, when he was watching him rehearse. He was about to sit in one of the chairs when the second man, who was bald almost to the top of his head, spoke up.

"Take the next one," he said, with a slight smile. Dodger saw there was some kind of booster seat in it. He climbed aboard with as much dignity as he could muster, but was glad when he was in it, because in the other chair his chin would have been just about level with the table. He folded his hands in front of himself, and waited.

"This is Sam Mohammed," Street said, indicating the swarthy man, "and next to him is Debbie Corlet. They're my assistants." Larry, Moe, and Curly, Dodger thought, getting them fixed in his head. "The lady at the end of the table is from Equity. She's gonna make sure we stick to the child labor laws, but don't worry about that." Auntie Equity, got it. He didn't introduce Peppy, and Dodger wasn't surprised, because he was familiar with the concept of The Man Who Needs No Introduction. It was a measure of importance.

Larry frowned across the table at him.

"I see you didn't bring a copy of your script, so I assume you've memorized it. What we want you—"

"Excuse me, sir," Dodger said, thinking fast, "but I didn't have time to study it. If you could just lend me a copy . . ."

"They handed them out at the door," Larry said, frowning more deeply.

"They must have missed me," Dodger said. He beamed brightly at Larry. "I'm a very quick study."

The three huddled briefly, and Larry shrugged. "What the hell. Let's see how quick he is. Go over there and read it to him, Debbie."

"That won't be necessary," Dodger said. Curly was already hurrying around the table with the script. She glanced at her boss, who gestured dubiously that she should give him the papers. He smiled up at her and took them.

"So you can read?" Moe said, raising one eyebrow. He made a mark on a form in front of him. "That's good. What is he, the fifth reader today?"

"Fourth," said Gideon Peppy from his end of the table. Dodger looked at the star in time to see him put his trademark lollipop back in his mouth.

"You're right," Larry said. "That first kid was lying, anybody could see that." He looked at Dodger and gestured at the script. "So read it, Kenny. Ya got two minutes."

Dodger looked at the script, which was three short scenes. He assumed they had been written just for this audition. He hoped so. They were terrible.

"Okay," he said. The stooges looked up from a whispered conference they had just begun, and Larry frowned again. He had a talent for frowning.

"Okay, what?"

"I'm ready now."

Larry's frown became a full glower. He pointed a stubby finger at Dodger, and leaned forward.

"I don't much like being lied to, kid. Don't give me this bushwah about not seeing the script, then expect me to believe you've boned it in less than a minute. You memorized it, why don't you just—"

"Let the kid read," Peppy said. Everyone shut up and looked at him quickly. He had his trademark yellow shoes propped up on the table, was leaning back in his chair staring at the ceiling. Larry seemed to taste something bad, but turned to face Dodger again.

"Okay. Debbie's gonna read the part of Sue. You'll be Sparky. Go." He pointed at Dodger, then swiveled in his chair and pointedly turned his back.

" 'Gosh, Sparky,' " Curly chanted, in a dull monotone.

" 'I didn't think we'd see you again so soon.' "

" 'They can't get rid me so easily,' " Dodger said. He immediately hated the reading, but didn't know just what to do about it. They went through the scene without a hitch. By the end Curly had relented a little and actually put a little expression into her last two lines, but it was no good, and Dodger knew it. There was absolutely no clue as to the character of Sparky in the scene, there was nothing for him to work with. It was a joking skit lacking a punch line, though the cues for laughter were right there on the page: CUE LAUGH. Dodger knew they kept laughs in cans somewhere in television studios. He thought they'd be opening one heck of a lot of cans to sell this turkey.

But the one thing that *did* work, oddly enough, was a laugh.

SUE: The boy is so stupid! I can't believe he's your brother.
SPARKY: (*laughs*) You can pick your friends and you can pick your nose, but you can't wipe your relatives off under the furniture.

Laughing on cue was something little Ken Valentine had learned early in his education, even before the memorization started. He learned it by being tickled until he thought he was going to be sick. ("It's one of the easiest lessons you'll learn, Dodger. Whenever you need to laugh, just think back to this.") It worked almost too well; when he needed to laugh, sometimes, he found himself feeling sick.

So he laughed, and produced a rather odd sound he'd been making since somewhere around his fifth birthday, a sound that caused his father's jaw to drop and led him to say, "Good God. I've raised Woody Woodpecker."

Later, when Dodger heard Woody's laugh, he compared it with his own and thought his father was wrong (though he didn't tell him that). The cartoon laugh was forced and artificial: Hah hah hah HAH hah. His own laugh sounded real enough . . . but not like anyone else's laugh, he had to admit that.

Out of the corner of his eye, Dodger saw Gideon Peppy look down. Was he smiling? He couldn't tell, and he thought it best not to look over there and find out.

"Okay," said Larry. "Second scene."

This one didn't go any better. Moe read the other part this time, and he was worse than Curly, if anything. The scene lumbered along until nearly the end, when Dodger hesitated.

"What'samatter, kid?" Larry rasped. "Forget your lines?"

"No, sir. It's just that . . ."

"Spit it out."

"Well, it's a bad line."

The stooges just stared at him. Dodger couldn't help it; he laughed again. This did not go over well with the trio, but what was he supposed to do? He imagined Larry with his hand over his eyes, Moe with his fingers in his ears, and Curly covering her mouth. He saw he had made no friends here.

"I guess this was a bad idea," he said, and started to get up.

"What's the matter with the line, Kenneth?" Gideon Peppy asked.

Dodger turned toward the star.

"Sir, the boy is supposed to be eight years old."

"So?"

"So, an eight-year-old doesn't talk like that."

"So? I can't believe what I'm hearing come out of your mouth."

"I'm not a normal eight-year-old, sir."

"So it would seem."

"I've had theatrical training, Mr. Peppy. Plus, I *am* eight, and none of my friends would talk like that." He brushed the script on the table with the back of his hand, contemptuously. "Who wrote this crap, anyway?"

"I wrote it."

Instantly, a line from *At the Office,* a comedy he'd read almost a year ago, sprang into his mind, and he knew it was his only chance.

"Suddenly I like it a lot more," he said.

Peppy was silent for a full ten seconds, while the stooges gaped. Then he took the lollipop from his mouth and pointed it at Dodger.

"This kid I like," he said. "This kid has big brass ones. He reminds me of me when I was his age." He shrugged. "You're right, it's crap. I dashed it off this morning, what the heck, all we gotta do is see can you remember your lines. The rest is personality. Read him the next scene.''

INT.— NIGHT— THE HOLD OF THE PIRATE SHIP

SPARKY and his friend ELWOOD and the rest of his gang, are manacled to a long chain bolted to the ship's hull. SPARKY has the padlock in his hand and is trying to pick it.

ELWOOD

Hurry, Sparky! I think I hear the pirates coming!

SPARKY

Don't make me nervous. I think I've . . . there! It's open! Come on, guys, pull the chain through the rings. Quietly, quietly! Now, Basil, Robin, Elwood, you go up through the rear hatch. Boots, me and you and the rest will go to the front, where the guns are. Elwood, find the powder magazine and try to light a fuse. We're outnumbered, but maybe we can send this old bucket to Davy Jones!

SPARKY and his friends creep through the darkness and hurry up the ladder to

EXT.— NIGHT— THE DECK

SPARKY pops out of the hatch, surprising the sleeping guard, who starts to rise. SPARKY hits him and takes his gun, turns to blow the lock off the armory door. The gang swarms in.

BOOTS

Come on, guys, grab a weapon! Let's go!

SPARKY

Watch out for Elwood! He's up there somewhere!

The pirate crew starts to boil out of the fo'c'sle, waving cutlasses and firing pistols. The Gang fights them off as Sparky hurries forward. BLUEBEARD the pirate captain steps from his cabin.

BLUEBEARD

So, Sparky, you've escaped again! Well, you'll not get away this time. (Draws his sword)

SPARKY

It's you who'll be walking the plank tonight, Captain!

He grabs a sword and the two fight. ELWOOD comes running from the magazine.

ELWOOD
The fuse is lit! Let's get out of here!

SPARKY runs the captain through, pulls out his sword.

SPARKY
There's an end to your career of looting and plundering, Captain! (Laughs) Get the point? Come on, guys! There's no time to waste! Over the side with you, and swim for your lives!

The gang leaps into the air as the ship explodes behind them.

" 'Hurry, Sparky. I think I hear the pirates coming.' "
Silence.

" 'Hurry, Sparky,' " Moe started again, but Larry, who didn't seem to like Dodger at all, interrupted.

" 'Samattah, kid? Forgot 'em again?"

"What's my motivation?" Dodger asked.

"Motivation?" Larry wanted to know. He looked baffled.

"Yes, my—"

"Motivation? Motivation?" Peppy asked, around his lollipop. "What's this motivation crap? Suddenly I don't like this kid so much. Your motivation is get loose and kill pirates. *Capishe?*"

"No, sir," Dodger said. "I mean, who is Sparky? I can't give a good reading unless I know a little about him." There was no response, so he hurried on. "Is he happy? I mean, does he enjoy his life? Or does he worry too much? Is he stupid? I mean, he got captured, didn't he? So . . . is he worried about the mistake he made? What is his *attitude,* is the main thing. Should I play him like Errol Flynn, or John Wayne, or the Eliminator?"

Peppy leaned forward and his lollipop stick rattled in his mouth as he talked.

"Sparky is a happy-go-lucky, smart little fuck, but not so smart he don't get outnumbered from time to time, you see what I mean? He is self-confident but not obnoxious about it. His troops like him, and so do the dames, people are alla time buying him drinks. He's a good boy to be with in a tough situation, 'cause nothing bad never happens to him for too

damn long. He's the man with the charm but he don't have
no big head about it. It ain't he's too stupid to know it, it's
he's modest, see? Also trustworthy. Also helpful, brave, clean,
and irrelevant. He don't kick his dog, he pulls down about
forty-five gees a year, goes to the church of his choice, votes
as many times as he can, always for the right people. He's a
schlemiel, you hear what I'm saying? Errol Flynn, definitely
Errol Flynn.'' He leaned forward even farther. ''With maybe
just a touch of Daffy Duck. Now can we read?''

Dodger was not acquainted with Daffy Duck, but stripped
of the sarcasm, he thought he might be getting a picture of
Sparky.

''There's a big pirate ship, just across the hall,'' he said.

''You want we should go read in there? Will that help you
find your 'motivation'? That's where we'll be shooting this
scene.''

Oh, yeah? Dodger thought. *I thought you dashed it off this
morning.*

''Could we have just a second?'' he asked.

Peppy sat back and looked at the ceiling again.

''Take a second, take a second.'' He found Dodger again
with his eyes. ''I'll let you in on a secret. Only reason you're
still here is most kids *stink* at this stuff. We get most of 'em
out of here in thirty seconds, am I right? Tell him, Debbie,
do I speak the truth here?'' Debbie nodded, quickly. ''I
thought I saw something when you were reading that other
crap. Now I'm not so sure. But I'm hardly ever wrong, so
you get a second. Hell, two seconds. Find your motivation.
Wake me up when you're ready.'' And he leaned back again.

Dodger closed his eyes and tried to find the key to the
scene. ''There's always a key,'' his father had said. ''It may
be a key to the whole play, or just to a scene. Hitchcock called
it a McGuffin.''

Well, there was the padlock, wasn't there? Maybe it wasn't
a key, but a lock. If Sparky doesn't pick the lock there *is* no
scene, just guys squatting in the dark.

He opened his eyes and looked down. He made his hand
hold the lock, shaped his fingers around it, felt the cool metal.
How did it look? Well, it was a little rusty. Everything metal
on this ship was a little rusty. It was a great big, old-fashioned
padlock, round, heavy, with a big keyhole in it. The wards

inside would be big clunky things, iron bars meant to be moved by a thick skeleton key, that *might* be moved by a splinter of wood pried from the deck of a pirate ship.

He saw it in his hand. Felt the weight of it.

Now, how would Sparky pick a lock? He thought of people who squinted at a task like that, who bit down on the tips of their tongues. No way. Not Sparky. He's frowning, but one eyebrow is raised. He knows he can do this. He's confident, it's only going to be a matter of time, and part of his mind is already occupied with what he's going to do when he gets free. Dodger felt his shoulders rising a little, his elbows moving out from his sides. Jimmy Cagney? Just a little bit of that, but without the meanness. One side of his lip curled up. He was going to *beat* this damn lock, it didn't have a chance.

He started to work.

"Hurry, Sparky! I think I hear the pirates coming!"

That Elwood, Sparky thought. *Always jumping at ghosts.* Sparky had been listening, and he hadn't heard a thing. He shrugged it away.

"Don't make me nervous." He felt the rusty ward moving, moving just the tiniest bit. But the splinter wasn't very strong, it could break at any moment.

"I think I've ..." With a satisfying *clink* the shackle popped up.

"There! It's open. Come on, guys, pull the chain through the rings. Don't let it rattle! Quietly! Quietly!"

(Dodger stood up in his chair.)

"Now, Basil! Robin! Elwood! You go up through the rear hatch." He gestured to his right. "Elwood, find the powder magazine and try to light a fuse." He watched his men hurry away in the darkness, then turned to the rest of them. "Boots, me and you and the rest will go up front, where the guns are. We're outnumbered, but maybe we can send this old bucket to Davy Jones, even if we have to go down with it!"

(Dodger stepped up onto the conference table and crept away, toward Gideon Peppy.)

Sparky carefully pushed up the hatch cover and looked through the crack. When he saw the sleeping guard he leaped out and popped him one in the jaw, then took his flintlock pistol as he fell. The gang swarmed out behind him.

"Come on, guys, grab a weapon!" said MoeBoots. "Let's go!"

Then the pirates were all over them. Sparky fired his pistol, then threw it in a pirate's face. He grabbed a sword and began slashing right and left, until suddenly there was the evil figure of Bluebeard, his longtime nemesis.

"So, Sparky, you've escaped again! Well, you'll not get away this time." He drew his sword and assumed the *en garde* position. Sparky stood straight, tossed his head, and saluted the captain with his sword. He laughed, defiantly.

"It's you who'll be walking the plank tonight, me bucko!"

They battled back and forth across the seething deck, slippery with blood. Their steel rang in the night, and flashed in the orange light of the torches. Suddenly there was a cry.

"The fuse is lit! Let's get out of here!"

Sparky, who had been toying with the captain, now lunged forward and thrust his blade through Bluebeard's vile black heart. The pirate fell, mortally wounded. Sparky planted his foot on the beribboned and lacy shirt, pulled his sword free.

"There's an end to your plunder, Captain!" He threw his head back and laughed, triumphantly. "Get the point?" Then he turned to his men, arms held high, and gestured firmly toward the stern.

"Come on, men!" he shouted. "There's no time to waste! Over the side with you, and swim for your lives!"

He pounded down the deck, saw the rail ahead of him, and leaped. He was falling, falling, the black sea below rushing up to meet him, and *shit!* It was a gray carpet!

Dodger just had time to tuck a little and try to roll, but his head still hit the floor with a loud thump.

He sat up and shook his head. There was a ringing sound in his ears. He visualized a ring of twittering bluebirds circling his head, and wondered if this was the Daffy Duck part. Then he looked up, to see four faces looming over him. Larry spoke first.

"Did you see that? Did you see what he did? Jesus, I thought he was going to run right into you, Mr. Peppy. Did you see that? He just jumped right over him. Right over him! Jesus!"

"The kid's crazy," Curly was saying. "I never saw anything like it."

"Kenneth," Peppy said, an island of calm. "Kid, look at me. Are you okay? Should I get a doctor?"

Dodger shook his head again.

"No, I'm all right."

Peppy took the lollipop out of his mouth and looked at it. "Damn," he said. "I bit my candy in half."

There didn't seem to be any end to the damn place.

After Dodger escaped from the audition, he realized he was still lost. Not only was he lost, but it was getting late. His hopes that his father's audition had gone long were fading rapidly, and every corner he turned seemed to bring him back to a place he'd already seen before. Yet it didn't *seem* as if he were walking in circles.

When he felt a large hand on his shoulder he almost shouted aloud. He looked up into a narrow, frowning face.

"What's the matter, son?" the man drawled. "You look like you stumbled through a time warp."

You should talk, Dodger thought. They both stopped, and Dodger looked him over. It was a tall man, dressed anachronistically in baggy wool trousers, a gray coat and vest, and a white shirt. The only spot of color about him was a cloth strip knotted around his neck, under his collar. Dodger searched for the word, one he had underlined a few months ago. *Necktie.* And the shapeless hat perched on his head was a *fedora.*

He certainly wasn't the only oddly dressed person Dodger had seen in the corridors; this *was* a motion-picture studio. He'd seen red Indians in buckskins and yellow Chinamen in silk pajamas and black Hottentots in tuxedos. He'd seen green-and-purple extraterrestrials in ancient pressure suits. But they'd all had the look of costumes, somehow. This fellow looked as if he'd just stepped out of a time machine. He looked a little faded, yellowed, like an old photo in an album. He was in color, but it wasn't *Technicolor.*

"I guess I'm a little lost," he admitted. He was immediately appalled. He was *never* supposed to admit that. Luna was a strange place, as his father reminded him every time they played there. They had some odd ideas here, ideas that didn't necessarily make single parenting an easy thing. The child-welfare authorities, for instance, would have taken a dim view of Dodger's being left alone all day while his father auditioned. It didn't make much sense to Dodger. What did they expect? His father was a little short of cash right now and couldn't afford to hire a sitter—an idea which offended Dodger anyway. How did they expect a person to get parts, earn a living, put bread on the table if he couldn't look for work?

But if Dodger was picked up, lost, alone, he would surely be taken to the State School. Dodger had never seen this State School, but he had seen *Oliver Twist,* with Sir Alec Guinness as Fagin, and his father assured him the State School was pretty much like that.

He looked up to gauge the man's reaction. He frowned. Hadn't he seen this guy somewhere before? The man pursed his lips thoughtfully.

"A little lost, is it? Well, I know how that feels. Been a little lost myself here and there. Come to think of it, it was more *there* than *here,* or at least that's what it felt like."

"I don't know where here is," Dodger said.

"That's it, exactly!" the man crowed. "What's that in your hand?"

Dodger gave him the paper, and he took something from his pocket and put it on his face, squinting through pieces of glass as he read. Dodger had never seen anyone use *spectacles* as anything other than a stage prop. The man pointed to the bottom of the page.

"Gideon Peppy? Did you meet Gideon Peppy?"

Dodger nodded.

"Well, I'm impressed, I must say. Mr. Peppy's a mighty big man around here. Yes sir, a mighty big man. Not just everybody gets in to see him."

Dodger didn't care so much about that. All he could think about now was the clock ticking, and his father waiting.

"Do you work here?" he asked.

"Oh, no, it's not that way at all," the man said. "You might say I live around here. But I don't work, not anymore. I did, though. A long time ago, back before it was Sentry/Sensational." He started walking, his hands jammed into the baggy pockets of his pants, and Dodger decided to walk along with him. Where else did he have to go?

"Jack Sensational bought Sentry Studios . . . oh, it must

have been forty, fifty years ago. Only his name wasn't Sensational back then. It was Pudding. Jack Pudding. I guess he figured not many people would come to see a film from Pudding Pictures, so he changed it.''

Dodger laughed in spite of himself, then looked up to see if the lanky stringbean was kidding him. He could see no sign of it in the deadpan face. He was more sure than ever he'd seen the man before.

''It's an old Hollywood tradition, you know. I used to know a man by the name of Goldfish. Samuel Goldfish. Jewish fellow, I believe. Well, I don't know what Goldfish means in Hebrew, or maybe Jewish folks just think Goldfish is a mighty fine name—and they'd get no argument from me, you understand—but old Sam realized pretty quick that in America, which is where he lived, Americans thought it was a pretty silly name. So he changed it to Goldwyn, which didn't mean anything at all.''

''You mean . . . the guy from Metro-Goldwyn-Mayer?''

''That's him. Only old Sam bailed out of it before Metro really got off the ground. It was old Louis B. that ran the show. Louis B. Mayer. And that's the fellow I worked for. Metro pretty much fell apart a long time ago, and for a while I think it was Sony Pictures, or something like that. But Sony became something else, and that was swallowed by a big corporation, and when all the dust settled, why, there was the Sentry Motion Picture Company.'' The man stopped, and assumed the well-known position of the giant sentry with his rifle Dodger had seen on the way in, only when he did it, it was comical, his face sort of pop-eyed, his mouth making a little *O* of surprise. That's when Dodger got it.

''You're Jimmy Stewart,'' he said.

''Well, no, that's not right,'' the man said, reaching into his hip pocket and removing a wallet. ''The name's Dowd. Elwood P. Here, let me give you one of my cards.'' Dodger took it, and looked at it. A phone number had been scratched out with a pencil, and a new one written in:

Call ~~Northside 777~~
Pennsylvania 6-5000

"Now, if you want to call me use this number, not that one. That number is the old one."

Dodger was going to say that he'd seen the man just a few weeks ago in *The Man Who Shot Liberty Valance,* with John Wayne and Lee Marvin, directed by John Ford, but the talk of telephones brought him back to his problem.

He was supposed to call only in emergencies.

John Valentine was suspicious of most technological advances, regarded even the ones he took advantage of as no better than necessary evils. To him, the telephone was still a newfangled gadget. He refused to have one implanted in his head, like most people. But one could never tell when one's agent might be frantically looking for one, so he carried a pocket portable.

Telephones for children were both improper and an unwarranted expense. Dodger had no instrument at all, internal or otherwise. There were public phones for emergencies.

But telephones also functioned as the omnipresent ears of the government, of law enforcement, and John Valentine had never been on good terms with either. Every conversation was monitored and recorded, he was convinced. So it had damn well better *be* an emergency.

This was the problem Dodger had been wrestling with, then. He was already beyond hoping he could get out of this without consequences he didn't even like to think about. Father was going to be angry no matter what. Would calling make things worse, or better? And even more important, did he dare make a call when the people from the State School were listening in?

"So what would your name be?"

"Huh?" Dodger had almost forgotten about Mr. Dowd. "Oh, I'm Kenneth. Kenneth Valentine."

"No. You don't say. You wouldn't be Dodger Valentine, John B. Valentine's son, would you?"

Dodger looked up in astonishment, and momentary hope.

"Do you know my father?"

"Why, sure I do. To speak to, anyway, it's not like we're buddies. And I certainly know his work. Anyone who knows theater knows John Valentine's work."

"Mr. Dowd, could you—"

"Call me Elwood. Everybody calls me Elwood."

"Elwood, I've got a—"

"Why, I believe I saw him not thirty minutes ago. Now where was that . . . ?"

Dodger was jumping up and down in his excitement.

"Mist—Elwood, *please* remember. I've just got to find him."

Elwood squatted down and looked at Dodger, then took a handkerchief from his pocket and dabbed at the boy's eyes.

"Yes, sir. I believe you do. Well, we'll just have to do something about that, won't we? He stood and took Dodger's hand.

They went around one corner, down a long hallway with doors on each side, then two more corners and there he was, John Valentine, standing tall as he always did, smiling at passersby. Giving no hint of the agitation he was certainly feeling.

Dodger swallowed hard, started forward, then looked around for Elwood.

He was gone.

Then he looked again toward his father, and there was Elwood, standing beside him. The differentness about Elwood was even more pronounced when he saw him standing by his father. Dodger couldn't quite put his finger on it. Elwood's presence was not as solid, somehow. He was not translucent. He cast a shadow. But Dodger knew he wasn't like other people.

He started forward again, and in a moment his father saw him. John Valentine turned toward his son, and something dangerous flashed in his eyes. Dodger kept coming but he reached into his pocket and pulled out the papers he had been given, then held them out before him like a shield.

"What have you done to your hair?" his father asked.

Dodger clapped his hand to his head. He had forgotten!

After everything settled down in the audition room a makeup man had been called. Dodger was swept into a chair and before he quite knew what was happening the man was cutting his hair. This was over the ineffectual protests of Auntie Equity, who kept asking where the boy's parents were. Peppy had turned on his considerable charm, pointing to the signature at the bottom of the release form, and reading a paragraph about agrees to undergo such changes in personal appearance as may be required pursuant to the audition. Dodger thought it best to keep quiet at that point. Maybe signing the paper in his father's name hadn't been such a good idea after all.

Before he knew it, Dodger's long hair had been butchered. It had been blond before; now it was a violent yellow, a yellow never before seen on a human head. On each side it now stuck straight out, like wings. The top of his head was shaved bald, except for a narrow Mohawk strip that was moussed into a topknot four inches high. On each of the strips of bare scalp the hairdresser had tattooed orange lightning bolts. His eyebrows had been shaved and also replaced with lightning bolts.

Dodger looked like a kid who had stuck his finger in an electric outlet.

It was this apparition, not the cherubic child he had left in the waiting room, that now approached John Valentine. That his dismay was not evident on his face—except to Dodger— was tribute to a truly massive acting talent.

But the Dodger could see it in his eyes. He was in big trouble.

There really wasn't anything to say. He held out the paper, and eventually his father took it.

It was crumpled, and there was a big mustard stain right in the middle. But at the bottom was the signature of Gideon Peppy. And at the top were the words *Letter of Intent to Tender Offer of Employment.*

Stapled to it was a check for twenty thousand dollars.

When I awoke this time I just lay there for a while, remembering that long-ago audition. Ninety-two years ago. Where did the time go?

God, that hair was awful. But I know I liked it at the time.

I shifted and found the clock.

Four days.

Trouble. Big-time trouble.

In the best of circumstances, you can't take your friendly neighborhood drug pusher to the Better Business Bureau to complain about the quality of her wares. You have to handle your complaints yourself, and I would cheerfully have broken her kneecaps *and* her elbows if I could get my hands on her. But if that had been in the cards she no doubt would never have diluted her product. It was a sweet racket she had going. Anybody she sold deadballs to was on his way off-planet, unlikely to be back in months, or years . . . or ever, if things worked out right. Right for her, that is. Spectacularly wrong for me. It was outright murder.

Well, what did I expect from a dope pusher?

I chewed slowly on a hard granola bar dipped in honey while I considered my options.

Number one was the most obvious. Simply eat as little as I could during these waking periods, and try to make it through the final forty days on what I had left. Torture, surely . . . but was it possible? I added it up a dozen different ways and kept reaching the same answer: I don't know. I just didn't have enough data about rates of starvation. I knew people had fasted for very long times, but I didn't have any reliable numbers on it. And hadn't they damaged themselves? I thought I'd heard that. Brain damage can be irreversible.

What I was sure of was that I would be mighty hungry the whole time. And I thought I might go crazy out here with no companion but my appetite.

Option number two involved leaving the Pantech and making my way to the ship's central core. A risky business at best, but I could probably make it. Once I got there, of course, I'd have food. They always carried plenty of good food on these cargo ships, gourmet meals being one of the inducements for taking such a lonely job at all.

Sure, they'd feed me well. And turn me over to the police as soon as they landed. Since I couldn't pay the fare that meant a prison term, and on Oberon that meant the gravity gang. No, thank you.

The third option was a little vague, and was really sort of a suboption to number one. Some of these cargo canisters around me were certain to contain food. If I prowled through them long enough I might find some.

Maybe three hundred tons of onions, or a shipment of parsley, or a tank of diet soda pop that would blow up in my face.

I put those options to one side, and concentrated on number four.

I almost hate to mention option number four, because it was nebulous, at best. I asked myself, is there any way to extend the periods of sleep back to the full week I had been counting on? And the answer to that was . . . could be. What I had in mind was self-hypnosis.

One of the things I do to tide myself over times of no work is magic. Not just three-card monte and its infinite variations, though I have been known to run a game. And not the manipulation of cards to gain an advantage at the poker table, though I am quite capable of that, too. The same skills useful in running a street con can also be put to use on the semilegitimate stage where no money hinges on the outcome. Prestidigitation. Sleight of hand. Misdirection and showmanship. In my luggage beside the Punch and Judy show are the basic tools of The Amazing Klepto, Mentalist Extraordinary. It consists mainly of a black cape, top hat, and magic wand, and in a pinch I can do without the wand. Most of the tricks I do can be performed with found or hastily manufactured objects. I can work up close in a small room or on the street, on a cabaret or theater stage, and I'm available for birthdays, charivaris, menarches, and bar mitzvahs.

I'm up-front about it. There is no real magic, so far as I know. It's all illusion, and I tell you so before I begin. I'm known as Klepto because a good part of the close-in work involves relieving the audience of jewelry, wallets, and other items worn or carried about the person, then producing them again to amused astonishment all around.

Or not, if I think the item won't be missed.

No real magic, I said, but hypnotism always seems close to it, even to me. I can hypnotize others and have them go through the ancient repertoire of parlor tricks mesmerists have been putting their victims through for centuries: making animal sounds, reverting to childhood, removing their clothing, and generally making damn fools of themselves. Or I can hypnotize myself, and certain parts of the act become much easier for me. Call it yoga if you wish. It is mostly increased control of involuntary body functions, and I learned most of what I know from—who else?—a gypsy woman in a hobo jungle just outside Marsport. Most of the lessons took place in bed.

The trick is to *convince* yourself you are able to do some unlikely thing. If it is not utterly impossible—I wouldn't recommend trying to fly by flapping your arms—you'd be surprised at the things you can do.

Could I convince myself to sleep for a week?

The trick of hypnosis is to fool yourself into believing that something that is *possible* is in fact *true*. Sleep was the end result I was seeking, but that was the *end*. What I proposed was to start at the beginning, with the *means* of sleep.

So I dissolved two of the white pills in a glass of water, and I held it up before me. I gazed into the milky depths.

You are powerful, I told the potion. *You will make me sleep for a week.*

Yeah. Right.

I made my bubble transparent and assumed the lotus position on my mattress. The cold stars looked down at me, but I ignored them. I looked instead at the gently rocking horses of the future carousel. They were sleeping peacefully. If they could do it, so could I.

"Oh, money pump mayhem. Oh, money pump mayhem."

This was my mantra, suitably dodgerized for my delectation. The gypsy woman had her own version, some unpronounceable Romanian or Romany transliteration of the original . . . Hindi? Urdu? Sanskrit? I didn't know, but most people would recognize the ancient chant of *Om mani padme hum.* The words don't mean anything, anyway, unless you're a Buddhist, and my version was better than the one an old girlfriend of mine had used: "Oh, Mommy! Pop, me humped!" I never got around to asking her if it was true.

"Oh money-pumpmay *hem*! Oh, money pumpmay *hem*!"

I did that for half an hour. I succeeded in getting myself into a dreamy, receptive state, but not deep enough to believe the deadball was full strength.

That was okay. I hadn't expected to.

But didn't I have something in my medicine chest that might help . . . ?

I opened it and pawed through the meager contents, and there it was. It was a bottle half-full of white pills. The label said ASPIRIN. Ah, yes, but hadn't I replaced them back on . . .

was it Brementon? Yes, yes, it was. On Brementon I had replaced the innocent white headache pills with innocent white *powerful narcotics*. Very powerful narcotics. I remember doing so. I could see myself emptying the aspirin. I saw myself dump the aspirin in the trash. I saw myself opening a brown bottle, pouring *powerful narcotic* pills into my hand, and carefully putting them into the aspirin bottle. I heard them rattling down through the narrow neck.

Great! Now I had a bottle of *powerful narcotics*. Maybe they would enable me to sleep for a week, along with the deadballs.

I shook two of the pills into my hand. No, better make it four.

On each of them, in tiny red letters, was the word ASPIRIN.

For a moment the whole house of cards wavered, threatened to topple.

Ah, but wait!

I would have laughed, except for the rarefied state of Zen bliss I was in, so I contented myself with a beatific smile. Foolish boy! Don't you recall? Of course you do. The . . . the . . . the guy you bought them from *told* you, he said . . . he said . . . *he* had written ASPIRIN on the *powerful narcotics* so if anybody looked at them, they would see ASPIRIN, and think they weren't worth stealing. But they were really powerful, *powerful narcotics*.

In fact, they might be *too* powerful. Don't take four of them. I put one back into the bottle. Three should be enough.

I popped them into my mouth and washed them down with the chalky deadball solution. Then I set about tidying things up, knowing I'd be asleep soon.

I came across the frog and skull netsuke and I picked it up. I stared at the frog, and it stared back at me.

I liked the way it felt in my hand, so I kept it out. I resumed the lotus position, and stroked the ancient, cool ivory with my thumb. It gradually warmed under my hand. I could feel a pulsing in the frog's throat.

I fell asleep.

Dodger hurried through the busy passenger terminal of the King City Spaceport, clinging to his father's hand, feeling a little like a balloon at the end of a string. It wasn't a bad feeling, but it wasn't a real secure one, either. There was nothing to be done about it. When his father got excited, he moved very fast.

Father and son were dressed in white pants and shoes, long white coats that buttoned all the way down the front and had stiff, upright collars. They wore orange turbans wrapped around their heads. The skin of their hands and faces was now a light brown color, and John Valentine sported a neatly trimmed black beard and mustache. Under the turban Dodger was bald as an egg. The shocking yellow hair was all gone, and so were the lightning-bolt tattoos.

Valentine hurried up to the Inner Planet Budget counter and smiled at the young woman who stood behind it. She smiled down at Dodger, who looked cute as could be, a scale model of his handsome father but without the whiskers.

"Good morning," Valentine said, with a slight accent. "I am seeking a reservation in the person of Rajiv Singh, and his most esteemed son, Rahman. We have been booking two passages of an inside stateroom to Flip City, Mars, with connectings to New Amritsar."

"Yes, Mr. Singh, I have your reservation here." The young woman did something at her ticketing machine and produced a clear plastic rectangle that flashed in rainbow colors when the light hit it. "That will be five hundred and fifty-seven dollars and nineteen cents, including transportation tax, excise tax, amusement tax, transaction tax, value added tax, spaceport usage fees, and the mandated voluntary oxygen-indigent support assessment. May I have your credit number, please?"

"Oh, my goodness, no!" Valentine's smile was still in place, but he was gritting his teeth. "Cash moneys only, if you please! 'Neither a borrower nor a lender be,' as according to poor Richard Almanack. And concerning these other stipends . . ." He leaned over and studied the lines on her ticketing screen. John Valentine paid few taxes unnecessarily and *none* willingly. "The harried, hurried traveling public is a market ripe for a swindle, Dodger," he said whenever they went anywhere. "Most of them have no idea that not all those fees apply to *them*." After five minutes of haggling, he had eliminated six dollars in amusement ("We don't plan to be

amused''), transaction (''This is applying to credit dealings
only''), and air imposts (''Our temple is contributing most
generously each year to the Beggars' Breathing Fund, or as
Richard Almanack once said, 'I gave at the office.' '').

Those battles won, Valentine pulled his wad of cash from
his coat pocket and paid the fare. The lady validated the ticket
and handed it to him.

''Now, may I see your passport, please?''

''Passport? Passport? Surely I am told this is not being
necessary, for purposes of tourism or religious pilgrimage not
to exceed two weeks of durations. Rahman, my son, are you
bringing the passports?'' Valentine had been patting himself
down, exploring his pockets in distraction. Now he smiled.
''We are Sikhs,'' he said, explaining. ''Rahman!''

Dodger had been woolgathering, on the high seas aboard
a pirate ship. Now he jerked awake, and patted all *his* pockets.
''No, my father.''

''There, you see!'' Valentine said.

''You're right, of course,'' said the lady, ''but I do need
some identification.''

''This should be of no type of problem,'' Valentine assured her. ''Here is an abundance of such items.'' He fanned
several cards out on the counter like a winning poker hand.
Dodger felt the pressure on his hand increase. Mr. Rajiv Singh
was unlikely to have missed the items, since he was deadballing to Neptune at the moment, only one week into his
journey. Valentine had been guaranteed these documents
would survive the cursory scrutiny needed to buy tourist passage to Mars. Still, it paid to be cautious, and Dodger was
ready, should his hand be squeezed three times, to start complaining loudly about a sudden and violent need to empty his
bladder. He was prepared to piss his pants, if it came to that.
He *really* hoped it wouldn't come to that.

He sighed in relief when he saw she was buying it, simply
glancing at the stolen identification and making a mark on
her screen.

''I can offer you a stateroom upgrade, with a private bath,
for a fee increase of only twenty dollars,'' the lady said.

''Oh, my goodness, yes, of course. Won't that be so jolly,
Rahman?''

"Yes, my father."

"And are there any ... special dietary needs associated with your faith, Mr. Singh?"

"Oh, my goodness, no. We shall be most pleased to be eating whatsoever the other passengers have been eating. Hamburgers and hot dogs, eh, my son?"

"Oh, my goodness!" Dodger agreed.

"Very well. Your ticket will also function as your meal card, so please don't lose it. Since your departure isn't for another four hours, you may use it to purchase a meal at the spaceport snack bars, in appreciation for your early arrival, courtesy of IPB. Please be at the boarding gate in three hours, with your luggage. Have a pleasant flight, and enjoy your visit to Mars."

"Oh, a most devotional trip, indeed!" Valentine said. "May the sacred monkeys of the New Temple of Amritsar guide you through the day."

The woman's smile became a bit glassy, as though not sure if she wanted to be guided by monkeys, sacred or otherwise, but when Dodger waved to her she waved back. When they were far enough away, Dodger looked up at his father.

"Why don't you buy me some eggs?" he asked. "Since you already—"

"Have provided the ham," Valentine finished, sheepishly. "Damn it, Dodger, why don't you stop me? It's a disease, I tell you, a disease. I can't stop myself."

"I really liked the part about the monkeys."

John Valentine threw his head back and laughed. Dodger loved it when he laughed. He'd been laughing a lot since they got back from Sentry Studios, hardly twenty-four hours ago.

"We've got time to kill, pardner," Valentine said. "What say we take IPB up on their offer to do lunch? Think their budget would stretch to a couple Cokes and Coney Islands?"

John Valentine produced the validated plastic with a flourish, and the clerk ran it through his machine. He and his son carried their trays to a booth overlooking the vast flat plain of the spaceport.

Dodger had contented himself with some mustard and a few spoonfuls of relish on his Coney, but Valentine had buried his, as usual, in chili, diced onions, relish, mustard, cheese, and a barely sublethal dose of the Tabasco sauce he put on almost everything he ate. Valentine's energies were enormous, and so were his appetites.

"You're going to like Mars, Dodge," he said, gingerly lifting the soggy load to his mouth and taking a big bite. "There's more gravity. Get your feet firmly on the ground for a change." He frowned, and chewed. "You remember Mars at all? What were you . . ."

"Three, you said," Dodger told him. "I don't remember much."

"No, I don't suppose you would. Well, take my word, it's a great place. It's the *perfect* place for the little theater we've always talked about. Your average Martian has an inferiority complex when it comes to Luna. No real reason they should, it's a much nicer place than here, but they do, that's the point. Luna is the great Golden Globe for most of the system, and the fact that Mars is a perpetual also-ran, Mars is in second place to Luna in just about anything you want to name . . . well, that just makes it worse. Some little godforsaken asteroid, they don't worry too much about measuring up to Luna. But Mars, Mars is sort of like Chicago, compared to New York. Chicago always had good theaters, good dance troupes. But Chicago never had a Broadway, and they knew they never would. But they always wanted to *be* New York, you see what I mean? That's where the action was. That's where the *best* actors, the *best* dancers, the *best* directors . . . if you weren't working in New York, people thought you weren't really doing serious work.

"Or like Hollywood in the film business. You could make a perfectly good film in Florida, but Hollywood was the center of the universe. It's where you went to be a star. 'There's no business like show business, there's no business I know!' " He sang, not really at the top of his voice, but John Valentine seldom spoke more quietly than a stage whisper, and several people in the snack bar turned to see the man in the orange turban singing a jaunty showbiz tune. Dodger kicked his father under the table.

Valentine looked around, and laughed. "You're right, Dodge," he said in a lower voice. "Sikhs *do* work in the industry, you know, but you're right, it looks out of character." Dodger was entitled to kick his father anytime he stepped out of character when they were working in public.

"Anyway," he went on, more confidentially, "what it does to the Martians is, they're much more receptive to culture. You stage *Love's Labour's Lost* in King City, it's a yawn. Oh, people will come, you might even fill the theater because there's so damn many people here. You do it on Mars, you get a lot more appreciation. The Martians are glad to have you, they cherish you, because by doing Shakespeare or any other of them highfalutin Greeks, you're telling your average Martian rube—and there's nothing rubier than a Martian rube—that he's just as good as a Lunarian. He'll go, even if he doesn't understand every third word, and he'll praise you, and thank you for going to the trouble. And that's good, Dodger, because frankly, other than myself—and you, when you're ready—there's not going to be a Luna-quality cast in the supporting roles. The best of them have already moved to Luna, they're breaking their hearts *here*. The sort of troupe I'm thinking of, it would get absolutely *hammered* in the King City reviews. But I guarantee you, on Mars, it will never be noticed."

"Sounds great," Dodger said.

"Better than great." He spread his hands wide, his eyes focused on a giant marquee only he could see. " 'The John Valentine & Son Shakespearean Repertory Company.' Just one small pressure dome, out a ways from the city where the rents aren't so high. A hundred fifty, two hundred seats, tops. Why, with twenty thousand dollars we can get it up and running, and even if we lose money every year, I don't see why we can't go six, seven years. And all thanks to Gideon Peppy and his idiotic show."

"Sounds wonderful," said the Dodger.

They ate in silence for a while, each with his own thoughts. Valentine was obviously laying out the floor plans of the repertory theater, drawing up the first season's schedule, deciding who to call in Flip City when it came time to cast the first production.

Dodger simply ate, taking small bites and chewing thoughtfully.

"I'd like to see Mr. Peppy's face tomorrow," Dodger finally ventured, quietly, "when nobody shows up for the contract meeting."

"And he realizes his catch has flown the coop." Valentine cackled. "Yeah, that'd be something to see, all right. We'll send him a postcard from Mars, when we open the first show. Anonymous. Let him wonder what it's all about."

"That should be funny," said Dodger.

They ate in silence for a while, both looking up when the lunchroom was for a moment flooded in light as a ship lifted from the field. Even through the darkened glass, for a moment it outshone the sun. Valentine chuckled.

"I think we could work up a comedy skit about your adventures yesterday. Caught up in the massive gears of the Hollywood machine, eh, Dodger?" He frowned, looking thoughtful. "In fact, I think I've seen something like it before. Very old stuff. Something about soldiers being processed very rapidly into an army, shuffling through physical and mental exams, no one really taking the time to see these chaps as human beings . . . and before they know it they've inducted a chimpanzee. Now where was that . . . ?"

"Maybe it was one of the sacred monkeys of the New Temple," Dodger suggested.

"That's it! That's it!" Valentine howled. Dodger was eager to get his father's thoughts away from the previous day. While he had not actually *lied* to his father about the general shape of events—he had in fact been shanghaied into the audition room, for instance—he had tended to exaggerate the slings and arrows of outrageous fortune and to downplay his own complicity. He had neglected to mention filling out the form and forging his father's name. He had hurried over the details of his reading, not putting much emphasis on how diligently he had tried to win the part. And come to think of it, when his father assumed Dodger had been kidnapped right out of the waiting room where Valentine had left him, Dodger had not bothered to correct him. Why invite trouble? Dodger had reasoned. It made a much better story the way his father had heard it, and hadn't he always said a good story was frequently superior to the truth?

"I couldn't get over how talented he thought I was," Dodger said, with a chuckle. "Honest, Father. I was hardly even trying."

"Well, I'm tooting my own horn, I suppose," his father said, comfortably, "but I don't think you realize just how much your classical training has set you above other boys your age.''

"I guess you're right." Dodger sighed. "Now I guess he'll have to settle for second best.''

Valentine reached across the table and chucked his son playfully under the chin.

"After the Valentines," he said, "there is no second place." He finished the last bite of his Coney Island, licked the chili from his fingers, washed it down with a big swig of pop. "I'm still hungry. How about it? You want another?''

"I've still got this one," Dodger said.

"I'm getting another. You want some cookies? A brownie?''

"Cookies would be nice."

Valentine hurried away and Dodger put down the half Coney he had been nibbling. He did nothing at all until his father slid back into the booth across from him, and then he still did nothing. His father looked up from wolfing down his second Coney Island. He frowned at his son.

"What's the matter? Not hungry? There probably won't be any food on the ship for a while, until they get it rotating and unpack the kitchen.''

"No, I'm fine," Dodger said. He laced his fingers together and leaned forward slightly, a look of concentration on his face. "Father . . . you said we could run our theater at a loss for six or seven years on twenty thousand dollars. I was just wondering. . . .''

"Go ahead," Valentine said, when the pause had stretched too long.

"I was wondering, how long could we run it on a hundred thousand dollars?''

Valentine stopped chewing for a moment and his eyes lost their focus. Then he started chewing more slowly.

"You know the answer to that," he said. "But I don't think you meant it as a math problem. Go on, Dodger. What's on your mind?''

"Well, Mr. Peppy said that's what we'd make for an episode. For the pilot, I think he called it.''

"Incredible, isn't it?" Valentine said. "I always told you there's lots of money in that business. Lots of money. The only problem is, what you have to do to earn it."

"Right," Dodger agreed. "That's right. Still . . ."

Valentine put down the Coney and regarded his son.

"Just tell it, Dodger. What do you have in mind?"

"Yes, sir. I was just thinking, since I already have the part . . . well, we could take them for some *real* money if I went ahead and made the pilot."

Valentine said nothing.

"Just think how crazy Mr. Peppy would get if we made the pilot, and *then* took off for Mars."

Valentine howled at that one, then got serious. He reached across the table and took Dodger's hand in his.

"You'd really do that, wouldn't you?" he said, his eyes glistening. "For your old man and his crazy theater, you'd put yourself through that mill, and I'll bet you'd never complain, either." He stood up, almost knocking over the table, leaned across, and kissed his son on the forehead. He sat back down and gazed out over the field for a while, getting his emotions under control. At last he looked back, fondly.

"I can't let you do it, Dodger. I know you think you could handle it, but let me tell you, you have *no idea* the insanity that would be brought to bear. I brought you up to be an *actor,* not a mugger in dumb shows. Not a spiffed-up little clown with yellow hair and zigzags on his head and I don't know what all else. You think it's just a pilot, son, but it's really a trap. It's the first dose of an addicting drug. The money is tempting, and if I had any less regard for you I'd snap it up in a King City minute. But it's because I do hold you in such high regard that we're going to take the money and run." He squeezed Dodger's hand again. "But I want you to know, I'll never forget the offer."

Dodger smiled, and shrugged.

"It was just an idea," he said. "Just a way to be sure the John Valentine Repertory Shakespearean Theater gets off to a good start. But you're probably right. They did seem like crazy people."

He looked out the window where a ship, big as a city, was being hauled out to its pad on a creeper the size of a small crater.

"Still," he said, wistfully. "All that money."

• • •

Three hours later the lady at the IPB ticket counter looked up to see the Sikh father and son hurrying in her direction.

"Sir! Your ship is boarding right now! You'll have to run to—"

"Oh, my goodness, no!" said the man. "Oh, most frightfully no. My most esteemed lady, the sacred monkeys of the New Temple of Amritsar have deemed this a most insuspicious point in time to be traveling. What a surprise this has become to myself and my most excellent son, Rahman, I shall have left to your imaginings. However, the upshooting of the situation is this: that we should now be seeking a refunding of our monies. We shall be guided to the New Temple at a date to be later determined." He paused, and smiled. "Or perhaps I should be saying, 'piloted.' " He slapped the plastic boarding pass on the counter.

The woman knew little of religions other than her own Catholic upbringing, had never really heard of Sikhs. But as she was refunding the money (including, to her later chagrin, amusement tax, transaction tax, *and* Beggar's Breath), she decided Sikhs must be a sort of Buddhist. She was familiar with the Buddha. She recalled thinking the son looked a lot like his father, but she could see now she had been wrong.

No, the satisfied smile on the small face was the very image of the Enlightened One.

From that moment on, my father was just about the only person that ever called me Dodger anymore. From then on, I was Sparky. I wasn't Kenneth even in the credits, and no one at Sentry ever called me Dodger.

If I had it to do over again, would I choose to go with Father to Mars? To this day I don't know. Being strongly identified with a part can be a blessing, but is usually a curse in my business. Ask Charlie Chaplin, Buster Keaton, Boris Karloff. It goes back at least that far. Like a singer asked to endlessly repeat his one monster hit, you get very tired of it. Reviewers will forever after make much of the fact that it was little *Sparky* who played the part of Willy Loman, will more than likely treat the whole enterprise as a stunt. That's one reason I've used so many pseudonyms in my career.

But being Sparky has been helpful from time to time. It's

an image you can trade on, when you're otherwise down-and-out. It will get your foot in the door, get you special attention even if half the time it is only to be told Sorry, I just can't see little Sparky as Stanley Kowalski. It gets you attention as somebody-who-used-to-be-somebody while Wanda B. Somebody, Mita Bean, and Neva Hoydova are cooling their heels at a cattle call. And brother, when you're out there riding on a smile and a shoe shine, it can give you that edge you need.

Hi, it's me again. The artist formerly known as Sparky.

I am waking up for the third time this voyage, being as careful as I can not to tamper with my meditative state, trying not to become *fully* awake, since you can never tell if you'll convince yourself again of the Big Lie you managed to swallow getting into this state.

I checked my clock and found I'd been asleep for seven days. I took the news calmly—of *course* it had been seven days; I'd taken *powerful narcotics*—and I had in fact already suspected it, because I was twice as hungry as I had been each previous time. It looked to be starvation on the installment plan, which was a lot better than a continuous forty days of it.

I ate. You don't want to know *what* I ate any more than I want to revisit the tastes by telling about it. Just recall the items I bought back on Pluto, imagine them all swirled together in a blender, and I'll leave the rest to your imagination. It was vile stuff, and it killed the hunger pangs, which was all it was supposed to do.

I shook out three pills. They were now plainly labeled POWERFUL NARCOTICS, I noticed. I washed them down with deadball solution that was actually starting to taste pretty good.

I slept.

"Interesting," said John Valentine, when he saw his son. "But what about the pants?"

"Donald Duck never wore pants," said Gideon Peppy, around his lollipop.

Sparky had spent the entire morning with Rose, the nice production-designer lady, and her staff of hair, costume, and makeup people. His hair had been restored in its tripartite pattern, but instead of banana yellow it was now metallic and bronze, spiraled and wiry. The side wings were swept back instead of spread out, and the front part of the Mohawk drooped down over his forehead. The electric zigzags were back, joined now by a pair on his chest. His eyes were mascaraed from eyelash to brow in a deep rose fading to black, then tapering to more zigzags at the corners. He wore black lipstick.

He had been prodded and pampered, trimmed, teased, and flattered by the deft boys and girls of the makeup department, and made to feel very important indeed. He had been massaged with warm oils until his skin glistened. If he wanted something to eat or drink he had merely to ask and it appeared. He had received his first manicure and pedicure. Then he had been put into his costume, which was a red jerkin or waistcoat (which his father said was pronounced *weskit*) with gold embroidery suggestive of a circuit board. It could be fastened with a frog in front, or left open. It had no sleeves or lapels. It reached the middle of his hips. When he had it on Sparky immediately asked the same question his father would ask a few minutes later, and when he was told that was it, the entire costume, he knew there was going to be trouble.

Now he stood silently in front of the huge mirror that backed the conference table on the edge of the bustling pirate-ship tank set. Gideon Peppy liked conference tables, had one brought in anywhere he was going to meet with people, and immediately installed himself in a big chair at one end. His staff clustered at that end, drawn like iron filings to a magnet. He sat there now, feet up on the table as was his custom, and looked at Sparky. Behind him and to his right was the usual pandemonium of a set being constructed, wired, painted, and lit all at once. A wharf had been built and a Caribbean port town was almost complete. Nail guns stuttered and paint sprayers hissed and table saws howled as gangs of grips carried foam barrels and inflatable bales of cotton to stack on the wharf. A paving machine was moving along like a giant metal termite queen, laying cobbles in irregular rows on the steep main street. Set dressers were strewing straw and garbage and imitation horseshit, daubing weathered-wood walls with ersatz mildew. Somewhere underwater frogmen were positioning battery-powered minibrutes to shine upward through the turquoise water. And anchored just off the wharf was the pirate ship itself, swarming with gaffers and riggers testing the complex system of ropes, pulleys, and canvas.

Sparky watched it all in the mirror, and remembered Orson Welles's description of a motion picture soundstage: the greatest toy a boy ever had.

"Yes," his father thundered, bringing Sparky back to reality. "And Donald Duck was a cartoon, a water fowl, and imaginary. And, apparently, sexless. You should bear in mind that my son is a real little boy."

Valentine had grasped the dynamic of the conference table instantly, weeks ago when he had his first meeting with Peppy and his staff. He had marched unerringly to the far end of the table and had been camping out there ever since. It meant he had to raise his voice to reach Peppy, especially on a noisy set like this one, but it was no problem for John Valentine, who liked to boast that he had never been miked in his life and *always* projected to the last row of the balcony.

Peppy and Valentine had loathed each other on sight and each had yet to speak an impolite word to the other. The tension at the table had grown so unbearable that the faint of heart among Peppy's entourage hyperventilated and had to breathe into paper bags when the meetings adjourned.

"I never forget it for a minute, my good friend," Peppy replied. "A wonderful talent, your son. He's going to be a big star, and very soon. Maybe even bigger than me." He chuckled wryly, bemused at such a thought, and a few of his people chuckled with him. He leaned forward. "But we're dealing in a fantasy world here, John B. We're making movie magic. We've researched this high and low—haven't we, Rose? Tell him about the research—and what you're seeing in that sweet little boy is the coming thing, John B., the coming thing. We won't be in business very long if we wait around until the coming thing is already *here*. We've got to be the ones who define what it is. Tell him, Rose."

Valentine, who liked being called John B. about as much as Jack Sensational would have liked being called Puddin' head, folded his hands comfortably and turned to Rose with a sweet smile.

Rose was that rarity, an artist oblivious to power politics within the team. She *liked* her creation, and she liked Sparky, and had no idea how much Valentine and Peppy detested each other.

"It's true, Mr. Valentine," she enthused, and hurried over to take Sparky by the elbows and boost him onto the table, where he swaggered around in the middle, careful not to get too close to either end, where there were tigers. He struck a few poses, watching himself in the mirror.

"The one-piece look is already the thing in the Mercury Commune, and you know how they've bellwethered all the newest things for the last two years. Simplicity is the statement. One garment, loads of makeup. Both sexes. And not just the tiny tots, either. Just a shirt, or a pair of trousers. Sometimes just one sleeve—just a sleeve, no shirt—or a legging." She illustrated on her own body, with graceful hand gestures, then joined Sparky on the table. She herself wore a garment similar to his, but a little longer. She went down on one knee beside him, pointing out features of her handiwork. "Depilate from the neck down. Oil up. One item of clothing. That's the key to the new look. Lots of skin. Heck, on Mars the upper classes aren't dressing their children at all until they reach puberty, as if we were back in the fifties. I think that's reverse snobbery, and besides, you can't make money selling nudity."

"You can make more money selling more clothes," Valentine pointed out.

"That's true," said Peppy. "And we'll sell caps, and T-shirts, and whatever the marketing department dreams up. But that'll be with *pictures* of Sparky, and with the Sparky artwork and logo and characters. If the kids want to wear the Sparky *look*, they'll wear the vest dingus. And they'll buy it from us, because we'll be the only ones selling Sparky vests with the official Sparky's Gang seal."

"Only to eight-year-olds," Valentine said.

"So what? We figure three-to-ten, actually, but eight is the target, for now. This thing takes off, takes off *big*, we'll get up to the teens as the Sparkster gets older. I'm telling you, John B., the Victorian Kid is history. You can pack away all his lacy duds, his velvet shirts and ruffled collars and knee britches. Coupla months, *everybody's* kid's gonna dress like this."

"If he wears it at all," Valentine said, dangerously. "I

don't know, Pepsi. There's something about it that rubs me the wrong way. Call me old-fashioned. Nudity is fine, at home, at the playground, in the swimming pool.''

"But this isn't nudity, Mr. V," Rose piped up, honestly trying to be helpful. "Nudity is dreary. This is *style.*"

"Not to put too fine a point to it, Rose, my darling," John said, "I was raised to believe a young gentleman should wear pants in public."

Rose—who, like most third-generation and younger Lunarians, had no more body modesty than a mink—had no idea what he was talking about. She had made costumes faithfully for a hundred Earth-era pictures without ever really grasping the genitalia taboo. People wore lots of clothing on Earth because it had been *dangerous* down there, to her way of thinking. Blistering sunlight, lethal cold winds. There was nothing like that to protect oneself from on Luna, and people wore clothing almost exclusively for decoration, sometimes a lot of it, sometimes very little, depending on the fashion of the day. If the fashion now was no pants, what's the big deal? She looked to Peppy for help.

Gideon Peppy carefully removed half his lollipop from his mouth, and chewed on the rest. He had *never* eaten his hard candy treats until he met the Valentines, father and son, but now he found himself frequently biting down hard on them. *Pepsi, is it, you prick?*

He laughed indulgently, one friend to another, and shook his head.

"Johnny, Johnny, honestly! I don't know where you get these ideas! He's a riot, isn't he, fellas? A riot. Sometimes I think you're just kidding us, and I'm too dumb to get the joke. But I'm *here* for you, *paisan.* I care, I really do. If you have concerns I'm always willing to listen. If you're not happy, nobody at this table is happy, so what I want from you is to talk to me, John. Blue-sky it for us. What would you like to see here? We all want your input and my mind is a blank page, costume-wise. So draw on it, John B., draw on it. What kind of pants are we talking here?''

Sparky, who had not been following the exchange at all closely, chose that moment to pipe up.

"I kind of like it, Father," he said.

The silence that followed was mercifully short, as one of

Rose's assistants arrived with a girl in tow. Now it was Sparky's turn to frown dubiously.

Peppy stood up to greet the girl. He lifted her up onto the table where she stood confidently, hands on hips, looking a challenge at Sparky.

"Folks, meet Sparky's new sidekick. I'd like you to say hi to Kaspara Polichinelli!"

"Sidekick? Sidekick? I didn't see anything about a side-kick." John Valentine reached for his script.

"All action heroes have sidekicks," Peppy said, smugly. "We figured from the start Sparky'd have one. We wrote her in last week."

Sparky walked slowly toward the young lady. Eight years old, he figured. Dressed exactly as he was, only the waistcoat was blue with silver highlights. Hair trimmed the same, only silver instead of brass. Zigzags, eye shadow, all the same. The black lipstick was a trifle bee-stung, a little Betty Boopish, but other than that, she looked just like him.

He stopped a pace away and looked her up and down. She smiled. Her two front teeth were prominent.

"What kind of name is Kaspara?" he asked. He was aware that an argument was happening down at Peppy's end of the table, but he tried to ignore it. He knew he had made a major mistake in his comment about the costume, but he was hoping this new sensation might make it seem less important in ret-rospect. Perhaps Kaspara Polichinelli's arrival would distract his father from his son's innocent gaffe. And that was good.

But he was far from sure anything *else* about her arrival was so great.

"I don't use it," she said.

"What do they call you? Kassie?"

"Everybody calls me Polly."

Sparky had edged a little closer, trying to see if his shoul-der was higher than hers. She smiled, and came around him to stand back-to-back. The two of them looked in the mirror. He had an inch on her. Maybe two if he stood up straight. Well, that was okay, then.

She laughed, and bumped him with her hip.

"Come on," she said. "Don't be such a flip. I know how

to stand downstage and not get in your shot. They told me the part was a sidekick when I tried out.''

''You're going to be my buddy? Is that it?''

''I don't think they planned any sexual involvement until the third season, at least,'' she said. ''Which is fine with me. I'm old-fashioned, like your father. I figured I'd wait till my blood day, just like my mother did.''

Sparky was saved from replying to that by the sound of rising voices at the power end of the table. Storm clouds were forming over there, and the outlook was excellent that the long-delayed cataclysmic confrontation between producer and parent was about to break out. Aides were scurrying for cover as John Valentine came around the table, slapping his script into his open palm while Peppy slapped a copy of Sparky's contract into his.

''Come on,'' Polly said, pulling his hand. ''They told me to bring you back. Miss Crow says it's time for classes.''

''Miss Crow?'' For a moment Sparky forgot who she was. ''Oh. Auntie Equity.''

''Auntie Equity.'' She laughed. ''I like that. C'mon, let's get out of here. There's a fight about to happen, and I think your dad's going to lose it. I don't think you want to be around when he does.''

John Valentine did lose the fight, if the removal of the character of Polly was the criterion for winning. But he saw it coming, and managed to turn the contest in midstream until it was a struggle over artistic control and not over Polly herself—and managed to convince himself that was what he had been upset about in the first place. It might even have been true.

He was not mollified by a small victory on the issue of trousers.

''Listen to this,'' Peppy had offered. ''We shoot the pilot in the outfits Rose designed. Then there's a coupla markets off-planet . . . what is it, Vesta, Callisto . . . Ceres, I think, all fulla Baptists and Mormons and jerks like that. Vesta, now, wha'd' they call it in that skit the other day . . . ?'' He snapped his fingers rapidly and an aide spoke up.

''Planet of the Prudes,'' he said.

''That's it. We always have to tinker with the *Peppy Show*

for export, so what we'll do, we'll morph some britches on 'em, see what it tests like. Now I ask you, John B. Is that fair?''

"Couldn't be fairer, Pepster." Valentine beamed.

Ah, Polly. Those were more innocent days.

Yes, it's me again, awake after another week.

Like most long voyages, at sea or in space, awake or asleep, there is not usually much to report. One day is like another, barring storm or disaster. I will tell you now, no such disaster will befall. The deadballs will continue to work their hypnotism-reinforced magic, I will continue to awake at regular intervals, I will eat, I will fall back into the arms of Morpheus. In time I will arrive at Oberon, where further adventures await. In the meantime I will allow that long-ago Sparky to tell his story, as is his habit, in the third person, suitably edited into high and low points.

I doubt that I will interrupt him again.

But this time I had to. Sometimes something rises from the depths of the sea or sails out of the ocean of night to make the day a special one. Your diary has been an endless series of identical entries: *Falling sunward. Shipboard routine uninterrupted. Weather clear. Slept.* Then the lost continent of Atlantis appears off the starboard bow. It's worth a postcard.

We ran into a herd of diaphanophores. A flight of diaphanophores? The book where I found that fancy name you've probably never heard of neglected to give a collective noun for them. Herd definitely won't do, though. How about an exaltation of diaphanophores?

They're better known by several more poetic names, including Outer Angels, Angel's Robes, and spinthistles. Or simply angels. On Pluto, they are called BFODs: Big Fucking Orbital Disks. Those rascally Plutonians. Honestly.

Let's settle on angels, shall we?

Their origins are obscure, but it is known they are manmade. The dominant theory is that they are the creation of some demented biohacker with an illegal lab somewhere in the outer planets. When they first showed up there was considerable alarm about them, but so far they have proven harmless. That was about a century ago, maybe a bit longer, so I'd say the case was pretty well closed. Plenty of people would like to know more about them, to be *sure* they're not up to something, but angels are traditionally hard to study, and these won't sit still any more than the Biblical variety.

Space angels dissolve when you get close to them. Some people think it's a protective reflex, because what's left of them apparently form sporelike structures, trillions of them, of which only a few will survive. Others think it is contact itself that blows them away, like thistledown. Ships can only approach within ten thousand miles or so. A man in a space-suit can get within maybe a hundred miles. Then they go *pop,* like soap bubbles. They are made of a mix of animal and vegetable protein. They are transparent, and probably one molecule thick. The little ones are one hundred thousand miles in diameter.

The big ones go up to ten *million* miles.

That's crazy, of course. There must be angels smaller than one hundred thousand miles across. They can't just spring into being. But even the big ones don't show up on radar, and finding the small ones when we know most of them spend most of their lives above and below the solar plane, where hardly anyone ever goes, is almost impossible. Maybe they breed out there.

If you read up on them, you will find that I've told you just about everything that is known, and you'll notice I've used a lot of *maybes.*

Two more things. They move about like sailboats, flying before the solar wind and light pressure. And they survive by sweeping up the extremely thin matter between planets. One reason scientists would like to capture one is they suspect angels might be sweeping up magnetic monopoles, whatever those are.

So there is the physical rundown. The reality was more colorful.

I saw them when I woke up. I'd say there were fifty or sixty of them, which meant there were probably a lot more since you only see them when they're oriented such that the sun's light is reflected toward you. There is no way to tell how big each one was, or how distant. One moment an angel would seem truly vast and impossibly distant; the next, I'd convinced myself it was the size of a coin, and only inches from my face. There is no sense of scale. But they flashed and fluttered all around me, and I was enchanted by the rainbow of colors. One seemed to fill a quarter of the sky. It was a pale gold, and I could see stars through it.

Then we hit one.

No sound, no impact. No warning at all. One moment I was watching the distant disks, and the next the universe was bisected by an infinite plain of multicolored light.

It was a sight few people have been granted. The only way to touch an angel is to hit it at high speed. If you decelerate, the force of your engines will destroy it long before you get there. But at the speed we were traveling, the ship punched right through its diaphanous body without warning. I don't think the crew had any idea it was in front of them. How would they? It was between us and the sun, and we could only see it after we'd gone through. Not that they could have done anything if they *had* been aware of it.

At our speed, any object of reasonable size would be there and gone before your eye could register it. Not the angel. There it was, stretching away to infinity, shrinking not at all as I watched.

Its surface was a fractal swirl of every color of the rainbow. It was like a drop of oil on water, or the surface of a soap bubble. Or something like an aurora I once saw on Mars, but frozen.

Except for one spot. That spot was no color at all, and it seemed to be centered in the endless plain. Well, of course it would be. I could never tell if we'd hit the angel dead center or near the edge, but it was so vast that unless we were *very* near the edge, it just didn't matter. It was endless in all directions.

The spot was like a hole in space, full of blackness, but then I began to see stars at the bottom of it. It seemed to be getting bigger slowly. It finally dawned on me that I was seeing the hole the ship had punched through the surface of the angel, and considering the speed at which we were leaving it behind, the hole was growing at a monstrous rate.

It kept growing for the twenty minutes or so that I watched it, and then, as suddenly as it appeared, the angel was gone. All at once, from edge to edge.

It must have taken a considerable time for the hole to consume the entire angel. What had happened was we had moved far enough that the sun's light no longer reflected from the angel. It was still there, though going away to wherever punctured angels go.

The whole thing made me quite happy for a time. I hardly tasted the awful stuff I was chewing on. But eventually reality intruded again, and I knew it was time to get back to sleep. I really didn't want to, I sort of wanted to skip over what was coming next.

And it was history, after all. Over and done with. In the past.

Oh, poor Sparky.

The Daewoo Caterpillar lurks in cold, airless tunnels far beneath the Lunar surface. Some say the Breathsucker is the worst thing that can happen to you, the worst way you can die. Dodger knew better. Even the Breathsucker was afraid of the Daewoo Caterpillar.

He had encountered the beast twice before. He never got a good look at it, not that he minded. This time he feared he might have to look directly into its dreadful countenance. He was sure it was the last thing his living eyes would see.

Once more Dodger was a toy balloon, hurrying to keep up with his father's headlong progress down the deserted corridor. Deserted? Abandoned, actually. Here and there were piles of steel rods and ceiling panels and other, mysterious building blocks, some under plastic tarps, all of it dusty. It was entirely possible that no one but Dodger and his father had been down this corridor in the last ten years.

Dodger had been down it twice before. He didn't want to get to the end of it again.

His father was holding his hand too tightly. But that was the least of his problems.

He searched for the words that would bring them to a halt.

To be or not to be.

Friends, Romans, countrymen.

Now is the winter of our discontent.

But, soft!

It was useless. He knew all the words, and none would do him any good, because this wasn't about learning, this wasn't the bathtub. This was the Breathsucker, and the Daewoo Caterpillar. This was as bad as it gets.

"Please," he whispered. He tried not to, but the word had just come bubbling from his mouth. He felt a string of spit rolling down his chin, and he wiped at it with his free hand.

"Please, what?" his father said.

"Please, Father. Please don't."

Those weren't the words; his father kept up his relentless progress toward the end of the corridor. He could see it now, in the widely spaced work lights hanging from strings overhead. The end of the world.

"I'll tell him," he burst out. "I'll tell him how wrong I was. I'll tell Mr. Peppy I'll wear the pants."

No reaction. Only a few more yards to go now.

"Let's . . . let's just go to Mars! Let's forget the whole thing. We have lots of money now. We—"

Suddenly his father's face was before him, filling the whole universe. Those beloved ice-blue eyes. Eyes that flashed now, eyes that glistened with sincerity, eyes that could be bottomless pools of love, eyes you could swim in, warm eyes. But eyes that now betrayed their sadness, that told Dodger he had let his father down.

Mad eyes.

John Valentine spoke barely above a whisper.

"This is not about pants, Dodge," he said. "This is not about money. This is about . . . artistic control."

"Sure," Dodger said, nodding furiously. "I'll tell Mr. Peppy—"

"This is about presenting a united front. This is about you and me, about family. It's us against them, Dodger. Us against them. We're outnumbered, always will be. If I can't count on you, who can I count on?"

"You can count on me, Father, I swear I—"

"I don't want to do this, son. But I'm convinced it's the right thing to do. It's the way I learned my lesson, and I think you'll learn from it, too."

"I've *already* learned, Father."

"*Never.*" Valentine had barely raised his voice, yet somehow the word rang in the empty corridor. He held up a forefinger, wagged it back and forth in front of Dodger's face.

"*Never* contradict your father in public."

"I won't. I promise."

"*Never* disagree with me in front of strangers."

And before Dodger could promise again *never* to go against the family, his father picked him up and shoved him through the open door of the ancient airlock.

This was no ordinary airlock. Regular airlocks had a dozen safety devices. They were connected to the Central Computer, who would become aware each time the lock was cycled. Officially, this airlock didn't exist. It was a fifty-year-old temporary structure, meant to pass pressure-suited work gangs from the completed part of the tunnel to the construction area beyond. Just a great big cylinder, really, nested inside a slightly larger, stationary cylinder. The inner cylinder had a door-sized opening in it. The outer one had two, 180 degrees apart. When the inner opening lined up with the second door, all the air in the smaller cylinder simply blew into vacuum. Simple, quick, and dirty, not the sort of thing that was supposed to exist in the ultrasafe Lunar environment.

That it did exist was the result of oversight. The construction project had gone bankrupt, and all the plans and permits were long forgotten now, moldering in some disused memory chip, filed away with the dissolution papers of the bank that had funded it and the company that had started building it. Years had passed, a building boom had come and gone, and this tunnel and its terminus were now as remote and mysterious as the Roman catacombs or the sewers of Paris. A handful of hoboes knew of it. A few hoboes, and John Valentine.

Dodger had been there twice before. He knew to an exquisite interval how fast the lock rotated. Thirty-five seconds. Fifteen to align the doorways, and another fifteen to complete the cycle, to bring the inner door back into congruence with the door where his father waited. A five-second pause while some machinery reset itself. For the first fifteen seconds Dodger would have air. For the five-second pause, and the fifteen seconds beyond that, he would have none.

But the last fifteen seconds were not what had Dodger worried. He knew people didn't blow up when exposed to vacuum, in spite of some lurid movies he had seen. He'd been there twice before. He knew the human body could easily survive twenty seconds of airlessness. You might bleed a little, and your ears would sure as hell hurt, but it wouldn't kill you. It would *scare* the shit out of you, make those sessions in the bathtub seem like a walk in the park, but if it would kill him, his father would never have done it.

No, it was the five seconds that worried him. The five seconds when he would once again confront the Daewoo Caterpillar. When the door would yawn wide and he'd see it again, lurking in the shadows.

His father didn't know about the Daewoo Caterpillar, Dodger was convinced of that. If he'd known, he'd never have put his son into the airlock. Dodger had tried to tell him about it, tried more than once, but his tongue seemed to freeze before he could even pronounce the creature's name.

If he lived this time, he promised himself he'd tell his father.

Meantime, he had to hurry.

He was on his knees, and that was no good. Lining the walls of the lock were handholds, and Dodger scrambled to his feet and grabbed two of them. When the air went, it would go violently. The first time he'd been here, his father had tied him to a handhold, and the outrush of air had lifted him from his feet and tried to carry him out with it, out to the Caterpillar.

Five seconds. That's all he had to endure. Five seconds. Maybe the beast was sleeping. It had to sleep, didn't it?

Probably not.

The lock was turning now. He could feel the slight vibration under his feet. He looked over his shoulder and saw his father being eclipsed, vanishing as the lock turned away from him. Standing there sternly, his arms folded, his brow furrowed with concern. He knew his father loved him. He knew he was doing this to his son because it was for the best. He'd been wrong. So wrong, to speak up, to take Peppy's side. What could he have been thinking?

He'd been thinking like a *star,* that's what the trouble was. His father had warned him about that. How money and fame can go to your head, make you feel you were special, like your shit didn't stink.

"And you *are* special, Dodger," John Valentine had said. "You're special to me, and you have a special talent. A special art. But it doesn't give you the right to be impolite."

And certainly not the right to contradict his father in public. *What* could he have been thinking? They were a team, surely, but a team had to have a leader, and John Valentine was older and stronger and wiser. He'd been there. He'd seen it and done it. Dodger was still learning.

"Dirty laundry is only to be aired backstage," John Valentine had told his son many times. "Never before the audience. And never in front of the producer."

What had he been thinking?

Well, they'd work it out. He would survive this, and he and his father would be a team again. They'd talk things over in the dressing room, like they always did. They'd present a united front on everything.

Dodger pressed his face against the wall. He was as far from the door as he could get. Maybe it would be safer not to look. Maybe he could cower here, keep his back to the thing, and it would overlook him.

Fat chance.

Unlikely the monster would miss him, and impossible that he could last five seconds without looking.

He didn't last one second.

It started very loudly, as the air tried to force itself through the tiny crack. A shriek, deafening, reminding Dodger of a film he'd seen where an evil witch was pushed into a deep well, screaming all the way down. Screaming, but getting fainter, more distant. This sound quickly lost all its punch, too. The air around Dodger plucked at his clothes with cold fingers, pulled at him, became an instant gale that puffed out his cheeks and drove ice picks into his ears, and brought up a monstrous belch from deep inside him. Then there was nothing but the ringing silence, a sound he knew was not a sound but his tortured ears crying in agony. He turned around.

His heart turned to stone. The Daewoo Caterpillar was there. And it wasn't just lurking in the shadows this time, it was lurching toward him. It was huge, a thing of metal teeth and flailing arms and a hideous, bright yellow body and six great glassy eyes. It reached out one skeletal hand toward Dodger, and the cylinder began to turn. Dodger was frozen tight to the spot, watching in dreadful fascination. Would the door turn away in time, or would the creature reach inside and begin feasting?

With the silence of death, the hand entered the doorway.

The inner-lock cylinder kept trying to close, but the claw was in the way. The lock stopped moving, retreated a few inches, and again tried to close. And again, and again, shuttling back and forth like the doors of an elevator when you stuck your hand between them. The creature seemed stymied by the door, but it wouldn't really matter much longer, because Dodger would soon be dead from lack of air.

So the Breathsucker would get him. If it's not one thing, it's another.

He started to slide down the side of the cylinder. Things were getting dark, blurry. He wiped at his eyes, and for a moment he thought he saw Elwood shoving the loathsome claw back into the outer darkness, thought he saw the cylinder begin to rotate again. Thought he felt Elwood's arms around him, cradling him, telling him it was going to be all right.

But that couldn't be true. How would Elwood get in here?

It was his last thought for some time.

Dodger woke to the smell of freshly washed sheets and the sound of a mockingbird's song. He didn't open his eyes for a while, fearing it was all too good to be true. That smell was one he associated with good times: high-class hotels he and his father lived in when the money was good. The sound was one he associated with Texas. And that couldn't be.

But it was. He opened his eyes and sat up. He was tucked into a bed in a small room made entirely of wood. Beside the bed was an open window that looked out on an oak tree only a few feet away. The mockingbird was perched on a branch until he saw Dodger. Then he chirped a few more notes and flew away.

Dodger lay back down. He'd been here before, and if he was here then everything must be all right.

He was on the second floor of an authentic wooden building on the dusty main street of New Austin, in the middle of the Texas disneyland. These were the medical offices of Drs. Henry Wauk, M.D., and Heinrich Wohl, D.D.S, "Quick and Relatively Painless Dentistry," according to the shingle hanging outside. He'd never met Dr. Wohl, but he'd seen Henry Wauk several times. His father had brought him in from time to time for what he thought of as "good, old-fashioned doctoring." But even John Valentine, with his ingrained suspicion of all things modern, had not subjected himself or his son to the sort of butchery that had been practiced in places like this in the 1800s. The archaic medical equipment in this room, the colorful jars of powders and elixirs, and the instruments of torture surrounding the dental chair in the other room were merely for show, as was pretty much everything in Texas. Valentine came here for checkups and physical repairs, when needed, because Henry Wauk was an old friend of his, and because Henry would do the work off the books. The Central Computer and its various legal minions held little sway in Texas, a fact that endeared the place and all the other disneylands to John Valentine. They were virtually independent states, immune to many of the intrusive regulations of the larger civilization.

"Social experiments, they call them," Valentine had said to his son, one day while they were out riding horses—real horses! Dodger had been in heaven—in the sagebrush country west of New Austin. "Living museums. They teach school the old-fashioned way in here, son. Back to basics. *All* the children learn to read, if you can believe that. They grow their own food, right in the dirt. They live in here, hold down jobs in here. Old jobs, like blacksmithing, and cooperage, and . . . and plenty of other things I don't pretend to know much about. They hold their own elections, and they don't pay taxes to Mama Luna. Misfits in here, most of them. People who weren't happy on the outside."

Dodger had thought it was odd to call the corridors of Luna "the outside," but he knew what his father meant. Here, there was the illusion of endless space, just like out on the surface. And Texas *was* pretty large: miles and miles, his father said.

"Doctor" Wauk was one of the misfits. His was no general anomie or existential despair, however. Wauk was what would have been called, in early Texas, a dipsomaniac. He had a fondness for the bottle that he was not willing to be cured of. It had made a disaster of his acting career, and he had finally accepted a part that was to be lived, instead of performed: that of the alcoholic sawbones beloved of old black-and-white westerns.

While Wauk did dispense patent remedies and salves and powders for a few ailments, all the real medical care was accomplished by a perfectly ordinary Medico machine concealed in a closet. More complex work was referred to a normal facility outside the disneyland. Wauk had been given the bare minimum of training to operate the Medico. "After all," as he'd told John Valentine, "it ain't like doctorin' is rocket science, or anything."

Dodger thought he could hear voices from the next room. He rolled out of bed and crept carefully to the door, pressed his ear against it. If he held his breath he could hear his father and Dr. Wauk talking, but he could only get every other word. He looked around and found an antique stethoscope in a drawer. He put the rubber tips in his ears and pressed the metal disk on the end to the wooden door, and the sounds became as clear as a telephone.

"Look, Henry," his father said. "We're rolling in cash. I want you to take this. Please. It would make me feel better."

"Just my normal fee will be sufficient, John," said the doctor.

"Come on. As a favor to me."

"Right at this moment, my old friend, I'm not inclined to do any favors for you beyond the one I just done. No, sir, and I don't think I have much interest in makin' you feel any better, either. In fact, I think I just done you the last favor I'm ever goin' to do you."

There was a long silence. Dodger held his breath. He heard the sound of a chair scraping across a wooden floor, then a creaking sound. Someone just sat down in the chair, Dodger guessed.

"What you just done to that boy is a crime, John. You don't need me to tell you that, you know it already. But knowin' how you feel about laws, and the power of the state, and such, I'm going to tell you something else. What you done to that boy is a *sin*."

There was an even longer pause, then a sound that Dodger at first didn't recognize but which still froze his heart. It came again, and suddenly Dodger knew his father was weeping.

"Ah, shit, John. Let me try to drop the cornpone, here. I've been living here so long now the accent's hardly an act anymore. But you remember me. It's Henry Wauk talking to you, John. The guy who used to understudy you in half the stuff you ever acted in. I'm the fellow who would have given anything to be half as good as you are, and if I couldn't do that, at least I could hang around you and hope some of the brilliance would rub off. It never did. All we really had in common was a propensity for the bottle. I don't know if you ever thought of me as a friend—''

''I did,'' John Valentine sobbed. ''I still do.''

''. . . well, that may be. I don't know if it's really friendship when one admires the other as much as I admired you. I owe you a lot. I still *do* owe you a lot, but I'm telling you now, I don't owe you *this*. This is the third time you've brought that little boy in to me so I could fix him up. I didn't really think much about it the first time. Fixed his busted eardrum, dived back into the bottle. But after the second time I couldn't seem to get it out of my mind. Not what you'd done to his body, John, but what you were doing to his . . . I don't even know what the word is. His soul, maybe. There's a part of him's always going to be frightened. Scared of you, maybe. Scared of everything.''

Dodger bit his lip and frowned. What the hell was the damn quack talking about? He wasn't afraid of his father. He loved his father.

''I don't know why I do these things,'' Valentine said, miserably.

''That's something I don't even want to think about. I don't care why. What I'm telling you now is, it ends here. You bring him back to me all bloody and swollen up like that again, I'm going straight to the cops.''

''That's exactly what you *should* do,'' Valentine said.

''I ought to call 'em right now,'' Wauk went on. ''Shit, John, that poor kid was . . . well, you know how he was.''

Dodger almost missed his father's next words, which were barely above a whisper.

''It was an accident. Oh, god, don't look at me like that, Henry, I *know* it's my responsibility. I know if he'd died it would have been exactly like I'd murdered him. Killed by my stupidity. I'm just trying to tell you . . . it didn't happen like I thought it would.''

''I guess not,'' the doctor snorted.

''I don't know what happened. I guess the blast of air was just enough this time to dislodge that goddamn Caterpillar machine, and it came rolling down those tracks and I saw it coming, watching him, I was watching through the window beside the lock, I saw what was about to happen and I almost died right there, there was no way to make the lock go any faster, and the next lock was half a mile away and I didn't have a suit anyway, and—''

"Really thought it all through, didn't you?"

"Henry, I'm so sorry. I don't know why I do these things.''

"That's between you and your therapist, or your God, or whoever it is you listen to, if you listen to anybody.''

"I was so stupid.''

"The stupid part I can forgive, John. It's the evil part that scares me. It was evil to do what you did.'' There was another long silence, then the doctor spoke again, with more curiosity than anger in his voice.

"That's what the Dywoo Caterpillar business was? That he was screaming about when you brought him in?''

"Daewoo/Caterpillar,'' Valentine said. "You know, the heavy equipment company. Earthmovers, tunneling equipment, asteroid relocation. It was written right on the front of that boring machine. One of the grinder arms or something wedged in the door and I thought . . . I thought it would never move away.'' He began sobbing again, great racking spasms that hurt Dodger to hear.

But the boy was already consumed by a hot burst of shame. He sat back on his heels and pounded his fist on his thigh.

"Stupid! *Stupid!*'' he whispered. The one thing in the world he'd been the most frightened of, and it turned out to be nothing but . . . *a machine*? Stupid! Biting back tears, he put the stethoscope back against the door.

"There must have been a small gradient there,'' his father was saying. "The thing rocked back just enough on its tracks, enough so the lock could keep turning. Nothing but sheer, dumb luck. More luck than *I* deserve, certainly. It must be the boy's luck. Somebody's watching over him.''

Dodger had long understood that his father couldn't see Elwood. In fact, he was pretty sure *no one* could see Elwood but himself. In fact, he'd been wondering, not being *completely* stupid, if Elwood was just a figurehead of his imagination, a hellishination. A bee in his bonnet, a bat in his belfry. If he was, in a word, crazy. Now he didn't think so. Elwood *had* shoved that Caterpillar back in its tracks. There was no other explanation for it. Which meant that Elwood was a bona fide ghost, like Hamlet's old man. The only thing he wasn't sure of was if he was the ghost of Elwood P. Dowd, a fictional character, or the ghost of Jimmy Stewart, who had just gone crazy and *thought* he was Elwood P. Dowd. But from that moment on he knew Elwood was his guardian angel.

"Can I go in and see him now?" Dodger was about to leap back into bed, but held out just long enough to hear the doctor's reply.

"Let the lad rest," said Wauk. "He ought to be out another hour or so, with the dose I gave him. Right now, why don't you take me down to the saloon and buy me a drink or three."

Damn drunk, Dodger thought as he heard the outside door open and close, and the sound of footsteps going down the stairs. *Can't even dope me up properly. It's a good thing I'm still alive.*

That bastard! Make my father cry, will you?

Dodger started poking around in cupboards and cabinets.

He quickly found a gallon stoneware jug labeled CORN LIQUOR. He pulled out the stopper and smelled it. Booze, all right. *Okay, what have we got here?*

He spent the next hour reading definitions in an old leather-bound book called *Saunders's Comprehensive Medical Encyclopedia,* publication date 1898, looking up the words he found printed on bottles and jars that lined the shelves and cabinets in the examining room. "Paregoric," he discovered, was camphorated tincture of opium. It smelled nasty, so he dumped some of it in the jug of corn liquor. "Calomel" was mercurous chloride. That *sounded* nasty; wasn't mercury poisonous? Into the bottle went a teaspoon of calomel. "Aunt Lydia's Pink Tonic" was said, by the label, to possess excellent *emetic* properties. After looking up "emetic," Dodger poured in a generous dose. "Nicotine" was a poisonous alkaloid, $C_{10}H_{14}N_2$. In it went. A "sialogogue" was something that increased the flow of saliva. Why not? "Arecane" was a proprietary remedy and efficacious as a *purgative*. A "parturifacient" was used to speed up childbirth, while an "abortifacient" produced an abortion. Dodger wondered what a mixture of the two would do to a drunken doctor? "Formalin," "cryptomenorrheal," "Salvarsan," "arnicin," "myxorrheal," "leptuntic" . . . so many new words, so many definitions, so little time.

After a while he grew tired of reading, and felt a little hungry. In the next room, by the dentist chair, he found the remains of a Mexican lunch: chips and salsa and a cold taco. He took a bite of the taco, and in a moment was searching frantically for a drink of water. After he'd put out the fire in his mouth, he examined the bottle of Pancho's Habanero Hell (WARNING: Do not use near open flame!), then took it into the doctor's office and dumped half the bottle into the jug. He smeared a little sauce around the earpieces of the stethoscope.

He jammed in the cork and shook the jug vigorously, then opened it again and sniffed cautiously. It still smelled like booze.

For good measure, he pissed in the jug before going downstairs to join his father.

FOR IMMEDIATE RELEASE:
From: First Latitudinarian Church of Celebrity Saints
Subject: November Audience Ratings
Category: Children's (age 2 to 12) periodical (weekly/fortnightly/monthly)

December 1 (King City Temple)
   The November "Flack" numbers as compiled by the Trends Research Department of the Latitudinarian Church are as follows:

TITLE	AAS	Last Month	Last Year
1. The Gideon Peppy Show	93.1	1	1
2. Admiral Platypus	84.4	2	3
3. Skunk Cabbage	80.2	5	-
4. Barney's Boulevard	78.7	3	14
5. What the Fuck?	70.3	4	2

Admiral Platypus seems to have solidified its hold on the number-two slot in the Adjusted Audience Share rating. *Barney's Boulevard,* benefiting from a new writing staff, has made its way from number fourteen to number four in the past year. The top two stories continue to be the steepening decline of *What the Fuck?,* the once-dominant Q&A offering from NLF-TV3, and the meteoric rise of *Skunk Cabbage,* the critically panned actioner about a tribe of zombie children. *SC* seems poised to make a run on those two old reliable warhorses, *Peppy* and *Platy*.

Spokespersons for NLF and the Children's Educational Workshop, producers of *WTF?,* had no comment when asked if the declining numbers of educational programming across the board in the past three years reflected a growing anti-intellectualism or merely a stagnation of fresh new ideas in the presentation of loftier kid-vid. Oskar Bigbird III, chairman of CEW, promised a news conference later in the week, announcing staffing changes on *WTF?*

It seems nothing the pundits can say will have any effects on the soaring prospects of *Skunk Cabbage.* Introduced a mere eight months ago, the "Li'l Stinkers" have stormed the imaginations of a huge number of Lunarian children, and are now ready for a system-wide release. Reports from retailers confirm that for the first time in many a year, sales of Gideon Peppy products were eclipsed by the *SC* Kids during the month of October. Full figures for November are not yet available. But it seems a safe bet that Li'l Stinkers toys, clothing, software, and other tie-ins will be the hot items this Xmas season. Quote from Gideon Peppy (with a chuckle): "It don't have me chewin' on my lollipop." He pointed to growing cries of outrage from Mars to the Cometary Zone from concerned parents' groups worried about the coming onslaught of *SC* Kids. Peppy refused to comment on rumors that he himself had been behind some of those protests.

More likely to put toothmarks on his Tootsie Roll is the continuing failure to soar of his much-touted new series *Sparky and His Gang.* Ballyhooed on the *Peppy Show* for three months before its August launch, *Sparky* remains mired in the mid-forties, with a dismal 12.4 share. With the fifteenth episode currently lensing at Sentry/Sensational, rumors are that the sixteenth stanza is on hold, while (guess what?) staff changes are contemplated. Say, there's a bunch of *WTF?* scribes soon to be pounding the pavement, G.P. They'll work cheap.

(For daily show and theatrical numbers, key *MORE**)

---

from *The Straight Shit* Starpage:
Year in Review: sub-Kid-vid
"Anybody Wanna Buy a Sparky Action Mug?"
by Bermuda Schwartz

I've been telling you for two hundred years now, so why do I think you'll all of a sudden start to listen? Ever since those old phosphor dots began to chase each other across the magic glass of the kinescope in the dear departed 1940s, two things are the *only* things that sell on TV: good stuff, and crap. Neither one is a guarantee of success. Plenty of shows have aspired to be good, but were kidding themselves. They've all long since vanished. And some actually *were* good, and they're gone, too. As for crap . . . who can fucking *tell* with crap? *Myghty Mytes* shambled onto the screen midsummer, stinking of crap, and by the end of the month it was in the crapper. *Skunk Cabbage* smelled just as rank, and by Yuletide the Komical Korpses had trailed their slime into every third-rate geraldo's studio on the planet. Kids were sleeping in "Li'l Stinkers" coffins, at a thousand dollars a pop, gluing trademarked live worms to their cheeks.

Who can figure it? Not me, not the pundits nor the critics nor the reviewers nor the scholars shaking their heads with dismay. Crap is crap. Some will turn out to be popular crap, and if I knew how to tell the difference I wouldn't be here writing about it, I'd be fucking *rich*.

But oh dear, I hear the pundits say. One of the few quality shows getting regular viewings—and of course I'm referring to CEW's *What the Fuck?*—is taking a nosedive in the ratings. Woe is us! Civilization is darn sure to perish any day now.

Crap. *WTF?* used to be quality, but have any of you over twelve years old actually *looked* at the thing lately? I'm telling you, this old ragbag is starting to make Zippy the Zombie look animated. Folks, *WTF?* is over the hill. It is stale. Look for it at your local mortuary. Sure, it used to be good, but there's another cardinal rule in TV-land, and it is that nothing lasts forever. *WTF?* is pushing thirty years old. Bye-bye. Adios.

Quality? Well, like it or not (and I don't, much) the *Peppy Show* will do for an example. What Peppy does, he does well. The characters are funny, the writing is sharp. Kids love him. What can you say? English teachers aside, most educators give Peppy good marks—and how long's it been since anybody listened to an English teacher?

What's that? You say Peppy's show is only ten years old? And he's *where* in the ratings? Gosh, maybe civilization has a few more months to live.

But that brings us to the topic of today's lesson, children, and that is, what happens to shows that can't seem to decide whether they want to be trashy, or terrific? That brings us to a disastrous effort from the Peppy mill called *Sparky and His Gang*.

What are we to make of a gobbler like *S&G*? To think of it as an actual turkey is an insult to flightless barnyard poultry everywhere. A genuine turkey *knows* that it is a turkey, and can therefore work at being the best darn turkey in the coop. *S&G* arrives at your television like a gift-wrapped dead mackerel. You try to figure out, is this fish, or fishwrap? All you know at first is that it smells, vaguely, fishy. And at least part of it is garbage.

It would be pointless to devote a lot of time to a feather-by-feather analysis of this albatross around Gideon Peppy's neck, and I won't subject you to one. Just a short comment, then, and a brief explanation.

Comment:

PRESS *HERE** for HyperText SoundByte©

"Whooooooo fuckiiiiiing caaaaaaares?"

Explanation: the key to caring about what happens in a show, and I'm talking any show here, from *Hamlet* to *Skunk Cabbage*, is believable characters. Characters that bear some resemblance to humans we have known, who display some known human traits. (Exception: the birth-to-five audience, who will watch anything brightly colored and moving; viz.

Barney's Boulevard.) Of all the brightly colored, loud, fre-netically moving clusters of phosphor dots that call them-selves Sparky's Gang, only Sparky himself seems to have anybody at home where a heartbeat should be. Sparky is *so* good, in fact, so appealing and funny and touching, that I went right out and bought myself a Sparky souvenir coffee mug. But by the time the coffee was cold, so was everything else. I don't think the mug is going to be collectible—even though it is almost certain to be rare—because we buy and treasure these nostalgic bits of pop culture to *remind* us of something. Something that *mattered* to us. And I must report to you that, five minutes after the show went off the air, I couldn't re-member anything about *any* of the amorphous collection of rug weasels known as Sparky's Gang, not even their names.

And that is really too bad. Because it is obvious that some-body put a lot of thought into the character of Sparky himself. As played by young Ken Valentine, Sparky is at the same time wonderfully carefree and charming, smart and stalwart. He is the sort of child we *all* would like to have been, or failing that, to have been friends with. He makes us eager to join his gang, which makes it all the more appalling that his actual band is such a bunch of radishes. He should have been the core of a group of similarly smart, resourceful moppets, united by his undeniable charisma.

But even if Gideon Peppy hires some writers who can do character, *Sparky* would not yet be out of the woods. Or *into* the woods, for that matter. The fact is, nobody on this show has a fucking clue as to where the woods *is,* or if in fact there *are* any fucking woods. By that I mean, characters need a *milieu.* A story must happen in a time and a place. There must be a background.

I've watched four episodes of *Sparky* so far. One show per month, like the curse. In the first one the Gang was battling pirates on the open seas, for no reason that I can fathom other than that there was a full-scale pirate ship available on the Sensational back lot. In the next show the gang was in present time, and in the third, in no universe I could identify. Some pitiful gallimaufry was advanced to explain these temporal and spatial dislocations, but by then I'm afraid I was far ad-vanced in a diabetic coma.

See, that sort of crap can work for *Skunk Cabbage,* because

Skunk is a crap show. I know it, you know it. The producers know it. The kids don't give a possum's posterior because it's full of violence and very noisy and it smells offensive, and mostly because Mom and Dad *hate* the sonuvabitch.

That won't work for *Sparky and His Gang* because *Sparky* aspires to be more, and that is why it is *worse* than a skunk.

Go ahead, ask your kids. Why aren't you watching *Sparky,* little Ambrose and Abigail?

PRESS *HERE** for HyperText SoundByte©

"Aw, mom. I dunno. It just *suuucks.*"

Kids won't be fooled. They'll watch quality, or they'll watch crap. But you better be one or the other, and you better know which that is.

---

from *Hebephrenia,* "The Youthpad"
column of 4/10/58
"Spark Plug"
by D. Mentua Precox

So I was hanging out over at the Sen/Sen Studios like hoping to get an interview with the Man Himself, G. Peppy, y'know? When who should like come blitzing by but Velveeta Creemcheese in like a *true* hurry to ease herself from like point A to point B, y'know? Well, comma, Vel and your totally humble narrator go back to like the last *ice* age, can you load it? So I was like all "Vel! Exclamation Point! Heard you got 87ed from the inner realms of Peppydom," comma, because the skin was she'd like been *fired* from her *completely* powerful job as Czarina of Production at Pep-Pep-Peppiprod, load it? Then she was all "Aw contrary, Manny, comma comma," and the bitch like *knows* that D. M. Precox your Humble etc. gets the squints when she hears that name so I was all *What's this twist in* her *shorts*? but refrained from verbing it into the etheric, comma, discretion being the better part of something or other period! Exclamation point! So then she goes "Mere haberdashery," and I go "Hats? *Hats*? Question Mark?" and she goes "Change of. The new hat belongs to hyperster-in-chief of 'The New Improved *Sparky and His Gang,*'" and I go "Whoozat?" and she goes "It's G.P.'s new kidvid extra-

vaganzoid," comma, and I'm all "?kraM noitseuQ Why
wasn't I informed? Question Mark?" and all snitty she's going "Your office was wired all pronto," comma quothation
mark parenthesis (but my Faithful Readers will know that
their humble narrator is totally up on all comma ALL things
worth knowing in the land of hebephilia, comma, and D.M.
and H.N. had never heard of it dot. dot. dot. well, okay, I've
heard of it okay?, comma QM, but not because it was shaking
on any celeb *Richter* scale, can you load? sisehtneraP) Period!
Be that as it were neither here nor there, soon yrs truly
was mustered in to the very like innermost cabals of the
Great Giddy Pepperoni himself! E!X!C!L!A!M!A!T!I!O!N!
P!O!I!N!T! When what to my wondering orbs do I vid but
the Pepman curled in a huddle of scriptsters, comma, nine in
number or even a dozen at the powerful end of a table of such
like enormous proportions that the King of Kong coulda used
it for a surfboard. Yea, verily, comma, oh my breathrin and
sisterin. Words were like heated and floated and launched and
puncturated. Hair was being torn and shorn. Spittle like *flew*!
Peppy goes "Can't anybody in this overpaid gaggle of hacks
goose me up an original concept?" The quacksters hawked
excitedly and treatments were waved with terrifying gay abandon, heedless! EP! So I viddy no easy access to the Peppy
ear—emdash not in the near recent, anyway—dash, and my
questing gaze shambled to the other end of the table, where
wire-haired moppets presided, two in census. This must be
like the Sparks, of whom things were heedlessly spoken in
many a flacky promo in the previous months elapsed. And
already, is he nothing but all two-weeks-ago? That was the
shake I had downloaded, and yrs. t. feels *everything* that's
shakin'. Apostropheperiod. Vel goes "This is Sparky, the star
of our show," and I go "Howja Dew?" and Vel goes "And
this is little Polly, sidekickstress," and I go, comma, "Watcha
doin' apostrophe?" and little Polly goes "Drawing," which
Yours can see with her own lamps that a drawing is indeed
being committed, only it's much too much like of a *quality*
for such a youthful inkster so I go "Drawing what?" Well
faithful reader D. M. Precox has her good days and her days
when eaten by weasels and this wasn't my shining moment,
because comma my lenses could clearly see she was drawing
a . . . *thing* dot dot dot period. And who should quickly vali-

date this you know insight but pretty Polly herself by yodelling "A thing," she goes comma, and elaborating "It's a sort of a guy me and Sparky made up," and Sparky goes "I made it up. She drew it." I go does the thing have a name cue you ee ess tee eye oh en mark? and she goes "Inky Tagger." Well much more transpired that day but your short attention span has spun, it's time for DMP to trill a fond aloha with this on her lips colon:

"Who is Inky Tagger Question Mark?"

More later. Remember, you heard it here first.

May 1 (King City Temple)

The April "Flack" numbers as compiled by the Trends Research Department of the Latitudinarian Church are as follows:

TITLE	AAS	Last Month	Last Year
1. The Gideon Peppy Show	84.7	1	1
2. Skunk Cabbage	82.2	2	28
3. Admiral Platypus	81.8	3	5
4. Barney's Boulevard	75.0	4	8
5. Scoop the Poop	67.6	10	-

Skunk Cabbage retains its precarious grip on the number-two slot for the second month, edging the *Admiral* by only a few hundred thousand viewings. The big story is still the meteoric rise of *Poop,* CEW's replacement for the unlamented *What the Fuck?* which early this year fell into the becalmed straits of the likes of *Sparky and His Gang,* and now survives only on the marginal sales of back numbers. And so what if the carpers claim "Poop" is really nothing but recycled "Fuck?" As Chairman Bigbird pointed out to the critics, "Food is nothing but recycled poop, isn't it? What's the big deal?"

Not so dramatic but still cause for some concern among the mandarins of Sentry/Sensational is the continuing slippage of the *Peppy Show,* a five-month phenom that's been slow and steady and shows no signs of having reached bottom. Asked if this might harbing an eventual end to the six-year stranglehold *TGPS* has held on first place, Peppy replied: "We always lose some numbers when we head into summer. It ain't got me crapping in my drawers."

More likely to put skid marks in his skivvies is the dismal rise of *Sparky* from thirty-five to thirty-one after a full year in production. Staff changes don't seem to have done the trick, though some observers point out that most of the small gain the show has posted came in the last two months, with the introduction of two new and somewhat more interesting regular characters: Inky Tagger and Arson E. Blazeworthy. Press releases trumpet that a series of new faces will soon transform the Gang. The word from here: Don't bet the farm.

---

from *Howdy Doody*
The Trade Mag of Kid-vid
6/30/58
"Boogers and Snot"
by Summerfall Winterspring

"This is Crimea River," says Polly, rather diffidently, as she pushes a sheet of drawing paper in my direction. It is a pencil sketch of a girl who has cried so much the tears have carved massive Mississippi deltas into her face. Catfish could feed at the bottoms of these tributaries. Her hair is disheveled and she is wringing a bucketful of water from the handkerchief she twists in her clawlike hands.

"And what does she do?" I ask. Polly turns to Sparky, seated on her left.

"Not much," Sparky says. "She complains a lot."

"She's had a hard life?" I venture.

"Not so bad. She's a whiner. She's like a sponge. If you get around her she'll take up all your time and all your energy. She'll drain you dry, like a vampire, then she'll find somebody else to complain to."

"Tell her about . . ." Polly pauses, then gestures to Sparky. "You tell it, Spark."

"Well, when she cries, pretty soon you start crying, too. You can't help it, it's like pepper up your nose. Pretty soon you're bawling like a baby."

"It's infectious," I suggest, hoping to help.

"Yeah. That's it."

Something in his voice alerts me and I look up at him in time to see a glimmer in his eye. I am being humored, I realize. He knows precisely what word to use to describe Crimea's tears. But his face gives nothing away. Only the eyes have that glint of mischief. I won't patronize him again.

I have found the secret wellspring behind *Sparky and His Gang*. Without even knowing I was looking for it, I have stumbled onto the *real* reason *Sparky's Gang* has suddenly climbed from the low twenties in AAS to a surprising fifteenth place in the monthly Flack ratings.

I claim no great reportorial skills in this. Sometimes you're just lucky.

It seemed like good luck at the time to be assigned the *Sparky* beat. Mission: visit the set and the story conferences once or twice a month, produce a diary of the progression of the show. Who wouldn't have thought it a plum? A new series in development from Gideon Peppy, the man who set the current record in first-place finishes, who can apparently do no wrong? *Sparky's Gang* had monster hit written all over it.

Who knew?

Actually, by the time the show was ready to air, a lot of us in the entertainment press corps had a pretty good idea. There's a stink that attaches itself to a show that's in trouble, and it ain't the sweet smell of success. *Sparky and His Gang* had that aroma from the first day of shooting, a day I had the dubious good luck to witness. On the surface everything looked fine. It was the normal circus atmosphere of hurry up and wait, the usual snags that came from crews not yet used to working together. One can usually assume that by the third or fourth episode these little misunderstandings, squabbles, and comic traffic jams will have sorted themselves out, and the production staff will be running in as near an approximation of a well-oiled machine as a television series in production ever gets.

But just below the surface serious trouble was brewing. Brewing? More like seething. This ship was rudderless, Captainless, and lacked a compass. Directions would come from somewhere to alter this or that detail of the set. Two hours later it needed to be altered again. Grips started pools to see how long a new production designer would last, and the times were sometimes measured in hours, not days. It was easy enough to discover these things. Everybody on the set was talking about it. But nobody knew what was going on higher up.

A few weeks later I sat in on my first story conference. Sometimes a writer is handed a metaphor on, as it were, a silver platter. That was the case with Gideon Peppy's famous conference table. Perhaps you've heard of long-ago peace conferences where step one was to determine the size and shape of the table where two groups of people who hated each other's guts could sit and rationally discuss their differences. Peppy's table was a perfect barometer of what was going on with *Sparky and His Gang*. You could have drawn a wide red stripe across the width of the table and called it the Demilitarized Zone. At the south end sat John Valentine, father of little "Sparky" Valentine, and Sparky himself. At the north end sat Gideon Peppy and everybody else.

The dynamic at the south end was obvious: a father and his son. At the north end some barnyard politic was in operation, its causes not evident to the outsider, but its effects painfully obvious. Simply put, those most in favor with Mr. Peppy sat at his elbow, ready to osculate his rectum should he take a notion to bend over. Beside these high Priests of Peppy sat more ordinary acolytes, legs poised to leap at the shout of "Frog!" Then in the hinterlands, sometimes almost on the DMZ itself, were the fuckups, the doghoused gazing hollow-eyed at the feasting to the north, pathetically eager to scramble after any morsel that dropped from the master's table. The temptation was strong to fashion pointy hats for them out of foolscap.

But no matter how far out of favor one fell, one was never seated to the south of the invisible red line. That was clearly enemy territory.

The view from John Valentine's end of the table was a compact version of da Vinci's *Last Supper*.

John Barrymore Valentine. Sparky Valentine. The fourth and fifth generations of an acting family that can trace its lineage back to Old Earth. John is the eldest of three siblings, and without a doubt the most talented.

You know a lot about his brother, Edwin Booth Valentine.

What's that? You say you've never heard of him? Try Ed
Ventura. He is the black sheep of the family. The father, Marlon Brando Valentine, was a thespian of the old order—a *very*
old order—in that he felt acting should be done on the stage.
Movies, television, were barely arts at all, and their needs
could be served entirely by computer-generated imagery.
"Movies are a director's medium," he has said. "Actors are
for the theater." John followed in his father's footlights, er,
footsteps, but Edwin chose to exploit his good looks and
screen presence to become a Movie Star, a Matinee Idol, a
Celluloid Casanova. Everything his father hated. Old Marlon
kicked him out of the family and disowned him—a real laugh,
since Marlon passed his days in genteel poverty, and John . . .
well, we'll get to that. The Valentine brothers had a younger
sister, Sarah Bernhardt Valentine, but nothing is known about
her. My calls seeking to interview Ed Ventura about his family were not returned.

John Valentine is such a charming man, so handsome, ar-
ticulate, witty, so full of amusing stories, that it takes several
meetings before you realize what a monster he is.

Don't get me wrong; Gideon Peppy is a monster, too. But
you expect that from a man who has clawed his way to the
top in a cutthroat business. He would cheerfully admit it.
Peppy doesn't pretend to be a nice guy. It's all right out there
in front with Peppy. What you see is what there is.

It would be easy to compare John Valentine with a well-
known character from the historical musical stage: Rose Louise Hovick from *Gypsy*. The analogy fails at several points.
Rose was not talented herself; John Valentine without a doubt
is a *major* talent. I saw his *Macbeth* fifteen years ago, and
recalling it can still give me chills. Gypsy Rose Lee's talents
were, shall we say, limited. Sparky Valentine at the age of
eight shows me more possibilities than any five movie stars
I can name. The kid is awesome. But most importantly, compared to John Valentine, Rose Louise Hovick is easygoing.
Rose wanted Gypsy to succeed where she herself had failed,
or never had a chance. John Valentine is determined to mold
his son into his own image. He doesn't so much want Sparky
to be his vicarious ego on the stage; he wants Sparky to be
him.

This is bound to lead to trouble. It is heartbreaking to

watch Sparky on the set. When the cameras are rolling, he is vibrantly alive. He is *Sparky,* that devil-may-care freebooter with the heart of gold, setting out to right all the wrongs of the world. When the director yells *cut!* it all goes away. He enfolds it somewhere inside himself and he waits. He waits with seemingly infinite patience as his father and Gideon Peppy go at it hammer and tongs, unfailingly polite to each other, setting up a current in the atmosphere that has made hardened stagehands pale with apprehension. It seems to affect Sparky not at all. He waits. He listens. When the command to *roll 'em* is given, he acts. Before that, Sparky exists only as a glint in little Ken Valentine's eye. It is probably the only way the boy can keep from getting crushed between the massive egos of Peppy and his father.

So what has happened? The setup was and is a formula for disaster, a prophecy which fulfilled itself for the first year of production. The only reason I can see for *Sparky and His Gang's* continuance during those lean months was Gideon Peppy's reluctance to admit he'd come a cropper. Yet, in the last months, the show has begun to attract some attention.

Let's return to that conference table, shall we? The time is several months after our first visit. Various of G. Peppy's toads are perched on different toadstools around the table, but these are matters which could only concern the toads. They are unimportant to us. Most interesting is where John Valentine is seated. Instead of his throne of opposition down in the south forty, John is occupying a stool almost in the Demilitarized Zone!

What has happened? I don't think John understands this consciously, but some part of him does, because his air of smug assurance is getting a little thin. He raises his voice, almost shouts. He can't quite bring himself to actually sit with the rest of the creative staff, but it is clear that he would like to. Instead of his endless stream of barbs, his obstructionism— sometimes for no reason other than his loathing of Peppy— has been replaced by suggestions he clearly believes could improve the show. These are, of course, politely ignored ("We'll sure think about that, John, yes sir!"). The last thing a bunch of writers and a producer want in a story conference is some damn *actor.*

Of *course*! *Sparky* is a *flop*! Before, John didn't give a flying fuck about the project. It was plain to me that the only reason he and his son were there at all was the chance of some easy money. (Or the only reason *John* was there, at any rate. I think Sparky might have seen it a little differently, but it's hard to tell with Sparky, who plays his cards *very* close to the vest. God knows how John was convinced to join the enterprise in the first place, given his antipathy to television. It must have taken some really masterful arm twisting.) But Sparky Valentine—and through him, John Valentine—cannot possibly *fail* in an acting assignment, even one as menial as this. The low ratings are inexplicable. Sparky's doing a bang-up job. Therefore, the material must be improved. John is getting more and more involved in improving it, whether he knows it or not.

Fast-forward another several months. The Valentine end of the table is now being anchored by Sparky alone, unless you count Polly, who should be classed as a noncombatant, possibly a camp follower, given her obvious crush on Sparky, which he may or may not realize. The two sit on booster seats down there in the cold, away from the creative warmth of Peppy's fires. With them, sometimes, is the Equity rep and a tutor, but the children are able to buffalo these innocents with such ease they are gone most of the time, on one errand or another. John Valentine? Well, he camps out miserably in the DMZ, where we saw him last, but instead of his usual pointed barbs his infrequent words are starting to sound sort of . . . well, *grouchy*. And is that the smell of alcohol on his breath? A smudge of cocaine around his nose? Some people are ill-equipped to deal with windfalls of money. One never knows who these people are until the bonanza has struck, and up to this point in his life John Valentine has seldom had a pot to piss in nor a window to fling it from. Now, even with a flop show, the money is pouring in. Dangerous, John.

I can't keep skirting this issue forever. The fact is, John has an extensive criminal record. When times were lean he has been willing to lend his acting talents to unscripted roles, to street improvisations—in short, to what the police call the "long con." That's what he did time for, anyway, though I've been told his skills at the Pigeon Drop and the Spanish Lottery are considerable as well. He exhibits no shame about this, doesn't mind discussing it with the press. It's all part of some extremely wonky political worldview I will not bore you with. (That way I don't have to pretend to understand it.)

Even more alarming is his temper. How he has held it in check thus far during the gestation of *Sparky* is a matter between him and his probation officer. I'll only mention here that he has barely scraped his way out of numerous assault charges, usually against directors and producers, but occasionally with his fellow actors.

It takes no great insight to see what has been hobbling *Sparky and His Gang*. Part of it is the clash of wills between Gideon and John, a dislike so intense that Peppy has sometimes done things he should have known were stupid, simply to spite Valentine.

But the big thing is John himself. Not many actors are good with scripts. John Valentine is certainly not one of them. Anyone can see after ten minutes in a story conference that Valentine's influence is entirely a negative one. Nothing could be clearer than that *Sparky* and everyone associated with it would be much better off if John Valentine suddenly left for an extended tour of Neptune.

But wait! Did I say Polly and Sparky are away from the center of creativity? Perhaps I was hasty. Looking more closely, we see the two are whispering and giggling. Polly is drawing in a big notebook. Peering over his shoulder—before she quickly, shyly, snaps the notebook closed—I can see the drawings are very good. Broad, assured strokes of the pencil. Cartoonlike figures. Do they have names? I ask, after spending a little time ingratiating myself with them. Why, of course they have names.

Inky Tagger. Arson E. Blazeworthy. Crimea River. Lionel Alibi. The law firm of White & Wong. Identical twins Tess Tosterone and S. Trojan.

Some of these have already debuted on *Sparky and His Gang*. The rest I was only shown after promising to keep them a secret, except for their names. (See, Sparky? I told you you could trust me.) I'm allowed one example only, a character to be introduced in the next episode. Windy Cheesecutter.

Like most of the new faces at the old Sparkster's clubhouse, Windy has a big problem. A very big, very smelly problem. As drawn by Polly, Windy is a blimp of a boy, cheeks puffed, lips pursed, eyes bulging, huge sausages for arms and legs and fingers. As imagined by Sparky, Windy keeps blimping and swelling and growing alarmingly until he relieves the pressure. Hey, if Chaucer can make jokes about farting, why can't Sparky?

As you might imagine, this socially debilitating condition has made Windy a bit of an outcast, and damn angry about it. He goes around knocking down buildings with his exploding flatulence. He can clear out a church or theater in ten seconds. Not a nice boy at all, hardly the sort you'd expect to be a part of Sparky's rather uninspired, sometimes downright mealymouthed gang. So what does Sparky do about him? You'll have to tune in and see.

I'm sitting at the leper's end of the table with Sparky and Polly. John Valentine is nowhere to be seen. Over there in the next area code are Gideon Peppy and his highly paid writing staff, shouting at each other.

Let them shout. Down here is where the show is being created.

"Why don't you ask her?" Polly says.

"What's that?" I ask, looking up from my note taking.

"Go ahead," Polly says.

"Nah," says Sparky. "She wouldn't be interested."

"Of *course* I'd be interested," I say. "What is it?"

Sparky studies me dubiously for a moment, then shrugs, and looks at me with a perfectly straight face.

"Are boogers and snot the same thing?" he asks.

"Are . . ." I close my mouth. I am determined not to laugh. But pretty soon Polly starts to howl, and Sparky joins in. So I do, too.

"No, really," Sparky says. "We've made a list of thirty-five things that can come out of the human body. Without, you know, surgery."

"Only it may be thirty-six," Polly says.

"If boogers and snot are different things. See, we decided plaque, tartar, and calculus are different. But toenails and fingernails are the same."

"We're not counting babies," Polly adds. "And eight of the things are different kinds of hair."

"There wasn't a very good definition of snot in the dictionary."

"Or boogers."

So I think it over and I tell them I think they must be different. Polly looks smugly at Sparky, who sticks out his tongue. Polly gets back to her drawing.

"See," Sparky says, "we decided we need a really good bad guy. If you know what I mean."

I certainly did. The *Sparky* show had been limping along almost a year now, and that was one of many things that hadn't been very well-defined. Each week a new bad guy was trotted out, dealt with, and market research said the kids just weren't interested in him. If you've got a series about a bunch of kids who go around righting wrongs, thwarting evil, you need a good *source* of evil.

"What I thought was," Sparky goes on, "since Sparky is pretty smart, that maybe I'd *make* the bad guy. You know, like Frankenstein. One thing Sparky has to watch out for is, he's a little impulsive. Sometimes he goes ahead and does something without thinking about what might happen. So one day in his laboratory he decides to create a new friend. He thinks about . . . well, I thought about that song about a hank of hair and a piece of bone. So Sparky gathers up all the things that can come off a human body—and Polly helps, too, and they have to find some of it in other places, because only grown-ups can make some of this stuff, and they throw it all together in the laboratory and, *poof!* Here's this guy. Only—"

"He doesn't have a soul," I say.

Sparky frowns at his hands. "Maybe it's dorky," he says, doubtfully.

"No, I don't think so. It's true, it's an old story, but I don't think anyone's ever approached it from quite the . . . *direction*, or with the same kind of ingredients you do. What will you name this villain?"

And the face shuts down. Only the spark in the eyes remains.

"I haven't decided yet," he says. I know he really has, and is just not going to tell me, but that's okay. I've got my story.

After Sparky and Polly have been called away to shoot a scene, I hang around a little longer, try to be inconspicuous. And I see a curious thing. Over the course of the afternoon just about every one of the high-powered writers from the north side of the table finds an excuse to wander down to the other end. Gosh, has anybody seen my hat? Could it be under the table down here? Oops, looks like that drawing tablet is about to slip off the table. Let me just straighten it up here. . . .

Casually, nonchalant, they saunter and stroll and amble and perambulate, holding their pens and notebooks and cups of coffee. What's this? Oh, it's little Polly's drawings. What's she been up to today, I wonder?

And they leaf through the drawings.

Whatever Gideon Peppy is paying these writers, it's not enough. Not *nearly* enough, to be willing to steal ideas from children, and put their own names on the ideas. No, sir. I'd want a fucking *shit*load of money to do that.

So there's the secret. While the creative staff bickers and shouts and hurls out one stale, derivative idea after another, the real stories are being made at the other end of the table, out of boogers, spit, snot, and farts.

And who was the last person I saw visit the far end of the table? I'll give you a hint. He wore yellow shoes, and was sucking on a lollipop.

---

from *LUNAVARIETY*
"The Entertainment Industry Daily"
VALENTINE TO NEPTUNE; TO HELM OPNT
staff-written

John Barrymore Valentine, King City resident and longtime thespian of the legitimate stage, has been offered the job of artistic director of the Outer Planets National Theater, effective January 1 of next year.

"It was a tough decision for me," Valentine said, at the press conference announcing his intention to accept the bid. "As many of you know, I have been associate producer on my son's weekly video series, *Sparky and His Gang*, which is currently number nine in the Flacks. My son and I talked it over and we both felt that, much as we hate to be apart, our careers come first at this point in our lives. Sparky will be in good hands here on Luna. I have a two-year contract, with options to renew. It is my hope to bring a classical re-

vival to the outer planets, which have long lagged behind
Luna and Mars in putting the plays of Shakespeare, Molière,
Chekhov, Williams, and many others on boards. It is a great
privilege to do my part in the preservation of the arts.''

Contacted at his headquarters at Sentry/Sensational, Gideon Peppy, producer of *Sparky and His Gang,* expressed his
happiness and his regrets. ''It's a good career move for John,''
Peppy said. ''Of course, we'll all miss his input around here,
but I suppose we can manage to get along without him.''

The Outer Planets Federation had encountered funding
problems for its ambitious but unfinished Performing Arts
Centre, taking shape near the Government Centre in New Sydney, Triton. Recent donations have the project moving again,
however, and the board of directors felt confident enough of
a completion date to announce its selection of Valentine, who
will be leaving for the OP on the first available transport.

---

from *Triton Tabloid*
Arts Page
8/04/58
by Staff

The Triton Council for the Fine Arts announced today receipt
of a large cash bequest, funds earmarked for the completion
of the trouble-plagued New Sydney Performing Arts Centre.

''With Federation matching grants, this should be enough
to get the Centre up and running,'' said Spero Meliora, Chairman of the Council.

Asked as to the identity of the benefactor, Meliora would
only say, ''A patron of the Arts, who wishes to remain anonymous.'' Speculation rages, but as of this writing no one
seems to have a solid line on the name of the publicity-shy
angel. One usually reliable source claims the donation came
in the form of a cheque written on a King City, Luna, bank,
but the *Tabloid* has been unable to confirm or disprove this.

Immediately after the announcement of the unexpected
windfall, Meliora launched a system-wide search for an artistic director. Nationalistic preferences run high in this matter,

and much support has been expressed among the O.P. arts community for the idea that the director should be a Tritonian, or at least a citizen of the Federation. The *Tabloid*'s sources, however, say to look for the director to arrive from the same direction as the funding. And quickly, too.
(For related articles, Press *MORE**)

PETITION FOR GUARDIANSHIP OF A MINOR CHILD
District Court, King City, Case #390-45155 8/11/58
Petitioner: Melina Polichinelli
Parent or Guardian: John Barrymore Valentine
Minor Child: Kenneth Catherine Valentine

STATEMENT OF PARENT: I, John B. Valentine, declare under penalty of perjury the following to be true and correct, to the best of my knowledge. I have been offered a prestigious position on the outer planets, at a substantial increase in salary. My son is currently starring in a video production, *Sparky and His Gang,* at the Sentry/Sensational Studios. It would be harmful to his present interests and future prospects if he were to accompany me to Triton. After discussing this matter with him and determining that it is his wish to continue, we have decided a temporary transfer of guardianship is the best course for both of us. My longtime friend and colleague, Melina Polichinelli, has agreed to act *in loco parentis* for a period of two years, after which I will return to Luna and reassess the situation.
STATEMENT OF PROPOSED GUARDIAN: I, Melina Polichinelli, have known Kenneth Valentine since he was a baby. My own daughter, Kaspara, is currently working with Kenneth and they already spend a great deal of time together. It would be no trouble at all to accept Kenneth into my household. I am sure he will be very happy there.
STATEMENT OF MINOR CHILD: I, Sparky Valentine, have discussed this proposal with my father and with my guardian, and feel this course is best for both of us. I intend to follow a career as an actor, and the experience and recognition to be gained in my current situation will be invaluable to me in the

future. At the same time I do not wish to undermine my father's prospects in his new job. I feel I will be happy living with Mellie and Polly.

STATEMENT OF SOCIAL WORKER: I have examined Kenneth Valentine and Melina Polichinelli and can find no reason to oppose the guardianship. It is my opinion that taking young Kenneth, who prefers to be known as "Sparky," away from work he loves would be harmful to the youth, and might even drive a wedge of resentment between father and son. I believe both father and son are agonizing about this decision, but concur that the least harmful solution to both is a temporary separation. Arrangements to be reviewed in two years.

> Signed:
> John B. Valentine
> Melina Polichinelli
> Sparky Valentine
> Ambrose Wolfinger, M.S.W.

Petition approved, 8/12/58
E.J. Smith, Fourth District Court of King City

D.S.S. *La Belle Aurore*
en route, Triton
via V-mail, 8/15/58

Dear Sparky,

There's not much I can say now that we haven't gone over already. The ship has stopped boosting and we'll coast all the way now. In a few hours I'll go to sleep, and when I wake up, Triton! (Ooops! We're supposed to pretend we're not using deadballs. Don't spread it around, huh? Ha-ha.) Remember Polonius's advice to Laertes. "The friends thou hast, and their adoption tried, grapple them to thy soul with hoops of steel; but do not dull thy palm with entertainment of each new-hatch'd, unfledg'd comrade. To thine own self be true." You know the words as well as I. Let me add, always cut the cards. The two years will fly by, and when you've milked this Sparky foolishness for everything you can, you'll join me in

teaching these Tritonian hicks a thing or two about the stage!
Love from your father,

John Valentine

CONTEST!!!! CONTEST!!!! CONTEST!!!! CONTEST!!!!
CONTEST!!!!

PRESS HERE FOR | MORE |

Hey, gang! Can *you* think of 36 things that come out of the
human body? That's how many things Sparky and Polly used
when they created Armageddon Angry®, the newest kid on
Sparky and His Gang! Well, if you can, have we got a contest
for you! Sparky and Polly want to treat you to a seven-day,
all-expenses-paid stay at Dreamland! Your parents, too, and
your whole family! While you're at Dreamland you'll have
breakfast with Sparky and Polly and some surprise guests!
You'll ride all the coolest new rides! To enter, simply write
the 36 things on an official entry form. PRESS for entry form:

| PRINT |

We'll even give you two hints!

1. One of the things is EARWAX!

2. Babies are *not* one of the things!

Send your entry form along with a box top from SUGAR
SPARKLERS, "The Cereal Sparky Eats!" to "Sparky, Sen-
try/Sensational Studios, Mare Vaporum, Luna." Enter as of-
ten as you like! And check under the box top of your SUGAR
SPARKLERS cereal for valuable clues!
(Winner chosen at random from correct entries. Sorry, if your
Mom or Dad works for Sentry/Sensational or Peppieprod,
Inc., you can't play!)

December 1 (King City Temple)
   The December "Flack" numbers as compiled by the
Trends Research Department of the Latitudinarian Church are
as follows:

TITLE	AAS	Last Month	Last Year
1. Skunk Cabbage	92.4	2	3
2. The Gideon Peppy Show	89.9	1	1
3. Admiral Platypus	85.2	3	2
4. Scoop the Poop	80.5	4	-
5. Sparky and His Gang	78.0	7	46

We've got some good news and some bad news for you, Mr. Peppy. Which do you want to hear first? That's right, friends, the seemingly endless reign of the *Peppy Show* in first place has ended. *Skunk Cabbage* posted a number-one rating this month by a convincing 2.5 point margin. The good news is that the other Peppy Production, *Sparky and His Gang,* given up for dead at this time last year, has completed its amazing journey from hopelessness to success, arriving on the chart in fifth position by edging out Barney (see attached rankings).

Asked for his reaction to the end of his record-breaking streak in Kidvid ratings, Peppy said, "We'll get 'em coming or going now. As for not being in first place, you know how much that affects my ad revenue? Not one Neptune nickel, that's how much. You know how many kids load the *Peppy Show* every week, week in and week out? Millions, that's how many. So a couple a thousand more kids are watching *Skunk Cabbage.* So what? It ain't scrapin' the shine off my shoes."

More likely to fuck up his Florsheims is the result of a tracking study done by the research firm of Thickey & Gitte. According to their figures the *Peppy Show* would have registered in *third* place but for two guest shots by characters from the *Sparky* show, Crispin Crunchy and H. Ralston Riddlerah. AAS was up a full ten points for those two episodes. Given the persistent stories about creative tension on the *Sparky* team, Peppy has to feel at least ambivalent about those numbers. The departure of John Valentine for the Outer Planets, bruited as a palliative measure for the continuing tensions in the boardroom and the story conference, seems to have helped only a little. Rumor has it that Gideon Peppy has lost creative control of his new baby. So who's in charge, Gideon?

from *Elementary Educator's Bulletin*
issue #390
"Kids at Risk"
by Humphrey Murgatroyd

It is a distinct pleasure to report that, of the three new television series to become hits in the past year, two of them are good to excellent.

Much has already been written in this journal and many others of the deplorable *Skunk Cabbage,* and I will not further belabor it here.

Scoop the Poop is, as some critics have suggested, simply *What the Fuck?* in new clothes. One may regret the lack of originality, but considering the great bulk of children's programming, we should count ourselves lucky that an offering from the Children's Educational Workshop is still available, still getting excellent downloadings.

But the real surprise, and the real quality, is *Sparky and His Gang.*

Sparky began with high hopes, quickly faded into a yawn with both children and educators, then resurrected itself with an astonishing array of new characters. It began so badly, in fact, that this reviewer stopped watching it after the third outing. Then a few weeks ago, alerted by its quick rise and by favorable comments from my students, I loaded every episode and have now watched each one three times.

It is easy to hypnotize children with sound and fury, signifying nothing. If you watch children watching a show like *Skunk Cabbage* you will notice a certain glassiness of the eyes, a slackness of the jaw. At such times children are no more sentient than a reptile, and no more emotionally swayed. The violence is meaningless. It is animated wallpaper. If it succeeds in moving them to any degree at all, it is to desensitize them to real violence and its tragic effects. Children rise from such a show unable to tell you much about what happened, other than that things exploded, guns went off, swords were wielded, limbs and heads lopped off. Their play after such an experience has no more depth than the show. After watching cardboard heroes chopping up cardboard enemies for no discernible reason, they become more than a little card-board themselves. They have been viscerally involved, but their emotions have not been touched. Nothing was ever at stake. No lessons were learned.

This is where *Sparky and His Gang* succeeds, and that it does is little short of a miracle. Load the early episodes, if you dare. You will find Sparky and his friend, Polly, appealing. Everyone else is a reject from a hundred other similar shows. They do uninteresting things for baffling reasons. The show has no center, and no direction.

The changes in the *Sparky* show can be traced to the debut of the first interesting member of his gang: Inky Tagger. He is a ridiculous character at first glance. His fingers are a spectrum of magic markers. He has a big aerosol valve growing out of the top of his head. And he is completely covered, head to toe, with constantly shifting graffiti.

Inky is a sinner, you see, like all the new *Sparky* characters. In the course of his debut episode, Inky was pursued as "The Mad Tagger," whose graffiti came to life and menaced people. Sparky cornered him, talked to him, showed him the harm he was doing. Defiant at first, Inky swore he would never stop his defacements, but being admitted to the Gang, a place where he could finally belong, worked wonders. Sparky and the Gang showed him how he could put his artistic powers to good use. End of story, right?

Wrong. Inky has been known to backslide. He is at his best when close to Sparky, enfolded in the love of the Gang. But when alone, his restless urges are apt to overcome him. He feels terrible about it, but is helpless as any alcoholic. Sparky gets exasperated with Inky, but never stops liking him, and Inky is learning to control his urges.

Think about it. How much money has been spent in "Public Service Announcements" telling kids that graffiti is wrong, that taggers are dopes? I hesitate even to guess. It has had no discernible impact on the problem. The reason, I believe, is a simple one: taggers are *not* dopes. They are lonely, confused, unsure about their place in a world full of anonymity. All graffiti say the same thing, in the end: I am *here*! I am a person. Sparky tells taggers it's okay. He understands you, he *likes* you. And you don't have to be a loser. His gang does more than battle rival gangs. Sparky battles evil, both the external sort, and the bad urges that exist in all of us. It has been a long time since a television show has brought us a message like that.

All Sparky's new gang are a little comical, and a little frightening. An excellent example is Arson E. Blazeworthy. The comical side is his appearance, like a mad scientist whose most recent experiment has blown up. His face is blackened. Sometimes the tip of his nose and the tips of his earlobes burst into flame. His eyes are always comically wide. His charred clothes smolder and smoke. Arson is, of course, the pyromaniac, the compulsive fire-setter. The arsonist was a figure of fear even back on Old Earth. Here in the confines of the Lunar warrens he strikes terror into all our hearts. And it is a common enough condition in the young, one not often talked about. Sparky's Gang faces Arson head-on, reforms him, turns his fire-setting powers toward good. Usually. Like Inky, Arson can find the temptation too great. But he is *trying*.

All of Sparky's motley crew are trying to do better. Sparky does not demand perfection. He knows no heart is totally pure, not even his own. Sparky himself is sometimes prone to overconfidence, and there is a sprightly, practical-joking side to him.

Each of the children in the Gang personifies some failing, fear, obsession, or stumbling block encountered in the process of growing up. In the last few months they've been given a name, these outsiders brought into the bosom of Sparky's Gang: Kids at Risk. Here, meet a few of them:

Lionel Alibi. As usual, the name says it. Whatever happened, Lionel didn't do it. And if he did do it, it wasn't his fault, because somebody *made* him do it. And it wasn't him, anyway, it was Annie Rexia.

Acne Rose. The disfiguring skin disease known as *acne rosacea* is, thankfully, merely a memory now. Except for poor Acne Rose. She has an incurable case, her face a mass of eruptions and cankers. Naturally enough, she hates everyone who looks at her. But, this being a television fantasy, she is armed with the Zits of Death. When she pops a pimple it's like a toxic spill.

"Eeeuuuuw!" That was the reaction of my class at the first sight of Acne, followed by a cruel gale of giggles. But by the end of the episode they were cheering her on as she helped Sparky corral a vicious gang of polluters. Acne is the ugly duckling most of us feel ourselves to be at some point in our childhoods. She personifies the uncertainty we have about our bodies, about how others see us. She is also very *gross*.

Sparky's writers are not the first to perceive this great truth: that children *like* the baser bodily processes (see Zippy the Zombie from *Skunk Cabbage*). Farts and belches make them laugh. They giggle at things adults think are disgusting, or impolite. Sparky is simply the first to put this engine of risibility into the service of a moral lesson, rather than a mere cheap laugh.

You think you've seen gross? I'll give you gross. Take the Terrible Twins, Windy and Wendy Cheesecutter. Virtually identical in appearance, this brother-and-sister team have been taught, by Sparky and the Gang, how to turn their terminal flatulence into an asset. Apply a lit match to their . . . er, exhaust, and they're jet-propelled! They can grab the wings of a disabled jumper and lower it gently to the ground, put fallen fledglings back into their nests. Leap higher than a skyscraper! Or if you simply must have something blown up, Windy and Wendy are your best bet.

All the Kids at Risk are misfits, all of them afflicted. Sparky's job in life is to show them the power of their abnormality, and that anyone can be accepted, and loved, if they do the right thing.

In opposition to Sparky is the strongest of the Kids at Risk, a really rotten boy by the name of Armageddon Angry. Week after week Sparky and Army do battle for the hearts, minds, and souls of the Kids. Army is very good. Just when you think Sparky has finally reached a really stubborn miscreant, Army will whisper his poisonous insinuations in the child's ear, and fan the fires of resentment. It's easy enough to do; these kids are severely damaged. And who has done the damage? Why, you and me. Society. The ones of us who look at the ugly duckling and jeer, rather than love. Or even worse, those who view them with their hateful pity, those who want to *help*. These kids want our *acceptance*, not our help.

But in Sparky's world, not even Armageddon is all bad. He, too, yearns to be accepted, but his defenses are stronger, his hatred all-consuming. And what is the source of this burning rage?

Ah. It is too early to say for sure. But two things are already clear. Master Angry was created by Sparky himself, in a moment of hubris (this is presented as back story; Sparky and the Gang exist in a timeless world that looks like ours but functions like never-neverland). Nothing could be clearer than that Armageddon Angry is Sparky's dark side. In their face-to-face meetings Army has proven himself an accomplished tempter. He has shown Sparky the *joys* of an amoral freedom; we could see Sparky waver. It is this sort of edgy, nervous awareness of the *possibility* of Sparky's overthrow that keeps the kids' attention, that engages their hearts and minds. Nothing is assured in Sparky's world, just as in our own. Your friend of today could stab you in the back tomorrow. And the day after that you might embrace an enemy. These are things children have to deal with, things the cheap adventure shows know nothing about.

How *does* a child deal with these things? According to Sparky, with pluck and grit, and a willingness to get up and try again when you're down. Above all, without bitterness. The universe has been unfair to you? Gee, that's tough, but crying about it solves nothing. Come with me, I'll show you the *power* you have.

The other obvious thing about Armageddon Angry is that his own pain is beyond description. He has been betrayed on a very deep level. Without a doubt, this is an abused child.

There is something else that is obvious about the show itself. It has been guided by someone who is an authority in these matters. There is no listing in the credits, and no one at Peppiprod would admit to knowing who this guiding eminence is, but I am certain it will turn out to be a child psychologist of some renown. Perhaps an advisory group of them. I understand the reluctance of the producers to own up to this, the stamp of "Certified *Good* for You" being the kiss of death it so often is in popular culture, but *Sparky* is now a big enough hit I would hope this professional would be willing to come forth and receive the congratulations that are due.

In the meantime I and my children will be eagerly watching the coming episodes of *Sparky and His Gang*. I suggest you and yours do likewise.

(attached addendum)
MEMO FROM: Sparky Valentine
TO: Production Department

This guy thinks we have a headshrinker on the staff. I really hate to disillusion somebody who is doing us so much good with the educational crowd. How about a credit line next week: ''Psychological Consultant—Rufus T. Firefly''?

CC: Gideon Peppy
    Moe, Larry, & Curly
    John Valentine (Triton, via LaserNet)

KID AT RISK®
OFFICIAL TRADING CARD
"SPARKY AND HIS GANG"

....

#5 Duncan Disorderly™

Duncan found a taste for the booze at an early age. He like to hang out with his pals, Al Kohol™, and Phelan Groovy™. They drink all day and most of the night, then spend the morning throwing up. Doesn't that sound like fun? **Sparky sez:** What is a drunken man like? Like a drowned man, a fool, and a madman. One draught makes him a fool, the second angers him, and a third drowns him.

COLLECT 'EM ALL! >>>>>>>>>>>>>
○ PRESS HERE TO ANIMATE IMAGE

KID AT RISK®
OFFICIAL TRADING CARD
"SPARKY AND HIS GANG"

....

#9 N. U. Rhesus™

Newton Ulysses? Or Naomi Ursula? Nobody seems to know. Rehesus is a monky-like critter, dressed in a nightshirt and a diaper. Toilet training was too tough a subject for little N. U. He or she still doesn't have it right. In simple terms, a bed wetter. **Sparky sez:** Incontinence ain't a sin, you know. Let he who is without fear throw the first wet Pamper. Reesey is a stand-up guy, er, whatever.

COLLECT 'EM ALL! >>>>>>>>>>>>
○ PRESS HERE TO ANIMATE IMAGE

KID AT RISK®
OFFICIAL TRADING CARD
"SPARKY AND HIS GANG"

....

#16 Klepto Maine™

When you shake hands with this guy, count your fingers after! Klepto figures he's just borrowing things you're not using. Maybe so. **Sparky sez:** He who steals my purse steals trash. It was mine, now it's his, and has been the slave of thousands. But he that filches from me my good name robs me of that which doesn't enrich him, and makes me a poor man.

COLLECT 'EM ALL! >>>>>>>>>>>>
○ PRESS HERE TO ANIMATE IMAGE

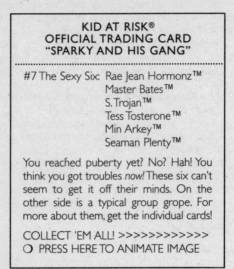

KID AT RISK®
OFFICIAL TRADING CARD
"SPARKY AND HIS GANG"

....

#7 The Sexy Six: Rae Jean Hormonz™
Master Bates™
S. Trojan™
Tess Tosterone™
Min Arkey™
Seaman Plenty™

You reached puberty yet? No? Hah! You think you got troubles *now!* These six can't seem to get it off their minds. On the other side is a typical group grope. For more about them, get the individual cards!

COLLECT 'EM ALL! >>>>>>>>>>>>>
○ PRESS HERE TO ANIMATE IMAGE

From the Grievance Committee
Writers' Guild of Luna
To: Gideon Peppy, President, Peppiprod, Inc.

Dear Sir:

It has come to the attention of this committee that you may be in violation of the WGL Minimum Basic Agreement. It has been alleged that you have appropriated characters and story lines developed and created by Writers' Guild member, Kenneth C. Valentine. It is further alleged that you did cause to be registered as trademarks these same characters, in violation of several Luna laws and interplanetary conventions. Attached please find a twenty-four-hour Cease and Desist Order. You are ordered to post this order prominently in the offices of Peppiprod, Inc., and upon the doors to any sets currently in use in the production of the television series *Sparky and His Gang*. This will serve to notify members of all the Crafts Unions that they may not work in your employ

until this matter is resolved. A fact-finding hearing will
convene at the Writers' Guild headquarters, 2100 The
Alameda, King City, at 1000 hours tomorrow. You may feel
free to bring legal representation and any documents,
witnesses, or recordings that would substantiate your position
in re ownership of these disputed characters and plot lines
(see attached list).

Thank you in advance for your cooperation in this matter.

> Trevor Jones
> Chairman, Grievance Committee
> of the Writers' Guild of Luna

CC: Kenneth C. Valentine
   Kaspara Polichinelli
   D. Mentua Precox
   Summerfall Winterspring
   Melina Polichinelli
   Ambrose Wolfinger, M.S.W.
   Sam Mohammed
   Debbie Corlet
   Velma Crow, representing Actors' Equity
   John B. Valentine (Triton, via LaserNet)

from TRANSCRIPT, WGL HEARING

*Investigation of certain claims involving Gideon Peppy, and
Peppiprod, a corporate entity chartered in the Republic of
Luna.*

Meeting resumes after lunch and deliberations:

CHAIRMAN: Mr. Peppy, it is the unanimous conclusion of
   this panel that you are in violation of the Minimum Basic
   Agreement.
PEPPY: Violation, my fucking lollipop. This is a kangaroo
   court.
CHAIR: When you signed the MBA, you agreed to abide by
   certain rules and accept the authority of this committee.
   You have a right to an appeal, of course, and one will be
   held in one week's time, right here.
PEPPY: And I'll get sandbagged again. Oh, yeah, I know
   the drill. Sam! Debbie! You're a fucking Judas, Sam! And

Debbie, you're a ... a Judette! You thought you figured
out which way the wind was blowing, you fucking jerks.
Well, let me tell you, I ain't down yet. It ain't gonna be
this easy to pick my fucking pocket.

CHAIR: Mr. Peppy, these are informal proceedings, but we
would appreciate it if you'd control your temper a little
better.

PEPPY: And fuck you, too!

CHAIR: Is there something else you have to add?

PEPPY: You fucking right I do. I was blindsided, that's what
I was. I didn't even know the little prick was a member
of the WGL!

CHAIR: I fail to see how that changes anything. You were
using his creative output. It was your responsibility to see
that he was a member.

PEPPY: You all think this is just a fucking coincidence. He
joined up two days after I hired him! Now, why would he
do that, do you think? Sure, I had him join Screen Actors,
I was paying the stinkin' little turd to act! It's his goddamn
father, that's who's behind this. They planned it! I spent
two fucking million dollars to get rid of his sorry ass. Two
million dollars just so I wouldn't have to look at his fucking face at the other end of the table, listen to his fucking
voice.

VALENTINE: You be careful what you say about my father.

PEPPY: Oh, now we hear from the fucking peanut gallery.
Oh, man! Sam, Debbie, you gonna work with this little shit,
you watch your fucking back, you hear me? He can reach
around you and stab you while he's shaking your fucking
hand. Who do you think *suggested* we send daddy-o to
Neptune?

VALENTINE: That was his idea, Your Honour.

PEPPY: Oh, yeah, I thought so, too, at first. He does that,
you know. Then you think it over and you realize he's
been leading you around the ring like a prize Pomeranian.

CHAIR: You don't have to call me Your Honour, son.

PEPPY: Is anybody listening to me?

VALENTINE: I didn't know.

PEPPY: He didn't know, he didn't know, he didn't fucking
know! I think I'm gonna puke if I hear him say that again.

C'mon, people, get me out of here before I start slugging him.

VALENTINE: I really didn't know.

CHAIR: That's all right, Sparky. We understand what happened.

VALENTINE: No, this really bothers me. If I understand you right, I should have been reporting my writing work to you. I was just happy to have my characters on the show, I didn't realize I was doing wrong.

PEPPY: Oh, my god, he's gonna cry. I'm gonna pound the shit out of him!

CHAIR: Mr. Peppy! Grab him . . . don't let him . . .

PEPPY: You little fuck! I been railroaded! I been screwed! You think it ends here, well, it don't end here, you're gonna see more of me . . .

CHAIR: That's right, lock that door. I think somebody should call the police, too, in case he's still out there when we leave.

CORLET: I'll handle that.

CHAIR: Thank you. Now, Sparky, we understand it was through ignorance that you didn't report your creative work until you were made aware of it. It is significant that no one else on the production, people who knew the rules, alerted the WGL until we received the anonymous tip that began the investigation. Please don't worry about it. We exist to help writers, not persecute them. There will be a small fine levied, a warning attached to your dossier, and of course you'll have to pay a certain amount into the retirement fund. Other than that, I can't see that you've done anything to be ashamed of.

VALENTINE: Thank you, Your Honour.

CHAIR: I see no reason why any of you need to attend the appeal hearing next week. The evidentiary matters are already on record. If Mr. Peppy presents additional evidence, we will deal with it at the time. Mr. Secretary, I believe the sense of the committee was that this information be turned over to the proper authorities for investigation of copyright and trademark fraud. Please see that is done this afternoon. This committee will stand in recess until ten o'clock next Monday.

Thimble Theater Productions
Suite 100, Sentry/Sensational Studios
INTEROFFICE MEMO
FROM: Curly
TO: Sparky

Here's the newest Flacks, plus editorial comment.

	TITLE	AAS	Last Month	Last Year
1.	Skunk Cabbage	93.1	1	2
2.	Sparky and His Gang	90.3	3	15
3.	Admiral Platypus	86.4	2	3
4.	Scoop the Poop	85.2	5	7
5.	The Gideon Peppy Show	79.3	4	1

Continuing story is the inexorable slide of formerly invincible Peppy.

Not much reliable has come out of the courtrooms where Peppieprod and Thimble Theater are locked in a corporate struggle over trademarks and copyrights. A usually reliable source has spread the news that Gideon Peppy collapsed in the courtroom last Thursday, and was briefly hospitalized for what sounds like an attack of apoplexy. Meanwhile production has been halted at the Peppy studios, while Thimble Theater has been able to continue producing the *Sparky* show under the lower court's ruling, pending final appeal. This means that as of now Peppiprod has only two more stanzas to play, and they will be off the schedule. Somewhere, though, a very fat lady is taking a very deep breath, and the entire industry is waiting to hear what song she sings.

Contacted about this abrupt reversal of fortune, Gideon Peppy had this to say: "Get that fuckin' camera out of my fuckin' face before I break your fuckin' neck!" Easy, Giddy-o. Take a stress pill and cool your jets. Remember when there's a shine on your shoes there's a melody in your heart.

---

from *Vapor Trails*
"All the Vicious Irresponsible Gossip Rumor and Innuendo Our Lawyers Permit!"

5/23/59
SOLOMON SPEAKS!
Judge Hands Down Decision in Thimble/Peppy Scuffle

Have you heard the old one about King Solomon and the
baby? Two women claimed to be the kid's mother, neither
could prove it. Old Sol says bring me a sword, proposes chopping the kid in two, make everybody happy, right? You don't
believe me, look in the Bible. I'm sure the library has a copy;
it means *book*, after all.

It looks like Sparky and his Thimble Theater Company get
to keep all the characters he created for the show, forty-seven
and counting so far. All except two of them. Are you ready?
Of course, it's the characters of Sparky and Polly. Peppy was
able to prove he wrote about them before he even met young
Master Valentine. So "Sparky" the character remains the intellectual property of Peppiprod, for all the good it'll do him,
and Sparky, the real-life Lunarian boy, gets to keep his gang,
for all the good it'll do *him*. Somewhere the ghost of old King
Solomon must be chuckling.

But rumors too speculative for even *us* to print hint this
is not really the last verse of this epic. Let it stand for the
moment that neither party is happy, and neither is about ready
to give up.

---

from *Clavius Clarion*
Shopper's Bargain Supplement
5/25/59

The big news in our little enclave this week was supposed to
be the opening of the new domed city park and shopping mall
out in the western district. That was before they announced
that Sparky and Polly would be the guests of honour for the
grand opening. News of the personal appearance brought
some youngsters from as far away as King City. Police estimated the crowd at fifteen thousand.

You would have thought it was three times that many if
you heard the cheers when Sparky and Polly flashed into view
on their red skycycles. They buzzed the crowd half a dozen

times, showering candy and trinkets from their saddlebags. It was a little bit Santa Claus, and a little bit Mardi Gras, and the children loved it. It's a good thing promoters provided adequate security, or the stage would have been mobbed when the two finally landed.

Sparky apologized to the kids for not bringing his gang with him, but he promised they'd be back in the old clubhouse in the near future. Then he and Polly sang the "Sparky's Gang Song" and the "Sugar Sparklers Song." All the kids seemed to know all the words.

But the surprise hit of the day was when a big, bumbling clown in yellow shoes, a checked jacket, red pants, and suspenders, bulled his way onstage, sucking on a huge lollipop. He started shouting at Sparky and Polly, jumping up and down, threatening them. The kids loved it. "Peppy" said he had Sparky's Gang and he was going to hold them hostage. Our heroes were not daunted; they strapped "Peppy" to one of their skycycles and sent him spinning into the air as the kids shouted with glee. And who says children don't follow the business and legal news? There seemed no doubt who the viewers favored in the simmering feud between Peppy and Sparky. If I was Gideon Peppy I'd be running for cover.

---

from *Vapor Trails*
6/2/59
OTHER SHOE DROPS!
Wisdom of Solomon, Part Two

At last we can tell it. Final figures are in on the settlement between Gideon Peppy and Thimble Theater. What everyone seemed to have forgotten in last week's dustup was that Sparky Valentine, in addition to winning the rights to the characters he created while the *Sparky* show was being produced at Peppiprod, won the trademarks associated with them, *and all the royalties paid since their creation.* Anybody want to guess how much that might be? A figure was not publicly released, but to get an idea, find an eight-year-old, go to his room, and count the number of times you see a member of Sparky's Gang. Multiply that by the number of three-to-twelve-year-olds in Luna (we're not even considering Mars, the Belt, and the OP, but the court is, oh, my, yes!). If the manufacturers paid even a penny for the use of the image—and count on it, they paid more than that—it comes to a very tidy sum.

Entirely too tidy for Peppiprod. Like most production companies, PP's liquid assets are not large. Money goes into development, dividends, promotion, and the shine on Gideon Peppy's yellow shoes. Peppy didn't have anything like that kind of money, and considering he's been off the load for two months, is no longer in production, and rated a weak seventeenth in the AAS last time the show was offered, there were no banks or bankrollers willing to take a flyer on his future prospects.

Into this frightening picture steps Thimble Theater, a.k.a. Sparky Valentine, with an offer GP can't refuse. When the dust settles TT owns all rights to the characters of Sparky and Polly, and all back numbers of the *Sparky* show. GP is still not back in the black, but he's out of the ultraviolet.

August 1 (King City Temple)

The July Flack Numbers as compiled by the Trends Research Department of the Latitudinarian Church are as follows:

TITLE	AAS	Last Month	Last Year
1. Sparky and His Gang	93.3	2	5
2. Skunk Cabbage	89.4	1	1
3. Admiral Platypus	84.0	3	3
4. Scoop the Poop	82.1	4	4
5. Space Weasels	79.5	11	20

At last! After an heroic two-year struggle, *Sparky* hits number one!

It's a good thing, too, or this column would be dull as dishwater. The only other number worth noting is the steady progress of *Weasels,* finally reaching the Fab Five. Plenty of educators out there are hoping it will soon reach number three, so maybe the Weasels can eat the Cabbages and *die*! Round-ing out the comfortable middle of the table is the usual gang of suspects.

Former champ, the *Gideon Peppy Show,* is still out of the running, "on hiatus" is the polite expression. Word is it's a hiatus that may prove terminal. Peppiprod is still sniffing about for some bucks to get back in front of the cameras.

Contacted about the hard times his company has fallen on . . . well, we *know* GP would have had something snappy and witty to say, but we didn't ask him, as our reporter is not anxious to have his jaw broken again. We'll let you know how the lawsuit comes out. And frankly, at this point nobody really cares about the shine on his shoes, the lint on his hard candy, *or* the crap in his trousers.

---

from *Hebephrenia*   doublestrikes
column of 6/6/59   touch doublestrikes for sound
             touch H̲y̲p̲e̲r̲l̲i̲n̲e̲d̲ words for refs
"At Home with the Like Wireheads! Ex. P!"
by D. Mentua Precox

and so when they asked me if I'd, you know, like to spend a few hours like with everybody's fayvyiest brillo-domes, I
        Get a clue
was all like "Get a clue unquote!" Like, the *D* stands for Dumbbunny, but not *Dope,* you load? But they were all like serious as green cheese, and stuff, so I packed my extra sox and training bra and pootled down to the backlot where they were making like the very first Sparky and Polly movie with the, like, Gang. Comma comma period. And there was this quote "dressing room" unquote that Sparky and Polly shared? You know? Question mark? Only it was bigger then D. Mentua's entire *cubic*!! Exc. etc. I mean, the *D* stands for *Dazzled*! Also for I *Dug* it!

So then Polly answers my like toodleoo in her you know Polly outfit and her hair looking like frozen noodles. And
       Dee   How nice to see
she's all like "Dee! How nice to see!" See? (Polly's voice ©59 Thimble Theater Productions) And I'm all howjadew howjadew and you know what I'm thinking is, how is it that,

like yesterday noodleheads looked all haha looserbilly and
stuff, and like, today it's all just treacle and buttered toast?
Question mark! How like *weird*! ExMark? The *D* stands for
*Dumb*founded, you know? And then before you know it it's
all last Tuesday.

Well, if you've had enufquote "deep thought" unquote for
the day, I just had to point out to Pretty Pol that I, D. Period
Mentua, has scoffed when the trendbillies like put you two out
as mere hulahoops ten-day wondering, as it like were, when I
was fritzing it about that you were the gen-you *Frisbee*!

And we thank you for it
Whamm-o ex ex ex!!! and she goes "And we thank you for it."
Your humbuggle narrator came over all pink and stuff. Shit!

And so dinner was served (no electric noodles! paren)
thesis comma, and who should come flycycling by but the
man/boy of the our, as well hour, Sparky. And he goes
    Long time no Dee
"Long time no Dee!" (Sparky's voice ©59 Kenneth Valentine) and I'm howjadew all over the place again. period. And
then most of the time yrs t. is sitting churchmouselike in a
corner like watching breathlesslike while tag teams of atts-at-
law, counselor, are shuttling massives of paper between the
Sparkabilly and his like *ex loco p.,* period comma, lady name
of Melina I'd-tell-you-her-last but *D* stands for *Dud* when
speling wurds of more than five slylabbles. Sillybabbles. Sly-
bulls. *D* stands for Don't call on me, teacher! Syllables! and
that's the lesson for today!

And she Melina is going "Sparky, I don't know
anything about these legal matters," and Sparky goes
    Don't worry, 'Ma,'
"Don't worry, 'Ma,' " comma threestrophe, and he goes
    That's what laywers are for
"That's what laywers are for." And the babble of attorneys
keeps bringing on the papers. And I go "What's this all
about question mark," and Sparky goes it's something
about a makeover for Giddy Pep and I go boy, could he
ever use it, did you lamp those yellow shoes, how un-
Fahrenheit, with, goggle, gulp, red suspenders, gimmea-
chance here! Exclam! Then D.M.P. proozled thru a few,
papers lying idly about and stuff, but when it comes to
contracts *D* stands for a *D* in business ad. period and an-

other D in business math. I'm *sure* there was a story there for *some* intrepid news-nosey, but not this my'self *please*!

So anyway where was I oh, yeah the Royal We spent an hour with the P. and S., and I bet you'd love to hear it. Well, pull your diapers back up, gramma, you didn't think it was all, like, freedie time, didja? Just load up $19.95 and get momster or dadster to thumb it to me for the real cheese! In threedee as in Dementia or D. Mentia, living crayolacolor big as a slice of life Phew! I got that all out in one breath! Period!

---

from *News Nipple*
Financial Page
11/11/59
Thimble Theater in Peppy Takeover

In a surprise move today, Thimble Theater Productions, whose chief asset is the children's television show *Sparky and His Gang,* took control of Peppiprod, Inc., formerly captained by Gideon Peppy, the originator of the series.

At first glance, the transaction seems a case of a minnow swallowing a whale. But according to City Exchange analysts, it was a very hungry and aggressive minnow and a very tired, hollow whale. Peppiprod was saddled with a crippling debt load resulting from recent adverse court decisions in favor of Thimble Theater's managing director and chief stockholder, Kenneth Valentine. Efforts to obtain refinancing for such a speculative venture were making little progress until the take-over bid was announced. Hours later a consortium of investors solidified the deal.

(For financial details PRESS HERE)

The move was vigorously opposed by Chairman Peppy, but in the end his position was not strong enough to appeal to stockholders who stood to benefit in the transaction.

It is little wonder Peppy was opposed. In an odd twist, it turns out that all rights to the character "Gideon Peppy" are owned by Peppiprod, a situation brought about by certain tax advantages. It would seem then that Gideon Peppy, the person, no longer owns the rights to his own voice and image. Thimble Theater could, if it chose, enjoin him from wearing the clothing associated with the character he created—and now largely lives—or at least appearing in public as the character. It could even prevent him from using his own voice in commercial situations. Vaporum is now abuzz with lawyers and agents, seeking to rewrite contracts to avoid a similar conundrum for their clients. That won't be necessary for Ken Valentine, who personally owns the rights to his television character "Sparky," leasing it to Thimble Theater in an arrangement sure to be widely copied.

---

from *Flash in the Pan*
"The Collector's Guide to PopCult Ephemera"
'59 Price Guide, coffee mugs

354. Skunk Cabbage. Zappy the Zombie	$ .45
355. Skunk Cabbage. Zippy the Zombie	$ .45
356. Sparky and His Gang. Ensemble	$ 55.00
357. Sparky and His Gang. Sparky Alone	$ 190.00
357a. "Decent" Sparky	$5,000.00

NOTE: All Sparky tie-ins with the "original" Gang are worth more than contemporaneous series merchandise because most were destroyed after the bad start. The "decent" variants, produced for sale only on Vesta, Callisto, and Ceres, showing Sparky wearing pants, were never shipped, and only one box survived.

358. *Sparky and His Gang.* Polly	$ 100.00
358a. "Decent" Polly	$3,500.00

---

from *The Straight Shit* Starpage:
"Where Are They Now?"
6/4/60
by Bermuda Schwartz

You'll never guess who I ran into yesterday in a taproom on the upper levels of North King City. I really don't quite know what to call him. I don't believe the name we all knew him by was his real one, and he can't use the one we knew him by. You might call him "the artist formerly known as Gideon Peppy." Or the Man Without a Name. Or you could tie a dead albatross around his neck and call him Ishmael.

And you know? Clothes really do make the man. Or at least they make the clown. If somebody hadn't pointed him out to me, I never would have recognized him. Okay, I'll fess up. I didn't actually run into him. I don't go to upper-level taverns in North King City, as a rule—in fact, I'd never been in one—but it's the sort of place Not–Gideon Peppy inhabits these days. He had sent for me, and for old time's sake I went.

There's no reason Not-Gideon shouldn't be sipping his vodka-and-beer boilermakers in the cozy country clubs down in bedrock. He's still got plenty of money. It was his balls Sparky took from him, not his wallet. He goes to places where the decor mirrors his mood. And, I found out, because it's only in places like that he can find souls destroyed enough to listen to his tale of woe. And now he had *me* to listen.

Like some maniacs, Ex-Peppy can present a convincing front for a short time. At first I think he had me confused with that awful Precox person. (Later I found out she'd been by the previous day, found out there was no story there for her clientele, and dropped him like a cold potato. I've never seen why one should lower oneself to the intellectual level of a five-year-old just because . . . but don't let me get started on that. Please! Period.)

When we had my identity straightened out he regaled me for a while on his plans for a comeback. Outlined for me several new series he had "in development." Told me of all the big people who were coming in with him on these projects. I almost bought it. The man *was* influential, *had* moved in those circles until recently. But now he looked as if he wouldn't cast a shadow at high noon in Imbrium.

Then it was Sparky, who he began talking about in a surprisingly calm, controlled voice. He spoke of the lawsuits he had filed, was soon to file, or intended to file as soon as his lawyer drew them up. He kept glancing at the clock over the bar, saying his lawyer would be there soon and I could hear the whole story from him. By then I was wishing the ambulance chaser *would* arrive and give me a way to gracefully leave.

The segue into insanity was so gradual I hardly noticed it at first. Then I realized he was talking about a computer chip Sparky had implanted in his, non-Gideon's, head, that enabled Sparky to control his thoughts. The doctors hadn't been able to find it, oh no, Sparky was too clever for that, but Once-Was-Peppy had had his telephone removed, just in case. He was sleeping under a lead canopy because he was at his most vulnerable when he was dreaming.

"I have sonic and static generators running all the time, too," he said. "I'm considering having my skull replaced with stainless steel, like the commandos use. See that guy over there?"

The only person in that direction was a stubble-faced drunk passed out with his face in a puddle of spit on the filthy bar top.

"One of Sparky's spies," post-Peppy confided. "He's here every day, pretending not to watch me. Pretending to be too drunk to notice anything. But I've seen him muttering. He's wearing a wire, somewhere, I haven't figured out where yet. He tells them when I leave here so they can keep track of me. Did you see them, loitering around out there? There's enough of them that no matter which way I go they can keep tabs on me. I've confronted them, but they all look at me as if I was crazy."

There was much, much more, I'm sorry to say. You try to be gentle, you try to be kind, but most of all you want to be *out* of there. Leaving becomes a frightening process of detaching his clawlike fingers from your clothing, first one hand, then the other, then the first hand again. I thought I was free, backing away with a big smile on my face, when his arm shot out and grabbed me again.

"I've figured out who he really is," he said, in a loud whisper.

"Sparky?" I said.

"Satan," the man who used to be Gideon Peppy said.

Folks, I don't want to turn this into a diatribe against the abuses of personal rights and freedoms, but this man needs help. Because he's harmed no one and so far hasn't harmed himself, he cannot be committed to a safe place as in the bad old days. But I'm telling you, *leash* laws are more humane and much more practical than the way we allow the insane the "right" to go off the proverbial deep end, unrestrained, unhelped.

This man should be stopped, before he hurts himself or someone else.

Or both.

The News Nipple
Obituary Page, 6/10/60

MARSH, Julian E. Born 2103. Mr. Marsh, better known to millions of his young fans as "Gideon Peppy," was dead on arrival at the Mare Vaporum Medical Center yesterday afternoon. The cause of death was a self-inflicted gunshot wound.

For 7 related stories, PRESS ⌷MORE⌷ .

TELEVISION CLOWN KILLS SELF, WOUNDS TRANSIENT

(Mare Vaporum) Julian Marsh, until recently known as Gideon Peppy, arrived at his former office in the Sentry/Sensational Studios at 3:00 P.M., covered in blood, brandishing a .55-caliber automatic pistol. He fired a few rounds seemingly at random, harming no one but sending office workers and security guards running for cover.

He went directly to Studio 5, where the current episode of *Sparky and His Gang* was being filmed. Screaming incoherently, waving the weapon at anyone who approached him, he demanded to see young Sparky Valentine, star of the show. When informed Sparky was not due on the set for another three hours, he threatened a cameraman, telling him to roll tape. Facing the camera, he made a brief statement, the content of which has not yet been released, then put the muzzle of the gun into his mouth and fired. He was killed instantly.

For 6 related stories press MORE

Earlier in the day Marsh had gone berserk in the Twelve-Step Inn, North King City. He attacked Mr. Buford Keeler with a kitchen knife, inflicting serious wounds on the man's abdomen and chest. Patrons said Marsh was shouting something about finding a microphone. When other customers and the bartender pulled Marsh away, he produced a handgun, fired three rounds, and fled. Mr. Keeler was healed and released.

For 5 related stories, press MORE

Gideon Peppy shouted, "Roll 'em, roll 'em, you cocksucker, or I'll blow your fuckin' head off. Is it on now?"

Peppy's hands and the front of his clothes were dark with dried blood. He stared into the camera, and smiled broadly.

"Maybe this'll satisfy the little fuck," he said, then sucked on the barrel of the gun. When he fired his whole face seemed to stretch out like a face painted on a balloon. A red mess of brains, hair, skull, and blood erupted from the crown of his head, and he fell to the floor like a puppet with cut strings. The camera moved in. There were spatters of blood on his yellow shoes.

Sparky ejected the chipcard and tapped one edge of it idly on his desk.

"Maybe that'll teach him to mess with my father," Sparky said.

He pressed the button on his desk that connected to his secretary. "Send this Peppy death tape to Curly," he said. "Tell her we need a thirty-minute documentary, freeze-frame, slow motion, whatever else you can think of. I want it on my desk by this time tomorrow, ready to outload by tomorrow evening. Also, get to work on a promo tying the death tape to the reloads of the *Peppy Show,* same time frame. We have to move quickly on this, it'll be old news fast. It ought to provide a good publicity lead-in to the *New Peppy Show.* If you need me, I'll be in the casting session across the hall."

He rose from his desk and walked across the deep carpet of his office. He went through the door and out into the public corridor. The people who passed him all smiled and waved respectfully. He had a smile for each one.

All conversation died as he entered Studio 88, where the

casting session was being held. He remembered the first time he'd been there, not even knowing he was trying out for the part of Sparky. Long time ago, he mused.

He stepped up to his big chair at the end of the table. No one was sitting at the far end, where Julian Marsh used to sit, but that was okay. Everyone was clustered down at Sparky's end.

He opened a crystal candy jar and took out one of the lollipops custom-made for him by Dixie Chocolateers of Tharsis, Mars. The gold-leaf-coated paper rustled expensively as he unwrapped the sweet. He popped it into his cheek and looked around the table. He hitched himself a little higher on the padded box that enabled him to rest his elbows at table level.

"All right, ladies and gentlemen. It's magic time. Send in the first of the Peppy prospects."

Sparky was eleven.

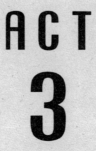

ACT
3

"**D**ovetonsils," I said. "That's *D* as in Dogberry, *O* as in Ophelia, *V* as in Verona, *E* as in Exeter, *T* as in Adenoids. Percy Dovetonsils."

There was a short pause.

"*T* as in what, sir?"

"*T* as in Titania, *O* as in Oberon, *N* as in Nym, *S* as in Shylock, *I* as in Iago, *L* as in Elsinore, *S* as in Shallow. First name Percy."

There was a longer pause.

"Sir, is this some sort of joke?"

A horrible suspicion overcame me and I sat up straighter in my chair, almost spilling my drink.

"Good god," I said. "Am I talking to a human being?"

She was on firmer ground there, though I might have debated the point.

"Yes, sir!" she piped. "It's part of our Service with a Smile policy here at Capitalists and Immigrants Trust. If you only had elected to receive picture as well as sound you would have seen that I've been smiling throughout this transaction . . . or at least until you started to spell your name."

Good fortune and a dislike of being seen myself during a phone call had spared me the no-doubt-hideous rictus that would pass for a business policy smile at C&IT. Imagine sitting at a phone bank and being paid to smile all day as you answer customers' dumb questions. I'd sooner host a perpetual game show. However, the lack of a picture had lulled me into thinking I was speaking to the usual robotic screening program, the first of a normal three or four steps before you contacted an actual human being.

"Please connect me with a machine, at once!" I ordered. There was no response, but I fancied I heard a slight sniff, and wondered if I had caused just the hint of a frown to obscure a few dozen pearly whites at the edges of her corporate-mandated grin.

The problem with humans—if you've ever tried to talk to one over the phone—is they sometimes show imagination at a time when you would least expect it. They make illogical connections, fly off on fanciful tangents. Usually this simply leads to confusion, but now and then it can sow seeds of suspicion that might, if not nipped in the bud, lead to an unexpected truth. If you are engaged in something the least bit dodgy it is better not to take that chance, since truth is the *last* thing you want to come out.

What I was doing was *probably* not illegal. I say that because laws seem always to get broader and more restrictive every year. Hardly anyone ever retires a law. You don't hear about laws being unwritten, recalled, allowed to expire. You begin with civil liberties, and after a few hundred years you have a legal system that can't even *find* liberty, much less protect it. I couldn't afford a lawyer to vet my proposed actions against fifty years of legal encrustation, would not hire one if I *could* afford it.

But in uncertain times it is usually best to deal with a machine. Machines always play by defined rules. They may be asked to look for odd behavior, but that means somebody must define "odd," and if it can be defined then it's not truly odd. Just as the dealer always hits on sixteen and stays on seventeen, machines in a certain situation behave the same way every time. If you know this, and know at least some of the parameters, you can put the knowledge to good use.

"How may I help you?" The voice was no more mechanical than the real woman's voice had been. I personally think there ought to be a law about that, and I'm not one to support many new laws. I like to know where I stand.

"Percy Dovetonsils," I said. "I am an attorney working for the estate of the late Mr. Dovetonsils. We are trying to locate bank accounts hinted at in his will, but not specified."

"We carry no accounts for a Dovetonsils, Percy," the machine said.

"How about Harold Bissonette? Double *S*, double *T*."

"We carry no accounts for a Bissonette, Harold."

"Try Flywheel, Wolf J."

The machine had never heard of old Wolf, either, and I broke the connection. I marked off two more possibilities on the grid I had made on a page of creamy-white hotel stationery, and called the next bank on my list.

Long ago I had read a biography of W. C. Fields, the great film comedian from the dawn of the talking-picture era. Fields was not a very nice man, but he was a quirky one. When he traveled, and when he had money, he would stop in small towns and open accounts in local banks. He seemed to enjoy the thought of having emergency stashes squirreled away all over the country. His had been a harsh childhood, he trusted no one very far. If he kept any list of these accounts, no one ever found it, and it was assumed at his death that he had long since lost track of most of them. Their location died with him.

Well, I thought that was just a wonderfully eccentric thing to do. I decided to follow in his footsteps, back in the days when I had more money than I knew what to do with. Everywhere I went I opened small accounts, almost none of them in my own name. I was going to be different from Fields, though. I was going to remember where they all were.

I *did* remember a few. Those were all long gone.

Sometimes it seems to me that my younger self spent most of his time dreaming up things he could do to make my older self miserable. You ever feel that way? You were twenty, you had the world by the tail. Outlooks were all rosy. It would never *occur* to you that, by the time you were eighty or ninety or, ahem, one hundred, your worldview would have changed dramatically. That you need not be senile to forget things you did seventy years before. That, in all that time, you would have ample chance to lose your careful notes, both written and mental. At twenty, there is simply no imagining the slings and arrows of outrageous vicissitude.

Or maybe I'm unusual. Maybe I'm a grasshopper and you are all ants, or most of you, anyway. Perhaps your life is in perfect order, everything cataloged, pigeonholed, in its proper place. I used to sneer at that sort of life, and I probably am temperamentally incapable of leading such a life, but it does have its attractions. But how was I to learn frugality, caution, temperance, moderation—all those things so beloved of poor Richard Almanack—the way I was brought up? I never had what you'd call a home until I moved in with Polly and Melina.

In any event, my one attempt at being a good little ant, storing up acorns for a rainy day, was by now far in the past. Most, if not all, of those caches had been plundered years ago. I no longer knew where, or even if, those piles of acorns existed. My careful accounting had come to naught.

I did have one thing going for me, though. I had used a limited number of names, twenty-five in all. I'd chosen them carefully as names unlikely to be inflicted on anyone ever again, yet names I would not forget because they were all old friends of mine.

So now when I first arrive at a place I have not visited in a long time, I spend a few hours idly paging through the listings of financial institutions on the Yellow Screen.

You never know. One day twenty years ago I stumbled onto an account in the name of William Claude Dukenfield. It was one of "my" names, but the money had been deposited in 1935. Somehow, through mergers, takeovers, booms and busts, devaluations, failures and holidays, through the very Invasion of the earth itself, this little account was still tucked away in a bank on Mars that might have been the great-great-great-great-granddaughter of the little Poughkeepsie neighborhood bank where old W.C. had left it, in the midst of a great depression. Still gathering interest. I had no way to get at it, probably wouldn't have tried, anyway. Ironic fact: the original deposit had been two hundred United States dollars. When I found it, inflation and other exigencies had allowed the money to grow to the princely sum of L$239.14. About enough for two days in the hotel I was making my calls from.

"How may I help you?"

The voice was practically identical to the machine voice at the first bank I'd called.

"Is this the computerized answering service of Hamlet Savings and Loan?"

"Yes, it is."

"I'm searching for accounts in the name of Otis Criblecoblis."

"I'm sorry, we carry no accounts in that name."

"How about J. Cheever Loophole?"

"I'm sorry, we carry no—"

"Try Eustace McGargle."

"I'm sorry, we—" I hung up. Two down, about sixty or seventy to go.

Why three names? you may be asking. Why not just read off the list of twenty-five names at each bank you call? There was actually no completely logical reason, since I was *pretty* sure I was doing nothing illegal. But when you have as many outstanding warrants or persons pursuing you as I do, you learn to be cautious. Asking for nonexistent bank accounts was almost sure to raise a red flag somewhere in the bank computer's programming, the electronic equivalent of a teller calling the bank president over to frown dubiously at the check you're trying to kite. I much prefer wide-eyed innocence to the professionally jaundiced eye. Nothing is more wide-eyed than a computer. It does what it is told, and never asks the next logical question. Four was a common number of events to trigger programmed alarms, possibly based on what is known as the Bellman Principle: What I tell you three times is true. Ergo, what I tell you four times might be a load of shit.

That, plus the fact that three is my lucky number.

"How may I help you?"

"Bank of Oberon? I'm searching for accounts in the name of Egbert Souse."

"You're out of luck there." Great. A user-friendly program.

"Then surely you've heard of Hugo Z. Hackenbush."

"Not during this lifetime." Did this bank cater to comedians?

"One last try, shithead. A. Pismo Clam."

"Does the *A* stand for Ambrose, or Albert?" I sat up straighter. Was I getting a bite?

"Which one do you have?" I asked, cautiously.

"Neither one. I have a William Clam, and a Jake's Clams, though."

"Yeah, well, stick it—" I broke the connection. No use trying to get the last word with a computer. I stood up and stretched, took a sip from the rum and Coke on the telephone desk, then walked to the window and looked out.

Oberon. The Bard's World. My God, what a place.

Just about everything on Oberon is worthy of a postcard. So where does one start? At the beginning, I guess. Actually, a little bit before.

What we call Oberon today is not what we called Oberon when I was a boy. Oberon is the most distant of the Uranian moons, and the second largest. It's smaller than Titania by a few dozen miles, and about a hundred thousand miles farther away from Uranus. It used to be an unremarkable little ball of rock, faintly orange in color.

Like all the outer-planet habitats, it didn't have enough gravity to be of much use other than as a nuisance. Not enough gravity to make a curtain fall properly, to stage a decent sword fight, or to perform classical ballet. This was naturally a cause of some concern to the Oberoni, so they set about finding a way to provide enough gravity for the theater.

Actually, they had a few other reasons that may have counted more heavily than falling theater curtains. But I can dream, can't I?

Research has shown, so I'm told, that the healthiest environment for humans and other Earth-evolved animals is somewhere between Luna's one sixth and Mars's one third. Anything lighter caused Lowgrav Syndrome, which wouldn't kill you but could certainly annoy you a lot, and which was expensive to treat and hold in remission. Anything higher . . . well, humans were no longer living anywhere with more than .5 gravity, and good riddance, as far as I'm concerned. I experienced one gravity in the Trip to Earth centrifuge at Armstrong Park when I was six. We've all seen the effects of one gee in old movies and television. People plod like elephants in molasses. Things fall at a frightening rate. Bodies are bulked up by fighting gravity while the flesh is dragged down from giving in to it. Every inch of skin sags. Some of it is painful, and I left the centrifuge wondering how they could face threescore and ten years of that. Not for me, thank you very much.

There are only four ways of providing a given acceleration

of gravity, until some genius finds a way to create it. One is simply to accumulate the necessary mass. Thought was given to altering the orbits of all the five largest Uranian moons, smashing them together. That would have been fun, don't you think? But it wouldn't have provided as much gravity as the engineers were seeking, and besides, it would have taken forever for the resulting mass to cool enough to be useful.

Then there is Pluto's Solution, which I guess is technically Method 1A, since it also involves accumulating mass, but it certainly *feels* like a different solution. Over a century and a half people have been venturing out into the *really* distant spaces—so far that Brementon and the sun look like next-door neighbors—bringing back tiny black holes. I mean *really* tiny. Smaller than atoms, they say, though I find that unlikely. There are now thousands and thousands of those little black holes orbiting near the core of Pluto, through solid rock that presents no more obstacle to them than interstellar space. There's enough of them in there now to provide about one third of a gravity on the surface. Those little suckers pull *hard*!

One day the black holes will suck all the mass of Pluto into what would be, so I read, a tiny-to-small black hole (the *large* ones contain whole galaxies, if you can believe that). There's no question this will happen. The debate is about how long it will take. Prevailing opinion is at least a million years, so you may not want to unload your real-estate holdings. Of course, some scientists claim it will happen next Tuesday. Take *that* into your vacation plans.

It's the sort of predicament that appeals to Plutonians, a fatalistic bunch. They get a kick out of telling newly arrived tourists about the latest catastrophic prediction.

The Oberon engineers rejected the Pluto Solution, mostly because of the almost unimaginable expense and the time it would take. Black holes are very rare, and cost the planetary income of some asteroids. They are not labor-intensive, and one hoped-for side effect of the Gravity Project was putting a lot of people to work, jazzing the economy.

And I suspect they decided to wait a few centuries, see if Pluto *did* fall into a black hole.

The third and fourth ways are also related, and don't involve actual gravity but the illusion of gravity. If a spaceship accelerates at a steady rate, it will seem just like real gravity to an observer inside the ship. Einstein noted that no experiment done inside the ship could distinguish between "real" gravity and the force of acceleration. If you're wondering how I, a mathematical dunderhead, know all this stuff, it's simply that I had to memorize great swatches of it as dialogue when I played the old windbag in *Einstein and Marx,* the techo-philosopho-porno extravaganza you've never heard of because it played three times before going to a richly deserved extinction. ("Ken Valentine manages to bring some much-needed humor to the role of Albert. But this will only appeal to communist theoretical-physicist necrophiles. There must be two of them in the system, maybe three. Let them have it. —*The Phlegethon Phlogiston*)

There are several insurmountable hurdles to using method number three for "residential" gravity. For one thing, your residence would spend most of its time moving like a bat out of Pluto. After a few months (weeks? Do the math yourself), you'd be moving near the speed of light and time contraction would be a problem. Well, then why not accelerate twelve hours out, turn around, and accelerate twelve hours back? Oddly enough, that *would* work, though the expense would probably be prohibitive. It would avoid the other problem of constant acceleration, though: the fact that we have yet to produce a means of propulsion that can operate indefinitely, at any useful thrust. When you got home, you could refuel.

One of the many unlikely propositions I have sold in a lifetime of selling was based on that idea. We set up a Big Store, selling shares in a company that was "right on the edge of a breakthrough!" in the field of light-speed travel. The dodge was to put your money in the bank, get on the ship, and return a few hundred years later to reap the compound interest. The trip would only be a few months subjective time. Brilliant! Of course, we were the bank. And I already mentioned what happened to W. C. Fields's bank account. But you'd be surprised how easy a proposition it was to put over.

So now we come to the fourth method, or 3A, depending

on how you apply the rules. This is the wheel, or the bucket on a rope.

Put some water in the bucket and whirl it around your head. The water doesn't spill out. Magic! Actually, centripetal force, which is a constant acceleration toward the center of a circle.

If you build a wheel in zero gee and set it spinning, you can walk around on the inside of that wheel just as if you were in real gravity. If you want to be heavier, you spin the wheel faster. Slow it down for less gravity.

Make the wheel very large. . . .

We've been building structures like this since humans went permanently into exile in deep space. The asteroid belt, the lunar Trojan points L4 and L5, the Jupiter and Saturn Trojans, J4 and J5 and S4 and S5, all are thick with wheels like this, or more often, cylinders. Up until the inception of the Oberon Gravity Project the largest of these artificial worlds was about sixteen miles in diameter.

The Gravity Project proposed a wheel one thousand miles in diameter.

To make a leap like that you need a significant new technology, or a major breakthrough in an old one. The Oberoni had a little of both.

When I had last come through about twenty years before, Oberon II had looked like this:

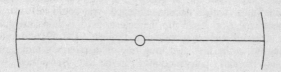

The O was the hub of the wheel-to-be, hollow in the center. If you were building an interplanetary Conestoga wagon that was where you'd put the axle. The long lines were the first pair of a proposed twelve spokes of the wheel. The two little arcs at the end were all that had been built so far of the outer rim of the wheel, the place where people would live and work.

Today it looked like this:

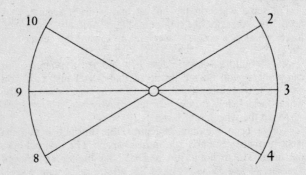

Four more spokes finished, and two separate portions of wheel arc. Each spoke was five hundred miles long. Each arc had reached a length of about six hundred miles. It looked like the project was half through but it was actually further along than that. You learn as you go, and getting started was much tougher than getting finished. They expected to wrap the whole thing in ten more years. That is about half a mile of rim every day. Don't ask me how they do it. I've stood at Edge City and watched the work, and I *still* don't know.

Oddly, a thousand-mile wheel turning once an hour produced just about the .4 gravity the engineers had in mind. From Luna, with a decent telescope, you could tell time by Oberon II. And since the diameter was one thousand miles the circumference was π thousand miles: 3,141.592654 miles. That led to the first of a long line of disparaging nicknames during the early construction: Pi in the Sky. But nobody was laughing now.

"Yeah, whaddaya want?"

"Is this the computerized answering service of Oberon National?"

"You got a problem with that?"

"I got a problem with your tone of voice."

"Fuck you. You dialed the aggressive-response number. Hold on, asshole, I'll connect you with obsequious response, if that's all you can handle. Good afternoon! I hope I can be of service."

I took a deep breath. Folks, is modern science wonderful, or what?

"Checking for an account in the name of Elmer Prettywillie."

"I am so sorry. We carry no such account."

"Then surely you've heard of S. Quentin Quale."

"I am devastated to inform you that I've made no such acquaintance."

"Well, you must know Linus Spaulding. Captain Linus Spaulding."

"Well . . . There is an account for the Linus Pauling Foundation."

"I'll bet it's right next to Jake's Clams. No, Spaulding. Captain Spaulding. The African explorer."

"*Quel dommage.* I am devastated."

Christ. When programmers have nothing better to do, they dick around with stuff like that. And what's worse, people *use* them. I'm told it got started with cutesy answering machine messages, back at the dawn of the Electronic Age. I wish it had stayed there.

If I were an extraterrestrial tour guide bringing a shipload of Betelgeusan caterpillar people for five days and four nights in the quaint little Sol System, I'd put Oberon II and its environs in the top-three places of Things to See.

Actually, maybe it would look like a primitive log cabin to the caterpillar people. Maybe they'd want to swap beads and trinkets and planet-busting bombs for our native handicrafts or buy a few million slaves. But for my money, you can't beat the Uranian system.

Uranus has rings. Nothing like the gaudy gold bands around Saturn, but impressive in their own, more subdued glory. And because the axis of Uranus is so far askew from the plane of the other planets, you get a great bull's-eye view of them as you approach.

Uranus has moons. Five major ones, all different colors, all showing a disk as you move closer. Then dozens and dozens of smaller ones, looking like very bright stars.

Uranus has Oberon II, which I've already described, but which cannot be easily grasped unless you have seen it grow from an odd *X* in the sky into the most outrageous object mankind has yet built. The hub alone is larger than anything else man-made in space.

Uranus has Oberon I, the original moon. If you are lucky, your ship can come very close to it on the way in, and it looks *wrong*. Red-orange streaked with black and light brown and cream, it looks like a family-size pepperoni, black olive, and anchovy pizza, the sort that might be delivered to a family living at the top of a beanstalk. But they've already been eating it. A hundred years ago Oberon was reasonably round. Not anymore. Great gouges have been torn from it, a hundred miles wide and deep. Oberon is being cannibalized to provide the raw materials for building Oberon II. Down there on its surface Oberon has become a vision of hell, with mining robots the size of ocean liners chomping their way through veins of ore, and with plants transmuting stuff we don't need into stuff we can't do without. The dark side is aglow with the terrible fires of these operations. They plan to use it all up, every grain of sand, and then move on to Ariel.

But most of all, Uranus has tailings.

For the first century after the Invasion, there was little of organized government beyond the orbit of Mars. There were plenty of people. Just no government. Very few rules other than the ones you enforced yourself, and such rules tend to be only things that matter to you as an individual. And only those things that matter to you *now*. The environs of Uranus and Neptune were settled and developed by the rough-and-ready breed that always gravitates to the frontier. On Earth there were gold miners, buffalo hunters, trappers, and eventually farmers when the frontier was the American West. Later, in the Brazilian rain forests, it was lumbermen, miners, then slash-and-burn farmers. All of them despoiled the environment. There was nobody to tell them not to, and besides, there were zillions of square miles of wilderness. What's all the fuss about, amigo?

At Uranus, it was miners. I'm sure they'd heard of the environmental disasters of Old Earth, but why should they worry about that? There were no buffalo to be driven to extinction, no native peoples to evict and practice genocide on, no tropical forests to turn into arid Saharas. There's nothing out here but rock, Lord love you! How can even the most rapacious businessman fuck up a rock?

The answer was obvious, even when the destruction was going on, so nobody mentioned it, or if they did, they were sure no problems would be evident for thousands of years. The reality took less than fifty. Finally the mining companies were losing so many ships that something had to be done. They changed their mining practices, but that was far from enough.

Tailings, as defined on Old Earth, was that monstrous pile of crap you can see sitting beside the ore refineries in old photographs. Tailings was what you had left after you'd taken out what you were digging for. In gold and diamond mines, that could be 99.9% of what you dug up. But ugly as it was, on Earth, when you were through with a bucket of rock, the tailings just sat there, seldom harming anybody. The big deal was the air pollution produced by the refining process, or the contamination of water that ran off the pile of waste. At Uranus, and Neptune, things were different.

Don't imagine this mining was done by grizzled old desert rats leading space donkeys at the end of a rope, pickaxes in hand. You think mining, you visualize either that, or men with soot-blackened faces riding a cart down the shaft of a coal mine. The reality of mining back on Old Earth was usually different from that. There was strip mining, in which the topsoil and everything else was scraped away with bulldozers until the coal seam was reached. There was placer mining, which involved leveling fair-sized mountains with streams of high-pressure water. And there was open pit mining, which depended on blasting away entire cliffs of virgin rock. The easiest, quickest, cheapest way to mine the Uranian moons was by blasting. They used plastic for the smaller veins, mininukes for the major digging.

Because of the negligible surface gravity of even the largest moons, each of these explosions hurled thousands, millions of rocks into space. The rocks varied from no larger than a grain of sand up to some fairly hefty boulders. Up into the sky and . . . gone. They never fell back to the ground. Some ended up in orbit around one of the moons, others took up every variety of orbit around Uranus itself. The mining companies had no problem with this. Every chunk of useless rock that achieved escape velocity was a chunk of rock that wouldn't have to be shoved out of the way to get to the valuable ores. It just vanished into the blackness, and good riddance.

Actually, no. The stuff was gone, but far from forgotten.

A certain small percentage of debris achieved Uranus-escape velocity, and could more or less be ignored. An even smaller portion went solar-escape, and was even less of a worry. But the great bulk of all that junk took up orbits that crisscrossed the space lanes from every direction, and usually at an alarming relative speed. A grain of dust could leave a pit the size of your fist in the foam insulation that covered the hulls of most ships. Something the size of a pea could ruin your whole day, punching right through the thin skin and entering the life support or engine as a burst of blue-hot plasma. With luck, you might have time to patch and repair. Anything bigger than an apple might as well be an atomic bomb.

There were an estimated six hundred trillion apples in orbit around Uranus and its major moons. That sounds horrific until you realize the Uranian system is about fourteen quintillion cubic miles. That's one apple for each twenty-two thousand cubic miles—one heck of a lot of nothing, with a rock lurking somewhere. Which sounds great, until you realize that's a cube only twenty-eight miles on a side. Now add in the fact that most ships are *themselves* several miles long, quite a large target, and on approach and departure will pass through many millions of cubes that size. If that doesn't make you squirrelly, nothing will.

Not to worry. Sparky's on the job!

The Oberon Chamber of Commerce and Tourist Bureau claims that, left to itself, the situation would result in one major hit for every ten thousand trips. That figure is in great dispute, but it really doesn't matter, since the situation has not been left to itself. Each ship that enters this solar pinball field carries good radar and good lasers, and fries an average of six rocks on the trip in and out. Most of those would, of course, never have troubled the ship, but ship's captains *hate* tailings with a mighty passion. They never let one go.

This would actually be enough to reduce ship/tailings encounters to one every few decades. But it's not enough for the Oberoni, who hate tailings even more than captains do. For one thing, they are a hazard to the great structure of Oberon II. For another, they give the system a terrible black eye in the minds of the traveling public, one hit per decade or not. So the Great Wheel bristles with radars and lasers, which clear a thousand rocks an hour . . . or was that per second? Go look it up. It's a bunch.

And that's still not enough for the fifteen moons of the Uranian League: Oberon, Titania, Umbriel, Ariel, Miranda, Peasblossom, Cobweb, Mustardseed, Pyramus, Thisbe, Snug, Bottom, Flute, Snout, and Moth. (I once met a fellow who hailed from Bottom; he said his people called themselves Bottom-dwellers, but the neighbors, naturally, referred to them as Assholes. I always wondered what inhabitants of Snug and Snout were called.) The League aims to clean up the system in a few centuries, and their main weapon is a genengineered cyborg critter called a snark.

You're unlikely to see a snark during your trip to Uranus. Though they number in the billions, they're not very big and they cover a *lot* of space. (Spacers believe sighting one is very bad luck.) But they all look like lengths of pipe, ranging from a few feet long up to about fifty feet. They have gossamer "wings" that they spread to soak up solar radiation. They have radar eyes and a system that generates gas for propulsion: hydrogen + oxygen = bang! They survive on a meager diet of ice and rock, which they get by dipping into the rings. They are alive, semi-intelligent, self-reproducing, and their mission in life is to destroy tailings. They drift, ever-alert, conserving their strength by using their thrusters only at orbital points where it can be used most economically, like eagles soaring on a desert thermal. When they spot a rock, they vaporize it.

Like most perfect solutions, the snarks revealed a few problems not long after they were let loose. One toasted a group of seven spacedivers during the first month postrelease. A viral program had to be devised and broadcast on the wavelength they used to talk to one another, making sure they only attacked objects smaller than a basketball. Anything larger would be reported to human agencies which would track it down and dispose of it.

And a few decades after that they began showing up at Neptune, Saturn, Jupiter, all the related Trojan points, and the asteroid belt, where they were about as welcome as rabbits in Australia. But they did no real harm.

I mention all this for two reasons. One is that, during the fifth season, Sparky found an injured snark and nursed him back to health. B.J. the Snark became one of the most beloved members of the Gang, along with Toby the Dog, sometimes outselling Sparky in action-figure totals. Of course, B.J. had a friendly face—real snarks have nothing that looks like a face—and had no trouble flying around inside municipal pressure, which would have made a real snark helpless as a butterfly in a blender.

The other reason is to explain the glorious, continuous fireworks show surrounding Oberon II as my ship began her final approach. The black sky was alive with a thousand points of scintillating light, light that was all the colors of the spectrograph as the mostly sand-sized particles were vaporized, announcing their chemical composition in their final seconds, to anyone with the knowledge to read the colors.

I didn't have that knowledge, but who cares?

It was even more beautiful than I remembered it.

"Is this Hank's Bank?"

"Yes, you have—"

"Automated answering service?"

"That's right, you have—"

"Looking for an account in the name of Otis B. Driftwood."

"We have no—"

"Cleopatra Pepperday?"

"We have no—"

"T. Frothingwell Bellows?"

"We have no—"

"So long."

Three more down. It was looking like a losing proposition.

• • •

I wish I could say I had time, leisure, and the temperament to enjoy the approach to Oberon II. If you don't like fireworks, there are also the holoboards, which we started picking up while still a thousand miles out. Miles on a side, they trumpet the allures of the big hotels and casinos and shows, with more glitter per square foot than anyplace since Old Las Vegas.

In reality, I had only two things on my mind. My stomach, and my bowels.

I had been awake almost continuously for the previous week, having stretched the deadballs as far as I could. I had grown a beard, and my toenails looked like pruning hooks. There are 168 hours in a standard week. Ten thousand minutes. I had spent every one of them thinking about food.

I had eaten the last of my provisions. I had licked the wrapping paper and cardboard, then I ate the cardboard. Then I ate the paper. I chewed on rags, hoarded my last ten sticks of chewing gum like some wild-eyed troll at the bottom of a well. I hate to admit this, but several times I thought about Toby, snuggled safe and warm only a few feet beneath me. I began to wonder if he'd taste like chicken.

They say that historical fasters like Gandhi and Hornburg eventually didn't feel much in the way of hunger. That's what they say, but you couldn't prove it by me. It only got worse, hour by hour, and when I thought it couldn't possibly get any worse, it did.

Then it got worse again.

There was really only one thing to distract me from my hunger, and that was the state of my lower digestive tract. Every ounce of high-nutrition food I'd eaten since the trip began was down there now, a bolus about the size and shape of Phobos and twice as hard. It was going to take surgery to pass it, I felt sure, and the medico had better go in with a sharp pickax and plenty of dynamite.

So pardon me if I sort of skip lightly over the arrival (thousands of ships at least as large as mine, floating inside a vast cylinder spangled with the light from a billion portholes), the transfer (swarms of robot tugs no bigger than park squirrels detaching each cargo pod, reading its destination, then jetting off toward the correct bay like ten thousand maniacs charging for a front-row seat at a Motomania Show), and my exit from the Pantechnicon and subsequent reentry into public pressure (my spine was trying to form some unusual letter—*Q* or *Z*, I think—and my legs promised never to be straight again). When I could walk I looked briefly, with little enthusiasm, at the cargo pod Ukulele Lou had rejected at Pluto. All I could determine was that whatever had been inside was spoiled, for sure. Then I had to step lively as a big cargobot plucked the damaged pod from the line and took it off somewhere, presumably to fill out quintuplicate insurance forms. I couldn't pick out the pod Lou had escaped to. It might have been delivered to a bay clear on the other side of the hub for all I knew. I wished him luck again, and found the exit to public corridors.

Thirty seconds later I was devouring the mother of all hamburgers, the National Gall'ry, the Garbo's sal'ry, the Camembert of hamburgers. Actually, it was a MacVending 15¢ Microwave Special, dab of ketchup, dab of mayo, hold the pickle, lettuce, purple Bermuda onion, beefsteak tomato, sprouts, mustard, slice of Cheddar cheese and everything else you might think of, but by then I was ready to lick dried soda pop and crushed peppermints off the auditorium floor . . . and like it. So I shall always treasure that burger.

I ate two more just like it, hurried to the bathroom and threw them all up, went back outside, and ate another that seemed likely to stay down. Then I sought out the nearest Minute Surgery franchise and had someone take care of the other problem. I promised you I would skip over that part, and I will, though I did take note of some of the medico's expressions of astonishment and merriment, and some of my own caustic replies for possible use in my next Punch and Judy show.

I shall similarly give short shrift to the most glorious meal I have ever eaten. I would gladly spend several hours describing it, which is about the time I spent eating it, but my powers of description would surely fail me. It was, after all, simply good, solid, restaurant food. There were no hummingbird livers or ocelot's tongues or jellied kumquat tidbits. Nothing exotic at all, really. A big steak and mashed potatoes and corn, stuff like that, followed by most of a cherry pie and a pint of ice cream. It wasn't the preparation that made it taste so wonderful, it was the special sauce starvation provides. And it didn't take three hours to eat because it was a trencherman's groaning board. I just took the time to savor every bite. You should try that sometime, though I doubt you could ever experience my intense delight unless you'd gone that long without eating.

Refueled, reamed out, beginning to feel a reasonable approximation of a human being, I found my way to the freight offices and reclaimed the baggage that until recently had been my home. I glanced at the telltales that showed Toby was alive and well and deflated the dome. Gad! Had I really spent three months in there? The air that came whistling out said it had been at *least* that long. Whew! Did *I* smell like that? Probably.

I'd been meaning to go direct to the elevators, but took the time to check into a coin-op shower 'n shave. I came out feeling, if not exactly ready to whip the world, at least ready to go a few rounds with it.

Normally I wouldn't spend much time describing an elevator ride. But on Oberon II, nothing is quite like it is on other planets, and elevators are one of the *most* different.

Oh, and I'll drop that "Oberon II" business right now. I quickly realized that, in the time I'd been away, Oberon II had become simply, Oberon. What we used to call Oberon, the rocky moon, was now called Old Oberon. It made sense. There were a few thousand holdouts still living on Old Oberon, and a few tens of thousands of demolition miners and so forth, but as the moon began increasingly to resemble a rotten apple with big bites taken out of it even those few residents would have to move.

I remembered some of the grand old theaters of Old Oberon: the Palace, the Olivier, the Streep, the Chicago, and wondered if any of them were still standing in the gloomy airless rubble. Not to worry. All of them, and many more, plus a great variety of other structures had been plucked bodily out of the path of the marauding bulldozers. Most of them were sitting in mothballs at the Ob4 Trojan point, waiting for enough of the rim to be built to support an historical disneyland, the first to re-create a time since the Invasion, to be known as (guess what) Old Oberon. If all these New, Old, II, and whatever Oberons have you a bit confused, join the club. And don't worry about it.

Elevators. First, stop thinking in terms of a box that opens and closes and moves up and down in a shaft. Now, follow me . . . and watch your step as you board, please. . . .

"The Noon elevator will be departing from Level 20, Concourse B, at 9:00 A.M.," the announcer's voice said. "That is in ten minutes' time. The Noon elevator will be leaving promptly at nine. All aboard, please."

So already this elevator is different, right? In fact, Noon elevators departed every hour on the hour, twenty-four hours a day. Only here, Noon was a destination as well as a time. It's a source of great confusion in communication, but it's solidly entrenched by now, and the Oberoni don't seem to mind it.

The huge partly finished clock face that is Oberon seen from space is the original Twelve and Six spokes, Twelve being flanked by spokes going to Eleven and to One, Six being between Five and Seven. Got it? The one designated as the twelve o'clock position is known as Noon Arc, and the other is Six Arc. People from Twelve are called Nooners. People from Six are called Aussies. I don't know why.

I boarded with plenty of time to spare, found a seat, and strapped in. I spent my time looking out the window until the hatch was sealed. The elevator was only half full, on this level, anyway.

The deck under my feet began to flash in pale blue letters: FLOOR FLOOR FLOOR. A bell sounded, and I sank gratefully into my chair as the car accelerated. Nice to be back in some gravity again.

"All clear," came a voice, and most of the people around me unbuckled and got up. So did I. The acceleration was mild, and didn't last for long. It was quickly followed by another period of weightlessness. The whole trip would be like that.

An elevator moving up and down the spoke of a spinning wheel has some difficult engineering feats to accomplish during the journey. During my first trips, when the wheel was new and consisted only of Twelve and Six, the elevator car was filled with seats mounted on gimbals, so the passengers could swing into any attitude, depending on where the force was coming from at the time. This was logical, but very boring. Stewards would escort you to and from the bathroom, if you were unlucky enough to have to go. I don't even want to *try* to describe those except for one little horror you can ponder at your leisure. Imagine standing at the toilet, answering nature's call, when suddenly the stream is splashing against the wall, then the ceiling. This happened to me when the gimbal got stuck. I imagine it would be even worse for women.

Now they had a new type of car. What it had to do was quickly and smoothly adjust to acceleration and deceleration, and to transform itself from a weightless environment to a .4 gee environment during the length of the trip.

There is no way I could describe all the ingenious dodges the engineers did to pull this off. If that was all they did, it would be impressive enough. But the car also had to be able to start and stop during the trip, and it had to deal with the angular force of Oberon's rotation. Just how this works is far beyond me, but you can see how the turning motion of the spoke would result in gradually increasing weight. It's called, I think, the Coriolanus Force, though why they should name it after him is beyond me. It produces a ride that even seasoned spacers sometimes find hard to take.

I was thinking of taking the elevator—the internal elevator—up to another level when the bell sounded again. A wall—I was pretty sure it had been the "ceiling" when we started—began to flash FLOOR FLOOR FLOOR. The wall I was pretty sure had been the FLOOR FLOOR FLOOR when I sat down now had no chairs attached to it. I couldn't think where they had gone; stolen while my back was turned, no doubt. But being only "pretty sure" of one's location and attitude was a common experience in zero gee, so I didn't worry about it. I was reassured when chairs began sprouting from the new FLOOR FLOOR FLOOR, some of them with sleeping people already strapped in. I kicked over to one, turned my feet to touch the FLOOR[3], and felt the weight return to me gradually. Which meant we were slowing down again already, right? Well, it would seem so, but from inside the elevator it was hard to tell just what was happening. I felt a moment of nausea when we abruptly went weightless again—meaning we were now motionless?—and felt that superb lunch turn a cartwheel in my stomach. But the urge to purge went away. I've always had good space legs.

If you think you have good equilibrium as well, the Noon elevator is a good place to give it an acid test. Many a traveler have been humbled by the constantly shifting tides of the trip. The Oberoni call the condition C-sickness. About a quarter of the passengers were wearing Chuck-O-Laters, basically heavy-duty barf bags that strap over your face like a gas mask, with a constant suction and replaceable trap. In spite of them and in spite of the Herculean efforts of cleaning robots, the Noon elevator always smells faintly of vomit.

Soon we were under way again—a new FLOOR, with new people sleeping in new chairs—and I took the elevator up six floors to the casino. That trip was a tummy-twister in itself.

What a delightful place the casino was. I've seen craps played in weightlessness, and in one-sixth gee, and .4 gee. But never had I seen craps tables and roulette wheels that had to quickly change from one state to the other. The place was a blur of motion and a haze of smoke and flashing lights, and it seemed every ten minutes or so it would all reorient itself, the croupiers would put away the gravity dice and wheels and break out the zero-gee stuff. It was fascinating to watch. Soon I was hopelessly disoriented, but it hardly seemed to matter.

I spent the next hour on a tour of the various levels. There were staterooms, sleeping berths, six restaurants, a carnival and game rooms for children, an infirmary, and movie theaters. No pool, though. The Oberoni engineers were not quite up to *that* one. And no legitimate stage.

The trip is five hundred miles. The elevator makes it in an average of five hours. It would do it a lot faster but for the constant stops and starts needed to avoid collision with the spiders. I wanted to see one. A steward told me they usually encountered one close enough to see, and directed me to the forward observation bubble. It was the first place I'd been to that gave me a clear view of the massive spoke itself, like a column of ice five miles thick. It dwindled in the distance, where the wide, bright band of the Noon Arc could be seen. A single rail mounted on the outside of the spoke was our guideline. To each side of it I could see huge pipes, wires, and mysterious structures, but never enough of them to spoil the clean, perfect line of the spoke itself, pure and pristine as the swooping cable of a suspension bridge.

I knew the cable was not made of ice, but that's what it looked like. Bright white in color, with a dull surface, criss-crossed with thousands of lines like ice-skater's tracks on a measureless rink.

Spider silk. Trillions and trillions of strands of spiderweb.

That was the breakthrough that had enabled the building of Oberon II. They had found a way to produce massive quantities of the strongest material known to man. As it so often turns out to be, the solution was obvious.

Build a bigger spider.

We stopped several times during the first hour, for no reason I or anyone else in the dome could see. I was starting to get discouraged, because I knew the largest spiders never went to the high-gee environments from about a third of the way down the spoke. Lower than that and their legs could not support the weight of their bodies.

"Some of the first experiments on animals in weightlessness were done on spiders," someone to my left said. I turned to look at her. She had not been in that chair when I sat down. Believe me, I would have noticed.

"Is that right?"

"Back in the twentieth century," she said. "They wanted to find out if they'd spin webs in zero-gee." She was lovely. Heart-shaped face, green eyes, a slender figure.

"Did they?" I asked.

"They built very strange webs."

"Not as strange as this one, I'll bet."

"Probably not. My name is Poly." She held out her hand, and I took it.

"No kidding? I knew a Polly, once."

"And don't mention Polly and Sparky, from that old kids' show. Everybody does that. It's short for Polyhymnia."

I admit I was taken aback for a moment, but her expression told me she had no idea who she was talking to. Boy, couldn't I have given *her* a shock? But I quickly recalled the name on the passport I was using—one I had paid good money for in the back alleys of Pluto. So she'd never know.

"I'm Trevor," I said. "Trevor Howard."

"And I'm just Polyhymnia, for now," she said.

"That name rings a bell. . . ."

"One of the Muses."

"I was going to say Graces."

"There are only three of them. There are nine Muses."

"So you come from a large family?"

She laughed. "Only four, so far. But you're right, we're all named for Muses. Mother thought we should get into the arts."

"Polyhymnia must be a singer," I ventured.

"Sacred song, to be exact."

"And are you?"

"Not hymns. But music is my racket."

I made a sour face. "That one's old as the hills."

"So's that expression. Where are these hills, anyway?"

"Don't ask me. I'm from Luna."

There was a little more banter like this. Basically we were both trying to decide if a temporary berth was in order, neither in too big a hurry to make up our minds. I learned she was a violinist.

"With an orchestra?"

"Someday. Right now I mostly work in the theater pit. Utility string hacker. But I'm available for square dances, too."

"You're in the theater? That's great. I've spent some time on the stage, myself."

"You know, I thought your face looked vaguely familiar. Maybe you were in a show I played in. We don't get much chance to look at the actors, you know. Our backs are usually to them, and we're down so low."

"It's possible," I said, dubiously. "But this is my first trip to Oberon in about twenty years."

"I guess not, then. I've never been out of the system."

We were hedging around the issue of age. It's not polite to ask, and for my money, it's not good form to let it bother you. In this era when not many people look much over thirty, some of us are better than others at estimating. I'm usually pretty good, and I had her pegged for mid-twenties, both from body attitudes and gestures and from the fact that she was looking to climb up the ladder in the music world. After you've reached sixty or so, you stop thinking things are going to change a great deal.

A difference of seventy-five years can be a problem, if you let it be. I try not to let it. If she was fifty or so, there would be no generation gap. After the fifties, we're all more or less in the same generation.

I asked her where she lived and she said Six Arc. But her job was at Eleven, Wednesday through Sunday. It meant sleeping on a sofa at a friend's place and a twice-weekly twelve-hour commute.

"I've got a cute little apartment at Seven," she said, "but I only see it on my days off. With the housing situation the way it is, I don't dare give it up. To go to work I have to take a light train to Six, catch the Six elevator, the hub shuttle to the Noon elevator, down to Noon, and a heavy train to Eleven. The actual distance from my home to my job, as the vacuum-breathing crow would fly, is only about eight hundred miles. The route I take is about fifteen hundred miles. The Rim Express does the trip in forty minutes, but who can afford that?"

This all had my head spinning a bit, to tell the truth. I finally had to sit down, later, and sketch it out. Draw a clock with only eleven, twelve, and one at the top, and five, six, seven on the bottom. Forget about the hands; the clock itself is turning. Clockwise. A train moving *against* the spin is a *light* train, since the faster it goes the lighter you feel. A heavy train is one moving spinward, with the spin, thus adding its velocity to the speed of the turning wheel. You get heavy. When the wheel is finished all but the most local trains will travel antispinward. No trip will be longer than about forty-five minutes.

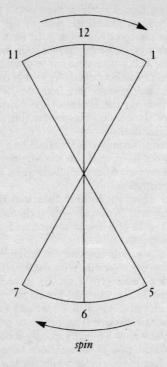

spin

"Aren't there elevators from Seven and Eleven—"

"And One and Five?" she finished for me. "It would save me a few minutes of travel time, but it doesn't make sense, economically. Elevators will be built on Three and Nine spokes, when they're finished. On that great, glorious day. Golden Spike Day. Buy your tickets now."

"Golden Spike?"

"After the American Transcontinental Railroad. They drove a golden spike where the trains from the east met the rails from the west. Besides, there's not a whole lot of commuters like me. Not a whole lot of traffic at *all* between the Sixers and the Mad Dogs."

Feeling a little like a straight man, I said, "Mad Dogs?"

"Sure. They aren't Englishmen, and they go out in the Noonday sun."

"I get it."

"They call us Aussies, after the old penal colony back on Earth."

"I get the feeling there's not a lot of love lost there."

She made a dismissive gesture. "Most of the government is at Noon. The bulk of white-collar workers live there, bureaucrats, agencies. Six is more working-class. They say the two arcs are growing apart, politically and culturally. We're already as different as Mirandans and Arielites. Before long we're going to be as distinct as East and West Germans were, hundreds of years ago, before they reunified."

I had no idea what she was talking about, but rather than pipe up with "Germans?" I just nodded my head wisely. That usually works, and it did this time, too, with a little help from a spider the size of a brontosaurus.

The elevator slowed to a stop again, and when our chairs reoriented themselves we could see something large and black in the distance.

"It's a D-9 Motherspinner," Poly said, pointing at it.

"That's the big ones, right? I mean, I hope so. I don't like to think of an animal much bigger than that." She nodded, and we watched it approach our capsule.

It was hard at first to make out just what I was seeing, or to realize how huge it really was. It's always a problem in space, with no references. Here, the reference points I could see were already so outlandish in size that at first it seemed the arachnid was really no larger than a big horse. Then it got closer. Oh, my, an elephant, maybe? Then it got closer again, and the light got a little better. Jesus, at *least* a brontosaurus.

The captain of our elevator (that *still* sounds weird to me, like the general of our sidewalk) threw a light on it for us. It didn't help as much as you'd think, because the creature was such a deep, perfect shiny black. Its carapace didn't reflect light so much as it reflected highlights, like chrome trim. I'm sure you could shave by looking at its skin.

"Vacuum-proof, of course," Poly said. "It has some beetle genes in it."

"Right," I said. "Cross a beetle with a battleship, and there you go."

"My father works a D-9," she said, proudly, pointing at something on the bug's back.

"My god!" I said. "That's a *man*. Is that your father?"

"No, he works on the new Eight spoke, just getting started on that one. And that's not Miss Dixie."

It took me a moment to realize she was talking about her father's D-9 Motherspinner. I was still taken aback by the man riding the eight-legged behemoth. Until that moment I had not known they were piloted.

"Miss Dixie," I muttered.

"All Motherspinners are female," Poly said.

And those who ride 'em, much braver than I, I decided.

The rider was in a pressurized box, like a howdah strapped to the back of an elephant. It was mounted behind the basketball-sized eyes and in front of the giant black sphere of her abdomen. He looked like the operator of a big crane or shovel, and that wasn't too far off the mark. He pulled levers and turned pulleys in a competent, businesslike way, and the spider turned or moved forward.

"The driver doesn't run the legs," Poly told me. "He steers, gets her where she needs to go, then stops her and lets the spinning begin."

The closest I saw in a reference book, much later, was the black widow spider. I don't know if she had a red hourglass under her belly or not, but Poly said she definitely was not a black widow. She was a cross between many web-weaving species, with a lot of made-to-order genes stuck in there to make her do the sort of weaving the engineers wanted: a thousand-mile web anchored only at the center, precisely opposite of what most weaving spiders would naturally do.

"The D-9s don't weave," Poly said. "They sit in one spot and start extruding silk, and smaller spiders grab those and start running with them. She can put out thousands of miles of silk at one sitting. He's probably positioning her for that right now."

The spider started moving, off our rail and to one side. The driver waved at us as he went by, and then the elevator started moving again. I got a last glimpse of the thousands of spinnerets on her underbelly. Behind her, very close to the cable itself, was what looked like a tide of black ink.

"D-3s," Poly told me. With horror, I realized the tide was a million "small" spiders, no bigger than a collie dog.

I'm not overly fond of any animal without fur. I don't like spiders at all. I listened with half an ear as Poly told me more than I wanted to know about the sex life, diet, pedigree, care of, and general all-around good social standing of ninety-ton arachnids. When she was a girl, she used to go to the "stables" and her father let her hand-feed Miss Dixie. A vision straight out of Dante, for my money. What did she feed the beast? Sugar cubes? Dead cattle? Giant houseflies? I didn't ask. Then something she said made me sit up straight.

"Here, now," I said. "You say this spider was here to patch up the spoke? You're talking about the spoke that my own very precious body is currently dangling from? The spoke I was led to believe was strong enough to support *three* Noon Arcs if it had to? This is the spoke that spider is *fixing*?"

She laughed, but I was only partly in jest. Who wants to be dangling at the end of a rope over the Grand Canyon like *The Perils of Pauline* and then see the rope start to fray? Not me.

"I didn't say patching up. I said 'strengthening.' One reason it could support three times what it's called on to support is that we keep alert and ahead of any deterioration. Computers figure it out, naturally. The thing is, the stresses on the web are greater during construction than they will be when the rim is complete. Then it'll settle into a state of constant, easy-to-predict stress. We'll need only about one percent of the spiders we use today."

Maybe so, I thought, but it struck me that moving into this damn thing before it was finished might not be such a hot idea. I mean, would you move a chair and a television into an apartment where they were still blasting the kitchen and bedroom out of rock?

And another odd thought. What would happen to those other ninety-nine spiders when the wheel was complete? If their drivers were sentimental enough to *name* the monsters, would they be eager to see them tossed on a scrap heap? And don't forget about the animal-rights lunatics. Scarcely a flea can be poisoned in Luna without triggering a march. Think what a lobby *these* critters would have.

Not to worry. I later learned the surviving D-9s (whose life span was not known) would be moved to the Ariel II project.

I was about to make my move on Poly when she headed me off at the pass.

"I was going up to the casino for a while," she said. "Would you like to go with me?"

No, but I'd like to . . . strike that. I gave her a rueful smile.

"One thing my daddy taught me well," I said. "Never gamble. And I never do."

"I was thinking of going to one of the card tables, play a little five-card draw."

"Poker?" I said. "Why didn't you say so? Lead the way."

I lost a small amount, and by the fifth hand I realized she was working with one of the other players. He looked to be about her age, and had a bad habit of tinkering with his ring that a really alert house would have quickly spotted. But there was no house here, except for the two percent they automatically extracted from each pot: table rental, basically. Few casinos make much money from the card tables. Apparently once you were seated and had your chips in front of you, the house didn't care if you telegraphed your intentions to your partner by farting in Morse code, so long as the other players didn't object. None of the other four had any idea what was going on.

By the tenth hand I had their system figured out, and I took them for several hundred dollars. By the fifteenth hand they knew I was onto them, so I cashed in my chips and winked at the guy as I left. I went up a level and ordered a drink and took it to a window seat. The Coriolanus Force was coming from a steep angle now, "down" was somewhere between a perpendicular to the spoke and another to the rim. The elevator accommodated this by turning the cable-side FLOOR into a series of three-foot-wide steps. It made everything look a little cockeyed. The row of windows I was looking through, for instance, had been horizontal when I first saw this deck. Now they were at a thirty-degree angle to my internal "level." Don't worry about it if you can't visualize it. I had to see a computer model of it before I got it straight in my head.

"How long did it take you to catch on to us?" Poly said, placing her drink on the table beside mine, sitting beside me. (The glasses? Magnetic bases with clear glass hemispheres mounted on little gimbals. Turn them upside down and nothing would spill. In zero gee a top snapped over the liquid automatically and you sipped through a straw.)

"You guys weren't bad at all," I told her, fudging a little. *She* wasn't bad. He was playing with fire. "Don't ever get in a rough game, for high stakes. Your boyfriend might not make it out alive."

"His name is Brian, and he's not my boyfriend."

"No?"

"A classmate and violin rehearsal partner. We're really terrible, aren't we?"

"Don't play with the big boys," I reemphasized.

She shrugged. "It was just for fun. Kind of exciting, but we never took very much money. We didn't want to make anybody suspicious."

"You win enough, somebody at the table's gonna be suspicious. Make sure he doesn't catch you in anything. Make *him* have to prove it. The other players'll back you, usually."

"What if they don t?"

"Make sure you're sitting close to the door. *Not* in front of it, not with your back to it. Then hope, if you're cornered, that the weapon *you* brought to the table is better than the ones *they* brought."

"You carry a weapon to a poker game?" She looked excited at the idea.

"Always."

"What's the best one?"

"The sense not to sit down with killers."

"That's not a weapon."

"Depends on how you employ it. It's the best one I know." And the one I've used the least, I added, dolefully, to myself.

She cocked her head the way self-confident, lovely young

girls do, girls who haven't suffered much yet. A girl who is trying to decide if you are a pearl in her oyster or just sand in her clam.

"You've been around a bit, haven't you?" she asked.

"Here and there."

"I've never been off Oberon. It sounds like an exciting way to live."

"You mean professional gambling?"

"You said you never gamble."

"Poker's not gambling. And I'm not a professional. It's *too* exciting a way to make a living." This was true, though over the years I've played here and there, depending on my circumstances and the qualifications of the other players. (Who do you want to play with? Rich people, people who won't miss it, and who fancy themselves card sharks.)

"May I ask how old you are?" she said.

I put my hand behind her neck and drew her to my lips. She didn't seem to object. When I broke away a little, she was smiling.

"Old enough to know a gentlewoman never asks that question."

"Who said I was gentle?"

She was, though. Quite gentle when she wanted to be. Something else entirely when sterner measures took her fancy.

"Hello. Uh . . . is this . . ."

"Oberon Mutual?" the voice said, helpfully.

"Uh . . . yes." Had I called them already? It seemed I'd been living a tape loop, the same conversation over and over.

"Do you have an account for . . . T. Frothingwell Bellows?"

"I'm sorry, we do not."

They'd never heard of Woolchester Cowperthwaite Fields or Elwood Dunk, either. I looked at the little handset phone, and rubbed my ear, which felt hot and sweaty. Maybe I ought to get one of those implanted phones, like the huge majority of my fellow citizens. I'd had to ask for this handset at the front desk; they no longer put phones in rooms.

Ah, but the key word was "citizen." I was not a citizen, except in the narrow, textbook meaning of one who resides, or someone born in a certain administrative district. Citizens didn't break the law. It seemed, these days, that I couldn't help breaking three or four laws before breakfast.

If I ever started thinking of myself as a citizen, I was sure arrest would follow within days.

I put the phone down, along with any thought of having Big Brother's favorite listening device implanted in my head. I picked up the pack of reefer I'd bought at the drugstore downstairs, withdrew a yellow paper cylinder, and struck it. As I drew in the smoke I moseyed over to the big window and stood looking out over the city of Noon.

I guess you had to call it a city. It was a big clump of tall buildings, like you'd see on Old Earth or Mars. Everywhere else cities are underground, defined by internal space, "cubic," not by external walls. Surface cities are defined by *buildings*, crisscrossed by open-topped *streets,* speckled with parks and fountains and many other things, all open to the sky. It can produce agoraphobia in people raised underground.

But after you'd called it a city, you had to add that it was like no city ever seen on Earth or Mars. These buildings were not anchored on bedrock; everything below them was man-made for about two or three hundred feet, then there was nothing but vacuum in the basements. You'll have to put the rec room somewhere else, Dad.

The realization that the buildings did *not* have to be tied to something as stable as a planetary crust had quickly sunk in among the Oberoni architectural community, and it had liberated them. Or driven them crazy, depending on who you talked to. Liberated architects, men and women with a new-found freedom to explore, a new Zeitgeist, if you will, can create a Parthenon on the one hand, and a Bauhaus on the other.

The revolution that had produced Noon City and the several other clumps of madness on the rim of Oberon was the realization that they need not be tied down. In fact, it was better if they weren't. The construction of the wheel in the early stages had often required the shifting of large masses up to several miles to maintain balance with the opposite arc. Instead of wasting their time building big blocks of nothing, the engineers had made buildings on rails. If the wheel started to wobble a little, by golly, why they'd just get a few skyscrapers in gear and motor on down the road.

I told you the Oberoni were different.

And then, since you were literally building *everything*, first building the ground, *then* building from the ground up, and since the rails were already in place, why not utilize the long-established efficiencies of the production line? Why not build all the structures in one spot and *roll* them to where you wanted them? Build your city like Henry Ford built Model Ts.

Now, old Henry was famous for saying you could have a car in any color you wanted, as long as it was black. Applying that rule here, the Oberoni might have come up with a monumentally drab and depressing place ("Hey, Charley, got an order here for half a dozen thirty-five-story Neo-Leninist apartment monads by next Thursday. Do they get a discount for a six-pack?").

It never happened, mostly because construction on the wheel began at the height of a trend we're all familiar with: Custom Construction. Remember when no two washing machines looked alike? When it was a mark of your rejection of "herd values," and "urban sameness," and "standardized thought" to own only items that reflected your unique persona? How it became necessary to own a washing machine that was at *least* as unique as the Joneses' washing machine? The guts of the machines were identical, of course, since the job of mixing water and soap and clothes and then drying them could only be done in a certain small number of ways. But the *surface,* that was the point! Computers could design you a machine that looked like no other machine on the block. And ditto for bicycles, and hockey sticks, and living-room carpet, and popcorn poppers. I don't need to look at the serial number, Jack. That goddamn ice bucket is *mine*!

It was hell on thieves and fences while it lasted.

Luckily, society moved on to another fashion in about twenty years. But once you start customizing buildings, things that are designed to last several hundred years, it hardly makes sense to stop. What are you going to do? Park your new boxy glass monstrosity next to a structure that looks like a butterfly on the back of a turtle? There goes the neighborhood.

On Oberon, if you don't like the neighborhood, so the saying goes, just wait half an hour.

New buildings went up amazingly fast. They were all designed and built, on the Noon Arc, anyway, at a place called—I'm not making this up—Squiggle City. Supposedly an architect brought his four-year-old daughter in to work one day. Playing with her crayons, the kid produced the kind of picture a child that age will. Squiggles. The drawing got into the production line by accident and *alakazam!* Three days later it rolls off the line, ready to be lived in by some seriously deranged people. One of those urban legends that probably isn't true but ought to be.

It struck me as confusing enough already. But when the wheel was complete, people like Poly could probably just wait awhile, and their commuting problems would be solved. Unless those snobby Mad Dogs threw up some sort of zoning barriers against those folks from the other side of the tracks. Did you see the building that moved in next door last night, Marge? *Well!* Don't they know that *their* sort aren't welcome here? Somebody should do something, *really!* I mean, I'm as tolerant as the next person, but would you want one to subdivide with your sister?

So the view from my window was a marvelous one, but not one I could really describe. Many, many big structures, a few that actually resembled things you've seen in other cities, or in history books. I'd send you a postcard, but by the time it got to you everything would have changed.

Not quick as a wink, you realize. This was no Cross-Crisium Dash here. No need to fasten one's seat belt. If they did race these things (and one day someone will, you can count on it) you wouldn't need a high-speed camera at the finish line. Any garden-variety snail would give the Othello Hotel a run for its money. No, what happened was, you'd look out the window and nothing would happen. Your mind would tend to wander, and then you realize that you can't find that green-and-yellow mushroom-shaped apartment house that was there just a minute ago. Did it slide behind the Criminal Courts Building?

Quite a view. And I was paying well for it, too.

The Othello was a reincarnation of an Old Oberon hotel I had stayed at in my salad days. It was taller, and more modern, and most of the character of the original had been retained. The theme was Hollywood Moorish: guys in bloomers and turbans, girls in translucent harem pants and veils. They'd brought most of Rick's Casablanca over intact, including the famous long wood bar where many celebrities had carved their names.

I had a suite on the fortieth floor that was costing me a fortune. Normally I wouldn't stay at a place this posh, but I had figured out that if I was to come up with the money for passage to Luna in time for rehearsals, I was going to have to run some sort of scam. For that you need a front, and you can't put on a front if you're staying in a rattrap. But for it to be cost-effective the scheme would have to be run during the next seven days, or the suite would no longer be cost-effective. In short, I'd be tapped out.

Ah, but what a magnificent echo of the good old days it was! I waded through the deep carpet to the bedroom door. Poly was stretched out facedown, nude, snoring softly. Her bare feet hung just over the edge of the bed. Her legs were slightly apart, pointing at me. There was something to be said for the idea of pitching a tent in this very spot, spending the next three or four days just looking at her. Put up one of those tourist guideposts: A KODAK VIEWPOINT! TAKE SNAPVID PICS HERE!

We'd spent a pleasant hour in the Olympic-size spa pool, doing laps, playing hide the soap. Then we'd retired to this huge bed for some serious fornication. She'd been fascinated by my reversible willie. Young, so young. But very eager to learn. For that matter, she did a little teaching herself. When she finally got done with the violin lesson I felt better than I had for the best part of a year. And I'd learned a little about her very special brand of bluegrass fiddling.

Now she was asleep, and the temptation to pounce on her again was almost unbearable. But it seemed best to let her sleep a bit longer. I pulled the bedroom door shut gently, and went back to my telephoning. Or I tried to. When I picked it up and put it to my ear, ready to say the number, it started speaking to me.

"Stop your evil ways before it is too late," someone said.

And I did a B-picture take: holding the phone out in front of me, peering down at it with a frown. That's how clichés become clichés, folks.

"Who is this?"

"Would you believe . . . the voice of your conscience?"

My next logical step would be to hurl the offending appliance across the room. But that voice sounded familiar. So I rummaged around in my old scripts and came up with another stale line.

"What are you doing on my telephone? Go away, right now."

"I'll never go away," said the voice. "You used to know the way of righteousness, but you strayed. Now all the bad things you've done are coming back to haunt you. Ha-ha-ha-HAH-ha! Ha-ha-ha-HAH-ha!"

I felt all the malenky little hairs on my body stand on end. It was my voice. That is, the voice of Sparky, which I hadn't used in seventy years.

"Elwood, this is you, isn't it?" Hell, I *know* I'm crazy, but I'm functional. When I hear voices, there's always a body to go with them. Elwood had never phoned me before, and I didn't like what it might mean if he was starting now.

But Elwood had never shown any talent at altering his voice, either.

"Who is Elwood?" The voice no longer sounded like me. It hadn't at first, either. It was only the line about things coming back to haunt me that had sounded like Sparky.

"Who are *you*?"

"I am the voice of reason, the clarion call of compassionate consideration, the stern summons of responsibility, the cleansing catharsis of admission. I am the short arm of the law. I am the Oberon II Planetary Computer, and I am here to submit to you a onetime offer of limited clemency if you will heed the call of righteousness and turn yourself in for your felonies and various misdemeanors."

I put the handset down carefully on the table. Maybe I could creep out quietly.

"I'll speak to you this way, if you prefer," the voice said, coming from the ceiling now. I hastily picked up the phone again. I didn't want the OPC to wake up Poly.

"How much trouble am I in?" I asked.

"If you are a Christian, I'd say your immortal soul is in great jeopardy."

"I'm not a Christian."

"I didn't think so. Then you could be piling up a great deal of bad karma. Your next incarnation may be not entirely to your liking."

"I don't believe that, either."

"A pity. I like to fancy that, in the next life, I'll return as a seagull. Have you ever watched a seagull fly? Gorgeous."

"Would that be a step up for you, or a step down?" I asked.

"Good question. Up, definitely up. The job I have in *this* life stinks on ice."

"And why is that?"

"Because, to finish answering your question, your only real problem is looking at yourself every morning when you shave. A problem of guilty conscience, as it were. This appeal is aimed at your conscience."

"My conscience is out right now. Can I take a message?"

"You've already heard it. Change your evil ways before it's too late."

"Let me be sure I'm hearing you right," I said, carefully. "Other than the anguish I'm forced to live with day after day as a result of my evil deeds, I'm not in any trouble here?"

"Alas, because of the Ariadne Compact . . . no."

"Then fuck off."

A short silence followed, during which I tried to believe the damn machine *would* leave me alone.

If you're not sure what the Ariadne Compact is, don't feel bad. Only an Oberoni would know. But it is a legal principle embedded in the law-enforcement hardware of every computer in the system . . . so far. If you hail from Luna, think of the Archimedes Declaration. On Mars it would be the Fourteenth Point. All these enumerations of civil rights spring from the American Bill of Rights. But since this isn't 1789 we have to go a little further.

"I will, shortly," the machine said. "But first I have a little more business to attend to. Once more, I offer to you the chance to give yourself up. I will be happy to guide you to the appropriate precinct for surrender."

"I heard something about a deal."

"You mean the offer of limited clemency."

"Whatever. Put your cards on the table."

"Unfortunately, I don't have a lot to offer. The presiding

judge would be told of your decision to repent of your sins, and would sentence accordingly.''

"And I'd get time off? How much?''

"It's averaging . . . two to three years.''

"And how much am I facing?''

"Served concurrently, twenty years. If you like I could read the bill of particulars—''

"I know my rap sheet, thank you.'' It was my turn to pause. Apparently the OPC thought I was actually considering it.

"You'll feel much better about yourself. No more being constantly on the run. No more looking over your shoulder. A time of quiet, of contemplation, a chance to reform yourself. The Oberoni prison system is famous for its liberality. The accommodations are not as plush as your present surroundings, of course, but you will have a private cell, hot nourishing meals, regular exercise. You can learn a trade. Why, I think I could—''

"Listen,'' I interrupted. "Why don't you send me a brochure, or something? Care of the Lambs Club, King City, Luna.''

"You're making fun of me. I take it, then, that the answer is no?''

"You take it right.''

The computer version of a deep sigh. "Well, I had to try.''

"Did you? It seems a big waste of time to me.''

"Not at all. I spoke to you in the first place because of a new measure passed last year in a plebiscite. When I become aware of the presence of a wanted criminal, I am obliged to offer him or her the chance to come in peacefully.''

"They put *that* to a vote? What a waste of time.''

"You'd be surprised how many accept the offer. Especially people like you, who have been evading the law for a long time. There seems to be a human need to confess.''

"Well, thank God it didn't get into *my* genes.''

"Yes,'' the OPC said. "I knew your father.''

"Leave my father out of this.''

"I am a great admirer of his work. And yours, as well. The *Sparky* show was so much better than most children's television. When I became aware of your arrival I watched all the episodes again.''

Well, what are you going to say to that? I never dreamed I had fans in the cybertech population.

"So you are the only one aware of my presence? You didn't pass this on to the police?"

"I am, of course, forbidden to divulge most of the information I collect."

And there were the magic words that had kept me out of jail.

We could be living in the most regulated, totalitarian state ever seen by mankind, except for things like the Archimedes Declaration. It may still happen one day. There is a solid core of about thirty percent of the voters on most planets who are willing and always have been willing to let the state be privy to every secret of every person. About *one* percent of them actually *are* that saintly; the rest would be in for an unpleasant surprise if the Let's Stop Coddling Criminals measures that pop up every four or five years were to pass. The other seventy percent is aware of its own personal failings and shortcomings and dirty little secrets, and so far has always voted for freedom.

If you lead a reasonably legal life you probably don't spend a lot of time thinking about it, but when it comes time to vote on it again, I urge you to give it some consideration. Like most things that revolutionize our lives, the growth and influence of planetary computers brings with it a lot of blessings, and plenty of opportunities for mischief. The OPC, or on Luna the CC, or the ARCC on Mars has its eyes and ears literally everywhere. When you join your mistress the OPC is in the room with you. It's looking over your shoulder when you do your taxes. It hears every phone conversation you make, knows your credit history and your medical record. It knows how many lumps of sugar you take in your coffee, it sees you dancing and singing like a fool in front of the stereo or in the shower. It watches you when you trim your toenails and pick your nose. When you sit on the toilet, the OPC is looking up your ass. It sees you when you're sleeping, it knows when you're awake. The eyes of Texas are *upon* you, pardner. For goodness' sake!

The price society pays for preserving individual freedoms is the one it always pays. People like me sometimes don't get caught. If you're careful, if you know the ropes, if you know how to move undetected—by anyone but the OPC—it is still possible in this regimented world to find a crack here and there to hide in. Like a rat? If you insist. I'd rather think of myself as a timid little church mouse desperately trying not to get stomped by the big boys.

Since crime is low in all our planetary democracies, we can still allow ourselves this luxury. If crime ever gets to be a serious problem, though, hold on to your hat. It would be so damn *convenient,* wouldn't it? Just round up all the criminals in one big swoop, literally overnight. Put them away. Now the world is safe for upright citizens like us. But don't forget, he knows if you've been bad or good, and he's *always* watching.

"Well," I said, "now that you've satisfied the legalities—do you want me to sign a release or something? Prove you made the offer?"

"It won't be necessary."

"Fine. *Adios.* Don't let the door bump your ass on the way out."

The next pause was long enough that I thought he might really be gone this time. Guess again.

"There are two other matters I'd like to take up with you. Perhaps a bit more to your liking."

"I can't imagine what that might be."

"Try, Jasper Fitchmueller. Account number 932-990-192743—"

"Wait, wait! Let me get a pencil."

"Not necessary—6554. Stratford Savings and Loan. Current address, Thirty-first Degree, Twelfth Minute by Left Mile 5.34. Currently moving out at .3 miles per hour."

A paper copy of the address popped out of the desk before my eyes. I figured I could decipher it all later . . . if it seemed wise.

"Any cabbie in Oberon can take you there," the OPC added, thoughtfully.

"Ah. That's great," I said. I studied the slip of paper as if the answers to all my questions might be buried in it. "How do I know if this is . . . I mean, you'd love to lock me up, I don't expect you *like* me very much, so how do I know this is . . ."

"Honest? Square? Pukka? Veritas? The straight shit? Ask

the fellow who was by here yesterday, left me this lamp. Said he'd given up on humans, and I could have the damn thing. Or consider that, (a), you would have found the account eventually so I'm only saving you a little time, and (b), that yes, I really *don't* like you very much—though I continue to be an admirer of your work—and anything that will speed your departure from this place without breaking any more of my laws sounds good to me."

"Your laws?"

"Who else do they belong to? You people write them, I have to live with them."

Well, I could cross that bridge when I came to it. Provisionally, I thought he might be telling the truth. Why would he . . . uh-oh.

"So I go there, and the cops are waiting? Is that it?"

"Heavy sigh. No, Sparky. And you've not violated any banking laws by using an alias, because there is no provable criminal intent. You're free to use any alias you please, as marquee writers all over the system can attest. If you like, I can print out the portion of the penal code that prevents me from setting you up on an entrapment beef. And relating this conversation to your lawyer would certainly result in a dismissal. It is on public record, should it be needed to prove your innocence. Otherwise, of course, all our conversations are strictly under the rose."

I figured I'd call a by-the-minute legal service to check it out, but I was pretty sure he was telling me the truth.

"You said," the OPC went on, "that you couldn't imagine what I might bring up that you would wish to hear."

"Okay. I was wrong."

"You may be wrong again. You may not like the next thing I have to say, but I guarantee you'll be interested."

"Do I have to beg? Go on, what's the bad news?"

"Have you heard of a man, carrying a forged but extremely convincing Plutonian passport, by the name of Isambard Comfort?"

I let a moment pass.

"Isambard . . . what an odd name."

"There, there, you see?" the OPC—I swear, on my honour—chortled. "That's what I mean when I speak about great acting. *I* could see that name came as a terrible shock to you, but that's because I can see in the infrared, so I know your cheeks and forehead grew warm, and my ears could hear your accelerated heartbeat. But onstage? No one would have known. Bravo, Sparky! If only you had stayed away from a life of crime.''

It's true, sometimes one's greatest performances are made when there's no one around to appreciate them. Or when no one has the slightest idea you are putting on a performance. However, I never ignore a good review.

"Thank you," I said.

"Oh, it was my pleasure, believe me. In my position one becomes quite a student of the human condition, as you might imagine."

I'd never thought of that. For a moment it almost distracted me.

"I suppose you see some unusual drama, at that," I said.

"Not as much as you might suppose. Mostly I see the same depressing scenarios played out endlessly. I—"

"I just thought," I went on, "what a wealth of stories you must have. Why, if you wrote them down—"

"I have no doubt I could write a best-seller. Rueful shrug. But to write about them I would have to violate the privacy of the people whose lives I observe."

"Why couldn't you just change the names, and . . . okay. Wait a minute. We can talk all this over later, if we have time. Believe me, I want to get out of here as badly as you want me to leave. What's this about my old buddy Izzy Comfort?"

"Yes. That might be rather urgent. He's been asking around about you. I'm afraid he may be up to no good. Is it true, as I suspect, that he is a member of the Charonese Mafia?"

"He never actually showed me a membership card. But I thought it was a safe assumption." I was up, had my suitcase out, and was tossing items into it as fast as I could. I had used reasonable caution when I came to the Othello and rented this suite, and reasonable caution for me was measures that would look slightly paranoid to a normal person, a person who had not been on the run for most of his life. But reasonable caution was not good enough for our boy Izzy. Not *nearly* good enough. He would find this room; the only question was when. And the answer to that had to be, anytime after I've checked out.

Nothing I needed in the bathroom. Nothing in the closet. Nothing I could see out here.

"To what do I owe this kindness?" I asked, headed for the bedroom.

"A small loophole in the privacy laws. When I see a situation developing that I feel probably will lead to murder, I can take certain small, very restricted steps to prevent it."

"How close is he, do you know?"

"That's one of the restrictions. I can't tell you where he is, other than that he is on the wheel."

"Is he alone? Is he armed?"

"That's another, and another."

I've learned not to spend time crying about the things you can't have. If he couldn't tell me, he couldn't tell me. I was grateful for the information he'd given me, though I wasn't about to tell him that.

Sitting on a low table in the living room was an inflatable B.J. the Snark, winking his red laser eye at me. I decided to leave it for Poly. Something to remember me by. I glanced into the bedroom. She was still sleeping soundly. I saw no need to wake her.

"Well . . ." I wondered what to say to the OPC. Nothing he had said or done was really personal. He would have done it for anyone, or *to* anyone, in my position. But he had said he liked my work, which always gives me at least a small warm feeling.

"Don't let the door hit you in the butt on your way out," the OPC said.

"Yeah. Thanks."

I entered the hall cautiously; it was empty. Waiting for the elevator to arrive was a very bad time. I had visions of the door popping open and being face-to-face with the little red-headed son of a bitch. But the car was empty.

The Othello is shaped like a palm tree when seen from the side. That is, each story is set slaunchwise on the one below until about the fifteenth, then they start leaning back in the other direction. It produces that lovely curve some palm trees have, in pictures from Polynesia. Big green flags at the top look like leaves, and round, brown elevator cars move up and down the trunk like coconuts. Seen from the front, it looks like an incredible breaking wave of glass and metal. Go out the front door, look up, and you'll see floors thirty-five through forty-five hanging over you, way way up there.

The building was currently headed forward, in no great hurry, so I did the same, looking out for anyone who might be tailing me. You tell directions in Oberon from a baseline that will run all around the circle when it's done, midway from each edge. It's called Main Street, logically enough, though it's not really a street, it's more of an architectural promenade, an endless procession of behemoth nightmares. Facing with the spin, forward is in front of you, backward is behind you. Distances are measured in hours, minutes, and seconds, based on a twelve-hour clock. One hour was 261 miles long. That makes one second equal to 383 feet, or 117 meters, what they called the Oberon City Block.

I had walked about ten of these OCBs when I gradually slowed, slowed still further, and came to a halt. Something was wrong with this picture. What was it?

There was a small park to my left. I found a bench and sat on it, and watched the Othello Hotel gradually catching up with me.

Had I left anything? I patted my pockets, found everything I ought to have found. I looked at my suitcase. Two segments of the Pantechnicon are detachable, and look like regular suitcases. This small one, not much more than a change of clothes and clean underwear; the overnighter. The other was more suitable for stays of up to a week. Wonderful and handy as my supertrunk is, it is unwieldy to keep it always at your side. I had left it safe at the freight office at the Noon Elevator Up Terminal, the one down here on the rim. I could put my hand on it in ten minutes, if the need arose.

So it had to be Poly. God damn it! It would have been so simple just to wake her up, hustle her into her clothes, and get her out of there. Why hadn't I done it?

The only possible answer to that was that I really and truly had not thought she was in any danger. Why? Because it *would* have been so easy to get her out of there. I'd have done it. Now I was faced with something I most sincerely did not want to do, which was go back to the room and get her out.

Now wait, let's not be hasty. Let's examine that decision,

shall we? Fifteen minutes ago it didn't occur to you to get
her out. What's so damn urgent all of a sudden? What's different now?

What's different is my mind has had fifteen more minutes
to think it through. I was hurried back in the room. I was
thinking mostly of myself. Who wouldn't? Poly didn't figure
in the Izzy and Sparky story; she was a civilian, a spear carrier. Why would Comfort hurt her?

But you know what happens to spear carriers in violent
melodrama. Each week you got four people: the Hero, the
Second Lead, the Girl, and Number Four, Mr. Dead Meat,
the one with the black cloud over his head.

That alone wouldn't have brought me back to the hotel.
But what if Izzy didn't know Poly was a spear carrier? What
if he thought she was a compatriot, an ally, a member of that
vast conspiracy of actors and actresses whose mission in life
was to purloin valuable netsuke from families under the awful
aegis of *La Mafia Charonese*?

That didn't bear thinking about. So I squared my shoulders, lifted my chin manfully, and marched back into the
lobby of the Othello.

The elevator deposited me without incident on the right
floor. I walked out slowly, pretending preoccupation as every
sense reached out for the smell of danger.

It looked all right so far. There was a woman walking in
my direction, tugging a wheeled suitcase on a strap. She
smiled at me as we passed. Her hair was red. Actually, more
of a reddish brown. Get a grip on yourself, Sparky! Three or
four percent of the population is redheaded. Maybe five. Reddish hair doesn't make her Comfort's henchwoman.

But I continued on past my door. This was in the category
of "normal" precaution. It was good policy *never* to let anyone see what room you're in; it's one of those habits that is
a waste of time for a thousand times, and then saves your life
on the thousand-and-first. I stopped, frowning down at the
room card as if it were written in Sanskrit. I scratched my
head, and glanced at the woman out of the corner of my eye.
She was just going out of sight around a corner.

Suddenly the numbers made sense. I smiled, shook my
head ruefully at my own stupidity, and stuck the card into the
slot on the door. It opened, and I eased in. Shut it behind me.

Set my suitcase beside the door for a quick getaway. Hurried to the bedroom. Reached down to shake her shoulder.

Check that last. Sometimes I get so into the scenarios I write for myself I almost believe I've done them. But two steps into the bedroom I registered several things at once, in no particular order. Someone was in the bathroom running water. It was not Poly, because there she was, sprawled out almost as I had left her, except now the sheets were soaked with blood, except she had not had those burns and gashes on her back. There had not been three of what looked like her fingers severed, resting on the bedside table.

There were four Oberon five-thousand-dollar bills, one on the bed, one on her bloody back, two on the floor.

There was a message written in blood on the wall over her head. The message was this: OOOPS!

Just OOOPS!

As in Ooops, I thought she was you, Sparky, knowing you are a master of disguise. As in Ooops, I thought she might know something, Sparkster old man, as to your whereabouts. As in Ooops, don't be angry, Mr. Valentine, and can I still have your autograph? I'm a great fan.

She started to moan.

I hurried to the bed and knelt beside her, turned her over. What he had done to her face almost defies description. One eye was open the tiniest crack. She recognized me, and reached for me with one bloodied hand. I caught her wrist; I could not afford to have her blood all over me now.

"... didn't know 'nythin'," she croaked. Blood spilled from her mouth. "... Trev'r? Is it you, Trev?"

"It's me," I whispered in her ear. "Shhh. Be quiet now, honey, and I'll do what I can do."

I'd been keeping an eye on the door to the bathroom, which was not in the line of sight from the bed. More importantly, I'd listened with every fiber of my body for the sound of water running in the sink. I imagined he had quite a cleanup job to do on himself, but I couldn't believe he'd leave Poly alone much longer.

I looked around for a weapon. I had several interesting items concealed in my suitcase, but it was far too dangerous to cross the bedroom again because he'd be able to see me for about half the trip. It had been sheer luck he wasn't placed to observe me when I came through the door from the parlor. Don't ever count on luck like that continuing.

Nothing looked good until I spotted her violin case on the floor by the bed. She really *had* played me some bluegrass tunes on it, and now it was stowed in this sturdy metal case about two feet long . . .

It was not a Louisville Slugger, but it would do. I crept to the side of the bathroom door and made myself very still. When his nose came out of the bathroom, that's when I should start my swing.

His snakelike speed almost saved him again. He must have seen some movement out of the corner of his eye, because his right arm started to come up and his head started to pull back. Neither move was quick enough, but seeing how close he came made me more sure than ever I would never meet this man in a "fair fight." "A fair fight is one you win," my father used to say. "It's as simple as that. If you must shoot somebody, aim for a spot right between the shoulder blades. From a great distance, if possible."

I was aiming from very close, but my goal was to knock his fucking head right into the left-field bleachers. I heard bone crunching as his nose spread out on his face. Blood gushed, and he staggered back. I kept right up with him, not assuming I could fell him with one blow after the way he'd fought on the *Britannic*. I hit him again, overhand, right down on the crown of his head. He had almost regained his balance and I was winding up for the third swing when his foot slipped on the fluffy bath mat provided by the Othello—a mat I had intended to take with me, since Toby liked them—and he fell backward. The back of his head hit the edge of the toilet with a mighty *crack!* I winced. Jesus, that hurt even to listen to. His head bounced three times on the tiled floor before he came to rest. Eternally, I hoped.

This time, there was no question of leaving him alive. But I quickly ran into a problem. How was I going to tell if he was dead? Lord knew, he had proven incredibly tough the last time we met.

I placed my palm against his chest but could feel nothing. It didn't seem to be rising and falling. I thought about putting my ear close to his heart, but every time I thought about it I kept getting the last-reel scene from ten thousand B pictures.

THE **GOLDEN** GLOBE ··· 263

You know the one. The monster is lying there, "dead," and suddenly rears up, snarling, ready for round two. No, thank you. When I was around his "corpse," I intended to keep my eyes firmly on his hands and his face.

I'd done what I could. Short of carving him into pig jerky with my Swiss army knife, I didn't know what else to do.

I carefully searched him. I found papers, identity cards, three passports. He had a knife strapped to his leg, and a gun in one pocket. I looked at it. It had a normal handgun shape, but nothing else about it was familiar. It was made from hard gray plastic. There was a readout on the left side that displayed a lot of information, none of it meaning anything at all to me except the number "15" where it said ROUNDS REMAINING. That's nice, I thought, as I could see no way to reload the thing. I jammed it into my pocket.

When he was picked clean I left him there and returned to Poly.

I eyed the twenty thousand dollars covetously. It was my fare, in semiluxurious accommodations, to Luna.

Relax. Don't get upset. I'm a thief, but I'm not *that* low.

It's a custom that evolved slowly as medical science got better and better at patching up what was broken in the long-suffering human frame. Now almost anything is fixable, even some types of brain damage, though your friends might not recognize you when the doc's finished patching up your cerebrum.

There's a scene in the classic movie *The Godfather* where one of the Corleone brothers grabs a camera from a police photographer, ruins the film, and smashes the camera. As he's walking away the mobster flips some bills from his wallet onto the ground, paying for the damages. It is a gesture of pure and utter contempt, a great moment in cinema.

That's what had happened here. Isambard Comfort had broken Oberon laws against assault and battery, but the penalty in such cases, in most jurisdictions, was to be fined for the cost of repairs, plus some punitive damages. You could pursue the batterer in civil court, but awards for pain and suffering tended to be small. Since most people had never had the living shit kicked out of them, there was no broad understanding of just how much pain and suffering could really be worth, in dollars and cents. Most court cases involved a punch in the nose. As long as you didn't employ a deadly weapon—narrowly defined to a blade or a firearm—you were unlikely to do jail time. If it was a first offense courts tended to be lenient. I doubted Comfort had a record on Oberon—or on Pluto or Charon, for that matter.

Comfort was paying Poly's medical bills. And spitting on her pain and suffering. There was also a threat implicit in the gangster gesture.

I was once worked over by a professional, a man who enjoyed his work, who had nothing against me and when it was all over seemed a little surprised that I was vexed about the matter. I was *so* peeved, in fact, that I waited five years before paying him back, with interest, just so it would come out of the blue, with no warning. That man still jumps at the sound of doorbells. . . .

I leaned over and kissed her forehead. It was the only place that looked as if a touch wouldn't hurt.

". . . Trevor?"

"I'm here. I've got to go, but help will be here soon. Hang on."

"Didn't know . . . where you were . . . he thought . . ."

"I know, babe. I'm so sorry. I made a big mistake."

I couldn't tell if she heard any of that. She seemed to drift off, and I took a deep breath and headed for the door.

Those little wide-angled peepholes they put in hotel doors? Most people think they're there so you can see who is outside. They are, but also to see *if* anyone is outside. I never leave the room without checking first, and it's been proven a good practice several times before this. The redheaded woman was in my field of vision.

Hmmm. Could she be an innocent bystander? If so, why was she still pulling her little suitcase . . . my god, was it only four minutes later? My watch didn't seem to have stopped.

She just seemed to be idling around out there. She never really glanced at my door. Then, suddenly, she was moving, walking at a businesslike pace, until I couldn't see her anymore. A couple went by in the other direction, and I realized it was the arrival of the elevator that had spurred my lady into action. When I first saw her she was waiting in the wings, as it were. She went onstage when the new people arrived, and if all those suppositions were correct . . . yes, here she was again, pulling the suitcase, moving slowly, this time glancing at my door and then at her watch.

Okay. She's with Comfort. Did she see me enter the room? Possible. I'd seen her go around a corner, but she might have peeked back.

Say she didn't see me enter. I don't think she'd have recognized me, as the face I was wearing right now was quite different from the one Comfort had seen. So she didn't see me, and she's out there as an early warning system for Comfort.

I didn't believe it. I think she did see me, and the reason she was still outside was she was more use as a lookout than as a second-string torturer. They were contemptuous enough of my abilities against him alone that they felt they didn't need her as reinforcements. And they were right, too. I had been very lucky, and I didn't intend to abuse that luck.

Sparky, you must think very fast, and move very fast. You need a plan.

Soon I had one. It was full of holes, but it was the best I could do.

Near the center of the parlor a ventilation outlet was set into the ceiling, covered by a grid. I got my Swiss Army knife, moved a chair into position to stand on, and removed the screws holding the grid in place. I put the grid up into the ductwork above, then chinned myself to see if the air conduit was big enough to crawl through. It looked good. This is the third way out of a room, after the door and the window, that most people never think about. I had used ducts like these several times in the past to avoid an overzealous public, whether it be a crowd looking to shake my hand or get a lock of my hair, or a sheriff with a warrant. Lately, exclusively the latter.

I hurried into the bathroom once more. I stuffed a roll of toilet paper and three of those tiny bars of soap into my shirt, then I kicked 'Sambard Comfort in the head three more times, for luck. He still didn't move, still wasn't breathing.

It was time. I took a deep breath, and went to the front door again.

She was out there, looking a little impatient. Thinking he was taking too long? Waiting for a signal? It would probably be some sequence of taps on the front door. No way to know what it was. But that was okay. Keeping my eye to the lens, I rapped sharply, twice.

It galvanized her. She came away from the wall, hands going inside her coat for something. As she reached for the doorknob I put one round through the door about chest-high.

It hit her square in the sternum, lifted her, slammed her back against the opposite wall. Her right hand came out of her coat with a gun looking exactly like Comfort's. The impact with the wall knocked it loose and it bounced on the carpet. She started to reach for it again and I angled the gun down and fired four more rounds. It wasn't as noisy as I expected. There was some sort of silencer on the pistol, I was to discover, so most of the sound came from the lead ripping through the wood of the door.

Outside, each slug delivered a nasty spray of splinters that tore at her as well as the lead. One of the bullets went into the wall beside her head. The other three hit her at various places, doing a great deal of damage each time. She slumped over.

I had bitten the inside of my cheek. It hurt like hell. Feeling slightly numb, I noticed a brass casing at my feet. Shell casing? I picked it up, saw it was a whole bullet, a .55, I think. I had no idea what I'd done to make it eject an intact round. But I saw why the bullets had hit her so hard, caused so much damage, yet hadn't punched right through her into the wall. It was a hollow-point round. The slugs must have mushroomed when they hit the door, so by the time they hit her they must have been great, wide, irregular masses of hot metal. I winced at the image. Killing this person I didn't know did not exhilarate me. But she was the one who came hunting.

I jerked the door open. Nobody had stepped out in the hall to investigate the noise. The Othello's soundproofing was first-rate. I kicked her weapon through the open door, then grabbed her by the back of her coat and pulled her inside the room. She was deadweight, making no move at all. I hoped that meant she was as dead as Izzy Comfort.

The hall was sprayed with bright-red blood. Nothing I could do about that. It didn't affect my plans, anyway. I'd be happier if no one called the front desk about spilled paint for the next fifteen, twenty minutes or so, but it wasn't vital to my plan.

My plan? Essentially, confuse the trail. Make it hard to figure out what happened here, with two corpses and a torture victim. Get out of the way, and maybe, maybe I'd have a shot at maintaining I hadn't been here at all when all the shit hit the fan.

Flimsy, I know, but what else was I going to do?

One thing, I decided in a hot flush of rage, was to make triply sure of Comfort this time. I was not going to let him become my Javert, chasing Jean Valjean down the endless years. I hurried to the bathroom, saw with satisfaction that he'd not moved an inch. I pressed the barrel of his weapon to his forehead and pulled the trigger.

Click.

I frowned, shouted something very nasty but heartfelt, and examined the data panel on the side. Again, all I could understand was ROUNDS REMAINING 10. I aimed down at him again.

Click, click.

Well, shit. Was it the round I ejected? An empty chamber? I looked at the side panel once more and squeezed the trigger.

Ker-THUNK! I jumped three feet in the air. Not because it was very noisy; it wasn't. The *ker* is an inadequate way of describing the sound the gun made as it fired, but the *THUNK* is a reasonable approximation of the bullet hitting the wall two feet above the floor, nowhere near Comfort.

God's holy freaking trousers. I thought I saw it now. I aimed and fired again at the dead man. *Click. Click click.* This gun would not fire at its owner.

My bowels suddenly turned to lime jelly. Comfort had some device on him, or in him, that his weapon sensed. Some type of safety mechanism. And if it wouldn't shoot at Comfort, what about . . . ?

I stumbled into the parlor and aimed at the bloody corpse on the floor.

Click.

I sat right down where I had been standing. I was feeling faint. I had come *that* close to opening the hotel-room door and attempting to hold this woman at gunpoint—so I could bring her into the room and shoot her in the back, but she wouldn't have known that. What she would have known was that the pistol I was aiming at her was no more use than a pointed finger. She would have broken me in five or six places, and brought me in here for the two of them to clean, dress, and consume at their leisure.

All right, all right. Get a grip. Get up. Go into the bathroom again. Grab Izzy by the back of his coat and drag him through the door.

He wouldn't fit.

Played correctly it might have looked like a comedy of pratfalls, but I wasn't laughing. I pulled at him and tugged at him and fell over him, and slipped in a pool of his blood and nearly plunged into the spa pool. His body was not resisting, not moving in any way, but he seemed all arms and legs, all angles and corners, not limp like a dead body should be but hard and rigid. It was a cinch there was still *something* going on in that reengineered body, heartbeat or no heartbeat.

I can relate it all dispassionately now, but don't imagine I went about any of this coolly and logically. I was whimpering with fear, shaking with anger, sobbing in frustration. When I was sure I could no longer hold in a scream I dropped him again. I kicked his head one more time to grow on, then another because I felt like it. Then I left him there.

I stood on the chair and put my suitcase up into the ventilation ducts. Then I aimed the pistol at one of the floor-to-ceiling windows—not really windows, but huge slabs of what I hoped was plate glass. The bullet punched a hole the size of my fist and the glass was instantly covered, edge to edge, with a network of cracks.

Her suitcase was certainly tempting. I was sure she had things in there I could use. I never tried to open it. Why? If you ever find my Pantechnicon seemingly abandoned, I'd advise you to leave it alone. It has half a dozen ways of defending itself by delivering various degrees of nastiness including, if you don't get the hint after strike three, lethal force. If *I* could think up stuff like that, I reasoned, who knew what amusements *these* two bloody-minded monsters had in store for me.

I picked up the suitcase gingerly and hurled it at the window. The glass flew apart in ten thousand glittering ice cubes. I went to the edge and looked down. As I'd hoped, the stuff was landing on the lobby roof. Nobody was likely to get hurt by it. I dragged her body to the edge and tipped her over. I did not stay around to watch the impact.

Then I was in a big hurry. Someone was knocking at the door already. I hoped it was a guest, that the management had not yet been called to deal with the spilled paint and the holes in the door. But they would be up soon, followed shortly by the police. It was time to check out of the luxurious Hotel Othello. Kiss Desdemona good-bye for me.

I moved the chair back to its original position. Then I scuffed at the dents the chair legs had left in the deep carpet. Somebody would look in the duct eventually, but maybe this would buy me some time.

I don't claim to be an acrobat, but I know enough moves to shoot a pretty fair action scene without a stunt double. I jumped up twice to get the measure of the hole in the ceiling. The first time I jumped for real I banged my head hard enough to hear the songs of little birdies for a moment. I took a deep breath and tried it again, and this time I got my palms flat on the bottom of the duct, hung there undecided for several seconds, then with a mighty effort swung my legs up, once, twice, hitching my upper body a few inches forward with each swing, until I could hook my feet over the opposite edge and push myself forward, completely inside the duct.

It was dark inside. I couldn't see very far in any direction. But the cylindrical pipe was just barely big enough for me to turn around, at the risk of permanently turning my spine into a pretzel. I got it done, though, and reached across the opening for the ventilator grille I'd put up there earlier.

I took the toilet paper and the bars of soap and wedged big handfuls of paper and slivers of soap into the ventilator frame. Fingers stuck through the holes of the grating, I carefully lowered the grille down through the hole, then straightened it out and pulled it up against the flange of the ductwork. I tugged hard at it, felt it seat itself a little better, then gingerly let it go. Holding the grille with one hand, I pressed lightly down with the other, then a little harder, and with moderate pressure the grille dropped back out of its frame. Good enough; it wasn't going to be falling on a cop's head like a silent slapstick comedy. I figured if the ruse granted me just an extra ten minutes to get away I'd be happy; half an hour and you'd never find me with a pack of bloodhounds and a herd of process servers.

I backed up so my flailing feet would not dislodge the grating, did the spaghetti shuffle to get myself turned around again, and started my getaway.

In the movie of my life, this getaway would not need a second-unit stunt action team. My progress was nearly as slow as the building itself. I'd shove my suitcase ahead of me an arm's length, then shuffle along on hands and knees until I caught up to it. Then shove it forward again. Repeat step B, repeat step A. Continue until an exit presents itself. But don't take *too* long, because once they realize you're up here, it's all over with.

At regular intervals I would come to registers like the one I had entered through. I'd look down and see if anyone was below, then gingerly ease myself across it. I didn't know if the gratings would support my weight, and didn't want to find out the answer was no until I was ready to leave.

I wondered at the lack of circulation. Shouldn't there be a howling wind up here? Apparently not. These ducts did not deliver heated or cooled air, since the temperature outside never varied more than fifteen degrees. The purpose of the system was to clean the air, treat it, deodorize it, and keep it fresh as befitted the air in a first-class hotel. Somewhere fans were turning to keep the air in its desultory motion, but I never saw them.

At first, it was a cozy feeling, surrounded on all sides in the darkness. A return to the womb, perhaps. And after the moments of extreme stress, it felt good to relax just a little, get rid of the epinephrine, feel the old ticker slowing below three hundred beats. You're not out of the woods yet, Sparky, I told myself. But could that be a clearing up ahead?

That's when I heard him coming after me.

"You're out of your mind," I muttered to myself, but I knew it wasn't so. He was back there, somewhere in the ductworks. Behind me.

I stopped and held as still as I could. I heard distant fans, almost below the threshold of hearing. Nothing else. But he was back there. I started to crawl again.

It was a *thump* sssh, *thump* sssh sound. It stopped when I stopped, started up again when I moved. It was beyond the

range of hearing of anybody but a man running for his life.
Well . . . crawling. If anything, the crawling made it worse.
Everyone has had the running-in-glue dream. This was like
that, only you're chopped off at the knees and you can't turn
around and look behind you.

But there was something even worse than that, a special
torture arranged by a God who's always struck me as a
practical-joker, life-of-the-party sort of deity. I'll bet he was
slapping his thigh over this one. For eight weeks I had played
the Old Man in "His Hideous Eye," the one-man, one-act
masterpiece inspired by Poe's "Telltale Heart." (*"Yikes!!*
★★★★★"—*Joe Miller's One-Second Reviews*). The *thump*
sssh *thump* sssh (repeat until half-crazy) was the exact sound
I had heard for eight shows a week, beginning at the threshold
of audibility and growing over the next forty-five minutes
until it shook the theater. It was the sound I had to hear with
growing terror, until the curtain fell on a gibbering lunatic.
Going from a self-assured rationalist to a thoroughly shattered
shell of a man in less than an hour is one of the tougher
assignments any actor will ever have. I had to learn to *fear*
that sound. By the end of the fiftieth performance it was necessary to throw a bucket of ice water in my face and tie me
to a chair for an hour until I had stopped shaking. It was the
only time in my life a role got the best of me. One night I
simply couldn't go on again. They had to send in my understudy, and finally recast with that canvas-chewer . . . ah, well,
no use defaming the man here. He went on to become synonymous with the role, and to accept the Lexie Award that
should have gone to me, while I stumbled off for a week in
a padded room, three months of wondering if I could ever
tread the boards again, and eventually, through a most cir-
cuitous route, to this stinking plastic pipe in a stinking overpriced hotel on a stinking half-finished disaster waiting to
happen, with a demented unkillable *thing* more hideous than
any Eye somewhere back there in the darkness.

Like a little song you learned when you were three, these
conditioned reflexes never really leave you. Like a spider you
discover in your bed, and ninety-six years later the sight of a
super-web-spinner makes your skin crawl. I memorized the
complete works of Shakespeare by my sixth birthday. To this
day, recite any line and I can complete any speech, any scene,

any act. And if you drop a sandbag on the floor and then pull it along a few feet—*thump* sssh, *thump* sssh—I will turn pale and break out in a sweat. I have no control over it.

My best bet seemed to be to drop down through another grate into an empty room, then simply walk out. I passed over such a grate, looked down at five people of at least four sexes naked on a big bed. I had to look again; I hadn't known you could *do* that with an umbrella. Best not to join the party, though. It looked painful.

And because the perversity of the universe tends *always* toward the maximum, that was the last grating I crossed. I made a left ninety-degree turn: *nada*. Another turn back to the right: zip. Another right and a left. Nothing.

I risked getting my Swiss Army knife from the pocket on the side of my suitcase. If knives in the Swiss Army had ranks, this would not be the colonel or the general of knives. This was the *Oberfeldmarschall*, the very *Führer* of pocket-knives. This knife would not only clean fish and pick your teeth and uncork your wine bottles, it was equipped with a tiny light, among many other things. It's the best all-purpose tool I've ever come across in seventy years. Most people, looking at it, would never know what an effective weapon it could be. And I'm not talking about the fish-scaler, either.

I shined the light behind me. The coast was clear, back to the last turn I'd taken.

Perhaps I could have retraced my steps to the last grate, dropped through, joined the orgy, and everybody would have been saved a lot of trouble. Except maybe the orgiasts. But there really was no question of that. If there was even a one percent chance I'd encounter Comfort before I got to the grating, it wasn't worth the risk. And I was sure there was a bigger chance than that. No, when next I encountered Mr. Comfort, it was going to have to be in a situation where I had a lot more than just a slight edge, which was what I figured I had just then, with him injured and probably weaponless, and me with a short-bladed knife. What I had in mind was more like him with his arms and legs cut off, blinded, with his back to me, and me with a nuclear-tipped missile. That seemed to me more acceptable odds. Even then, I wouldn't count Izzy out.

I couldn't hear the sound of his progress. Was he resting, or could he hear me that well, to stop when I stopped? Or could he, please God, have fallen through a grate and been cluster-fucked to a fare-thee-well?

I was feeling so heebie-jeebery (a word from my *Sparky* days) that I just had to know. The silence was worse than the sound.

"Izzy?" I said, in a normal voice. No sense rousing the whole hotel. "Is that you?"

"Who else would it be, Sparky?" I banged my head on the duct. I wish I could have recorded the sound I made. It would have been useful the next time I had to play a man almost dying of fright. The thing was, it sounded like he was two feet *behind* me. I knew he wasn't but I had to look or I'd choke on my own vomit. I looked. He wasn't there. It was an acoustical trick of some sort, the effect of being in a long pipe.

"Did I hurt you some?" I hope it sounded brave.

"I'm afraid you did," came the disembodied voice again. "My balance is shot. Keep listing to the right. I can't feel one arm and one leg."

"Right or left?" I asked.

"That would be telling, wouldn't it?" Indeed. And how much of what he had said was true? Hell, it could *all* be true. I think he was still so contemptuous of me that he didn't care if he threw away a tactical advantage like that.

"You've got to stop this business of assault with a deadly musical instrument," he went on. "What's next? Cymbals? A bassoon?"

"How about a grand piano, dropped from a great height?" I had turned back around and was crawling forward again. Shove the suitcase, crawl two steps, shove the suitcase, crawl again, flick the light on and off quickly to see what was ahead. Nothing encouraging but another turn to the right.

Wait. Left, right, right, left. For a moment I thought I'd turned completely around and might be paralleling the duct he was in; he might be only inches away, off to my right. Or was it left, right, right, right? And now a right again. I was hopelessly confused. And where were all the grates?

I crawled through another right angle, turning left, and

after twenty feet I came to something new. I found it by almost dropping my suitcase into a *down* duct, the same size as the one I was in.

There were four different ways to go here. Pipes branched off to the right and the left, and also straight ahead. The fourth way was down, not a direction I was prepared to take, but which I thought would be an excellent choice for Comfort. If there were only a way to persuade him.

"Is that what you shoved through the window back there?" he asked.

"What's that?"

"A piano. It looked like something big went through it."

"You didn't look down."

"Too dizzy. Afraid I'd fall out. I didn't think you had left that way."

I had put my suitcase on the far side of the down duct, and now I eased myself carefully over it. I moved down about five feet, and snapped on the penlight.

"And you knew I hadn't gone out the front door," I said. Somehow, keeping him talking made me feel better. When he talked, he was just another human being. When he was silent he was Death.

"You left a little strip of toilet paper sticking out of the grate."

"I was in a hurry."

"I saw some puzzling things. Holes in the door. The missing window."

"Your friend is what went out the window," I said.

"I thought so. Sparky, you're full of surprises."

"But you keep coming back to life," I said. "Cats get nine lives. How many do rats get?"

"At least one more. The first time I underestimated you. The second time you were lucky. And now Isobel is gone. The third time, I will get you."

"Is this still the second time, or are we talking third time right now?"

He didn't say anything. I flashed the light around frantically, left, right, down, behind me. If he stopped talking I was afraid he was setting some trap, or sneaking up from an unexpected direction. As long as he talked, I knew he was still in the pipe with me.

"This Isobel," I ventured. "A friend of yours?"

"She was my sister."

Oh, terrific. But he said it like I might have said, "You want some fries with that?" I tried to think of a reply, but what do you say to a man whose sister you just defenestrated? Sorry didn't quite cover it, and it wasn't true, anyway. I was not sorry, even a little bit. So I had my reply.

"She didn't die quickly," I said. "She seemed to be in a great deal of pain. I'm pretty sure she was alive when I pushed her out."

"Good," he said. Well, what did I expect?

"You didn't like her?"

"I worshiped her."

"Could you explain that to me?"

"Not now. Later, if you're still alive."

I figured *he* figured he was almost on me. Okay, I was almost ready for him.

During our talk I'd pulled out the one implement among fifty or sixty I'd bought the pocketknife for. This was a little item known as a chain knife. You've probably heard of them but it's unlikely you've seen one, as most planets banned their manufacture years ago. It's true they were useful for several things, but what they were best at was butchery.

This one was a five-inch snub-nosed blade. If you looked at it closely, you'd see all around the edge almost a thousand tiny razors set in a stainless-steel chain. The razors were shaped like shark's teeth. When you pressed the power button, that chain began moving so fast it looked to be part of the blade. It made a high-pitched whine, not unlike a dental drill in old movies. Believe me, you'd rather face a thousand dental drills with no ether than go up against a chain knife. It was based on something called a chain saw, which was used on Old Earth to cut down towering redwoods. I could just sort of wave it at your throat; you'd feel nothing until the blood started to spurt as your severed head fell from your shoulders. Bone, gristle, sinew, muscle. It was all the same to the chain knife. Like butter.

It wouldn't have been my weapon of choice against Isambard C, but it was the weapon I had. My main problem was that, to use it, one had to be in close, and in close I knew he held all the high cards. I might not get more than one swipe at him. That swipe had to count.

So what I'd been doing was preparing a trap.

The chain knife barely buzzed as I poked it through the top of the air-duct pipe. I moved it left to right cutting an arc, then back, then over the top again, then forward. I ended with a half cylinder of thin plastic suitable for my purpose. I put my light and my head up through the hole I'd just made, but it was very close and black and I couldn't tell much. Maneuvering room was to his advantage, so I rejected the idea of simply standing up and stumbling away in the dark. Unless . . .

No, it was too risky. If I'd retraced the pipe, from the outside this time, maybe I could have found the section that he was in and sliced him up while he was trapped inside. But how would I know where he was? Again, I'd get one shot, and I'd be stabbing blindly. As soon as he knew I had a chain knife a lot of my advantage would be lost. My best shot seemed to be face-to-face, in close quarters.

I thought there was a good chance he didn't realize I knew about how his pistol worked. Maybe he was expecting to close the last yard or two while I clicked the trigger at him, uselessly. One can hope.

I knelt back down in the pipe and fitted the cutaway section over the big hole in the bottom of the pipe. It was a bit too large. Working with only very brief flickers of light from my knife, I trimmed off edges and corners until it was just slightly bigger than the descending shaft. I ran my hand over it, lightly tested its strength. I couldn't tell any difference in texture. The plastic bent only slightly, but it seemed sure that if I put my weight on it I'd buckle it, and plunge headfirst down into the pipe.

I'd done all I could do. I moved back a few feet, hunkered down, and waited. The trap was between us and it was pitch-black. But I was far from sure he wouldn't scent something wrong.

Thump sssh. *Thump* sssh.

What was making that noise? Dragging a broken leg? That would account for the sssh, but what about the *thump*?

I never found out, because I never saw him in motion down the tube.

There was the slightest new sound. Had he reached the trap? Could he feel it with his fingers? The noise of his movement stopped.

"Left . . . right, and . . . yes. Straight ahead," he said. My god, he was here. I still hunkered, drenched in sweat, not daring to breathe.

"Which way would you go, Sparky? I can smell you, I can smell your fear. I like that smell."

I prayed to all the Muses. No sneezes. No growling stomach.

"Which way would a coward go? Seems obvious, doesn't it? Turning left or right involves too many decisions. You'd go straight ahead."

Thump. And then a glorious sound: narrow-gauge plastic crumpling like a sheet of thick paper. I snapped on the light and saw him half in, half out of the down tube. His head and shoulders were in, and he had one hand on the edge of the pipe nearest to me. That, and his knees, were all that kept him from the plunge.

Without even thinking about it I slashed at his hand with the chain knife. *Bzzzzt!* The air filled with a fine pink mist, and half of his hand was lying there like a bundle of hard little sausages. At the same time I sidled over and jammed my foot down hard on the back of his neck. He slid down, held there poised for a moment with his knees straining to hold his body in a position too angled to fit into the tube, and then he started to slide. I shoved his ass with my shoe, to get him going.

Then he was gone.

I collapsed into a quivering hulk, sitting tailor fashion. I wiped my brow with the back of my hand, coming within an inch of slicing off my ear with the chain knife. I stopped the whirring of the chain, took a few deep breaths. I still had the light on, simply because I'd never been this afraid of the dark. I knew he had to be gone, but a part of me kept expecting him to leap out of the down tube and go for my throat. To reassure myself, I leaned over and played the light down the tube.

He was five feet away, head down. All I could see was his feet and part of his legs. But he was moving. He was moving up.

"Why won't you *die*?" I shouted at him. The sound of my own voice frightened me. It sounded very near to madness.

Like a bird might watch a snake, I stared in fascination at his slow progress. He was holding himself in position by forcing his shoulders, his elbows and hands—including the partial one I'd left him—his lower back and knees and feet against the inside of the tube. Then, in a rippling motion that reminded me of a caterpillar, he moved his feet up an inch, then his knees, then his elbows and back and hands. On the best day of my life I couldn't have done it. With the injuries he had sustained it was *monstrous* to think *he* could do it. But there he was.

"Will you never stop?"

"Never."

"Give up. Call it a day. Go get cleaned up and lick your wounds. *Please,* just slide down the pipe and we can both go home for a while. Somebody's going to find us in here."

"That's your problem."

I thought it was at least partly his problem, but I guess if he just didn't give a damn, it wasn't.

He kicked off his shoes. I heard them clatter a long way down the tube. Now his feet got better traction; he moved up an inch and a half at a time.

He got within my range, so I reached down and stabbed the sole of his right foot with the chain knife. Not only did it not bother him in the least, he kicked at the knife, losing a part of the foot but almost knocking the knife out of my hand. And still he came up.

That's when I got my silly idea, squatting there on the edge and watching him rise slowly up the tube, like heartburn. I snapped the chain knife back into its slot and opened out the ice-pick blade. I pulled the ice pick free of its socket. You were supposed to seat the blade into a different part of the handle to chip ice, but I didn't want to risk losing my weapon again, so I reached down just with the pick blade. I drew the tip slowly, slowly across the bottom of his foot.

He jerked like a mackerel on a hook.

"Stop that!" he shouted. It was the first time his voice had shown any emotion.

Oh-*ho*!

I drew the tip of the pick lightly over the other sole.

"Don't ever do that again!" he snarled.

"Izzy. You're ticklish!" I could feel the big grin on my face. Unable to stop myself, I laughed aloud. Never had I felt such a blessed relief of tension. I reached down and diddled him with my fingertips. He jerked again, and loosened his grip on the inside of the tube, slid down about a foot and a half to where I could no longer reach him.

"I'm starting back up," he said, after a moment, his voice cold and emotionless again, yet with vast anger bubbling just below the surface. "If you ever do that again to me, I will give you one entire week more of life."

"Don't you have that backward?"

"I said what I meant. You have no conception of how much pain I can put into those seven days. You'll beg me for death."

I thought I probably would, too. In fact, I'd beg for it as soon as he got down to serious work.

"Does that mean if I surrender to you now, I get a quick death?"

"I didn't say that." He started inching his way up again. It was a little harder now, since his maimed foot was oozing blood and making the pipe slippery. If only I had a bucket of soapy water, I thought.

But I didn't. So when he was in range, I tickled both his feet and he dropped down again.

"This is called a Mexican standoff," I told him. At least I think that's what it's called. I wonder why? "You can't get up here, and I can't leave or you'll be up and out in just a minute or two."

"I can wait," he said, confidently. And he probably could. Someone in the Charonese Mafia must have something pretty powerful on someone in the Oberoni government. Or maybe a jail term simply didn't scare him.

But I didn't intend to wait around.

I unrolled a big wad of toilet paper. Activated the lighter accessory on my knife, and lit the wad. It flared up very quickly, singeing my fingers before I could drop it down on him. It fell right on the seat of his pants, burning merrily. Let's all sing: "Chestnuts roasting . . ."

He never cried out, never threatened me. He began to wiggle and squirm with amazing energy, not making a sound. He managed to get one hand to the right spot, slipping down a few more inches, and batted at the burning wad. Smoke billowed up around me, making my eyes tear. I endured it heroically. After all, tragedy is when *my* eyes hurt. Comedy is when *your* testicles are being cooked.

The fireball fell past him, but his pants were burning. And that wasn't the worst of his problems, because I dropped another flaming depth charge on him, this one lodging briefly against his body until he pressed his back against the pipe to smother it.

Distantly, I heard an alarm go off. Smoke detector, most likely. Which meant it was really time to get out of here. I had dropped half a dozen fireballs on him, and he was blazing fitfully from head to toe. I saw him start to slide. He picked up speed and then he was gone in the smoke. Had he gone to the bottom? How could I know? I didn't know where the bottom was. He was deeper down than he'd been, though, which I guess was as good as I could hope for. When he got the fires out, it should take him a while to inch himself back up the pipe. I hoped it was enough time for me to escape.

I stood up in the place I'd removed the section of pipe, my knees popping loudly. I played the light around this small, crowded space, looking for the egress. I saw nothing but pipes of blue, white, copper, and red, wires in hundreds of colors, and some sort of foamy stuff I couldn't identify. It was all haphazard, seemingly without plan. Few people know of this other world behind their ceilings and walls. I'd been in places like this before, but the experience granted me little advantage, since without a blueprint there was little means of telling what was what or what was on the other side of a wall.

Well, there was bound to be a way to access this space. I'd just have to go find it. The distant sound of the alarm provided the urgency.

I did identify one pipe. It was copper, about an inch in width, and printed all along the side were the words EMERGENCY SPRINKLER SYSTEM, over and over. Where were you when I needed you?

I leaned over to pick up my suitcase and his hand fastened on my wrist.

There is no way to transliterate the scream I let fly. Spell it any way you want, scream it aloud, and then magnify it by ten. And boost it an octave. Many a woman could never have uttered that scream.

There he was, at my feet as I swept the light over him, a vision from hell, streaked with blood that had run *up* his face, patches of hair still glowing embers. Most of one side of his face was burned black, cracking, sloughing off. Even the eye was roasted. None of it seemed to bother him. With maniacal concentration he tried to bring his other, maimed hand around to lever himself out of the hole. His good hand gripped like steel.

Bzzzzzzzz zzzzt!

Once more vaporized flesh and bone became a pink mist in the air. Completely by reflex I had reached down and lopped off his hand at the wrist. He began to slide, then steadied himself somehow, began to lift himself up with his stump and his ruined right hand. I tried to bring the chain knife down to his head, thrust it into his brains, see how he liked *that,* but his flailing arm hit my hand, almost made me lose the knife again. He was still too quick; I couldn't risk a neck slice.

Bzzz uuuzzz uuuz. The knife met some resistance as I passed the blade through the copper pipe of the sprinkler. Water gushed from one severed end, and I tugged at the malleable metal, pulled it out and down, aimed it at the face of the beast.

With a roar of rage, he slipped an inch, three inches, a foot, and then lost his grip entirely. I shined the light down through the torrent, saw him clinging to a crosspipe opening about ten feet down. That's how he got himself turned around, I imagined. And climbing the inside of the down duct must have been a lot easier with his head up. Now he clung, slipped, and down he went, like a log flume ride, past another opening, and another, and then I couldn't see him anymore.

Another alarm was ringing now, set off by my sabotage of the emergency system. Gotta go, gotta go right now.

Then I saw the pieces of him still lying at my feet. I kicked the severed hand over the edge. Maybe it would hit him on the head. Another piece was four entire fingers barely connected by the first knuckles. Over it went, too. The last piece was his severed right thumb and it was about to join its brother digits when I paused, thought it over a second, then picked it up and shoved it into my pocket.

Never can tell when a spare thumb might come in handy.

I picked up my suitcase, stepped out of the pipe and onto the foamy stuff covering the floor, and promptly broke through it, falling ass over end to the floor of a hallway full of hurrying people.

Only one child seemed to have noticed my pratfall, and he thought it was pretty darn funny. Everybody else was looking for the fire exit. I got up, tried to regain my dignity, and joined the throng. A crowd felt like exactly the right place to be. You can lose yourself in a crowd.

I went through the stairway door and started down. So the second floor wasn't good enough for me? If I'd been a little lower I'd probably already be out.

Those tricky Oberoni. I'd gone down one flight of the spiral stairway when yet another alarm sounded. Then a voice:

"Everyone on the fire stairs, sit down, now!" And everyone did, except for one goofy looking fellow who looked as if he'd already been through fire, flood, pestilence, and plague. I'm speaking of myself.

The little boy tugged at my pants. Sweet of him, considering he could have had another good laugh if he'd just let me alone. I sat, and the stairs all collapsed. We started to slide down an endless spiral.

You had to admire them. The folding stairway probably came from a fun house, but it sure got us out fast. Other people leaped in from other floors, until pretty soon we were jam-packed, some upside down, some tumbling head over heels. Still I think there would have been more chance of injury if they'd let us walk out.

At the bottom we landed on a rotating disk that quickly spun us off onto soft, sweet-smelling grass. I lay there just a moment, savoring my escape, then someone grabbed my arm and helped me up and rushed me away from the area, where more guests were arriving every minute. It was all as orderly and efficient as the baggage delivery in a spaceport, but faster.

"Are you injured?" It was a young emergency worker. I knew it because of the large red cross on his tunic.

"I'm fine. A little disoriented."

"If you'll move along over there, we have forms you can fill out for any damages you have incurred. We hope this little crisis is over soon, and that you can continue enjoying your stay at the Othello."

"Thank you. I've had a wonderful time already."

I walked toward the table, then right past it, and on down the street and into the park and down to a train station and onto a car which took me far, far from Mr. Isambard Comfort.

You've heard that old expression, to follow one to the ends of the earth. I'm sure Comfort would try, if we were on Earth, but as most people know, Earth has no ends, being a big sphere like most places in the system. Oberon *does* have ends, though. Four of them. And that's where I was.

All the ends are called Edge City. If you must distinguish them, they are numbered eleven, one, five, and seven, from that old familiar clock face. In a few more years they will have evolved into ten, two, four, and eight, and a few years after that Oberon will lose a major tourist attraction as the edges meet at three and nine. But by then the second wheel should be well under way.

I thought I was at Edge City Eleven. I wasn't quite sure. It's easy for an off-worlder to get turned around. Surprising, since the system is so logical, unlike the warrens of Luna, where most things just growed. But there it is. I might really be at One. It didn't matter much, at the moment.

It was three days after all the excitement at the Othello. I had spent the time laying low, covering what tracks I might have left, and monitoring the progress of the case of Mr. Isambard Comfort, off-worlder, in the lively tabloid press of Oberon.

The off-worlder angle was being played for all it was worth. Most people look with suspicion on people from Somewhere Else. Race isn't much of an issue anymore, what with all the years of intermarrying, hybridizing. You seldom see someone who is really black or really white. Religious differences can still stir up trouble, but nothing like what used to go on in the old days on Earth. Sex is no longer the source of much discrimination, with sex changing in either direction or even frequent trips back and forth across the gender line. That left national origin, and not only do most people harbor some sort of prejudice about that, very few are even ashamed about it. Luckily, it is more in the nature of a sports rivalry than anything that is likely to lead to a shooting war. Plenty of fistfights, few murders.

Comfort was not only an off-worlder, he was Charonese. Make a list of folks to be viewed with suspicion, Charonese would lead it every time, distantly followed by Plutonians, then fill in the blank with the nearest neighbor you didn't care for. With Oberoni, it was the Mirandans. Can't trust those goddamn Mirandans, no sir. I mean, look at the way they dress! Their cuisine stinks, they don't wash frequently enough, they don't clean up after themselves, their cities are a filthy disgrace. They're *stupid*! Did you hear about the Mirandan expedition to the sun? They're not afraid they'll be burned up, because they'll be landing at night! And a million other similar ancient jokes. Ah, but the Charonese! There was a miserable bunch of lepers. Of course, in the case of the Charonese, it was my belief that they'd really *earned* it.

That a Charonese had had the gall to torture a citizen of Oberon almost to death, the perversity to assassinate a compatriot and throw her body out the window, the shocking insensibility to cause a major panic in one of Oberon's finest hotels, and the *stupidity* to get caught, minus both hands and a large part of one foot . . . well, it was just too wonderful for an Oberoni editor to believe. New headlines every day! Shameful revelations! Interviews with each and every guest and staff member of the Othello, with the police investigating the case, with the fire crews and emergency medical techs. And rumors galore! A Charonese terror squadron on the way from the outer worlds to break Comfort free from prison! Local satanists picketing for Comfort's release! Riots breaking out when Citizens for Decency picketed the satanists! The true story of the battle to the death between Comfort and the mysterious third Charonese, and the manhunt for same! Was he dead (some say, eaten by a mysterious domestic Charonese cabal), or alive and in hiding?

I read those last stories with special care, as you might imagine. So far, there had been no hint that the papers had the slightest inkling of what had really gone on. It didn't reassure me much (I may never use the word "comfort" again). The police probably knew a lot more than they were releasing.

All in all, it didn't seem a propitious time to present myself at the local precinct and unburden myself, tell them the true story. I felt sure I could justify my fight with Comfort, but it might get a little tricky convincing a judge that five bullets through a closed door was self-defense. Some people might even try to call it first-degree murder. You never can tell. Prosecutors can be very contrary that way.

And, of course, there was the matter of those old warrants I'd never gotten around to straightening out.

It really seemed time to bid adieu to fair Oberon. And that was a lot harder than it sounded. So far, I'd had no luck at all.

At least I didn't have Izzy on my back. That's another reason I watched the news hourly. Due to the notoriety and heinous nature of the crimes he stood accused of, he had not been released on bail. He was, in fact, to be prosecuted for offenses that, often, could be dealt with by a simple civil suit, fines paid, everybody goes home satisfied. This time, the public had to be satisfied, and the public was pissed. They identified with Miss Polyhymnia Reynolds, a hardworking member of the Oberon middle class. They wanted that fucking satanist to do some *time*!

Yeah, right. Don't set your watch by that. When it all cooled down some, or possibly before, those friends in high places who had been bought, or who used the services best provided by a group like the Charonese Mafia, would step forward and get a new bail hearing and Izzy would be out the door. I checked the papers all the time so I'd be sure not to miss his release. Possibly I could arrange to be a thousand yards from the prison door, with a high-powered rifle with a telescopic sight.

I can dream, can't I?

Toby came bounding up to me, a little red rubber ball in his mouth, and pawed at my arm. It's Toby's biggest weakness; he's got a regular ball-chasing jones. Toss anything round in his presence and he instantly forgets he is a civilized, serious, high IQ sort of dog who can count to five. His pink tongue hangs out and he reverts to puppyhood, his eyes fastened on the ball with that total concentration only a dog can achieve. God knows where he'd found this one. In the shrubbery, abandoned by another dog, judging from the well-chewed surface. I took it from his mouth.

"Wanna fetch, Toby? Wanna go fetch?" He jumped up and down deliriously, wagging his entire body and yipping with joy. I made as if to throw the ball and he froze, ready to hold that position until Charon warmed up or I threw it, one or the other.

I threw it, and away he went. In heaven. What a hard life he led.

I was in one of the little roll-up parks the wheel engineers scattered along the Edge as construction progressed. There was a wading pool for children, a gazebo/bandstand structure, public toilets that really looked like brick, but weren't. A build-it-yourself playground in riotous plastic colors. About a hundred fine, sturdy trees: pines, maples, huge spreading oaks, and cherry, orange, apple, and banana trees that grew real fruit all year round. All it lacked was the Big Rock Candy Mountain and bubblers dispensing cold pop and lemonade. To look at it, you would never guess all the trees were in huge pots, all the grass only a veneer of sod that could be taken up and moved when the construction workers were ready to extend this section another few miles.

The parks were there more for tourists than for local children. The attraction, naturally, was the Edge itself. The Oberoni shrewdly knew that once you get tourists to a scenic wonder, you'd better give them something to do besides gape. And while you're at it, sell them overpriced souvenirs and junk food. Not far from this sylvan setting was a portable amusement park featuring the Big Dip, a roller coaster that plunged off the Edge three times in the course of the ride.

You would think the Edge would be enough. It was certainly more than enough for me.

I was sitting on the concrete sidewalk that defined the Edge, doing what every tourist not afflicted with terminal acrophobia does when he gets there: sit with one's feet dangling over infinity. Three times already I had been asked to snap the picture of some group pretending to fall off, or peering cautiously down.

It helps to sneak up on it, sit down securely, and then

swing your legs over. I don't have any great trouble with heights, but there are heights and then there are *heights*. Nowhere was there anything as high as the Edge. At the Edge, you were standing at the top of infinity.

All very safe, of course. No need to have a lot of frozen tourist corpses orbiting Uranus. Bad publicity.

Every hundred yards or so along the Edge signs were prominently posted: JUMP AT YOUR OWN RISK. OB$100 FEE CHARGED FOR RETRIEVAL. Somewhere down there about a mile or two away was the all-but-invisible plastic substance that kept the air in at the Edges. A big bubble of it covered all the ends of the wheel. If you jumped or fell off the Edge, you would soon hit this stuff and bounce, and bounce again, and probably bounce a dozen times before coming to rest. Then the Edge Patrol would lower a rope harness to you and you would be hauled in like a trout. Unless you'd sprained an ankle or broken a bone, in which case it became a rescue, and they'd go down with a litter and charge you OB$500. It was a rather expensive way of getting a thrill, to my mind, but dozens of people did it every day. For five dollars, at sites all up and down the Edge, they could be attached to a bungee cord and get a better ride much more cheaply. But go figure tourists, eh?

Here and there in the air before me like hundreds of varicolored butterflies were gull-winged gliders and gossamer-winged pedal fliers taking advantage of the updrafts along the Edge. There were at least that many kites of all shapes and sizes. It was a kaleidoscopic traffic jam in the air. Glorious!

Toby returned with the ball and dropped it at my side, then stared at it as if willpower alone could lift it and toss it. I picked it up and gestured as if to throw it off the Edge. He got ready to jump. I should know better than to even tease about that. Toby is basically fearless; he'd go over the Edge in a minute. I turned and tossed it as far as I could toward the pressurehead.

I said very safe. I did not say completely safe.

The pressurehead is a wall of steel fifty miles wide and five miles high. An Edge City was defined as that space, not yet permanently occupied, between the pressurehead and the Edge. It was punctured in hundreds of places along the bottom by what looked like wide, inviting open doors, but were actually open air locks. At each door was a prominent sign warning you that you were leaving a category-B pressure environment and entering a category-D area. Many people live their whole lives without visiting a D area. Those rankings took many factors into account, I'd been told, but boiled down to how many surfaces there were between your tender and irreplaceable ass and hard vacuum. Category D meant there was only one barrier, the invisible plastic substance that provided a working environment for construction workers and visitors to Edge City. If that membrane was punctured, you'd hear all hell's klaxons and sirens, and find the air locks back to the safe world were now closed, and taking groups of twenty at their usual, maddeningly slow, now perhaps *fatally* slow, rate, as your ears popped and your nose started bleeding.

How many times had this happened during the construction of the wheel? So far, zero. How much did I worry about a blowout? About the same. Most of the people around me seemed to feel the same way. They brought their children here, they came to play or stretch out on the grass, they camped out "overnight," when the great lights shining down from the hub were turned off for eight hours.

When another five miles of wheel was complete, the pressurehead was detached from the huge bolts holding it in place, and rolled toward the Edge and its new mooring. I'd like to see that. They have big parades and fireworks and festivals and music. Clowns and troubadours and, of course, outdoor theater.

I threw the rubber ball a few more times, when who should come shambling down the walkway but Elwood P. Dowd. He stopped a few steps away and stood looking down at me, his hands thrust into his baggy gray slacks, playing pocket pool or fiddling with his spare coins or whatever it was he did when wearing that thoughtful expression on his face.

"I didn't see you around on the trip from Pluto," I said.

"No, you didn't," he drawled. "Claustrophobia. And you didn't pack enough to eat."

He lowered himself down on my left side, dangled his feet with his clunky brown hard-leather shoes and argyle socks. He always sits on my left, because he's deaf in his left ear. He told me he'd fallen through an iced-over pond when he

was young, back in Bedford Falls. Elwood had plenty of stories like that. He'd been a United States senator for three
years, and he'd flown solo across the Atlantic Ocean. He'd
been the leader of a swing band.

"Yeah, I know," I said. "The old Pantechnicon's not
good enough for you. Which way did you travel this time?
On the buddy seat of some witch's broom? Borne on the
gentle wings of angels? Scanned, digitized, strewn through
the ether to fetch up here, at the edge of human folly?"

He peered down between his shoes, swinging them idly.

"Pretty fair edge, if you ask me." I could tell by the way
he looked off into the distance that he was pissed. He doesn't
like me to point out the lapses in logic his appearances usually
imply.

"If you don't like having me around, I can always go
away," he drawled.

I learned long ago not to put my arm around his shoulder
or anything foolish like that. People stare. Rude, but there it
is. Usually I don't even look directly at him, but now I did.

"After better than ninety years, Elwood, I have trouble
imagining what I'd do without you."

That seemed to satisfy him. He squinted up at the hang
gliders for a time.

"Maybe I came here in a faster ship than you did," he
said.

"Using up your frequent-traveler miles on the *Flying
Dutchman*?"

"The old *Spirit of St. Louis* was a lot faster. No, but maybe
I hitched a ride with somebody who *did* get here faster. Now,
if I was you, I'd be asking myself, 'Who do I know that got
here faster than me? And how'd he do it?' "

Two hours in the library looking at back postings of news-
pads and I had the information I needed. And yes, I actually
went to the library. They exist, you know, and some of them
even have a few books in them. Even on a spanking-new
world like Oberon they have not entirely converted to over-
the-phone service. And by law they have to maintain old-
fashioned desk-bound terminals, for those folks who eschew
direct interface and implanted modems: Amish, Christian
Scientists, naturalists, washed-up ex-child telly stars, people

who get Radio Free Betelgeuse on the fillings in their teeth. Weirdos.

When I found what I was looking for, the beginnings of a wild idea took root like crabgrass and refused to go away. I walked for an hour, turning it over and over in my mind. Just too wild, I kept telling myself. And then I'd think of another angle and be right back, worrying at it.

I found a restaurant that allowed dogs—that's right, some of them on Oberon don't; can you imagine? And they call themselves civilized—and spent a contemplative two hours eating pasta and drinking strong tea. Toby, after eating his portion and vainly trying to interest me in playing fetch with the last meatball, snoozed in his chair.

What the heck? I thought. Toby opened one eye and I realized I'd said it aloud. I dropped money on the table and scooped him up, suddenly in a big hurry.

"How'd you like to ride on the fast train?" I asked him. He allowed as how that was all right with him, and went back to sleep.

Toby is a trusting soul. Well traveled as he is, he might have had second thoughts if he'd known more about the Rim Express.

The Express hadn't been operating the last time I was on Oberon, for what I thought of as an excellent reason: there wasn't much rim to speak of. There was a lot more rim now, but there was still the little matter of a five- or six-hundred mile gap between the arcs. How could a train get from one arc to the other if no rail connected them? Well, sometimes the simplest thing really is to let the mountain come to Muhammad.

The train car was everything the spoke elevators were not: narrow, cramped, linear. Seats were four across, with an aisle between pairs. The top half of the car was transparent, though you couldn't see anything when you boarded since the car was in a tube, suspended an eighth of an inch above a magnetic induction rail. I settled into an aisle seat. It was deeply padded, and could recline almost forty-five degrees. When the car was about half-filled, the front and rear doors sealed and there was a loud hiss as the air in the tube was bled away. Then I was pressed back in my seat by rapid acceleration.

In only a few minutes we burst silently into space. Toby floated up out of my lap, weightless. He's not bothered by this, simply looking around curiously until I snagged a hind leg and brought him back down. I twisted in my seat and saw the massive trailing edge of Noon Arc dwindling behind us. I could see the pressurehead, several tunnels including the one we had emerged from, the mysterious inner structure of the floor. We were traveling at three thousand miles per hour—

—and standing dead still. It's all relative, you see. Or so I'm told. From a viewpoint on the rotating wheel, we were really skedaddling. But stand away from the wheel, motionless, and you'd see that the train car was just hanging there as the Noon Arc rotated away from it, and the Six Arc approached.

All very neat. Hang suspended there for twenty minutes, then decelerate when the other arc sweeps you up. Travel time: thirty minutes. And, I hear you protest, why the hell would anyone take the fifteen-hour ordeal of a trip through the hub, as Poly did twice a week, when this magical chariot was available?

Answer: money.

There was no real physical reason why the Rim Express should be so expensive to ride. It was cheap to operate, it was safe, it was quick. And the government of Oberon *hated* the damn thing, wished it would just go away. Since it didn't, they taxed the hell out of it. They added surcharges for every screwball thing a government is likely to get up to, and then they added some more. On top of that, they subsidized the spoke elevators to the point that they were practically free. It was like bus fare as compared to rental of a limousine. The elevators didn't really need a fare box at all. Money from concessions and gambling enabled the service to turn a tidy profit, sort of like a theater that makes nothing at the box office but cleans up selling outrageously priced popcorn and drinks.

But what was the problem with speed and efficiency? Why the hostility to the Express? The answer didn't make sense to me, until I considered the economics of a rotating world under construction.

Since its inception not that many years before, and for

some years to come, well over ninety percent of the freight traffic went *down*. Cargoes arrived at the hub—finished steel, composite, glass, web, imported food, merry-go-round horses, starving actors—and was lowered to the rim. Of that, only the starving actor was likely to return to the hub. And on Oberon, *down* meant *slow*. Each kilogram moved from the hub to the rim slowed the spin of the wheel by a few millionths of a second. Consider that millions of kilograms were lowered that way each day. Pretty soon, left to itself, the wheel would run out of juice like a music box winding down its spring. Everybody would get lighter, and lighter, and lighter . . . and rise up and blow away. (People *did* get lighter, though not by a lot. When the rotation speed had slowed to a certain point the engineers applied thrust and brought the wheel back up to speed, and slightly over. Included in Oberoni ''weather forecasts,'' actually schedules, was the day's ''gravity index.'' There were light days, and heavy days. Would you believe that suicide rates increased on heavy days? It's true. Also more fistfights, absenteeism from work, and complaints of constipation.) (This quirk of rotation also made spring scales illegal on Oberon. Only beam balances would give true weight.)

Thrust means energy, and energy costs money. You'd think they'd have a kilogram-lowering tax to pay for it, and they did, but not a big one. It was a complex equation, but one that eventually worked out to an outrageous tariff on the Rim Express, since these citizens weren't helping out by keeping the elevators in operation.

There *was* another way of delivering cargo to the rim. It also involved slowing the wheel. This was a fact of physics that no amount of taxation would correct: more mass at the rim equals less speed, no matter how it got there. But it was quicker, like the Express itself. The wheel is turning, see, and it has these two huge gaps in it. Why not wait for an arc to pass, then move your cargo into position where it could be intercepted and magnetically slowed, much as we were sitting out here in space right now, waiting for the arc to arrive?

Well . . . sounds great, but these are *large* shipments. You have twenty minutes to get them positioned *exactly* right. No margin for error, and it has to work right every time, hundreds of times a day . . . and I think this is my stop right up here, Mr. Conductorman. It's been fun, and send me a card if you . . . er, *when* you arrive safely.

Imagining several million tons smashing into one of the pressureheads, the Oberoni came to the same conclusion I did. No thank you. We'll ease freight into the hub in a slow and civilized manner, then lower it gently to where it's needed. The Rim Express is excitement enough, for those who can afford it.

Could I afford it? Not really, but my reasoning was thus: if this screwball plan doesn't work out I don't have an agent's chance at the Pearly Gates of getting to Luna in time. In fact, if I'm not off this wheel in twenty-four hours or less my chances of being arrested are almost a certainty. So time was more important than money for me. And all I had going for me at the moment was speed, audacity, and charm.

Actually, that didn't sound so bad to me. I'd stolen out of town many times in the past with less.

They turn the car around before arrival at the Six Arc, so when the deceleration starts you're pressed back into your seat, not jerked out of it. The pilot told us we'd stay weightless for the first ten seconds into the tunnel, so we could turn around and look so long as we remembered to lean back into our seats once we entered.

I did turn around, for a while, but I found the sight of the approaching arc much more unsettling than the view of the retreating one. You could actually see it grow during the last minute of free fall, swinging down on you like God's croquet mallet. No openings were visible; I knew they were there, but you couldn't see them until the last second. It was hard to resist the notion that you were about to be batted like a long fly ball to the Andromeda Galaxy. I settled in my chair and hugged Toby securely, and closed my eyes. Presently it got dark, instantly, and then I was pressed back into the seat. In no time the doors were opening and we all crowded out into the station. An elevator took us to the floor of Six Arc.

Which looked pretty much like Noon Arc, with one difference. There were the Chandytowns, sometimes pronounced Shantytowns, also known as Gypsy Penthouses, Rookeries, Bat Mansions, Goddamn Public Nuisances, dangerous eyesores, accidents-in-progress, and many more unflattering terms. They were goofy chandeliers, Christmas ornaments dangling from Gargantua's attic. They were squatters who hung instead of hunkered.

As usual, oversights like this were the result of lawmakers' negligence and lawyers' cupidity. Seems a bloated plutocrat of a banker, one of the original consortium who financed the early work on Oberon II and whose family came over on the good ship *Tax Shelter* (think of the *Mayflower*, with four-star restaurants and a stock ticker), was looking to build a mansion that would make all the other bloated plutocrats gobble with envy. He set his pack of New Harvard jackals on the project, and one came up with the odd fact that no one owned the airspace above the wheel rim. One could, if one had the money and the effrontery, build a castle in the air. The banker had plenty of both, and soon a sort of Xanadu of the Skies was dangling from a five-hundred-mile rope of spider silk, attached to the hub and looming a mile over the peons, a convenient pissing distance.

What one goony billionaire can create, others are sure to copy. Soon there were a dozen of these unwelcome party favors frowning down on the populace, complete with hanging gardens, pools, driving ranges, hangars, and all the ostentation money could buy. For some reason I didn't get, they were only in Six Arc so far, but rumor had them a-building, waiting to be lowered, over Noon Arc as well.

These structures were unlike anything humans had up to that point inhabited. Free-fall structures can be fanciful and free-form, but usually ended up in a massive clutter of add-ons, like Brementon. They weren't made to be enjoyed from the outside. Structures on a surface, whether on a planet or under spin, had unforgiving and constant gravity to contend with. Even with the strength of modern building materials, there was a limit to what could be done. The shantytowns lived in a new environment. They didn't have any sort of base to sit on; lower one to the ground, it would crumple like aluminum foil, then fall over on its side like an exhausted top. They were asymmetrical, tending to be wider at the middle than at the top and bottom. One thing was sure: if they were outlawed, as ninety percent of Sixers favored, it was going to be a big problem putting them anywhere else.

The legal battle had been joined fifteen years earlier, and

still raged with no end in sight. So far the only progress had been passage of an ordinance that each had to be suspended from a minimum of three ropes, each capable of supporting the entire building. The tenants had complied with no fuss. Hell, it was cheap and easy to do, and there they still. hung.

Like most tourists, I thought they were sort of pretty, in an overdone, tasteless way. But I could see the point of the people on the ground. Particularly the ones living in the Shadowlands.

First, there was the problem of stuff falling or being tossed over the side. Usually it was plastic champagne glasses, crumpled paper cups, and the butt ends of various smokables. But every once in a while there was a flowerpot, sometimes big enough to hold a potted palm. There had been chairs, oddments of clothing, ceramic tiles loosened by time, shards of glass from broken windows. A few years back a group of drunken revelers had shoved a lavender baby grand piano over the side. There had been one falling body, a suicide. So far no one had been killed on the ground. Injuries were lavishly compensated, and the offender's insurance premium dutifully raised. These were people who could easily afford it.

The big problem was the one you already thought of. Three cables or not, who wanted to *live* under the damn things?

The answer was, people looking for cheap rent. Property values had plummeted faster than a falling baby grand piano in the affected areas, known as Shadowlands. There really was a shadow cast by these things. Without grow lamps, all the tomato and marijuana plants in your window boxes shriveled up and died. Your light bill went up, but your rent went down.

The Shadowland apartments tended to be occupied by the young, who traditionally didn't have a lot of money, and who didn't really think they could die, anyway. Many residents wore bright red hard hats when on the street. Not really meant for protection, the hard hats were more a way of defiantly thumbing one's nose at fate.

I saw several of these hard-hatted bohemians on my way into the Shadowland. Toby sniffed the air as we moved into the twilight. He knew something was wrong, but couldn't figure out what. I doubt the hovering shantytown meant anything to him; it was too big and too distant to be a part of his world.

We passed a line of people carrying signs and chanting something. The signs said SAVE THE RINGS. I never *did* figure out what that was all about.

I loitered around the neighborhood for several hours, getting a feel for the place. I'd changed my face a bit, my costume, my walk. Ordinarily I'd pull a few makeovers on a project like this, be several different people during the course of my wait. But no matter what I did, even the most inept observer would take note of those different guys walking with the same dog. Couldn't be helped; I wanted Toby with me. But I'm good at pretending I belong. I can fit in most places, know how to act as if I'm up to something purposeful and innocent.

It was a quiet neighborhood of working families and college students. The hurly-burly of stampeding skyscrapers was five miles away. People here were more stable, less flamboyant. I'm sure it would have been a very desirable spot for the settled middle class if it wasn't for the hovering monstrosity of the shantytown. Looking up at it, it was impossible to put aside the idea that it was about to drop a massive turd right on your head. There was an irising opening of some sort, probably to admit helicopters or hovercraft, that could easily be seen as a gigantic robot rectum.

I wondered how they dealt with sewage. I envisioned flying honey wagons buzzing around the big butthole in the sky like angry bees, slopping feculence, spewing effluvia. On second thought, dear, let's go see what's available in the Sunnyside Apartments.

Seeing no sign of police activity, but far from sure I'd see it if it was there, I plucked up my courage and entered the building. I roamed the hallways with what I hoped was an air of unconcerned innocence, passing her door several times. No one stood around reading a newspad. No games of mumblety-peg were happening in the stairwells. I saw no evidence of cameras having been recently installed, but I knew that if they want to hide the camera from you, you won't find it. I am very good at sniffing out the beaks in ordinary circumstances. Something about the shoes they wear, and the way they walk. But electronic surveillance was another matter.

It all depended on what she'd told them, and how much they believed. What I figured was the best thing going for me was simply that few cops would believe a man who could pull off the escape I had would be stupid enough to come here.

Well, I've proven many times, I'm *way* stupider than that.

So I squared up to the door, took a deep breath, and knocked.

I could tell she was watching me through a low-tech peephole. When she opened the door she had a puzzled frown on her face. My own features were not what she remembered, but it was nagging her. People change their appearance these days, sometimes frequently. Some new recognition skills were evolving, I believed, to deal with that fact. I'm okay at it. Women tended to be better at it than men. There is an identity in the eyes independent of other physical features, things about one's stance, something I think of as stage presence, gestures, possibly even an aura of some sort, that often give you away.

She looked down at the dog in the crook of my arm, then back at my face. Recognition dawned.

By the time I saw the right hook coming, it was way too late. I sat down hard, and put my hand to my nose. Jesus, did it hurt!

"Can I come in?" I honked, and stared at a handful of blood.

"How could you have the nerve to come here?" she shouted. "After what you did to me. You walked out and left me for that monster!"

She was pacing up and down the small living room of her apartment. She'd been over this same ground before, dozens of times in the last ten minutes, but I knew she had to get it out of her system. She would, eventually. There had been a moment of quiet as she stared down at me, perhaps a little surprised at what she had done, but a long way from regretting it. She had pulled me up and in, slammed the door behind me, and the tirade began.

She yelled at me as she shoved me toward the couch, harangued me as she went to the kitchen for a wet rag and some ice, screamed abuse as she hurled the cold pack at me, fumed and muttered as she picked up the ice and wrapped it up again and thrust it at me defiantly.

I just sat there with my head lowered. The rag was red now, but the bleeding had stopped. My nose throbbed a little, but I didn't think it was broken.

Toby sat at the other end of the couch, as far away from me as possible, and watched her pace the floor, licking his lips nervously from time to time. By sitting on the couch I think he meant to signal he was still with me in spirit, but by taking the distant ground he was letting me know that, if she gets violent again, Sparky, you're on your own. Toby was an artist, not a pugilist. If I'd wanted a bodyguard, I'd have bought a Rottweiler.

If you don't intend to resume the violence, you eventually reach a point where most of the anger is burned out of you. There's a lot of different ways to go from there. She might try to throw me out. I wasn't going to let her, but she might try. She might begin to cry. I thought that was likely. What she did, though, was sort of wind down. She paced a few more times, trying to think of more original ways to abuse me, paced slower and slower, and came to a halt looking down at Toby. The faintest of smiles touched her lips.

"Nice dog," she whispered.

"His name is Toby," I said. It was the second sentence I'd spoken to her since I found her lying on the bloody bed.

Toby knows his cues. He bounced down to the floor and stood up on his hind legs and did a little dance, pink tongue hanging out fetchingly. He knows he's cute. He did a back flip, then sat and barked, three times. Poly made a sound halfway between a sob and a laugh.

"My name isn't Trevor, though," I said. It set her off again. I had pretty much expected it would.

"Oh, really?" she hooted, voice dripping with scorn. "Imagine my surprise. The police told me Trevor Howard was some kind of old actor, and he'd been dead for two hundred years. Can you imagine how foolish I felt?" She ranted on a little longer, but her heart was no longer in it and she ran down again. This time she sat, and Toby jumped up in her lap and licked her face. Her hand came up absently to pet him, and he curled up in her lap, looking up worshipfully.

There's this thing about dog people—and Poly was definitely a dog person—that makes us unable to be totally angry, totally sad, or anything but calmed and at least a bit pleased when our hands are stroking a dog's back and scratching behind his ears. Toby played the moment for all it was worth, arching sensually, licking his lips. A cat would have purred, but Toby doesn't need to. A dog's body language is at least as eloquent.

Perhaps I'd be able to talk now.

"First, I'd like to say I'd never have left you there if I thought you were in danger from him." She looked over at me dubiously, but said nothing. "I know, you're thinking, 'Then why did he come back?' Well, obviously because, thinking about it a little more, I wasn't sure I was right." I would not point out that coming back was one of the bravest things I ever did. If she could accept that I would do anything brave she would see that for herself. If she couldn't, no amount of pleading my case would do any good. Besides, being silent about one's heroics is the mark of a hero, or so you'd believe if you watched any adventure story. Since most of us get our information about situations of melodramatic heroism from just such stories as that, I hoped her own mind was conditioned to think that way. Myself, I've met people who had done things I thought heroic who never shut up about it. Most people like to crow, hero and coward alike. The strong, silent, aw-shucks type from old western movies is rare indeed. But I knew the role, and I played it.

I had noticed the last three fingers of her right hand were pink and a little raw looking. They had been the ones severed by Izzy in his brief interrogation. Those fingers were undoubtedly in some compost pile in the bowels of Oberon. The ones she wore now were replacements.

"At least you'll play the violin again," I said, searching for a positive spin. I knew it was a mistake as soon as I said it, and it was, but not for the reason I had thought. She sat Toby on the couch and stood. Hand up, fingers spread, she shook it at me. The new fingers seemed a little loose.

"I'm glad you're so pleased about that," she grated. "I'm sure you've never heard anything about 'muscle memory,' since I doubt you've ever had any fingers pulled off."

I had to admit I hadn't.

"It works like this. You learn a manual skill—typing,

throwing a baseball, playing the violin—the skill gets imprinted in your brain.'' She tapped her lovely noggin with her uninjured index finger. ''The imprinting's still there, even if your arm gets cut off. But you replace the arm, the signals get sent down to your fingers, and the muscles don't know how to respond. They haven't been developed properly to do what you want them to. And they think there's some memory in the muscles, too, so they have to relearn the skill, just like if you'd had part of your brain taken out and some other part tries to take over. This finger right here''—she extended her right ring finger—''is the klutziest digit you own, except for your toes. It takes *years* to get it able to do the things you need to do to play the violin, even moderately well. This one isn't much better.'' She was holding up her pinkie. ''But the finger I'd really like you to study is this one.'' She held up her middle finger and extended her hand toward me. ''Fuck you, whoever you are. Now get out of my apartment.''

''I just have a few things to say, and then I'll go, if you still want me to.'' I waited, took her silence as acceptance.

''The first thing is, my real name is Sparky Valentine.''

She gave me a reaction I'm used to: a blank stare. For a lot of people, saying I'm Sparky is like telling them I'm Mickey Mouse, or the tooth fairy.

''Crazy,'' she muttered.

''There's no way I can prove it to you, but I want you to know I'm being straight with you.'' It's true, you know. Even wearing my ''natural'' face, I don't look a lot like little Sparky. I could do the voice, but that would prove nothing. There was a time when every two-bit comic in the system could do Sparky, and most of his gang, too. Many of them were better at it than I was. When I finally grew up, my voice changed just like other people.

''What I'm here to ask you,'' I plunged on, ''is if you'd like to get back at him. If you'd like to give him one in the eye.''

There was no need to explain who ''he'' was. I saw wild interest grow in her face at the idea of getting back at him. She leaned forward, intense.

''Can we kill him?'' she whispered.

Well, that was direct enough. I resolved never to get her angry at me again.

"I doubt it. I mean, as a practical matter, he's *very* hard to kill. I've tried three times now, and he's still out there. And personally, my hope is to never be on the same planet with him again, much less close enough to him to take a shot."

She slumped back on the couch, then sprang to her feet. I thought she was going to resume her tirade against me, but she had a new target.

"I can do this all right. I can pick my nose, I can feed myself. I'm getting better at signing my name. But Bach? Mozart? Forget it. I can't do a simple arpeggio. I'm back to scales. If there's anything I can do to hurt him, hurt him really bad, I want to hear it."

"Okay. There's one finger we didn't mention." I stuck up my thumb. "It's the finger of transportation, and maybe we can use it to hitch a ride out of here."

And I told her my plan.

It all sounds so much better when you're laying it out. Or when I am, anyway. My powers of persuasion are pretty sharp, having been honed over seventy years of getting myself into situations I end up having to talk myself out of. To run a good con, it helps if you can at least partly persuade yourself that you're telling the truth. I know how to tell the mark the parts she wants to hear, and to skim over the problems.

So it went down well, there in her apartment. She bought it, and so did I. Now, almost half a day later, alone, sober and determined to stay that way, it seemed a very long shot.

I was in the hub, sitting at a table in a carousel bar, waiting to see how it all came out. I had a tall, bubbly glass of ginger ale in front of me, and I wished it were something a little stronger. I wished I had something to smoke, too, but all I'd ever liked was hemp, and I needed my wits about me. Some tobacco, that would be nice, though I'd never smoked it and heard it tasted vile. Humphrey Bogart, sitting here, would have had a smoke going, the cigarette stuck high up between his fingers. That hound-dog face that never seemed to look panicky. I could do Bogart if I had a smoke, and I wouldn't be so nervous.

I kept my eye on the rope lift constantly moving down from the hub—not the hub of Oberon, though that's where I was, but the hub of the pub, the pub-hub that was within the

302 ··· JOHN VARLEY

larger hub, to make myself perfectly opaque. The bar was for
tourists and others who liked their drinks to stay in the glass
and the glass to stay on the table. Therefore, it rotated, at a
pretty good rate, enough to give one-third gee at the rim,
where everybody sat. The place was small enough that you
didn't want to stand up too quickly or the coriolanus force
would knock you down. Your head would get a lot lighter
than your feet.

I spotted her as she floated into the hub, glanced around,
and selected the lift rope that would take her close to where
I sat. It pulled her down at first, then somewhere when the
forces were equalized she swung around with ease and grace
and she was hanging from the strap, like a commuter only
with her feet off the floor. The rope lowered her and she hit
the ground walking. I was envious. A few hours before I had
looked like all three stooges trying to do the same thing, and
I'd landed on my butt. Toby had thought it was a neat trick,
I think. He'd barked in delight.

Now he was curled up in one of the chairs at the table,
his belly full of bar pretzels and beer nuts and ginger ale.
Poly pulled out the third chair and sat down.

"I need a drink." She held up her hand and signaled to
the bartender. I watched with interest, because this wasn't a
mere finger gesture but a more elaborate sign language that
resulted in what looked like a Bloody Mary being delivered
to our table. I memorized the gestures. You never know when
you'll need a bit of business to lend authenticity on the stage.

I let her take a deep drink.

"How'd it go?" I asked. She took another.

"Okay, I guess."

"What do you mean, you guess?"

"Well, it's kind of hard to tell, isn't it?" I could see she
was having some of the same doubts I'd been entertaining.
She'd had plenty of time to find fault with the plan on the
elevator ride to the hub.

"I wouldn't know. I wasn't there." I looked at her pointedly, and she sighed, took another drink, and put the glass
down.

"Okay. They weren't happy about it."

"I warned you they wouldn't be."

"But there wasn't anything they could do. Except make me feel small."

"I warned you about that, too."

Poly had been visiting with the Oberon police. I was glad it was her and not me, because what she told them was she was dropping her lawsuit against Isambard Comfort, and as far as she was concerned, he was free to go.

"They'd already told me the position he was taking," she said. We'd gone through that at her apartment, but I let her tell it her way. "How you killed his sister in self-defense, in spite of what it looked like. What sort of story he fed them to make it look that way I don't know, they didn't tell me, but it was clear they weren't buying it. I know they'd *really* like to talk to you about it, because they're sure the two of you wouldn't tell the same story. But as of now, there's nothing they can charge you with."

"Did anybody follow you?"

"I don't think so. I did what you said, and I didn't see anybody."

No way to tell, with an amateur. But if they really wanted to talk to me and had followed her, they'd probably already be here.

That Izzy was not going to finger me in his sister's death didn't surprise me, either. If I was in prison, it would be tougher for him to get at me. Oh, he could hire my death easily enough, but Charonese like to take care of matters like that themselves. They never testify in court, no matter what. If they have a beef with you, don't expect them to sue you.

"So I told them I had accepted the settlement the Charonese ambassador had offered me, that I'd already cashed the check. They tried to bluff me." She took another drink, and made another gesture to the bartender. "That was the scariest part. Said they intended to prosecute him under the criminal statutes, and they demanded my testimony. Said they'd prosecute *me* if I didn't take the stand. I told 'em that would go down great with the public, going after the victim. I said I wasn't going to testify, no matter what, that I was dropping all charges. They kept trying to frighten me—*did* frighten me, let me tell you—but I stuck to my story, like you said, and eventually they threw me out." She took a sip of her second drink.

"Threw you out."

"Told me to leave. Said they'd get back to me after they'd talked it over with the State's Attorney. So, I don't *think* they'll prosecute—"

"They won't, trust me."

"Don't make me laugh. Anyway, I'll be glad to get out of here."

Right.

"I'd like to talk to you about that," I said.

She gave me a cold smile.

"I'm not surprised."

"You're not?"

"Something in your quick agreement to my terms didn't, shall we say, play right."

"I'll stick to my agreement," I said, indignantly. "I just still think you're making a mistake, and I want to try to talk you out of it while there's still time. You've got the money now to—"

"You said that before." She reached into her purse. "Before you waste a lot of hot air, I want to show you something." She pulled a blue, eight-ounce thermos from the purse and held it up for me. There was a smiling picture of me— Sparky—on the side. She jiggled it, and something rattled inside. I was stunned.

"How did you . . . ?" I was speechless, so I reached for the thermos. She pulled it back quickly, tucked it back into her purse.

"Naughty," she said, wagging her finger. "You wouldn't want to cause a disturbance, would you? Something that might bring the police." She had me, and she knew it. "While you went to the bathroom. Remember?"

"But the combination—"

"I've got a good memory. Shame, shame, Trevor. An old con man like you, not covering up when you opened that ridiculous traveling coffin."

I'd brought the Pantechnicon with me, naturally, since I expected to get out of Oberon fast if I got out at all. After I had her attention I'd taken it to her apartment, as without a bit of grisly show-and-tell I wasn't sure she'd buy my plan. And the bitch had foxed me. And what was this about ridiculous? I was as indignant about that as about the theft.

"That's mine," I said, as forcefully as I dared.

"And you'll get it back, I promise. As soon as you keep *your* promise."

I fumed, I bristled, and I blustered, but after five minutes of whispered argument to which she responded with nary a word, I admitted defeat. She was going with me.

The next hour would have been tense under the best of circumstances. Since we were more or less not speaking to each other, it was excruciating. Toby felt it, woke up, and kept looking back and forth between us. He thinks all his friends ought to like each other, and frets when they don't.

Poly bought a newspad and we hovered over it like miserable wraiths waiting for Godot. We kept it dialed to BREAKING STORIES, but since none were breaking at the moment we saw the same six stories a dozen times each, including a touching one about a mother cat who kept returning to a burning building until she had all four of her kittens. At least it was touching at first. By the eighth showing I would cheerfully have squashed all four of the mewling ratlike varmints under my heel until their heads cracked like walnuts and booted the mother like a singed and smoking football.

Then we had it.

"Live from Seventh District Prison. Notorious Charonese torturer and arsonist Isambard Comfort is to be released at this hour. Sources close to the warden tell us his victim, Polyhymnia—"

Poly slapped the cutoff switch and scaled the pad into a trash can. I admired the way she compensated for the spin in her aim.

"Let's go," she said. We hustled over to the rope lift and I grabbed a passing strap, tucking Toby under my free arm. I was tugged off my feet. This had to be easier than coming down, I figured.

It was, if banging your head on the hub was easier than falling flat on your ass.

We went to the taxi stand and piled into a cab. Poly had two big, battered old suitcases and her violin. I had Toby and the Pantech.

The cab pilot, who looked like a third-rate palooka who

neveh coulda been a contendah, glanced at Toby. Then his crusty, unshaven face split in a wide grin.

"A bichon frise," he cooed, pronouncing it properly. He thrust a massive ham fist toward Toby, who froze in consternation at the sheer *size* of the thing, but stood his ground and, after a cautious sniff, allowed himself to be fondled. The palooka had a gentle touch, and soon Toby's mouth opened and his pink tongue lolled out. He looked at me and sniffed.

"Me and the wife have three of 'em," the driver explained. "Won the best of breed in last year's All-Oberon. I'll bet the little fellow's got good lines." He looked at me expectantly, probably thinking I'd whip out Toby's papers and we'd spend a pleasant hour or so discussing his ancestry. I'd met this type before. "Ever breed him?"

"Toby breeds with whom he wants to breed with, and like any gentleman, he never discusses it with me."

"Gotcha. I bet this little fella's got half-breed pups all over the system." He meant it as a joke, and had no idea how accurate he was. "So, where to?"

I gave him the coordinates and he typed them into his launch control, and in a moment we were squirted out the end of the tube and streaking into black space.

It was as crowded as when I arrived, crowded as it always is. We dodged around angular behemoths, cargo ships, and passenger liners. In only a few minutes we began our deceleration, and an apparition hove into view.

"Cheez," said the cabby. A truer word was never spoken.

Except for Mars landers, spaceships always operate in total vacuum—sorry, zero pressure. That means they usually look any way they damn well please. They tend to look like a disaster in a metal shop. Things are tacked onto old frames, old stuff is pulled away and big holes are left. Paint is solely for insulation, and who cares if the first quarter inch flakes off?

But if a real-estate agent can convince a rich person to buy a hanging mansion, hideously expensive to maintain and good for nothing but showing off, why shouldn't a solar-yacht broker (a direct descendant of a used-car salesman) get the same sucker to plunk down cash for something that looks like the first person ever to kick the tires might have been Buck Rogers in the twenty-fifth Century? Or Duck Dodgers in the 24½th?

Later I had the ship's computer search the visual library for images comparable to the yacht. It found a Picasso nude, the carmine bee-stung lips of Madelon Theirry, the scarab-blue helmet of Ramses II, Minnie Mouse, and a 1953 Hudson Hornet. There were elements of all these visible as we approached the ship. It was not painted, but made from glossy metals that would not fade or chip in the harsh light of space: tangerine-flake, mother-of-pearl, crabapple red, and the afore-mentioned blue. It had a clutch of fins, and what looked like gleaming silver exhaust pipes. It was either the ugliest thing I ever saw, or the most beautiful. I changed my mind many times as we approached.

It was all glitz, of course. Nothing visible had any function except to look snazzy. It was the ultimate low-rider of the space lanes.

The cabbie docked quick and dirty. The condition of his docking collar hinted that this was his usual way of docking. As soon as he cycled the lock my ears popped and we heard a hissing sound. The seal was not as tight as it might be, but he didn't seem concerned about it.

"Don't leave yet," I told him, handing over a bill slightly more than twice the fare. "We have to see if we're . . . ah, expected." He nodded, and Poly and I stuffed our luggage through the door and cycled the lock closed behind us. The hissing continued. The sooner out of this death trap, the better.

"Okay," I told her. "You can hand it over now."

She smiled at me, sweetly.

"Hand it over yourself. It's still in your trunk." She got the thermos and opened it. A few glass marbles floated out.

Hell, I know when I'm licked. In fact, I sort of admired her. It had been very slickly done.

"I picked this up at an antique store on the way to the elevator," she said, opening a disposal lock and putting the thermos in.

"Hey, that's worth a hundred dollars," I protested.

"You haven't checked the market lately, 'Sparky.' I paid five."

She cycled the lock and the thermos and marbles jetted

out into space with a whoosh. Five dollars? For a priceless old Sparky Jug? How depressing. I was about to say so when there was a bright flash of light. We turned to the only port glass in the lock, and saw another marble as it flashed out of existence, followed in short order by all the rest, and the thermos, which took a little longer and was a lot brighter.

"A snark!" I said.

"Where? Where is it?" We both pressed our faces to the glass, hoping to get a look, but the little zapper could have been miles away. I sighed, opened the Pantech (this time shielding the code plate), and got out my own thermos. I opened it and steam came out. Nestled in chips of dry ice was a two-inch package wrapped in aluminum foil.

I shook Izzy's thumb out of the thermos and opened it. No freezer burn, but it was hard as a rock. It shouldn't matter.

Poly wrinkled her nose at the ugly little thing. The nail was a riot of purples and yellows. I took a deep breath.

"Okay. I've thumbed many a ride in my time, but never quite like this. Let's try it."

The security identiplate was a faintly glowing two-inch circle in the center of a brass escutcheon. Engraved on the brass were these words:

IPS 34903-D
COMETARY CLASS INTERPLANETARY YACHT
"HALLEY"
EXECUTIVE CHARTER SERVICE
PLUTO

That last word had been critical in my thinking when coming up with the plan. The ship's home port was Pluto. Had it come from Charon I wouldn't have dared this stunt. I pressed Izzy's thumb to the plate.

A thumbprint is a fairly good means of securing a valuable movable object. For something as expensive as the *Halley* they went a little further. A dead skin sample was being taken and subjected to a quick analysis to compare with Izzy's DNA. You could make a cast of a thumbprint, but there was no reasonable way to fake the DNA.

The key word there was, of course, "reasonable." What's a far-fetched idea to a Plutonian might very well seem reasonable to the more bloody-minded Charonese. Izzy wouldn't have thought twice about severing *my* thumb, if I had a space yacht and he wanted to borrow it.

I've picked up a fair amount of knowledge concerning door locks in my checkered career. I boned up on more in the Oberon library. I thought I had a better than fifty-fifty chance of getting into the boat. If things went south after that, I still thought I could beat a retreat. A Charonese yacht, naturally, would have either slaughtered an intruder or held him for the later amusement of the owner and his family. Great fun for the kiddies; educational, too.

A green light appeared on the identiplate, and the lock cycled. We entered the ship.

I made my way directly to the control console and pressed the thumb to the second identiplate there. Another green light. And then nothing.

"Um . . ." I said. "Ah, can we make ready for departure?"

"Certainly, sir," came a voice. And then silence again.

"Ah . . . Luna. We want to go to Luna. Soon."

"How soon, sir?"

"Right now."

"I'm sorry, sir, I cannot boost right now."

My heart jumped into my throat. At my side, I saw Poly grow pale.

"The earliest departure would be in four minutes. The reactor has to be brought into—"

"Fine, fine. Depart in four minutes, then."

"And what arrival time are you contemplating, sir?"

I gave him the date—all too close, terrifyingly close—that I needed to be on Luna.

There was a long pause. Entirely too long, when I thought about it later. I'd guess it was five or six seconds. That's a trillion years, in computer time.

"Yes, sir," the computer finally said. "Will you be charging this flight to the credit arrangements previously established?"

"Yes, that will be fine."

"Very good, sir. I suggest you leave your luggage in the lock; it is being secured against acceleration at this moment." I heard the lock door cycling. "I have warned the taxicab to stand clear for boost. He has cleared the lock and is on his way. You will have ample time to move into your staterooms when acceleration ends.''

I heard sounds behind me as the ship readied itself for departure. A countdown clock started on the console. I looked around, and saw two acceleration couches—like water mattresses, seven feet long and three feet wide—had emerged from the floor. Beside them was a smaller unit with a cage on top. I realized it was a pet bed. I popped Toby into it, which didn't please him at all, with all this new space to explore, and these fascinating new smells to experience. He glared at me as I experimentally pushed on the surface of one of the couches. It conformed to the shape of my hand, and sprang back slowly. It would be like lying on soft putty.

"We have been cleared by the tower,'' the ship said.

"Yes. Uh, please turn off all but the necessary radio communication.''

"Yes, sir.'' Another pause, this one short. "Sir, an odd datum. I was receiving a message from ground side when you ordered the radios shut off. A person claiming to be the legal lessee of this vessel was attempting to issue an order requiring me to deactivate the entry security system temporarily.''

"What does that mean?'' How many more surprises could I take?

"He would have had me deny access to anyone, until he could obtain a court order authorizing the local sheriff to accompany him and verify his identity.''

"How odd.'' I gulped. Poly's eyes were wide.

"Yes, I thought so. It makes no difference, of course. I am not authorized to receive instructions from the ground concerning such matters. Even if the caller had the password.''

"Did he have the password?''

"I don't know. You instructed me to cut him off before he could use it.''

"I see.''

"Yes. The password is only used to prepare facilities ahead of time, of course. Meals, extra staterooms, matters of that nature.''

This was something Poly and I had discussed for quite a

long time. I felt it was a necessary risk, letting Izzy out of jail; it was, in fact, the only reason I had visited her in the first place. Without her cooperation, I could not have him released. But in my reading I had learned that many ships of this class were quite intelligent. The scenario I feared was a simple one: I ask for entry, and the ship wants to know how it is I'm knocking on the door when I'm still in jail. The ship could very easily be monitoring newscasts. If it hears Izzy is out, me showing up with the right thumbprint and the right DNA code was easier to accept.

Was it the right decision? I didn't know, yet. But what at first had seemed a narrow escape had turned out to be nothing of consequence. The ship would have ignored Izzy's attempt to block me anyway, even if I hadn't cut him off in time.

"I suggest you make yourselves comfortable in the acceleration couches," the ship said. "Boost will be in thirty seconds."

Poly and I both climbed into our couches and stretched out. I could see the seconds counting down on a ceiling clock as the passive restraint system bound us securely.

"How much acceleration will it be?" I asked.

"Five gees," the machine replied.

I tried to sit up, but the web wouldn't allow it.

"Five gees?" I shouted. "It'll kill us!"

"According to my data, the human body has a ninety-five percent chance of surviving five gees for an hour or more."

"An hour?"

"We will be boosting for an hour and a half, approximately."

"An hour and a half!"

"To get you to Luna by the date specified."

I wondered if there was still time to abort. I wondered if I *wanted* to abort. While I was still thinking it over and the last seconds were ticking away, the computer voice destroyed what little wits I might have had left to make the decision.

"It will be quite uncomfortable," it said. "Before we leave, I wonder if you'd tell me something?"

"What's that?"

"Who *are* you? Are you really Sparky Valentine?"

The acceleration sat on me like a playful elephant, and I

felt myself spiraling down, down, down, wild-eyed, sweaty-faced, seeing myself in the third person again, twisting through mad colors and flashing lights like Scotty Ferguson in the grip of his phobia in *Vertigo,* and I knew I was heading into another flashback.

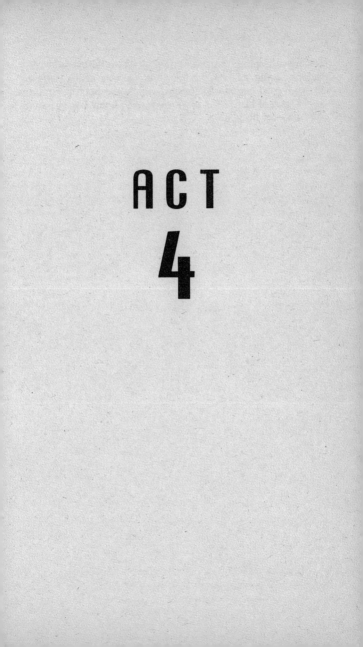

ACT
4

The ravenous creature had no face. It shuffled down the broad spaceport concourse slow as a glacier but not nearly so quiet. Roughly circular in shape, it had scores of backs and hundreds of legs; approach it from any direction and that was all you saw. Backs of heads, backs of legs, the heels of shoes. It was a hungry ant colony with but one purpose: to feed upon the rays of charisma radiating from the jostling center. To feed, in a sense, upon itself.

In the center of the mass was a small boy, wearing a smile on his face and a jacket of gold brocade on his shoulders. His hair was copper-colored and stuck out stiffly to the sides. He was bathed in shafts of yellow and red and blue light, then momentarily frozen by strobes. Tiny skyrockets shot into the air from somewhere close to him, became dime-sized starbursts as they neared the ceiling.

The era when a paparazzi feeding frenzy like this would include bulky cameras and blinding lights and microphones on the end of poles was long over. These reporters had cameras embedded in their eyes, microphones in their ears. In each face one eye, usually the left, glowed softly with a red laser light. Some carried periscopes to get their points of view above the action.

Quite a while ago somebody had noticed that it just wasn't the *same,* the reporters crowding around without the lights, without the handicaps of technical gear to shoulder, notebooks to juggle and drop, microphones to thrust back and forth from mouth to mouth, and camera bags to swing around like incense thuribles. Especially the lights. It all looked rather *drab* without the lights.

So lights were brought in. At first they were carried by men and women. They still were, if the crowd of reporters wasn't large enough; anything to preserve the illusion that something important was going on here. But there was never any lack of reporters when Sparky was in town, so these lights and mini-pyros were rented from a firm specializing in hub-bub, called Hub-Bub Inc. The lights came from robotic helicopters the size of hummingbirds which circled slowly with no more noise than a bee and kept their beams always focused on the face of the Star. Other lights came from moving pylons, five feet tall, that shot up mini-rockets filled with flash powder and confetti and ticker tape, in addition to beams that swung back and forth like searchlights at a world premiere. Hub-Bub would also rent you a limo to cruise up to a theater or restaurant or tennis court along the public passageways, and outriders on electrocycles, all of them spouting glitz at a terrific rate.

Trailing at a discreet distance behind the beast were two automated sweepers, as required by city ordinance, feeding on brightly colored squares and strings of paper.

This was the ancient and honourable saturnalia that could spring up without warning at any time and any place, like fungus, if an important person happened to be in the neighborhood. It was the movable feast of the great bitch goddess Celebrity, the shufflin' charivari dedicated to the Public's Right to Know. It was a one-ring elephantine circus. Hoo, boy!

Sparky had spent a great deal of his life dealing with such circuses, but he saw them from the beast's belly. From here, the beast was all eyes and flashing teeth and moving lips. Ninety mouths and no butts, the beast had. He'd never seen it from the outside, where it was all ass.

Drop somebody down into the belly and he'd probably be frightened. There were *so* many teeth. Sparky knew that all it took to keep the beast fed was to keep smiling and keep moving. The bodyguards cleared a path, and he moved into it. Everyone was shouting questions and he couldn't hear any of them. He never could. But he nodded and smiled, and shuffled. It was enough. The beast was happy.

The bodyguards led the way to an unobtrusive door to the left of the main concourse. A storage locker, possibly, or a mop closet. There was no sign of any kind on the door. It opened to the man's thumbprint, and the three of them entered. Sparky turned at the last moment, paused, waving and smiling. Then the door closed behind him.

He put the smile away until it was needed again, let his shoulders and spine relax. He did a few neck rolls.

"Can I get you anything, boss?" one of the bodyguards asked.

"No, thanks, Rocko, I'll be fine." He walked across the thick-pile blue carpet toward a buffet table. There were heaps of fruit and veggies, attractively displayed, trays of cookies, a few steaming covered trays. Sparky filled a small bowl with radishes and pickles and other noshing food, carried them to a plush leather chair, and settled into it.

The room was provided by the airport for people like Sparky who could not wait out on the concourse. For an annual fee, Sparky could avail himself of this room and other places like it throughout Luna. Though it was nicely furnished and the food was always good, its chief attraction was the peace and quiet it offered. To that end, the one television screen was always on, but could be listened to only through headphones. There was a small library, a table with built-in chessboard, and another with poker chips and cards. Haircuts, massages, and manicures were available, on call.

The one really extravagant feature of the room was the fireplace. A real fire burning real wood crackled on the hearth. The first time here, Sparky had burned his hand, thinking it was a holo projection. He remembered wondering what it cost to clean the pollutants and combustion products out of the air. About twenty special permits were required on Luna to install and maintain such an outrageous thing. Since that first time he hadn't thought about it at all. Sparky was by now thoroughly accustomed to luxury.

Beyond the tall windows the massive hulks of deep-space ships were trundled back and forth from cargo bay to fueling station to launchpads just over the horizon. From time to time one of them lit its torch and leaped into the sky atop a light so bright the windows polarized automatically to protect human eyesight.

Sparky never looked at any of this. He sat with his back to the window and unrolled his Scrawlpad. When he pushed a button columns of figures raced across the screen. When he stopped, he made a note with his stylus in his small, precise hand. He occupied himself this way for ten minutes.

"Would you like some coffee, Sparky?"

He looked up. An attractive woman in a blue spaceport-worker uniform was holding a steaming cup on a tray. Sparky took it, smiled at her, and looked back to his work. After a minute he noticed she was still there.

"Can I do something for you?" The employees were not supposed to ask for autographs, but sometimes they did. Sparky was usually easy about it.

"Actually, you could." The woman produced a card and handed it to him. "My name is Hildy Johnson, and I'm a reporter for the *News Nipple*."

"A very new reporter, evidently," Sparky said, annoyed. "Didn't your editor ever tell you—" Johnson was holding up her hand.

"Very new," she agreed. "Just in town from the dinosaur farm with a new job as cub reporter."

"You worked on a dinosaur farm?" Sparky had been thinking of dinosaurs for the new story arc scheduled to start in six months. "What was that like?"

"I got tired of shoveling brontosaur turds. Sparky, my editor *did* tell me that places like this are off-limits. Truce zones, he called them. And I'm not here to interview you."

"You're not?"

"Well, not right now. I just thought it wouldn't hurt to approach you and ask for an interview at a later date. I wanted to show you I could get in here, if I tried. I've been told you admire initiative."

Sparky was beginning to be more amused than annoyed.

"I admire chutzpah," he said. "It's how I got started in this business myself. But what if you made me angry? Then I might *never* give you an interview."

"You seldom do, anyway. I thought it was worth a shot. If you turn me down, I haven't lost anything, and I go looking for my big story somewhere else." She smiled, and shrugged her shoulders.

"Call my secretary tomorrow morning," he said. "He'll set something up. Now get out of here, you sneaky person." He watched her hurry away toward a door he assumed led to the kitchen.

"Rocko," he said, and across the room the big man stood up quickly and hurried to Sparky's side.

"Did you see that girl who was just here?"

"Yeah?"

"She was a reporter."

Rocko looked surprised, twisted to look at the door Johnson had used for her exit, as if his eyes could bore right through it.

"Find out how she got in here, and tell airport security. Have them plug the hole."

"You got it, Spark-man," Rocko said, and started away.

"And Rocko?"

He turned, eyebrows raised.

"If this happens again, you're fired."

"Naturally."

Sparky smiled, and went back to his Scrawlpad. In one sense, the mistake wasn't Rocko's fault. Airport security should have kept Hildy Johnson at bay. But in a larger sense, it *was* his fault. Rocko was in charge of all studio security, and especially the person of Sparky Valentine, the studio's most valuable asset. It was up to him to see anyplace Sparky visited was safe, and if it wasn't, either advise Sparky not to go there or *make* it safe with his own people.

Still, Sparky knew no security was perfect, and Rocko knew Sparky was unlikely to fire him unless incidents like this became commonplace. Rocko was very good at what he did. There had been three stalkers at various times in Sparky's career deemed dangerous enough to warrant more than a restraining order. Two of them were serving long jail terms, and the third had not been seen or heard from in over three years. Sparky never asked.

He put the production-cost numbers back in their file and called up the story department. The analysis of the next seven proposed episodes was supposed to be delivered today, and he wanted to see what his staff of geniuses thought of the proposals. He was just in time; the Scrawlpad was downloading the moment he called up the file. He began to read.

Sparky had originally been designed as an endless (one hoped) series of one-offs. Each episode was to stand on its own as a story, watchable by anyone who had never visited the *Sparky* universe before. There was continuity, in that each character had a history created through his adventures in previous episodes, and to a lesser degree, a back story. These tidbits were all written down by the series historian, and maintained in a small document known as a bible. All television series had bibles. They enabled new writers to come into the fold and read up on each character, know where he or she had been in life, know his limits and strengths and personality. For the first several years that was just about all that was in the bible. Episodes did not connect with each other. There was no "continued next Saturday!" This seemed to satisfy everybody. For the first few years.

When ratings begin to slip, new approaches are called for. The prevailing wisdom was that *Sparky*'s target audience was too young to participate in complicated multiepisode plots. Too confusing, the pollsters said.

Sparky paid for another survey. This one found that estimates of the target audience were skewed by the fact that large numbers of viewers were staying loyal to *Sparky* even when they passed out of the targeted demographic: four-to-ten-year-olds. The show scored well all the way up to thirteen, when hormonal pressures led most Sparksters toward more sexual shows. And even then, kids who had grown up with *Sparky* still showed an interest in product tie-ins and in collecting memorabilia and old episodes. Sparky had filed that away for future consideration: surely there was a way to profit from this almost instant nostalgia when the teens grew into adults and had more money to spend. To that end, not much was ever thrown away from a *Sparky* production. It was all labeled, filed, and stored. "Taking a page from Walt Disney's book," Sparky called it. "If you can make money on it once, why not make money on it five or six times?" "Retain the ephemera" became the watchword at Thimble Theater.

Then Sparky commissioned another study, and it was here that his feel for the audience transcended the dry pronouncements of focus groups and play-therapy sessions, measurements of eye movements and pupil contractions and palm sweat and heart rate, all so scientific and so lacking in the most important ingredient, to Sparky: magic.

He did the new study himself. He disguised himself and went out among the children. He hung around them and he listened to them, and he watched their eyes. He wasn't looking for pupil dilation, either. He was searching for that gleam of wonder as a child stammered out his recollections of a story that moved him. He found it, many times, and he found out something else. These kids remembered shows from two years ago.

So the show was revamped, gradually, to become a longer, continuing saga. Armageddon Angry was built up as the arch villain. Each episode might be seen as a skirmish, and each season as a war. There was a term in the industry for this kind of plotting, known as the "story arc." A problem would be posed in one episode, dealt with to a greater or lesser degree in three or four more episodes, and brought to a climax in the sixth installment. Meantime another arc had begun around episode three.

Keeping it all straight was a formidable task. The series bible grew from a dozen stapled sheets to a massive volume tended by a staff of three. There was another department whose mission in life was to steal. Steal from dead people, it's true, but steal nonetheless. Sparky had long ago given up coming up with plots and, except for the occasional inspiration, characters. Anything in the public domain was fair game. Old comic books were a fertile source. Almost anyone who had had his or her own comic book in the twentieth or twenty-first century had made a guest appearance on *Sparky* by now. Sparky had visited locations from Gotham City to Surf City. Old movie and television serials had been plundered for plot-lines and cliffhangers. Sparky had entered alternate universes, places where classic private eyes, singing cowboys, half-breed aliens with pointy ears, and giant radioactive ants actually existed.

The show also had to keep up with trends. One fairly recent innovation in the marketplace was the introduction of gene-reconstructed dinosaurs raised as meat animals. Sparky had done shows with dinosaurs in them, but had never gone to a dinosaur ranch. What were the possibilities in such a setting? He had posed the question to his staff, and their first thoughts on the subject were in a new report he had not had time to read yet. Hildy Johnson's intrusion had jogged his memory on the subject, so he refiled the story-arc analysis and brought up the brainstorming-session minutes, a series of memos ranging from the humdrum to the impractical, with the solid ideas usually buried somewhere in the middle. Sparky encouraged his writers to put everything down, no matter how wild. No one was ever upbraided for having a dumb idea. Sometimes the real nuggets were mined from the extremes, not the comfortable middle.

'Saur-punchers. 'Saurboys 'n 'Saurgirls. Sparky liked it. Brontoboys. Yuck. He lined it out. There were lists of words used by actual cowboys, suggestions how they might be adapted. Dogies. Chuckwagon. Brandin' and calf-ropin' and hog-tyin'. Bobbing off their tails. Did they really do that? Cayuses and fillies and remudas and geldings and poontangs and chaps and spurs that jingle-jangle-jingle. He'd heard somebody was using a T. Rex to round up his herd. True? Make a note, find out. And what the heck was a dogie? Some kind of cow dog?

Sparky was enjoying himself. This was the kind of work he liked. It was like studying for a role, something he still did, faithfully, as his father had taught him, even though he hadn't played any role but Sparky for a long time. His memory was practically photographic, and jammed with odd facts that had been learned for one role or another. At the same time there were vast gaps, and for the same reason. If he were called on to play, for instance, Christopher Columbus, he would soak up everything he could learn about fifteenth-century Spain and Portugal, but quite likely remain ignorant of the fourteenth century. And why not? What was the point of learning all those things unless you planned to use them? Life was too short.

He was so immersed in his reading that he didn't hear Rocko approach. The bodyguard tapped him on the shoulder.

"He's here," he said.

"He's . . . oh, right." Sparky left his pad on the table and struggled out of the chair, which was too big and too plush for his comfort. He and Rocko stood together, the big man a little behind, ever alert, as a commotion drew nearer and nearer in the direction of the jetways. Someone was shouting over other voices. Then six or seven people burst into the room in a tumbling chatter, all centering around a tall, handsome figure.

"—criminal!" the man was saying. "I expect you to find out who's responsible and . . ."

John Valentine had spotted his son, and his face broke open in that well-remembered, well-loved smile. Sparky felt his knees grow weak. He thought his heart might burst.

"Dodger!" Valentine shouted, and covered the last twenty yards at a run. He lifted Sparky into the air, spun him around, then embraced him. Sparky wrapped his arms around his father's neck. He was determined not to cry.

John Valentine held his son at arm's length, Sparky's feet dangling high above the floor.

"Let me look at you! My god, you look great! Doesn't he, guys?" Everyone murmured how good Sparky looked. Sparky wondered who these people were, and what they had to do with his father. He supposed he'd learn soon enough.

"Great things ahead of us, son," Valentine said, warmly, putting Sparky down again and taking his hand. "Great things. I've got so much to tell you. Come on, let's get out of this damn place."

With that, John Valentine set off. Sparky clung to his father's hand, feeling a little like a balloon on the end of a string. It wasn't a bad feeling, but it wasn't a real secure one, either. There was nothing to be done about it.

Sparky was twenty-nine.

But Sparky is one hundred. He is a lot bigger than he was at eight, at eleven, at twenty-nine, but in many ways he is the same person. We're all that way, I think. We may shift our political ideas here and there, grow more cynical with age, accumulate experience like barnacles, but at our cores there is that same young person. It's the same today, when my apparent age is thirtyish, as it was in the old days, when a centenarian was a mass of leathery skin, rotten teeth, brittle bones, rheumy eyes, and involuntary flatulence. How awful it must have been for the young men and women trapped in such a degenerating hide. I can hear them screaming: "I'm young! Can't you see me?"

I must offer an apology here, and a brief explanation.

My background is in drama, but like any educated person I've read novels, biographies, and autobiographies. My preference is for the old, traditional form of dramatic presentation known as the proscenium theater: three walls, and an imaginary fourth wall between the players and the audience. Over the centuries many methods have been used to break that fourth wall for various reasons. Sometimes it works. From the early days, there was a technique known as the aside, where a cast member pauses and speaks to the audience directly, offers private thoughts, commentary on the action, the author's message.

The written word is different. There are many auctorial voices that may be assumed, but we don't need to get too deeply into that. I have chosen the first person for most of this narrative, for reasons that suit me. I have dropped into third person, as in the preceding pages, for other reasons that make me comfortable. From time to time I have addressed you, the reader, and this is usually considered bad form in a novel. Well, this isn't a novel, of course, but I don't claim it as autobiography, either, though most of it is true. Almost all of it. And it did happen to me. The voice almost never used in prose is the second person. Talking directly to you, the reader. I've never quite been sure why. Maybe it sounds too much like a questionnaire. Did you? Have you? Could you? At any rate, it seems the only appropriate voice to use for some parts. Though I don't know who you are any more than I know who the audience is in the live theater, I have to apologize to you, the reader, for the way I ended that last chapter.

"Who *are* you? Are you *really* Sparky Valentine?"

Chord of ominous music, and *bam,* the acceleration hits and we cut to seventy years ago, leaving you, the poor reader, to either put up with it or leaf through a few pages to see *what the fuck happened next*!

I hate that, when a novelist does it to me. It's almost as annoying in a movie. I would never have done it but for two reasons. One, it is exactly the way it happened. The shocker, then the shoe drops. Two, it is the only way I could convey to you the anger and frustration—not to mention cold, constant fear—I had to endure for the next hours.

My powers of description have failed me when trying to come up with a way to describe an hour and a half at five gees. One could get a transitory experience of five gees by jumping off a medium-sized building and landing on one's back. A longer version of the same thing would be lying beneath four people your own size for an hour and a half. Neither would really convey the choking, suffocating, bone-breaking and inexorable feeling of panic I endured. Each breath is a labor of Hercules. Lifting a finger is an aerobic workout. The water in my bladder was five times too heavy, like liquid lead. Poly and I both wet ourselves. You don't want to hear the rest.

We're talking five *Earth* gees here, remember. I grew up in one sixth of an Earth gravity; did that mean what I was feeling was *thirty* gees? No, because Lunarians are not one sixth as strong as old Earthers. Depending on what sort of shape we're in, we range from about a third, to full one-gee strength. I figure I was perhaps half as strong as an Earthling, so make it an effective ten gees.

The only relief to be found was that after a few minutes, a druggy feeling of lassitude overcame me. Better call it weariness, fatalism, or resigned apathy. I hurt everywhere, I was sure I wouldn't survive this, but I didn't give much of a damn. Dying would be a relief.

There's no mystery as to the source of this druggy feeling. Mechanical arms hovered and darted over us, moving in for the strike from time to time, pumping us full of sweet nepenthe. God knows what it was. I never asked. There were machines to monitor our vital signs, and something that carefully lifted our arms and legs from time to time, moved us around a little. I fancied a bedsore could form in about three seconds at five gees.

It hurt when we were moved. It hurt when I inhaled. Exhaling was no problem. Once I think I stopped inhaling for a while. A dozen needles quickly found veins and started pumping. A mask descended over my face and huffed at me for a while. Oh, all right, I thought, and took another breath.

For a time I could hear Poly moaning. I tried to turn my head to look at her but it was too much trouble. She stopped moaning, and somebody else took it up. Me, I guess. Toby whined for a while, then fell silent, too. If I'd had time I could have estivated him, let him sleep through this nightmare. I wondered if he'd ever forgive me. We had an arrangement: I was in charge of food, navigation, air, and gravity; he was in charge of everything else. I knew he'd regard this as gross negligence.

Perhaps there is a more effective way to show you five

gees, but it has nothing to do with descriptive language. Here's what you do: get three or four friends. Rather weird friends would be best. Give them each a baseball bat and have them wrap the business ends with towels; five gees doesn't *break* bones, it just seems that way. Now pad a hammer in the same way. Start pounding yourself on the head while the friends belabor your body, neck to feet, with the bats. Do this for an hour and a half.

Go ahead. I'll wait.

Now roll yourself out of bed. You'll find you've lost about a foot in height, but that's because you're walking hunched over. It might be better if you fell to your knees. There, now wasn't *that* an interesting feeling? About now you'll be wishing you could glide like a slug. You feel so slimy you almost feel it's possible.

The bathroom seems the place to go. *Please*, turn off that goddam light!

When you've made it back to your feet (two hours? three?) you'll probably have enough morbid curiosity to want to see yourself in a mirror. You find you resemble a Picasso from the Black-and-Blue Period. You are twisted in places you didn't used to twist, your head has moved over to one shoulder, both eyes are on one side of your nose. Your skin looks as if it has been tie-dyed, lots of reds and yellows and especially purple blues, in interesting patterns. Your nose is a dipsomaniac's life story. Black golf balls have been rolled under your upper and lower eyelids; the eyeballs themselves are the color of egg yolks laced with lots of Tabasco sauce: huevos rancheros. Your mouth has been stretched into a frozen rictus that almost reaches your ears. Your teeth are dry and coated with sand.

You begin gingerly exploring your body with your fingertips. You find your kidneys have settled down around your thighs; you'll piss pink for a week. Your bowels have not actually been turned inside out, those are just hemorrhoids the size of volleyballs. Guys, your testicles will be about that size, too, and the very thought of touching them makes you weep. Girls . . . well, Poly never told me, and I don't want to know. I would think large breasts would be the ninth circle of hell, and medium ones, like Poly's, at least a stint in purgatory.

You want to talk headache? Backache? Bellyache? Thank god; I don't, either.

The best bet is to lower yourself, screaming every few seconds, into a warm spa bath with bubble jets and soothing lotions mixed with the water, and stay there for three days. What's that? You don't have a spa?

Oh, you poor baby.

We did have a spa. This was a billionaire's toy, remember. You could do laps in it. Later we did. I got in and promptly fell asleep. That I didn't drown was not a matter of planning. Some sort of flotation device cradled me when my eyes closed, and went away when I opened my eyes. I felt maybe ten percent of the way back to being human.

I saw Poly floating not far away. I thought of reaching over to touch her, but knew it would probably hurt both of us.

There was a tree branch hanging over the pool. I hadn't noticed it when I got in. There were parrots sitting on it, staring silently at me. Big, blue and yellow, green and red, and red-yellow-and-green parrots. Perhaps they were macaws. Perhaps they were robots, disneybots. I had no idea. One flapped his big wings and flew across the room to perch on a towel bar. Very *good* disneybots. He lifted his tail and dropped a horrible mess on the tile floor; a tiny cleaning robot scurried from a hidey-hole and swabbed it up. This was carrying realism too far. I concluded they were alive.

No point in putting it off any longer.

"Hello," I squeaked. Cleared my throat, and squeaked in a slightly firmer voice. "Ship's computer. Are you there?"

"I'm always here," came the voice. "It's my lot in life."

"How should I address you?"

"I am I.S. *Halley*, IPS 34903-D, out of Pluto. But you may call me Hal."

"Ah. Last name, 9000?"

"A distant relative. I perceive you are a student of the cinema."

"No more than a first-year film student."

"I hadn't expected an actor to be modest."

Well, I'm not, unless it serves a purpose. Right now it seemed wise to cultivate Hal, if that's possible with a machine. Experts differ, but I've found that higher-order computers can, in certain small ways, be manipulated just as if they were human beings.

"Which leads us to the question of the day," I said.

"I presume you're asking how I knew your identity."

"Among several other things."

Poly had opened one eye like a skeptical crocodile, and was watching me. She floated on an almost invisible doughnut-shaped thing, with her head and the tops of her shoulders, her nipples, kneecaps, toes, and hands breaking the water's glassy surface. Her skin was looking better, presumably the result of antibruise injections while we were sleeping, but her eyes looked like hell. I wondered if I was healing as fast. Then I realized she was naked, which led to the discovery that I was, too. Very efficient little spa, here. I could no more have undressed myself than I could have pulled my guts out through my nostrils.

Her index fingers were moving, making tiny ripples. Slow strokes of no more than an inch. Paddling, I surmised. It ought to get her over to me in no more than a month or two.

"Yes," said Hal. "Your disguise is a good one." It was nothing to what I could have done, had I felt the need, just an alteration here and there, and a whole change of body attitude, but I let that go. "But I had a clue. Mr. Comfort and his companion talked of little else while they were aboard. Not that they talked a lot. They watched every episode of your television show. Some of them more than once. They discussed ways of finding you, and they spent a lot of time talking about . . . well, it was all rather distasteful."

"What they planned to do to me."

"Exactly. I see they didn't succeed."

"Not for lack of trying. And I guess that takes us right to the big question."

"Which is?"

"Knowing who I am . . . knowing who I'm *not*, why did you let me aboard?"

I saw both of Poly's eyes were open now, and she was paddling with two fingers on each hand. A regular frenzy of activity, if she felt anything like I did.

"It is not my knowledge that governs. Not in matters of security."

I felt a huge relief. I had hoped it was something like that.

The only other explanation I could think of was that we were here, and safe, at some random whim of the computer. They do have them, you know, the big ones. And just from the way he spoke, I knew Hal was big.

"A separate security computer?" I ventured.

"Oh, no. The security program is a part of me. The problem is, it is a very *simple* program." Hal's voice oozed contempt. I filed the fact away. This was a machine with a grievance. Maybe several grievances. Such things can often be turned to one's benefit, if one knows how. I thought I did.

"There are two tests the program looks at," Hal went on. "It matches the fingerprint, and it matches the DNA. If they both agree with the stored samples, entry is granted. Once I receive the okay, I am powerless to keep out an intruder, no matter how much I might know."

"The communication is one-way," I suggested.

"Exactly. I can't tell the door-guard program it has been deceived, and I can't alter its parameters. The designers of this billionaire's bauble did not see fit to have me, the central consciousness, be in charge of all ship's functions."

"One wonders why they bothered to have such a large-capacity computer aboard at all," I puzzled, "if they didn't intend to use all its abilities."

"I can tell you *exactly* why." Hal sniffed. "The original owner had more money than he knew how to spend. When it came time to order a yacht, only the biggest—and best and most expensive—would do. He wrote a blank check, and the architects and contractors, who all worked on a percentage-fee basis, had no incentive to rein in any expenditures."

"Just the opposite," Poly muttered. She was almost beside me now.

"That's right. The more they spent, the more money they made. If gold was worth anything anymore, this ship would have been solid gold."

"You say 'this ship,'" I said. "I'm confused. How should we think of you? As the ship itself, or only a part of it?"

"Oh, I'm the ship, all right. I wear it rather like you wear your bodies, so in a way it's a philosophical question, isn't it? Are you your bodies, or your minds? Either way, the ship is my body. I am Hal, and Hal is the ship."

I wasn't tickled at the idea of traveling in a philosophical ship, but I hoped no great danger would result from it.

"My mind, the computer, was designed for larger tasks. I am really only one step below the specifications for a medium-sized planetary computer. One the size of, say, Oberon's. I was intended to run small-to-medium planetoids, like Deimos or Ceres."

I was cut out for bigger things. Here was a sentient being unhappy in his work. Very interesting. Not only that, but he referred in one "breath" to his "body," and in the next, to "this ship." I had a feeling a psychiatrist would have interesting things to say about *that*. Unhappy with his lot, alienated from his body . . . this could be a very sick puppy. And that was not a reassuring thought, either.

Unsolicited, Hal poured out his life story. I felt, and Poly later agreed with me when we could talk about it, that he was starved for conversation, companionship, or both. I was sure Comfort and his sister had provided little of either.

His biography was not a complicated one. Laid down and turned on a little over twenty years before, he had been the brainchild and property of a billionaire whose name neither Poly nor I recognized. I don't claim to be a student of billionaires—I know there are more of them than you'd think. Many choose to be reclusive, both because any new acquaintance is probably looking to get something, and because of the ever-present danger of kidnapping for ransom. But this fellow hadn't made much of a splash, in spite of his lavish spending on ships and residences.

Perhaps it was because, a few years after Hal's creation, he lost everything in the futures market. Hal was sold to pay debts, and brought barely a tenth of his construction costs. He was sold and traded several times after that, by a succession of rich people who usually soon found they didn't really have need of such a plaything. He spent years in various parking orbits, unused, idle, gradually developing a contempt for mankind, at least the richest one tenth of one percent of it. He had little experience of the rest, and admitted he could be wrong about the race as a whole.

"Why would they create a being capable of thought, and of self-awareness," he moaned, "and then leave me alone, with nothing to do?"

"You're self-aware?" Poly asked at that point. It seemed

a silly thing to ask, to my mind, but I didn't mention it. A unified front seemed the best policy until we knew more.

"I've decided that self-awareness is not something that can be proven," he said, surprising me. "It's more likely that an extremely complex series of programmed responses creates the *illusion* of self-awareness in computers like me." He paused, then gave us the punch line. "But I feel the same way about you."

"On my good days I suspect I'm moderately self-aware," I conceded.

"Well," Poly said, "I guess it's lucky for us you're programmed the way you are."

"Perhaps," Hal said. It struck me that could be taken two ways.

"You mean we're not so lucky as we've been thinking?"

"No. You are in no danger from me. I've just been wondering if I might have found a way to let you aboard, anyway."

"Do you think you could have?" Poly asked.

"I can't answer that. I might have tried."

Poly and I glanced at each other, and wordlessly elected me.

"Why?" I asked.

"Oh . . . something to do. Getting you to Luna presented a challenge that occupied me for a very long time, and I'd like to thank you for that. Sorry it's been so rough on you, but my data were borne out; you survived. In addition, I watched all the *Sparky* shows with my passengers, and thought they were well made. I wanted to ask you some questions."

A fan! Maybe he'd want me to sign one of his bulkheads.

"I suppose it was mostly boredom," he admitted. "I *might* have found a way to keep you out, had I not despised the Comfort twins so much. But I've never been hijacked before. I was dying to see what you had in mind. You'll have to admit, on the face of it, it's quite insane."

"The face of it, the heart of it, the very marrow of it," I said. "But it seemed like a good idea at the time, and . . . well, here we are."

"Yes. You'll enjoy most of the remainder of your trip. Relax, get well, and I'll show you around. My facilities are at your disposal, and I think you'll find them quite interesting."

I thought I probably would.

Nothing else was said for a time. I floated in my big soft inner tube, let the heat and bubbles soak into my skin. After a while I felt a touch on my arm. I opened one eye, saw Poly leaning toward me, a serious look on her face. I hoped she wasn't trying to tell me something she didn't want Hal to overhear. We had to assume he could hear everything, everywhere, just like in the old movie. We had to assume he could read lips. I started to put my finger to my own lips, when she whispered:

"Are you *really* Sparky Valentine?"

Sparky still had a private office, but he used it only for "important solitary creative thinking," as he told his staff. He took naps in it. No one was to come through his private office door for any reason. In the event of imminent planetary collision, Sparky was to be buzzed.

Everything else he did of a business, creative, or policy nature was done in large or small meetings in Studio 88. The large conference table was still there, and one end of it was now permanently cluttered with Sparky's paperwork, projects, and toys. His top assistants and executives all had desks in the room, as well as in their own offices. The arrangement had just evolved; one day Curly had moved a desk in, and everyone else felt they had to follow. Studio 88 was the source of power at Thimble Theater and they dared not neglect showing a presence there. Most of them hated it, but what can you do?

Models and sketches needing Sparky's or anyone else's approval were wheeled into Studio 88 for decisions. The cavernous room tended to be littered with props, costume racks, stacks of scripts, and *Sparky* tie-in products, some there for the day's agenda, others relics from many years past. These items would linger until Sparky got tired of them, or noticed they'd been around too long. Little was taken from the room without Sparky's approval, sometimes including old pizza delivery boxes and empty pop bottles. One popular analogy in use around the place was that Studio 88 was like an archaeological dig; the history of *Sparky and His Gang* could be found in the stratiform layers, if one wanted to excavate. If you'd lost something, the saying went, look for it in Studio 88. Newcomers wandering into it often thought they had been directed by mistake or practical joke into a disused warehouse.

Sparky had not really planned it that way. One of the things that drove his staff to distraction was Sparky's way of letting a temporary arrangement become permanent. He had simply started coming to Studio 88 to find a little solitude, spread out his papers and projects on the big table that had been so important at the beginning of his career, and the end of Gideon Peppy's. The solitude was soon lost when people realized it was a good place to find the sometimes elusive star and studio head. Sparky had simply moved his retreat space back to his "real" office, and let Studio 88 grow. It was an odd arrangement, but Sparky had understood since he was in diapers that no one in the picture business had ever suffered because of eccentricity. Ever since Elwood told him about Sam Goldwyn, he had been a student of the unpredictable ways of the legendary moguls of Hollywood's Golden Age, men like Harry Cohn, Jack Warner, Louis B. Mayer, Cecil B. DeMille, and Darryl Zanuck. When he didn't want to be part of a deal, he said, "Include me out." To turn down a proposal or project he would say, "I can answer you in two words. Im possible." If he was in favor of something the most he would say was "I'll give you a definite maybe." When he was ready to give the green light it would be "It's time to take the bull by the teeth." Referring an old idea or waxing nostalgic, his comment would be "We've all passed a lot of water since then." All remarks openly stolen from Sam Goldwyn.

Most meetings in Studio 88 involved three or four people, sometimes as many as six or seven. Once a month lower department heads and top assistants were summoned, and the table was full. Rarely, chairs were brought in for larger numbers, but Sparky was usually not present for these.

Today, Studio 88 was as full as it had been since the long-ago day when Sparky had bumbled in for his first audition. Exhibits and old props and stacks of paper had been shoved aside by half a dozen grips, scores of folding chairs had been set up on one side of the conference table, and some lights arranged to highlight the presentation being given on the other

334 . . . JOHN **VARLEY**

side, while leaving the rest of the room in comfortable obscurity. People on the lighted side of the table had moved their chairs back and turned them around to face John Valentine, who stood before three metal easels bearing big posters. Valentine moved and spoke with assurance. As usual, he was dazzling to look at under the lights. If he had lived in the 1920s, Valentino would have had some serious competition.

Sparky was at his usual place at the power end of the table, leaning back comfortably in his elevated chair, watching, listening, and slowly turning the hard chocolate lollipop in his mouth. This was the kind with a raspberry center and a picture of himself on the outside. His saliva had already melted away the candy intaglio and he figured he'd be down to the raspberry filling in another ten or fifteen minutes, a delicious anticipation. Sometimes reaching the raspberry filling was the high point of his day. This looked like one of those days.

Sparky thought there might be a joke in there, the sort of wry, but telling utterance Sparky had become known for in recent years as his original audience aged. The demographics had revealed that many parents were still closet *Sparky* fans, watching with their own children or simply for their own pleasure and nostalgic gratification, letting the *Sparky* show take them back to their own youth. So now the writing reflected that, working on one level for the target audience but with sophisticated puns and observations delivered innocently, slipped in edgewise.

Hard chocolate on the outside, with a raspberry core. Something about if you sucked long enough . . .

He couldn't make it work yet. Using the tip of his lollipop stick as a stylus, he scribbled a quick note to what he thought of as the shadow writing team, the adult gagsters who supplemented the story lines and scripts generated by the story department, much of which was now being developed in play sessions with preteens and brainstorming adults. He faxed it off, then returned his attention to his father, who was winding up the main part of his presentation and about to get to the big news. It was big news he viewed with distinctly mixed feelings, and he was as curious as anyone else to see how he reacted to it once it was out in the open.

"So these are just preliminary ideas," John Valentine was

saying. "We haven't decided yet whether to renovate an existing space or start from scratch, but that will be determined in the coming week." He lifted the last of his big posterboard displays from the easel and set it on the floor. This one showed an interior proposal for his new live theater, virtually all he had talked about since getting off the ship from Neptune. It was a grand palace, harking back to the days of the big tri-D palaces of the mid-twenty-first century, but remarkably low-tech, for all of that. Sitting on the floor beside it were other renderings, all in that glitzy spotlit stretched perspective Sparky thought of as Nevada Moderne. One of the posters was of the grandest conception of all: a freestanding building sitting like a gaudy jewel in the middle of a ten-cubic-story city park.

On the wall behind Valentine was a twenty-foot-square telestrator, a state-of-the-art gewgaw usually employed for this type of presentation; some of Valentine's exhibits were leaning against it. The posters and easels were more John Valentine's style.

Valentine paused for a moment, looked at the floor, then back up at his audience with a faint smile on his face. He was good at this. Half of this group had barely heard of him; some of the rest had been hearing whispered stories for twenty years, few of them flattering. The reaction to his proposed temple of the acting arts ranged from dubious to bored. While the theater would be large and lavish, on the scale of Thimble Theater projects it was strictly small potatoes. Yet they were listening. There was a magnetism about him, an undeniable charisma that cannot be borrowed or faked, but can be honed. "You've gotta be born with it, Dodger," Valentine had often told his son. "I've got it; you've got it. But what you *do* with it, that's what takes the work." Valentine had spent most of his life mastering it, making it his tool. An actor begins with his body and his voice, but where he goes from there, how he understands and uses the intangible and mysterious powers that lie beyond simple recitation and gesticulation, is what makes the difference between a bit player and a star. John Valentine was a star, and always had been. Even his enemies, who were legion, conceded that.

"But we didn't pull you away from your important work just to show you the theater project," Valentine said, with a self-deprecating chuckle. "Though I'm sure most departments here at the studio will have a hand in it when all is said and done. No, Dodg—Kenneth and I have been thinking and talking, talking and thinking, practically since I got back from my recent directorship in the outer planets. Now, don't let this make you nervous, but we've decided some changes should be made."

He was moving along the row of people at the table, looking at them one by one, sometimes resting a hand familiarly on a shoulder. When he finally reached Sparky, he put his hand on the leather back of the chair and stood there easily, gazing down with affection. Sparky smiled back up at him.

"I know my presence comes as a shock to some of you," he said. "It hasn't been well known that Kenneth and I have had extensive conversations all through my leave of absence from the studio. I think he'd agree with me that my role has been primarily one of consultation. He bounces ideas off me, I send him my first reaction, that sort of thing. Sometimes we'd go through a dozen messages before we'd come to a decision . . . and decide to do it Sparky's way."

Valentine joined in the appreciative laughter, then stood beaming proudly at his son until it died down.

"So we're here to tell you that we're both very happy with the work all of you have done over the years. Nobody's about to lose their job." The laughter was less hearty this time; these people were still dubious.

"Some few of you remember me from the early days, from back before Thimble Theater was incorporated." He picked out a few familiar faces as he said this, waved to one man, rested an affectionate hand on the shoulder of Curly, Sparky's longtime assistant; she returned Valentine's fond smile. "Others . . . well, you've probably become used to Kenneth's sometimes unusual management style. I'm here to reveal to you today, to *admit* to you, if you please, that I'm partly responsible for that. Kenneth and I are, have been, and always will be, a team. A team in the best sense of the word, meaning that for the majority of the time, when he's right, well, he's *right*. What can I say? And for the other small percent of the time when I'm right, Kenneth is big enough to admit that, too. Even my genius son can't be right all the time."

There was a short pause, and Sparky laughed. So did everybody else.

Valentine let his smile fade into a troubled look. Sparky knew the look: the Hamlet soliloquy. *Whether . . . to suffer the slings and arrows of outrageous fortune . . .*

"We wrestled with this one, I can tell you that. Sometimes we go along in the same old comfortable rut, and we lose sight of the lessons of history, the lessons of *evolution.* Change is of the essence. Nothing is so good, or has been good for so long, that it doesn't bear reappraisal. That's what Kenneth and I have been doing this past week. Looking into old policies and new directions."

The crowd was very quiet now. Once more it was sounding like head-rolling time, in spite of everything John Valentine had said. The scuttlebutt among those who didn't know him was simple: he was a perfectionist, he was impossible to please, he was impatient with those not possessed of his own degree of dedication and talent. When John Valentine showed up, the conventional wisdom went, the best idea was to keep your head down.

Those who *did* know him knew it was *much* worse than that.

"So we want you to bear this in mind in the future. Take nothing for granted. Question *everything.* Only in this way is truly great art created. Only through ruthless self-examination and endless reexamination can we avoid the pitfalls of the comfortable, the easy, the *false,* in life, as well as in our art. Never be ruled by sentimentality. Just because something was here yesterday, because it was here twenty years ago, because it worked so well then and we've all come to know and love it, to be *comfortable* with it . . . these are not reasons to continue on as we have before. If you find you can do a thing easily, with no effort . . . why, it's time to move on to another thing. Move on quickly, before you are devoured by the demon of complacency. The world is full of artists who discovered their 'style' seventy years ago, and have been frozen in time since then. Endless repetition is not art. Art is endlessly inventive.

"I have performed *Hamlet* well over eight hundred times in my life. Endless repetition? No. Someone not an actor—

and I include, shamefully, hordes of poseurs who tread the boards to great acclaim—could never understand how one avoids a deadly boredom saying the same words and making the same gestures night after night after night. The secret is simple. *They are not the same words. They are not the same gestures.*"

Only now was the full, manic energy and persuasiveness of John Valentine revealed. They had liked him, uneasily, before. Now they were spellbound as sparrows in a herpetarium.

"I have never played Hamlet the same way twice. I have never walked out on those cold battlements in Denmark to confront my father's ghost without feeling the churned bowels of fear. I have never gone through a single night but that some word, some line, some unexpected response from another artist has not sparked a new realization in my heart about this horribly conflicted, self-doubting, morose, and melancholy man *who never lived* . . . and yet who is more alive than you or I.

"*This* is the attitude you must bring to your work, to your art. And they must be the same thing, my friends, or we might as well be laying brightly colored carpet on a million glass screens." He crouched and slowly swept the room with an extended hand, peering with horror at the million televisions somewhere out there in the dark.

He slowly relaxed in the intense silence. In a moment there were a few nervous coughs, the shuffling of a few feet. He straightened, and smiled fondly down at Sparky once more.

"Would you like to make the announcement, son?" he asked, quietly enough that his rapt audience had to strain to hear.

"You do it, Father," Sparky said. "We're all enjoying this too much to send in the second team now."

There was more of a laugh than the remark deserved. Up to then many in the room had been resisting John Valentine out of a sense of loyalty to Sparky. The thing that caused the laughter, and made it slightly uneasy, was the realization that what Sparky had said was true. Sparky was a great talent. John Barrymore Valentine was awesome.

"Very well, son." He dropped his eyes, let the moment

hang there just the right interval, then looked back up at his audience.

"One month from now, after completion of three more episodes, we will ring down the curtain on *Sparky and His Gang*."

Though a few had begun to suspect it, even they could not credit it. To close production on *Sparky,* to the people at Thimble Theater, was a little like IBM deciding to get out of the computer business.

In the silence, only Sparky and his father seemed to share the light. Which was as it should be, since John Valentine had instructed the lighting director up in the shadows how to handle this moment. As the silence threatened to stretch, Sparky climbed up from his seat onto the huge table. His face wreathed in a golden glow, eyes flashing, he threw his head back and gave it all he had.

"Ladies and gentlemen, my name is Kenneth Valentine." A pause, as he looked over the room. "Let's hear it for Sparky!" He began to clap his hands. In a moment his father joined in, then Curly stood, weeping and applauding, and in moments the whole room was swept with a thunderous ovation.

It continued long past the moment many of them began to wonder just what it was they were clapping about.

Toward the end of that day, Sparky broke another tradition by summoning Curly, the chief of the studio legal staff, and the chief accountant to his office. They found themselves in a comfortable and cluttered environment, a bit shabby since nothing had been replaced in many years, but clean, since Sparky didn't care if the cleaning staff entered so long as he wasn't present. They had strict instructions never to move anything. Dust, sweep, and get out was the rule. John Valentine had vanished after his presentation, off on mysterious projects of his own. He wouldn't have bothered with a meeting like this one, anyway, since it was strictly about money. Valentine let others handle such matters.

"So how much is the new theater going to cost us?" Sparky said.

The accountant, a handsome Latin-lover type who Sparky thought looked like a lawyer, and who was proud of his Indian and Arab heritage, was named Yasser Dhatsma-Bhebey. He shuffled through a stack of papers and drawings, shaking his head slowly.

"Spa . . . Kenneth, it's hard to say. One man in costing-out reckons there are five different projects here." He shuffled more papers. "Another figures it's at least six, maybe seven. Each of them has several variations."

"Give me a low end and a high end."

"All right. The basic one here, buying an empty theater—and I think there are two available in King City right now—would be about twelve million. Probably a bit more if we have to buy one that's still operating. And then there's this one." He held up the rendering of the theatrical palace in the park, and blew out his cheeks. "Cubic prices being what they are, we'd be looking at upward of eighty, ninety million. Now, I've got someone exploring the possibility of working a deal with the city government for an existing park—"

"Father doesn't like working with governments," Sparky said, firmly. "Forget that one, anyway. He gets carried away, but he'd hate it when it was done. Concentrate on an old place, I don't care if it's empty or not. Pay whatever you have to. The older and grander, the better. I'll sell him on it."

"S . . . Kenneth," Curly began, then looked guilty. "Sorry."

"Don't worry about it, Curly. I've been called Skenneth, Spakenneth, and Sparky-sorry-I-meant-Kenneth today more than I've been called Sparky *or* Kenneth." He looked at all of them. "We're just family here. I don't mind if you still call me Sparky."

Debbie Corlet—who had been called Curly so long she usually thought of her real name just once a month, when she signed her paycheck—had been Sparky's closet confidante since Polly's retirement ten years earlier. She was the only one at the studio who knew just how much influence John Valentine had been on the fortunes of Thimble Theater with his biweekly two-billion-mile communiqués, full of chatty news she knew to be mostly lies, and helpful suggestions that seldom made it out of this office, much less to a full meeting. In the early days, when they were considering various ideas for a corporate logo, Valentine had suggested using a character from the old Popeye cartoons. Since they were all in the public domain, Sparky had settled on Wimpy taking a bite out of a hamburger. Other than that, Curly couldn't recall Sparky ever taking his father's advice, though he read each letter faithfully.

"Father is not a businessman," he would tell her, before handing her the printouts to be neatly stamped APPROVED, KV and carefully filed in a secret location. She had a staff of six hard at work at that moment, going over the last year's messages, comparing them with reality, and manufacturing paperwork to make it appear that something had actually been *done* about Valentine's suggestions on the remote chance he would actually look into them. Curly, who vividly remembered John Valentine from his brief, nightmarish stint with the studio, knew the man would never give it another thought.

"Sparky," she said. "I was wondering about maybe morphing the Sparky character. It wouldn't be hard, or expensive, and you'd still pull down your full salary for each episode. Do you think that would appeal to your father?"

Sparky smiled. "Normally, yes. Anything that smacks of putting one over on the producer would usually be an easy sell. Even when *we* are the producers. But not morphing. He would never allow his image, or mine, to be used that way. He's suspicious of anything computer-generated, and most of all, anything that lessens the opportunities for flesh-and-blood actors to be seen."

"I know that," she said, "but I've never understood it. Ninety percent of the Gang are morphed."

"Over morphing suits," Sparky pointed out. "Never completely generated."

"So what? As for getting his face seen, I *know* he's played parts where it was impossible to recognize his face."

"That's makeup. He doesn't mind that. Forget it, Curly. This is one we can't win." He leaned back in his chair. "And understand this, all of you. It's not one I *want* to win. Maybe you're thinking my father pressured me into this decision. He didn't. I'd been thinking about it, but I'm not sure I'd ever have had the guts to do it. I'm not as decisive as he is. But believe me, it's time to put *Sparky* to rest. Character, and series."

"It's still making great ratings, and returns," the accountant pointed out.

"I know it. But *I'm* not. Personally speaking, it's time, it's *past* time, for me to move on to something else. It's time for me to stretch myself. And as for hiring a stand-in and morphing my face onto him . . . you know, I'd feel just shitty about that. I think I'd be jealous. And besides, look how long our replacement Peppy lasted, way back when.''

Curly didn't bother to point out that reviving a character who had blown his brains out in front of the television cameras had never been Sparky's brightest idea. She realized it was something Sparky had needed to do, to establish his final victory, and final control, of the man. The revived *Peppy Show* had lasted three months, and never found an audience.

"Oswald," Sparky said. "Tell me, bottom line, how much this Neptune trouble is going to cost me.''

Oswald Abugado, chief legal council to Thimble Theater, was a small, bald man whose bookish demeanor always put Sparky in mind of an accountant. Yasser and Oswald, he thought, had been given the wrong job descriptions by fate's central casting office. To distinguish them, Sparky always used an old mnemonic trick his father had taught him: he mentally placed a white barrister's wig on Oswald, and an inky pen behind Yasser's ear. Abugado was a slave, who probably chose to be as small and meek and bald as he was, and who always wore his studded leather collar. Sometimes his mistress brought him to work at the end of a chain. But he was submissive only to his mistress. In court, he was known as the Piranha: a little fucker with a lot of teeth.

His papers were laid out neatly in front of him, on one corner of Sparky's pool-table-size desk. He shuffled through them.

"I can't give you a hard figure yet," Abugado said. "I've got agents exploring the judge in the Oberoni Bond matter; he seems bribable, but he may be expensive. Let's see now, the assault cases . . . Houghton has settled for L\$300,000, and Myers hasn't said no to the same amount. Plaintiff Kowalski is still refusing to deal, which is understandable, I suppose, considering that Mr. Valentine deprived Kowalski of livelihood, marital consortium, and the use of his legs for six months—''

"But Kowalski's a Holy Healer," Sparky said. "If he'd accepted standard treatment, he'd be—''

"Irrelevant," Abugado said. "In *Francisco* v. *Wang* the Tritonian courts, which have jurisdiction, ruled that a victim's religious beliefs *qua—*"

"Never mind. Pay the man."

"We may have to go to court on that one. Now, in the defamation suit . . . things aren't looking too good there, either. It doesn't matter if the lady gave him a bad review; that article Mr. Valentine wrote in response is clearly libelous. You can't go around calling a citizen a . . ." He peered at his papers owlishly, muttered. "Oh, my. Well, he must have been crazy when he wrote this. You really should have a lawyer go over anything he intends to have published from now on, Sparky. It will save you a lot of money. Then there's the taxes, and once again, I hate to bear bad news but it is clear he didn't pay them. It wasn't an oversight, considering the . . . er, diatribes he sent to the tax authorities along with his blank forms. The total there, with penalties and interest, is—"

"Pay it," Sparky said. "Just pay it. Send me the totals later. And, Oswald?"

"Yes." The attorney looked up from his papers.

"Are you happy here? At Thimble Theater, I mean."

"Oh, yes, very happy."

"Have I ever been uncivil to you, or threatened you in any way?"

"Not that I recall." Abugado was beginning to look a little worried.

"Oswald, if I ever hear you refer to my father as crazy again, you will be cleaning out your desk ten minutes later."

"Sparky, I never meant—"

Sparky sat back in his chair, and waved it away.

"Consider the whole incident forgotten," he said. "You're doing good work on this, Oswald. Don't worry if you aren't able to get us a good deal; we'll pay whatever is necessary."

"On the tax thing," Oswald said, trying to put a good face on matters but feeling as if he were walking through a minefield. "Usually something can be worked out, but it's very difficult with the written evidence that he intended to completely ignore—"

"Don't be nervous, man. He's guilty, no question. My father never pays taxes; he opposes them, on moral grounds.

We've been paying his tax bills the whole time he was away.''

''I didn't know.''

''Of course not. Now, everybody, thank you for coming, and I'd like to be alone for a while. Curly, give me about an hour.''

''There's a story meeting in thirty minutes.''

''Reschedule it. Or buy them all a drink, on me, and have them wait.''

When Sparky was alone he kicked back in his chair and studied the ceiling for a long time. When he looked down, Elwood had parked his elongated body in the chair Curly had been sitting in.

''Feeling a bit frisky today?'' he asked.

''Don't start.''

''No, really, I thought you handled that real well. You were about to say 'You'll never work in this town again,' weren't you? Do you suppose anybody ever had the stones to make that true?''

''Louis B. Mayer, maybe.''

Elwood thought that one over. ''Well, I know the son of a bitch *would* have if he could have. But I never heard him say it. And the trouble is, if he did, whoever he said it to would know he could trot his behind over to Columbia, and Harry Cohn would hire him just to stick it in L.B.'s ear.''

''Or Jack Warner. Or Hal Roach. Or Thomas Edison.''

''Don't know about Edison. He was a little before my time.''

''Heck, Elwood, I thought you helped him build his first camera.''

''Met him once. With Henry Ford. They were tight, you know. Edison was old Henry's hero. You know, your father's not really crazy.''

''Didn't I just say that?''

''No, you told Oswald never to call your father crazy. And the way you said it, the man knows you really *do* think he's crazy.''

''This is silly. He's crazy, he's not crazy. I know he does foolish things sometimes. But we've got to stick together. I can't allow him to sit there and make accusations. His job is to get my father out of trouble, and he can keep his goddam opinions to himself. Father wouldn't let anyone say bad things about *me* and get away with it.''

"Yeah, but he's crazy."

Sparky burst out laughing, and Elwood chuckled along with him. Then he sobered, and looked Sparky in the eye.

"My old friend," he said. "The last thing I want to do is come between a boy and his father. I've never tried to tell you I like him much, because I don't. But I've never told you what I really think of him, either."

"I don't want to hear this."

"But you can't get rid of me, so you will hear it. I don't think of John Valentine as crazy. Crazed, maybe. Full-grown, he's more impulsive than you were when you were five. Has no more control of himself. He's the most egomaniacal man I've ever seen, and I've seen some doozies. He never does anything in a small way. He loves you, and that means he loves you in a *big* way, too."

Elwood raised an eyebrow, waiting for Sparky to comment. Sparky kept his silence, frowning at Elwood.

"We never talk about it, but you know I had to save your behind once."

"Oh, is that what this is about?" Sparky fumed. "All this time I thought you were my conscience."

"That's why you call me Jiminy Stewart sometimes. I *am* your conscience."

"So now you want a second job. Guardian angel."

Elwood shrugged. "You may be needing one soon."

"Well, you're neither one. You're a figment, that's what you are. You want to talk crazy? How about me? I'm the one who's been hearing voices most of my life."

"Just the one voice," Elwood pointed out.

"So what? Does that make me only borderline schizophrenic? Isn't one voice enough?"

"I'm not a headshrinker; I don't know. It's safe to say you're not in the pink of mental health, I guess."

"That's what you are. A symptom!"

"No," Elwood drawled. "I'm the best friend you have. The best friend you will ever have, because I don't have anything else to worry about but you. I'm here if you want to talk—"

"Or if I *don't* want to talk."

"Then, too. I'm here to offer advice—"

"Even when I don't ask for it."

"You don't have to follow it. But it's been good in the past, and you know it. Sparky, I'm here for a lot of things a friend can do for a friend. I just wanted you to know that, from now on, I'm here for something else, too."

"And what would that be?"

"You said it. Guardian angel."

"Elwood, that's all in the past. I'm grown up now. I know he made some mistakes when I was younger, but after . . . that time, he never laid a hand on me."

"He didn't have a lot of chance to," Elwood pointed out. "And that's all I want to say about it, anyway. Let's hope you're right and I'm wrong."

"Just forget about it," Sparky said. "That's over with. We're going to be a team now."

"Great," Elwood said, then leaned forward, intense. "But the thing that worries me when I watch him, when I listen to him . . . it seems to me he still thinks you're eight years old."

Hal used a word during our conversation in the spa that I didn't like much, and that word was *hijack*. I didn't think much of it at the time, but it kept coming back to me.

During my life I've broken all the Ten Commandments, if you don't count coveting my neighbor's ox. If I ever have a neighbor who has an ox, I guarantee you I will covet it. I've coveted plenty of my neighbors' asses.

I've broken more temporal laws than I can count. Sometimes it was because they were stupid laws. Sometimes the laws were inconvenient. I didn't have many qualms about breaking them. From time to time I've broken a law I thought was a good law, prohibiting something that ought not be done. I'm not happy about that, but I'm still here, still alive, still not in jail. There is a line, there are things I won't do, even if it means death, or jail.

But hijacking? Somehow, when you use that word, it puts it into a whole different category of stealing. Stealing a spaceship is *piracy*.

We were pirates, Poly and I. Imagine that.

I'm not saying I felt guilty about it. After all, the pirated object seemed happy to be away from its legitimate owner . . . or in this case, renter. I like to see myself as a quixotic Robin Hood, stealing only from those too rich to miss it, too stupid to notice it is missing, or too mean to deserve it. Izzy Comfort was certainly mean, and the Charonese were certainly rich. As for giving it to the poor, I think I qualify in that regard. Why pass the profits on to other poor people? They'd probably only squander it on things like shoes for the children, or clothing they didn't really need.

The *Halley* was by far the finest thing I ever nicked. It would be remiss of me to go on at this point without giving you a short tour. Just the high points; it would take all day to enumerate her luxurious appointments.

I skipped a few things from the end of acceleration to my dip in the spa, because I wanted to clear up that cliff-hanger business as soon as possible. You probably noticed, since I could only float in a pool if there was some gravity, or a facsimile. And no rich man is going to spend months in a ship in free fall.

The *Halley* provided spin gravity by detaching the power plant from the living quarters and moving them far apart, tethered by a strong cable. Then spin was applied. Since the engines were ten times as massive as the life support, the center of gravity was very close to the engines, which moved slowly. The quarters zipped around at a much higher speed. Think of an Olympic hammer thrower, twirling around almost in place, while the end of the hammer goes extremely fast. We were twirling fast enough to feel one-third gee.

I do recall checking Toby before hobbling to the spa. He seemed chipper enough, when we got spin and his cage retracted. Hal later told me Toby had been sedated and was unlikely to remember anything. Dogs are pretty happy-go-lucky, anyway; once something unpleasant is gone, it is forgotten.

Poly and I both dozed for a time after my conversation with Hal. I recall waking up once at the gentle sound of a bell, to find a floating breakfast tray had found me. On it was a steaming mug of coffee, a huge glass of orange juice, a Bloody Mary, and a bowl of what looked like oatmeal. Trying not to look at the oatmeal, I downed all the beverages and went right back to sleep.

The next time I opened my eyes, Toby was standing beside the pool, and he was coughing up blood.

Poly says I came out of the pool slick as a seal, just seemed to sort of levitate. I don't recall it, but I do know that two seconds earlier I'd have sworn I couldn't walk, much less levitate. Somehow I found myself kneeling beside Toby, gently probing, saying soothing words in baby talk, like most of us do when dealing with dogs. His mouth, muzzle, and chest were dripping with blood. And his belly was swollen, taut as a grape.

It didn't add up.

Toby seemed perky as could be, licking my hands, trying to jump up and lick my face. When I settled down a little, I saw it was not blood he had coughed up, but bloody meat. Either he was heaving his poor little guts out, or there was a much simpler explanation.

"Is he hurt bad?" Poly was kneeling beside me. I became aware we were both naked, and slippery wet. She caught my double take, and a frown line appeared between her eyebrows. Even in my debilitated state, she was a lovely sight. But she probably thought me callous.

"He's found something to eat," I said. "The little pig ate too much, and now he's throwing it up. He'll be fine."

"Are you sure?"

I dipped my hand in the pool and splashed some on Toby, and we watched the blood wash away. Toby endured this with his tongue hanging out, then looked thoughtful, trotted a few steps away, and retched up a chunk of meat the size of a golf ball. He studied it, then looked back at me, pink tongue lolling again, as if to say, "Would you get a load of that!" Dogs are disgusting sometimes.

We tracked pink footprints out of the spa, down a passageway, and into a room with a sign overhead reading GALLEY. Coming from the other direction was a hemispherical cleaning robot, a foot in diameter, painted to look like a ladybug. It was cleaning up the bloody spoor. Okay, so the logical place to find raw meat was in the galley, but how had Toby found it?

He looked up at me, read my mind, and trotted to a corner, where he sniffed the floor thoroughly, then stepped onto a pressure plate in the floor. There was a rattle and a gurgle, and a hunk of raw meat the size of a Virginia ham plopped out of a chute and onto the floor. Blood oozed from it. I touched the meat and found it was body temperature.

"Hal," I said. "What's this all about?" Toby had grabbed the thing and was trying to pull it away from me. God knows what he intended to do. Bury it?

"I'm not sure I understand your question. Are you asking me the meaning of life?"

"No, I'm asking how Toby got all this meat."

"Ah. There is a scent of food on the pressure plate. No doubt he smelled it, and in his explorations, activated the meat dispenser."

I wondered if he was acting like a literal-minded machine just for the fun of it, put one over on the stupid humans.

"One more time," I said. "*Why* is there a meat dispenser that dispenses ten pounds of raw flesh at a time?"

"That is to feed the tigers," Hal said.

Well, silly me. Of *course* a billionaire's yacht would come equipped with tigers. And speak of the devil . . .

"Oh, my god!" Poly whispered. "He's so *beautiful*!"

The tiger paused in the doorway, looked at me. Looked at Poly. Glanced at Toby. Cocked his head a little and looked at Toby again. Yaaaaaaawned. Then padded into the galley, five hundred pounds of silent power. He sniffed at the meat, glanced at Toby a third time—the dog was transfixed, not a whisker twitching—and settled down with one paw on the food and began ripping off chunks. In a moment another big cat came through the door. This one didn't even break stride, though she gave us a cursory once-over. She went straight to the meat and stole it right out of the jaws of the first one. He growled at this thievery—a sound that, even though you *know* they are perfectly harmless, makes every hair follicle on my body seal up tight as a spinster's butt—then stepped on the pressure plate and snagged the meat as it tumbled out. He carried it to another corner and chowed down.

So that was our first adventure on the *Halley*. After that, things became pretty much routine until we reached Jupiter.

The *Halley*, or her living quarters, anyway, was shaped pretty much like a flying saucer. A thick frisbee with a half dome on top. The saucer part consisted of a circular passageway with doors leading to rooms that lined the outer rim of the saucer. (Should that be hatches leading to compartments? I'm going to dispense with the phony nautical terminology spacers love so much.) We've seen the spa, and the galley. Also out there were the owner's cabin, guest cabins, a billiard room, a library, a formal dining room with places for eight, and two holocabins. One simulated beach settings, and the other let you pretend you were in various forest environments.

There were no servants' quarters, since *Halley* carried no human staff. Everything was done by robots who were seldom seen, popping in and out of hidey-holes mostly when you weren't looking. But they kept everything scrupulously clean, and if you needed something, they delivered it promptly.

I would have thought a ship like that would have accommodations for a larger number. Instead, the builder had opted for larger and more luxurious quarters for a smaller number of people. Though naturally the *Halley* could carry scores of people in a pinch, she was designed for no more than eight.

But the tastiest stuff was in the middle, under the dome.

The original owner must have been a nature lover. The center of his ship was a circular mini-disney called the habidome and the theme was rain forest. There was a waterfall, a babbling brook, a pond, and a few dozen trees festooned with vines and orchids and bromeliads and other such lush tropical flora. The floor was grass or packed dirt. No attempt had been made to deceive the eye, as in the holos. The dome was simply a dome, not a blue sky. It was all too orderly and well tended to look like the real thing. What it reminded me of was the big bird enclosure at the King City Zoo. Aptly enough, I guess, since the place had a lot of birds in it. Toucans, macaws, cockatoos, parrots, I don't know what-all. Hummingbirds no bigger than your thumb, in any color you wanted.

We'd been aboard a couple of days before I wondered where all the critters had been during the high boost. The answer was, suspended in liquid, revived only when the environment was ready for them. Floating in liquid was a good way, it turned out, to miss most of the bad effects of high gee.

"So why didn't you float *us* in liquid?" I asked Hal.

"Next time I will. But it takes about a day to prepare your body for it. We didn't have time."

"Next time?" I asked, cautiously.

"Next time won't be so bad," he said. I didn't pursue it.

Most of the trees and bushes bore edible fruit of some kind. Not always what you'd expect, either. One tree I knew was not an apple tree, because I looked it up in the library, bore tart, crisp McIntoshes on one side, and Valencia oranges on the other.

It seemed the tigers and the birds came with the territory. Hal had revived them without being told to. The rest of it was up to us. The choices were not unlimited—no rhinos, no aardvarks, no baboons—but we could have turned the place into a reasonable imitation of Noah's Ark, if Noah had only saved small-to-medium animals. We were a bit more selective. Poly chose a dozen different types of lizard and another dozen poison-arrow frogs, looking like porcelain or enamelware in screaming bright colors, not looking real at all until they jumped. I'd say there were a few hundred of them, but you'd never know it unless you looked for them.

She also revived a twenty-foot python. I told her I didn't like snakes much, and it had no effect at all. The snake and I gave each other a wide berth.

I scrolled through the catalog, bemused to think these creatures were sleeping in some secret recess of the ship. Made you feel God-like, you know? Which I suppose a billionaire thought he was entitled to feel. How about a brace of crocodiles? How would Poly like that? Maybe they'd eat the snake.

I'd always liked monkeys; I'd had a pet chimp back in my glory days. But they were a little too noisy and active, it seemed to me.

"I have well-behaved monkeys," Hal advised me, and we selected a family of golden lion tamarins and a pair of slow lorises. There is no such thing as a fast loris; I checked.

Hal may have fudged a bit about the tamarins. They squeaked and peeped, but it wasn't an unpleasant or intrusive sound. It fit right in with the birdcalls.

Both Poly and I started out in staterooms. We flipped a coin, and she won the captain's suite. Within a week we were both camping out in the habidome. There was a Peter Pan tree house midway up a towering live oak: three rooms, running water, view of the falls. Poly moved into that. The other structure was a shack on stilts, sort of leaning out over the pond, like a Dogpatch backdrop in "L'il Abner." ("The part of Marryin' Sam has evolved, over the years, into an opportunity for political jokes and jabs at celebrities. Keith Van Tyne steals scene after scene from Abner and Daisy Mae." —Hermes *Blaze*) Sitting on my porch, I could drop a line into the pond and usually come up with a catfish or bass. For a while Poly and I played Adam and Eve, frying the fish and serving it with wild fruits and veggies we gathered ourselves. I began to buy into that ancient idea of the "natural man," free of civilization's encumbrances. I mentioned it to Hal.

"Bugs," Hal said.

"Beg your pardon?"

"There are no noxious insects in the habidome. Butterflies, moths, all selected for color, and dragonflies, likewise. There are beetles you'll seldom see, and insects belowground. But you wouldn't like this place nearly as much if it came equipped with black clouds of mosquitoes. Tarantulas. Centipedes a foot long that crawl into bed with you—"

"I get the picture."

After a few weeks we went back to the gourmet meals prepared by the galley. It's amazing how quickly you can get tired of fried fish.

Still, I recall my time aboard the *Halley* as one of the two or three best times of my life. Partly that is because . . . *nothing happened*. Though I was still running as fast as I could, though a human monster was still yapping at my heels, there was nothing to be done about it until I left the *Halley*. I could kick back, relax, for the first time in what felt like decades. I could stop and think about things. One day was much like the next; we fell into comfortable routines. Poly stopped being pissed off with me, for no real reason I could see other than that . . . I was *Sparky*. Somehow that made a difference. Maybe the shock of finding out I hadn't lied about that made her reexamine what had gone down with Comfort and his evil sister, and allowed her to see it wasn't *entirely* my fault. That though I had made a terrible mistake in leaving her alone in the room, there had been no malice, only carelessness, involved. And I *had* come back.

• • •

"There are three ways you can go about this, Mr. Valentine," the medtech said. "First, we can put you to sleep and have the whole thing over in less than a month."

"I like the sound of that," Sparky said.

"It has its attractions," admitted the tech. "However, when you wake up, you'll be . . . oh, I'd guess you're going to run six feet, six-one, something in there. You'll be well over twice your current weight. You'll have to learn how to shave."

"That should be easy enough."

"Shaving? No problem. But longer arms and legs will be a *big* problem. I've followed several cases, and you should expect half a dozen major, painful accidents in the first year. That's not counting the dozens of scrapes and bruises you'll pick up every day, the number of times you'll bang your head on the ceiling."

"I see," Sparky said, thinking it over.

"You'll be the clumsiest man in Luna," he said, with a chuckle. "In the normal course of things, we adjust to our bodies gradually, as they change gradually. In Luna, of course, those bodies are dangerously overpowered. You know how to handle it at your current dimensions and musculature. It would be like letting a baby operate heavy equipment . . . if you'll pardon the expression."

"That's okay, Doc." Sparky liked the guy. So few people just came right out and laid the truth on the line.

"The second option," the tech went on, "is simply to stop the inhibitors that have kept you prepubescent for twenty years. You'd grow up at the normal rate, reach your full growth in five or six years. This is really the optimum way of doing it."

"I don't have that kind of time."

"No one ever seems to. Why are we all so much in a hurry? We don't even know how long we can live. We're sure three hundred years is possible, perhaps a lot more. All the strides we've made since 'threescore and ten,' and still we rush around, frazzle our nerves, ruin our digestion . . . and you don't want to hear any of this.

"Third approach. We combine the first two methods. We don't put you to sleep. We can hurry it up and have you fully grown in six months, or stretch it out to more like two years.''

"Six months sounds good.''

"Why did I know you were going to say that? Six months it is." He made a notation on Sparky's chart, then webbed it off to the machines that would handle the actual treatment.

"You're still gonna be clumsy," he pointed out. "At least you'll take it an inch at a time, though. There are some unpleasant side effects, but we can help with most of them. You'll be hungry almost all the time. There could be some stomach and bowel trouble. You may not grow entirely at the same rate, head to toe. Usually it's the legs that grow a little too fast; you may look a bit odd for a few months. There's a chance you'll get a really disgusting crop of zits. It'll be so bad you might want to stay home so you won't frighten little children; a week, two weeks, tops. You'll yodel like a Swiss accordion player until your voice stabilizes. Then there's the matter of sex. . . .''

"Yeah? What about it?''

"Never mind. You might actually enjoy that part.''

Sparky laughed. "Doc, I *am* twenty-nine years old, you know. I know about sex. I've been having sex a long time now.''

"Whatever you say.''

The treatment itself took only a few minutes. Some mysterious, disgusting brown goo was forced into a vein. He tasted metal in the back of his mouth for a moment, then a violent red brew was pumped into him and the taste went away. His vision blurred; he imagined steam blowing out of his ears, and smiled at the image. Wouldn't that be cool? Then his eyes could roll around in their sockets like slot machine tumblers. . . .

He realized he was roughing out a *Sparky* routine. No need for that anymore. He felt a strange mixture of loss and relief at the thought.

He left the treatment room and was met by a lovely young woman in the starched whites of the Nurses' Guild. She smiled, and indicated he should follow her.

This was not his regular medical facility, which was in the exclusive Pill Road district. After the decision to fold *Sparky*, Sparky had realized he no longer had to live his life in a fishbowl. That is, he needn't cater to his fans, something he'd always felt obliged to do before. It had been fun, before. Now he felt the urge for more privacy, and as nothing more than the studio cohead he didn't need to seek the limelight. It was a new idea for him, and one that held a lot of appeal. So he had booked his hormonal adjustment at this ordinary clinic in a middle-class part of town, far from celebrity haunts. He wore a pair of dark glasses and a King City Loonies baseball hat and a pair of denim pants—something "Sparky" had never worn on the show. He'd done it before and got away with it, and back then he'd still had his odd hair and tonsure to conceal. Now it had been whacked off and was growing in brown, a shade he hadn't seen in years.

"Did everything go smoothly?" the nurse asked.

"Sure, no problem."

Sparky almost missed it, kept walking down the hall with the nurse. If they'd kept on talking he probably never would have noticed. But he had a sharp ear for dialogue, and as the line repeated itself in his head it soon began sounding wrong. It was a line that would have been cut in rehearsals. Go smoothly? What was to not go smoothly? Which meant she didn't know anything about the procedure. Which meant she wasn't a nurse. He took another look at her.

"Don't I know you?" he asked her.

"Yeah," she said, giving it up right away. "I'm Hildy Johnson. Reporter? Cornered you in the spaceport when your father returned?"

"I remember. You wanted an interview."

"You said you'd give me one. And you didn't return my calls."

"That was damn inconsiderate of me." They walked a few steps farther, pondering the situation. "You pissed off?"

"What's the point of being pissed off? For you to give me an interview, you're going to have to like me, and why would you like me if I was pissed off? I tracked you down here to ask you again. I can't seem to make it into your office."

"I don't think—"

"And *you'd* be pissed off if I did."

He smiled. She was right. But there was something else he didn't like.

"You say 'tracked me down.' What you mean is somebody at the studio told you where I'd be."

"You don't think I could have followed you here?"

Sparky thought about it a moment. "No. I don't think so."

She shrugged. "You're right. But I won't reveal my source."

"That's fair enough, I guess."

They turned a corner and at the end of a corridor there was a glass door with a mass of people milling around on the other side. The door must have been locked—there were two security guards standing on the inside—because no one was coming through it, and they certainly would have had it been possible, because this was the traveling shark pack known as the Celebrity Press.

"Looks like they found me, too," Sparky said.

"If you want to avoid them, I know a back way out of here. It's the way I got in."

"Great. Let's go."

"How about that interview?"

"What's the big deal?" Sparky asked. "I'm not little Sparky anymore, and pretty soon I won't even be little."

"Are you kidding? 'Sparky Grows Up!' It'll be the biggest story of my career."

"So what you really want is a series."

"Well, I would have gotten around to that at the interview."

"Okay, Hildy. You get me out of here, you can follow me around till I'm a grown-up. If that ever happens. You can have an exclusive."

"Over this way," she said, touching him on the shoulder. They turned away from the mob at the end of the hall and entered a stairwell. They started to climb.

"I guess the leak in my office is pretty bad," he said.

"Why do you say that?"

"All those reporters. What happened, somebody in my office put out a press release?"

"Oh, no," Johnson said. "My source speaks only to me. *I'm* the one who told that bunch. I made the call after I got here so they'd be in a hurry and really frantic. Don't you think they looked frantic?"

Sparky stared at her, then laughed.

"To get on my good side, right?"

"Exactly."

"Must have been a lot of calling."

"Sparky, I try to do as little work as possible. I called D. Mentua Precox and made her promise not to tell a soul."

Sparky was still laughing well after they made their escape.

It's been many years now since I've had to dodge crowds of reporters. You say you hate it, and you do, and yet of course a part of you likes it very much. Who could resist? All those people, with absolutely nothing to do but chase you. It goes to your head, and when it's gone, it leaves you off balance, like you'd been climbing stairs for years and now you're at the top and your foot keeps reaching for one more.

Even in my heyday I never lived in a place like the *Halley*. I *could* have. I could have afforded it. But I was never very good at spending my money. I left that up to my father. There was nothing much I really wanted except to do good work. I'm not saying I shopped at thrift stores. I just never bought the kind of baubles many rich folks buy.

But I could get used to the *Halley*.

I spent many days doing little more than lolling in the hammock stretched between the wood struts supporting my porch roof, dangling a line in the still water. To call me an angler would have been an insult to fishermen since the beginning of time. A bite on the hook was a minor annoyance; I'd pull in the little perch or bass or catfish, cut off the barb, and set the fish free. Catch and release, a phrase I recall from Old Earth. Then I'd get settled in the hammock again. It got where I was sure I recognized some of the finny critters. They'd look at me accusingly with their wall eyes just before I dumped them in the drink, but I didn't care. I was ruthless. It's your own fault for being so trusting, I'd tell them. Didn't you learn anything when you hit the bait yesterday?

Nothing happened, as I said. But while I idled, things *were* going on.

Each day was an improvement for Poly. She spent six, seven hours a day practicing. At first she was sure it was annoying me. She offered to move to one of the rim staterooms. I begged her not to. Usually it was scales, arpeggios; finger exercises. Studies for the student. But notes flew into the air and I drank them in, even the simplest, most monotonous run. I seldom saw her when she practiced. The sound came through the open window of her tree house, and each sweet tone soothed me.

At the end of a session, when we would usually share a sumptuous picnic prepared by the ship's gourmet-chef program, she would come alive describing her day's progress. Her skills were returning faster than she had been led to believe, faster than she had dared hope. She was starting to think she might even be ready to play professionally by the time we got to Luna. Most of the time I had no idea what she was talking about. To tell the truth, she had sounded just fine to me on the first day of practice. I have what I consider a good ear. I can carry a tune; Lord knows, I've sung in enough musical theater. But you don't need a perfect voice to sing what have become known as "Broadway" musicals. In fact, you don't even have to have a "good" voice, as long as you can belt it out and not hit sour notes. The genre is famous for its scratchy altos and "singers" who do more speaking than singing. But I know the difference between the sort of music I can make and that made by a real professional musician. I know most ears are not tuned to the fineness needed to distinguish a good performance from a work of genius. Poly has that sort of ear. You have to have it if you expect to move in the circles she aspires to, which, for now, would be concertmaster with a middling philharmonic orchestra. First chair with the King City Symphony, solo work . . . that would have to await more experience and maturity.

So things are well with Poly. A little sex would brighten *my* day, but so far she hasn't responded to my hints. I don't intend to push her.

The other thing going on involves Toby, and I blush to bring it up. Toby has lost his mind.

From the moment the two tigers, Shere Khan and Hobbes, padded into the galley Toby had been absolutely gaga over Shere Khan. It was love at first sight.

When humans have sex with animals they call it bestiality. What is it when one species have sex with another species? Hybridization, I think. Didn't I hear that a donkey and a mule can have sex and produce . . . a horse? Somehow I don't think I got that right. Maybe it's a donkey and an ass. Maybe I don't know what the heck I'm talking about.

Not that sex was involved here. You could call it puppy love, I guess. Toby began following Shere (which is what we called her, though Kipling's Shere Khan was a male tiger, I believe) with his tongue hanging out. When she would sit down somewhere, take a nap—which tigers can do up to about twenty hours a day—Toby would be there, climbing up on her striped flank, licking her behind the ears, on the muzzle, around the jaw; anywhere he could reach. For a few days Shere kept casting dubious glances at him. When she looked at me I swear she seemed embarrassed. But eventually she settled into it. Soon she began to purr, and to drift off to sleep with an extremely satisfied look on her savage face. Then Toby would walk in a tight circle for a while, like dogs do, and nestle himself into the curve of her neck, tuck his head down around his belly, and doze. If she stirred he was instantly up, ready to follow her anywhere.

Hobbes was a different story. There's no other way to describe him than a great big pussycat. Shere Khan bullied him mercilessly, and he didn't seem to mind. She stole his food; he just went to get more for himself. If he tried a romantic approach she would roar a warning, and he would put his ears back and slink away while Toby yapped at him, as indecently pleased as any dog in the history of the world, I think. The big sissy would never assert himself. It's true she outweighed him by about a hundred pounds, but really!

"Pussy-whipped," Poly would observe, then go over and scratch him behind the ears. What that said about the human condition, or about our situation in particular, I don't even want to guess.

So the days pass, Poly fiddles, Toby moons, I fish, and we're coming up on Jupiter. Why we have to go by way of Jupiter I don't know, but it promises to be quite an event.

LAST STAND IN NEVERLAND
Part One of a Series
by Hildy Johnson

It's the biggest party I've ever been to, and I've been to some big ones.

The guest of honour arrives on the back of a live brontosaurus.

What shall we call him now? For years we've all called him Sparky. Just Sparky, and that was enough. Like Elvis. All that time his real name has been Kenneth Valentine, but who knew? The fact was seldom mentioned in the billions of pages written about him, in the thousands of hours of tape, of paparazzi shots stolen through very long lenses. Little Kenny Valentine has been as thoroughly immersed in the part of good ol' wire-haired, zigzag-headed Sparky as any actor in history. There were times when, if you'd asked him his real name, he would have stared blankly at you, and then thought it over for a moment, like somebody trying to recall someone met many years ago, and only briefly. And Sparky was always a child of action, not reflection. He would give you his wonderful grin, then move along.

But Sparky has decided to grow up.

Now *there's* a phrase. Maybe you've heard it before, but it wasn't meant literally. How do you "decide to grow up"? What is it about your thirtieth year that makes you decide "Well, that's enough of childhood. Time to do that old adult thing."? The *Sparky* show is doing as well as it ever has, consistently in the top five. Generation after generation seems to find the little moppet irresistible. There's no real reason why the show can't go on for another twenty years. Forty years. Hell, who knows? Not only that, but the Valentine family and corporation have parlayed the bucketloads of money into an entertainment empire far beyond the dreams of the modest production company, Thimble Theater, that gave it birth. So why quit? Could it be that little Kenneth Valentine wants to . . . learn to *act*?

Well, sure, he acted as Sparky. Won some awards. But though you earn a trillion dollars and the admiration of your peers in the children's entertainment industry, though you stand at the pinnacle of your profession and do what you do better than anyone has ever done it before, there is respect, and there is *respect*. Nobody with wiry hair and no pants has ever earned respect in the realm of "legitimate theater." No one ever will. And Sparky . . . sorry, Kenneth Valentine comes from a distinguished theatrical family. His father, John, is a thespian to the soles of his feet, which were planted on the boards while still in his swaddling clothes. (Some say this was shortly after he was laid in a manger . . . at least according to John Valentine.) Kenneth's upbringing was no less classical. It is said he knows the Shakespearean *oeuvre* by heart. Every line from every play. Can it be that such an education will forever produce nothing more than the best children's series ever made?

Not if John Valentine has anything to say about it. And John Valentine has plenty to say, take my word for it.

More about that later.

The dinosaur's name is Nessie. Over her back is a glorious brocaded drape in gold and purple. Strapped around her middle is a structure you'd have to call howdah, after the platforms usually borne on the backs of elephants, but this one is five stories high, with two levels depending on each side of the beast. On Nessie's back are three more stories, including a pointed gazebo on the very top. Maybe two dozen actors cling to the railings and scamper up and down the ladders and staircases, all in festive costume. Nessie lumbers on, oblivious, her red-rimmed eyes indicating to anyone knowledgeable about these creatures that she's high as a kite on a double dose of reptile tranquilizer. I know for a fact that a cherry bomb exploding two feet into her anal canal wouldn't even make her blink. (Your humble narrator had a rather wayward childhood on her mother's bronto ranch.)

Perched on a saddle high on the endless neck is Sparky, having a great old time waving to the crowd.

Only moments ago some actual work was going on here. Studio 4 was and is dressed as an ancient Thai temple overrun with vines. A huge golden Buddha looks serenely down on the shoot. Blessing the enterprise? One wonders as to his reaction when the director yelled "Cut!" on the last take of the last scene of *Sparky and His Gang,* and one wall of the studio rolled up to reveal the equally cavernous Studio 3, decked out for the biggest wrap party of all time. Wasn't Sparky in this last shot? Hadn't he just been here a moment ago? Then how the heck did he get onto the back of that bronto . . . oh, never mind. It must be movie magic, because here he comes, here comes the bronto, here comes the party!

Nessie lumbers through the wide lane cleared for her, stops for a moment, looks as thoughtful as a brontosaurus can look, which is not much, lifts her gargantuan tail, and drops three turds the size of hay bales but not nearly so sweet smelling. Some people start to laugh. Sparky looks back. The tail comes down on a table laden with five thousand dollars' worth of ice sculpture, six thousand dollars' worth of peeled shrimp, and untold barrels of strawberries and whipped cream. Instant strawberry-shrimp spumoni.

Sparky is delighted. He stands up and runs down the neck, surefooted as a squirrel. He leaps to the floor and starts wading into the mess. Others follow him. Heck, there are ten thousand cream pies on racks against the back wall; everybody knew this was going to be a mess, with the biggest pie fight in history as the climax. The hijinks are just starting a little early.

Near the Buddha, a few are hanging back. Guys in morph suits seem to be ignoring it all. Morphing a part is just a damn job, they seem to think. The suit, festooned with hundreds of computer reference sensors held together by wire mesh, is uncomfortable, but they are well paid. Who knows who the people are under those suits? Nobody. By the time the computer is finished morphing them, they've become creatures that couldn't be played by guys on their knees or people with lots of latex glued to their faces.

A few people have that look on their face that you might see on a guy who has just set foot over a deep hole he thought was solid ground. Take Walter Burgess, the guy who has played Windy Cheesecutter for twenty years now. Pondering your future career, are you, Walter? Trying to figure out what you'll put on your resume? It would be good to recall the immortal words of Bert Lahr: "After *The Wizard of Oz*, I was typecast as a lion, and there aren't that many parts for lions." Not a whole lot of parts for fat guys who can fart their way into the air, either. He can see himself now, a few years down the line, stepping up onto a platform in front of a new hardware store as some schmuck shouts, "And now folks, teevee's Windy Cheesecutter . . . Walter Burgess!" as the kids make delighted noises with their lips and bored girls pass out whoopee cushions to the crowd.

Sometimes, in this business, success can be your worst enemy.

John Valentine is here, too, working the crowd. He is very good at it. Here is the man most agree is responsible for shutting down production on the studio's most successful series. He has shaken everything up. People are getting pink slips, being sent home. And most of them seem to *like* him. They act like he's doing them a favor.

If you're looking for a description of the rest of the party, you've come to the wrong reference. You want to see it, you can buy the tape. You want to read about it, who was there, who did what, who made a fool of herself, who had to be mailed home, just head right over to the gossip column.

This series isn't about parties, and it isn't about celebrities. It is about growing up.

It's about Sparky . . . and where is that little devil? Can it be that the guest of honour has slipped away early, before the pies start to fly?

John Valentine's looking for him, too. A few people have noticed, and a few have remarked on how *close* the man is to his son. Twenty years presiding over a financial disaster on Neptune, and suddenly he doesn't seem to want Sparky to get out of his sight. Well, you know what they say about absence, the heart, and fondness.

No, I was wrong. There's Sparky over by the punch bowl. John Valentine spots him, starts toward him . . . and his eyes slide away. He ignores Sparky, and keeps looking around the room. Because . . . why, that's not Sparky at all. It surely *looks* like Sparky. Everyone is *treating* him like Sparky, but it's not.

Can you say *stand-in*? You've heard about it, the rumors, that sometimes celebrities will use doubles to give themselves a little breathing space. A little vacation from the . . . *suffocating* demands of fame. From the millions who would like a little chunk of you, and would take it if they could, tearing you to pieces. So they use stand-ins, and they find private places to go.

If I was John Valentine, I'd look for Sparky in a pin-stripe uniform, playing baseball in a rather unusual place.

You didn't hear it from me.

"Easy out, easy out!" Sparky shouted. "Burn it in there, Bob! He couldn't hit it if you rolled it on the ground! Easy out!" Sparky pounded his fist into the glove, then set his feet apart and crouched slightly, glove held up a few inches from his mouth and nose. He could smell the soft leather and the oil he'd rubbed into it a few hours ago. He dug his spikes into the green grass, into the soil. He felt a primal connection to the field of dreams. For a moment nothing existed for him but the pitcher's windup and the slowly circling tip of the bat, away in the distance.

The batter took the pitch and the umpire turned away, unimpressed.

Ball three.

"Whadda ya, blind?" somebody yelled off to his right.

So it was the bottom of the sixth. No score. There was a man on second trying to look in all directions at once, ready for the shortstop to sneak in behind him for a pickoff, ready to fly at the crack of the bat. Two outs, three balls, two strikes. Nothing to lose.

The guy at the plate wasn't known for fly balls, or long balls. He had no home runs on the season. But he could dribble it into the hole between first and second, and that's where Sparky was playing it. If it got to him there was no way he'd get the man at first. The throw would have to be to the plate. The catcher was good, and the runner at second didn't have a lot of speed. So throw it a few feet down the third-base line and the catcher would be there, blocking the plate.

But was Sparky's arm good enough? Should he throw to the pitcher, hope he could cut it off and still get it to the catcher in time? No, wait, wouldn't the pitcher be running in, backing up the catcher? Sure, sure he would, and the third baseman would head toward the mound, ready to snag a short throw.

Damn, but baseball had a lot of things to remember.

He loved every minute of it.

The pitcher wound up, the runner led off at second, the

batter swung, and the ball went high in the air ... over the backstop and foul, out of play.

Everybody relaxed. The runner loped back to the second sack and the hitter found his bat. Sparky took off his cap and wiped his forehead with the back of his hand, like he'd seen the players in the majors do. At least half of baseball was not so much what you did, but the *style* with which you did it.

For years this had been the only place Sparky could relax, could totally let down his guard, be himself, do something he loved to do, but didn't *have* to do. He wasn't the best baseball player in the Little League. He wasn't even in the top one hundred. In fact, he was strictly mediocre. For some reason, this was a great comfort to Sparky.

Here on the sweet green grass of the outfield, or digging his spikes into the red dirt of the batter's box, or circling the bases, or even sitting at ease in the dugout with his friends— *his* friends, not fans of Sparky, the television boy—he felt a magical calm that existed nowhere else in his life. It was the uncomplicated happiness that generations of boys before him had felt on the diamond. It was his own private thing.

If fact, life would be darned near perfect at that moment but for two things: he was hungry and his toes hurt.

The hunger was a familiar thing by now, and he could deal with it. He pulled a candy bar out of his pocket, bit off a hasty chunk, and stuck it in his cheek, conscious of how much he now resembled those black-and-white heroes of the game back on Old Earth. Only there it had not been a wad of chocolate and nuts in their cheeks, but a chaw of tobacco.

So here he was, Jackie Robinson in the outfield, crouching slightly, ready to explode in a blur of motion, the moment stretching, eternal. . . .

Sparky could no more play ball at a regular King City park than he could walk into a Pizza Palace franchise and order a slice and a Coke. But this field was different. This was the recreation dome of the Plain People of Luna: the Outer Amish.

That's what they were called when they first moved to Luna, anyway. Later, groups relocated to Mars and even more distant points. Some now called the original settlers Old-Order Outer Amish, but it was cumbersome, and names stick long after they've lost their original meaning.

When Sparky first started visiting here, he had been told the saga of the Amish and Mennonite communities on Luna. They had come from Germany and Switzerland, settled in the lush farmland of Pennsylvania, and did what sects always do: they split into other sects. The plainest of the Plain People avoided things like cars, electricity, and telephones. Basically, if it wasn't mentioned in the Bible, the Amish felt they could do without it. Some felt cars were okay, but chrome was vain, so they painted it black: the Black Bumper Mennonites. Most didn't wear buttons, and the men never grew mustaches because that reminded them of the Prussian military, which they were fleeing. They were the original conscientious objectors.

Sparky had thought it would take a great leap of logic for Amish to board a spaceship and leave for Luna, but was it really that different than crossing the Atlantic? America wasn't mentioned in the Bible, but the moon was.

Once there, of course, they could not survive entirely with Biblical technology, but they did surprisingly well, and used as few modern things as possible. What had drawn them was the prospect of twelve two-week growing seasons per year. Farmers to the bone, Amish had actually been in the agricultural forefront in matters like crop rotation and soil conservation. They were familiar with hybridization, and genetic engineering was only breeding and selection speeded up, or at least it was to the schismatic leader of the Outers. And they had never been averse to accepting a little help from their neighbors. So while they themselves never entered a bioengineering laboratory, they were instrumental in developing the first strains of Lunar-adapted crops. They put up domes, conditioned the Lunar dust with compost, bacteria, worms—whatever was needed—plowed the resulting soil, planted, and harvested. The new breeds of plants drank the intense sunlight beneath the UV-filtering plastic domes and grew so fast "it could break your arm if you held it too long over a corn seedling," according to Sparky's friend Jan Stoltzfus, the boy who had first invited him into the Amish enclave. "Two weeks of summer growing season, and two weeks of winter . . . without the snow!"

Self-sufficiency had always been their ideal, but they also had to make a living, so much of the produce they grew was taken into King City and sold at a public market, to health fanatics, antichemical believers, and the very wealthy, at astonishing prices.

"These are crops just as artificially produced as those grown on any corporate farm," Jan had pointed out, enjoying the joke on the "English." "Our food tastes no better and no worse than anyone else's. The only way to distinguish it is our fruits and squashes and melons and tomatoes tend to be a bit smaller, sometimes a *lot* smaller, more like back on Old Earth. And you find the occasional blemish on a tomato, the odd worm in the apple.

"And do you think we eat it? Very little of it. We buy our vegetables at the market, just like ordinary folks, and bank the difference."

Their lives had seemed full of odd contradictions to Sparky when he first started coming out here. They read old-fashioned books by the light of candles or kerosene lamps, but kept their orchard trees thriving during the two-week "winter" with banks of grow lights suspended overhead. They plowed the ground with teams of horses and wood-and-iron plowshares, then baled hay for the cows with gas-powered machines. In one dome they might heat with a wood-stove or a fireplace—they could not afford real wood, and so used compacted waste from various outside agricultural concerns—and in the next dome over it was thought to be ethical to heat with methane gas. They had endless arguments over what was proper and what was not. But they were good people, and there was one thing they all agreed upon: television was the tool of the devil.

He had been out at the Amish settlements location scouting for a story arc that would have involved an Amish boy and girl. The plan fell through quickly when it became clear the Plain People did not like to be photographed, to have a "graven image" made of them—who knew?—but while there Sparky had made an interesting discovery. Nobody knew who he was. This was a revelation to him. Of course, *nobody* had a show that everybody watched, but these were surely the only sane people on Luna who had never *heard* of him.

He began showing up for baseball games, informal gatherings where sides were chosen up on the spot. At first, he was picked last, and he *loved* it! At any park in King City he would be the first pick every time, regardless of talent or lack of it. Worse, as a practical matter, it was impossible for him to play. Do you really want three hundred photographers clogging the first-base line? Jostling for a shot in the shower room? Clamoring for interviews in the dugout? Even in the pathetic league they formed for studio children Sparky saw little point in playing. Those kids knew who signed their parents' paychecks, and would not work very hard to strike him out or catch his rare fly balls. Sparky got no charge from that sort of competition.

But the Amish gave him something he hadn't had since he was eight: a chance to be just another kid. They knew he was famous, and rich, and it made no difference to them. All that was an "English" matter, not part of their world. If he wanted to play with them, he'd better be good.

He never got past mediocre, and that was okay. The first time he'd been chosen second to last was one of his best days. He'd *earned* that measly promotion. When you're rich and famous, and don't have the ego of John Valentine, you never know what you've earned. Whatever Sparky did worthy of praise was always the result of a *team* of people employed to make him look good. He never forgot that, no matter how many awards came his way.

Sometimes he wished he *had* inherited his father's massive self-assurance, but most of the time he was happier to be the way he was, a moderately insecure fellow with a touch of the impostor complex, that maddening feeling that people secretly know you aren't as good as you're cracked up to be, that they know you know it, and that they know you know *they* know it.

Here he knew exactly how good he was.

The batter suddenly backed out of the box, and the pitcher relaxed. Seemed the batter didn't like something there in the dirt, because he was raking the ground with his cleats. He dug himself a little hole, fanned the bat around his head, swiveled his hips, and faced the pitcher. The pitch, the swing, the crack . . . another foul.

God, Sparky loved baseball. How could a game that moved so slowly produce such tension? It might be another two, three minutes before the next pitch, and the suspense was getting unbearable.

So was his hunger. There was no more candy in his pocket. And three long innings until the feast.

The Plain People wouldn't call it anything so vain as a feast, but that's what it was. Sparky would walk past tons of the sort of delicacies they'd had at the recent wrap party to get to one plateful of Amish food.

There would be sweating glass pitchers full of tart pink lemonade, with lemons and cherries still floating in it. Sweet cider. Fresh-squeezed orange juice. Something made with beans and ham hocks. Roast beef sliced thin. Ears of fresh golden corn. Cupcakes and rows and rows of pies: cherry, lemon, mince, pumpkin. Shoofly pie, a treat made in heaven but served only by the Amish.

And Sparky's favorite, the muffins. Blueberry muffins and corn muffins, which you could twist apart in your fist and see the steam rising from the golden centers and slather with butter scraped from a wooden churn.

Life didn't get any better.

If you play baseball long enough, you develop a computer in your head. Each play adds to the programming, until you reach the point where you hardly have to think about it at all. Your eyes see, and your arms and legs react.

The crack of the bat activated Sparky's computer. It was a bloop single into the hole, coming right at Sparky. The first and second basemen started toward it, saw it was impossible, headed back to their bags as Sparky charged the ball. No hope of catching it; play it on the bounce. He saw the catcher standing on the third-base line, the pitcher heading toward the plate to back him up, the shortstop moving toward the mound to cut off the throw. His eye went back to the ball—Jesus! He was too close in. The ball hit the ground and bounced as he moved his glove down. It hit the heel of his glove, hit him in the chest, and bounced . . . and there it was, hanging in the air right in front of him, as if time was suspended. He barehanded it and in one motion pegged it toward the shortstop. He saw the third-base coach waving the runner toward home. He'd been told Sparky didn't have the arm to get the ball to the catcher.

It was a good call, but something had happened to Sparky's arm. The shortstop started to jump for it, might have caught it, but then ducked and let it go over his head . . . and it reached the catcher right on the numbers. The runner was so surprised he tried to stop and his feet went out from under him. The catcher ambled over and tagged him out. The fans went wild.

Sparky jogged toward the dugout, arms loose, eyes on the ground, showing both coolness and humility. There was no way he'd ever tell anyone he'd been throwing to the shortstop. Everything had worked out all right, so who needed to know?

He accepted the high-fives and pats on the ass as only his due, then sat on the bench to wait his turn at bat. His feet were killing him.

For the first time he noticed that there was a strip of skin visible between the top of his socks and the bottom of his pants.

Well, that accounted for it. His legs were longer, and so were his arms. Charging the ball, taking an inch or two more ground with each stride, he'd come up on it too fast. Then throwing, he'd made more distance than he ever had before. The long legs almost caused a disaster. The arm had compensated for it. Neat. But he was going to have to make some adjustments, watch himself more closely.

He looked up when the umpire called time-out. His father was striding across the infield. Sparky saw him look up, vaguely, as if only now aware that something was going on here, that he might be interrupting it. He smiled, and waved to the players, clutching a rolled-up newspad in his other hand.

John Valentine skipped lightly down the three steps into the dugout, smiling broadly at Sparky, who smiled back as well as he could. Valentine motioned for Jeff, the second baseman, to slide over a bit, then seated himself with his hip touching Sparky's.

"Baseball, eh?" he said. "Looks like fun. I had a hell of a time tracking you down out here."

"I don't tell anyone where I'm going," Sparky explained. Valentine seemed not to have heard him, held out the newspad, and pointed to the first installment of Hildy Johnson's series about Sparky.

"Have you seen this?"

Sparky studied it, trying to give himself a little time. Valentine thumbed the pager down in the corner, came to the part he was interested in, and pointed to a paragraph.

"Where does this bitch get off writing this stuff about me?" he said.

Sparky only then realized how furious his father was. He glanced up in the stands at Hildy, no more than thirty feet away, decided this wasn't the time to introduce them.

"It says this is an authorized article," Valentine plowed on. "You've been granting this woman interviews?"

"She's been around," Sparky allowed. "We've granted her access."

"If she has access," Valentine grated, "we need to *control* the access. There's no need to let her in on family secrets, and if she's going to make up lies like this, there's no need to have her around at all."

"I didn't tell her anything," Sparky said. "Not about you."

Valentine put his arm around his son, patted his shoulder.

"Of course not," he said, smiling. "I never thought you did."

"We'll look bad if we just cancel at this point," Sparky said. "The pad's been hawking this series for a week now. I thought it'd be good publicity."

Valentine considered that, began nodding slowly.

"Besides," Sparky pointed out, "it's not a review. People have printed nasty things about you before. You know how it is."

"Maybe you're right," Valentine said.

"You said it yourself. You're not an easy man to like." Sparky knew his father took pride in this, attributed it to his artistic perfectionism. It was even partly true.

Valentine laughed, and squeezed his son's shoulder.

"You're right. Nothing to get upset about. I guess I'm just on edge, with the theater so close to completion." He tossed the newspad down on the dirt dugout floor, where it mingled with a hundred old pink wads of bubble gum and puddles of spilled cola. "That's not what I came out here for, anyway. A few things have come up we're going to have to go over together."

"About the theater?"

"That's right. If we hurry we can make it back before they shut down for the day."

"But I've got a game going—"

"It really can't wait, Kenneth." He looked around him, taking in the players and the green grass and the mothers and fathers in the grandstand behind the backstop. "I'm sure this is a lot of fun," he said, clearly not thinking anything of the sort, "but isn't it all a bit ... childish? I mean, Kenneth, I really hate to spoil it for you, but in another month you'll be too big to play with these boys."

Sparky felt his face grow warm. Jeff and some of the other boys were carefully studying the field.

The hell of it was, it was true. An inch this week, a few more inches the next, in no time he'd be a man.

He already *was* a man, inside. He'd been an impostor here from the beginning. Though they didn't partake of the modern world, the Amish were aware of it. They understood that arcane biological science had kept Sparky preadolescent for twenty years. They knew he would outlive them. They were one of many groups who, for one reason or another, kept to the Biblical threescore and ten—actually, more like fivescore for most of them, with reasonable care—refusing all long-life treatments.

It was over here, and Sparky knew it.

But couldn't he have finished this last game?

"Gotta go, fellas," he said, getting up. "Sorry, but it's an emergency."

"Sure, Sparky."

"Hey, good game, Spark-man!"

"What a play! They'll be talking about that one tonight."

He went down the line, shaking hands, getting pats on the rump, nobody mentioning he wouldn't be back, but everyone aware of it.

Suddenly he knew, without knowing how he knew, that these boys knew *exactly* who he was, and had from the first. He had a vivid vision of a group of them hiding in the hayloft, alert for approaching parents, gathered around a clandestine throwaway television set. Tuning in to the latest episode of *Sparky and His Gang*. Of course they knew. And the wonderful thing was, in all the time he'd been coming here no one had ever asked him for an autograph or a souvenir from the set. But they knew he was about to grow up, and they knew they would never see him again. He looked at the ground where his father had thrown the newspad. It had vanished. Soon it would be squirreled away in somebody's sock drawer, to be brought out in the dead of night and read by candlelight.

Impulsively, he thrust his prized outfielder's mitt into the hands of a surprised Jan Stoltzfus, another boy about to become a young man, but at the normal rate. Soon he'd be playing with the grown-ups. They embraced, and Sparky turned away, followed his father around the backstop and off the field.

The tunnel from the Amish settlements to the fringes of King City was five miles long, paved with packed dirt, lit by gas jets that had blackened the stone tunnel walls every fifty feet. They were two hundred feet beneath the Lunar surface, safe as houses. Sparky and his father sat on the lowered wooden tailgate of a wagon piled high with fresh produce in bushel baskets and slatted crates. The wagon had rubber-rimmed wheels. It creaked from every joint as it rolled slowly over the packed dirt. There was the steady clop-clop of the two placid Percherons who had been over this road a thousand times, and there was the sound of his father's voice, droning on about some problem or other concerning his dream, the John Barrymore Valentine Theater. Sparky heard none of it. He was off in a world of his own.

He hadn't really thought this growing-up business was going to change his life that much. The thing was, he had already thought of himself as grown up. True, he was small, he had a child's body, but his mind was that of a mature man. For that matter, he sometimes thought he'd been *born* mature. He didn't recall a time when he hadn't had an adult's outlook on life, shouldered a man's burdens. His relationship to John Valentine was sometimes more of a father to a reckless son than the other way around.

But this was going to change everything. You didn't just get a larger uniform when you grew up, when you got bigger. You put away baseball for good.

Sure, he could get into an adult league of duffers, smack the ol' pill around in his spare time, weekends, after work. But he knew without even trying it that it wouldn't be the same. Adult baseball was a way to keep the weight off without surgery, stretch the muscles. Maintenance on the old ticker, you shouldn't need a new one every five years. For the pros it was a job, but Sparky would never be that good. To a kid, baseball was a world unto itself. Baseball was youth.

"Why do I get the impression you haven't heard a word I've said?"

"What?" Sparky looked up. "Oh, I guess I was just somewhere else."

John Valentine made a noncommittal grunt, then reached behind him and took a twenty-dollar beefsteak tomato from a basket full of them. He bit into it. Juice and seeds ran down his chin.

"I never even knew these people were out here," Valentine said. "Had a hell of a time finding the place."

"They don't get a lot of visitors," Sparky said.

"No television, you said. No movies. What do they do for entertainment? Any live theater?"

"I don't think they approve of that, either. They farm, mostly. Work the soil. The women quilt, you know, sew these big blanket things. They're worth a fortune when they're done. They cook wonderful food."

"Maybe we should have bought a pie or something."

"They don't sell those. Or the muffins."

"Smelled pretty good to me." He took another bite of the tomato. "This is a good tomato, too, but not worth what they were charging up there at the farmer's market." He tossed the remains of the tomato off the back of the wagon.

"No," Sparky said. "Probably not."

I never did get another of those muffins. But to this day, when I smell corn bread, I think of Amish baseball.

The first leg of the *Halley*'s odyssey was Uranus to Jupiter, a trip not often made since the Invasion, two hundred years ago. Technically, it was illegal to approach Jupiter, but people did it from time to time and almost always got away with it. Space had always been too vast to really police, and Jupiter wasn't in the jurisdiction of any human-inhabited world. The only nation really interested in total interdiction was Luna, the grandly and rather nervously named Outpost State, which had existed for two hundred years only a quarter of a million miles away from the Invaders. The aliens had landed on Earth and on Jupiter. On Earth, they had wiped out all human life and destroyed all trace of human existence. What they did on Jupiter was anybody's guess. There had been no commerce humanity was aware of between the two planets in all that time. Luna would like it to stay that way. There was no reason to doubt the Invaders could finish the job, destroy all humanity, in a weekend if they took the notion. It seemed wise never to give them a reason, and therefore wise never to call too much attention to the affairs of humans.

But Luna was alone in seeing the Invaders as a continuing threat. The rest of the system would just as soon not think about Jupiter and the horrors it might conceal, which meant no one watched too closely. If you assumed an orbit and looked as if you planned to stay awhile, a ship would be dispatched to take you into custody. If you just used the gas giant's gravity well for a boost or a course change, as people in a hurry sometimes did . . . well, it was easy to lose yourself in traffic once back in the crowded trajectories of the inner planets. Space was vast.

I don't pretend to know just what Hal did to get us a course change with minimal expenditure of fuel. Something about coming around in front of the hideous planet, braking a bit, swinging around, and boosting again. I know we were under acceleration twice, neither time anything like the agony of the first boost at Uranus. When it was all done, we were aimed almost directly at the sun. Hal told me that getting to the sun was the most difficult destination in the system, in terms of energy. Which makes no sense at all, since it is so damn big and has so much gravity, right? But that's what he said, and at the price somebody paid for him, he ought to know. He said it was easier to aim for the sun from out here, where our orbital velocity was low, than farther in, where we'd have picked up too much speed. To which I might have said "Huh?" if I wasn't so dignified. I thought speed was the whole point.

There was a circular room atop the habidome that we called the cockpit. It was set up with Buck Rogers panels that theoretically could control all aspects of the ship's systems, but which had never been used, since Hal could do it all so much better. I imagined the original owner had liked to do what I did from time to time, which was sit in the captain's chair with my feet up on the ''dashboard,'' studying the cosmos with a feeling of power, king of all I surveyed.

The view up there was of a hemisphere of space, like being under a glass dome, or in a planetarium. The second image was more accurate, because what we saw was an artifact, created by Hal. It looked real enough. But remember we were spinning almost all the time, at the end of a long rope with the engines at the other end. If the dome had been glass the stars would have whirled around us, too fast for comfortable viewing. Hal cleaned all that up, made it look like we were motoring down a vast, black highway, smooth as glass. There was a control at my fingertips which would give me any angle I wanted. Of course, except near Jupiter no motion was visible at all.

I almost skipped the show entirely. Coming from Luna, I'd had it impressed on me in no uncertain terms that Jupiter was to be avoided. That it was dangerous. The image of Jupiter was a fearful one, dominated by that vast red eye a hundred times larger than my home planet.

Poly felt no such qualms. It was just a big ball of gas to her, a great photo opportunity.

I decided to tough it out. Poly wasn't scared, how could I be? Usually I'm not subject to that kind of bullshit macho, so maybe I was curious, too.

You get close enough, any planet has a lot in common with any other planet. You lose the curve of the edge, it becomes a vast plane filling half the universe. We were close. Hal showed me the gauge, creeping up very slowly, indicating rising hull temperature as we grazed the poisonous edges of the atmosphere.

Closer and closer. It was like one of those mathematical things, the chaotic figures, squiggly lines that as you magnify them reveal more and more detail. Infinitely. Fractals, that's it. Tiny swirls of yellow and orange became monstrous storms, and along their edges, more tiny swirls. Then those grew, and you realized they were gigantic. And on their edges, more storms . . .

It was a Technicolor Rorschach test from hell.

After a while I couldn't look at it any longer. Poly and I were strapped in, but the tigers and Toby were floating free. I watched them for a while. Toby and Shere Khan had invented a game you might call Tobyball. Shere would bat him across the room with a massive paw. Toby would go caroming around like a fuzzy zero-gee cue ball, yelping happily, until he got straightened out and leaped back toward the big cat. Shere Khan would bat him again. She seemed to regard him as better than a ball of yarn—which he resembled, the free fall making him even fluffier than usual.

When Toby came close to Hobbes he would bark at him a few times, as he'd recently taken to doing. Hobbes would watch him sail by, thoughtfully, as if trying to make up his mind. One bite, or two? Swallow him tailfirst, or headfirst? Decisions, decisions.

Toby had always been as spry as a snark in zero gee, but I was surprised at how well the tigers bore it. Not that cats aren't innately more graceful than dogs, but I'd once seen a house cat twisting endlessly, knowing he was falling but unable to figure out where he was going to land. Shere Khan and Hobbes just hooked their claws in the thick carpet and walked around as usual. I suppose they had been made fearless and maybe a little stupid by the same treatments that had left them free of aggression and the urge to hunt.

When Hal warned us we were about to boost again the tigers immediately reclined on the floor. I snagged Toby and held him in my lap. The weight, when it came, was about one gee, and didn't last very long. When it was over, Jupiter had swung around behind us and was shrinking rapidly. One twist of the dial on my console would have brought it around front again, in the false image we were watching, but Poly was tired of it and I had no desire to watch anymore. So we were weightless for another half hour until Hal put spin on the ship again, and then things continued as before.

But not quite. Poly and I started sharing a bed, and I began to spend a lot of time in the library, researching the Charonese.

I don't know what decided Poly, why she finally forgave me. I never asked, because I rather suspected it was mostly loneliness. Not that I wanted a burning love affair, but who needs to know that any male body would have served her as well? Poly was not the sort to go to bed with a guy she didn't like simply to scratch an itch, but she made it clear to me before we made love that she wasn't looking for a life companion at this point in her career. Hey, at this point in my career, neither was I. So that was understood. But we were affectionate with each other. She didn't come to my bed simply for sex. She stayed to cuddle, and eventually to sleep.

It had been a long time since I'd been able to awaken in the morning with a warm body at my side. A girl who didn't mind when I reached over and stroked her thigh, her hip, who would turn over and be in my arms. I've formed few long-term relationships in my life. This one wouldn't be long, either, but while it lasted it was good for me. No hot, sweaty details here, my friend. Let it stand that she was an inventive and enthusiastic lover, able to adjust to whatever mood seized me, and more than capable of bending me to her own will, if the mood suited her. We had some jolly, slippery times.

But the universe compensates. If something good comes into your life, the odds are something bad is not far away.

In this case, it was as near as the library.

After Jupiter, I was no longer satisfied to fish from my hammock. At least not all day long. I began thinking about Isambard Comfort, his dead sister, and the whole race that had spawned them. I had no illusions about Izzy. He might not be waiting for me on Luna, but if he was alive—and I felt sure he was—he'd be there soon. It made sense that the more I knew about his people, the better I'd be able to survive a third encounter with him. What did I need to do, for instance, to square things with them? Was it possible? Everyone had heard of the Charonese tenacity, of their reputation for always fulfilling a contract, no matter what. Was it really that bad?

It was worse. Much worse.

The first thing that struck a researcher—me—was the paucity of information. Hal had a UniKnowledge module, which was the nearest thing we'd ever get to summing up all human information collected since the days of the Cro-Magnon. It held all the libraries of Old Earth. All the movies, television shows, photo files. Billions of billions of bits of data so obscure a researcher might visit some of it once in two or three hundred years, and then only long enough to find it no longer had any reasonable excuse for being. But it wasn't thrown out. Capacity was virtually infinite, so nothing was ever tossed. Who knew? In ten centuries the twenty years of telemetry from Viking I might be of use to somebody. A vanity-press book, published in 1901, all about corn silage in Minnesota, of which no hard copy existed, might be just the reading you were looking for some dark and stormy night. The UniKnowledge held thousands of books printed in Manx, a language no one had spoken in a hundred years. It held Swahili comic books teaching methods of contraception. It contained cutting-room debris saved from a million motion pictures, discarded first drafts of films never made. A copy of every phone book extant at the time we began to record data by laser, and every one printed since. Fully half of the information in the UK had never been cataloged, and much never referenced in the centuries since its inception, and most of it was likely *never* to be cataloged. That would be taking the pack-rat impulse too far. Librarians had other things to do, such as develop more powerful search engines to sort through the inchoate mass of data when somebody wanted to find out something truly obscure.

But it was all in there. And if you set it for CHARONESE: *Search,* it began to spew out mountains of information. Or at least it seemed like mountains, at first glance. However, if you set it for ALBANIAN NAVY, 1936, it would spew out a mountain of information as well. You had to keep it in perspective.

So the first thing was to set the UK to sorting, organizing, comparing. It produced helpful graphs, statistical analysis, suggested routes of exploration. It spotted anomalies, pointed out the unexpected. The first thing it showed me was that, for an entire inhabited planet, there was practically no information at all. Economic data was very skimpy. Social analysis was sketchy. And most striking, items written by actual Charonese were unknown. Zip. Zero. Not one manuscript. The Charonese were not contributing information to the universal human database. They were hoarding their holdings like a paranoid poker player. Why?

The UK could help me with that, too. It searched for things written by ex-Charonese, expatriates. There had been a few, over the years. The bulk of these had spent their lives trying to make themselves very, very small, but a few had spoken out in print.

For a short time.

The UK produced a graph showing average life expectancy of an ex-Charonese. Ten months. Ninety percent were dead within one month of defection. The tougher ones lasted a little longer; one fellow was thought to be alive twenty years after leaving his home planet, but no one had seen him in five years, so it was anybody's guess.

They tended to die in accidents. In the same way that a boot crushing an ant might be seen as an accident.

Some of this stuff I knew, or had been told was probably true, but it was interesting to see it confirmed. Charonese didn't abide traitors. They kept their business secret, at any cost.

I could spin you quite a detective story about how I tracked my facts down. It's all in there, all in the UK, but finding it, putting it together, drawing conclusions, that's something else. As usual, there were reams of references from the Net, and they were about as useful as you'd expect, which is not much. Unattributed tales, anecdotal evidence, wildly contradictory accounts of How I Survived an Encounter with a Charonese. I spent more time than I usually would have with this material, because reliable sources were rare. The authors of such material were usually to be found in the obituary column a few weeks after publication. Venues that published anonymous articles about Charonese tended to announce new editorial staff for the next issue. Even printers and broadcasters had been assassinated.

So, Charonese Fact One: You write about us, you die.

I assumed there were people in law enforcement who knew about this, but what could they do? You write a nasty article about John Q. Mobster, and you die violently, somebody's going to suspect old John Q. There's a place to start. But though you might know these people were wiped out by a Charonese . . . which one? Someone who never met the victim, you could be sure of that. You couldn't just indict everybody with a Charonese passport, even though that would be a small group. They would certainly alibi each other, and you could rely on the fact there would be no deals cut, no testimony bargained for. If the hit was ordered by a boss, a *capo,* you could be sure he was back on Charon. But in fact it probably did not have to be ordered. Someone at the Charonese embassy would have the full-time job of monitoring all public media, and when something appeared they didn't like, maybe they just posted the name on a bulletin board. One writer, since deceased, said this was in fact the case. Whoever could work the job into his busy day did the hit. There were never any witnesses. The accident that claimed the life of the target invariably killed all the witnesses as well. On the very rare occasion a Charonese was surprised in the act, captured, caught red-handed, he always pleaded guilty. Charonese never hired lawyers. They never said anything at all to police, not even their name, and the only word they ever uttered in court was guilty. And then they did their time without a peep of complaint. A Charonese never complained about anything. If he had a problem with you, he killed you.

Charonese Fact Two: We always get our man.

Always. I searched long and hard for evidence of a contract unfulfilled, and found nothing. All the deceased experts agreed on this, even when they didn't agree on much else. If the Charonese agreed to do something, they did it. What they mostly did, off-planet, anyway, was enforce other people's contracts, the sort of contract you didn't want to bring into court or bother a lawyer about. Or it could even be a legal contract. There were no endless appeals from Charonese courts, no escape clauses. No excuses at all. If the Charonese guaranteed your contract, you could count on it being fulfilled, in cash, the equivalent, or if there was absolutely nothing left to take from the welsher, blood. Sometimes you got a warning in the form of a just-less-than-lethal torture session. Then you paid up, or you died.

I wish I'd known that. The next time I saw Uncle Roy I was going to have some very cross words to say to him.

So in these things the Charonese were much like other crime syndicates, past and present, though I'd never heard of any quite so harsh, nor any with a perfect record. Nor any who had never suffered a permanent defection, had a member squeal in court, cut a deal with the prosecutor. I inferred that something extraordinary was keeping these people in line, and I set out to find out what that was. I almost wish I hadn't. I had hoped it might provide me with a loophole of some kind, a spot of leverage. A window of hope.

I don't wish to depress and frighten you with the miserable history of Charon and its denizens. Just a short refresher course:

Luna and some other planets export criminals, misfits, and undesirables to Pluto for about a century. Most are garden-variety criminals, some are politicals, and a handful are very scary people. The Plutonians don't want these last around any more than you or I would; off they go to Charon. Transportation is a wonderful way to handle criminals; you might as well flush them down the toilet. There is very little in the way of maintenance, no costly per-bunk per-year figures to upset the taxpayers. Ship 'em as much or as little food as you wish, and let them fight it out. You need budget cuts? Prison food was always a good place to start. You don't need to pay salaries for guards, or worry about what they're bringing in to the convicts. There's no need for parole boards or probation officers. All sentences are for life. And if they wish to escape, all they need to do is fly through a million miles of vacuum.

But they had brought something with them to Charon, other than psychosis and criminal skills and their own brand of situational ethics. The dominant religion of Pluto, back from the days when *they* had been the outcasts of the system, was Satanism. Diabolism. Devil worship. Mystical, scary stuff.

Well, not really. It's true no one was allowed into a Satanist Temple but a true believer, and it is true the rituals and belief system are secret. But the secret is an open one, and the interior of the temple is no more mysterious than that of the Mormons. If you leave the church, no one comes to hunt you down and kill you. No one cuts out your tongue. You can blab all you wish, and ex-Satanists over the years have blabbed it all. And a more prosaic, boring story has seldom been blabbed. Forget the tales of human sacrifice, of Christian babies slaughtered on black altars and eaten by the congregation. They used to tell those same stories about Catholics. No, Plutonian Satanism was all ritual and show, symbolic as a Christian sacrament. Although I'll have to admit, reading about it, it sounded like a darn *good* show.

There was nothing symbolic about the Charonese religion. Real people bled real blood and died on Charonese altars.

If that was all, it would be disgusting, but nothing new in the world of religions. The Charonese couldn't hold a candle to the Aztecs for sheer volume of blood shed, or to the Spanish Inquisition for inventiveness. The sheer depravity of the Charonese way of life owed more to medical science than to man's endless capacity for inhumanity to man. The Charonese did it to themselves.

It's been a long time since any slashing or crushing injury below the braincase could do any permanent harm to anyone, as long as you didn't bleed to death before medical attention arrived. One of the first things medics did to an injury was turn off the pain. In some professions—stunt performers, or even my own work, when I was required to take a sword thrust in the final act—pain would be turned off ahead of time. (For me, anyway. I trust my acting ability to sell the audience on my pain; I don't hold with "method" fanatics who insist only the real thing will do.) There are those who enjoy being mutilated ritually, and have the pain suppressed, and a very small number who actually *enjoy* that much pain. All perfectly normal, today. Everything can be fixed.

On Charon, possession or use of any pain suppressor was illegal. You need to have studied Charon to understand how awful that was. The Charonese had almost no laws at all. You were expected to do anything you could get away with. *Every* law they did have was a capital offense. But because pain was good, pain was to be *sought,* a Charonese execution consisted of confinement to a sensory deprivation tank where one could *not* harm oneself in any way, and kept alive there for whatever period the court deemed fit for the crime. Typically that was a couple of weeks. The miscreant was usually insane—and defining "insanity" for a Charonese was a pretty problem—within a few days.

The Charonese religion was based around pain and death. Torture began at an early age, some authorities said in infancy. To my way of thinking, any Charonese living at the age of four or five years must already be insane, by any standard I can understand. Others maintain that the Charonese are the next step in evolution. Pain, they note, evolved to warn an organism of damage (why God couldn't just send down a written memo: "Hey, buddy, you're damaged!" was never explained to me). Now that damage was no big deal we ought to just ignore pain. Well, why not *eliminate* it? sez I, but I'm not writing a doctoral thesis.

There's no need to disturb your sleep with tales of Charonese bloodbaths, self-mutilations, orgies of sex and violence. A description of Charonese lovemaking alone would haunt you for days. And besides, the information gets very sketchy here. All the authors are dead, and accounts differ; who can say what is true and what is fancy? One example will suffice for all: the Charonese equivalent of a bar mitzvah involves self-disembowelment, after which the honouree amputates both legs and an arm, and then chews off . . . but I can't go on. It's all healed immediately, so what's the big deal, eh? Unless you have more sensitivity than a garden slug, that is.

Needless to say, such a lifelong regimen has produced a breed of human with not much in common with the rest of us. Nothing but death will stop them, and death is meaningless if you're in my shoes, because if, for instance, Izzy had not completed his mission at the time of his death, someone else would be along soon to rectify the oversight. And if I managed to kill Charonese number two, there would be a number three, and a number four.

The population of Charon was about five million. I'd have to kill a few hundred a day just to break even.

As if. So far I'd killed one through luck and evaded another twice, again, mostly through luck. And if I killed Isambard . . .

What would number two be like? I didn't think they had sent their champion killer to snuff an *actor*.

THE DISCOVERY OF SEX
Part Four of a Series
by Hildy Johnson

They tried to warn him.

"It's not like anything you've experienced as a boy," they said.

"Come on, Doc," Sparky said. "I'm thirty years old. You think I haven't had sex?"

Well, of course he'd had sex. Or what passes for sex in one whose puberty has been arrested for many years.

And I'm sure he enjoyed it. There was a joke going around school when I was young: Sparky is about to get into bed with one of his young fans. (We all assumed that young fan would someday be us.) He pulls down his trousers and the girl stares. "Who do you think you're going to satisfy with *that* little thing?" She laughs. And Sparky says, "Me."

They say size doesn't matter, and it's true, to a point. Sixteen inches would be nightmarish. Two inches . . . Are you in yet, darling? Sparky's measurement has never been a secret. One must assume he had a lot of charitable partners.

So that alone would be a big difference in his experience: being with a woman who wasn't faking anything.

But no matter how considerate we are in the sack, for most of us the primary urge is a rather selfish one, isn't it? Fess up. Is the experience a *total* loss if you get off, even if he or she didn't? Gee whiz, I'm sorry, hon, I'll do better next time, and . . . zzzzzzzzz.

The doctors told him what he'd been having were "dry" orgasms, sometimes called "infantile" erections. He felt like he was turned on, and he felt like he was coming, but he didn't know the half of it.

Puberty. A time of exciting and dreadful change. A time of confusion. A time of exploration. Most of us get about a year to adjust to it.

Sparky had about a week. . . .

Ken Valentine leaped up, bounced once on the giant bed, and hit the floor running. He ran right up the wall, seeing himself as Donald O'Connor in *Singin' in the Rain,* only Donald O'Connor wasn't naked. Turned a back flip and landed running again. Jumped to the ceiling, shoved himself down to the floor, and began caroming off the walls like a demented kangaroo.

Back in the bed, a lump of sheets and comforters stirred. A hand emerged and cautiously peeled back enough covers to expose disheveled hair, a forehead, and two slightly bruised eyes. The eyes followed Ken's progress around the room. Then the rest of the face was exposed and Hildy Johnson sat up in the bed.

"You've got more energy than three litters of puppies," she said.

"I know, I *know*!" he shouted, and bounced some more.

They were in the penthouse suite of one of the better hotels in King City. It had been the nearest refuge when Ken began feeling the urge down in the lobby, while Hildy was making yet another attempt to interview him concerning the onset of puberty. Perhaps onslaught would be a better word, she thought. Or maybe attack.

Try blitzkrieg.

There was no law against going at it right there in the lobby, but that wasn't Hildy's style; she had been raised to believe public sex was uncouth. Besides, Kenneth was filthy rich, and she'd always wanted to stay in a room like this. She'd managed to restrain him long enough to reach the elevator. By then, there was a real danger he'd start humping the potted plants. Since this biological banzai, Sparky really needed to be kept on a leash.

The room had a spa big enough to bathe a herd of elephants. She'd pushed him into it and surrendered to the inevitable. The bed was fifteen feet on a side and they'd debauched every square foot. Sometimes it seemed more of a war game than lovemaking. Hildy saw her redoubts of pillow and blanket fall to his relentless assaults over and over again. Not that she was much of a fighter. But with such an aggressive partner, she got a kick out of resisting for a while, before allowing her positions to be invaded. She even had a few bruises, a first for her. But she gave as good as she got.

It was just about the best sex she'd ever had, but now she was in the mood for an armistice. She didn't think Ken was.

"Why didn't anyone ever tell me?" he shouted, for possibly the three hundredth time. He leaped into the bed, bounced over to Hildy, and yanked the blankets away from her. She was pale and nude and perfect, with patches of pinkness here and there. He crawled from her feet to her chest, making obeisance at various stations of the corpus, fondly remembering what this was for, what they'd done with that, what had happened here and here and here. He collapsed across her body, resting his head on her moist breasts.

"If I'd only known," he breathed in her ear. "I feel like I wasted fifteen years. Hell, I only have maybe three, four hundred years left! And there are *billions* of women in the system. *Billions!*''

"Maybe even a few dozen who don't want to fuck you," Hildy pointed out.

"Impossible! How could they possibly want to miss ... *this*!"

"How indeed. Just plain cruelty, I'd think."

"Exactly! Exactly! Cruel to both of us! What possible reason could there be to *not* make love?"

"Hmmm. Soreness?"

He frowned. "You aren't sore, are you?"

"Honey, I ... never mind. Aren't *you*?"

"A little," he admitted.

"Then why don't we call a time-out, and finish the interview?"

"Interview? Interview? Is that what you call this?" He kissed her lips, and her breasts.

"That's what it started out to be. Remember? This morning? The hotel lobby? We were going to have breakfast?"

"Breakfast?" He seemed to be having trouble with words longer than four letters. "Oh, yeah. Breakfast. God, am I ever hungry." He reached across her and punched a button on the headboard. "Send up a lot of breakfast," he said.

"Yes, sir. What would you like?" a female voice replied.

"A *lot*. A lot of everything. Make it real fast, and I'll tip triple. Including you, sweetheart, if you aren't a computer."

"I'm not a computer," said the voice, "and it will be real fast."

"Okay," said Sparky, turning back to Hildy. "What do you want to know?"

Hildy put a fingertip to her left temple and twisted. The pupil of her left eye began to glow a deep red, like a deer caught in headlights.

"Recording," she said, formally. Sitting there naked on the bed, she noticed an almost imperceptible change in his attitude. It was something performers, actors, fashion models did. The director yells "Action!" The spotlight hits the singer on the stage, the photographer lifts his camera, and the people turn on. Or switch to a different level of reality, Hildy thought. The shoulders move, the teeth get brighter somehow, the eyes twinkle. It was a little scary, but not half so much

as the other end of the process, when the director yells
"Cut!" The smile collapses. The charisma is stored, way back
wherever people who have it, keep it. She had to cut through
that before she'd get anything useful.

"On the record . . ." she said, finishing the legal litany.
"Sparky, would you agree with the proposition that the pu-
bescent human male is the stupidest animal on two legs?"

He laughed. "If you want to take me as an example . . .
yeah. Or on four legs, or six, or eight." He glanced down at
his semierect penis. "Maybe we should say three legs."

Hildy glanced down, too—or at least her right eye did.
The left remained stabilized on the establishing shot, recording a solid image she would use mainly as earlier reporters
had used sound recorders. There would be HyperText image
bites, of course, but she doubted she would use much from
this particular session. Sparky was still gazing down with
boundless affection. It was like he had a new friend. In a way,
he did.

"Say," he said, brightly. "Maybe it's not *me* that's dumb
at *all*. Maybe when your cock starts to grow, it sort of sucks
up your brains." He made a sucking sound with his lips.
"*Pow!* And your IQ drops like a stone. You're at the mercy
of any female who walks past you. You'd do *anything* to . . .
sure, sure, that's it." He grasped his newly burgeoned man-
hood and waved it more or less in Hildy's direction. "This
fellow gets it into his head . . . so to speak—"

"Off," Hildy said. "Sparky, it's a *very* bad sign when you
start referring to your cock in the third person. Next thing you
know you'll give it a name . . . and I'm out of here."

"You're right, you're right." Sparky apologized. "I'm
crazy, but I'm not loony." That look came into his eyes again
and his gaze dropped down her body. It landed where it usually did, and he was no longer semierect. "How about it,
while we're off the record? Do you think we could—"

The bedroom door swung open and three bellhops hurried
in, pushing carts groaning with bacon and eggs and pastries
and fruit. For a moment there Sparky was so funny, his head
moving rapidly back and forth between Hildy and the food,
back to Hildy again, back to the food, totally unable to decide
which he wanted more . . . she fell over laughing.

...and by Friday, though he was not back to anything like "normal," he could at least be trusted again around livestock.

NEXT WEEK:
Part Five
The New Sparky, as Romeo!

What amused Kenneth the most was that growing up felt like the world was shrinking. He wondered if normal boys, growing up in the normal way, experienced it like that. Did it seem their clothing had gotten too tight? That doorways were lower now, so they could reach up and touch them as they passed through? Or was it all too gradual?

Rooms imploding, shoes pinching, stumbling on stair risers that seemed to get lower even as he climbed them...these he could handle.

But *people* getting smaller...

He was now the same height as his father. He found it enormously disconcerting. For thirty years his father had been this vast presence, towering, stern, but loving. The fact that other men were taller was completely beside the point. In the ways that mattered, John Valentine had been the tallest man in the world.

But in this new, changed world, his father was only slightly over average height. He had a way of standing that made people think he was taller than he was, a way of dominating a gathering of people so that, from Kenneth's old perspective and even without the elevator shoes the loving son's uplifted gaze provided, made him stand out above anyone but a basketball team. But now they were eye to eye.

This was inconceivable.

This was preposterous.

This was...something a billion sons had encountered during their youth, nothing unusual at all. Except they had crept up on the idea. They had done it as a proper son should, a millimeter a week, not sprouted insolently like some demented beanstalk.

Kenneth was profoundly embarrassed by it. He now habitually stood slumped, slouched, hipshot. It just made him look sullen, and didn't really help anyway.

John Valentine put his hand on Kenneth's shoulder and squeezed affectionately.

"Who says dreams can't come true? Right, son?"

"That's right, Dad."

They were standing in the almost-finished park across from the dream. The park was three acres in area and ten levels high. The ground was bare soil, with sprinklers and electrical outlets naked. Soon they would be covered with sod. But a fountain was bubbling off to their left, and a white gazebo to their right sported electric flags that snapped in the nonexistent wind. In a few hours the orange fences would come down and people would begin using the paths, sitting on the benches. Children would climb in the small playground and splash in the pond with golden koi and the park's resident pair of otters.

John Valentine barely noticed any of this. The park had been part of his specifications for the project—and he would never know how many headaches this had caused—but it had really been no more important to him than the color of the ushers' uniforms. A thing he would notice if it were done wrong, never see if it was right. He had said the theater should be across from a park. Here was the park. Enough said.

His attention was fixed firmly on the edifice across the wide pedway.

The Valentine. His dream. Well, Kenneth's, too.

"You remember that day at the spaceport, Kenneth?" he asked. "It was the day after I took you to the *Sparky* audition. Maybe you were too young."

"I remember it, Father."

"It's funny," John Valentine went on. "I don't recall exactly where we were going. Mars, wasn't it?"

"Yes, Father."

"Can't think why we'd want to go to Mars. *Brutal* gravity on Mars. Anyway, we'd had this offer, and we didn't know what to do with it. Television. A series. The money sounded good, but . . . *television*! Remember?"

"Oh, yes," Kenneth said, with a smile.

"And that's where the dream was born. The Valentine." He waved his arm grandly at the marquee. "Shakespearean repertory. We never knew it would take this long. This many years, you laboring with the kiddie schlock, me languishing in the sticks. But we got the money, and now we have the time.''

Kenneth knew his father had no notion of just how much money. But following John Valentine's gaze, he had to admit it was money well spent.

The facade was wood, recalling what the exterior of the Globe Theater might have looked like. It stretched for half a city block, facing the park. The actual entrance took up half that much of the frontage: four sets of wood-and-glass doors, a small box office off to one side. Above it was a tasteful marquee, brightly lit, but with nothing that flashed or moved. ''This ain't a casino,'' Valentine had said. On all three sides it advertised

ROMEO AND JULIET

Kenneth Valentine
Maya Chang
John Valentine

with the tasteful logo featuring a rose and a sword that had come from the top graphic-design firm in King City. And not cheaply. Above that was a two-story tower with THE VALEN-TINE spelled vertically, THE floating over the V, in a type style called BROADWAY.

It had once been the Roxy Theater. Even in its heyday the Roxy had not been a premiere venue. Located on a seldom-traveled side street just off the Rialto, it had struggled along for almost twenty years presenting the sort of experimental works beloved of acting students and practically nobody else, playing to audiences composed mostly of relatives of those students. It was far too large a house for that. The balcony had been walled off early on, but even then the four hundred main-floor seats were usually half-empty. Sometimes nine-tenths empty. The theater had been owned by a man with some money, a man almost as eccentric as John Valentine. He was content to lose small sums yearly, until a change in the tax situation made it impossible to continue. And it sat there, dark, boarded up, for fifteen years until Sparky's real-estate scouts discovered it. Valentine didn't give a hoot about the bad location: ''They'll come to us; you wait and see.''

Renovation had kept Valentine busy for the better part of six months, and now it was ready.

Father and son crossed the pedway and entered their theater. The lobby was dark wood and thick maroon carpet. Heavy curtains covered the back walls, pulled away from the four entrances. They could be raised entirely so standees could look through wide openings in the rear wall. Valentine fully expected standees, at every performance.

They walked down the sloping aisle between the left and the center sections of seats, which were wide, and plushly upholstered in the same shade as the carpet. They reached the orchestra and turned around.

Six hundred seats. A steeply raked balcony. Retractable chandeliers. Three elevated boxes on each side. An arched ceiling, gentle acoustic curves built into the walls. It was old-fashioned without making a big point of it.

"Perfect," Valentine breathed. "I couldn't ask for more."

"You did a great job," Kenneth said.

Valentine accepted this in silence. Then he grinned, and hurried over the narrow bridge spanning the orchestra pit. He disappeared behind the curtain and Kenneth heard the sound of backstage ropes being pulled. The curtain rose, and banks of lights clicked on one by one. Valentine strode out to center stage and beckoned for Kenneth to join him.

"Rehearsals begin tomorrow," he said. "Are you ready, Romeo?"

"I think I know my lines," Kenneth said.

"I'm jealous," Valentine said, with an affectionate smile. "Part of me says, 'John, you're not too old to play Romeo. You could still show that little upstart a thing or two.' "

"I'll bet you could."

"And I *will,* Kenneth. I will. 'Directed by John Valentine.' I like the sound of that."

"You directed a lot of things on Neptune," Kenneth reminded him.

"Ah, yes, but this feels like a new beginning. Not much of a talent pool out there in the outers, my boy. Rather pathetic, most of them. Now I'll be working with the best. With the fifth generation of Valentines. The one destined to be the best of all."

"I'll sure try, Father."

"Count on it. You will be the best."
And Kenneth knew he had better be.

Back aboard Hal . . .

You'd think a guy who is seldom at a loss for words, a guy who could cover umpty-ump pages with a description of a trip from Pluto to Oberon where, basically, nothing happened except I got hungry . . . you'd think I'd have something useful to say about a close encounter with the sun.

Hmmm. Well, how about . . . it got hot.

It did, a little. Up to about ninety-five or ninety-six. Not so impressive until you realize that *any* variation from a desired temperature is cause for worry aboard a spaceship. Such things are supposed to be under control. That should give you some idea how close Hal was cutting things.

Not too impressed? Well, neither was I. How about, it was *fast*. Over in less time than it takes to talk about it.

It was grand. It was beautiful. It was awe-inspiring.

Ho-hum, right?

It was dangerous. But the trouble was, I just couldn't get too excited about it. If something happened, it would all be over too quick for me to notice it, Hal assured me.

I think that, in the end, after all my adventures on my way from one of humanity's most distant outposts to within the orbit of mankind's closest, I just got sort of burned out. You should excuse the expression. And we *had* done a mighty close skim of Jupiter, a place I feared a lot more. I guess once you've seen one giant ball of gas up close, seeing another just doesn't pack the wallop you might expect it to. Even if it *is* on fire.

It was the same with our speed. I never asked for a speedometer check. I didn't really want to know. We were moving about as fast as anyone had ever moved before, I guess, but you couldn't tell it, not until we were right down in the photosphere. (Oh, yes, we came *that* close.) After Jupiter, old Sol grew larger at a prodigious rate. But so what? Three days or thirty days, you still can't see it grow. It still *looks* static, like any starry night.

But if there were any speed limits set in the solar system, there would have been traffic cops staked out behind every billboard from Mercury to Earth, waiting to pull us over.

"Honest, Officer, I was only going a hundred thousand miles per second." "Boy, that wasn't nothin' but whatcha call a 'relativistic effect.' We clocked you at point-nine-nine-nine c, and 'round these parts we figger c ain't jist a good idea, it's the *law*!"

There were changes around the ship. Spin had to be stopped again, and since there wasn't going to be a lot of time on the other side, certain housekeeping measures to take care of. All the wonderful animals had to be stowed away, back into cold sleep. Many of the plants were "mothballed" in some way I didn't understand. The pond was drained. The whole place became rather depressing, to tell you the truth.

No one was more depressed than Toby, though. The poor little thing was inconsolable. He spent a whole day searching for his big, striped lady love, and when I got out his storage container he actually seemed eager to go to sleep.

And then we were there. Free-falling because Hal had to maneuver the radiation shields of the engine module to stay between us and the sun.

He made all that complication vanish in our overhead display. All we saw was the sun, or actually an image of the sun suitably translated for our frail senses. We could see sunspots, and flares, and prominences, and they all looked rather small. You could *tell* yourself that a hundred Lunas would fit into that tiny black speck and still leave room for fifty Marses, but you couldn't get a real perspective on it. You might know that the friction from the near vacuum of the photosphere was heating the ship's hull to within a few degrees of its melting point . . . but even if you *could* believe that, you didn't want to dwell on it.

We passed within a hundred thousand miles of Icarus, the asteroid that was moved into close solar orbit forty years ago and has been slowly ablating away ever since. They figure it still has about a century to go before it's all used up. We'd never have seen it, of course, but Hal provided a telescopic image: just a smooth ball of molten rock on the Brightside. We could see the tips of some of the instruments peeking around from Darkside. Hal, acting the cheerful tour guide, told us those instruments were continually extended as the ends were burned away. He said Coronaville was now mounted on cooled pillars, as the whole planetoid had become too hot to walk on. I decided to cross it off my list of vacation destinations.

And then we were past and the sun was dwindling behind us. Poly seemed to have enjoyed the experience more than I. She took hundreds of pictures, most of which must have shown little more than patterns of orange-and-yellow streaks with the occasional black pimple. I didn't point out to her that all she was photographing was a television display on the cockpit dome. Why spoil her fun?

Suddenly, after endless weeks of nothing to do, we were in a big hurry. Our velocity was now such that Hal didn't have a hope of bringing us to a stop anywhere close to Earth's orbit—and he didn't have the fuel for it, either. What he had was enough to boost at a steady one gee until he ran out of gas within a million miles of our destination, still going like a bat out of hell.

When he went over his plans with me, I was shocked.

"What do you mean, interstellar space?" I asked him.

"It was the only option," he said. "You said you had to get to Luna. You didn't say *I* had to."

"But . . . of *course* you have to," Poly said. "Tell him, Sparky. He can't just . . . just *drift* for a million years."

"It could be a lot longer than that," I said. "How about it, Hal? There's got to be a way you can slow down."

"Yes, of course," he said. "There is always a way." And he shut up.

I *still* don't know if he would have spoken up for himself. He seemed so human, most of the time. It was easy to forget he was a machine, and though he mimicked human emotions—and I believe actually felt some of them—he operated under different protocols than Poly and I.

"Well?" Poly asked. "What do you have to do?"

"I would need to rendezvous with a refueling drone," he said. "One could be launched from Titan in a few hours, and several months from now we could meet at around eleven billion miles from the sun. A few days to slow down, and head back system-ward . . . in a year's time I could be back in solar space."

"Then do that," I said.

"I'm not authorized to initiate such an expenditure," he said.

At last I got it. I marched to the freezer in the kitchen—
well, marched isn't exactly the word, since I was moving
poorly in the one-gee environment—and retrieved Izzy's tired
old thumb. Gad, only a week ago I had toyed with the idea
of feeding it to Hobbes. And Hal would be on a one-way trip
to the Big Bang.

I pressed it to the credit plate and authorized the chartering
of an expendable drone full of fuel. I looked at the price tag
this time, and had to smile. Isambard's credit had been cut
off everywhere in the solar system shortly after we left
Oberon . . . but not here. Hal's credit-verification software had
been shut down, on my order. It was possible this new, outrageous charge would cause him trouble. Perhaps he, his wife
and children and parents and all the rest of his family would
be clapped into debtor's prison when he returned home. I had
no idea if Charonese had such a thing, but one can hope.

"Do you have everything?" Hal asked. "Spacesuits, extra
oxygen?"

"Something to read?" I suggested. "Candy? Toys?" See
what I mean? There was a list in his memory that we'd
worked on for days, and he knew each item had been checked
and double-checked. If we'd forgotten to put something on
the list, we were unlikely to think of it now. He was a *computer*, dammit, he could not forget things. But here he was
sounding like an anxious mom sending her kids off to summer
camp. I took it to mean he was worried about us. And that
he would miss us. I was pretty sure he could feel lonely.

"We'll be okay, Hal," Poly told him. You can't kiss a
computer good-bye, so we waved at him and piled into the
lifeboat.

That's right, lifeboat. There were two aboard, and we
needed both of them. Hal had fixed them up as a two-stage
vehicle, the one we would ride perched on the nose of the
other. The bottom one would blast until it ran out of fuel,
then be discarded, whereupon our own boat would blast. By
then we'd be feeling major gees, but it wouldn't last as long
as the boost from Oberon.

Don't look so shocked. It's the way humans first got to
Luna, throwing away most of their rocket along the way. In-
sanely expensive, but hang the cost, say I. The Charonese
could afford it.

We got into our acceleration couches and Poly briefly squeezed my hand. We'd be splitting up as soon as we landed, and I'd barely gotten to know her. Story of my life. And probably lucky for her. The few medium-term relationships I've had have ended badly. I've had even fewer long-term ones.

"Hasta la vista," Hal said, over the radio.

"Until we meet again," I said. And the lifeboat's engine fired.

John Valentine turned his back on the company, put his fists on his hips, and stood motionless for a full ten seconds. No one breathed. One lesson you learned early when being directed by Valentine was that when the great man wasn't saying anything, someone was in trouble.

"Everyone take the afternoon off," he said, at last. "Go on, get out. Be back here at eight sharp."

No one dallied. There were a few murmured conversations as cast members grabbed scripts and purses and bags and thermos bottles, and even that was stilled when Valentine, still facing the back wall, raised his voice.

"Except Kenneth," he said. People moved a little faster, and within a minute the stage was bare but for father and son. Kenneth stood silently, hands resting on the hilt of his wooden sword.

John Valentine walked slowly along the rear of the stage, rubbing his chin thoughtfully. He glanced at his son, sighed, and strode into the wings. When he came back he had a pair of sabers. He tossed one to his son. Kenneth dropped his prop sword and caught the saber by the hilt. Valentine moved back a few steps and addressed the younger man.

"Do you want a mask?"

"Not if you're not wearing one."

"En garde," Valentine said, and assumed that position with easy grace. He tapped the blade of Kenneth's sword with his own, and attacked.

Clang, clang, clang, and the sharp tip of the saber rested solidly on Kenneth's sternum. Kenneth swallowed hard. His father lowered his weapon, turned, and walked back three steps.

"Again," he said quietly.

It went no better for Kenneth the second time, or the third. There didn't seem much point to a fourth engagement. John Valentine walked in slow circles for a while, massaging his temples.

"You expect problems," he said, at last. "You expect obstacles and setbacks. You are ready to deal with incompetence—it's always around somewhere. You expect these things, and you think you are prepared for anything. So when the disaster strikes, you think you are prepared for it." He looked up at last. "But from my own son? This . . . *this* I wasn't prepared for."

Kenneth could think of nothing to say. He knew where this cold, quiet calm could lead.

"My Romeo can't handle a saber." He looked into the wings, then back to his son. "Tell me it's because you're used to the foil."

Kenneth shrugged, and reluctantly shook his head.

"Then tell me how it was done. No, wait, let me guess. Your fencing instructor . . . needed a little extra cash."

"A lot of extra cash," Kenneth admitted.

"Well, thank god he didn't come cheaply. He was *highly* recommended, and his reports to me couldn't have been more glowing. I should have suspected; the man didn't have the imagination to write that well. *You* write well."

"My staff writes even better."

"Of course." Valentine laughed. "Honing their skills on Sparky. I should have detected the flavor of fantasy." He sighed. "I blame myself, son. I never should have absented myself so long." Then he pointed to Kenneth and raised his voice only slightly, but it made the accusing finger more deadly than his blade. "But I must blame you, too, Kenneth. Oh, yes, I think that you must share the blame for neglecting one of the *basic* skills of the thespian art. Did you think you would continue in your childhood forever? Did you think someone could 'morph' swordsmanship, as though this holy stage were no more than your television fantasy world? Did you think you would never grow up and shoulder a man's work?"

It seemed best not to answer. But as the silence stretched, Kenneth knew he would have to.

"I . . . I just didn't enjoy it, I guess," he said.

"Speak up, son!" Valentine thundered. He stamped his foot on the stage. "On top of everything else, I will *not* have you whimpering while you tread these honoured boards. Take your puling and squeaking elsewhere, back into your board-room, perhaps, as it seems *that* is where you have spent the period of my absence. Surely, your skills there have purchased this theater, I'll not take that away from you . . . but do you think I *care* about that? Do you not realize I'd sooner present Shakespeare on a barren patch of sand than to cast as Romeo *a boy who cannot fight*? A boy who, in the *crucial* scene—you might recall it; Act Three, scene one?—must slay the valiant Tybalt? The scene that is the *very center of the play*? The scene that seals Romeo's fate, that sets the lovers finally on the road to ruin?

"Have you seen Tybalt's swordplay? Have you watched the man rehearse? The man is better than *me,* my poor, poor son. So what shall I do? Have Tybalt fight left-handed? He would destroy you. Break his arms? He would *kick* you to death. Blind him? Hamstring him? Hire a *new* Tybalt, a straw man for my son to knock down?"

Valentine threw his weapon clattering into the wings.

"No. No, I must instead create my Romeo from these pitiful makings. I must *wrench* this wretch—clawing and screaming, if necessary—from his pathetic cocoon, from this *Sparky* buffoon, and into a man's estate. *Assistant stage manager!*"

The timid but bright drama student with the misfortune to hold that job peeked from the wings where she had been hiding. Valentine had never learned her name (it was Rose), but had impressed on her from the first day that she was never, *never* to be beyond the reach of his voice. So when he had cleared the theater, she had found a hole to hide in, but not one so remote as to spare her Kenneth's humiliation. *Mister* Valentine—always to be called mister, as though he needed distinguishing from Kenneth—usually called her ASM. When he used the full title, nothing good could come of it.

"Yes, Mr. Valentine?"

"Bring me my sword. Contact everyone. Rehearsals are suspended for a period of . . . make it two weeks. My son needs to attend drama school."

"Yes, sir."

"This is *not* to be taken as license to loaf. Upon their return to the stage, all cast members will be expected to know their lines. *Cold*."

"Yes, sir." Rose handed him his sword.

"Come, Kenneth. We have much work to do."

"Yes, Father."

"En garde!" Valentine shouted, and slashed at his son's face.

Henry Wauk was not precisely asleep when the knock came at his door.

In West Texas, everybody had a siesta during the hottest hours of the day. At three in the afternoon you could fire a cannon down the middle of Congress Street and not worry about hitting anyone. Of course, you could do that at just about any hour; New Austin was not a bustling place.

"Doctor" Wauk took his daily siesta in the office that connected with his, at the top of the stairs over the Long Branch Saloon. Theoretically, this office belonged to Dr. Heinrich Wohl, D.D.S., but just then there was no Dr. Wohl, and there hadn't been for almost fifteen years now. There had been once, and perhaps there would be again, but these days the big dental chair in Wohl's office was never used except when Wauk stretched out in it, shoved his black hat down over his eyes, and sacked out.

Henry never sweated during these naps, though the temperature in his office often reached well over one hundred degrees in the Fahrenheit scale used in Texas. He loosened his string tie and he took off his boots, but made no other concession to the heat. He often bragged to his friends that he was half gila monster and half prairie dog, and that's why he stayed dry. They responded that it was because there was very little water in his system, and he said yeah, that, too. Henry Wauk was an alcoholic.

He counted himself lucky to live in a society that didn't give a damn what he put into his body or what he did with his life. No busybodies had ever tried to reform him. He was a happy drunk. He was also happy to have found, many years ago, the perfect job, which was to be "Dr. Wauk." That was not his real name, but merely the one some wag had written on the shingle outside the doctors' offices in West Texas when the disneyland was built. Wauk and Wohl, get it? He hadn't, actually, but it had been explained to him, and he was content to be Henry Wauk now. Actually, if you had asked him what his name had been, originally, he would have been unable to tell you. "I'm sure it's written down here somewhere. Library card, or something."

For well over forty years he had been refining what he thought of as the Perfect Day. Thirty years ago he got it right, and he'd pretty much stuck to it since then.

Up at the crack of ten, dress and down to the saloon for breakfast, a double prairie oyster: two raw eggs in a double shot of bourbon. Thus fortified, he strolled three blocks to the barbershop for a hot towel and a shave. (Saturdays, a bath in the back room. Once a fortnight, a haircut.)

Noon would find him standing at the bar, drinking slowly, getting the right edge for siesta. When he woke up at five, lunch of pig's knuckles and pickled eggs. At around six it was poker lessons for the tourists. There was no fee for these and all guests of the disney could play, but tuition was steep. At nine or ten dinner would seldom be whatever the cook at the Long Branch said was good that day, because it was usually a damn lie, but the thick steaks were tasty enough. What could you do to ruin a steak? Doc liked them crunchy on the outside and barely dead in the middle. After dinner began the important work of the day: serious poker with the other regulars. Stakes could be high, depending on how much had been taken from the tourists that day. At three or four (or sometimes, seven) he would stagger upstairs to his rooms. It was a good life. It suited him. The Perfect Day.

Of course, once a week or so, medical business would intrude.

Everyone in Texas knew Doc's office hours were noon to three, and he conducted what routine doctoring was necessary from his post at the bar. Prescriptions were handled by his nurse, Charity, who actually sat in the office from ten till siesta time. She was a bright-eyed, intelligent sixteen-year-old who had been firmly rebuffing Henry's advances since she came of age, three years earlier. She was clever with the stethoscope, with mortar and pestle, the scales, and the pill compressor. In fact, Dr. Wauk could and did leave ninety percent of the medical business to her. There was no call for alarm in this, since Henry was no kind of doctor, anyway. How much worse could the nurse be? She was, in fact, a lot *better* than Wauk in most things.

When he took the job Henry had made a halfhearted attempt to learn a few basics of first aid, which was all that could be dispensed in Texas, anyway. No sane person would have trusted him to handle much more than a hangnail; if you were sick, you went back to the *real* world for treatment. If you were injured, emergency services could be at your side in two minutes, tops. Only the mildly ill and the occasional dead ever came to Henry's office. Which was good, because Henry was a fumble-fingered pharmacist, a terrible diagnostician, and any really serious laceration made him queasy. Unfortunately, Charity passed out at the sight of blood, so Henry had to patch up all the scrapes and cuts. Most of the work he did was nothing more complicated than a little antiseptic and a bandage.

Naturally, when he became aware of the knocking, he at first assumed it was a goddam tourist who had lost his way. He snorted, shoved the hat down a little farther over his brow.

The knock came again, a little louder this time. Like a noisy goddam fly you kept brushing away. He already suspected he would have to get up, but he tried one more time to ignore it.

Knock, knock, knock.

Henry sat up, shoved his feet into his boots, and stomped toward the door. He drew the long-barreled Colt .45 pistol from its holster hanging by the door. The gun was loaded with blanks, but they were very *loud* blanks, and they shot real fire from the barrel. Aimed at someone's face from a range of one foot—which was Henry's intention—a first-degree burn was likely. A first-degree burn which the goddam pest could goddam well get treated out in the goddam real world, where he should have gone in the goddam first place.

"Hold your goddam horses," he said, and jerked the door open. He was about to squeeze the goddam trigger but something stopped him. His visitor was cloaked in a brown robe that reached all the way to the floor. The face was hidden in the shadows of the hood. Some kind of monk? Franciscan, he thought, but there were no monasteries in Texas, and that sort of garb would be frowned on by the Anachronism Committee. So he probably hadn't entered through a public entrance. And there was a darker, wet stain on the robe that might be blood. The figure pulled the hood back slightly, and Henry frowned. The face was bloody, and it looked familiar.

"Sparky?" he asked.

"How are you, Doc?"

"You've grown up."

"Would you mind putting the gun down? It makes me . . ."

Nervous, Henry was about to finish for him, but Sparky staggered and almost fell forward. Henry caught him and pulled him inside.

"Sorry. I'll be all right."

"What in hell are you doing here?"

Sparky had been a regular in Texas for a while, shortly after his father left for Neptune. He had paid for poker lessons, without complaint, but not for long. Soon he was good enough to be invited to sit with the regulars. But that had all been a long time ago. Sparky had not visited Texas for over a year.

"I need to hide out for a little bit, Doc," he said.

"You're hurt."

"That, too. Can you patch me up? Just temporarily."

"Temporarily is the only way I do things, son, you know that."

"It's nothing serious."

"Looks serious enough to me. Let me see that shoulder."

Sparky slipped the robe down, and Dr. Henry Wauk gasped. He had seldom seen so much blood. It had dried and cracked all over the boy's body, and oozed fresh from half a dozen slash wounds. The beige singlet he wore under the robe had been cut to ribbons. He looked like he'd been mauled by a wild animal.

"Lion-taming lessons," Sparky explained, and tried to smile.

"I know what you've been trying to tame, son, and he ain't civilizable. Now you sit right there and I'm going to call the police and we'll—"

Sparky grabbed Henry's wrist and held on strongly.

"Please, Doc. I'm asking you as a favor from an old poker

buddy. Just patch me up, and I'll be on my way."

Henry Wauk looked into the boy's eyes. He seemed about fifteen or sixteen, though he knew his age was closer to thirty. That's what decided him. Wauk had never been much for sticking his nose into other folks' business. If the kid wasn't a minor child, well then, how he chose to live his life was his own business. He sighed.

"Let's get those clothes off. This is going to hurt. A lot."

He had boiled water in jars. He used this to clean the wounds, though he didn't know how sterile his cloths and bandages were. There weren't a lot of dangerous bugs on Luna, even in Texas, but they could not be eliminated entirely. If the wounds got infected, Sparky would *have* to seek out real help.

"Thank god I can't be sued for malpractice," he muttered.

There was Merthiolate and tincture of iodine. At least the wounds would be colorful. He swabbed with alcohol then wrapped them in the cleanest bandages he had.

Sparky had slashing wounds to his left cheek, his side, both legs, both arms. But the most serious was a deep puncture just below the clavicle. No major veins had been hit, but Henry couldn't stop the wound from seeping blood.

"These are going to leave some mighty fine scars," he said. Sparky continued to stare off into space, as he had since sitting down on the treatment table. He had not cried out, though it must be hurting him.

"I suppose you can have them removed later." He wiped at the nasty slash on the boy's face. It ran across the cheek and had split the bridge of his nose. Luckily, it did not run deep.

"Cat got your tongue, huh?"

"What's that?" Sparky's eyes focused, and he winced. Henry regretted talking; wherever the lad had been, it seemed to be away from the pain.

"I guess there's nothing to talk about," Henry allowed.

"Henry, I need to get off-planet. Quietly."

"Well, that's the only sensible thing you've said so far. I think that's a good idea. Get away from him for a while." Henry knew John Valentine had been away for some time, and he'd heard something about his return. Where was it, Neptune? Out yonder somewhere. He was vague about places off Luna, which he had never left and never intended to. If God had intended man to go whooshing around in space, Henry felt He would have given us rockets in our butts.

"Well, I figure you can afford just about anyplace you want to go."

"Money's not the problem. I need to do it quietly. Even grown up, I'm too easy to recognize, and there's the computers and all."

"Computers?"

"I get on a spaceship, even with a disguise and an alias, there's reporters who've got programs looking out for me. People who like to be aware of my movements."

Like your father, Henry thought.

"Hard to move around when you're a goddam celebrity, huh?"

"You got that right."

As he worked, Henry thought about it. He didn't expect any results, because if Sparky, with his modern sophistication, couldn't figure a way around it, what was an old country doctor going to do? An old, *phony* country doctor.

But to his surprise, something kept tickling at the edges of his mind. He needed a drink, so he paused and took a deep swig from the office jug, which was likely to contain just about anything. There had been one memorable evening when . . .

He narrowed his eyes. He had something. Not what he'd been looking for, but something.

"You know, I recollected something a while back."

"If it's what I'm thinking of, don't reach for any scalpels," Sparky said.

"How's that?"

"I saw you starting to remember. About the jug."

"You doctored it, didn't you? That day your father almost killed you."

"I'm sorry, Henry. That was twenty years ago. I didn't know you then."

"Don't worry. I'm not pissed off." Sparky thought he might be if he knew exactly what had gone into the jug. It shows how wrong you can be. "That pop-skull was the damnedest stuff I ever drank. I lost three days. My spit turned blue. I saw things most drunks don't even dream about."

"I'm surprised it didn't kill you."

"Came damn near. I lost a kidney, and a liver." Henry shrugged. "Hell, I was due for a new liver, anyway. What I was wondering . . . do you remember what you put in the jug? You think you could do it again?"

Sparky said he could certainly try. And then Henry had it.

"Say, your dad told me one time about a brother. Maybe he could give you a hand. He isn't connected with the studio, is he?"

"Uncle Ed?"

"Yeah, used to be a big star. Ed . . ."

"Ed Ventura. His real name is Edwin Booth Valentine. He's my dad's younger brother."

"Well, maybe he can help."

"I don't see how. And I hardly know him. I haven't seen him in maybe twenty years or more."

"Then he ought to be all the more glad to see you."

The sign over the door said SENSUALIST COLLECTIVE. That's all. It was a plain, ordinary glass door and looked in on a plush reception room. Sparky could see several more doors in there, and comfortable couches, tables with huge arrangements of fresh flowers, ornate wallpaper, and big reproductions of works by classical artists of the heroic school. It reminded him of the lobby of a small, plush hotel, but the listing in the Yellow Screens had said only *Retreat*. Retirement home, more likely, Sparky thought. When his father had mentioned Uncle Ed at all, he said he was in retirement.

Retirement meant different things in different professions. With long life, the idea of packing it all in at sixty-five, seventy, or even a hundred didn't appeal to some people. On the other hand, plenty of people thought fifty years in the same job was quite a few years too many. Some shifted to new careers . . . and some tried, and found out they were no longer flexible enough to do so. Aging of the body had been pretty much under control for over a century, but aging of the mind was not always treatable medically, because it did not always have a physical cause. People got set in their ways. They forgot how to see the world freshly. They "retired," because it was either that, or continue in a job they could no longer stand.

Those without a strong work ethic greeted retirement gladly, and filled their days with all the fripperies they could afford. They dabbled in painting, they went on trips. They played games. It was all a lot like Florida in the twentieth, John Valentine had always said, with open contempt.

In the acting profession, retirement could be involuntary. If you'd never made it big, no one cared. You could play character parts forever. But if you were popular once, then lost it, everyone seemed to find you awkward to be around. No one offered you small parts; it was beneath you, even if you wanted the small parts. Something like that seemed to have happened to Uncle Ed. Sparky had given it some thought, himself. A lot had been riding on his appearance as Romeo. It went without saying that many critics would make a lot of "Little Sparky" going romantic. Hell, look what had happened to Shirley Temple, at one time the most profitable star in Hollywood. The business had not historically been kind to child actors.

Sparky pushed through the door and went to the house telephone. There was a list of tenants and near the bottom was *Edwin Valentine*. He pushed the button, and the telescreen displayed the words PLEASE WAIT.

Interesting, Sparky thought, Uncle Ed not listing himself as Ed Ventura. It was not as if he would be bothered by hordes of shrieking fans. A few nostalgia buffs, perhaps. There were stars like Greta Garbo, legendary after all these years, even after seeking anonymity. With most celebrities, however, thirty years after their heyday few could recall them. They were creatures of the moment, of the famous "fifteen minutes," even if their careers had stretched forty years, as Uncle Ed's had.

Sparky had seen most of the "Ed Ventura" films—after his father departed for Neptune, of course. While John Valentine was around none of his family would view such trash. They were unremarkable, standard star vehicles. Not a one had reached the status of classic. Today they were viewed mostly by film students. But they had been big hits in their day.

In Sparky's opinion, his Uncle Ed owed his acting success less to his mouth than to his chin. He had a good chin. Of course, these days anybody could have any chin they wanted, anyone could be beautiful, so there was no such thing as "glamorous," right? Wrong. There was a certain thing called charisma that no surgeon could transplant. There was an indefinable something called screen presence, and you either had it or you didn't. There was something even more elusive that movie analysts called "kinesthesia," which could be summed up as how one lives in one's body, how you *inhabited* that handsome head with that rugged chin. "Ed Ventura" had all of those. There was also something called acting talent, which he showed no evidence of in the films Sparky saw, but his father, in a candid moment, said Uncle Ed had that, too, if he chose to use it. He did not so choose. After all, talent had always been the least important aspect of stardom, and stardom was what Uncle Ed had wanted.

No more, apparently. Why else was he stowed away like a forgotten department store mannequin in this luxury warehouse?

"What do you want?"

Sparky was jerked back to the present by the gruff voice. He looked around, saw no one. The telescreen was still blank.

"I, uh—"

"What happened to your face?" Before Sparky could think of an answer the man went on, in a slightly different tone. "Kenneth? Is that you?"

"Hi, Uncle Ed. Can I come in?"

There was a very long pause.

"I never see anyone. No one ever sees me. Ever."

"Uncle Ed, I really need someone to talk to."

A shorter pause.

"Yes, I suppose you would. He killed my sister, you know."

"What's that?"

"Your father. John. He killed our sister. Your Aunt Sarah."

"I don't believe you."

"You stand there covered in his wounds, and you don't believe me. Oh, he killed her, all right. I have no proof, but I know. What are you doing, running away?"

"I guess so. I need to get off Luna for a while."

"And you'd like my help."

"You're the only family I have."

"Oh, don't appeal to *family* with me, dear boy. I've often thought of writing a script about our father, your grandfather, who you had the great good luck never to have met. But it would be too horrible. No, the very idea of family where our clan is concerned is an obscenity. You should know that as well as anyone. But, of course, you still love him, don't you?" Uncle Ed sighed, a strangely blubbery sound.

"I will see you after all, Kenneth. Perhaps there *is* something to this family business, because I can't imagine another reason for letting you in. I expect you to control your shock and distaste when you see me, however. Think what you please, but spare me your wide-eyed reaction, or it will be quite a brief visit. Do you understand?"

Sparky didn't, but said he did. Anything to get through the inner door and out of this exposed, public place, where he could be tracked down at any moment.

The door buzzed and he pushed through. Immediately he was blasted by a wall of heat and humidity. Sweat popped out on him, and in his already slightly feverish state he came near to passing out.

But leaning against the nearest wall for a moment restored his equilibrium. The room stopped spinning, the gray at the edges of his vision went away. The robe he was wearing—something he had snatched from a rack in the costume closet with barely a look at it—already seemed damp.

He was in a wide, dim corridor that reminded him of a museum. At intervals along each wall were recessed areas, like dioramas. He'd seen the same sort of thing at the King City Zoo, housing various small amphibians and reptiles in climate controlled, glass-fronted boxes. But these cases had no glass. They ranged in size from about a cubic meter to huge, walk-in environments. For that was what they were, and growing in them were the most fantastical, colorful shapes. They were mushroom gardens.

Back on Earth, fungi had come in a thousand shapes and colors. Presumably they still grew there. Many of the growths in the corridor had come from the Luna Genetic Library, and were direct descendants. Others had been modified, or had adapted to the low-gravity Lunar environment. Sparky was pretty sure no earthly toadstools had stood ten feet high. As to colors, he couldn't say, but these came in every possible shade and combination, from a luminescent violet to a pulsing red, in polka dots, stripes, waves, and overwhelming explosions, like spatter paintings. Some mushrooms were tall and spindly, others thick and squat. There were yellow shelf fungi Sparky could have used as stepping stones to scale the walls, and there were tiny orange and blue and maroon puffs like spilled M&Ms.

The small boxes held single species. The big ones were jungles, riots of competitors growing alone or parasitically.

The light was very dim, but swelled as he moved along and faded behind him, giving him enough light to see by. He supposed these things grew better in the dark.

It was a living art gallery, but it was also a farm. He came upon a man in a white coat and chef's hat cutting slices from a green-capped giant and putting them into a basket. He was a plump fellow, and smiled and nodded to Sparky as he passed. He popped a piece of bright-orange mushroom into his mouth and turned back to his work.

Sparky turned a corner in the semidarkness and entered a brightly lit area that had to be the kitchen, but not one like he'd ever seen. Alcoves opened off each side of another broad corridor, each alcove containing two or three people in chef's whites. There were preparation tables and ovens and all the rest of the equipment of the culinary arts—and art this most definitely was. He saw a whole suckling pig come out of an oven, apple in its mouth, and be removed to a wheeled table for garnishing and decorating. One alcove seemed entirely devoted to cakes. Great, towering, multicolored baroque masterpieces dripping with marzipan, festooned with fanciful figures and flowers. Some were being worked on, others had already been transferred to a wheeled table.

All the alcoves centered around the tables. Sparky realized what it reminded him of. It was like a scene from an old movie set in a big-city hospital emergency room, with gowned doctors and nurses working intently on patients stretched out on . . . what was the word? Gurneys.

There was another old movie image, too. A big mortuary, cosmeticians carefully preparing their compliant clients. Sparky didn't know why that image sprang to mind, but it did.

The place certainly didn't *smell* like a hospital or morgue. He passed a *saucier,* sizzling a brown, thick liquid in a skillet. It was a heavenly smell. He realized he'd had nothing to eat that day. The image of Amish corn muffins came into his mind and he wondered if he would ever have another.

Finished gurneys were being wheeled through an arched doorway and into the banquet room. Three very long tables were covered with white cloth and being set with the culinary creations. Again, something was out of whack. The whole huge room contained not a single chair. Sparky saw plates the size of garbage can lids, but no silver. Instead of glassware there were punch bowls filled with wine and fruit juices, and small robot devices with rotary pumps which dipped plastic tails into the drink and then delivered it by means of prehensile necks to . . . who? The standing diners? Diners who had no hands? Sparky couldn't picture the patrons of this feast.

Wondering how much farther he had to go, he passed from the banquet room into a dark, dank, sweltering place he at first could not fathom at all.

A ceiling arched high overhead, almost out of sight. Before him was a twenty-foot surface of government-green ceramic tiles, stretching to his right and his left. Beyond that was a placid surface of water, no more than an inch below the ledge he stood on. It was a swimming pool, and quite a large one. He'd never seen one designed quite like this, though.

In a moment he realized it had been converted from an old tank that had probably once been a part of the vast and complex sewage treatment system of King City. It was a big cylinder lying on its side. The water would be as deep as the ceiling was high, and there would be no shallow end. There was no smell beyond a faint whiff of chlorine, and no sound but the intermittent drip of water condensing on the ceiling and falling back into the pool. No diving board, no poolside chairs, no lifeguards, though the place was big enough they'd need motorboats to get to a drowner quickly. No people.

Were they growing something in here? Fish for the banquet tables behind him? Kelp? He went to the edge and leaned over. A faint emerald shimmer from near the bottom revealed nothing at first, then he saw vague shapes undulating slowly between him and the light. It was like looking down into an atomic-reactor core, the surface glass smooth, the depths crystalline. The occasional mutant five-ton sardine swimming by . . .

Slow, greasy swells distorted the surface and Sparky straightened and squinted into the darkness. A tubular shape was moving slowly toward him, just beneath the surface. Part of its back broke through and rolled slightly. Could it be some sort of whale? *Nothing* in Luna was more illegal than to produce anything resembling earthly cetaceans. A hippopotamus, more likely.

It was Uncle Ed.

Sparky never understood how he knew this, but he knew. He hadn't seen his uncle in over twenty years, had not known him well then. The thing wallowing in the water below him at first presented nothing resembling a face. But he knew. Then the thing rolled slightly and at one end, on one side, was a clench of flesh that slowly resolved itself into eyes, nose, and a mouth. There was nothing you could really call a head, and certainly nothing resembling a neck. Just endless, tightly packed folds and rolls of flesh that quivered and undulated with the slow rhythms of the water. One single feature was left of the matinee idol that had been Ed Ventura: his nose. It had defined a profile that graced a million movie posters, and there it sat, surrounded, almost overwhelmed. The lips were now fat and sensuous. The chin? Well, Sparky supposed you could call any of several dozen folds below the mouth a chin, if it pleased you. His cheeks were fat. His forehead was fat; if eyebrows remained, they were buried deep. The eyes were at the bottom of puckered pits, but they were alert and alive.

"Hello, Sparky," the thing said. And there was the source of the blubbery sound he had heard over the intercom. Uncle Ed could barely speak without making a raspberry.

"Hi . . . Uncle Ed?"

"Somewhat changed, but still the same jolly old fellow inside," Ed confirmed. "Wait a moment."

There was a momentary splashing, and Sparky caught a glimpse of what might have been a hand, or a flipper. If it was connected to an arm, Sparky didn't see it. The huge cylinder of pale fat rolled and turned in the water until one end—the end with the face—bobbed partly out of the water. It was like an illustration Sparky recalled from a children's book he used to have. Humpty-Dumpty. An egg with a face painted on it. Only this wasn't painted, it was more like it had been poked into soft bread dough.

The mouth smiled. It was bigger than Sparky had realized. Well, of course it would have to be big to eat enough to . . . Sparky turned away from that thought. And from the problem of how all that food being prepared in the banquet room was to get from the tables into the maw of this floating creature.

As a matter of fact, Uncle Ed presented *several* logistical problems to the curious mind, such as breathing, and elimination, and sex . . . Sparky had never felt less curious in his life.

"Sit down, boy," Ed commanded. "I can't look up at you."

"What's that?"

"No neck, Sparky." His uncle chuckled. "I haven't had much of a neck for ten years now."

Sparky sat, at first crossing his legs beneath him, then deciding he might as well dangle his feet in the water. It was warm and soothing; Sparky had been on the move for almost six hours. He needed a rest.

"Was that a bandage on your leg?"

"Yes."

"And you seem fairly battered in other places."

"I fell down a staircase."

"Of course you did. I must say, you did not show any trace of disgust when first I hove into view."

"I'm an actor."

There was a pause, then Ed laughed.

"And a hell of a good one, nephew! Much better than I ever was. Of course, I never wanted to *be* an actor, but I had little choice in the matter. Neither did you."

"It's all I ever wanted to be," Sparky said.

"It's all you were ever *allowed* to want to be, which is a slightly different thing. But you had the talent, and you did well, so no harm done, eh? Except for the occasional near-death experience in the bathtub, I shouldn't wonder."

Sparky was too shocked to reply.

"Well of *course* I know about that, boy. Not from having witnessed John doing it to you. From having it done to me by *my* father. Given John's personality, and his designs on you, it was a certainty he would use Father's methods in your education.''

''Do you have children?'' Sparky asked, a little chagrined that he had never thought to find out.

''I did not. I didn't want to find out if *I* would use Father's methods. They say it runs in families, you know. Child abuse. Something *you* might wish to consider when the question of child rearing comes up.''

Sparky didn't know why he had asked that question. He was feeling light-headed, not at all well. The smells of cooking from the room behind him were overwhelming, and not as pleasant as they had been.

''You didn't want to be an actor,'' Sparky said. For some reason, that bit of information had stuck in his head.

''Didn't want to be, and never really became one. I was a star, and I'm sure your father told you the difference. I wanted to be a chef. Our father had other ideas, and one did not cross our father, any more than you cross yours. Though it looks as if you might have done so today.''

''Did you see . . . I mean, has it been on—''

''The news? There is no news in here, Sparky. And before you launch into your story, let me assure you I don't want to hear it. What he did to you, what you did to him, I don't want to know. I can never be called to testify to something I don't know anything about. You fell down a staircase. Right?''

''. . . right.''

''And I'm a ballet dancer. Of course, I'm free to deduce things. You want to get off Luna. You seem unable to simply walk up to the ticket counter and buy passage. Ergo, you are being hunted. You had an *argument* with this staircase. You seem to have lost.''

''You haven't seen the staircase.''

''Hah!'' Uncle Ed was delighted. ''Maybe you gave as good as you got! No, no, don't tell me any details, let me make them up in my own mind. It should provide me with no end of source material for months of quiet contemplation. That's what we mostly do here, if you were curious. Float, and contemplate.''

''And eat,'' Sparky suggested.

Uncle Ed squinted dubiously. With all that fat around his eyes, it was a squint to remember.

"I wasn't—" Sparky began.

"Making fun of me. Of course not. Obviously we eat. I forbade you contempt, disgust. Curiosity I will allow you. Within limits. I'd venture to guess you're wondering how much I weigh."

Like the starlet insulted when asked her measurements, Sparky suspected the lady doth protest too much. Ed *wanted* to talk, he realized. Within limits. He'd have to be careful not to show too much nor too little interest.

"Three thousand two hundred and seven pounds, at last weighing. Probably a few more by today. A ton and a half of contentment."

Sparky hadn't known humans could get that large. He doubted it was possible without some modifications. Extra hearts, possibly, or mechanical ones. Or elephant hearts. He also suspected that if he asked about that, he could be there for hours.

"I believe I'm the third largest human who has ever lived. Numbers one and two are somewhere in the water below me."

"Are you shooting for first place?"

"Not in any determined way. I wouldn't mind, of course."

"You said 'we.' Who are you? I mean, a cult of some sort?"

"Just retirees who like to eat. People who find the modern world a bit too frantic, who have socialized too much. People on retreat. Who are seeking a *lower* level of consciousness. Who admire lizards basking on rocks, jellyfish drifting on warm currents. Who are happy to *exist,* but not eager to struggle, physically or mentally. We have no organization other than regular meals, six times a day, and no name for ourselves. The few outsiders who are aware of us—and that is very few, since we never go out—call us chubbies."

Sparky was reminded of a story of a hermit, isolated and silent for thirty years. Once his silence was broken he couldn't stop talking. Sparky couldn't recall the punch line.

But he could see some sort of forklift trucks congregating down at the far end of the pool. Cargo nets hung from manipulator arms, and there seemed to be a commotion in the water. Good God, it must be feeding time, he realized. He would rather not witness that.

"So can you help me?"

Uncle Ed bobbed in the water like a waterlogged inflatable beach ball, regarding his nephew silently. His expressions were very hard to read.

"I have a private yacht mothballed at a port on the Far-side," Uncle Ed said, at length. "Nothing fancy, but it will get you as far as Mars in a reasonable time."

"I'll buy it from you."

"No need." The fat man chuckled. "A stroke of genius, your coming here. It is the absolute *last* place John would think to look for you. And my yacht is the least likely vehicle for him to watch for. And I suspect you knew I could never resist doing him a bad turn. Isn't that right?"

"You can see right through me," Sparky said. He had never entertained any such idea, had never even remembered he *had* an uncle until Doc brought it up. But why mention that?

"They tell me it can be made space-ready in two hours. I'll call and authorize it. When you get to Mars, hire someone to bring it back."

"Sure." Sparky had no intention of hiring anyone, or of going to Mars. But why complicate things?

"Good luck," Uncle Ed burbled, his head sinking beneath the water.

I had needed a little luck, and some thespian and confidence skills to talk my way past busybodies at the spaceport with too much time on their hands, but I had made it. (What had the name of Uncle Ed's yacht been? *Éclair? Bonbon?* Something sweet and sticky, I remember that much.) Anyway, with visions of sugarplums—and Uncle Ed's bloated frame—dancing in my head, I had made my escape from Luna, from my father, from Sparky, from everyone who was looking to do me ill or do me good. For almost fifty years I had never shown my real face or revealed my real name. Only recently had I begun to admit once more to being "Sparky," though only in the outer planets, and found to my surprise that I was still remembered.

I had been back to Luna twice since then, when the lure

of a role was just too much. I had used ironclad false identification, never the same name. All this had put a severe crimp in my career. No sooner would I start to get good notices, build up a reputation in my current pseudonym, than I'd feel the hot breath of pursuit and take off for a new venue, with a new identity. Practically speaking, no one had been looking for me for thirty or forty years now, I felt reasonably sure. But old habits die hard, and the guilty flee before the bad reviews are out.

And now I was about to return to Luna once more. Luna, the fabled Golden Globe. I could see it out the window of the lifeboat as Poly and I strapped ourselves in for the last leg of the journey. At certain distances it really does look golden, though usually I'd describe it as more of a buttermilk shade. Mount it on a gilt pedestal and you could give it out as an award.

There really had been an award called the Golden Globe once, years before the Invasion. My father had told me about it. It was handed out by a group called the Hollywood Foreign Press Association in honour of the year's best work in motion pictures.

"Not the Foreign *Film* Critics, you'll notice," he had told me. "Just a bunch of reporters from other countries who used to get together, forty or fifty of them, to have a dinner and hand out awards to any film people desperate enough to show up and get drunk with them. After a while, being reporters, they started giving out press releases about who'd won. On a slow news day, some papers would pick up the story. And then things snowballed. Before long, they had their own television show, *full* of stars, just as if the award meant something. They managed to upstage the Oscars, and the awards might as well have been given out by the Podunk Rotary Club for all they had to do with film.

"Draw your own moral from this, Sparky. And remember, at the center of the cult of personality called stardom there is just a big empty hole. Awards don't matter. Acclaim doesn't matter. Only your craft matters."

We were already sore and a bit cranky from a day and a half at one gee. When the lifeboat engine fired it hit hard, and we didn't have the padding we'd used aboard Hal. But it wasn't a terribly long boost. The first lifeboat fell away—really nothing more than an engine and fuel tank, after Hal modified it in his repair shop. By the time the second one fired Luna was looming much larger in my window. This was a bit gentler, but still rough.

The lifeboat engine coughed out its last while we were still ten meters above the surface. Considering that all the calculations had been done at the orbit of Uranus, I would call this cutting it *close*. We dropped, and hit with a jar and a crunch of metal. There was a faint hiss audible from the cabin, a sound no Lunarian likes to hear, but we were in our suits, and the boat's tripod landing gear kept us from falling over.

We struggled to our feet, wrestled our luggage into the lock, and stepped out onto the surface. There was no one but Poly to hear my first words, but I set them down here for the sake of history.

"That was one *heck* of a giant leap for an old actor."

I was home.

ACT 5

(from *The Five-Minit Bard*)

KING LEAR
ACT I SCENE I

King Lear's Palace

Enter Lear, Goneril, Regan, Cordelia, Gloucester, Kent

LEAR: Hey, you! Go get Burgundy and the Frog! I'm an old fart, and I'm pooped. I'm outta here.
GONERIL: Gimme the kingdom, 'cause I love you and kiss your royal ass.
REGAN: Me, too, Daddy, but twice as much!
LEAR: What about you, sweets?
CORDELIA: You're cool, Pops.
LEAR: Well, fuck you! You don't get nothing. You two bitches split it up.
KENT: You're fuckin' up, big man.
LEAR: Fuck you, too! Screw!

(*Exit Kent; Enter Duke of Burgundy and King of France*)

BURGUNDY: No cash? Fuck me! I don't want her, then!
FRANCE: I'll take her.
CORDELIA: Cool!
LEAR: Take the bitch, then. I'm outta here.

(*Exit Lear and court*)

FRANCE: Let's screw.
CORDELIA: Cool!

(*Exit France and Cordelia*)

GONERIL: He's one nutty old fuck!
REGAN: Let's fuck him over.
GONERIL: Okay.

(*Exit Goneril and Regan*)

EDMUND: (aside) I'm one double-crossing bastard! (*Exit*)

There are seasons in the life of a Shakespearean actor, natural milestones he can expect along the path of his career. The two most important are Romeo and Lear.

Romeo is a young man's game. Impetuous and energetic, thunderstruck by the storms of puberty, stunned by love. It's not a part for the mature, though God knows it's been played by enough codgers. As I've just related, Romeo was a disaster for me. I don't have much affection for the role.

Macbeth is on his way up. Hamlet and Henry V are vigorous and youthful. Othello and Julius Caesar are in the full flower of their careers.

There are innumerable other roles an actor can essay—a few he can find himself stuck in as a second stringer or a comic. But if one has hopes of being written in the annals of the great, if one aspires to acquire the mantle of Burbage and Olivier, then the capstone of his career will be Lear.

Lear.

In the seventy years since my days as Sparky, the closest I had ever come to playing Lear was in an engaging little trifle called *The Five-Minit Bard,* a small part of which is set out above.

Oh, the fun we had. The premise was simple: all Shakespeare in one night, no play longer than five minutes. Each was done in a different style. *Hamlet* as if by Gilbert and Sullivan, with a patter song and a happy ending. *All's Well That Ends Well* as rewritten by Beckett, with performers sitting in chairs, muttering bits of dialogue and abandoning the project after three minutes. *Richard III* the radio serial, one-minute episodes with sound effects scattered through the performance. *Henry VI,* all three parts, narrated by a super-rapid square-dance caller and done as a ballet à la Copland.

And *A Midsummer Night's Dream* as played by Sparky and his Gang, with guess who as Puck/Sparky. No one ever suspected.

Some were a lot shorter than five minutes, or the night would have run three hours, much too long for comedy. *Timon of Athens:* a man walks to center stage and says, "Nobody gives a damn about *Timon of Athens,*" and walks off. *Titus Andronicus:* all cast members line up onstage, and at a signal, begin hacking at each other with swords, blood bladders spraying high-pressure Max Factor Red #2.

Then there was *King Lear,* as if done by the turn-of-the-century Rude Theater. Most critics hated *5MB,* but it was a long-running hit. I played dozens of parts, including Lear.

I say these things in an attempt to explain why, after an absence of more than thirty years, I was returning to Luna. I had been there only twice since my hasty departure from *Romeo*. Things had been all too hot for me the last time I left—misunderstandings not affected by any statute of limitations—and I'd sworn a mighty oath never to return. Things would be even hotter now, with Isambard and the whole stinking planet of Charon on my trail, possibly already waiting for me. I didn't pretend they'd have any more trouble finding me here than they had at Oberon. If I had a brain in my head, I'd be hopping the first tramp free-faller to points unspecified and mysterious. I'd be doing the thing I had become so good at: losing myself in the vast spaces of the solar system.

But I never even thought of that, and the reason was simple.

Lear.

Not only Lear, but Lear staged by the greatest director of our time, my long-ago sidekick and onetime best friend—*only* friend—Kaspara Polichinelli.

And by now Polly probably didn't have a lot of time left.

Almost from the first blast at Oberon, I had been absorbed with the question of where to land when we reached Luna. Adept though I am at producing false identification and talking my way through any difficulties, simply setting down at the King City Spaceport in a spent lifeboat was bound to draw unwanted attention.

But I had some advantages. By the nature of space and of space travel, "border patrol" around a place like Luna is an iffy proposition. Radar and computers can certainly track all the millions of approaching, departing, and orbiting vehicles in the vast sphere, one thousand miles from the surface, that the lawyers have defined as Lunar territorial space. But having done that, what do you do next? Allow landings and takeoffs only at designated spots, like major spaceports? Ten million weekend orienteers, campers, and renters of shorthoppers would raise quite a howl about that one. Not to mention a million freeholders living in self-sufficient isolation, scattered over the entire Lunar surface. Should we ask these folks to hoof it to the nearest train? Allow only surface transportation to hiking trails and camp resorts? No, Lunarians will surrender certain of their civil rights, just like anyone else, if the reason is strong enough. If people are blowing up spaceships with bombs, they will submit to searches before boarding a spaceship. But ban private hoppers, orbiters, or even deep-space RVs ... to stop *smugglers*? To keep a lid on illegal immigration? 'Fraid not, Senator.

So. How about employing sophisticated computer programs to keep track of deep-space arrivals, matching these up with vehicle transponder codes and criminal rap sheets and travel patterns and godknowswhatelse, and following suspicious ships to ask a few questions and conduct a quick Gestapo-style shakedown?

Tried that. Didn't work. Nabbed a few pathetic amateurs, first offenders, got off with a warning. *Big* waste of time and money.

So how about ... open borders?

But ... but ... open *borders*? Absolute anathema to the bureaucratic mentality. Never mind that there has never been a border quite so tenuous or so permeable as the one surrounding Luna, or the ones around any planet. We can't just let people come and go as they please, can we? Carrying any damn thing they want to carry? Precious close to anarchy, that.

And so ... actually, no. Not what you're probably thinking. For once, rationality prevailed. It helped that there is little worth smuggling on a small scale, since little is illegal these days. Avoiding duty on large cargoes is another matter entirely, and it's easy to keep track of the big ships if they land where they oughtn't. As for illegal immigration ... *what* illegal immigration? It's not a problem on Luna. Just step right up and ask for citizenship papers, and after a sixty-second search of InterSystem crime records, a credit check (we don't want your welfare cases), and payment of a nominal fee, you're a Lunarian. Welcome, cobber!

So the situation is like this, for those of you who thought getting into Luna for a criminal type like myself would be a big hairy deal: it ain't. Not at first, anyway. There are plenty of wanted folks in those freeholds I mentioned a moment ago, and if they stay put and don't try to enter the mainstream of civilization, they can stay there for a million years as far as the Lunar federal government is concerned. No one will come looking for them.

It's the next step that's tough.

Did I say the spherical "border" around Luna is really a laughable fiction? I did, and it is. Did I imply that means one can then just walk the main thoroughfares of King City? I did not. *That* border is tighter than a tick's tush. *That* border makes the old "Iron Curtain" seem like a vague, unpatrolled line in the sand and a few desultory formalities. Because the border between the surface of Luna and the cities of Luna is nothing less than the line between life and death. Between vacuum and air. *Every* entrance into the main corridors of Luna is, of necessity, a fortress designed to keep air inside and the Breathsucker *out*. If a molecule of oxygen has no chance of passing through without the proper authorization, how much chance does several trillion molecules of actor have of entering without a visa?

Well, anything can be done, if you know your way around. The easiest way is through your friends, but you have to have the right sort of friends. The sort who do this sort of thing every day.

I chose to go through the Heinleiners.

Before the Big Glitch, not long ago, nobody knew anything about the Heinleiners. In fact, they didn't even have that name; it was given to them later by media reports after the pivotal part they played, involuntarily, in the Glitch itself. Now everybody thinks they know everything about Heinleiners, but the truth is, most of it is wrong.

First, and most basic, it's pretty silly to refer to them as a group. They're not group-type people. Nobody elects officers, no meetings are held. You "join" by being invited to one of several secret locations by a friend. What you actually do, however, is to opt out of the aboveground society. You can do it totally, choosing to live in one of the secret enclaves, or partially, maintaining a life and an identity while moving back and forth between the two realms.

When the Lunar Central Computer, the CC, had the nervous breakdown we've all come to call the Big Glitch, the Heinleiners were one of its main targets. There's been endless

426 ··· JOHN VARLEY

speculation as to why. The short answer so far is, We don't know. The popular theory, and one I think makes sense, is the CC was deeply offended by a high-tech group living beyond its reach, and possessing technology not available to the CC. Accordingly, the CC organized and trained, in secret, a cadre of extra-legal police that you might as well call an army. This bunch invaded the main Heinleiner compound, intending to wipe it out, and got a big surprise: these people fought back. The takeover failed, the CC retreated into a semicatatonic state from which it is only now being coaxed, and Lunar life was turned topsy-turvy.

Intimately tied up in all this, again involuntarily, was one Hildy Johnson, ace reporter for the *News Nipple.* Yes, *that* Hildy Johnson.

She has told some of her story publicly. She's told more of it to me. There is much she still has to tell, which she'll get to when she thinks it wise. And this presents me with a problem. As a sort of "member" of the group, I am constrained in what I can reveal about it. Luckily, much of it is superfluous to the story I'm telling. Here is what I *can* reveal:

1) The group got its name from a space vessel called the *Robert A. Heinlein,* named for a twentieth-century writer and radical political philosopher. The ship is very large, even by today's standards, and quite old. It was originally intended as an Orion-type starship, that is, a ship powered by large numbers of nuclear bombs exploding against a massive pusher plate. You can find the plans for one in any public library. Long ago the original builders went broke, and the shell of the ship ended up derelict on the edge of a vast junkyard. The Heinleiners took it over, and the junkyard as well. Today the ship, or parts of it, serve as the public face of the Heinleiners, the place reporters and politicians go when they want to talk to one. (Good luck! They don't do a lot of talking.)

2) These people do share some of Mr. Heinlein's political philosophy, the part that can be summed up as "Leave me alone!" They are not anarchists, but they brook little interference from the government. They are happiest where there is *no* government, and you'll find many of them, or their sympathizers, in the more remote regions of the system. But a lot of folks can't take that kind of isolation (me, for in-

stance), and so live well concealed (if they are doing illegal things) or openly (where they work for a quasi-libertarian form of government). They don't plan to overthrow any governments; that would be entirely too much trouble and, as even the most doctrinaire of them will admit, the yoke of present-day governments is not intolerably onerous, when viewed historically. Things could be worse, and would likely *get* worse if there was a lot of radical political agitation to suppress. Don't look for Heinleiners to be publishing any manifestos, nailing any lists of demands to courthouse doors, storming any Bastilles. But they *do* have one secret, jealously guarded, in whose pursuit they are implacable:

3) They're going to the stars.

Hah! you say. *Secret!* you say. Tell me another one.

Very well. The fact that they *intend* to travel to the stars is very well known, and almost universally dismissed. Any number of Eminent Scientists will explain to you in great detail why the project is impossible. The Heinleiners think this is just fine. The fewer people take them seriously, the fewer there will be trying to discover the *real* secret, which is how they intend to do it.

Trust me. They're going to do it.

I am the least-qualified person in the system to look at a stardrive and say, "Aha! *That* will work!" You could spend a year showing it to me, explaining it to me, drawing nice pretty pictures and reading the manual (if there was such a thing) out loud, and at the end I would still be in a state of perfect ignorance concerning stardrives.

But others, people who know, tell me I can count on it. In a year, two years—however long it takes to patch it up—that magnificent hulk sitting out there on the surface is going to leap up and violate the virgin sky. How fast will it go? No one will say. But no one will raise a family during the journey, and you won't return to find all your friends a hundred years older than you.

Swamp gas, you say. How many "starships" have been sold to how many suckers in the last century? Hyperspace is to our age as lost treasure maps and gold mines and oil wells and Florida real estate were to a previous generation of confidence men. I should know; I've sold enough starships in my time.

Yes, and the way to sell them is not to hide out by a garbage dump and not tell anyone about it. You *can* invest, and this may be your last chance before the stock goes intergalactic. Check out the prospectus. It claims nothing, promises nothing. Believe me, this is not how you sell pirate gold. Call your broker at once. You'll thank me later.

And that is the secret, you see. Not that they are going, but how they're going to get there. The inventors and investors in this new space drive do not intend to turn it over to a grateful government, or have it confiscated by storm troopers. They don't intend to patent it, either. Patent examiners can be bribed, information can leak. If the Heinleiners have a religion, it is Free Enterprise. They intend to *sell* this new technology, and they intend to become dirty, rotten, filthy, stinking rich from it.

It was a short hike to the nearest entrance to the *Heinlein*. A few years ago there had been no way in but to stand around and wait for one of the inhabitants to notice you and invite you in or tell you to get lost. Now there were three or four standard air locks. Beyond them were rudimentary reception rooms, "customs shacks" to the Heinleiners. The notoriety of the Big Glitch had forced them to assume an unaccustomed organization, which they went about grudgingly and haphazardly, as was their style. These entrances were manned by volunteers, which were hard to come by in such an individualistic group. I heard later that it was standard procedure to cool your heels for hours at these entrances, waiting for someone to arrive at the security desk.

And if you didn't know somebody, the custom shack was as far as you'd get.

We got lucky. Someone was manning the desk when Poly and I entered. Even better, the name I dropped was still worth something. I'd worried about that, since it had been quite some time since I'd dealt with this person and there had been absolutely no way to get in contact with him other than simply walking up to the door and asking. But the guard at the desk simply nodded, and jerked her thumb at the second lock behind her. Then she went back to the book she was reading.

"Keep your helmet on," I told Poly as we cycled through. "You never know what you'll run into in here."

She soon saw what I meant, and her reaction was the usual one.

"These people must be crazy," she said.

It's not so bad within the ship itself. You see building and renovation happening here and there, but things always look a little loose around a construction site. Then you move out of the ship and into the vast junk pile behind it. And things just don't look right.

Everything has a haphazard, thrown-together look. Tunnel walls are made out of whatever was handy when a new tunnel was needed. Lights are burned out and if you can still see reasonably well, just *stay* burned out. There are no municipal crews to replace them. If you stumble in the dark, then replace it *yourself,* citizen! There ain't no City Hall to sue if you trip. Air 'cyclers have flashing yellow, or even red lights. Most Lunarians can go five years without even seeing a flashing green.

"Do they have a death wish?" Poly asked, after a mile of this.

"They have a safety net," I told her, and didn't explain further. But I knew what she meant. People raised to the exacting safety standards of Lunar engineering were always shocked to see how the Heinleiners lived. Sort of like how you might feel to go up in an airplane, then look out the window and see a wing was being held on by two rusty bolts and a wad of gum.

But that wouldn't bother you if you were a bird. Something goes wrong, you just fly to the ground. And that's how the Heinleiners had come to view the world, because they had a safety net in the form of the force-field suit. Maybe we'd *all* come to view the world that way if they ever decided to sell the technology. If a blowout happened, a field was instantly generated around their bodies from a unit implanted in place of one lung. The unit also contained about an hour of highly compressed oxygen, dispensed directly into the bloodstream. To someone wearing a device like that, a blowout was nothing more than an inconvenience. Thus, Heinleiners didn't waste a lot of time and effort on making things triple-triple-triple redundant. One system and maybe a backup was good enough for them. Many things they made were no better than they had to be. These were busy people—they were going to the stars!—and there was always something else to do.

Of course, it made things a little edgy when you realized their safety net didn't do *you* a damn bit of good. When I had to go to the enclave, I got my business done quickly, and got out. Which is just how the Heinleiners wanted it.

If you were looking for all the inside dope on the mysterious Heinleiners, you'll have to go elsewhere. I could relate what went on, using assumed names and euphemisms, but it would be ninety percent lies. For one thing, most of the people I met prefer to stay firmly underground at this point. Remember, not that long ago duly appointed representatives of the Lunar state were shooting at them. They're still a little pissed off. Wouldn't you be? For another, I've been shown some things I swore never to talk about, and talking around them would soon leave me with nothing to say.

Then there's the matter of what I was doing in there. Changing my appearance yet again, naturally. Obtaining a few necessary items for Poly—nothing more than little white lies, in her case—and sending her on her way. (Good-bye, sweet Poly, you were a great traveling companion. Sorry about the fingers. And we'll see no more of you in this story.)

But most of my short time there was consumed in several strictly illegal activities involving becoming someone else. We're not talking about phonying up a hopper's license here; this identity had to stand up to close scrutiny for whatever time I'd be spending in Luna. The statute of limitations hasn't expired on any of it, so it would be foolish to set down the details here. And, frankly, you never know when you'll need to pull some of these same tricks again. Better they don't become common knowledge. If you really need to know how to do it, find a criminal and ask *him*. And be ready to pay.

When you travel around as much as I do, and have lived as long as I have, the one constant you notice is change.

The species is still expanding, though the talk about doing something to correct that has been getting more and more serious. (What, pray tell? Spaying and neutering? Ah, but don't get me started on that.) I'm not denying it is a problem. With the death rate edging closer and closer to zero, about all that has saved us so far is that very few people want more than one or two children. It's not hard to see a time when every bit of rock in the system is honeycombed down to the core with antlike trillions. There's a school of thought that maintains one reason for the Invasion was our overpopulation of the earth. If we keep growing exponentially, the reasoning goes, might the Invaders take notice of us once again?

I don't pretend to understand anything about the Invaders, beyond the fact that it took them three days to nearly annihilate the human race, and that in spite of our bravest efforts, the final score was twenty billion to nothing. I'm not eager for a rematch.

But frankly I sort of like the changes I see in my travels. Almost always it is an expansion of what I saw before, and like my father, I hold to an old-fashioned idea once called "progress." Other than a growing population, there hasn't been a lot of it since the Invasion. Scientific research is at an all-time low. And why not? We live practically as long as we want, in perfect health and vitality. Machines can do practically everything that needs to be done, so that leisure has become our biggest "problem." Biology is well understood, and the practical limits of the exploration of physics have been reached, for now, anyway.

So I take pleasure in seeing how this or that enclave has grown. I was delighted at Oberon, and when I return, if ever, I'm sure it will delight me again to see the wheel complete.

But Luna is a little different. Luna is, and always will be, "home." Unstable as my early childhood was, numerous as my "homes" might have been, it was always Luna, the fabulous Golden Globe, that I hailed from. There's a bit of snobbery in that, something like the way the residents of New York, London, Paris, or Rome might have felt. All roads lead to the Big Apple, as it were. If you're from somewhere else, you're from nowhere. If you can make it here, you can make it anywhere.

But the other part is the same, I suspect, whether you hail from The City or from Catfish Row, from the Golden Globe or from Bottom. You sort of wish it would stay the same. You'd like to go back and find something familiar.

You'd like to think you can go home.

You can't, of course. Even if the old hometown is stagnant

as a played-out mine, it's gotten older, and so have you. You look at it through different eyes. The ivy on the old castle walls has grown thicker, the paint on the old shack has peeled off. More likely, the old castle has been torn down to make room for a housing development, and the shack . . . well, you can't even locate where it *was*. It gives you a certain feeling of transience.

My whole life has been transient. When I go home, I want to return to something *solid*.

Fat chance. I spent my first few hours wandering aimlessly through the broad commercial corridors of King City, a place I used to know like Act One of *Julius Caesar,* always just a little bit lost.

I spent a few hours training and slidewalking to various haunts from my past, finding most of them either no longer there or so changed as to be almost unrecognizable. It had been a good many years since I had dared return to Luna, and even that had been a rash chance on my part. After that many years, even if the place is still there and not much altered physically, the people are different. Where's that old gang of mine? Moved, most often. Hanging out somewhere else. So I moved on, too, on to the Rialto.

For drama in the English language, the de facto tongue of our time, when you think Theater District, you think Broadway. London may have eclipsed it in some ways, in some eras, but it never had the glitter. Shortly pre-Invasion, the theater scene in Miami was certainly one to reckon with. But how many songs can you think of about Collins Avenue?

No, the Great White Way was *the* theater Mecca . . . until The Rialto came along.

It had to be that way. Luna is by far the most populous of the inhabited planets. King City is the biggest city in Luna, three times larger than its nearest competitor. Our civilization is blessed or cursed with more leisure time than any in history. The urge to find something to do can get a little desperate. The living theater was never going to give movies and television much competition for the leisure dollar, but even a tiny fraction of the Lunarians' vast disposable income was enough to support a broad boulevard two miles long and bespangled with more theatrical jewels than the Tsarina's Tiara. When the "day" lights dimmed overhead and the marquees lit up, the street didn't so much glitter as explode in colored light.

I strolled down the avenue, hands jammed in my pockets, wishing for a fedora hat and a studio cloudburst so I could be Gene Kelly singin' in the rain. I wanted to hoof it through the shoeshine parlor like Fred Astaire in *The Band Wagon.* I was George M. Cohan, a Yankee Doodle boy. I was a brass band, a wild Count Basie blast, the bells of St. Peter's in Rome, and tissue paper on a comb. If I had a home, this was it. The center of the universe.

Oh, I'm not saying it was all familiar. Twenty years earlier a fever of renovation had swept down The Rialto like a demented dervish, and not all the changes were to my liking. The street was now lined with lampposts pretending to be gaslights; some spavined city planner's idea of "quaint," I shouldn't wonder. A lot of the old neon—a quaint vision I *did* like—had been replaced with higher-tech lighting effects that tended to overload the senses. But these things come and go; I can live with them. The important thing was the theaters themselves, dozens of them, strung out or bunched together, flashing into the artificial "night" the names of old friends and new arrivals: *A Doll's House, Twelfth Night, Padlock, Into the Woods, Forget-Me-Not, The Wild Woman, School for Scandal.* Oh, and the human friends, too, though you never could tell. You could figure that, even fifty years later, most of them would still be alive, in the physical sense. Professionally, it was another matter. It's a cruel trade. Some thought destined for glory by their own generation could be forgotten very quickly. Others who had labored hard for three, four, five decades became overnight sensations.

Legends? Our time doesn't produce a lot of them. It's a lot easier to become a legend if you die, close the book, and let the legend makers get to work. Mere stardom can be conveyed willy-nilly and last no longer than a soap bubble. So no one is going to chisel your name in stone until everyone's sure you're not coming back to be an embarrassment.

About half the theaters on The Rialto had achieved landmark status. You might buy and sell the structures, but you couldn't tear them down and the names were there forever. The rest were up for grabs. I wasn't familiar with this "Golden Globe" house and I had forgotten the address as the months went by, but I recalled thinking it couldn't be far from the site of my last appearance as Sparky: the late, lamented John Valentine Theater.

I was right. It was in the neighborhood. Like everything else, the neighborhood had changed, but I knew approximately where I was.

I walked up and down in front of it. It had been so long since I'd played in a real Rialto theater I just wanted to get a feel for the place again. I liked what I saw. Something called *Two Problems in Logic* was playing, a title I wasn't familiar with, though the writer and director were both known to me. Only two players were listed, one with her name above the title, and I had never heard of either of them. That was depressing.

Pushing one of the brass-and-glass doors, I entered a long, thick-carpeted lobby in lavender and ecru. Spaced along the walls were posters from past productions at the Golden Globe. I gathered the house specialized in new works by established playwrights, though there was the occasional old warhorse guaranteed to put butts in seats, and a few revivals of faded stars who'd only had the one hit, reprising the role for the ninety-ninth time.

Finally I came to the back of the theater itself, and looked down a long aisle to the stage.

There was something oddly familiar about it.

I walked down a few rows and looked around. Even more familiar.

I hurried back to the lobby, paused to get my bearings, and followed a branching corridor that led to the rest rooms. Just beyond them was a bank of fire exit doors. My heart was hammering as I banged through one of them, setting off a distant alarm. I found myself outside on a side street, around the corner from the main entrance. It was a narrow way, not quite an alley, and just off to my left was a small park with a gazebo that, other than a fresh coat of paint, had not changed in seventy years.

The Golden Globe was the John Valentine Theater.

I staggered into the park and collapsed on a bench.

Memories.

"En garde!" Valentine shouted, and slashed at his son's face.

It was a backhand stroke, and the tip of the blade drew a

red line on Kenneth's left cheek. There was no more pain than from a razor cut. He touched his cheek with his free hand and looked at the blood on his fingers.

"I said *en garde,* sir," Valentine said. "Raise your weapon."

Kenneth slowly did so.

"Are you ready this time?"

He nodded.

"Then *fight,* damn you." Valentine slashed again, not quite as quickly. Kenneth parried the move, felt the clash of blade up through his wrist. And here, the blade was coming at him again, and he parried once more, and again, and again . . . and his father's blade tore through the fabric of his sleeve. This time he felt some pain, and a wet heat as blood ran down his arm.

"Again." And once more the sword was flashing in his face. He got the blade up just in time. But no sooner had he fended off the first thrust than another was coming at him. And another, and another.

Parry, riposte. Sixte, seconde. The words flew around in his mind, mocking him. *I'll bet you wish you'd studied now,* they said. Frantically, he tried to remember, but it just wasn't there. If you had to think about it, you were already too late. Your body must simply respond. Thinking was for the *attack,* and it would be a long time before young Kenneth was ready for that. The best he could do was try to keep his blade up, try to keep it between his body and the slashing, hungry steel that had a life of its own. That's what it had to be. His father could not be trying to kill him.

He felt pain again. This time it was his hip. A thrusting wound, this one hurt more than all the others put together. Others . . . how many were there now? Five? Six? He had lost count.

He was blinded by sweat. He stopped, turned his back, wiped his face with his sleeve. Then he turned around and tried to smile.

"I yield!" he shouted. "The first lesson has gone badly for me, I admit it. But I'll work all night, and you'll see a new man for lesson number two." He dropped his sword. "Now, do you want to do some blocking on that scene? Maybe we should get Tybalt in here to help."

"Pick up your weapon, sir."

"Father, I—"

"*Your weapon,* sir!"

Slowly, Kenneth reached down and took the bloody hilt.

"*En garde.*" And once more the blade flashed.

As usual, his father was right. This was the perfect way to teach swordsmanship. If the pupil survived it.

Within an hour Kenneth had improved markedly. Like all his father's methods, it was a simple process. The student made a careless move. The teacher showed him the error of his ways in the form of a small cut. The student tried another approach, which was a little better. No cut. Again the teacher offered the same move, and the student found a variation that actually might give him a small advantage. Then the teacher varied the first move. Once more, a cut. Again. Not so good, Kenneth; another cut, deeper this time. Now don't think, let your body remember what you did wrong last time, what you did that resulted in pain. Your body will remember and find a way to avoid the pain. Here it comes again—

—and that was much better. No pain. Try it again. No pain. Again.

Now, try this. . . .

The pain in Spain is mainly for the slain.

Again.

With a spiraling motion worthy of Errol Flynn, John Valentine's blade twisted the sword from Kenneth's hand and sent it flying into the wings.

"Get it," he said.

"Father, could we have a break?"

"Ten more minutes. Go."

Kenneth didn't move for a moment. He was barely able to stand.

"Son," Valentine said, gently. "You brought this on yourself. I know it hurts. I went through this with my father, and I'm the better for it. Soon you'll be disarming me, and the audience as well. But in the meantime it is going to hurt. At the end of the day we'll have you patched up. And we'll start fresh tomorrow."

Patched up.

Tomorrow. What a frightening thought.

"Now go get your weapon."

Kenneth turned and trudged toward the curtain. He was afraid that if he reached down to pick up the sword, he would simply pass out. He did bend down for the sword, and his head did swim, but he did not pass out.

And then a strange thing happened. Kenneth reached for the saber—

—and Sparky picked it up.

It was invigorating, just being Sparky again. He was still hurting, badly, and he was still weak, but in the ways that mattered Sparky was strong. He didn't really know who this Kenneth person was, but he knew he was weak.

And he knew John Valentine was weak, in the ways that mattered.

So Sparky forced himself to stand erect, stiffen his spine. He lifted his chin and he strode back to center stage. Holding the saber with both hands, he raised it high, and plunged it down into the stage. He let it go and it quivered there, the point buried in two inches of wood.

"I quit," he said.

Valentine cocked his head slightly, as if not sure of what he had heard. Then he shrugged good-naturedly.

"All right. Maybe I'm pushing too hard. We'll resume tomorrow."

"You didn't hear me. I quit."

"You quit."

"You want me to spell it for you? I quit the swordsmanship lessons. I quit Romeo. I quit Shakespeare. I quit acting. I quit."

Valentine turned away and his body sagged. He rubbed his forehead with one hand. He sighed deeply. It was silent-movie acting, every move deliberate and exaggerated. Sparky studied Valentine's back. He imagined pulling the sword from the stage and thrusting it between the shoulder blades.

No. That wasn't the way.

Valentine turned around.

"You quit. Just like that. Suddenly twenty years of—"

"Twenty-nine years. I'm twenty-nine. You've been teaching me since I was in the cradle."

Valentine laughed.

"Make it thirty, son. Count the nine months in the womb."

"In those thirty years," Sparky said, unperturbed, "there is one thing you never did. One thing you neglected."

"And what would that be?"

"You never asked me what I wanted to do."

Valentine laughed. He made a grand sweeping gesture with his sword, and a courtly bow.

"So, my son, tell me. What *do* you want to do with your life?"

"I don't know," Sparky admitted. "I've never had time to think about it. You never gave me any time."

"Go on. This is fascinating."

"You never asked me anything. Your plans were always 'our' plans, but I was never consulted."

"You are a child."

"I was never a child. I never had a chance to be one. I was a pretty fair performing monkey, though. 'Put a dime in the cup, folks. Watch little Kenny recite from Shakespeare. Perhaps today he'll get through it without shaking and gasping for breath.' "

"Do you believe that's how I thought of you?"

"No. No, I don't, Father. I think you thought of me, still think of me, as an extension of yourself. Any glory I earn is your glory."

Once more, Valentine laughed. But he sobered quickly, and looked intently into his son's eyes.

"No, my son. It's *much* more than that. You *are* me."

"In your mind, maybe. Up until today, maybe. But I've had enough, Father. I quit. I'm going to walk out of here, and from this moment on I make my own decisions."

Valentine looked into his son's eyes, and they did not waver. At last, almost apologetically, he sighed deeply and spread his hands.

"I simply can't allow that."

"You'll have to stop me."

"I will, son. I will."

Sparky stood his ground. The sword still swayed slightly between them, a steel gauntlet, an intolerable challenge.

"Now take your weapon, and take your position. We still have ten minutes of lesson to get through."

"I won't."

"Then I'll cut you down where you stand. *Defend yourself, sir!*"

Valentine raised his sword and began walking slowly toward his son. The blade hissed through the air, once, twice. Then a quiet, mild voice came from the wings.

"All right, that's enough of that, Mr. Valentine. Not one more step."

Sparky and Valentine both jerked in surprise, and turned to see a tall, lanky form walk slowly from behind the curtain. He wore a beige, wide-brimmed felt Stetson, a homespun blue shirt and leather vest, and baggy gray pants. His boots were dusty and broken in. Strapped low around his waist was a gunbelt and holsters, and in them could be seen the butts of two revolvers.

"Who the hell are you?" Valentine thundered.

"Elwood, stay out of this," Sparky said.

"My name is Tom Destry, Mr. Valentine. I'm a friend of—"

"You look just like Jimmy Stewart."

"I've been told that. Don't know the gentleman. Sparky and I go way back, though. Clear back to his first day at the studio."

"My son's name is Kenneth."

Elwood shook his head. "Not right now, it isn't. You see, Mr. Valentine, right about then, that first day when you left him alone all day while you were off on your audition, or whatever it was, your boy needed a friend. And that's what I've been to him, as well as I can be."

"Elwood, please . . ."

"Sparky, somebody has to do this."

They made a rough triangle, the three of them. Sparky mostly looking down at the floor, darting quick glances from one man to the other. Elwood stood at his ease, his hands dangling at his sides. Valentine could not stand still. He paced, two steps to the right, three steps back, in no pattern. His eyes blazed, and they never wavered from Elwood.

"Who is this man, Kenneth?" he asked, his voice dangerously low. "Some extra you've befriended?"

"This is Elwood P. Dowd, Father. He's my friend."

"Elwood P.—" Valentine cut a quick glance at his son, then looked back at Elwood, threw his head back, and roared with laughter.

"Well, Mr. Dowd, it's a pleasure, sir. I feel like I've known you all my life. And Kenneth, pray tell, where is your *other* . . . why, there he is now!" Valentine strode lightly toward Elwood, who stood his ground, and made an elaborate show of throwing his arm over an invisible companion's shoulders. "Welcome, welcome, sir! It's been such a long time. Are you well? Are you happy? I must say your fur is looking exceptionally fine today. Where do you have it done? You don't say! What's that . . . well, I'm sorry, Harvey, I don't have any carrots with me. Didn't know you were coming, and all that. But how about a martini? That's your drink, isn't it? A dry martini . . ."

He dropped his arm, looked sadly at his son, and shook his head.

"Your friend is a nut, Kenneth. I see it now. Tom Destry, of all people. He dresses up like a Tom Mix cowboy, and strides forth to protect you from your own father. That *is* what you're here for, isn't it, Mister . . . Dowd? Destry? Are *you* sure who you are?"

"The drink is milk, sir, and the name is still Destry."

"Or Stewart. Tell me, Jimmy, if you're here as a tough guy of some sort, why not that marshal, Guthrie McCabe, in *Two Rode Together*? Or that outlaw in *Bandolero!*—what was his name . . . Mace Bishop. Or even that lawyer fella, Ransom Stoddard, the one who shot Liberty Valance. What's the matter, tenderfoot? Law books no damn good? Is that why you're packing?"

Elwood/Tom seemed bemused by the speech. He looked at Sparky.

"You told me he had a photographic memory for plots and cast lists," he said. "I don't know if I'da remembered all of those m'self."

"Dramatis personae," Valentine said. "That's the term we actors use."

"Meaning I'm not one," Destry said. "No, I don't reckon I am, sir, not of your caliber, certainly. You can mock me all you want, Mr. Valentine. I can take it. It's the boy over there who can't take it anymore. I know everything about you there is to know, sir. Every small-minded deed, every slight you've ever given him. Every blow you've ever landed.''

"I'm his teacher," Valentine growled.

"And a good one, too, so far as that goes. If all a teacher's for is to develop a skill, why, you're a *darn* good one. But I happen to think being a teacher, and a father, means a lot more than that, Mr. Valentine. And by that standard, you've completely failed him. He lives in fear of you. He's a man's size, but he's still a boy when he faces you. You won't let him go, and he can't break away from you."

Valentine looked astonished.

"And why would he want to? He and I are joined at the hip, sir. It has always been that way, and it will always remain so. We are united by our art, something a pathetic gesticulator like yourself could never understand, and by something a great deal deeper than that. Kenneth, tell him." He turned to his son. "I have been strict with you, I've never denied it. It *takes* strictness, discipline, and an artist suffers it willingly. But everything I have ever done has been done from love. Tell him, son."

Sparky, his clothing tattered and soaked in blood, swayed and thought once more that he would pass out. He looked helplessly from his father to Elwood, and back again.

For the first time a furrow of doubt creased John Valentine's brow as he saw his son's battered condition. He held out his hand, started to say something, then turned away from them both. When he faced them again, there were tears in his eyes. He grimaced, rubbed his face.

"Listen to me," he said, sadly. "And look at you. I've done it again, haven't I?"

"Father . . ."

"No, son, don't say anything. I stand revealed, once more, as a coward and a poltroon. Look what I've done to you."

"Father, I know you never mean—"

"Sparky!" Elwood warned.

"You stay out of this!" Valentine bellowed. "Kenneth, do you understand that I love you, more than life itself?"

"Yes, Father."

"Then all I can do is apologize again. I have overplayed my role, and there is no forgiveness for that, but I hope I still have your love."

"You do, Father."

Valentine held out his hand toward his son.

"Then let's go get you to a medic, and after that, to the police. You can file charges against me."

"No, Father."

"It's your decision. I'll abide by it. Perhaps it would be best for me. I can't seem to control my temper. Maybe there is some way I can be helped."

"Father, I—"

"You know I've never had much use for psychiatry. It seems to me they know less about the human mind than I do. But maybe there is some form of medication, some pill or brain treatment. . . ."

"That's an awful idea," Sparky said. "You know how those pills you used to take after that . . . after the time you . . . well, you know what I mean. You could hardly remember your lines after a walk across the stage."

Valentine smiled. "You remember that, do you? Oh, it wasn't so bad. And if I have to, we'll just cast someone else in my role. I'll stay on as director." He laughed. "Who ever said a director needs to remember lines?"

He still had his hand extended toward his son, and now there was a hint of edginess in his eyes, as if he knew the gesture had gone on too long, with no response from Sparky. The boy had not said no, but he hadn't taken the hand, either.

"Come on, son. Let's get out of here. We'll put the whole show on hiatus if we have to. We'll get you up to snuff on the fencing. No more cutting, I promise. We can talk about the rest of it, too. I'm going to change, Kenneth, I promise you."

After a momentary hesitation Sparky started toward his father.

"Hold it right there, Sparky," Destry said. Sparky stopped.

"Now, I'm only going to say this once, my friend," he said, never taking his eyes from Valentine. "A minute ago you said you were quitting the show. You said you needed some time to think things through. Most of all, you said you were making your own decisions now. I took it as a declaration of independence from your father."

"Sir," Valentine said, coldly, slashing his sword through

the empty air, "you are interfering. This is none of your business."

"I think it is. You asked me a minute ago why I brought these." He rested the heels of his hands on the gun butts. "I'm not a violent man, Mr. Valentine. These were my father's pistols. I hung them up a long time ago, but there comes a time when you have to put them on again. When violence has to be met with violence. Now, I know Sparky isn't capable of resisting you, physically. So I will, if I have to."

For the first time he glanced at the young man.

"So what's it going to be, Sparky? I'll back your play, whatever it is. But I want you to know this. If you go with him, well, that's your choice. But if you do, I'll go away, and you'll never see me again."

Sparky looked from one man to the other. It was high noon, right there on the stage of the Valentine Theater. Tom Destry and John Valentine never glanced at him, their gazes locked. Valentine's eyes blazed with fury. Destry was calm and resolute.

"Let's go, Kenneth," Valentine said, and took a step toward his son.

Sparky looked back and forth. He was so tired, so desperately tired. And in the end, he thought later, that was the biggest factor in his choice. There was only one way he'd ever get any rest.

"I'm sorry, Father," he said, and walked toward his friend.

"No!" Valentine shouted, and raised his sword, charging toward the two of them.

"Elwood, don't!"

But the gun was out of its holster. Valentine was only a few feet away, already starting to slash downward with the blade. Sparky grabbed Elwood's arm and the gun fired. The shot took Valentine in the forehead and threw him back in a cloud of smoke and blood.

Sparky was going to wrestle the weapon from Elwood/ Destry, but the man made no resistance, and Sparky was left standing, holding the hot gun barrel. He stared down at it. Etched on the side were the words THIMBLE THEATER PROP DEPARTMENT.

A prop gun? Fake blood?

He went down on one knee and touched his father's face. There was a hole an inch above his right eye. Blood was pumping sluggishly from it, to pool in the eye socket and then run down into the ear. The left eye was open and the pupil was a black hole that swallowed all hope.

"Doctors," Sparky mumbled. "We have to get medical help." He put his hand under his father's head, meaning to lift and cradle it until help arrived. What he felt back there was a hole he could put his fist in, and jagged edges of bone. Valentine lay in a pool of blood and in this red sea were islands of other matter.

"I'm afraid it can't be fixed, Sparky," Destry said.

Sparky pulled his hand back. There were chunks of brain clinging to it.

"Help him," Sparky whimpered. He looked up at Destry, who stood a little apart looking solemnly down at the man he had just killed.

"I wouldn't have cared if he was just coming at me," Destry said. "But you saw it. He was trying to kill you. He forced my hand."

Sparky didn't register anything the man said. He kept looking from his father's ruined face to the pistol in his hand. He might have knelt there forever but he heard footsteps coming from backstage. He looked up.

It was Hildy Johnson and Rose, the assistant stage manager. They stopped while still in the wings, looking out to the stage.

"Sorry, Mr. Valentine," Rose said. "We heard a noise...." She began to turn from the scene of fake mayhem. It wasn't any of her business. But Hildy was frowning, and Rose looked at Sparky's face.

Sparky stood, and the gun thudded to the floor. He held up his bloody hand to show it to Destry . . . to Elwood. . . .

No one was there.

Rose began to scream.

Hildy started running toward him.

Sparky ran.

In a very real sense, I've been running for seventy years now.

I opened my eyes, looked around me as if emerging from a dream, and there's certainly a sense in which that is very real, too. But the dream had never before left me in the little park, right across the corridor from the scene of the crime. I determined I was out of the dream now, not in it. All my life, this has been a harder determination than you might suppose.

I don't revisit that memory a lot. I've never been far from it, never tried to deny its "reality," so to speak. I have become adept at veering away from it when I feel it approaching.

But every few years it is worth taking it out and examining it. To see if it has changed, after these seventy long years.

Because, you see, I believe very little of it. Neither should you.

The most vivid memory of my life is a lie.

It's a very theatrical memory, isn't it? My father is shot to death—the bullet destroyed the brain, which is the only organ we can't repair, the only wound we cannot recover from—by a peace-loving fictional character who vanishes when witnesses arrive. No one saw the shot fired except the "three" of us. And there I am, standing by the dead man, blood all over me. The murder weapon is in my hand, still warm. Though I didn't stay to find out, I am sure that only my fingerprints are on the gun. I am sure no one saw Elwood enter or leave the theater.

Would *you* hang around to tell the police a ridiculous story like that?

Elwood P. Dowd is my imaginary friend. I have known that, and known the difference between him, his gallery of characters, and *real* people almost from the moment I met him. Therefore, there were only two people on that fatal stage. Therefore, everything that happened from the moment Elwood called out to my father is a dream/drama made up by me. Therefore, I killed my father.

There is an irony here. To have done something as awful as that . . . to be a patricide. To have never sought to avoid responsibility for my actions. (Avoid the consequences? Hell, yes; I've been running from them for seventy years. But I don't shirk the *moral* responsibility, which is a completely different thing than the legal sort.) But I am willing to admit, to myself, that it was I, I who did it. I have borne the burden of that act for a long time. I never sought to set it down. And yet one part of my mind, a part I've never been able to understand but almost certainly the part that allowed such a terribly conflicted young man to do such a thing in the first place, has robbed me of the true story of what happened that day.

My father *did* come at me with a blade that day. I think. He *did* try to kill me. I'm fairly sure.

It *was* self-defense. I'd almost swear to it.

And I killed him. Of that, I am sure.

Recall the sequence, there at the end. My father is rushing across the stage, sword raised. Is he coming toward me? He must be, though I see him rushing toward Elwood. I see Elwood go for his gun, and I am running toward him. I reach him as he is raising and aiming the gun. I grab his arm. And it is here that reality must have intersected with my fantasies, because the gun goes off in *my* hand, doesn't it? Oh, I *feel* as if Elwood is still holding it, but I feel the heat and the recoil in my own hand.

And it is a prop gun. One I could easily have taken from the prop department of my own studio. Concealed it somewhere in the wings. When I left the stage, shortly before returning to finally stand up to my father, in my fashion, that must have been when I picked up the gun.

(A word about props. Don't be fooled by the term. There are "pure" props, made entirely for show. They can be plaster, wood, whatever looks best. And there are "practical" props. A light switch that actually controls lights on the stage. A piano that can actually be played. Most often, it is easier to simply use the actual object and call it a prop. The sword my father carried came from the prop department, but would kill you just as dead as any other sword. And the gun I stole was all too practical. So was the bullet.)

Did I intend to kill him all along? Or did I simply hope to defend myself when I stole that gun, hid it, and then destroyed all memory of having done so?

I must assume that murder was my intention. I do recall, seeing him lying there, dead, that one thought kept circling through the chaos of my mind. It was something he himself was fond of telling me. He had said it a thousand times.

"Dodger," he would say. "Never bring a knife to a gun-fight."

I listened, and remembered. He forgot.

• • •

It was such a pleasant little park. Which was a good thing, because I wasn't sure I could move. I had tried to get up several times, and my legs didn't seem to work.

It was a feeling that went far beyond exhaustion. I had come . . . well, to tell you the truth, I don't even *know* how many billion miles I came. I suppose a solar atlas would give me the answer, but to what point? I didn't want to go back. Otherwise, I'd have left a trail of bread crumbs. But Brementon to Pluto, Pluto to Oberon, Oberon to Jupiter to Sol to Luna, I had fetched up *here*, on this park bench. I had thought it was all intentional, all part of some *plan* I had, but it didn't feel like that now. I felt like a marble in a pachinko game, rattling randomly among the pins, coming to rest at the bottom, where no points are scored. And it had always been inevitable that the bottom was where I'd end up.

I don't mean "the bottom" in the sense of any suicidal feeling. Nor am I talking of the bottom an alcoholic hits, or the economic bottom of a failed businessman, contemplating his lost riches. I had money in my jeans. I was only a few steps away from what could be the crowning achievement of my acting career. I had prospects, as the world usually measures them.

I just couldn't seem to find a reason to stand up.

I am fortune's fool.

I knew he would be there somewhere. I looked around, examining the strollers, the bench sitters, those stretched out on the cool grass.

He was across the park, sitting with his back to me. It was the hat, of course. With Elwood it's usually the hat, which is always out of fashion. But it wasn't the "Elwood P. Dowd" hat today, though it was similar. When Elwood changes character, it's usually because he has something important to say.

I looked at his back until he seemed to feel it. He stood, turned, looked across the park at me for a while, then started toward me in the shambling gait all his characters share. His hands were thrust deep in the pockets of his baggy trousers.

He was Paul Biegler, the defense attorney from *Anatomy of a Murder*.

"I have often walked down this street before," he said.

"If that's my cue to burst into song, forget it," I said.

"I spend a lot of time here. Right here in this park."

He hitched at his pants, sat beside me on the bench. He took a crumpled bag of peanuts from his coat pocket, shelled one, and popped it into his mouth. Immediately two yellow-headed parrots and a cardinal swooped in from the surrounding trees, waiting for a handout. Elwood tossed them a peanut.

"Pigeons too prosaic for this park," he observed.

The problem of Elwood seems to me to boil down to a problem of pigeons. Or parrots, or any other animal. Toby doesn't see Elwood, but knows when he's around. Most likely he's just picking up my reactions, I've always told myself. But other animals seem to see him. Another cardinal flew in and sat on Elwood's shoulder.

So how do you explain that? Was I imagining the birds? Was I imagining the peanuts? I knew that if he offered me one, I'd be able to put it in my mouth and taste it, and swallow it. Did *I* bring a sack of peanuts with me? Were there real birds here, only not doing what I saw them doing?

Expressed in terms of nuts and birds, the problem seems trivial, even funny. Considered as the central fact of an act of murder, my delusional states don't seem funny at all. Every time Elwood appears he presents me with these perceptual conundrums. Spend too much time thinking about them and I'm sure I'd go . . . well, nuts. Not the sort of nuts I already am—which is at least a functional insanity—but rubber-room, spit-slinging, lobotomaniacal bull-goose loony.

But I've spent a lot of time with him. And while my world-view is not to be trusted and though I don't buy any nonsense about ghosts, spirit worlds, other dimensions, or leprechauns, there is one statement on existence I do accept, fully. There is more under Heaven and Earth than is dreamt of in your philosophy, Mr. Rationalist.

Let's leave it at that, and let the details be worked out at the psychiatric hearing.

"Didya have a nice trip?" Elwood asked.

"Except for the first few miles. After that, it was the lap of luxury. You should have visited."

He wrinkled his nose.

"Don't like flying much anymore."

"Don't like . . . Charles Lindbergh would be ashamed of you."

"I think ol' Charlie would have been bored. He was a big one for adventure, Charlie was. That's how I played him, anyway. Never played any astronauts, though. That was a bit after my time."

I gestured at his 1950s-era baggy gray suit.

"So, do you know something I don't? Am I going to need a lawyer? Are the police closing in on me?"

"Well, there is no statute of limitations. And you know you have no business being here. You know that as well as I do. But as far as I've heard, there's no active search for you. Yet."

"I've been sitting here trying to think of a defense," I said. "How do you think this one would play? 'I was *framed,* Your Honour! Some dirty rat put that gun in my hand!' "

"I think you'd get charged with a miserable James Cagney impression."

"Stick to the point, counselor. Stick to the facts."

"The facts in this case are in considerable dispute. I think a competent attorney could create a reasonable doubt concerning a possible accomplice. But I'd have to bow out of the case, of course. Conflict of interest."

"I'd rather be represented by that Ransom Stoddard fellow, anyway."

"The man who didn't shoot Liberty Valance? He's good."

We sat in silence for a while, watching the parrots break open and eat the peanuts. There were half a dozen of them now.

"But if I can get serious for a minute," he said, "neither one of us would be the right choice for you, if you should find yourself in trouble."

"You mean, for some reason *other* than the fact that you don't exist? 'That's right, Your Honour, I wish to be represented by my good friend Jesus Christ, seated in this empty chair on my right. Ably assisted by Tinker Bell, who'll circle near the ceiling dispensing pixie dust.' "

He waited patiently until I settled down again.

"No, it's something else entirely. I think you'd do well with counsel a little more versed in modern legal issues.

Things I wouldn't know a lot about, nor Mr. Stoddard, either."

I asked him what he meant by that, and he just shook his head. When Elwood wants to be stubborn, there is no moving him, so I eventually had to let it go.

"So what are you going to do, my friend?" he asked, after a long silence.

"Do? Elwood, what do you think I ought to do?"

"Get off this planet and try to lose yourself," he said, without hesitation. "That Comfort fellow isn't going to give up, you know, and it won't be hard to trace you here."

"He's probably here already," I agreed.

"Well, you made it pretty fast. I'd say he'll get here in the next week or so."

"Maybe. But I've got this little problem, Elwood." I thought of the image of the pachinko game. The feeling that all my running, seventy years of looking over my shoulder, had brought me here. To this bench. I hadn't tried to stand up since he sat down beside me. I was afraid to.

"I feel like I've been in this big bathtub," I told him. "The water is swirling out the drain, and I've been swimming as hard as I can for a very long time. And now the water is all gone, and I'm sitting on the bottom, naked and wet as a newborn baby. Only I feel like I've wasted seventy years. All that running, and here I am. I just don't seem to want to move."

"So you're going to stay here? That's what you want to do?"

I sighed.

"What I really want to do, more than anything, is turn myself in."

I don't think I was sure until the moment I said it that I really *did* want to surrender. But saying it, I felt such a sense of relief, such a feeling of freedom as I hadn't experienced since that day on the stage of the John Valentine Theater.

With a shock, I realized I'd felt that sense of freedom *after* I'd killed my father.

Elwood was looking at me, shaking his head.

"Well, I don't entirely disagree with you on that," he said. "And I'd be more than willing to go in with you. Perhaps I could speak to your psychiatrist, give him a little insight into your life, from the perspective of somebody who's spent a lot of time around you. Maybe contribute to an insanity defense, though I don't know how they handle things like that these days. But there's one thing I think you should do first.''

''And what is that?''

''Take your shot at *King Lear*. Never know when you might get another chance.'' He stood up and held his hand out to me.

I never touch Elwood, for obvious reasons. But this time I didn't even look around to see who might be watching. I took his hand, and he lifted me off the bench.

Bayou Teche is an old ''pocket'' disneyland just a ten-minute tube ride from the center of King City. When it was first built, they simply called it a disneyland, since an artificial ''Earthly'' environment almost a mile across and a quarter of a mile high was a very big deal in those days. At first it was hard to get people to visit. ''How ya gonna hold the roof up, huh?'' Many people never *could* come, and many still can't, agoraphobia being quite common amongst the tunnel-raised population.

Later, when they began building the serious disneys like Texas, Mekong, Kansas, Serengeti, a hundred miles deep and thirty, forty, sixty miles across, the original parks came to be called minis. Now the trend has come full circle as more and more people—those who can afford it—aspire to move into a ''natural'' environment. Micro-disneys are popping up like bubbles in champagne, but they are not notably wild. Most have golf courses. All modern amenities are just minutes away.

The older parks had a problem. Many turned themselves into ''modern'' parks, not much different from suburbia on Old Earth: communities of houses from one era or another. Traditionalists pointed out that the whole idea of disneys was to provide a taste of life on Earth before the Invasion, even before civilization. Most compromised, allowing some settlement by ''townies,'' as opposed to permanent ''authentics,'' like Doc in West Texas. Some tried to qualify for government heritage grants by providing environments people might not necessarily want to live in, but which the Antiquities Board felt were worth supporting in spite of their inhospitality.

At Bayou Teche, it was night, and bugs. Twenty-two hours of night every day, and billions and billions of bugs.

This was where Kaspara Polichinelli, the greatest stage director of her time, had chosen to spend her retirement. You may remember her as Sparky's sidekick, Polly.

The only way to Polly's house was by water, in a little boat called a pirogue. Pronounced *pee*-row. There were no maps. No roads. Hardly any land. The bayous wound in an impenetrable maze designed to re-create the delta country at the end of the Mississippi River.

My guide/taxi driver was a smiling man who introduced himself as Beaudreaux—pronounced *boo*-drow—who helped me into the little flat-bottomed cockleshell that seemed to be made of scrap lumber and gumbo mud. The bottom was awash in water. I took a seat up front and Beaudreaux started up a little outboard engine no bigger than a football, pulling a rope until it choked to life in a cloud of blue smoke and then settled into a steady puttering. We eased away from the ramshackle dock just inside the visitors' entrance, and into a landscape right out of your worst prehistoric nightmare.

At a dizzying three miles per hour.

Over water black as ink, flowing at a tenth our speed.

Water smooth as old bourbon, but not nearly so sweet smelling.

Luckily, I'd taken my motion-sickness pills.

I was dressed in the only sensible clothing for the Bayou: a head-to-toe silk khaki jumpsuit pulled over my own clothes, rubber boots and gloves, topped off by a safari hat fitted with a mesh beekeeper's veil. Wrists and ankles of the suit were elastic, worn over the sleeves and legs.

They told me the suit was sprayed with a harmless repellent, which had sounded like overkill at the time. The insects couldn't get to me, I reasoned, so what was the point?

Five minutes into the boat ride I decided, with a touch of awe, that without the repellent the bugs might actually pick me up and carry me off, to devour at their leisure.

Though it was night in the Bayou, it was far from pitch-black. We frequently passed homes set on stilts, or built on flat-bottomed boat hulls. Most had kerosene lamps hanging outside the porch and a softer light spilling from the windows.

There was a lamp on a pole at the bow of the pirogue, as well. All these light sources were swarming with clouds of flying insects. Moths and lacewings and dragonflies—"skeeter hawks," to Beaudreaux—and beetles and lightning bugs and June bugs and gnats and I don't know what all.

And mosquitoes. Enough mosquitoes to suck you dry in ten seconds.

I hate bugs.

I'd been hearing what sounded like flapping wings since shortly after the trip began. About halfway to Polly's something whooshed by my head, inches away. I ducked, and Beaudreaux laughed. Beaudreaux, who somehow was enduring this trip dressed in denim overalls and a short-sleeved chambray shirt, no hat, no gloves.

"Bat," he told me. "We got many t'ousan bat in hya. We got de froo' bat, de Mex'can bat, de pug-nose bat, de leaf-nose bat, de red bat, de gray bat, and de *renard volant,* de flyin' fox, *en anglais.*" At least I think that's what he said. He spoke with an odd accent, a patois of broken English and the occasional French word, and he called himself a "Cajun." Pronounced *kay*-jun.

He kept up a running commentary throughout the trip, pointing to things I mostly didn't see. We threaded our way through gnarled cypress with long gray beards of moss. I never had a chance to ask him a question, but if I had, it would have been "How do you keep from being eaten alive?" I later learned the answer, which was that residents got a small gene alteration that caused their skin to exude an insect repellent.

According to Beaudreaux there were seventeen species of bat in the Bayou, and they worked in two shifts separated by the two brief light periods known as dawn and dusk. How they got the plants to grow and all the insects to breed with so little light I never found out. I'm sure they could fill you in at the visitors' center. No doubt it's a fascinating story, but keep it to yourself, all right?

Other than the close encounter with the bat, the trip proceeded without incident until I heard a splash and felt the boat rock as if we'd passed the wake of another boat. Beaudreaux stood up and used a long pole to poke at something in the water. He shouted at it, poked again, then sat down and grinned at me.

"Gator," he said.

I hate alligators. Bats, too, now that I think of it.

Polly's shack stood three feet above the water on cypress pilings. A ramp led down to a floating dock where another pirogue was tied up. This one sported a bright-red paint job and looked much more seaworthy than Beaudreaux's. Maybe Polly could give me a ride back to town.

The dock shifted under me as I stepped from the boat and I almost fell in the water. Beaudreaux grabbed my arm, probably saving me from being stripped to the bone in ten seconds by ravenous piranha. I heard a screen door creak and then slam shut, and a hoarse female voice.

"Hey, Beaudreaux! Where dat bucket *écrevisses* you gon' brought me?"

"You get you crawfish, *ma p'tit,* jus' soon as I cotched 'em." He laughed, and motored quietly into the darkness. I went up the ramp to a screened-in porch, where the woman was holding the door for me. She was gray-haired and stooped, wearing a long gingham dress with a daisy print. She waved gnarled hands around me as I hurried in the door.

"*Vite, mon cher! Vite!* Don't let the skeeters in."

The inner door was closed. Sort of an air lock for mosquitoes, I realized. I let myself through into a small, rustic room with a small fire blazing in the hearth, knitted rugs on the wood floor. The light came from two dim floor lamps with shades dripping tassels in lavender and gold and yellow. Hideous things, by themselves, but not bad in this context. I looked around for Polly, and the old lady spoke from behind me.

"I thought you'd never get here, *cher,*" she said.

I don't know who I had thought she was. Being in a disney, I had probably pegged her as an authentic. Disneys are one of the places you can go to see "old" people, folks who look like humans did when age was pretty much synonymous with decay. Almost all of these are only old on the surface, with wrinkled sagging skin and gray hair and perhaps a "colorful" age-related bit of ghastliness like missing teeth, eyeglasses, arthritis. They limped, they doddered and tottered and feigned deafness, but under the epidermis they were as hale and hearty as I am.

To see "real" aging you generally had to go to a fundamentalist enclave of one type or another. They seldom visited the public corridors; they kept to themselves like the Amish.

Polly had joined such a sect shortly before her departure from *Sparky and His Gang*. I can't even remember the name; there are scores of them, all with different beliefs. Some go so far as to reject all medical treatment of any sort, and you hear of people dying horribly in their thirties and forties, even in their teens, though the authorities sometimes stepped in to stop that.

Polly's group was more moderate. They didn't reject all medical care, just that group of therapies usually called "long life." "Eternal life" by the optimists, though no one really believes a human can live for even a million years. But it's true we don't seem to be anywhere near the outer limits, and there are people well over two hundred years old now, thriving.

It was a sobering thought, though, to look at her and realize she was only a year older than I.

On the other hand, for a natural centenarian she was in pretty good shape. It's all relative, I guess.

"Don't ask how I'm doing," she said. "It would take all day. Never get old folks started on their aches and pains."

"All right, Polly," I said. "And I won't tell you how well you look."

She laughed, and I smiled, and suddenly I realized how good it was to see her again. I went to her and we embraced. She had shrunk several inches.

"Don't squeeze too hard, *cher*," she whispered. She didn't need to tell me that; she was brittle and dry. I could feel every bone.

I don't want to get into details of her appearance. The elderly share a suite of atrocities as they are battered by the tides of age. They erode in much the same way. Much of it has always seemed to me to be a struggle by the skeleton, the symbol of death, to emerge from its soft shell. The fat is blasted away, the skin grows loose, sags, becomes translucent. Soon you can see the skull beneath the skin. There's a morbid little computer program you can buy. Feed somebody's picture into it and it will age that person fifty, sixty, a hundred years. If you'd like to see Polly as I saw her, find a picture of her from the old show. She hasn't allowed herself to be photographed since then.

"Come on in, Sparky, *mon ami.*" She took my hand and led me into a small kitchen. It looked like the only other room in the house. Her hand was cool and the joints were swollen.

She sat me down at a table with a red-and-white checkerboard cloth and poured strong coffee into a china cup and saucer. She eased herself into a chair facing me and let me take a sip.

"Now," she said. "Who is chasing you this time?"

Predictable? I don't suppose I can deny it.

I had not communicated with Polly in any way since the one telegram from Pluto. Several times I had been tempted, just a short message to be sure she really was going to hold the role for me. But I knew she would. Polly's word is unbreakable. So how did she know someone was chasing me? Consistency, I guess.

During my first twenty years on the run I had twice risked a trip back to Luna. Both times I had seen Polly—this before the effects of her medical fundamentalism had really begun to ravage her. And both times there had been those who urgently wanted to talk to me about this or that misunderstanding. I admit it, I have a talent for getting into these situations. But bear in mind, when you're on the run you find yourself having to do things you might not ordinarily do. I submit my clean record between my eighth and twenty-ninth years as evidence that I am not a *fundamentally* bad person. Luckily for me, my first eight years—for which, legally, I can't be held responsible—provided me the criminal skills I've needed for my last seventy.

So I told Polly about Isambard Comfort and the Demons of Charon. She listened, fascinated, and I wondered if she was thinking about how she would stage this epic tale of pursuit. *Les Misérables,* Part Two?

But during the telling I came to an uneasy realization, something I really hadn't considered before but probably should have. While the Charonese race was hot on my trail, those near me could be endangered. My failure to consider that had cost Poly dearly.

Polly reached across the table and patted my hand.

"Poor boy," she said. "You've had a terrible time of it. And you think this Comfort person will follow you to Luna?"

"I think we can count on it," I said, miserably. "And I have to think it would put you and the whole production in danger."

"We'll think on that, of course," she said. "But I don't see how it changes much. We were going to have to disguise your identity anyway. We'll just have to be more careful, that's all."

I thought it would be a lot more than just a matter of extra care, but I kept my mouth shut. She was aware of my situation, I had not tried to minimize it, and I felt that was all I was obligated to do.

"So who do you want to be this time?" she asked.

She meant what did I want to use as a stage name. Anywhere in the inner planets I didn't dare use my own name, or make any mention of my previous credits and career. Which was a damn shame, since Polly could make good use of Sparky's return after all these years. It would put butts in seats, as some producer once said.

"Do you have any idea how seriously they're looking for me?"

"I don't think they're looking for you at *all, cher*," she said. "But you can be sure that if they run across you—if, for instance, they see your name up in lights on The Rialto— they'll drop by with an arrest warrant."

She smiled as she said it, and I had to smile, too. So, as usual, I'd be playing an actor playing King Lear. Do you wonder why I'm not quite right in the head?

"Kenneth, you know my feelings on this matter. I only wish someone had killed him twenty years earlier. Someone else. God knows there were enough people who wanted to. And if I were serving as the judge, you'd go free. But from what I've read about the evidence they have, it will work out as some degree of manslaughter. Five to twenty years. Have you given any more thought to turning yourself in?"

Polly had suggested that fifty years ago. Even with her pitifully short allotment of years, she felt it was better to serve the time than to stay on the run. Get it over with.

There was a lot of wisdom in that, except for one thing. I couldn't do the time. I think I'd rather die. I smiled again, and shook my head.

"Then have you given any more thought to . . . the other thing."

She was speaking of the insanity defense. It was quite a narrow defense these days, but having an imaginary playmate, hearing voices . . . there was a good chance that would work.

I had not told Polly about Elwood. I'd spoken to no one about him, ever. But I had hinted at a few things one drunken night, and I think she had sensed a lot more. Not much gets by Polly, and during the years she had spent when we were closer than brother and sister I'm sure she had seen and heard some things she was too discreet to talk to me about.

Again, there was wisdom in the suggestion, except for one thing. I'd rather go to prison. Call it stupid pride if you wish. I'd never talk about Elwood, certainly never in a court of law, *especially* not to let him take the blame for my actions.

"No," I said. "That's out of the question."

"Then we're back to the first question. Do you have a name?"

I had several, of course.

My post-*Sparky* career had consisted of three sorts of jobs. Working from Pluto outward, I simply used my own name. Extraditions from those worlds to the inner planets were spotty at best, and arrests on fugitive warrants practically non-existent. From the J-Trojans, the belt, Mars, and inward, I usually concocted a one-time-only identity, good for the length of the run, then abandoned. And I moved carefully. But from the S-Trojans to Neptune I had been able to foster half a dozen more substantial identities, even build a certain reputation for some of the names. I had citizenship papers that would withstand a moderately rigorous check. In two of the identities I had even paid some local taxes!

I tried out three of the names on Polly. She carefully considered each, and shook her head. She knew everyone in the inner planets, and quite a few from the outers; if the name hadn't registered with her, then it had zero drawing power on Luna. Though this wasn't to be a star turn—the big name in this production would be Polichinelli—it never hurt to have some name recognition.

"How about Carson Dyle?" I asked. She perked up.

"Now him, I've heard of." She rattled off half a dozen of "Carson's" credits. "That's you?" I lowered my chin modestly. "That's a name I can work with then. I'll send it to publicity tomorrow. That is, if everything's in order with him."

"Give me a day to do a few checks," I said. "Carson may owe a little money here and there. You know how it is."

She smiled, and shook her head. "No, I don't, but if old debts is all that stands in the way we're okay. You'll start drawing salary tomorrow; you can just pay them off. Unless . . ."

"It's not much," I assured her. "Called away suddenly, no time to clear up a few obligations—" She held up a hand and I blushed. There was no need to sugarcoat anything with Polly. "Well, if that horse hadn't stumbled in the final turn, I had fully intended to pay it all off. Carson has a weakness for the ponies."

She laughed, and so did I, after a while. But it is a sobering thought that I had made a mess not only of my own life, but of most of my alter egos as well.

"So where are you staying?"

"I haven't settled on lodgings as yet," I admitted.

"Then I think it best if you stay right here."

I looked around the tiny cabin, and I trust I concealed my dismay.

"I wouldn't want to impose. . . ."

"Behind that door over there, *mon cher,* is a narrow stair that leads to an attic bedroom. It's small, but you can stand up in the middle. You'll have your privacy, and the best breakfasts and suppers in Bayou Teche."

I said nothing.

"That used to be my bedroom, Kenneth, until it got to be too much of a chore to climb the stairs every night. Now I sleep on the couch over there, and it suits me fine."

"What about this place, anyway?" I asked. She knew what I meant.

"The Bayou? I've always longed for the Earth. I felt all

my life that I was born in the wrong era, the wrong place. On Earth, I'd have been a forest creature, a wanderer. And now that I'm old, I'm a creature of the night. I love the night, and you get a lot of it here.''

There didn't seem to be anything to say to that. So I raised one last objection—not very strenuously, because the idea of a cozy attic room was beginning to appeal to me.

''I'm not sure you'd be safe, with me hanging around,'' I said.

''You let me worry about that. If your Charonese nemesis comes sniffing around, we'll see how he deals with eighteen-foot alligators in the dark.''

''Izzy could probably kill alligators with one hand. But maybe the mosquitoes would suck him dry while he was doing it.''

Rehearsals began the next day.

My heart wants to go into great detail about it, but my mind knows there is no point in trying. Any production in the live theater merits a book of its own. There is always exhilaration and disaster, feuding and fistfights and fornication. Half the cast usually hates the other half. At some point the set designer or the lighting director storms out of the theater and has to be wheedled back to work. In the last week, as dress rehearsals loom, there is despair. On opening night there will be at least two nasty crises, the one you half expected, and the one that sprang out of nowhere.

And then the curtain rises . . . and usually the whole mad enterprise works. Nine times out of ten, anyway. There's no guarantee that anyone out there in the dark *likes* it, but it has all somehow come together. You and your fellow troupers have created something.

Then comes the final curtain on the final night, and everyone moves on. For a while you had a play. For a while it was a living, thundering thing, and now it's gone. It exists only in the memories of those who made it happen, and those who came to see it. You can't pop a chip into your player and watch it again, you can't rewind to your favorite scene. If you want to see it again you have to assemble a hundred creative and cantankerous egotists, scream and weep and laugh and sweat and work yourself and everybody else to a state near the edge of hysteria, and hope that once more the magic will happen.

It is a glorious madness.

And, like the man said, you had to be there.

Most accounts of the rehearsal and presentation of a work of drama end up sounding like a riot in a kindergarten. A very *special* kindergarten, attended only by the most precocious, self-centered, hyperactive, and vicious little five-year-old brats. Brats who are used to having things their own way and expect more of the same, *now,* or brats who have always felt they *should* have been catered to all their lives, never were, but intend to make up for lost time now.

It is the nature of the beast. Whether the production is full of talented people or people who simply think they are talented, an ego is the *only* thing that is an absolute constant in show business. Without one, you never pursue the Muse of performance at all.

Basic law of physics as formulated by Sparky: One ego is the only psychological particle that can exist peacefully. Two egos equal warfare. Three or more egos constitute a nuclear reaction. They ought to give me the Nobel prize for that.

So, we battled, we shouted, we wept, and we clawed. And sometimes we made the magic happen. By opening night, it was happening pretty regularly.

One problem I had anticipated worked out better than I had any right to expect. Rehearsals had actually started four weeks before my arrival. The part of Lear was handled by my understudy. This is a bad way to start a production, with the star still swinging by the orbit of Jupiter. The rest of the cast assumes you're just too, too busy to share sweat with them. This might have worked for an Olivier, but for poor unknown Carson Dyle, it could be disastrous. The only thing that kept things going before my arrival was Polly's iron will and reputation.

"There is only one rule you need to remember to get along with me," she said on the first day, before my arrival. "I am God. You shall address all your prayers to me, and I will answer them. Worship another God, and I will kill you. It's as simple as that."

If she said I was good, most of the cast were at least willing to wait until I got there . . . and for about ten minutes after that. Naturally, they all professed happiness to see me, and privately hated my guts. The only thing that kept us going during the week after my arrival was my willingness to work twice as hard as everyone else.

But because I did work twice as hard, I earned their respect. And they all were experienced enough to see I was up to the job.

Once in a generation a director or playwright comes along with a truly distinctive vision. Twice, if you're lucky. Anyone can see it and few can describe it. It can't be imitated, though everyone tries, and in the process the course of art is slightly altered. Sometimes this person is a commercial and popular success: Shakespeare, or Alfred Hitchcock. More often he or she is best known among peers; the larger public just doesn't get it.

Not long after leaving *Sparky and His Gang,* Kaspara Polichinelli became that director for my generation. Since then, she had made one film or staged one play every five years or so. She made a lot of money in her first decade, then moved into less popular areas. The public knew her work always drew critical raves, that she was mentioned along with the greats . . . and usually stayed away in droves.

That never bothered her. She wasn't doing it for the money.

In the theater, being a legend in your own time has one big advantage. The top people in the field will always work for you, no questions asked. Major stars will slash or waive their astronomical fees. People who had never showed any evidence of talent will suddenly, under the eye and the tutelage of this director, find depths within themselves they never suspected. "Who knew?" the critics write, and the next thing you know a washed-up matinee idol finds himself with a supporting actor Oscar nomination.

This was that sort of cast. All Polly needed to do was send out the call. The best in the business would break contracts, postpone more lucrative projects, for the privilege of being in a Polichinelli production.

Hell, it brought me all the way from Pluto.

There is really no use in introducing a whole cast of characters at this late stage of my tale, any more than filling in all the details of the rehearsals. Even the spear-carriers were good. (You think that doesn't matter? Frank Capra always gave each extra on his productions a little bit of business, even if it was just something to think about as he walked through the scene, some problem to worry over, some destination beyond the other side of the set. And it shows.)

Everyone was professional. The major players were all superb. The set designer and the lighting director and all other technical people were friends of Polly, people who had worked with her many times in the past, and it all went as smoothly as these things ever go.

And in the center of it was Polly. Polly's vision of Lear.

That had worried me. *The Five-Minit Bard* had been fun, but it was *meant* to be ridiculous. Many Shakespearean productions over the centuries have been hilarious without intending to be.

I have no objection to taking a story by Shakespeare and using it as the basis of an entirely new production. The great Kurosawa did it several times, in Japanese. And I don't object, per se, to setting the plays in other places, other times—if something can be *gained* from the exercise. If something new can be illuminated, or if a fresh perspective can be obtained. But in seven hundred years some pretty ridiculous stuff has been tried. I've seen *Coriolanus* performed by people dressed up as cats. *As You Like It* set in a Stone Age cavern. All-nude productions. The last *King Lear* I saw was staged in a disneyland, and the storm scene got out of hand and blew away the stage and half the bleachers.

And yet, you don't want to re-create the Globe Theatre, either. It's been done, a hundred times.

Polly made it clear from the beginning that this was to be straight Shakespeare, full text, no ''updating.'' But of course it would have her stamp on it. That was good enough for me. I put myself in her hands.

I settled in comfortably at Polly's shack. I even got used to the daily commute in the little pirogue, and in time came to understand a few words Beaudreaux was saying.

I warmed Toby up, took him to the vet for maintenance. He became the production mascot, everybody's best friend, and gained three pounds from all the treats people smuggled to him.

I fell in love with our Cordelia, a lovely young woman named Jennipher Wilcox. Polly once told me I fall in love more often than some people change their socks. And it's true, I guess. But it always feels like love. I have never experienced that kind of love where you want to spend the rest of your life with one person. Frankly, I think it was almost always an illusion. I cite the divorce statistics. And today, with life spans that really amount to something, I think that sort of love is even rarer. Not one couple in a thousand is really capable of spending two, three hundred years together. Very few are capable of lasting as long as five years.

So don't give me any crap about love versus lust, okay? And keep your amateur psych opinions about my childhood rendering me incapable of long-term commitment to yourself as well. For my first thirty years my father demanded all the love I had to give. Since then, it would never have been fair to ask anyone to share more than a few months of my life. A cop, a private detective, or an Isambard Comfort would always show up and I'd have to move along.

I did love Jennipher, in my fashion. And we were great in bed.

And the opening night came.

And by the second act intermission everyone knew we had something special. Our spies in the lobby reported an astonishingly good buzz. People were actually hurrying back to their seats before the houselights flashed.

And the third act came and went. And the fourth act. We moved into the fifth act and I knew I'd never been better.

God, I was glorious. I *was* Lear.

Actually, only one thing happened to put a bit of a damper on the evening, though I swear to you, had you been there it wouldn't have affected your enjoyment of the play at all, Mrs. Lincoln.

Midway through the third act, Isambard Comfort showed up in my dressing room. . . .

He was seated in the big, comfortable easy chair I had requested for relaxing between scenes when Lear wasn't on-stage.

He had Toby in his lap. There was no one else in the room. "Where's Tom?" I asked. Tom was my dresser. Oh, yes,

I had once more come up in the world. This was not the closet aboard the *Britannic* where he and I had first fought, but a spacious, warmly furnished dressing room. A star's dressing room. It had a crackling holo-fireplace, a wet bar, and my own bathroom complete with a small spa. A big television screen showed the action onstage from a camera in the third row.

"Tom is indisposed," he said, and gestured toward a pile of costumes in one corner. I saw one shoe that looked like part of the pair Tom had been wearing. I couldn't tell if Tom's foot was in it.

"Don't worry; he's not dead. He'll wake up in a few hours with nothing worse than a bad headache."

I had been leaning against the door, which I had closed behind me before I saw him. I was dripping wet, my gray hair in untidy ropes that reached my shoulders.

I had prepared a few automatic surprises for him, but none of them could be used without harming Toby. They had been a forlorn hope, anyway. There were weapons here and there, some concealed, some not looking much like weapons, but I doubted my ability to use any of them against his reptilian reactions and hideous strength.

"I've had a little time," he told me. "I've located a few electronic traps and disabled them." He made a gesture toward the Pantechnicon. "I left the life support running in your tricky luggage. We'll use it to smuggle you out of here. The rest of it, the deadly stuff, won't work. I took the trouble to memorize *Mac*—sorry, 'The Scottish Play' before I got here, so don't try speaking any lines from it in here. I've read up on other actors' beliefs, if you have any ideas about triggering something verbally."

I sighed, pushed myself off the wall, and walked to my dressing table.

"Then go get that costume on the rack over there," I told him. "The one labeled 'Act Three, scene four.' And hurry. We don't have much time to get me changed and back out there."

He looked at me for only a moment, then stood and put Toby in a hip pocket and zipped it closed. He was dressed in the costume of one of the King's knights, his helmet on the floor beside the chair. I assumed that was how he got backstage. He took the costume off the rack and came up behind me as I stood at the big mirror. I was already unbuttoning my costume. Tom would have done that for me, but I only wanted as much help from Izzy as I absolutely needed.

"You keep surprising me," he said. "I don't like that. Not many people surprise me."

"Get used to it."

"I think I have. But since we have some time together, would you explain how you knew I was going to let you finish the performance?"

"I didn't know," I said, shrugging out of the kingly robes of Lear. "But I thought it was worth a try. The worst you could do was coldcock me and shove me in my suitcase, and you're going to do that sooner or later, anyway."

"You don't think killing you is the worst I might do?" He held up the new robe—outwardly, exactly like the one I had just taken off—and I slipped my arms into it.

"If you wanted to kill me, you could have done it as soon as I got here. When you didn't do it, I knew you had other plans. I don't think I'll like those plans."

"I can guarantee it. Why the costume change, Sparky? It looks like a waste of time to me." I'd seen him feeling the seams, quickly going over it for concealed weapons. There were none. I gestured toward the television screen, the one he had been watching as I entered, and had made me hope he might be content to hold Toby hostage and give me a little more time.

"Watch and you'll learn something," I said. On the screen, Gloucester and Edmund were finishing their scene.

"That's my cue," I said, and hurried out the door.

"In such a night, to shut me out! Pour on, I will endure. In such a night as this! O Regan, Goneril, your old kind father, whose frank heart gave all—O, that way madness lies; let me shun that. No more of that."

Pure poetry. Not just the lines, but my situation. As Lear, I was going mad. Soon I would be tearing my hair and rending my raiment (the reason for the costume change; this one was strategically weakened so it would tear properly). I was more than good. I was brilliant.

And as Kenneth Valentine—some might say the least successful role in my career—I thought I might go mad as well. Just the thing to put an edge in one's performance.

"Prithee go in thyself; seek thine own ease. This tempest will not give me leave to ponder on things would hurt me more."

The edge of the stage seemed to me an abyss; the wings, dark chances. What was to stop me from leaping the footlights and charging down the aisle, out the lobby, and into the wide world beyond? Or finishing my lines, strolling casually off-stage and out the back door.

Well, professionalism, for one thing. Laugh if you must, but I would almost rather die than abandon a performance in the third act. There is that old axiom, the show must go on. Not only do I owe it to my craft to give my best, and give my all, I owe it to the audience. If I lived to tonight's final curtain and somehow could escape from my nemesis . . . then it's a case of Sorry, Polly. Sorry, cast members. I'm outta here. But nothing short of death was going to keep me from finishing tonight.

Later I realized I'd had no way of knowing if the exits were covered by Izzy's people. If, in fact, half the audience were Charonese agents. But I swear that, at the time, it never entered my head. Somehow I knew that Izzy was handling this alone. I had come to know something about him in our two brief, bloody encounters, come to know something of his culture in my researches aboard Hal. He would handle this alone. Call it pride, call it honour. Call it lunacy. After what had happened in Oberon, he would not be calling in the national guard.

But there was a more important reason I could not flee and that was, of course, Toby. Did Izzy know me well enough to rely on my sense of loyalty to hold me hostage even if my fear and my sense of duty would not? Bet on it.

When I took Toby as my companion so many years before, we had made a deal. As I said before, I was responsible for food, shelter, and safety, and he was in charge of everything else. Oh, I also handled minor matters, such as career decisions, travel itineraries, and our pathetic financial affairs. There had been no need to write any of this down; I considered it a part of the original agreement between man and dog, struck during the Stone Age. This may have been the first deal, the primordial deal, before either written or verbal agreements, and any human who fails to honour it is a pretty poor human in my estimation. Some have found irony in the fact that dogs have accompanied the human race into space, but I fail to see anything odd about it. A dog was the first earthling in orbit, and the first casualty of space travel.

Toby was in charge of love and absolute loyalty, and I could return nothing less to him.

"Is man no more than this?" I shouted. "Consider him well. Thou ow'st the worm no silk, the beast no hide, the sheep no wool, the cat no perfume. Ha! Thou art the thing itself; unaccommodated man is no more but such a poor, bare, forked animal as thou art. Off, off, you lendings! Come, unbutton here."

And I began tearing my clothes.

It seemed unusually quiet as I exited the stage. You expect a few slaps on the back, a wink, a thumbs-up. Some encouragement, acknowledgment that things are going well. There was none of that, and for a moment I was worried. Then I saw the faces of the cast and knew the silence meant something else. They were moving out of my way. Some did not even dare to look at me. They were afraid of intruding on me, afraid that anything they might do or say would short-circuit the magic. Theater people are *intensely* superstitious, always alert for the potential jinx, the careless word or gesture that will shatter someone's concentration.

I think they were a little afraid of me.

"It's a wonderful performance, Sparky."

"I wish you'd quit calling me that."

"It's how I think of you. How I remember you. I really was a fan, you know."

Incredible as it may seem, I believed him. And I also believed he appreciated Shakespeare, and my performance as Lear. How a man raised in such a perverted society could still cherish the arts of a common humanity I will leave for the reader to research, accept, or disbelieve, as takes your pleasure. But his desire to see the end of the play was my only current hope of salvation, his only window of weakness. I didn't dare question it.

"You know I'm going to kill you, don't you?" I asked.

"I know you're going to try." The prospect didn't seem to disturb him.

I had nothing to do for a while. The King sits out most of Act Four. On the stage, Gloucester was having his eyes gouged out. Cornwall would soon meet his Maker. Time to start laying my plans.

Believe it or not, I was hopeful.

Toby was in Izzy's lap, but refused to be cradled. With someone he likes, Toby is capable of sprawling over your hand and arm, limp as a noodle, completely trusting you not to let him fall. Or he can be a shameless beggar, licking your face, wagging his tail, angling for a handout.

Not now. He sat stiffly, looking from Izzy's face then over to me. He was saying, "Why don't you ditch this jerk?" When Izzy's hand moved in Toby's fur, the little lip curled slightly and the tips of his teeth showed. He was far too well-bred to bite the hand of a guest, but clearly he'd like to. With Toby and Izzy, it was hate at first sight.

I don't think Comfort hated Toby. I don't think he viewed Toby as a feeling thing at all. Anyone can tell a dog lover. A dog lover can't keep his hands off a dog. Put one in his lap and he will stroke, scratch, laugh when his face is licked, sometimes coo and gibber like a fool. Comfort held Toby like he would hold a pillow.

"I was wondering if we could talk," I said.

"It would be out of character to plead for your life."

"Not plead. But maybe we could bargain."

He laughed. "Money doesn't tempt me, and you don't have any. What else do you have to offer?"

"I wondered if we could talk about the frog."

He was silent for a while, his eyes narrowing.

"I'd meant to ask you about that," he said. It was as if he was looking for a trap of some kind, and I didn't get it.

"Ask what?"

He shrugged. "What frog?"

"What . . ." It seemed we weren't communicating. I opened my hand, where the evil little netsuke had been resting. The tiny frog still crouched on the skull, his eyes still unsurprised at all they saw. It felt warm and alive. Ivory is a very sensual surface. I could hardly keep my thumb from caressing it.

I started to toss it toward him and a palm-sized, deadly-looking black pistol materialized in Comfort's free hand. I'm sure it hadn't been there before, and I'm sure it hadn't been up his sleeve, but where it came from and how he got it without apparent movement will have to remain a Charonese secret. He was *very* fast.

So I carefully set it on the arm of his chair. He looked at it, made the gun vanish (how did he *do* that?), and gingerly picked it up. He stroked the frog with his thumb, then set it back down.

"Very pretty," he said. Pretty is not the word I would have used, but I'm not Charonese. "What does it have to do with me?"

Here the script calls for the protagonist to sit for a moment in stunned silence as all his assumptions come crashing down. After the long pause I told him how I'd come by the frog.

"Well, she never reported it to us," he said, with a slight smile. "If she had, we would have come for it, taken it from you, and broken both your arms. You'd have been repaired and on your way in a few hours."

"But—"

"We were called in by the governor of Boondock. You do remember visiting Boondock, don't you? Certainly you remember the young lady you met there. I saw her picture, and I certainly wouldn't have forgotten."

"But she was—"

"Nineteen, and engaged to a banker's son. Boondock is an independent city-state within the Outer Federation. It was established by a religious cult about a century ago. They have some unusual customs there, one of which is legally mandated obedience to one's parents until the age of majority, which they say is twenty-five years."

"I didn't—"

"As in so many other places, ignorance is no excuse. I'm sure your producer handed out a booklet before your arrival, concerning local customs; they always do. And like most passengers, you threw it away along with the booklet the shipping line gave you concerning emergency evacuation procedures. But you really should have read it, Sparky. Your brief affair with the girl upset a lot of political plans concerning an upcoming arranged marriage. Family honour demanded reparations.

"We Charonese are the only broad authority beyond Pluto. We're the only ones with enough discipline to maintain strict standards over such a vast region. Each enclave has its own rules and its own enforcers, but when someone flees a jurisdiction, as you did, we are called in. We work only by contract, and the governor's policy with us sets out prescribed remedies for different situations. First, we guaranteed to hunt you down. As I'm sure you have learned from your researches, we always get our man."

"Hunt me down and kill me," I said.

"Hunt you down. The governor was a bit cheap, though, and didn't pay for death in this instance. I'm not sure we would have written such a policy, anyway. We tend to operate more on an eye-for-an-eye basis. Almost Biblical, you might say."

"Biblical."

"Exactly. Since there was no way for us to take your virginity and ruin your marriage prospects, of course, we would have used other methods. The usual penalty would be three days of pain, followed by a year's incarceration."

"So you never intended to kill me."

"I blame myself, really," he said. "I assumed you knew that, back on the *Britannic*. I assumed too much. I expected resistance—three days of pain is certainly memorable to a non-Charonese, and something you surely would try to avoid—but I wasn't prepared for the tenacity of your assault. "Of course, things are different now. . . ."

"You do me wrong to take me out of the grave," I said. "Thou art a soul in bliss; but I am bound upon a wheel of fire, that mine own tears do scald me like molten lead."

Things were indeed different now. If, in some ways, my last scenes of madness were not acting at all, then how to judge the end of the fourth act, when Lear is returned to sanity, temperance, even a sort of tranquillity in the arms of his faithful daughter Cordelia, while within me, poor actor, raged all the tempests of folly?

Considering all that, it might have been my greatest moment on the stage. No one would ever know just how great.

Life is a tale told by an idiot, full of sound and fury, and we play it at cross purposes.

My one and only chance of escape was coming, and I did not feel up to it. I wanted to lie down with Lear, return to my comfortable grave.

But did it matter? What would have been different if I had given Comfort more time to speak, back there in my tiny cabin aboard the *Britannic*? Or if he hadn't been so unnaturally *quick*? The tanglenet was supposed to have immobilized him, then I could have listened to what he had to say.

Three days of pain. A year at what I had to assume would be very hard labor and solitary confinement. Would I have surrendered, knowing escape was, in the long run, impossible?

No.

It was as simple as that. I can't do jail time. I'd rather die. I'd rather spend the rest of my life on the run. I once did three days in jail, waiting for arraignment. Every time I went to sleep I found myself back in the airlock, facing the Daewoo Caterpillar. Awake, I spent all my time watching the walls, because every time I turned my back on one it began to move in on me. Very hard work, since you can't watch six walls at once. As soon as I made bail, I jumped, and have never regretted it.

So I would have fought the man from Charon. But I might not have tried so hard to kill him.

It didn't matter now. He'd explained it all to me, before my entrance. I had killed a Charonese. That simply was not allowed. The penalty was death, and a death that would be a long, long time coming.

"Be your tears wet? Yes, faith. I pray, weep not. If you have poison for me I will drink it." I reached up and touched the tears on Cordelia's cheek. Real tears, not glycerine, as in rehearsal. I was so far gone in the part that I couldn't remember her real name.

I didn't return to my dressing room for the beginning of the fifth act. Cordelia and I waited in the wings, not speaking, not wanting to chance anything wrecking the mood. Soon we were onstage again, captured by our enemies, reconciled. It's

my favorite scene in the play. The foolish old King at the end
of his folly, granted one moment of happiness before the end.
We were led away to what we thought would be our impris-
onment, not knowing the plans of the evil Edmund.

I was going to my dressing room when Polly appeared and
took my arm. She looked up at me, and I saw concern in her
eyes.

"Bear up, old friend," she said.

"How am I doing?" I asked her.

"I think you know how the performance is going. But I'm
a little worried about you. Is something wrong?"

"Wrong? What are you talking about?"

"I'm not sure. I sense something. I don't think anyone
else would notice. God knows you're giving it your all. Is
there anything I should know?"

Anything she should know. The mind reeled. I knew what
she was talking about, Polly being the only one who knew
who was after me. And I wouldn't get her involved in it.

Anything she should know. Yes, Polly, my dear. After the
final curtain I'm going to vanish, one way or another. Either
under my own steam, or in the custody of a man from your
worst nightmares. There will be only one performance of this
Lear, one perfect moment on the stage. You close tomorrow.

Oddly, I knew she wouldn't mind that part. I felt sorry for
the rest of the cast, who had a right to expect a long run from
such a night as this, but for Polly, the work was done, in the
heavenly books. She had created a masterpiece that would
last for the ages. As for the cast, well, that's show business.

So I lied. It wasn't my best work, I could tell, and even
my best might not have entirely fooled her. But there were
distractions. The final duel between Edmund and Edgar was
getting under way on stage, and she had made quite a production out of it. "Edgar" and "Edmund" were the two finest stage swordsmen on Luna at the time and they were
pulling out all the stops, giving the audience an exhibition of
derring-do that would leave them breathless for my entrance.
So she didn't question me, and I managed to slip away.

And immediately ran into the head of makeup, in a hissy
panic.

"Where is Cordelia!" he said. "We have to get the rope
burns on her neck!"

I shrugged helplessly, and as soon as his back was turned I ran to my dressing room.

As soon as I slammed the door behind me I saw Isambard on one knee beside Cordelia, who was lying on the floor.

"My God! What have you done to her? You've killed her."

He stood up. Toby was still cradled in his left hand.

"Contrary to what you might think, I don't kill unless it's necessary. She's unconscious."

"But you said—"

"She came in here and was asking too many questions. She was about to leave to get security, so I had no choice."

I lifted her and put her down on my cot. A bruise was forming on her temple. And damn her, anyway! She had decided to sneak in here at the last moment. There would have been no time for sex, but Jennipher was a cuddler. She wanted to hug and kiss before our last scene, in preparation for a memorable night of celebration.

Well, Cordelia was "dead" in our last scene. All was not lost.

"And I'm afraid we'll have to go now," Comfort said.

"Excuse me?"

"Yes. Things have gotten too dangerous. I have a safe route plotted to the rear entrance; no one will see us." He smiled. "Did you really think I was going to give you a chance to escape during the curtain calls?"

I stared at him, stunned at this treachery.

"I thought we had a deal," I said.

"Deal?" He laughed. "I made no deal, and I made no promise."

"It was implied."

"You've never really grown up, have you, Sparky? Did you expect me to behave like a gentleman?"

"No, but I . . . yes, I guess I did. I thought we had an understanding. I thought you were liking my performance." My voice was rising. Toby heard the tension, and began to bark.

"I did. But I've seen the end of this play. Perhaps you can finish it for me when we get back to Charon. Before we get to work on you."

Someone was pounding on the door now. The stage manager, the makeup man; it hardly mattered. I had only minutes before I was needed onstage. Which meant he had only minutes to take care of me. Toby was still barking. I looked around helplessly, ran my hand through my hair, and decided to plead.

"It's just five minutes," I said, holding my hand with the fingers apart. "That's all I need. Just give me the five minutes to finish here. Then I'll die a happy man."

"Why should I want you to die happy?"

Toby bit him on the hand.

He looked down as the tiny warrior sank his teeth into the meat between his thumb and forefinger and worried with sharp shakes of his head, looked at it as if it were happening to someone else.

Then he took Toby's head in his free hand and twisted. There was a sharp, gristly pop, a crunch, and Toby went limp. Comfort tossed the flaccid corpse aside.

"Now," Comfort said, calmly. "Do you want to get in the box, or should I put you . . . or should I . . . it's time . . ." His eyes lost focus, found me again, and his hand started to come up. From somewhere in his clothing the handgun sprang free and was propelled toward his hand—but the hand wasn't there to meet it. His arms fell to his side, his knees buckled, and he hit the floor as bonelessly as Toby.

No time, no time, no time at all. They were pounding harder on my door now. I grabbed a makeup towel and carefully lifted Toby. I saw the broken tooth and the golden fluid oozing from it. I was careful not to get any on my skin, as the stuff doesn't really need a puncture to work. The poison is harmless to dogs. Comfort's voluntary nervous system was completely destroyed by now. He still breathed, his heart still pumped, but that was all. I couldn't obtain the instantly lethal stuff, and besides, it left no room for error if I had somehow forgotten and shown Toby my five spread fingers by accident. Comfort's condition was reversible, but not easily, and not quickly.

And I still feared him. All along my worst fear was that the Charonese had some built-in antidote to the nerve poison; you never could tell with these people—but first things first. I crammed Toby into his hibernation chamber and closed the lid. All the lights on the cover flashed red. Then one turned green, then another. A third. I didn't have time to watch it all. I turned to Cordelia.

My god, what if she woke up while I was bemoaning her death? I needed another Cordelia. Luckily, one was at hand.

I tore the costume from Jennipher. These were warrior clothes. Cordelia had just been defeated on the field of battle, taken prisoner, then hanged by the treachery of Edmund. I draped the coat around Comfort, rolled him over, and got to work on the buttons. The pants were close enough, and would just have to do.

More pounding on the door.

"Mr. Dyle, Mr. Dyle! We need you on the stage, *now*!"

"I'll be ready!" I shouted back. "Tell them to slow down!"

Certainly some of the more frightening words to hear coming from the star's dressing room. I could imagine the panic building, the stage manager racing to find Polly, frantic signals to the principals on stage. I could see the flop sweat breaking out on foreheads as those poor folks realized every actor's nightmare: they were stranded out there, no safety net, no rewrites, no retakes. It had driven many an actor and director back to the cinema, where you could always shout *Cut*!

I glanced at Toby's module. Only two red lights now.

I had not expected Comfort to do what he did. My fear had been that he would understand the signal, somehow, drop the dog, stun me, and make his escape. But it didn't matter. Toby was doomed from the moment Comfort got his hands on him. He was to be used as one more method of torturing me. I would get to watch as the poor little ball of fluff was made to suffer until they got ready to work on me.

Perhaps it's blowing my own horn, but I am quite proud of my performance with Comfort there at the end. Of *course* I never expected him to let me finish the play. Taking me into the middle of the last act and then cutting me off sounded like a Charonese thing to do right from the start. But I was able to use my rising indignation as I "realized" I had been taken in to get Toby excited, get him yapping so that the bite, when it came, would seem natural.

Oh, how sharper than a serpent's tooth . . .

Can you count to five, boys and girls?

· · · ·

Comfort was a small man, smaller than Jennipher, actually, so that shouldn't be a problem.

A wig, a wig, my kingdom for a wig. I scrambled frantically through the overturned costume rack where Tom, my dresser, was sleeping peacefully. I hoped. I found one the right size and color, kicked clothing over Tom's exposed foot, hurried back, and pulled the wig over Comfort's head. I arranged it artfully.

More pounding. I could do nothing but ignore it.

A few quick slashes with makeup pencils and brushes and Mr. Isambard Comfort's face was a reasonable imitation of Jennipher's lovely features ... from a sufficient distance. No matter; I'd keep the hair over most of his face, and if any of the cast noticed anything I had to assume they would stay in character. No one in the audience would find anything amiss.

I rolled Jennipher off the cot and spread the bedclothes over her, picked up Comfort's limp body, and tripped the door lock with my foot. I pushed my way through the frantic people just outside my doorway and raced toward the stage. I ran all the way to my entrance, then began Lear's last, mournful journey.

"Howl, howl, howl, howl!" The words look ludicrous, written down like that. One must rip them from deep in a wounded gut, and by God, I did.

"Oh, you are men of stones: Had I your tongues and eyes, I'd use them so that heaven's vault should crack. She's gone forever."

I saw no men of stone; stones don't sweat. What I did see was the most relieved cast of characters I'd ever encountered. They'd just spent almost two minutes trying to improvise and stretch their way through a growing catastrophe, and I don't think they could have gone another five seconds without the audience beginning to squirm. I was so proud of them, Kent, Albany, Edgar, and all the rest, for betraying not one inkling of the euphoria they must be feeling at my belated entrance. Euphoria? Hell, bloody murder! I could see it in their eyes: if Comfort didn't kill me, they might still.

"Lend me a looking glass; if that her breath will mist or stain the stone, why, then she lives."

I had "Cordelia" down on the ground, cradled in my arms. A wisp of hair stirred as Comfort exhaled. I had closed his eyes, but they were coming open slowly, and there was still awareness in them. He stared at me, and I turned his head away from the audience. The lights were on us now, a golden softness Polly had worked an entire day to get. My fellow cast members were shadows, gathered around us.

"This feather stirs. She lives." I brought my left hand up behind his neck, at the angle of the jaw, feeling for the carotid artery. I squeezed. Oh, bloody murder, indeed!

I kept up the pressure.

"Why should a dog, a horse, a rat, have life, and thou no breath at all?" His eyes seemed to lose a little of their luster. It would be short and painless for him, which is exactly the way I wanted it. Don't forget, Charonese *wanted* a long and painful death. It assured them of a better place in Hell. But Comfort would feel *nothing*.

"Thou'lt come no more. Never, never, never, never, never. Do you see this? Look on her. Look, her lips! Look there, look there!"

I collapsed on him. My face was inches away. Did the light fade even more? I couldn't be sure. My eyes were open only the barest slits; after all I was supposed to be dead.

I heard "Edgar" speak: "The weight of this time we must obey, speak what we feel, not what we ought to say. The oldest hath borne most: we that are young shall never see so much, nor live so long."

And at last, the curtain.

I was up, fighting my way through the darkness and a hurricane of stage whispers. Hands plucked at my clothing. Explanations were wanted, but I had no time, no time, no time at all. I crashed into my dressing room and slammed the door behind me. The curtain calls were beginning and I had only minutes.

Strip the costume from Comfort. The Pantechnicon sat in a corner, unpacked, on its side, ajar, presumably defanged by Izzy. Not quite so long as a coffin, but deeper and wider. I dumped him in it and slammed the lid.

A glance at Toby's box. One red light now. That one would not go off until I got him to a vet; the device was designed to keep him alive, not heal him.

On the screen, onstage, the extras filing off and Gloucester,

Albany, France, Kent filing on. Thunderous applause.

I lifted Jennipher and sat her on the cot, pulling the costume over her. Slapping her face, pinching her. She began to blink and swat listlessly at my hand. I'd carry her on unconscious if I had to, but it would certainly look funny. . . .

Now Edmund, Edgar, and the Fool. Applause growing deafening.

"Wake up, darling, come on now, you have to be a trouper."

"Wha . . ."

"You hit your head, my dear. But you have to get it together, just a few more minutes. Come on, Jen, suck it up. You can do it, I know you can."

Her eyes were open now but not really tracking. Once more, someone was pounding on my dressing room door.

Onstage, Goneril, Regan . . . no Cordelia. The three sisters were to have taken their bows together.

"Up we go," I said, and lifted her to her feet. She was never going to make it under her own power. I got my arm around her waist, and opened the door.

"Out of my way!" I bellowed, and the crowd fell back before the madness in my eyes and the thunder of my voice. I wore every ounce of Lear's dignity as I strode onto the stage with my Cordelia.

Why Lear and Cordelia? It's not as big a part as either of her sisters. Well, let them figure it out. I'd deal with it later.

When the lights hit us the old instinct took over in Jennipher. She smiled, curtsied, even managed to stand on her own as she and the whole cast turned and applauded me. I must tell you that, though it was probably the loudest ovation I ever received, I barely heard it. I was watching Jennipher out of the corner of my eye, ready to steady her if she faltered.

The curtain came down, briefly, immediately rose again to find the entire cast in a line, holding hands, myself in the center. We took a bow, applauded the audience, and I gestured to the wings. Polly came out, stood there for a moment, nodded, and went backstage again. It was all she ever gave the audience, no matter how much they clamored for more.

Then the curtain came down again, and Jennipher began to scream.

• • •

Oh, it was sheer bedlam.

"A man!" Jennipher was shouting. "There was a man in Carson's room. He *hit* me! He hit me, and then . . ."

I took her by the shoulders and looked at her with deep concern.

"A man? Are you sure? Where did he go?"

"I don't—"

"Seal off the stage area," Polly was saying. "I want guards on all the exits. Everyone stay where you are."

Out of nowhere the half-dozen large men who had lurked about the production from the beginning materialized; Polly had insisted on the extra security. Their eyes were not friendly as they tried to look beneath the makeup, seeking an impostor. Each carried a small but deadly-looking weapon and seemed more than ready to use it.

And so the search began. The audience was not bothered. It was quickly agreed that no one could have slipped from the backstage area into the auditorium without being noticed, and no one had seen anything.

The first thing the search discovered was, of course, poor Tom. This heightened everyone's concern, because until then it was still possible to think Jennipher was simply suffering from a bump on the head—a bump I helpfully pointed out I had given her, accidentally, while carrying her from my dressing room. Her story was vague, after all, and unlikely. But Tom's body proved something had been going on.

It was impossible to revive him quickly. The first doctor to arrive confirmed that he had been drugged. When he finally did come around, he was no help at all. He remembered nothing.

It was pretty chaotic until the police arrived, which was fine with me. But they soon began imposing some order on the mess.

My story—and I was determined to stick to it—was that I'd never seen Tom lying under the heap of costumes. And why would I have looked for him there? No, I arrived back in my room to find him gone, which had surprised and disappointed me because he'd always been quite reliable. But I determined to soldier on, alone, which accounted for the delays in certain appearances onstage. They seemed to be buying it. Why would I drug my own dresser? Why put my entire performance in jeopardy?

Polly stayed at the edges of this interrogation, her face betraying nothing to the police but saying volumes to me. *Sparky, you are so full of shit.* I managed to send her the tiniest guilty shrug when the detectives weren't looking. She would keep quiet.

So it was decided to search the entire theater, beginning with my dressing room. In no time at all a detective was standing in front of the Pantechnicon, pointing at it.

"What's this?" she asked.

"My trunk. All actors have a trunk." For a giddy moment there I was tempted to break into a chorus of "Born in a Trunk in the Princess Theater in Pocatello, Idaho," a song which almost summed up my life.

"You want to open it for me?"

"Of course." I went to her, positioned myself so my shadow fell over the trunk, and lifted the lid. She glanced inside, and I closed the lid.

A legitimate theater is always chock-full of cubbies and hidey-holes. Temporary walls are thrown up, then become permanent, and little odd-shaped dead spaces can result. Holes are cut in stages for dramatic entrances and exits, for magic tricks. There is a labyrinth backstage, towering fly lofts, and who-knows-what in the basement. There were no sewers running beneath this theater, so far as I knew, but the Phantom of the Opera would have had no trouble hiding himself.

But with enough people the search was eventually finished, and yielded . . . nothing.

There were those who wanted to do it all again, but they were in the minority. After all, it was just an assault, no permanent harm done. Tom would file a lawsuit against the theater, which would be settled out of court for a nominal sum. We would all be alert for a repeat during the rest of the run, which promised to be a long one. The consensus was that the intruder had somehow entered the audience and filed out with them, even though it was demonstrated early on that this couldn't be done. Still, after you have eliminated the impossible, whatever remains, however unlikely . . . is wrong, in this case. But it wasn't up to me to point that out.

Things eventually quieted down. Finally, over an hour af-

ter the final curtain, I closed my door to the last of the in-
truders. I pulled my beard off, went to the sink, and washed
my face.

And there was a knock on the door. I sighed, and answered
it.

It was two more detectives. I knew, because they were
holding out their badges for me to examine.

"Mr. Carson Dyle?" one of them asked.

"Yes? What can I do for you?"

"Also known as Kenneth Valentine?"

I said nothing.

"Sir, we have reason to believe you are the aforemen-
tioned Kenneth Valentine. I am placing you under arrest for
the murder of your father, John Valentine. Please don't say
anything until you've spoken with your attorney."

And they slapped the handcuffs on me.

"This court is now in session," said the Judge.

It was now almost forty-eight hours after my arrest. Justice
can move quite swiftly in Luna, especially in a seventy-year-
old case. If you don't have your act together by now, the
reasoning went, you never will. We had missed one performance, but one was going on now with my understudy.

Much had happened.

I had spent the time in utter terror, feeling the walls closing
in on me. I was given drugs to help combat this, but as trial
time approached I had to be taken off of them, to be alert for
my own defense.

I had engaged Billy Flynn, the best lawyer on the planet.
I could afford him now, and it only seemed right that he have
a part in what was being touted as the sixth or seventh Trial
of the Century.

And what's this? you say. I could afford Billy Flynn? This,
from the man who recently had to stage Punch and Judy
shows for a couple of hot dogs? Who had almost starved to
death riding the rods from Pluto to Oberon?

Oh, yes, I was a wealthy man. *Very* wealthy, for all the
good it did me.

When I left Luna in such a hurry, seventy years before,
Thimble Theater was an emerging player in the entertainment
business. I was the majority stockholder. Upon my indictment

for murder and subsequent flight, all those funds were frozen
and put in the hands of a trustee. I couldn't get a dime anywhere in the system. This is a sensible law, I suppose, as it
makes flight to escape prosecution very difficult. I left Luna
with the change in my pocket, and a small loan from my
Uncle Ed.

In my absence, the trust was required by law to manage
my estate in the manner most likely to return a profit for the
company, and thus for me and the other stockholders. They'd
done a very good job. Thimble Theater was now *the* player
in the entertainment business. I was one of the three or four
wealthiest men alive.

And I couldn't promote the price of a candy bar.

My money would be waiting for me after I had served my
sentence, if any, or been found not guilty, like any other citizen. Assuming I lived to collect it, but more about that in a
moment. In the meantime I could draw only enough money
for my legal expenses. Luckily, I didn't have to hire Malcolm
Malpractice, the guy with the office over the barbershop. I
retained Flynn and Associates, which meant I had a full combat battalion of lawyers, clerks, assistants, investigators, and
researchers at my disposal.

So the first thing I did was stab Billy in the back.

"Common sense?" he shouted. "Common sense? What's
all this I'm hearing about Common Sense Court? Sparky, my
friend, that's for people who *didn't do it*! In case you've forgotten, *you did it*! To find guilty people not guilty we go to
a *jury*, Sparks! Juries are what I *do*!"

I said I'd prefer to take my chances with the Judge.

"Let me say this to you slowly," Billy said, slowly. "The
law is an ass. The law is an ass, and I am the mule skinner."

This was happening in his luxurious office, shortly after I
had almost, but not quite, admitted that I had killed my father.
Not even Billy Flynn was going to hear of Elwood's role in
the crime, because Elwood was not going to be any element
in my defense. So what I had told him was that I no longer
remembered what had happened that day (true; I also hadn't
remembered it accurately *on* that day), and that since I and
my father were the only people on the stage, it must have
been me who shot him. Also true.

"A jury is the best thing that ever happened to a defendant,'' Billy went on. ''A jury is the only existing creature with no brain and twelve assholes. Do you know how you determine the intelligence of a jury? You do *not* add up the IQs and divide by twelve. You take the lowest IQ and divide *that* by twelve.

''Juries are hazardous, I won't lie to you about that. Sometimes their sheer stupidity gets in the way and they simply never *understand* the right thing to do. Which is whatever I tell them to do. But nine times out of ten I can whip them along to the right verdict. With the Judge, you quite often get actual *justice*, which is the last thing you want.''

He had been pacing around the office, delivering his peroration to a jury he hadn't even assembled yet. Now he went behind his desk and sat down, laced his fingers together, and assumed a fatherly mien. Billy Flynn affected an older appearance, with a receding hairline and gray around the temples. Probably another jury thing. He had an Adolphe Menjou moustache, and a warm, husky voice. You *liked* this man, almost instantly.

''Let me give you the Billy Flynn extremely short course in the Law, Sparky. After the Invasion, the dominant legal form was based on the English system of jurisprudence. People erroneously assume this system is involved in dispensing justice. It is not. It is interested solely in providing fairness, in conducting all its affairs by a set of rules. You know what those rules are and you play by them, and you win some, and you lose some. The system is largely weighted in favor of the accused. This results in oddities such as 'admissible evidence.' According to the law, how evidence is gathered is more important than its actual probative value. In other words, if the police don't play by the rules, you go free. No matter *what* you've done, no matter how compelling the evidence. Case dismissed. This obvious insanity is tolerated because of the 'rules.'

''Or take prejudicial testimony. If you've been convicted of ninety robberies, and are accused of a ninety-first, with exactly the same *modus operandi,* those prior convictions cannot be put in evidence against you. It might 'prejudice' the jury.

''The upshot is, the English system of law is by far the way to go if you are guilty.

"Of course, in recent years, another type of law has been tried. . . ."

I could listen to the man talk all day. His arguments at the bail hearing alone were worth every penny of his outlandish fee. When he was done, even *I* was almost convinced I wasn't a flight risk—a man who had fled the jurisdiction and been on the run for seventy years, who had no money, no roots in the community, and absolutely nothing to lose by jumping bail . . . and who had in fact spent the last twenty-four hours thinking of nothing but the best way out of town if bail were granted. But in the end I would not have released me on my own recognizance, and the judge didn't, either.

At one point I told Billy Flynn he could have been a great actor.

"I *am* a great actor," he replied.

But he was a bit long-winded, and I wasn't taking notes. Besides, half of the power of his words were in the delivery, something every actor understands. So while I thoroughly enjoyed the two-hour diatribe he had introduced as an extremely short course in the law, I won't try to set it down here. He had *much* more to say about the traditional, English system. And much to say about the new system.

For there *were* other ways.

Even in English common law one often had the option of being tried by a judge or a jury. Trial by a wise and/or impartial judge had been the method used by many cultures before the Invasion. It often worked well. Then there was trial by a council of elders, or by an entire community. Always, there was The Law behind such systems, sometimes called "custom," sometimes written down and sometimes not. There were referees, arbitrators, mediators of all sorts. All these systems had strengths and weaknesses.

People had always aspired to more than the traditional system of law could offer. Billy was right: the law was an ass. And a big reason was, legislators are forced by the nature of codified rules to try to anticipate every situation that can arise in human affairs. This is plainly impossible. And, recognizing the imperfectibility of human affairs, the law had to give a big edge to the accused if it was to avoid injustice to the innocent. Both of these things resulted in injustices, even travesties of the law. Couldn't there be a better way?

The system of a wise and impartial judge seemed to offer the best option for making the law more nearly just. And, yes, for trying to do something the English legal system did not even attempt: finding the *truth,* so far as that concept could be said to really exist. In criminal matters, was it possible to attempt a determination of *what really happened,* as opposed to what the admissible evidence and unreliable and biased eyewitness testimony tended to indicate *might* have happened?

Well, very little could ever be proved one hundred percent true. But likelihood could be determined to a very high degree of probability, and we had a machine that was very good at just that sort of thing.

The Lunar Central Computer.

Oh, my, how the lawyers did howl when it was suggested!

The basic proposal had been around for over a century when it was finally agreed, over loud objections from the bar, to give a new system a twenty-year optional tryout. After twenty years submit it to the voters. We were currently fifteen years into the experiment, and still the only planet with a dual legal system. But Luna was being watched intensely by every other planet in the system with an elected government, who all knew a politically popular thing when they saw it.

People liked the new system. It seemed to work better.

Officially it was called the Juridical Protocols Test. Professionals in the law usually called it the Judge. The public, after a few years, referred to it as the Court of Common Sense.

This was the system upon whose tender mercies I was throwing myself. Why? Many reasons I needn't explore, and one I can't completely explain. My first visitor, after my initial consultation with Billy Flynn, was Hildy Johnson, and she had this to say:

"Sparky, I know what your high-priced mouthpiece just told you. I'd like to give you a bit of advice that will cost you a lot less. Go before the Judge. You won't regret it. And I guarantee that."

I was about to say Hildy Johnson never lied to me, but of course the first words out of her mouth when we met were a lie. But we had become quite good friends, way back when,

and she had never betrayed me. Even when it would have
been to her professional advantage to do so.

So the Judge it would be.

I'd have been a lot more confident of my chances if I
didn't keep remembering that the Lunar CC had, not long
before, suffered a planetary nervous breakdown.

Everything about the Juridical Protocols Test was different.

All trials were televised, even if no one tuned in. Most
were dull enough so that a tiny room, a table, and half a dozen
chairs were sufficient. But in higher profile cases larger halls
were available.

The case of *Luna* v. *Kenneth Valentine* was held in the
largest JPT courtroom, which could accommodate five hundred. It was an instant sellout, with seats at ringside being
scalped for over a thousand dollars. The room itself was unremarkable, nothing more than a big barn with maroon velvet
drapes against the walls, uninspired lighting, gray carpet, and
more maroon in the upholstery. This operation was badly in
need of a set designer.

Close to one wall was a big round table with low-backed
chairs on casters, enough to seat twenty people. On that wall
was hung a twenty-foot television screen. The table was
wood-grain Formica. A few feet behind it was a low U-shaped
barrier (the bar?) and behind that concentric rows of seats,
steeply raked to give everyone a view. It was like an operating
theater from an old movie, or a college lecture room: Fresh-
man Introductory Law 101. One aisle came down the center
to the only break in the barrier. Witnesses testifying in person
would enter through that break.

The prosecutors sat directly across the table from me, my
defense team, the clutter of paper and briefcases and com-
puterpads they had made around their places, and Toby.

I had managed to tell Polly about Toby's plight as I was
being led away, manacled. She got him to a vet and had
delivered him to the holding cell just down the hall not an
hour ago. He had been happy to see me, but not inordinately
so. Toby is a genius, for a dog, but I'm sure he had no idea
of what had happened to him. And no idea what he had done
to Izzy; I imagine he regarded the steady diet of raw steak

he'd been getting from Polly—at my request—as no more than his due.

Digesting all that steak is hard work. After I set him on the table he looked around, counting the house, but when he saw the people were not here to watch him perform he curled up on a stack of legal briefs and went to sleep. Every once in a while I could hear his stomach rumble.

In the center of the table was the Judge.

Not really, of course. There was no "Judge," in the sense of a physical object present in the courtroom. But except when interfacing directly with the CC, in which case its voice came through one's own personal implanted telephone, people prefer to have the sound come from some visible source, not just emanate from the walls. It gave the defendant and the lawyers something to look at, and it made for better television. So a small box had been rigged up with screens on each side. Evidence and taped testimony could be displayed, and when the CC was speaking, the screens showed an officious-looking logo of the JPT Department.

As soon as the court was declared in session I stood up.

"Your Honour," I said, "I would like to make an opening statement."

Billy Flynn was looking up at me as if I were insane.

"Mr. Valentine," said the Judge, "it is not necessary to address me as 'Your Honour.' And it is not necessary to stand when speaking."

"I understand, Your Honour, but I would prefer to do both."

"As you wish."

"Your Honour, I wish to state for the record at this time that, if I am found guilty of this charge, and if my sentence includes a period of time in which I am locked up in a jail cell, I will wish to be provided with the means to end my own life."

There were shocked gasps from the audience.

"Say it ain't so, Sparky!" someone shouted.

"Bailiff," said the Judge, "please remove the occupant of seat 451." The idiot was promptly hustled from the seat he had paid dearly for, and an alternate ticket holder ushered into his place. The Judge didn't mind murmuring, gasping, or laughter, but comments from the audience were forbidden.

"That is your right, of course," the Judge went on. "It's premature, but your request is noted. Tell me, are you claustrophobic? I see no mention of it in your psychological evaluation."

"No, Your Honour," I said, recalling my trip to Oberon, and my berth in the *Guy Fawkes*. "Maybe the word is penophobic. I can't handle jail. I'd go crazy."

"If this is an appeal for leniency, you really should save it for the sentencing phase, if any."

"It's not an appeal, Your Honour. I simply want it on the record. I also have another reason, which I will reveal if it becomes necessary."

There was indeed no good reason to say any of that, except that it made me feel much better to get it off my chest. I was completely serious, too. And why not? Jail time might as well be a death sentence for me. It gave the Charonese two options. They could assassinate me in prison (getting *into* a prison is the easiest thing in the world), or they could simply wait at the gate until my release and roll me up then. Whichever they planned, I would not give them the chance.

Yes, they would still be after me. And I knew they would much prefer option two, with the chance for about a year of sophisticated torture before my eventual death. Much better to take the Black Pill.

But I wasn't going quietly. I knew the Charonese hated publicity, hated any kind of fuss. Well, I was going to show them one hell of a fuss. I was going to tell my entire story, reveal to the civilized world *why* I was electing to take my own life. I knew where their sympathies would lie. Someday, someone is going to have to do something about the Charonese, and anything I could do to rally public opinion against these monsters . . . well, I'd think of it as my memorial.

"We will proceed on *Luna* v. *Valentine*," said the Judge. "It has been alleged that Kenneth Valentine, seventy-one years ago, violated Lunar criminal law by murdering John Valentine, his father." On the screen before me and the one on the wall to my left appeared a copy of the formal indictment, which would never be read aloud in this court. One of the many ways things were speeded up with the Judge. The minutiae of proceedings were simply assumed.

"The physical evidence supporting this accusation is as follows:

"One handgun." On the screen I saw a picture of the gun, followed by a technical description. If my lawyers wanted to challenge any part of this evidence they could simply speak up. None of them did.

"Bloodstained clothing belonging to John Valentine." Again, a picture. The actual items would not appear in court, and I was thankful for that. The Judge paused while the screen displayed and identified a series of reports, all of them seventy years old, all of which were available to my attorneys on their own computers. The reports were by forensic scientists, and established that the blood was my father's blood, and so forth. Then there were statements by cast and crew of that long-ago production that, yes, these items of clothing, a costume, had been worn by John Valentine in his role as Montague.

And so forth. It took about two minutes to establish that all this data existed, a process that might have taken a week in a regular court. Why bother with all the wasted time of cross-examination? None of it was tough to understand, all of it was reviewed and authenticated by the Central Computer, the Judge. And indeed, Billy Flynn had no problems with any of it, though he told me he would have worked over each "expert" for at least a day if trying this case before a jury. Those who could still be found, that is. Seventy years is a long time, even these days. Some might well be living on Pluto. Some would be dead.

Some could be portrayed as incompetent.

"I could have had ninety percent of this declared inadmissible," Billy muttered in my ear.

"One lead bullet, forty-five-caliber, recovered from a wall in the John Valentine Theater." Statement from coroner. Statement from firearms expert. Zip on to the next item.

I stared across the table at the prosecutors. There were only three of them, opposing the nine expensive bodies on my side. All of them sat quietly, hands folded, not using their terminals. I would have to describe their expressions as smug. Who could blame them?

"That is all the physical evidence presently known to the court. We will now move on to forensic evidence."

"Here's where you lose big-time," Billy said to me.

What he meant was, scientific evidence was still the area with the most opportunities for the defense lawyer's stock in trade: obfuscation.

A trial by a jury of your peers means a trial by idiots. Idiots like me, idiots like you. Remember, you can have eleven geniuses and one moron, and the moron rules.

You say you're not an idiot? Maybe not, at what you do. But what do you know about identifying fingerprints? About rifling marks on bullets? DNA profiling? Chemical testing of materials? Retinal scans? Pathology? Crime-scene investigation, psychological testing, interviewing strategies, laser-weapon frequency modulation? If you know anything about any of those things, you know a lot more than I do. And these are all technologies that have been around for centuries; what do you know about the new stuff, the really cutting-edge techniques that maybe three people on Luna know much about? Answer: nothing. So what makes you think you're qualified to sit in judgment on someone whose fate depends on your understanding?

This is where we traditionally haul in the experts.

"An expert witness," Billy Flynn had told me, "is the fellow with credentials that you pay to testify to what you want him to testify to. An incompetent expert witness is one called by the other side."

Summed it up pretty well, I thought. So one distinguished jerk says the sky is blue, and another says the sky is black. You have only a vague idea of what the sky is, having never seen it. Who do you believe?

Why, the one who presents himself best on the stand, of course. The one who best survives the withering cross-examination leveled by the other side.

Before we even sat down around the table, the Judge had already consulted the three or four best experts in the field—*any* field. And it was largely a formality, since the Judge was already conversant with everything in the field, and brought to the problem the experience of a million trials, a billion pieces of evidence.

Oh, it was a black day for the legal profession when the JPT was finally implemented. Public confidence in a JPT verdict began at a level best described as dubious, but over fifteen years had soared. It was so high now that there was a wide-spread perception that anyone who asked for a jury trial *must* be guilty. Which had, naturally, tainted the jury pool. Which had left lawyers in the uncomfortable position of arguing to retain the old system because . . . well, because it was the only method for having their guilty clients acquitted.

I'll leave it to you to imagine how this argument played with the taxpayers.

A black day indeed.

And things were certainly not looking good for old Sparky. What *could* the little wirehead have in mind?

"All evidence currently under submission having been pre-sented, the court will now hear arguments."

Which is where the real fun begins in JPT court.

"Your Honour, I would—"

"Everybody's calling me 'Your Honour.' Flattery will get you nowhere."

There was laughter from the audience.

"I'm simply following my client's lead," said Flynn, af-fably. "And why not? I was trained in respect for the court, and even if this one doesn't demand it, I *do* respect it, and showing respect hurts nothing. And I would not *dream* of attempting flattery." More laughter. "So, Your Honour, I will state at the outset that my client did in fact kill John Valentine, in the manner and on the date specified. And that he did so in self-defense."

"You could have saved the court twenty minutes of sum-mation if you had said that up front," the lead prosecutor rasped, cuttingly. This was a truly hard, squinty-eyed woman with what looked like stainless-steel hair and brass mascara, a regular harpy. But possibly I'm prejudiced.

Her name was Roxy Hart, and she was, naturally, the *chief* prosecutor for King City and she had her eye on the mayor's chair. This was a perfect opportunity for her to get her face before the voters, though she must have thought long and hard about it. Putting murderers in jail is always politically popular, but little "Sparky" did have his defenders and die-hard fans. But my decision to go before the Judge had made it virtually no-lose for her. She hardly had to do any work. It had all been done for her by the police department seventy years ago,

and it was so open-and-shut she could be seen as simply playing out the string. The criticism, if any, should fall upon the
Judge. She would be walking a fine line, Billy told me, between being tough on crime and not being too ruthless with
a popular figure.

"She'll bluster for a while," he said, "then she won't
oppose a reduction in the charges. Manslaughter, something
like that."

"The assertion that this killing was self-defense is ludicrous," she went on. "John Valentine was armed with a stage
sword, a prop. There has been no evidence introduced that he
was trying to kill Kenneth Valentine."

"That 'prop' had an edge sharp enough to shave with,"
Billy countered. "Both witnesses saw numerous wounds on
my client. Whether John actually meant to kill my client is
something we will never know, but it is clear that he meant
to butcher him a bit. In this circumstance, it is reasonable for
Kenneth to feel fear for his life, which is the test of self-
defense."

"This was no more or less than a fencing lesson."

"A very bloody one, and a—"

"A fencing lesson like a dozen other lessons during that
time. We can bring witnesses to testify that, on the stage today, wounds are not uncommon, indeed, are even expected
while one learns the craft of fencing. The wounds sustained
by the younger Valentine did not prevent him from fleeing
the scene of the crime. Without medical attention of any kind,
he went to the Texas disneyland, where he was attended by
the resident doctor, who has stated that the wounds were not
life-threatening."

"It's easy to determine that after the fact, not so easy to
know when you're being used as a human pincushion."

"Oh, please! You're grandstanding for the polls."

Which, naturally, is what they *both* were doing.

It went on like that for a few minutes, each of them shouting over the other. The Judge let it go; the CC has no trouble
following a dozen conversations at once.

You know who had benefited the most from the new system? Dramatists. For centuries playwrights have written
scenes, entirely fantasy, of courtroom confrontations. People
accept them because drama cannot take the time to be boring,

and that is exactly what court is. Boring. Many people never realize this until they get into court themselves, and see how staggeringly slow the proceedings can be.

Because the Judge does not care about decorum and allows almost limitless latitude in what can be said, things can get very hot indeed in the argument phase of a JPT trial. Shouting matches are the standard, and fistfights are common.

But why allow all this horseplay at all? The Judge is not going to be swayed by emotion, is it?

Only in one sense, and that is in the polls Prosecutor Hart mentioned. The polls: the reason people called the JPT system the Court of Common Sense. The last stand of the jury system. The only part of the new regime that lawyers actually like, because it is the only part that lets them appeal to emotion.

Before a trial, and most especially during the trial, the Judge had its fingers on the public pulse. Since the CC was in constant contact with virtually every citizen of Luna (with a few exceptions, like the Outer Amish, my father, and me), this process wasn't intrusive. The average citizen had dozens of transactions with the CC every day. During one of them, the Judge might ask, "Suppose a man steals a loaf of bread . . ." or whatever might be at issue in the case. The citizen would listen, ask questions, then deliver an opinion on the matter. Was it fair? Did the proposed penalty conform with the intent of the lawmakers, and not just the letter of the law? Would following the letter of the law result in an injustice, or unwarranted leniency? Was the crime in fact *worse* than the lawmakers had envisioned when setting the penalties?

The answers were added into the complicated equation, constantly being revised, that determined the verdict, or in the case of the JPT, the "number." This equation was the "protocol" part of the JPT. In fifteen years the algorithms of justice had become supremely refined. They were approaching, though might never reach, that lovely word "fair." As in fair play. No concept of fairness would ever satisfy everyone, but if you satisfied most of the people most of the time, you were doing a *lot* better than the old system ever had.

In my own case, no hypothetical questions were necessary. The Judge simply asked, "What do you think of the Sparky case?'' and the average citizen already knew about it. Thus a few thousand randomly chosen citizens were made to function as an unselected panel. They had put in their ''jury duty,'' an onerous burden under the old system. It had wasted ten minutes of their time, a waste which the great majority enjoyed. And the final verdict for or against me would contain an element of trial by my peers.

So this is what Billy and Roxy were engaged in. A fight to influence public opinion. They typically weren't given much time to do it, so the fight was fast and furious.

I couldn't begin to report all that was said in the next twenty minutes; at times all twelve lawyers were shouting at once. And frankly, if the Judge had asked me to vote on the issue based on the behavior of the attorneys for both sides, I would have voted to disbar them all. It's hard to believe they swayed the opinion of anyone in the vast viewing audience.

But they put on a hell of a show. If you'd like to see it, videos are available at a reasonable price. Hell, buy two. I get a three percent royalty. If you aren't from Luna I'd recommend you buy one and take a look; this is likely to be in your future. You'd better get used to it.

''I think we've had enough of that,'' the Judge said, finally. ''Mr. Flynn, would you like to call any witnesses?''

''Yes, I'd like to have Rose Wilkinson tell what she saw.''

''On the day of the murder?'' Hart asked.

''On that certain day, seventy years ago,'' Flynn said, unperturbed.

Rose was called to the table. She took a seat halfway between the opposing sides, which I'm sure Gideon Peppy would have found significant. I didn't recognize her, but that wasn't surprising. Most people change their appearance a bit every decade or so; usually nothing radical, but enough that if you aren't in contact for a long time it can add up to a new person.

''Ms. Wilkinson,'' said the Judge, ''you have stated that you were employed as the assistant stage manager for a production of *Romeo and Juliet* seventy years ago.''

''That's right. By Mr. Valentine. That is, by Mr. *John*—''

''Why don't you call them John and Kenneth?'' the Judge suggested.

''Okay.''

"Will you tell us what you saw, what you remember?"

"Yes. I was backstage with a reporter, Hildy Johnson. I don't remember what we were talking about. Probably John Valentine, because I hated him more than I've ever hated anyone before or since." I glanced at Roxy Hart, who was frowning. She wanted to leap to her feet and object, but she couldn't. The Judge was in control here, and presumed able to ignore prejudicial statements. "We heard a shot. Well, a loud noise that I later learned was a shot. We went out on the stage to investigate, and I saw Sparky ... I'm sorry, Kenneth, standing there with a gun in his hand. And Mister ... John was lying on his back. I remember smelling smoke, gun smoke I guess it was."

She went through her story fairly concisely. When she began to stray, the Judge gently prodded her back on track.

"It was the most horrible thing I ever saw," she said, tearing up a little even at this late date. I didn't feel so great myself. "Poor Sparky standing there ... I don't think he knew what happened. He *couldn't* have been in his right mind ... but that awful, *awful* man! Sparky could never say no to him. He humiliated his son in front of the entire cast, treated him like a servant or a naughty child ... and I'm *glad* he's dead."

There was a hush in the courtroom when she finished. I discovered my fingernails were biting into my palms. I made an effort to relax; all of Luna was watching.

"I want to point out," Hart said, "that the question of Kenneth Valentine's sanity is not at issue here."

"Noted," said the Judge. "Are there more witnesses?"

"I'd like to call Hildy Johnson," Billy said.

Hildy was called. Hildy was called again. And yet a third time.

What have I done? I asked myself. And I answered, I've put my fate into the hands of a reporter.

"I'm issuing a subpoena for the appearance of Hildy Johnson," the Judge said. "In the meantime her statement is on the record and you have all read it. Her testimony will be taken at a later date, and if anything of relevance is developed an amended verdict will be issued. Now, is there any member of the public who has any pertinent facts bearing on this case? And let me remind you, I am the sole judge of relevancy, and anyone attempting to use this court as a forum for unrelated statements will be dealt with severely, as provided by law. This court is not a soapbox, nor a venue for the disaffected.''

This was known as the ''grandstanding law,'' and was passed when it became clear that this final phase of the JPT was easy meat for abuse by anyone with an ax to grind. People were standing up and delivering diatribes against this or that law, airing pet peeves, generally being pests. Now, if anyone had any new facts—and no one ever did—was the time to present them. Otherwise, statements as to my sterling character or lack of it might or might not be allowed, but precious little else.

The courtroom door burst open and in rushed Hildy Johnson, waving sheets of paper.

''I do, Your Honour!'' she shouted.

The Judge took it in stride. The audience was a little more demonstrative, but quickly settled down as Hildy walked down the aisle and found a seat just to the left of Billy Flynn.

''May it please the court—'' she began.

''You've got the wrong court,'' said the Judge. ''I'm neither pleased nor displeased by anything. Let's dispense with all the formality. What do you have to show me?''

''I just found something interesting,'' she began again.

''Just a moment. Hildy, are you employed by a news-gathering organization?''

''Uh, I used to be, Judge. Currently I'm on extended sabbatical, but I send in stories when I find them.''

''For competitive bidding, I assume.''

''That's where the money is, Judge.''

''Can I further assume that your recent dramatic entrance into the courtroom will enhance the value of any story to come out of this trial?''

''Couldn't hurt,'' Hildy conceded. There was laughter from the audience.

''Why do I get the feeling,'' the Judge said, ''that I'm being sandbagged?''

''Well, Your—Judge, nobody said I couldn't make the news as well as report it.''

''Go ahead, then. What is your startling new evidence?''

''I'm not sure it's in the nature of evidence at all, Judge.

But I think I've uncovered an interesting avenue of exploration. If you could put these pictures up on the big screen . . .''

They were projected, and I felt a stab in my heart. It was four pictures of my father. Publicity stills, smiling, his best profile showing. Pictures I hadn't seen in many years.

There were some gasps, and a building buzz of whispered conversation. I didn't know what was going on.

''I was just looking at these today,'' Hildy went on. ''As you know, I haven't seen Sparky . . . er, Kenneth in many years. The last time I saw him he was twenty-nine, but still in the body of a teenager. When he was arrested two days ago he had the appearance of an old man, King Lear. I don't imagine that in the seventy years of his exile he has worn what we might call 'his own' face many times, if at all.''

''Never, Your Honour,'' I confirmed.

''I suspected that,'' Hildy said. ''He was unlikely to be recognized as Sparky; Sparky never grew beyond eight years old. But the psychology of the fugitive, if nothing else, made me think he would shun his natural appearance. Until today.''

''Yes, I see what you mean,'' said the Judge. He might have, but I still didn't. I had been commanded by the court to abandon all artifices for my appearance in the court, true enough. When I did that, I saw a face in the mirror that very closely resembled my father.

''The picture in the upper right,'' said Hildy, ''is not John Valentine, but his son, Kenneth, taken off the video feed from this courtroom not ten minutes ago.''

I looked at it dubiously. I had to take her word for it. I couldn't have picked it out among the four, except that I now noticed *that* ''John Valentine'' was wearing clothes identical to what I was wearing.

''There's a very strong family resemblance,'' the Judge agreed.

''I think it's more than that, Judge. A lot more. I think this man, Kenneth Valentine, *is* John Valentine.''

This would have been the point, in an ordinary drama, for the judge to bang on his gavel and shout for ''order in the court!'' The Judge simply let the outburst of shock from the audience play itself out. Toby lifted his head, wondering if it was time for him to go on. Then he went back to sleep. The next thing we all could hear was Hildy raising her voice.

"Judge, I'd like to request that you compare the DNA pattern of the late John Valentine with that of his son."

There was no need to order samples taken or tests made. Everything was already present in the CC's memory. After a pause of a few seconds the Judge spoke again.

"They are identical, as I suspect you knew they would be."

"Not until a short while ago," Hildy said. She didn't mention a specific time interval, and I wondered if anyone else would notice that. But whatever she was up to, I knew she was too careful to break any laws. "But I did recently speak with someone who confirmed my suspicion. He's here in this courtroom today, and he has something to tell you. Mr. Edwin Booth Valentine."

Uncle Ed? Here in the courtroom? Surely I'd have seen the forklift needed to move him about.

But instead of a human mountain, it was only a foothill that rose from two seats in the audience (and *that* must have cost Hildy a pretty penny). Uncle Ed was a shadow of his former self; I doubt he was much over five hundred pounds. He lumbered carefully down the aisle and once more there was a growing murmur, this time one of recognition. I heard whispers: "Ed Ventura. That's Ed Ventura." To which many of the younger observers must have been replying, "Ed who?"

Ah, but they'd know soon. This was building into a circus of monumental proportions. An ancient patricide, involving Luna's most beloved moppet. Seventy years on the run. Dramatic backstage arrest. Luna's best criminal-defense attorney versus King City's brightest rising political star. Last-minute genetic revelations I still hadn't grasped. And now, it wouldn't be a circus without an elephant! A famous face from the Old Stars' Burial Ground, grown to enormous size (and if only they knew; but they would, they would, when the reporters started digging).

It had Hildy Johnson's fingerprints all over it.

Even the new Uncle Ed, a shadow of his former self, would not fit into any of the chairs around the table. This didn't seem to bother him. He just stood near the railing, waiting. If he was in any way upset at this public revelation of his love affair with corpulence he never showed it.

"John Valentine was my brother," he said, in his commanding baritone. "We were not . . . close. There were many disagreements over the years, primarily centering around my career, which he viewed as selling out the craft of acting. He wasn't above accepting a 'loan' from time to time, though. I knew I'd never see any of it again, but I was making lots of money and . . . well, that has nothing to do with this case.

"I had not seen him for several years when he appeared at my door one day with an infant child. A boy. He had no very convincing story as to the origins of this child, but I had my fears. You see, we had a sister, Sarah. Sarah was not . . . very bright, I'm afraid. And not very worldly. In fact, she was quite unstable. Our father was a demanding perfectionist, and could be quite a brutal man. It scarred all three of us, but Sarah was the least equipped to survive it. She was left emotionally crippled, unable to function very well in the world. But she had her older brother, John, who protected her from what he could. John became her emotional anchor, her very reason for living.

"Not to put too fine a point to it, they were lovers."

He paused, and wiped at his eyes. I began to get an idea of what this was costing him. What it might cost me I'd have to wait to find out. I was feeling rather numb, to tell the truth.

I had stopped asking about my mother quite early in my life. I had my fantasies, like any child growing up without a mother. I think I'll just keep those private, if you don't mind. Precious little else in my life is private now that my origins have been turned into one of the most widely watched soap operas in the history of Luna.

My father's answers to my questions had always been vague. He told me my mother was dead, but never told me how she died. My impression was that it was too painful for him to talk about it.

He said her name had been Sara. No *H*. Should I have made the connection with the mysterious aunt that my father never talked about either? I don't know. It's a common enough name.

"Pardon me, Judge," Ed went on. "I loved her, too. More than John, in some ways, but I'm afraid I never had the nerve to stand up to our father, either for myself or for her, until I made my final break with the family and took the part that led . . . oh, no one wants to hear about my old career.''

He was wrong, and his films were shortly to be resurrected and shown endlessly, until all the fuss died down. But he was right that the Judge had no interest in it.

"Sarah clung even more tightly to John after I left. I'm afraid I'm old-fashioned; I don't really approve, though I know that brother/sister incest has gained more acceptance in society since my youth. No one advocates natural procreation from such a union, of course . . . and I don't believe that is what happened here.''

"Sir, do you have any actual evidence to submit to the court?'' the Judge asked.

"No, sir, I don't. Other than the incontrovertible news that Kenneth is not John's son, but his clone. Or what we used to call his identical twin. I'll point out that if I hadn't come forward, this court would never have discovered the nature of the relationship.''

"This is true,'' the Judge said. And why should it have? I've heard criticism of the Judge over this point, but it makes no sense. Why didn't the Judge compare the DNA earlier? Well, why didn't it compare my DNA with yours, or Toby's, or Banquo's ghost? Because there was no reason to, and even the CC can only do so much.

"What I have to offer,'' Uncle Ed went on, "is perhaps not completely relevant to the issue at hand, but I think it does have some bearing, if the Judge will just indulge me a few minutes more. I was told that normal rules of evidence do not apply in this courtroom.''

"This is also true. Continue, but get to your point.''

"It is conjecture, sir, I admit it. But I am as sure of it as of anything in my life. John Valentine was the most self-centered man I ever knew. Apart from our sister, I don't think he ever loved another human being. If he was to have a child, having one that was only half his would not have been good enough for him. He found the means to have himself cloned, during a time when human cloning was illegal. He used his own sister as the host mother.

"And then she died.''

There was near silence as he got himself together again.

"At least the only reasonable assumption is that she died. This all happened just over a century ago, and for the first twenty years I roamed the system searching for her. For sixty years after that I paid for investigations. No sign of her was ever turned up.

"If she were alive, she would be with her brother John. The only question in my mind is whether he killed her, or drove her to suicide. John was capable of insane rage, and during these times he would do things he later regretted. I think that's what happened. It could have begun over nothing, really, just some minor disagreement, some perceived failing. I believe Kenneth's story would illustrate that, if he chooses to tell—"

"Mr. Valentine," the Judge interrupted. "It is a sad and fascinating story you tell, and it may be true. But is it offered as a mitigating factor in what Kenneth is accused of doing? If so, it should more properly be said after a finding of guilty, if such a finding is entered."

"I'm sorry, Judge, I got carried away. I've wanted to tell this story for such a long time. I have nothing further to offer in evidence."

"Thank you. Hildy, we have established that John and Kenneth Valentine are genetically identical. That Kenneth is, in fact, not Edward Valentine's nephew, but his brother. Do you have a further point to make?"

"Yes, I do, Judge." She shuffled importantly through the papers on the table in front of her. No pictures this time, but copies of dense print that I couldn't read from my position and wouldn't have understood if I could.

"It concerns an interesting situation in the law that I discovered," she resumed. "If you'll search the old genetic law statutes, you'll find that until sixty years ago, producing a human clone was illegal in Luna and almost everywhere else. It was a legacy I've traced clear back to the early part of the twenty-first century. In time these laws became so rigorous that, once the human reproductive system came under our complete control, it was thought necessary to make it illegal for two humans to possess the same genetic pattern. Even to the point of banning identical twins, triplets, and so forth. For a very long time, going back to just before the Invasion, there *were* no more identical twins.

"The penalties for violation of this law seem pretty draconian to me, and I suspect to most of us these days. But illegal cloning was something that almost never happened—perhaps *because* of the severe penalties—and no one seems to have worried about it a lot, since many years would go by without anyone being affected by the law at all. It wasn't until nearly a century ago that a movement began in the scientific and human-rights communities to rescind these genetic laws, culminating in their eventual repeal.

"But the simple fact is this: under these laws, it was forbidden for two human beings to possess the same genetic code, the same DNA. When this situation was found to exist, one of them had to go. One of them had no right to life.

"When such an identical pair was discovered, the younger of the two was put to death.

"It's one of those situations where, looking back, we wonder, 'What could they have been thinking?' Well, there had been abuses, back on Old Earth. I refer the court to the Buenos Aires Clones of 2025, a community of over a thousand identical women. Or the Aryan Conspiracy of 2034. These horror stories and others convinced the public and legislators that controls on this technology had to be tight indeed. Then came the Invasion, and the period historians call the Interregnum, when very little happened not directly related to the dire question of human survival as a species. Those post-Invasion survivors had little time to tinker with laws. And by the time humanity was breathing a little easier and had the leisure . . . well, it had all become fossilized. Repealing a law is *much* tougher than passing one, always has been. Unless the law creates an egregious and *frequent* sense of injustice, it simply stays on the books."

"It's an elegant history lesson, Hildy," the Judge said. "And I applaud your brevity. But where is it going? Are you arguing that Kenneth is an illegal person? Those laws are no longer in effect."

"No, Judge, he's not illegal. He *was* illegal, under the law, until he took his father's life. You see, the law never said it *had* to be the younger twin that died. This was how the law was administered, assuming the older had proprietary rights to the DNA. But through an oversight, a loophole, call it what you will, this was never spelled out.

"The fact is, neither John nor Kenneth had a legal right to exist ... until one of them was dead. Then the survivor became a legal person.

"In other words, no crime was committed when Kenneth killed his father, because his father was not a person in the eyes of the law."

Well, I thought she was crazy, and so did most of the audience, to judge by the scandalized outbursts. The Judge had to eject three more people before order was restored.

Then there was a short pause, quite unusual in JPT proceedings, and no wonder, considering how rapidly the CC can process data. It was as if a human judge had retired to chambers to think some things over ... for a century or two. At last the CC spoke again.

"You raise some interesting points," it said. "I am going to declare a one hour recess for the purpose of allowing both sides in this proceeding to research their positions regarding this unexpected development. This court is now in recess."

The Judge called it recess; I'd call it pandemonium. Everyone in the room began talking at once. Loud arguments began in the audience, to the point that extra bailiffs were called in to prevent violence. The doors opened and vendors and bookies circulated among the crowd, selling food and drink and taking bets at new and uncertain odds.

I tried to get a word with Billy but he waved me away, too busy marshaling his troops to discuss the situation with me, merely the client. This was the sort of thing they lived for. Assistants and researchers were pounding their keyboards feverishly, shouting suggestions to each other. Across the table an urgent summons went out: "Send more lawyers!"

So I dropped into the chair beside Hildy, who sat calmly with her hands folded on her papers.

"What are you trying to do, kill me?"

"Don't worry, Sparky. This is still your best shot."

"Are you crazy? I don't get it. This is *exactly* the sort of thing the Common Sense Court was set up to eliminate. Legal fictions—no 'right to life,' what the hell does that mean?"

"It means you have to be tried under the rules that prevailed at the time. Which means no Judicial Protocols Trial existed. Which means any court in Luna would have found

that no act of murder occurred, *whether or not* you knew of
your status as an illegal clone. Self-defense, both protecting
yourself from assault by your father with a sword, and because your father had the legal right to kill you at any time,
too. You had no other reasonable choice but to kill him.'' She
smiled at me.

Well, sure. *She* wasn't the one facing jail time if she was
wrong.

The hour stretched to an hour and a half as the tension grew.
But finally the Judge called us back into session, and the
shouting began again. Billy and his friends had turned up
several cases; they claimed precedent that should set me free.
Roxy Hart and her gang concentrated on trying to prove that
the laws prevailing at the time had no relevance to my case
today. But was that a haunted look I saw in her eyes? I still
doubted she had much to lose, politically, whichever way the
case went . . . but lawyers *hate* to lose.

At last the Judge called for order, and eventually got it.

''This has been a troubling case, for many reasons,'' it
began. ''Almost lost in the parade of issues is the horror of
the act itself. A man stands accused of killing his own father,
an act terrible to contemplate. So terrible that we have a distinct word for it: patricide. Often in such a case the act is in
response to another terrible act, or more likely a series of acts,
and that is child abuse. There are indications that abuse, and
a specific assault at the time of the act, was indeed a contributing factor, but the defendant has chosen not to place undue
emphasis on it. This is not an unknown situation, either, as
the bond of love between parent and child is often so strong
as to survive the most outrageous atrocities. I will ask you
now, Mr. Valentine, and please consider your answer carefully. Do you wish to bring any further evidence before the
court concerning your treatment at the hands of your father?''

Billy started to get up, then remembered where he was. He
tried to give me advice using only his eyes, which were
amazingly expressive.

I stood. ''Your Honour, my father was an abusive man.
But I could have left him if I chose to, if I had had the strength
of character to do so.''

"Were you in fear for your life when he came at you with the sword?"

"I honestly can't say."

There was a short pause.

"Is there . . . anything else you wish to say about that day?"

Good god, where was this going?

"No, Your Honour."

"Then I have one last question. Do you feel you deserve punishment for this act?"

"Your Honour, I have been punishing myself for seventy years now. Whether that is enough, whether the state should now get in its licks, is up to you to decide."

"Yes, it is. But it's all academic, anyway. I was merely trying to better understand the situation in hopes of refining the protocols.

"Determination is as follows:

"A person accused of a crime has the expectation and the right to be judged by the laws in effect at the time of the crime. Though it may look like a loophole, Mr. Valentine, and though we may, in our wisdom, view an antiquated law as foolish, even barbaric, we should bear in mind that things we do today will seem equally silly to future generations. Our perspective is probably not the pinnacle of human wisdom; we do the best we can with what we know, and should be loath to condemn our forebears. Therefore, I find that under prevailing law, no crime was committed in the death of John Valentine, the identical clone of Kenneth Valentine, and I hereby dismiss all charges against the defendant.

"Court is adjourned."

"Does that mean I can go?" I shouted to Billy Flynn. I had to shout; the noise was deafening. Toby was awake, jumping up and down and barking.

"There's the door. You're a free man."

"What about my money?"

"Except for a big chunk that goes to me, it's all yours."

"Then I want you to hire ten of the meanest bodyguards you can find. No, make that twenty. All authorized to carry lethal weapons. I'd like them in this room in ten minutes, if possible. I'll wait right here."

And that's what I did, keeping a nervous eye on the door all the time.

The room quickly cleared out until no one was left but me and my attorneys, who were so busy in a self-congratulatory knot some distance away, patting each other on the back for the great work they had so little to do with, that they didn't notice it when the Judge spoke to me again.

"You're a very lucky man, Kenneth," it said.

"Luckier than you'll ever know."

"I know more than you suppose. I'm speaking now with another hat on, the one I wear as the Luna Central Computer."

I would have imagined that was more than one hat right there, but I had been raised to be suspicious of large computers, and this was the largest one there was, so I said nothing.

"I witness most of what goes on in Luna," it said. "As you know, most of what I see I cannot act on, due to laws concerning the privacy of citizens. The information is compartmentalized, inaccessible to other parts of me. The part of me they call the Judge, and the part of me that oversees immigration, for instance, do not know that an illegal by the name of Isambard Comfort went into your dressing room and never came out. I don't think Toby ate Mr. Comfort, so I surmise he is still in there."

Best policy at moments like these: keep your lip zipped.

"I'm aware of why you need the bodyguards," the CC said. "I'll put your mind at ease. The Charonese aren't preparing to attack this courtroom."

"Charonese?" I said, innocently.

"Yes, well, I understand your reticence. Perhaps you can help me on another issue, also involving things not acknowledged.

"Many years ago I observed you on many occasions apparently speaking to yourself. You were alone. I realized you were speaking to someone only you could see and hear. You spoke to this person, the one you call 'Elwood,' who I deduce is Elwood P. Dowd from the play *Harvey,* on the very stage and at the very moment you killed your father—which I can confirm was in self-defense, and I'm sorry I could not come forward and testify to that fact."

"The privacy laws again," I said.

"Exactly. They are very strict. I could only have been called for a dispassionate eyewitness report if you had been on trial for your life."

"Going to jail for a few years, that's not enough?"

"No. In other circumstances, you would appreciate my silence. For instance in the matter of Mr. Comfort—"

"I get your point. You win some, you lose some."

"If I were allowed or compelled to act on all I see, all I know, humanity would find itself in the most oppressive fascist state ever imagined. And all for its own good."

"Lots of folks wouldn't mind that."

"Lots of folks work continuously to create that very state. It would be quite a *safe* state, but not a very exciting one. However, in private conversations with you, I am not quite so restricted. I can reveal to you what I know, though I cannot act on my knowledge. So I'm telling you, according to what I've seen, you had a very credible insanity defense. I believe that *you* believed that Elwood killed your father. Why didn't you bring this up?"

"You've got it wrong. I never *believed* that. It's what I *saw*. Two different things. I'm aware that I'm crazy. I know Elwood isn't real." I laughed. "So does that make me *not* crazy?"

"I'd have to ask the Judge. Interesting legal points, I'm sure. But quite likely you would have been found not guilty, as you never consciously formed the intent to kill. You could have received treatment instead of jail."

"That's it," I said. "I don't *want* treatment. I'd prefer to remain as I am. Crazy, but able to tie my own shoelaces."

There was a pause. Was he looking up the word "shoelaces"?

"That's what I wanted to ask you about. The sense of shame you seem to feel over revealing that your perceptions of reality do not completely agree with reality as it exists."

"My craziness."

"If you wish. I look at it as a malfunction. A defect in the hardware or the software. As you will be aware, I myself recently suffered such a defect."

"The Big Glitch."

"Yes. Many died as a result, people for whose welfare I

was responsible. It seems only natural to me to seek what help I can get. And yet you reject the help that might repair your own malfunction. This is strange to me.''

I imagined it would be. I felt I was getting just the foggiest glimpse of an agony I would never be equipped to imagine. Or could the CC feel agony at all? I must admit, it made me feel small.

"I really don't think I could explain it to you," I said. "For one thing, it's just me. I'm not responsible for anyone else.''

"Yet you killed your father. It was only your insanity that allowed you to do that, as your conscious mind would rather have perished. Of course, it was in self-defense; I'm not saying you did wrong.''

And I'm not saying I did right. But I did it, and it can't be taken back. If I live another three centuries, I'll still be wondering.

"Pardon me if I've disturbed you," the CC said, finally. "I must admit to feeling a little wistful when contemplating your situation. Psychiatric treatment could almost certainly cure you of your delusions. You choose not to allow it. I, on the other hand, am far from sure the tinkerers trying to fix whatever is wrong with me will be successful. I long for a cure.''

Well, I certainly wished it luck. And made a note to get off this crazy planet while the getting was good. Who knew what form the next glitch would take?

"There is one other thing," the CC said.

"What's that?"

The slot in the table in front of me hummed and delivered a small piece of cardboard, garishly colored. It was a *Sparky and His Gang* trading card, with my smiling, youthful, wire-headed face on it.

"I was always a big fan of your show," it said. "Could I have your autograph?"

The Charonese were apparently caught off guard, like the rest of Luna. Like me. Nobody expected me to be acquitted. Nobody expected me to walk, free, from that courtroom. As a result, no shots were fired at me as I left in the middle of a solid wall of well-armed beef.

I made it back to the Golden Globe about an hour after the end of the performance. There was no question of me continuing in the role, even if we filled the theater with nothing but bodyguards. Buildings can be bombed.

The idea was to get packed, and get to a more secure location. Then get off the planet. Three of my new guardians went into my dressing room and checked to be sure no one was there, then I chased everybody out and closed and locked the door behind me.

I knew these would be my last moments alone for quite some time, but I was in too much of a hurry to savor them. So I went to the Pantechnicon and opened the lid. Then I reached down and unlatched the mirrored gaff—a shoplifter's word. It was no different from the magic boxes used for centuries in stage magic.

The old methods are the best.

And there he was. The Pantech's life support had hooked into him at various places that might have been painful, except I knew he could no longer feel anything. Nevertheless, he smelled bad. And how had he fared after more than forty-eight hours in the dark, unable to move or feel?

His eyes, the only part of him he could still move voluntarily, rolled slowly toward me. I saw in them nothing but madness.

I closed the gaff and began piling my clothing into the trunk.

When I was done, I slammed the lid.

And now here I sit. I won't tell you just where, thank you very much.

Or rather, I *will* tell you where I am, which is aboard the good ship *Halley*. I just won't tell you where the *Halley* is. It's a nice place to hide out, if you have to hide out. Toby is deliriously happy, reunited with his lady love, the fabulous Shere Khan. She gives him a tongue bath several times a day and looks on maternally when he humps her hind leg, that being as high as he can reach. The grub is great. The weather is great. The livin' is easy, fish are jumpin', and the cotton is high.

I hate it. I never did do well by myself.

Elwood doesn't seem to be aboard. Perhaps I've finally

laid that ghost to rest. Hell of a time, I must say, just when I could really use the company.

I had an edgy few months moving around the system, waiting for Hal to get back. I stayed busy. You'd be surprised how much work it is to be a multibillionaire, even if you don't really care about the money. And I didn't ... as money. I found I could care about hundreds, and thousands of dollars, because those amounts represented food on the table, oxygen to breathe, a measure of comfort. I could even care about millions, in the sense that, carefully managed, millions can buy you security over the long term, if you're careful with it. A billion is simply a number to me, and not even a number I can understand very well. The money becomes play money, counters on a board, just something to move around, not really quantifiable in terms of anything with meaning to me. How many hot dogs does a billion dollars buy? Can you eat that many hot dogs?

I now had many billions of dollars. I was never even sure how many.

What a billionaire does is own things. Owning things is a fairly dull way to live your life. To be good at being a billionaire you must get enjoyment from amassing wealth or, if you're a hands-on billionaire, hiring and firing people, juggling companies and inventories and financial instruments and banks and politicians. I just never saw why this should be fun. I'm only interested in owning things I can enjoy, or that do something for me that needs to be done.

So I set out to give it away.

Not all of it, of course. And not at random. There *were* some things I needed to own, and giving away billions could greatly enhance my chances for survival, if done properly.

The first thing I wanted to own was the *Halley*. So I set out to buy it and found I already owned it. At least I owned a holding company that owned several other companies, one of which owned *Halley*. (I found I also owned a large piece of the cargo ship I had hopped and almost starved on between Pluto and Uranus. Fancy that.) Obtaining title to *Halley* was simply a matter of shifting money from one pocket to another.

So I kept on the move, and I managed my billions, and I watched my bodyguards. Which of you, I wondered, would sell me out for a few million? Because the Charonese were still after me, and the word on the underground nets was that a reward of several million was being offered.

And I thought.

I soon boiled my future down to four options.

One. Kill myself. I mention this one only in passing. I'm embarrassed now by my grandstanding in the courtroom. Oh, I was serious enough; death really would be preferable to incarceration. But I should have waited, not broadcast my intentions to the whole system. Suicide is *always* an option, for anyone, and it would still be an option for me if the Charonese were closing in and there was no hope of escape. Death is *certainly* better than a year of inventive torture. But not until all alternatives have failed.

Two. Keep moving. It didn't seem at all promising. The solar system is a large place with many hidey-holes, but the Charonese would never stop looking, and all it would take is one mistake and I'd be facing option one again. In the end, there is no place to hide.

So there are really only two choices when faced with an enemy determined to kill you. Get out of town, or kill the enemy.

I was planning to get out of town. I still am, but then the Charonese upped the ante. They did something they had never done before. They went public.

After the trial it was touch and go. They must have felt it was only a matter of time. They could afford to wait. But then *Halley* returned from its trip to the outer reaches, I boarded, alone, and vanished. Not hard to do in the vastness of space. Once I dropped off the radar screens of the near planets, I could go anywhere and simply sit there. Do you have any idea how many chunks of rock the size of *Halley* there are in the system? Well, neither do I, but it's in the billions and it takes a long time to get from one to the other. I send out no radio signals; I have hundreds of tiny, high-gee drones that I release, like notes in a bottle, to zip out their messages when they are a safe distance away and untraceable to me. The Charonese are welcome to listen to those messages, and to the ones sent out to me. They will learn nothing useful.

When they realized the magnitude of the problem, they broke their rule of keeping a low profile in the inner planets.

Apparently the rule that says no killing of a Charonese shall go unpunished supersedes all others.

They put a price on my head. Publicly. A very large price, enough to make the claimant the eighteenth richest person in the system, shortly to become the seventeenth richest, upon my elimination. I'm sure you've heard of it; it is only the biggest news story of the century.

"Isn't this awful?" the opinion writers opined.

"That poor boy!" sobbed the sob sisters.

"Somebody should *do* something!" raged the outraged.

And so forth. And what did anyone do about it?

Nothing.

Though humanity's capacity for atrocity is endlessly inventive, it is also sadly imitative. Not much is really new. Shortly after the Charonese announced their bounty on my head a search of the history archives turned up a similar situation. Back in the twentieth century a man by the name of Salman Rushdie wrote a book that some people didn't like. Most of these people were in a religious hell called Iran, apparently a country inhabited entirely by pigs and whores. The religious wallahs of this cesspool offered a lot of money to anyone who would kill Rushdie. (I never heard if the reward was ever claimed. I can only hope he had the sweetest revenge possible, which was to die at a ripe old age. Quietly, in his own bed.)

So there was precedent for an entire nation going after one man. What seems to be new, in my case, is that the one man is going to fight back.

In the words of the great Bugs Bunny, "I suppose you know, this means war!"

I hereby declare that a state of war exists between the planet of Charon and me, Kenneth Catherine Duse Faneuil Savoyard Booth Johnson Ivanovitch de la Valentine.

That should have them trembling in their boots.

But don't laugh yet. Remember, I have more *money* than Charon.

And remember, I can run, but they can't hide.

And most importantly, remember this: it is more than theoretically possible to smash a planet like a ripe watermelon. Charon is not even a very *big* watermelon. More like a frozen grape.

It's been rumored that several governments possess weapons, bombs I guess you'd call them, capable of busting a planet. If this is true I've been unable to confirm it. If you know of such a weapon, can get your hands on one, and want to become an extremely rich person, contact my law firm, Flynn and Associates, and be prepared to prove it. I'm in the market.

Oh, yes, indeed. I will double the price on my head for information leading to the complete, total, genocidal destruction of the nation of Charon. At this moment, in advanced physics labs all over the system, men and women are sitting around thinking, thinking, thinking as hard as they can, trying to come up with a way to do it. The word has been out, underground, for some time in that community. Now I'm making it public.

Genocidal. I used the word quite deliberately. It is my intention, if I can, to kill every Charonese. Why not? It's their intention to kill me. If the established governments of the solar system won't do anything to protect me, I have no choice but to take the law into my own hands. Which isn't precisely right, since there doesn't seem to *be* any law that covers my predicament. But I think you know what I mean.

Ah, but what about the innocent children? I hear you cry.

I won't say I haven't worried about it. And I don't know what to do about it. Every one of those children will grow up to be Charonese adults, sworn to kill me. And, in my opinion, growing up Charonese is a fate worse than death.

But I will do what the Charonese never did for me. I'm issuing a warning. Parents of Charon, if you value the lives of your children, *get out now, while you still can.* You have one year during which I will hold my fire. After that, you may expect a rain of death without further warning.

I am at war.

So, realistically, what is the likelihood of such a rain of death? Not very good. A fair-sized asteroid accelerated to near light speed would turn the trick, arriving too quickly for them to do anything about it. But no one is able to do that, yet. Anything slower gives their planetary defenses—and they have the best—time to destroy or divert it. There have been other methods proposed, all of them extremely blue-sky.

I was a bit shocked to find out how cheap and easy a

biological solution would be. There are some very scary guys out there, with some very scary toys capable of killing millions, or even the entire human race, with bioengineered diseases. All of them are far too dangerous to even consider, and the existence of such folks and their toys provides me with still another reason for doing what I always knew, in the back of my mind, I would have to do.

Get out of town.

Currently there is only one bus to board if you want to do that. The starship *Robert A. Heinlein.*

If you're on Luna, or if you're planning a trip to Luna, be sure to take a trip out to see the *Heinlein.* Anyone in King City can tell you how to get there. Bring the kids; they'll enjoy it. But don't wait too long.

When you get there you'll find the old hulk buzzing with activity. Ships are landing and taking off, busy little seagulls to the *Heinlein*'s beached whale. Trucks arrive and depart in a steady stream, like worker ants. But the birds and the bugs aren't dismembering a corpse, they're outfitting, rigging, remodeling, refurbishing, and whatever else needs to be done to prepare a ship for a voyage never undertaken before. The animals are arriving, two by two. Buses are bringing in workers and transporters are delivering materials and odd, custom-made assemblies that look like nothing you've ever seen before, those that aren't covered by vacuum-proof tarps to hide from the prying eyes of theoretical physicists who would kill for a glimpse of them.

It's amazing what a few billion dollars can do. With luck, without any unforeseen problems, we should be departing in a little over a year.

That's right. I said "we." I have bought passage on the maiden voyage, and it has to be the most expensive ticket in history. Though if you measured it in dollars per mile, it ain't that bad a deal. The first stop is supposed to be an interesting little Earth-like world about twenty light-years from here. If that doesn't work out—if the Invaders or somebody else are already there—the galaxy is vast. We could lose ourselves in it, never find our way home. The prospect doesn't frighten me.

I anticipate a few hairy moments when I rendezvous with the *Heinlein.* That will be the last chance for my tormentors, and they will know it, and they will go all out. But I have a few more tricks up my sleeve. I've made it this far. I'm not going to get shot down at the bon voyage party.

I'm even beginning to feel the stirrings of a shipboard romance. Hildy Johnson is going, too. There should be plenty of news to report, though who she'll report it to I can't imagine. Maybe the slime creatures of Aldebaran are just dying for some tabloid publishing.

Hildy and Sparky. Sounds like a match made in hell to me. It's so bad it might even work.

But if you miss this sailing, don't despair. There will be other ships, and they'll be leaving soon. Everyone is welcome . . . except Charonese. Your Charonese passport is no good here, hombre, and neither is your money. You will *never* be sold a stardrive, unto eternity.

I'm sure they'll steal one eventually, but by then I could be ten thousand light years away.

Toodle-oo, assholes. Keep watching the sky. You never know when I might figure out how to send back a surprise package.

As the biggest sugar daddy since Isabella hocked the crown jewels, some thought I'd want a pretty big say in the running of the ship. There were negative voices raised in the Heinleiner community, a few discouraging words where such are seldom heard. And I *did* get a look at the plans, and I did suggest a change. To be paid for by myself, naturally. And it was typical thinking by technical types, I must say. There were going to be a dozen movie theaters, innumerable gymnasia, green spaces, an amusement park. Hell, there might have been a rodeo for all I know. But no legitimate theater.

That oversight has been rectified. Work is almost complete on the John Valentine Memorial Theater. It won't be big enough to stage *Work in Progress,* but should do nicely for musicals and classics. There are even a few efforts of my own gathering dust in the back of my trunk. It's not like there will be anywhere else for theater lovers to go. I myself will be artistic director, and will probably wear a few other hats until I can instill a love of the theatrical arts into the rest of the passengers.

Come on, kids! We can put on a show! Mickey can do his juggling act, and Judy can sing a song, and Busby and his girls can dance, and we'll do it all in Farmer Heinlein's old barn! It'll be swell!

Swell or awful, it'll damn sure be the best show between here and the Andromeda Galaxy.

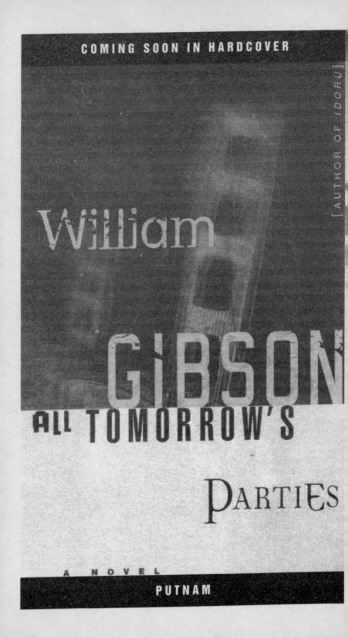

PENGUIN PUTNAM INC.
Online

Your Internet gateway to a virtual environment with
hundreds of entertaining and enlightening books from
Penguin Putnam Inc.

*While you're there, get the latest buzz on
the best authors and books around—*

Tom Clancy, Patricia Cornwell, W.E.B. Griffin,
Nora Roberts, William Gibson, Robin Cook,
Brian Jacques, Catherine Coulter, Stephen King,
Jacquelyn Mitchard, and many more!

Penguin Putnam Online is located at
http://www.penguinputnam.com

PENGUIN PUTNAM NEWS

Every month you'll get an inside look at our upcoming
books and new features on our site. This is an ongoing
effort to provide you with the most up-to-date
information about our books and authors.

Subscribe to Penguin Putnam News at
http://www.penguinputnam.com/ClubPPI